Prai[s]

Song in the Dark

"Jack Fleming has proven to be the most enduring of the vampire detectives, and Elrod has managed to keep his story and circumstances interesting from volume to volume."
—*Chronicle*

"Elrod knows how to pace the action without resorting to caricature. These characters, including the vampires, are believable and—for the most part—a pleasure to know."
—*Library Journal*

"There are enough plot twists and turns to keep the reader entertained right up to the end and looking for more... It's a treat to return to Fleming's humorous, slightly earthy take on the world and dealing with unique problems posed by being a vampire. If you enjoy vampire books and are searching out something different, check these out; you won't be disappointed."
—*Monsters and Critics*

Dark Road Rising

"P. N. Elrod ups the stakes (pun intended) in this latest, and best, installment of the Jack Fleming saga. Chills, thrills, and dark doings in '30s Chicago, heralded by the arrival of a darkly fascinating new vampire character with a deadly secret. Elrod takes her universe into unexplored territory with *Dark Road Rising*."
—Rachel Caine, author of the Morganville Vampires series

"The book is as dark and decadent as blood and chocolate. The writing pops, and Jack Fleming is a narrator to die for."
—Caitlin Kittredge, author of *The Nightmare Garden*

"*Dark Road Rising* is a refreshingly different vampire novel. The setting is captivating, the characters are original, and the plot will leave you hungry for more."
—Lori Handeland, author of *Crave the Moon*

"*Dark Road Rising* kept me up all night. A satisfying, smart, genuinely savvy read—with a lot of bite."
—Lilith Saintcrow, author of the Dante Valentine series

⧾ The Vampire Files ⧾

VOLUME FIVE

P. N. ELROD

ACE BOOKS, NEW YORK

THE BERKLEY PUBLISHING GROUP
Published by the Penguin Group
Penguin Group (USA) Inc.
375 Hudson Street, New York, New York 10014, USA
Penguin Group (Canada), 90 Eglinton Avenue East, Suite 700, Toronto, Ontario M4P 2Y3, Canada
(a division of Pearson Penguin Canada Inc.)
Penguin Books Ltd., 80 Strand, London WC2R 0RL, England
Penguin Group Ireland, 25 St. Stephen's Green, Dublin 2, Ireland (a division of Penguin Books Ltd.)
Penguin Group (Australia), 250 Camberwell Road, Camberwell, Victoria 3124, Australia
(a division of Pearson Australia Group Pty. Ltd.)
Penguin Books India Pvt. Ltd., 11 Community Centre, Panchsheel Park, New Delhi—110 017, India
Penguin Group (NZ), 67 Apollo Drive, Rosedale, Auckland 0632, New Zealand
(a division of Pearson New Zealand Ltd.)
Penguin Books (South Africa) (Pty.) Ltd., 24 Sturdee Avenue, Rosebank, Johannesburg 2196,
South Africa

Penguin Books Ltd., Registered Offices: 80 Strand, London WC2R 0RL, England

This is a work of fiction. Names, characters, places, and incidents either are the product of the author's imagination or are used fictitiously, and any resemblance to actual persons, living or dead, business establishments, events, or locales is entirely coincidental. The publisher does not have any control over and does not assume any responsibility for author or third-party websites or their content.

THE VAMPIRE FILES: VOLUME FIVE

PUBLISHING HISTORY
Ace trade paperback edition / March 2012

Ace trade paperback ISBN: 978-1-937007-12-6

Library of Congress Cataloging-in-Publication Data

Elrod, P. N. (Patricia Nead)
   The vampire files / P. N. Elrod.
      p. cm.
   Contents: v. 1. Bloodlist ; Lifeblood ; Bloodcircle
   ISBN: 0-441-01090-3
   1. Fleming, Jack (Fictitious character)—Fiction.   2. Private investigators—Illinois—
Chicago—Fiction.   3. Detective and mystery stories, American.   4. Fantasy fiction,
American.   5. Occult fiction, American.   6. Chicago (Ill.)—Fiction.   7. Vampires—Fiction.   I. Title.

   PS3555.L68V36 2003
   813'.54—dc22   2003045118

PRINTED IN THE UNITED STATES OF AMERICA

10   9   8   7   6   5   4   3   2   1

CONTENTS

THE VAMPIRE FILES

VOLUME FIVE

SONG IN THE DARK

To my good friends
Ian Hamill
Roxanne Longstreet
Roxanne Longstreet Conrad
Roxanne Conrad
Rachel Caine
AND ESPECIALLY
Julie Fortune!

Stand-up buds, all!

1

I slouched in the backseat of Gordy's Cadillac, the one that had just slightly less armor than a German tank, keeping clear of the rearview mirror out of habit, not because I cared one way or the other. The driver, a stone-faced guy named Strome, probably wouldn't have said anything about my lack of reflection even if he'd noticed. He almost certainly had other things on his mind, like whether or not he would be the one delegated to kill me tonight.

It was really too bad for him, because I got the idea that he'd begun to like me. I already had his respect.

A scant few nights ago Strome had seen me apparently dead, an ugly kind of dead, then had to contend with my quick and mystifying return to good health. I gave no explanations to him or any of the others who were aware of my experience, and soon he'd accepted that I'd somehow survived. So far as he knew now I was still healing from that bloody damage, yet able to walk around and carry on with what passed for normal life, which in his eyes made me without a doubt the toughest SOB in Chicago. Strome couldn't have known about my supernatural edge; anything to do with vampires was well outside his view of the world, which was fine with me. Like others of his ilk, even if specifics about the Undead escaped him, he was aware that I was dangerously different. He knew which questions *not* to ask, and that made him a valuable asset to the mob. And me.

Most of the time he and his partner, Lowrey, were bodyguards to their gangland boss and my friend, Gordy Weems. We all tripped and fell down on the job a few nights ago, leaving Gordy with a couple of bullets in him. He'd survived, too, barely.

While he'd been out for the count, his lieutenants decided that someone had to step into his shoes to deal with the running of their mob during the crisis and elected me to take his place. I thought it to be a singularly bad idea, but took on the burden for Gordy's sake. I wouldn't have been any kind of a stand-up guy to have ducked out when he needed the help. I'd been too cocky assuming the mantle, though. Because of my edge, I'd come to believe in my own indestructibility. I thought I could handle anything.

Circumstances and a drunken sadist named Hog Bristow taught me different.

I got my payback on him. Bristow was dead. Ugly dead. I'd killed him, and now I had to give payback to someone else about my actions. Even Gordy couldn't get me out of this one. It was serious gang business, the resolution of which would take place in his soundproofed upstairs office at his nightclub.

Or the basement. I'd been there once or twice. Not on the receiving end.

"Turn on the radio," I told Strome.

He obliged. Dance music flowed from the speaker grille. "You want this or something else?" he asked.

"That's fine." Music helped to distract me, to seal over the fissures inside. I had lots of those going deep down into blackness full of sharp, cutting horrors along the way. If I focused on the radio noise, then I didn't have to think about certain things, like what Bristow had done to me after hanging me upside down from a hook in a meat locker.

That's what this ride was about: the repercussion over what I'd done to him once I'd gotten free.

It wasn't fair that I was being called on the carpet for that bastard's death, but the mobs had their own rules and ways of doing things. Bristow had powerful friends back in New York; they'd give me a few minutes to give my side of the story—Gordy had wrangled that much for me—then I'd die.

Strome drove to the back-alley entrance of Gordy's club, the Nightcrawler, which was the normal ingress for bosses. The front was for the swells come to see the shows and try the gambling in a strictly private section of the club. The gaming was the main difference between my own nightclub and this one. If the stage shows were a bust, then Gordy was still guaranteed to make a ton of money from tables and slots. He thought I was nuts not having some as well as a backup, but I chose early on not to take that road. Sure, I had an accountant who could cook the books to a turn and, with Gordy's influence, could manage bribes and all the rest, but I wouldn't risk it even for that kind of money. All it'd take was one raid, one arrest, one daylight court appearance with me not there, and that would be the end of it. Maybe I did some sweating when profits were thin or nonexistent, but that was better than losing the whole works.

Not that any of it mattered much to me now.

Strome parked. I quit the car, sliding across the seat to get out on the driver's side, slamming the door harder than was necessary. It drew attention. Despite the cold there were a number of guys hanging around the Nightcrawler's back door. Two of them were Ruzzo, brothers in Gordy's outfit, strong arms, bad tempers, and not much brain. Being too hard to tell apart, they went interchangeably by the one name.

A few nights back, in order to assert my authority as temporary boss, I'd had to punch them both out to make a point. Now they lurked close enough to force me to notice them. Both looked like they'd shared the same bad lemon. Ruzzo the Elder had a split lip; his brother had a black eye. Two ways to tell them apart. They must have thought my number was up and were already figuring how to get me alone for some payback of their own before the boom lowered.

Ruzzo the Younger showed an exceptionally hard glare. It effectively distracted me from his brother.

Who threw a punch toward my ribs as I walked past.

Bad move.

I took it solid, but didn't collapse the way I was supposed to; instead, I sliced out sideways with my forearm and slammed him broad across the middle. I'd seen something like it on a tennis court, only you're supposed to use a racket.

The Elder staggered backward halfway across the alley, folding with an *oof* noise onto the cold pavement. The Younger blazed in to kill, pulling out a gun.

Which I plucked away from him almost as an afterthought.

He stared at his empty hand.

Strome finished up. He had a blackjack ready and swiped it viciously behind the man's left ear. The Younger dropped.

I held the gun out to Strome, addressing him loud enough for the others to hear. "These dopes shoulda kept in school. They could have found out how rough the big boys in first grade played. Maybe learned something."

His turn to stare. "You okay? He caught you a good one."

I pretended to shift uncomfortably. "Yeah, he did. Let's go."

We climbed the loading-dock stairs to the club's kitchen, but instead of turning toward the stairs up to Gordy's office, Strome led the way to

the main room of the club. Band music, live, played there, though the
place was still an hour or so from opening. A last-minute rehearsal for
their big star seemed to be going on.

"Have to wait here," said Strome, gesturing at a ringside table. It was
the one usually reserved for special guests of the boss. It was also the
farthest from any exit, and my being placed here was no coincidence. A
glance around confirmed I was expected to stay put. All the doors were
covered by at least two mugs, armed, of course. Strome sat with me,
keeping his hat and coat on. I did likewise.

"How long?" I asked.

He gave a small shrug. "Donno."

No need to inquire whether word had been sent up about my arrival.
That would have happened the instant we parked. I was supposed to sit
there and stew about my fate.

Instead, I watched the rehearsal. Nothing else to do. As with the
radio, the music kept me from thinking too much.

Things seemed to be running late and going badly. This week's big
star was Alan Caine. I'd heard him on the radio, and he was a popular
name in Broadway revues. He'd done speciality numbers in short-subject
films I'd never seen. He had a stadium-filling voice and was presently
using it to hammer at the red-faced bandleader.

"Three in a row—you going for some kind of record? Read the damn
music, if you can, and give me the right damn cue!" Caine wore his tuxedo pants and suspenders, an undershirt and dress shoes. He was so
handsome that even men looked twice at him, and with women it was a
foregone conclusion they'd faint if he gave them a half second's glance.
The line of dancing girls behind confirmed it. Instead of being put off by
his tone, they all looked to be in a giggly, flirty mood, eyes bright.

He eased into a gap between two of them, pasted on a huge, absolutely sincere smile, and froze, waiting.

The band, for the fourth time, swung into the prologue for his number, and must have gotten it right. Caine and his leggy troupe stepped
and strutted smarter than smart for eight counts, then the girls retreated,
leaving him out front to sing the rest of his song. I didn't like him on
sight, but he had a hell of a voice.

"Wanna drink?" Strome asked.

He got a blank look from me. Taking requests from the condemned
man? Or was he in need of fuel for what was to come? So far as I knew
he would be the executioner. He was like Bristow, a killer. Unlike Bris-

tow, Strome didn't make a big thing of it, and if he enjoyed the work, kept it to himself.

"No thanks."

Strome signed to someone I didn't bother to look at and got a draft beer, the glass opaque with frost. They knew how to serve things up right at the Nightcrawler: song, dance, drinks, girls, gambling, and death.

Alan Caine broke off in midnote. The dancers continued their routine for a few steps; the band continued as well until the leader caught on that he'd committed another sin. I'd been listening and hadn't heard anything wrong. Caine heard different and laid into him on the brass being too loud.

"They're paying money to hear *me*, not you," he stated, his sincere smile on the shelf for the moment. "What the hell do you think you're doing trying to drown me out? That's *my* name on the marquee, not yours. Get your people in line or get another job."

I waited for the leader to lay into him right back, but he just nodded and began the play again, starting a few bars before the interruption. This time the horns were softer, and Caine's voice went right to the corners of the room.

"Is he always like that?" I asked Strome.

"Since he got here."

"Why does Derner put up with it?" Derner was another of Gordy's lieutenants and also the general manager for the club.

"The guy packs in the crowds."

"No one's worth that kind of crap."

"This one is. He gets every seat filled and has a standing-room line at the bar. Even on the weeknights we can charge a two-fifty cover, and they come in herds."

"Two-fifty?" That was unheard of; some clubs in New York got away with charging so much for their cover, but less so in Chicago. You only did that on weekends and only when it was a real Ziegfeld-style spectacular. Nothing so elaborate was going on here with just Caine, the band, and eight dancers. There was no stage decoration, either, just the usual long curtains backing the musicians and someone to man the lights and keep the spot on the star. "He's worth it?"

"Depends who you talk to. The bookkeepers say yes, the performers say no. Bookkeepers win."

"He must be blackmailing someone."

"Hey!" Caine stopped the show again, this time his attention squarely on our table. He broke away from the dancers, striding over to glare at us. He was teeming with sculpted cheekbones, graceful jaw, and a perfect nose. Anger on him didn't look at all threatening. Maybe a little with his baby blues steaming up. He narrowed them, arching a too-perfectly shaped eyebrow. "I'm trying to *work* here. If you two can't put a lid on it, take your romance to the men's room."

A week back I might have reacted to him; tonight I had no reaction at all, just stared. I chanced to take a breath and caught a powerful whiff of booze from him, as though he'd just gargled with it. "Just do your song and dance, Caine," I said, hardly raising my voice above a whisper.

"Do I know you, punk?"

He was in his late thirties; I looked to be in my twenties. I was well used to the penalty of perpetual youth. "Be glad you don't."

"A tough guy, eh?" He could belt a song, but delivering dialogue didn't quite work for him, especially when it came out of the wrong kind of films. He should have stuck to showbiz stories and not tried imitating movie gangsters.

"That's right. Go back to work."

"Where's Derner?" he demanded, switching focus to Strome. "I want this punk tossed out on his ear. Go get him."

"Sorry, can't do that, Mr. Caine. I'm working, too."

Caine saw the beer at his elbow. "Nice job." He swung around, eyes searching. "You there! Go find Derner and bring him here."

The mug he addressed registered puzzlement at being ordered around by the stage talent.

Strome craned his head. "Never mind, Joe. Mr. Caine was just joking."

"Joking? We'll see who's laughing before the night's out."

Caine didn't appear to be drunk, but my instant-hypnosis act likely wouldn't work on him; besides, he wasn't worth the headache. I looked past him, hoping to spot the stage manager, but no such luck. However, a fierce-faced woman in a poisonous green dress and black fur-trimmed coat came barreling toward us from the front entrance. It was still too early to open. I wondered how she'd gotten in.

So, it seemed, did Caine. Genuine surprise flashed over him. "Jewel, what the hell are you doing here?"

Her lip color was so dark a red that it looked black, matching her hair. Two lines framing her mouth cut themselves into a deep, hard frown of contempt. Her eyes were wild, the pupils down to pinpoints. She braked to an unsteady stop. "The alimony is three weeks overdue, why do you *think* I'm here?"

He recovered composure, shifting to pure smarm. "You'll just have to wait till I'm paid."

She went scarlet, her whole body seemed to swell from outrage. "That's what you said three paychecks ago, you bastard!" She hit him with a green purse the same shade as her dress. He got an arm up to block any blows to his face and unexpectedly started laughing like a lunatic, which just made her madder. She cursed, he giggled. Funny on a movie screen, not so much ten feet away when all parties are dead set on inflicting damage, each in their own way.

It went downhill from there.

Not inclined to interfere, I watched the domestic drama with an equally unmoved Strome, content to let other guys rush in to bust things up. Several of the bouncers who'd been on the exits moved remarkably fast for their size. That would have been the ideal time for me to make an escape, just dart to the front lobby, duck around the corner phone booth, and vanish. It was one of my specialties. Instead, I kept my seat and wished I could still drink beer. A cold one would have gone down good about now.

It took three bouncers to remove Jewel Caine: two on her left side for her shoulders and feet, one on her right for her middle. She didn't make it easy for them, bucking and cursing the whole way as they carried her bodily from the room like a log, green purse and all. So far Lady Crymsyn, which was my nightclub, had suffered no drunken rows on this level, only comparatively mild, easily dealt with skirmishes. I could count myself lucky.

Alan Caine, grinning wide, called after her: "Why don't you get a job?"

She heard. "I'll *kill* you, you son of a bitch! I'll cut your throat if you don't pay what you owe me!" The rest was incoherent and, from the tone, likely obscene. Closing doors spared us from more opinions and threats.

One of the chorus dancers trotted up. "Alan, that was awful. Are you okay?"

"Yeah-yeah, Evie." He waved her off. "Back on your mark, let's get this over with."

She seemed disappointed he wasn't making more of a fuss over the disruption and visibly swallowed back the load of comfort and sympathy she must have had ready to pour out. Evie was just about the cutest little doll I'd seen in many a week and affected a tiny Betty Boop voice. I thought she could do much better than Caine. "Well . . . if you're *sure* . . ."

"I'm sure. C'mon, bub." He turned her around and gave her a light swat on her nicely rounded rump. This cheered her up, and she went trotting back to her envious and/or amused sisters. They formed their line again. Caine called a cue to the band, and they began in midstanza, this time making it to the end. He cut an exaggerated bow to them. *"Finally!"*

"About damn time," muttered Strome. He wasn't one for offering much in the way of comments. His beer, which he'd drained off, must have loosened him up.

"How's that?" I asked.

"He's been at it all day. If he was a dame, he'd be one of those primer dons. He better pray he don't ever lose his voice. That's all that's keeping him alive. Derner's been busy just holding off people from busting him one."

"Yet he packs the club?"

"He keeps that mean side away from the audience. With his looks they think he's an angel. People in the business know he's a jerk-off but they put up with it. He's got enough push from bringing in cash to get them fired."

"Or tossed out."

Strome spared me a look. He must have thought I was referring to myself, not Caine's ex-wife. "Derner woulda talked him out of it. Caine don't know who's who in this town yet."

"In my case it doesn't matter."

His stony face had almost become animated, but shut down at the reminder of why we were here. "It's just the business," Strome said. This was the closest he would ever get to making an apology to me for whatever was to come.

"Yeah."

A business where a guy like Strome could come up to me, his former temporary boss, and tender an invitation to take a ride that I had to accept. He'd been so sure of the end result that he'd left the motor running in the car when he walked into Lady Crymsyn to deliver the summons. We eyed each other in the yet-to-open lobby, as though either of us had options. He had to bring me in, and the gun he carried under his arm was the last word on the subject. I glanced around at my people, who were getting things ready for the evening, oblivious of any threat. Strome shook his head, letting me know they weren't on his list.

He wouldn't use them against me. I liked that.

I got my hat and coat and went along, turning the opening of Crymsyn over to one of the bartenders. There was no point putting things off. This way I had some control over the situation. If the bad guys insisted on killing me for killing Hog Bristow, it would be at a safe distance from friends who could get in the cross fire.

The men who took away the acrimonious Jewel Caine returned, two of them resuming their posts, the third pausing to glare at the empty dance floor. Caine and the chorus line were backstage, getting ready for the night's performance. The third guy shifted his glare toward me, but whatever bothered him was none of my doing, and he got a blank look in return. I was getting good at those.

His name was Hoyle, and like the brothers Ruzzo, I was not anyone he liked. He'd resented my taking over for Gordy. Hoyle thought he should have been the one to pinch-hit, but his name never once cropped up. If I'd turned down the job, then Derner would have taken in the slack. Hoyle didn't see it that way, and I heard he'd started blaming me for everything up to and including the Depression itself.

Some people have too much time and not enough to do.

After a minute Hoyle got tired of trying to intimidate me and moved on to the bar, snapping his fingers for a drink.

Strome's partner, Lowrey, emerged from a door with a PRIVATE sign on it and came down to us. He was shorter and wider, with a cast to one eye and few enemies. Live ones, that is.

"Boss wants to see you, Mr. Fleming," he said.

I was surprised. "Gordy's here?" He was supposed to be anyplace else, resting, healing from his gunshot wounds.

"In the casino." He jerked a thumb over his shoulder.

The two of them followed as I hurried though the door into the Nightcrawler's illegal but extremely profitable gaming room. The lights were low, the place gloomy and strangely quiet, like an empty church. I spotted Gordy at the far end by the back exit, seated in one of the semiprivate alcoves favored by the cardplayers. He was fully dressed, and his girlfriend—nurse for the time being—was nowhere in sight.

My escorts hung back as I went forward and slipped into a chair on the other side of his table and nearly echoed Alan Caine's question. "What the hell are you doing here?" I kept my voice low, swallowing anger. Shouting didn't work on Gordy.

His skin was sallow, sagging, but his eyes were clear. I didn't like that. His doctor had him on pain pills, and they tended to dull everything about him. Clear eyes meant he was hurting. "It's business," he said.

"You can deal with things on the phone, and Derner and I do the rest. You're still supposed to be in bed. Where's Adelle?" She'd been looking after Gordy since the shooting.

"She went to the stores to get some stuff, so me an' Lowrey scrammed to here. I had to give her the slip for a couple hours. Makes me crazy, lying around and her playing nursemaid like I was sick."

Adelle Taylor, actress on stage, screen, and radio, and sometimes a headliner singing at my club and his, would throw a fit when she found out. I said as much to Gordy, who gave only the smallest of shrugs. He was a big man and didn't have to move much to make a point. "I left her a note."

"She'll come straight down here. Loaded for bear."

"I'll be done by then."

"With what, exactly?"

"You. Maybe."

"If you wanted to see me, I'd have come over, there's no need to—"

"Wasn't my doing bringing you here. I've been stalling them. They wouldn't stall no more."

"What? Who?"

"New York. Bristow's friends."

"You been running interference for me? In your condition?"

"I'm better off than you were, kid." Gordy knew my real age, which was about the same as his, but sometimes he seemed a lot older. When it came to mob business, he was decades my senior.

"What do you mean?"

"I got from the boys what happened to you. What Bristow did."

I felt my face go red. Mortification does that to me. "I told them to keep shut about it."

"They did, until I woke up enough to ask."

"Gordy, you don't need to be bothering with this. Just go back to bed and get better. I'll take care of things and no problem, okay?"

He just looked at me, eyes sleepy-seeming, but still not dull. "You up to it?"

"Of course I am. I appreciate what you've done, but—"

He raised one hand, shutting me down. "Fleming, I know Bristow put you through something worse than hell. A man don't get over that in a couple days, not even you."

"I'm *fine,* everything's healed up. Really."

Another long look and a twitch of his lips. He was usually as poker-faced as they come.

"What's wrong?" I asked.

"There's a hammer about to fall on you. It should have happened days ago, but I put them off."

"New York?" Gordy's bosses.

"I got my orders. I'm supposed to kill you."

"Yeah? So?" I'd been half-expecting that for days. If Gordy thought I'd get upset at the idea of him having to kill me, he'd have a long wait to see it. Besides, he knew what I was. Maybe he would have to do his job. It could be arranged. Wouldn't be the first time I'd died.

"I put 'em off, did some talking, bought some time, but stalled them too much. Another guy's doing the job. I gotta stand aside while he deals with you or get rubbed out, too."

If my heart had been working, it would have stopped. "Another like Bristow?"

"No. Smarter."

It wouldn't take much. Bristow had been dumb as an empty box. Maybe this guy would be sober for longer than five minutes, and I could evil-eye whammy him into changing his mind.

"He's the one who sent Bristow in the first place. One of the big shots. Name's Whitey Kroun."

The big boss himself. One of them, anyway. "Why should he come here? He couldn't phone?"

"He had enough of you over the phone."

I supposed he had. Our conversations during the turmoil following the murder attempt on Gordy had been brief and curdling, and I'd not made any friends. Kroun didn't know me from Adam and was already allergic. He'd been one of the brains who, in a fit of idiocy, sent Hog Bristow to shake things up in their holdings here. The idea was to make Gordy turn over the Chicago operation to Bristow, only that didn't happen. Of course, it was clearly all my fault.

"Kroun . . . he doesn't much like me."

Gordy almost smiled. "You should try harder to make more friends."

"Not with my smart-ass mouth. Listen, I'll face the music, get the heat off you, off us both, but you *gotta* get home and let Adelle spoil you for a couple more weeks." Gordy was doing a decent job of hiding it, but was visibly weak to my eyes. And ears. His heartbeat was up, and a sheen of sweat was on his forehead. He'd gotten out of bed too soon, pushed himself too much, and there was no need. "When's Kroun due in?"

"He's here now. Waiting upstairs. My office."

Oh, great, fine, wonderful. "Got any advice?"

"Don't get killed."

Huh. Easy for him to say. "What's he like?"

"Scary."

He got a double take from me. Gordy using a word like that? "In what way?"

He shook his head. "Just tell him the truth. Play straight with him."

Strome came forward. "Boss?"

Gordy and I looked his way at the same time. I'd gotten used to answering to the title at Crymsyn and again from being in charge of Gordy's mob. The first time Strome had addressed me as such I nearly told him to stop, but held back. It was a show of respect, for the office if not also for me, and however much I hated to think of how I'd won both, I accepted the dubious honor. Once I completely stepped down he could go back to calling me "Mr. Fleming," or "Fleming" or, like a few others in the organization, "that creep son of a bitch."

None of them called me "Jack," and I was glad of it.

I was conscious of my face shutting down, slamming into the deadpan frown Gordy's kind of job demanded, and replied for both of us. "Yeah?"

"Mitchell's here." He jerked his chin at the back exit, where a man stood in the doorway.

Who the hell was Mitchell? He seemed almost familiar, but wasn't local. I knew most of the boys here by sight, and he matched their type. He stood motionless, hands in his coat pockets, giving me the hard eye, shifting his hostile gaze for a long moment to Gordy—no love lost there, I thought—then back to me. Not the genial sort, but few of them are.

Gordy motioned him over, moving just his fingers. Saving his strength, I hoped.

Mitchell came close. Hands still in his pockets. If he'd had a gun in each one, I would not have been surprised. He would be from New York and represented the big guys, the serious hoods who gave Gordy his orders.

Strome did the honors. "Mitchell . . . Mr. Fleming."

"You kiddin'?" Mitchell asked no one in particular. My apparent youth must have been working against me again. On the other hand, it was often a good thing to be underestimated. He stared like I was a bizarre zoo specimen.

Strome, stony-faced, reiterated, "This is Jack Fleming—the guy who took care of Hog Bristow."

"New York?" I asked. Just to be sure.

Mitchell's gaze flicked in Gordy's direction. "It's time." He said it like an executioner might. One who enjoyed his work.

Gordy started to get up, but I stopped him. "It's okay, I'll see to this on my own."

"You sure?"

"Go home. Look after yourself, would ya? I gotta see a man about a hog."

Easing from the table, I followed Strome to the back hallway, with Mitchell right behind us. Strome looked over his shoulder at me as though trying to figure out a tough problem. I was unafraid when I should have been puking my guts out. It seemed to bother him. I could still feel fear, but not just now. For the last few nights I'd been working at not feeling much of anything if I could help it. That's why pretty-boy Caine had been so unsuccessful at trying to embarrass me. After what I'd been through, his guff was less than a kiddie game.

We had to pass close to the backstage area to get to the stairs leading to Gordy's office. There was some kind of ruckus going on. The bulk of the gathered crowd of chorus girls, kitchen help, stagehands, and tough guys blocked the view, but I did hear a thump and grunt. The sounds of a basic beating going on, nothing I'd not heard before.

"Now what?" asked Strome. He pushed his way through. At the sight of one of Gordy's lieutenants, looking pissed, most of the people melted off, finding better things to do. A few mugs hung around, including Ruzzo. Both of them. Recovered from the alley dusting, they hadn't noticed me yet.

The hall was more spacious than normal since it served the stage. Dressing rooms opened to it, their doors wide, including the one for the star, Alan Caine. He was pressed against the wall next to it, held in place by Hoyle. His forearm was braced on Caine's chest; his other arm was free and swinging. He landed what was apparently another punch into Caine's breadbasket. Caine *oofed* as all his breath left him, but couldn't double over.

"Hey—what gives?" Strome demanded.

Hoyle barely noticed him. "He owes money."

"So collect after the show, we need him tonight."

"This is just a warm-up, so he knows it's serious." Hoyle started to back off, but I heard a quick march of little trotting steps, and, tricked out in her brief dance costume, Evie the chorus girl burst out of nowhere and jumped onto his back.

"Leave him alone—oh!"

That's as much as she got out before he threw her off. She landed on her perfectly padded duff, stockinged legs all over, and still full of fight.

She rolled and grabbed one of his ankles and pulled, throwing off Hoyle's balance. He staggered, threw a hand on the wall to recover, then hauled back his other foot to kick her.

I don't know how I got into it so fast. I wasn't aware of moving. No decision to take action went through my brain, suddenly I was just there and throwing the punch that took him down. Almost as part of the same movement I bent and lifted Evie, quickly passing her to a startled Strome. Only then did I stop to look around and wonder what the hell . . . ?

Hoyle was quicker on the uptake, realizing a new player had crashed his game. He got up and shook his head like a boxer, fixing his gaze on me. "You—? This ain't your business."

"We don't hit ladies around here," I said.

"Lady? You calling that piece of—"

He didn't finish. My fist derailed his train of thought, knocking him sideways and down like hammering a nail the wrong way. I was holding back, and it was hard going. Something thick and black and vile in me was just short of exploding, and I didn't know where it'd come from. Instinct told me it would be a very bad idea to let it get out.

I flinched when Strome dropped a hand on my shoulder. He flinched in turn when he caught my look, but didn't back off. "Is the show over?" he asked.

Hoyle was on the floor with a bloody nose and likely to stay there for a while. Ruzzo (the elder) bent over him, checking for permanent damage; Ruzzo (the younger) gave me the eye, hand in his pocket where he kept some heavy and no doubt lethal object in place of the gun I'd taken away. Alan Caine had wisely removed himself from the field of combat and stood next to Mitchell, who almost looked curious about the proceedings. Evie, white of face, stared at me. Feeling perverse, I winked at her.

"Yeah, show's over," I said.

Caine stepped forward. "Then someone remove *him*." He indicated Hoyle. "If that fool has damaged my throat, I'll see him in jail. And then I'm suing this place for every penny it's got. To hell with that, I'm suing anyway."

Strome said, "You. Put a lid on it."

"How dare you talk to me that way—I'm the one who pays you."

"Caine"—this from Mitchell, who apparently knew him—"shuddup and go to work before you get a spanking."

Caine's attention shifted quickly, and he grinned. "You'd like that wouldn't you?" He stole the idea from me and winked, too.

Mitchell's eyes sparked murder, but before he could respond, Evie rushed in and took Caine's arm, pulling strongly.

"Come *on*, Alan. Don't waste your time on them. The show's gonna start soon . . ."

He laughed like a jackass, but she was insistent and succeeded in getting him into his dressing room where she could fuss to her heart's content.

She glanced once at me before going in. "Thanks, Mister."

What the hell did she see in that guy besides the pretty face?

Then I caught a whiff of something that froze me out of distracting speculations. Bloodsmell. It was all over my knuckles, Hoyle's blood. Now that there was time to notice, the living scent of it flared through me, abrupt and too harsh to tolerate. I wasn't hungry; it was the memory of a different place strewn with bodies and awash with their blood and mine that made such a strong reaction.

It took a moment, and in that time I was oblivious to everything else, which was damned careless.

It took only a moment, and these were the wrong circumstances to let my mind wander.

Blinking hard, I wrenched back to the present, hoping no one had noticed.

There was a washroom on the left. I pushed my way in and shut the door. Cold, cold water straight from the cold, cold lake. Sluice that over the stained skin, scrub and scrub with the harsh green soap and hope its chemical stink would win out over the bloodsmell.

I suppressed a groan, feeling my corner teeth emerging. I wasn't hungry, dammit. *Not* hungry.

A shudder went through my whole body, and for a second I felt falling-down sick, but kept to my feet by hanging on to the washbasin. Something was *wrong* inside me, and I didn't know what.

I stared at the empty mirror, trying to hold steady. This had happened before. The last time I'd been in the throes of shock and quite insane. Another me had been there then, a me who had been visible in the mirror. He'd been ironically amused by the whole business.

He wasn't here tonight. I had to deal with this alone.

Another tremor started, turning my skin to ice, but I fought it off, panting, though I had no need to breathe. When I got control again I slapped cold water on my face, hardly feeling it for the inner chill. The runoff in the basin was pink.

I was sweating blood. Bad. Very bad.

Knock on the door. Strome's voice. "Mr. Fleming?"

"Yeah, yeah, gimme a minute."

Teeth receding. Good. Water running clear. Better. The fit passing off, leaving me shaken and trying not to shake. I dried and swallowed back the fear, trying and for the most part succeeding in shutting down the emotions. For me more than for anyone else, I couldn't let them see me scared.

The hall was clear, the lights down, and the band out front playing to the now-open club. How long had I been in there? Just Strome and Mitchell were left, the latter looking impatient.

"Trying to put it off?" he asked.

That didn't warrant a reply.

Strome went ahead of us. Mitchell kept close to my heels. We marched through the kitchen, stopping work for a moment as awareness of our presence rippled through the place. The noise picked up again as we reached the back hall, and I trudged upstairs, taking it slow. They seemed steeper than I remembered.

More mugs lounged about the upper floor. I walked the gauntlet. Did everyone in Chicago know about this? I nodded to a few, gathering dark looks or grim curiosity in return. Some respected me, others were like Hoyle and resented the punk kid clumping around in Gordy's big shoes.

Oddly enough, the attention revived a strange kind of confidence inside that I'd not felt in a long, long time. I speculated on whether this surge was what happened at the last moment for some prisoners as they took those final steps to the guillotine.

Probably not.

2

GORDY's office was several times larger than mine and filled with lush furnishings in black leather and chrome. He liked lots of cushioning on stuff sturdy enough to hold his big frame. In contrast to the streamliner-inspired couch and chairs were several wall paintings of soothing landscapes. The vivid greens, blues, and browns were like suddenly discovering a park in the middle of a concrete sea.

There were more guys here, but they moved, clearing my view to Gordy's massive desk. Behind it, sitting easily in the huge chair, was the man I assumed to be Whitey Kroun. He was lean and long-boned and even at a distance I felt a powerful presence about him. I tried not to let Gordy's summing up of "scary" influence me, but it was hard going. What I picked up the strongest came from the men around him. These were some of the toughest guys in the mob, and they were giving Kroun plenty of space.

He focused wholly on me as I crossed the room to stop before the desk. There was a radio on it playing dance music. It was out of place, and I questioned why it was there now, then remembered it was a way of foiling eavesdropping microphones. Some of the smarter guys in the gangs knew that the FBI tapped phones. It was illegal as hell, but still went on. If the phones had wires, then so might the walls. That made Kroun smart or paranoid or both.

I couldn't tell what kind of impression I made. His eyes were warm brown, a solid opposition to the cold cast of his craggy face. He couldn't have been much into his midforties, his brown hair going iron gray except for a surprise streak of silver-white that cut oddly across the left side of his skull, obviously the source of his nickname. He spent a long slow time scrutinizing me, which I imagined was supposed to be unnerving, but I'd long grown immune to that kind of thing.

Certain protocols were to be observed, though. He was the big boss. So as not to let down Gordy in his own place I had to show respect.

"Mr. Kroun." I took off my hat, holding it straight at my side. Humble.

"Fleming," he said. No "mister" in front, but that was all right. I knew his voice, which was deeper for being undistorted by the long-distance wires.

"Glad to meetcha."

"We'll see."

Opening courtesies—such as they were—finished, the guys standing nearest made more space around me. There was one chair square in front of the desk that was evidently to be my very own hot seat. It put about seven feet between me and Kroun, hardly suitable distance for a private conversation. Maybe he was going to go for a public dressing-down. It didn't seem to suit the situation unless he wanted plenty of witnesses to see me killed as an object lesson.

Hoyle and Ruzzo were nowhere in sight for the show, but I spotted Derner, who was the club's general manager and also in charge of the day-to-day running of this mob's business. Since the run-in with Bristow, Derner and I had had discussions over what to say about it. Derner would stick to the script we'd agreed on; it was in his own best interest to let me take the fall for him, too. He'd probably already been questioned thoroughly while I'd been down in the main room. He was projecting total neutrality. Smart guy.

Strome stood off to my left, hands clasped in front of him. Mitchell was behind me.

"Sit," said Kroun. To me.

I unbuttoned my overcoat, put my hat next to the radio, and took the chair. The immensity of the desk was before me, and looking across that dark ocean of wood, I realized that Kroun was not overwhelmed by it; he had a surfeit of authority packed into his lean frame. It wasn't anything physical, but you could feel it coming from him like the low hum a radio gives when the sound is down.

More staring. He was good at it. No one moved. It was disturbing, like being in a zoo cage with a lot of meat-eating animals who'd figured out I was on the menu.

"You're just a kid," Kroun finally said. To someone with his no-doubt colorful past giving him more than enough experience at life and hard times, I would be young—ridiculously young—to have been placed in charge of Gordy's organization.

I lifted one hand a little, palm up. "I've proved myself. Ask them."

Some of the men stirred, possibly reluctant to admit anything in my favor.

Strome jerked his chin. "'S true, Mr. Kroun." That was a surprise. He'd been told to keep shut, the same as Derner. I'd not expected any volunteered support. "He's stand-up."

"Oh, yeah? How so?" Kroun continued to study me, his dark eyes almost hypnotic.

"He took the worst Hog Bristow could dish and came back swinging."

"So I heard. Swung so hard he killed him. The other guys, too."

"Hog went buckwheats on him. I saw. Fleming—"

"Buckwheats," Kroun repeated.

"Yeah. Ugly."

This was news to a few of the men and sparked a whispered reaction among them. Giving a guy the buckwheats treatment was to kill him slow and painful. It was an object lesson, not so much to the victim, but to others who might dare to cross the mob. But sometimes it was for the satisfaction of the killer.

Bristow had thoroughly enjoyed trying to turn me into a permanent corpse. My changed nature had worked against me, keeping me screaming and aware long after a normal man would have found merciful release in death.

I could almost smell my own blood again. I flexed my hands, but they were quite clean and whole, not the skeletal claws I'd used to drag myself across the slick concrete floor to . . .

Bracing inside, I waited for the wave of nausea, for the shakes to return. Now would be the worst, the absolute worst time, for them to hit, so of course they would. There'd be no sympathy from this bunch. They'd see my real face, learn firsthand what Bristow's knife work had done to me. . . .

"What's the matter?" Kroun gave me a narrow look. "You sick?"

"Not much."

I breathed in warm air that smelled of booze, stale smoke, sweating bodies, bay rum aftershave . . . and blood. Not a ghost scent from my imaginings, nor the fresh stuff of a flowing wound, but the muted kind that lurked beneath the skin. It was always present, but I wasn't always aware, like the way you ignore traffic noise. For a few deep and profound seconds it struck me that every one of the tough guys crowding this room, the muscle, the sharps, the thieves, the killers, from Strome to the boss in charge, were all little more than walking bags of blood. I could feed myself sick on any of them. They had no way to expect it, no way to stop me if I made up my mind to do it.

Even the biggest, deadliest, meat-eating predator was my *food*.

So it had proved at the end when I'd killed Bristow.

I held on to that most interesting thought, sat a little straighter, and slowly breathed out again.

Well. How about that? Not one hint of tremor in my whole body. Skating so close to the memory should have had me doubled over and whimpering again, but it was like a switch had been flipped, and I was in control.

For how long I couldn't say.

Kroun still watched me, hardly blinking. "He doesn't look like he's got so much as a stubbed toe."

"He was hurt bad, Mr. Kroun," Strome continued. "Derner saw, too."

"I'm a fast healer," I said.

"Convenient," said Kroun. "What'd you do to get Hog Bristow pissed enough to go buckwheats?"

"Being stand-up for Gordy. Hog jumped things when he shot him out of hand like he did. I stepped in. Hog didn't like it much."

"What'd you think to get out of it by helping Gordy?"

"I wasn't thinking to get anything. I stepped in because that's what you do for friends."

"You had a two-grand hit out on Hog."

"Not a hit. That was a reward for *finding* him, nothing more. If you'll recall, I told you several times over the phone I wanted to keep Hog alive. I knew what kind of trouble it would make if he got killed. But at the end he didn't give me any choice."

Kroun's brown eyes were odd in this light, hard to look at, with strangely dilated pupils like holes into hell. He must have known their effect and used it plenty. "And that may just be something you came up with to cover yourself with me."

"You talked to Derner? Then you know it's what happened."

"Doesn't matter. Someone has to pay for killing Bristow. You're it."

Still behind me, Mitchell shifted, and I felt something pressing cold against my skull. I turned only enough to confirm it was a gun muzzle. One trigger pull and my brains would be all over Gordy's rug.

I nodded. "No problem."

"What?" Must have been a disappointment to Mitchell, me not being terrified. I just didn't give a damn. After surviving Hog Bristow there was little that could scare me these nights. Just myself.

My reply was to Kroun, not the hired help. "I know the rules."

Kroun watched me closely. I still had that strange serenity gripping me. He was food. Walking, talking food.

I smiled at him.

"You think I won't?" asked Kroun.

"You'll do what you have to do. But one question: after I'm gone is Gordy still running things? I'd hate to think I went through all that shit with Bristow, then got scragged by you and it be for nothing."

No one spoke, but another murmur ran through the room about that fine point. I could feel all of them looking at me. Impossible to tell what they might be thinking.

The simple response for Kroun would be something smart-sounding and harsh, but he didn't do it. "You're ready to die?"

I shrugged. "During my time with Bristow I kinda got used to the idea. If you need to kill me, there's nothing I can do to stop you. I just want to make sure Gordy gets something out of it."

His dark eyes flickered once. "You sound like you got an angle to bargain with."

"Maybe."

"What would that be?"

"Nothing you'll want to share with so many ears flapping." Even with the radio to mask most of our talk, there were plenty of listeners at hand. Too many for a paranoid man.

He thought it over. They'd seen Jack Fleming the wiseacre, not the wiseguy, called on the carpet and giving respect to the boss. Kroun had made his point. He shot a look to Strome and signed to Mitchell. The muzzle went away. Strome told the boys to leave.

There were protests from those who knew the best part of the show was about to take place. Others flatly refused, standing firm, arms crossed.

Kroun stood up. There was nothing threatening to his posture, and the lines of his natty brown suit were undistorted by hidden firearms of any size. Many of the guys here were taller or wider or both, but to a man, they fell silent. He didn't make a sound either, just looked at them while the radio blared. He was quite still, just his head moving enough so he could rake them with those intense dark eyes.

Damned if it didn't work. Some grumbled as they left, but they filed out. Derner, Strome, and Kroun's man Mitchell remained.

"Private enough?" Kroun asked. He turned those eyes on me.

"If you trust your guy like I trust Gordy's."

He gave a short grunt. Couldn't tell if it was a laugh. He came around the desk to look down at me. "What's your angle, kid?"

"You. You being smarter than you let on to me over the phone."

"Oh, yeah?" He hitched one hip onto the desk.

"For which I want to apologize. I got a mouth on me, nothing personal. Whenever you called things were running tense on this side, so I was talking short without much time to think things through. But that's changed, and since then I've seen what was going on more clearly."

"Which was . . . ?"

"For starters: why your boy was sent here in the first place. Gordy told me Bristow had powerful friends he'd convinced that he could do a better job of running the Chicago operation. Gordy was expected to hand it over. If he didn't, he'd be killed or in the middle of a gang war. That, Mr. Kroun, was . . . extremely brainless."

"Uh-huh." He wasn't agreeing, only encouraging me to continue.

"You guys had to know Gordy would never roll over for the likes of Bristow. Now it was either New York being stupid and for the hell of it putting him and Gordy in the same pen like a couple of fighting dogs just to see what happens or . . . you had something else going."

"Which was?"

"Playing Hog Bristow to the limit. You sent him out here, apparently to give him what he wants, then Gordy does what he's best at: listening, collecting information. He got plenty out of Hog every night until the guy was too drunk to talk. And all that time Hog is feeling sure of himself because he has New York to back him up and thinks Gordy's got no choice about handing over the operation. But I'm betting that every night Gordy called you up afterward to give you an earful."

"This is what Gordy told you?"

"All I heard from him was the first part, that Bristow takes over or Gordy dies, which struck me as fishy. I went along with it since Gordy's a friend, and the talks were taking place at my club. He probably thought that was all I needed to know. The rest of it . . . well, Hog Bristow was a loudmouthed drunk and dangerously dumb, certainly the worst kind of man to put in charge of anything. Guys like him are a liability and never last long. You either let them go—one way or another—or send 'em someplace where they can't do any harm. But for some reason you couldn't do that with Hog. You had to find a less direct means to bury him. My guess is he's got important relatives protecting him, or he had to know a lot of stuff, damaging, dangerous stuff. The only man you could trust to shake it out of him was Gordy."

"Maybe." There was a subtle change in Kroun. He gave no clue on whether I was hitting home or not, but was listening hard.

"Gordy did his job, but Hog got impatient and frustrated. He set deadlines, forgot them, then set more, but eventually he had enough and made his hit. He wasn't supposed to, but someone back home knew him well enough to gamble he'd sooner or later go over the edge. Gordy must have known that would happen, but not when. The night of the shooting we thought Bristow was too drunk to know which end of a gun to point. Maybe he had one of his boys do it for him, but the result was the same. He'd overstepped the rules and could be considered a legit target in turn."

"Gordy put himself in front of a bullet so as to do all that?"

"He didn't *intend* to get shot; he'd have some alternative planned out, only Hog threw a wrench into the works, surprising everyone. Then I got into the middle of things—"

"Yeah-yeah, and he went buckwheats on you. Except you don't look hurt."

"I'll be glad to show you my scars when the bandages come off. In the meantime, I get a cigar for hitting the bull's-eye."

"Ya think?"

"I know."

"It's a sweet story, kid, but that's not enough of an angle to get you off the hook. We wouldn't like any of it generally known, but blabbing it around won't help you."

"'S nothing I wanna do. Your boy came out to take over this town, and him being stupid got himself and the others killed. Someone's supposed to pay for it. Gordy's in the clear, which is fine with me, so I'm the one who's elected. I get that."

"What if Gordy was the one who set you up from the first to take the fall?"

I laughed out loud. I laughed long and heartily, right in his face. And damn, it felt *good*. "Oh, no. That was my *own* doing. Before I ever got involved, Bristow didn't like my looks, and things went bad from then on with us. If I'd been more on the ball, I might have sidestepped him, but it didn't work out that way, which was my own bad luck. Well, I took it on the chin good and hard, and what I am thinking is that I've *paid* for killing him and his boys. I've paid several times over. What he put me through has to count for something. I survived it; I've earned the right to live."

"If he went buckwheats on you even halfway," said Mitchell, bending close, "you wouldn't be sitting here. And you sure as hell wouldn't have done what you did downstairs." I'd forgotten he was behind me. As if that mattered.

"What happened downstairs?" Kroun asked him.

"He punched out a guy who was getting rough with one of the chorus girls. Never saw anything move so quick."

"*That* was adrenaline," I said. "I paid for it afterward, which is why I was in the john for so long, or did you forget that part?"

Mitchell wasn't buying. "From what we heard Bristow skinned you alive. Even if you got through it, you should still be laid up in a hospital."

"What d'ya want from me? I said I healed fast."

"Prove it."

"Okay. Seeing's believing." I stood and shrugged carefully out of my overcoat as though I were in discomfort and stiff. "Mr. Kroun? In the washroom, if you don't mind. These mugs don't need to gape at the freak show." Without waiting for a yea or nay, I moved slowly toward a door that led to the toilet. I went in, swatted the light on, and stood well out of their view. It was a big room, bright, black-and-white tile, a hefty tub. Gordy occasionally stayed over when work demanded, and he liked his comforts.

In the office the radio volume went up. Loud. Good. We'd have privacy from the boys listening in. Hopefully, they would stay out. All my worst scars were on the inside, but that wouldn't count with this bunch.

After a minute, Kroun came to the door and stepped through. He'd produced or borrowed a gun from someone and held it ready in one hand. Talk about being cautious. He waited, head tilted slightly, and holding very, very still. He didn't need a gun to fill the place with himself.

"Well?"

"No tricks," I said wearily. "Just the truth."

"Which is . . . ?"

"That Bristow chained me upside down from a meat hook and . . ." I stopped there, the words clogged in my throat. Weakness showing. Not something I intended. "Oh, jeez."

"Just show."

I had my suit coat open, but my hands hung straight at my sides as I looked steadily into his eyes. "I want you to *listen* to me, Mr. Kroun. Listen hard . . ."

He wasn't the only one with an effective stare.

It didn't work immediately. He might have had a drink earlier. He stared in puzzled annoyance for a moment as I focused hard on him and kept up the soothing drone that would put him under. Then he gave a small headshake and blinked once, twice, before his eyelids sagged to half-mast. I had him hooked, landed, gutted, cooked, and on the plate. His gun was pointed in the wrong direction, at me. I calmly told him to please put it away, and without fuss he shoved it into a pocket. His eyes were flat and dull. Perfect.

But inside my skull things began to thump badly, a building thunderstorm. I had to make this quick. Very fast and intense, I whispered some choice and vivid word pictures about what damage my torso was supposed to have. Kroun's face went the same color as that white streak in his hair. For a moment I thought he might be sick, which meant I'd overdone it.

"Take it easy," I murmured. "Nice and easy. We're friends now. You remember that. Remember that you look after your friends and help them. Watch out for me, I'll watch out for you. I just want out of this alive and no problems for Gordy, okay? None at all. He's been loyal."

Though positive I could have ordinarily talked him out of killing me, this would speed the process. I was fed up having a death sentence hanging overhead. But the thunder in my brain was starting to boom. Insistent, distracting. I licked my lips and tried to concentrate.

Kroun nodded agreement to my suggestions, his eyes still empty.

I had plenty more to say to him, only it never came out. A pain like nothing I had ever known before blasted through my skull. For the briefest instant I thought I'd been shot, but no one else was with us. Kroun stood motionless and staring. That was the last glimpse I got before the agony doubled me down. I clutched my head with both hands, biting off a cry. They couldn't see me like this. God, what was *wrong*?

The pain rose, tripled, tripled again. My head would explode from the pressure if I didn't—

Then peace, sudden as flicking a switch, plunging me into sweet gray nothingness.

I'd vanished.

Sometimes that happened to me involuntarily when I got too badly hurt to control the reflex. How I'd wished for it when Bristow had been skinning me, but a piece of ice pick buried deep in my back prevented that escape.

This was like heaven after hell. The pain went away, but not the memory or the fear that it might be waiting to fall on me again when I went solid.

I'd have to risk it, though. If the others got too curious and came for a look-see . . . I told myself it would be all right. Vanishing always healed me, bullets, paper cuts, even headaches went away. So it was now.

Melted back slowly. If Kroun was aware he didn't show it, continuing with the empty-eyed gaze into the distance. That was good. Hypnotizing people had always made my head hurt, but the pain had gone way out of hand now. *Why*, though?

Solid again, I moved away and sat on the edge of the tub, biting off the groans because I couldn't afford to give in. But for an awful second I actually felt on the edge of tears. My face twisted, and I rocked back and forth, arms wrapped tight around myself, resisting the urge.

My *body* was just fine. Healing had taken place. The head agony was gone, but inside I was a train wreck.

"God, I'm so tired." I was unaware of speaking until the words were out. I hoped the overly loud radio covered it.

There would be no more evil-eye work for me tonight. Maybe I was too nerved up for it. Kroun would come out of the trance on his own in a few minutes. I'd better use what was left of them.

"Okay, Mr. Kroun. You know Bristow hurt me. I just want to go back to my job and forget any of this ever happened. Keep Gordy in charge and go on your way home and no harm done, okay?" I did not look too directly at him.

He mouthed the word "okay." That's all I needed. The suggestion would last for a few weeks—months, even—after that, if I was lucky, he'd have other things to concern him, shoving out any second thoughts over tonight's "decision."

By the time he surfaced I was pretending to settle my coat and tie back into place. I walked past him into the office and slowly resumed my chair.

Kroun emerged from the washroom after a few moments, face still pretty pale. "He got the buckwheats treatment all right," he announced.

Strome and Derner gave me bleak looks, the closest they could come to sympathy. Mitchell was clearly mystified and stepped in front of me.

"Lemme see."

He got a glare instead. I was careful not to put any power into it.

"Come on."

"No." Absolutely, categorically.

"Boss." He appealed to Kroun.

Kroun waved Mitchell down and sat behind the desk. "Lay off him. That's Hog's work for sure. You don't wanna see, trust me. Fleming, how the hell are you able to walk around like that?"

I eased carefully onto the chair. "I got a good doctor. Jabbed me full of some *great* medicine. It blunts things. It's no circus, but I can do my job. I'm about ready to go for another shot, so if you don't mind, let's wind this up."

"How?"

"Like I said—I've paid for Hog Bristow's death. You can convince New York of that. Go back home, tell 'em I'll finish out my turn at watch nice and quiet. When Gordy's fully on his feet again I'll fade away and just pretend none of this happened. You guys forget about me; everything goes back to normal. Upheavals are bad for business. It's time this one blew itself out."

He thought it over. The new attitude that I'd forced on him would hold firm, but he still had to work out how to square it with whatever orders he'd have from his pals back home. "I should be able to do that."

I hoped so. I didn't want to have to hypnotize every mobster in New York into leaving me alone. It'd kill me. "I would be very appreciative."

"You'll get it. But there's other things I gotta straighten out."

"Name 'em. I'll help if I can."

"Where's Bristow? I need to know."

I glanced at Strome.

"He and the rest are in the lake," he answered.

"The lake." Kroun frowned, and I got the idea he hated watery graves as much as I did. "That's not good. Bodies always float to the surface no matter how much weight you use."

"Not these guys. We know how to do it here so that don't happen."

"And how do you do it here?"

"You get a really big oil drum, bigger than you think you need. Put the guy in it and pour in cement good and tight, no air pockets. The trick is to make sure the cement weighs more than twice what the guy does. You punch a hole in the lid to let the gas escape, then take 'em way far outta sight of land and dump 'em."

"That's the trick?"

"Yeah."

"Huh."

"It helps if you cut the body up and use two drums, three is even better . . ."

"Strome," I said, correctly reading the look on Kroun's face. He'd had enough.

Strome shut it off.

I'd been told in only the most general terms of what he and a couple of other carefully picked cleanup men had done to get rid of Bristow, and wanted to keep it that way. The bodies had been in a meat storage locker, and there must have been butchers' cutting equipment conveniently at hand . . . I gave a headshake to try to jostle that picture out of my mind, with indifferent success.

"Anything else?" I asked Kroun.

"I wanna know about this Dugan bird that you got it in for."

He'd taken his time getting to that one. Hurley Gilbert Dugan, society swan, blackmailer, murderer, kidnapper, and all-round useless bag of poisonous air, held a unique place in my life. He was the one man on the whole planet I wanted dead. I wanted to kill him the way Bristow wanted to kill me. I'd put a bounty on him, and had every gangster in Chicago and beyond looking for him.

"No one's told you?" I would have thought Derner might have filled Kroun in.

"Only that you want him alive, and you'll pay ten grand to anyone bringing him in. That's as much as Hoover put up for Pretty Boy Floyd."

"I didn't know that. The reward on Dugan could be a lot less than ten by now. He took off with that much cash on him. I let the boys know whoever brings him in alive gets to keep what's left, and I'll make up the difference out of my own pocket."

"Why you want him?"

"Personal matter."

"Details. Give."

I pretended a sigh. "Maybe you didn't get word of the society kidnapping case we had here. Gilbert Dugan was the big mastermind, killed some innocent people that didn't need it. He's garbage. I tripped him, made an enemy. It was because of him Hog Bristow was able to get me, so I owe him for that. When Bristow and the others died, Dugan was there. A witness. Neither of us needs him running loose. The cops are looking for him for the kidnap and murders. If they get him first, he could and would try making a deal that puts us all in the clink."

"Dugan saw you kill Bristow?"

"And what they did to me before that. Everything. If you thought Bristow was a liability, then don't meet this guy. He's a thinker. He can talk his way out of just about anything given the chance. He's full of more shit than a goose, but smart. People *trust* him. Even ones who should know better."

"You want him bad."

"Just looking after the company's best interests."

"Why you want him alive?"

"To prevent mistaken identity."

"What do you mean?"

"If the boys found someone who only happened to look like Dugan and killed him . . . not good. I don't want accidents on my watch, so I'm making it worth their while to be careful."

"How long's he been gone?"

"About a week. He could be anyplace." Each night right after waking, my first phone call was to Derner for a report on whether Dugan had been found. So far, no good luck.

"You'll never catch him now."

"I'm hopeful." But I thought Kroun might be right. With his head start, Dugan could be nearly anywhere. If he was ever found, it'd be by accident. "He's got smarts, but not for practical stuff. I heard that Einstein guy wears loafers because he can't figure out how to tie shoes. The same goes for Dugan. All he has to do is hide out in the wrong flop, and one of the boys spots him."

"What'll you do if you get him?"

"Depends on the situation, but . . . I'll maybe need a couple of oil drums."

That amused him. Kroun's frown lines eased a bit. "I'm seeing why you got put in charge."

"It's also because I don't want to keep the job. Gordy knows I won't get attached to it. It won't be for long. He's getting better every day." If he took care of himself. I hoped Adelle had tracked him down and hauled him off to sensibly rest.

"I can offer you another job when this one's done."

This guy was full of surprises. Maybe I'd laid it on too thick about us being friends. "No thanks. I don't belong. That's why some of the guys kicked such a fuss. They know I'm not one of them."

"Oh, yeah, you are." Kroun actually smiled. On him it was damned unnerving. "You just don't know it yet."

WORD of my reprieve spread fast.

By the time I'd wound things up with Kroun, put on my hat and overcoat, shook hands like we were dear old pals, and left, the guys waiting in the hall had either magically vanished or were lying in wait to congratulate me. How they learned was a mystery unless they were the ones with a microphone hidden in the office. Not that it would have worked with the radio on in there and Alan Caine's show playing downstairs.

Or they'd just pressed ears to the door and, when no shots were fired, figured it out.

One of the hall mugs pumped my hand and made to thump my back, but Strome got in between.

"The boss needs to leave," he said, and ran interference for me through the rest of the gauntlet.

Belatedly, I reminded myself that I was still supposed to be healing from Bristow's torture and should act accordingly. Strome was trying to protect my hide from further damage. He must have thought I had a truly amazing painkiller working away. I considered asking him what he thought was going on, but I'd have to hypnotize him afterward. Not worth it. Let him think what he liked.

We emerged from the kitchen entry into freezing night air. It was heavy with damp from the nearby lake and seemed much colder. The wind was up and on the hunt, knifing through my coat. That I was able to notice the chill told me I was tired, the weariness wholly mental and emotional. The interview with Kroun and reaction to the hypnosis had wrung me out, but I'd not been hung up to dry. Not as bad as it could have turned out.

Of course, there were still guys who thought that had been a cheat. Ruzzo, for two.

They were standing by a fat panel trunk parked behind Gordy's car, and their mad must have been pretty serious to keep them out in this wind. Moving like one man, they straightened to face me as I descended the loading dock steps. Strome started to move past, but I stopped him.

"No. It's got to be from me, or they won't learn."

He grunted displeasure toward them and hung back. I could be reasonably certain that he had a hand closed around the gun he kept in his overcoat pocket.

I decided to steal from Kroun's bag of tricks by going up to Ruzzo and stand in place and not say anything. It would get a rise of one kind or another.

"You lettin' him get away with it?" Ruzzo the Younger demanded of me.

The problem with some guys is that they will chew over whatever's bothering them, be extremely familiar with every tiny part, and fully expect you to know exactly what the hell they're talking about when they finally blurt it at you. This was out of the blue. I thought they'd be challenging my right to be their boss.

"Let who get away with what?" I asked patiently.

"That singer you're soft for. He owes."

"Yeah, owes," echoed the Elder. "You make bets and lose, you pay the markers."

Cripes, I should send them off to Tierra del Fuego to breed wombats. "Not my business," I said.

"You stopped Hoyle from doin' his job."

I'd have to use small words with these two. "Hoyle can collect from him *off* the premises—after Caine's done his act. If Caine can't sing, he can't pay."

"That's bullshit."

Dangerous words in this gathering, meant as a challenge; I couldn't let them go by. "You're calling me a liar," I carefully informed him. Them. I hoped theirs was a very small family.

"The singer *owes*. You talk to Hoyle. He'll tell you. You don't know everything."

"Neither does Hoyle."

"*He's* the boss on this."

"Sez him. I'm running things, not Hoyle."

"Sez you." Ruzzo grinned. Both of them.

Then they stopped being there. Both of them.

I couldn't understand it. Had the night swallowed them up? Were they like me and had disappeared into thin air? What the hell . . . ?

I was lying on my face on cold metal, which was moving under me. Rumbling through my body was the throaty noise of a truck motor going at a good clip.

Ow. Head pain. Not right.

What the hell . . . ?

Ow. Bad now, very bad.

What the hell? Again.

I repeated that several times, eventually working out that I'd been bushwhacked. While Ruzzo kept me distracted someone must have come up behind and . . . ow . . . yes, the back of my head. A familiar tenderness, bruising, and a knot. That's where he'd got me. With wood. *Had* to be wood. It was the only thing that could put me out without causing me to vanish. So . . . was it dumb luck or had someone known what would work?

Strome? Sure, he was a killer, but he had no reason to lay me flat. Unless he had special orders from Kroun. But I'd neutralized the threat.

Hoyle. Much more likely. He wasn't the forgiving type, not that I'd have apologized to him for busting him one over the dancer. He and Ruzzo were shoulder-to-shoulder apparently. Against me. Despite Gordy. Despite Kroun.

Oh, hell. This crap I didn't need.

▲
3
▼

I blinked against blackness. Very little light filtered through the painted-over rear door window, just enough for me to ascertain I was alone in the back of the panel truck that had shared the alley with Gordy's

Cadillac. No one had bothered tying me up. Chances were, after clobbering me they noticed I wasn't breathing and assumed I'd been killed. Which would leave them with a body on their hands. Better to get rid of me and delay the news of my death than have someone from the Nightcrawler's kitchen staff stumbling over the corpse a few minutes later.

Feeling queasy, I thought of how Strome had sunk Bristow and his boys in the water to lose them. Nope. That wasn't going to happen to me. I'd had too much of that damned lake already.

When I felt steady enough to get up I damn near cracked my head on the low ceiling. Not much space in here for a tall guy. On hands and knees I worked over to the windows, finding my hat along the way. My head wasn't to the point of supporting that much weight yet. Hell, even my hair was too heavy. I folded the thing and stuffed it in a pocket, glad it wasn't one of my fancier fedoras. Lately I'd taken to wearing only my second- and even third-best clothes, fearing (rightly) that something like this situation might drop itself on me like a net. If I didn't take things in hand with these mugs, I'd end up with a pawnshop wardrobe.

I pulled out my keys, using one to scrape away paint from a corner of the window. When I had a peephole I looked through.

Not a lot to see. Flat, snow-crusted fields. Farm country. How long had I been out? I held my watch up to the feeble light. An hour? The way I felt it had to be more than that. The watch still ticked, though, the time correct. No one at my club would miss me until closing, which was in the wee hours. It was still well on the right side of midnight, though to me it felt much later.

The rumbling changed in tone as the driver made a sharp turn. The truck shook like an earthquake, indicating unpaved road. I braced, holding on to a length of wood bolted to the metal side. Damned wood. Why couldn't they have just shot me? It'd have ruined a suit, but I could have taken care of them back in town. Idiots. Both of them. And Hoyle.

I deliberated about vanishing and sieving through to the front compartment to surprise the driver.

Not at this speed. The peephole showed an undistinguished country lane of frozen churned mud that made the truck bounce and skid erratically. This kind of road at this time of year tolerated sturdy vehicles going no more than ten miles an hour, if that much. We were moving considerably faster. I didn't care to be in a crash and have to walk home.

And if we were an hour's drive from Chicago, meaning a *long* walk, then I wouldn't be seeping my way out the back to escape, either. If my luck ran bad—and lately I had no reason to expect different—I'd have to improvise shelter from the sun. That meant spending the day away from my home earth, which meant I'd be a prisoner of whatever nightmares my brain threw out. After Bristow's work on me, it'd have plenty of horrors to draw upon. No, I wouldn't put myself through that. Better to wait until we stopped, then hijack the truck, leaving *them* stranded.

And roughed up. A lot. Yeah, I liked that idea.

We slowed somewhat. I took another look out the back. Lots of snowy acreage, twin furrows of tire tracks leading back the way we'd come and . . . headlights in the distance. Someone following? Maybe it was Hoyle in his own car, taking it easy to keep from breaking an axle. I'd break his head given the chance.

A shift in the gears and the truck's voice. Slowing even more, then finally coasting to a stop.

We were in an open yard by a low metal barn. A single electric light burned bluely against the dark. It was on a tall, lonely pole under a shade shaped like a Chinese hat. The cone of light from the oversized bulb covered a wide area before the barn. A car was already there, and four men emerged from it. One of them opened the trunk and handed out . . . what? . . . baseball bats? . . . to the others.

The truck doors in front slammed shut almost in unison, and Ruzzo joined their friends getting something swingable. They must have thought I was still alive, then, or they'd have been hauling me out instead.

I'd heard about this kind of send-off. Find a deserted spot for some batting practice on some poor son of a bitch, then either leave what's left in the cornfield for Farmer Jones to find come harvest, or make a shallow grave in the stalks. It was too late in the season for that; harvest was long over and the ground frozen, but they might not care. Just leaving me under a drift of snow would be enough until spring. Scavenging animals would do what they were best at and . . .

Shut the hell up, it's not going to happen.

The star-filled gray sky layered the surrounding landscape in a silvery sheen, turning it to day for me. In that soft dream-glow the electric light sparked brighter than a diamond. So, just how would I take out half a dozen guys armed with something that could actually stop me? One at a time? Sounded good.

A car horn blared in the distance. The six men all looked back the way we'd come, their attention on the approaching headlights I'd seen. Just how big a party was this?

Well, since they were distracted . . .

I vanished and slipped out under the door. A smooth, invisible tearing over open ground to the count of five, then I slowed to wash gently against the very solid side of the tin barn. Jeez, this was perfect. I glided on, keeping the flat surface of the barn's wall on my left, reaching an opening, and going in. An instant later I was solid again, standing upright in brisk freezing air I barely felt. I was in time to take in the show.

Hoyle, Ruzzo, and four other guys I knew by sight were less than twenty feet away. The start of a nice little gang.

The second car was Gordy's Cadillac. It braked majestically; the motor cut. Strome got out. He didn't look too good, seemed to carry himself gingerly. Though he wasn't obviously showing it, I got the impression he was pissed off.

"Hoyle," he said, by way of greeting.

Along with a baseball bat, Hoyle had a gun ready in his other hand. "What the hell are you doin' here?"

Strome would be armed, but made no move for his shoulder holster and the semiauto .45 he kept there. He looked around the yard, probably for me. My broken body was not lying out in the snow. Was *he* in on this? When Gordy got shot Strome had been more than ready to leave for greener pastures, but I couldn't think why he'd throw in with Hoyle.

Hoyle repeated the question. He tossed the bat to one of his men, who caught it neatly and held it ready to use.

Strome was able to summon some cold-eyed threat to pass around, enough so four of the mugs backed off a few steps. He was still one of Gordy's lieutenants, after all. "Whatever you're doing here, you stop."

"Not doing nothing, Strome. Just a little batting practice." Hoyle's smile was ugly. There was nothing specifically wrong with it, and that's why it made my back hairs rise.

"You boys pack it up and go back, and I won't say nothing to the boss."

"Which boss? Gordy or Fleming?"

"The boss what's in charge. The boss who will see you here next if you cross him." He nodded toward the group in general.

Hoyle and some others snorted. "Fleming, then. We don't take orders from that punk bastard."

Strome went patient, reverting to ingrained habit. "Gordy put him in charge. Every one of you knows that. Ain't for us to argue with Gordy."

"Yeah-yeah. *If* we can believe that it was Gordy who said so. All we know is what you and Derner let drop, and you guys got plenty reason not to rock the boat."

"So do you. You mess up on this—"

"Aw, screw it. You wanna run errands for that punk creep, fine, but we got regular business to do, an' it's gonna get done. Gordy'll agree with me on this, and the hell with Fleming."

They'd formed a rough half circle around Strome, but it was ragged, with four of the guys having drifted outward. Their collective attention was on him. I hoped he was deadpan enough to not react as I stepped clear of the barn.

If he did, I got too busy to notice, swiftly coming up behind the nearest man holding a baseball bat. I pulled it casually from his hand, slammed a left into his jaw as he turned, then swung the bat smartly into the next guy's gut. Both men dropped just that fast, and I rounded on another, giving him a low and mean bunt just under his rib cage. Half the opposition now lay on the snow, either unconscious or gasping for air. Hoyle had been alert for trouble, though, and spun with his gun raised. A joyous sneer lit up his narrow mug as he recognized me. I had a perfect view directly up the short barrel of his gun. At ten feet it was a cannon.

He immediately fired, point-blank. Three shots as quick as he could pull the trigger.

He had good aim, holding the muzzle steady on my unmoving form, the sound sharp yet toylike under the wide sky. The smoke was swept away by the icy wind, and for a few crucial seconds I had to fight its force to keep from being carried off as well. I'd surrendered just enough solidity so the bullets passed right through my near-ghostly body, spanging hollow into the barn's tin walls behind. Being just outside the nimbus of the light, I gambled that I could get away with such a risky stunt in front of witnesses.

Strome belatedly grabbed Hoyle's arm, and they wrestled and danced, cursing. The remaining two guys, Ruzzo, stared at me, probably because I should have been falling down and wasn't. Instead, I charged them, yelling and swinging the bat and moving a hell of a lot faster than anything they'd ever remotely experienced. Then they were also on the ground with their friends, not being any further problem.

I stepped into Strome and Hoyle's rumba and plucked the gun clear before Hoyle could shoot either of them. That didn't stop his fighting. My cracking one of his legs with the bat did. He broke off fast with a high scream, clutching his shin. It wasn't broken, but the bone would be bruised. I'd felt the impact through the length of the bat and judged he'd be limping for a week. Good payback for the knock he must have landed on me earlier.

"You summabitch, you busted—ah, Jesus God!"

He went on like that for a while, loudly expressing pain and outrage. Strome, huffing to get his breath back, kept an eye on him while I made the rounds of the others. One of them was recovered enough to fumble for his gun, but I whacked his wrist with the bat, then tapped him lightly on the forehead. Lightly for me, anyway. He hit the snow and stayed there. It was obvious they were in no condition for a counterattack.

I shoved Hoyle's gun into my belt. The barrel was hot. It struck me then just how quick he'd been to shoot. There'd been no hesitation, no thought of the consequences to hold him back from killing me. He either had a grudge on that was beyond restraint or must have done his thinking beforehand and made up his mind then what to do if we ever crossed. I barely knew the guy, so it was disturbing to have inspired such a reaction in a stranger, but not unexpected given this kind of work.

Hoyle sat flat in the snow, clutching his leg, still cursing, but in a lower, more dangerous voice. Having passed through the initial agony, his invective was for me, not his pain. His threats were basic and brutal and nothing I'd not heard before from other guys. He was a rangy, long-boned specimen whose loose-jointed manner of walking might be mistaken for clumsiness, but he was one of the rare ones who could instantly pull himself in quick and tight to surprise an overconfident opponent. I'd heard from Gordy that Hoyle had been in the ring about ten years back, but got thrown out because of a betting scandal. It left him soured on boxing, but he'd never forgotten his training and still looked fit and granite-solid. Strome had taken a hell of a chance mixing with him.

I looked down at Hoyle. He shot pure hatred right back. I grabbed hunks of his overcoat and hauled him up. He piled an iron fist into me. It was a short swing; he didn't have enough room to really get behind it, but sheer muscle made the blow sufficiently powerful to send anyone else reeling. I took the impact like a heavy workout bag, swaying a little, but not really moved. Before he could go for a second punch I lifted him right off his feet and thumped him bodily against the truck. Several times. I'm tall, but on the lean side. I don't look to have the kind of muscle to deal so easily with a 200-pound man. It stole the fight out of him and, once he shook his head clear, had obviously surprised him. Apparently Hoyle wasn't used to being thrown around.

He smothered his shock with glowering resentment but didn't attempt any more punches.

"You," I said, holding him upright, "are annoying me. Which means you are annoying Gordy."

"Go ahead and tell 'em, I ain't afraid of Gordy."

"Then you damn well better be afraid of me." I emphasized my words by smacking the side of his head with the flat of my hand. It must have made his ears ring, for his eyes went dull for a few seconds. I waited until he was able to pay attention again. "Gordy put me in charge for a reason. He knew I'd be able to squash bugs like you with no problem if there's a good enough excuse. You've given me a hell of an excuse with this stunt."

"You are screwing up business! That singer shit owes me money!"

"So beating him to death will get it for you?"

"It's to learn others!"

I cracked him again. "School's out. Gordy put me in charge to hold things, and I am holding things until he's back full-time. Everyone else is clear on that except you and these gutter bums. Your second mistake was going after me. You got one chance to stay alive. Get clear of town by morning."

"Or what?"

"Or I take you and all your apes apart like a Sunday chicken, only slower, and they'll be finding your bones over these fields from now until next year's harvest."

He held to a snarling expression, but his eyes flickered. He must have picked up from my voice that I was being literal.

"You got lucky, Hoyle. You didn't kill anyone, so I don't have to kill you. But I *am* annoyed. If I get even a hint that you're only just *thinking* about being stupid again, you will be walking on stumps. Now pick these saps off the mat and stay outta my way."

"Or what, you tell Gordy?" He'd reduced serious business down to schoolyard-level snitching.

Logic would never work on him, only pain. I knew a lot about pain. I hit him again, plowing tough into the hard shell of his middle. A strike from a bare fist is different from the boxing gloves he'd been used to; the force is more concentrated. Some men hold back to spare their hands. That wasn't anything I needed to worry about. I stopped short of rupturing his insides, but only just.

"Or," I said, talking quietly right into his ear, "*I* will kill you, Hoyle."

He was doubled down, and when he managed to suck in air, it came out again as profanity. Weak-sounding, though. No breath for it.

Couldn't let him get away with even that much. I dragged him up again and pulled his gun from my belt. He favored a revolver. I clapped it against the side of his skull to get his attention, then shoved the muzzle into his nose.

"I will kill you, Hoyle. Same as you just tried on me—only I won't miss."

To drive the point home, I threw him on the ground and quick-fired close to his head, using up the remaining three bullets. The gun didn't seem to make any sound at all, but for Hoyle it must have been a hell of a roar. Arms up, he convulsed away from where the lead struck snow inches from his face, then held still, staring at the gun, not me. He must have known it was empty, but a jolt like that is not easily shrugged off.

"What will I do, Hoyle?"

Trembling, he looked up blankly.

"*What will I do?*"

"Y-you'll kill me," he whispered.

"You're gonna remember that every time you think of me, every time you say my name, every time you *hear* my name, that's what you will remember. I will kill you."

I broke the gun open, tipping the cylinder clear. Shell casings rained out. Grasping it in one hand and the frame in the other I gave them each an opposing twist that hurt even my hands, but it was worth it. The metal held for a second, then abruptly snapped. I dropped both pieces on either side of the astonished Hoyle.

"*Every* time."

I slouched across the Caddy's backseat for the return trip to Chicago, a strange reprise of how the evening had started, just a different mood. Playing tough was getting easier the more I did it, but afterward the reaction would set in, leaving me surly and almost as torn up inside as the people I'd leaned on. Of course, I couldn't show any of that to Strome. My breaking the gun in two had breached even his expressionless reserve, and I didn't want to lose what awed respect had been gained. Not that I didn't already have it in spades.

I wanted Gordy on his feet again real soon. Some number of the boys in the gang were like Hoyle, resenting an outsider giving them orders, but they'd behaved themselves out of respect for Gordy. That Hoyle had a grudge against me for taking the big chair wasn't news, but he'd given no hint till now about making an open challenge. It wasn't only against me but Gordy as well, which was a few miles past stupid, but brains were in short supply for some of them. Hoyle had thrown down the glove, mob style, and I'd beaten him silly with it. Would that and my promise of death be enough to hold him in place?

"Is Hoyle going to be smart?" I asked Strome, interrupting the long silence of the drive.

Strome didn't answer right off, which boded ill. He thought it over a while. "He might."

"But . . . ?"

"He might not." He gave a minimal shrug, which reminded me a lot of Gordy. "He could get over his scare and try something else. You shoulda scragged him. Or at least sent him onna vacation like you done others."

I had a reputation for persuading stubborn people to do very unlikely things, like suddenly running off to Havana. None was aware they'd been forcibly hypnotized. It was part of my edge. I used it to get out of troublesome situations, like earlier tonight with Kroun. But after that head-busting agony I wasn't about to try anything fancy so soon. Hoyle wasn't worth the pain. I'd broken the gun to keep from breaking him. Which I could have done all too easily. It's a frightening thing to find out what one is capable of when the restraints are gone. Hog Bristow taught me that.

"Keep an eye on Hoyle," I said. "See to it he leaves town and have someone keep tabs where he goes and what he does when he arrives. If you think he'll step out of line, I wanna know before he does. The same for his goons. You tell me, and we'll take it from there. If I'm not available, use your best judgment and take care of 'em yourself."

"Right, Boss."

"And don't get caught."

"Right, Boss."

It was just that easy to put a death sentence on people. God, what had they twisted me into? I wasn't supposed to be like this. I was a normal guy with parents in Cincinnati, friends, a girlfriend, my own business. I liked flashy clothes, reading dime magazines, and was trying to turn myself into a writer one of these nights. So what that I was also a vampire? Killing people wasn't part and parcel with the condition. Hell, I didn't even have to kill to eat, just drain a little blood from cattle that could spare it . . .

Bad line of thought, that. Head it off. Quick.

"Strome. What happened back at the club? How'd you know where to go?"

"One of 'em clobbered me from behind, only he didn't make a good job of it. Knocked me down but not out. I saw them toss you in the back of the truck, then some piled into a car with Hoyle and took off. Good thing it was Ruzzo driving the truck, too."

"Why's that?"

"They got into a fight over who'd drive. By the time they figured it out I was able to get up and into Gordy's car. Then I just followed."

"You did good, Strome. Thanks."

"No problem."

"Your head bad?"

"I'll live. How'd you get outta the truck?"

I stole the idea from him. "With Ruzzo driving? I just let myself out when we stopped. I kept low. They didn't see a thing."

Thankfully, he accepted it. He nodded. "Before all that, I was gonna say something to ya about Mitchell. That you should look out for him."

"Oh, yeah?"

"He didn't like what Kroun did. Letting you off."

Mitchell had been poker-faced and then some through the whole session. The only time he showed anything was when I refused to display my war wounds. Such as they weren't. "How could you tell?"

"Used to see him around. Here. Back when Slick Morelli ran the business."

I did my damnedest not to react. Morelli had been one of the bastards who helped murder me. "How far back was that?"

"Couple years. When Gordy took over, Mitchell left for New York. He didn't mind being third fiddle when Slick was in charge, but he wouldn't stand for being second fiddle to Gordy."

Strome was revealing new depths. I never thought the man was so musically inclined. "He was that high up? Third in line?"

"He was in there, but mostly in his own head."

"Was Mitchell ever up for Slick's job?"

"Not that I heard. There was a hell of a mess with Slick and Lebredo suddenly both gone, but Gordy stepped in and kept things smooth, and that's what the big bosses wanted. No waves. Mitch didn't like how it turned out, so he moved to greener pastures."

So there was a very good possibility that Mitchell remembered me from then, which might better explain his initial reaction. It wasn't my looking young, but that I was the same Fleming who'd been around when Slick Morelli and Lucky Lebredo killed each other.

That's how we made it *look*, anyway.

I didn't specifically remember Mitchell from my encounter with Morelli's gang. Aside from Gordy, who was too big to ignore, I hadn't paid much attention to the muscle. The most I could say now was that

Mitchell probably hadn't been one of the guys who actually crowded me at the time, though he might have been on the fringes looking on.

"Gordy can tell you plenty on him," said Strome. "More than me. He knows the real dirt."

Gordy could have mentioned something when we'd been talking in the casino. On the other hand he hadn't been feeling so well. He couldn't think of everything, and when Mitchell arrived it'd been too late to give me a heads-up. Then again, Gordy might have held back so my attention would be on Kroun, not his lieutenant and bad memories about my own murder.

"So I should keep an eye on Mitchell?"

"I was just sayin' he didn't like what happened up there. Don't see what diff it should make to him. It's just something to know."

"You talk like Gordy."

He took it as a big compliment, nodding. "Thanks. You worked it okay with Kroun. I didn't think you'd get out alive."

"Neither did I."

"Sure you did. You knew before going in you'd walk clear. I could tell. I thought you was wrong, but you knew."

"The power of positive thinking."

"Maybe. But you got Kroun on your side pretty fast. He's seen men hurt before. Looking at what Bristow did to you ain't gonna bring a guy like him out in hearts and flowers. How'd you do it?"

I gave a minimal shrug like I'd seen Gordy do a hundred times. "There was stuff going on under the talk. I could see Kroun didn't want me killed. That would create more problems he didn't want to bother with. He just needed a reasonable way out and took the one I offered."

"Who'da thought it?"

Me. Just now.

"Radio," I said, not wanting more questions. "Put it on."

"Got it."

Strome turned the knob and fiddled the tuning until I said stop when he found a comedy. We listened to the remaining ten minutes of Jack Benny. The stuff was funny enough that Strome actually smiled once. I thought his skin would buckle and crack under the strain.

I lay back, well out of range of the rearview mirror, and shut my eyes against the growing brightness of Chicago. The jokes and puns and sound effects washed over me, and I didn't have to think about anything.

I couldn't sleep, of course, not until sunrise, and then it's a different kind of sleep, a shutdown of everything, dreamless, silent, too peaceful to last. I longed to be able to voluntarily conk myself out like that whenever I wanted, but the night wouldn't let me go.

The next program was longhair music, so I had Strome find a station with another comedy going. It was good to hear familiar tinny voices talking about ridiculous situations that had nothing to do with my own personal disasters. I was too isolated inside myself to be able to appreciate the humor just yet, but maybe in a couple weeks . . .

Or months. A couple years. Maybe never. But could I live with never?

My girlfriend, Bobbi, one of the reasons I was still more or less sane after Bristow's damage, would have something unsympathetic to say about that kind of thinking. She had plenty of caring for me, but no patience for self-pity. It was sometimes hard to know the difference between it and honest pain. I used Bobbi's probable response to my unspoken thoughts as a way of keeping the balance. Angst or honesty? Hell, she'd just tell me to flip a coin about it, then walk away from the result without looking.

Sensible gal, my Bobbi.

We were well into Chicago when the comedy ran out, replaced by a weather report. The announcer mentioned sleet, which roused me enough to look outside. Yeah, nice and wet and miserable, cold, but not to the point that the frozen rain glazed the streets yet. The stuff was smaller than rice grains, ticking gently against the windows, clinging for a moment, melting, sliding down, gone. This was a night to be inside next to a fire. I could arrange it, but couldn't trust that the thoughts keeping me company would be the warm and cozy kind.

I asked Strome to find another radio show. A broadcast of *The Shadow* was on, so we listened to it. I liked that guy. Life was simple for him. All his troubles could be solved by clouding a man's mind or shooting him— the kind of stuff I'd fallen into—but Lamont Cranston always made a fresh start with each episode. He didn't have to think about consequences to himself or others in between or carry them along all the time with him like a lead suitcase full of bricks.

We headed north a few blocks until I directed Strome to go east.

"You wanting Escott's place?" he asked.

My occasional partner's office was in the right area. Close enough. It didn't surprise me that Strome knew the location of the business. "Yeah, there."

The Caddy had special modifications to support the extra weight of the bulletproof windows and armor, but you could tell from the ride there was something different about the car, especially the heavy way it had of taking corners. That gave a nice feeling of security. Escott's Nash was similarly smartened up, but not to this degree. I'd have to take him for a ride in this one while the opportunity was available and watch his reaction.

Despite the fact the car was half tank, Strome took short cuts, moving quick enough for the evening traffic because of the powerful engine. It swilled gas and oil like a drunk guzzling cheap hooch, but daily stops at a filling station seemed an even trade for the smooth running and safety.

There seemed to be a lot of stop signals, and they were all against us. Being a man of careful, attention-avoiding habits Strome didn't miss any of them or go over the speed limit. He braked in midblock before the stairs leading up to the Escott Agency.

This was where my friend ran a business that was a close cousin to private investigation, though Charles W. Escott insisted he was not a detective but a private agent. He sometimes referred to himself as a glorified errand runner, doing odd jobs for people who would rather not touch the chore themselves. The private-agent angle earned him a living, and I helped him out on cases when he needed it.

I got out, walking around to the driver's side. The sleet dotted my back.

"I'll be a while," I told Strome. "Doctor's appointment." Whether he believed that excuse or not didn't matter. The abuse I'd taken tonight certainly justified my going in for treatment.

"You want I should circle the block?"

All the parking spaces were filled by local residents. "Yeah. Do that. Take your time."

"Right, Boss."

"Just a sec—find a phone and call Lowrey. Gordy will want to know how things went with Kroun."

"He'll already know."

"Oh, yeah?"

"One of the boys will have told him by now. Maybe Kroun himself."

"That's fine, then."

"What about telling him about what Hoyle tried with you?"

"It's not important enough. Derner should know, then maybe tomorrow for Gordy. Let the man rest."

"Right, Boss."

Strome took himself away, bits of paper and stray leaves kicking around in the departing Caddy's exhaust. Midnight was still in the future, but the street was wee-hours empty. The neighborhood was mostly small businesses, marginal manufacturing, and cheap flats. Few of the shops were open much past eight, except for an all-night drugstore in the next block and the nearby Stockyards.

Once the Caddy made its turn at the corner to head north again, I walked south, cutting over a couple streets until the lowing of cattle added a somber note to the night wind. Their accompanying stink made for a whole nasal symphony, though the freezing weather mitigated the worst of that. Breathing wasn't a habit for me, but I could still take in a potent whiff of concentrated wet barnyard when the motion of walking caused my lungs to pump all on their own.

I went invisible some distance from the first fence, floating purposefully forward and sieving through, holding on to the sweet and easy grayness until I was well inside. My corner teeth were out when I went solid again. After an anxious, dry-mouthed moment to find a likely animal, I ghosted into the holding pen. A last quick look to make sure I was unobserved, then I literally tore into my meal.

I couldn't feel much of the cold, but I was totally aware of the living heat swarming into me. The cow made a protesting sound but held still. Its blood pulsed fast and strong. Maybe I'd bitten too deeply; it could bleed to death afterward. That hardly mattered since it was headed shortly for slaughter anyway. I was just one more confusing, frightening incident in its horrific trip from pasture to plate.

Feeding doesn't take me long, even when I'm hungry, but I stretched it out. There seemed a boundless supply in that open vein, so I took more than I needed, filling up forgotten corners until it hurt.

Then I fed some more. Far more. Gulping it down.

Fed. Until it was an agony.

Fed. Until it was *past* agony.

And then beyond that.

When I finally broke off and reeled away I had to grab the fence to keep my feet. I held on like a drunk, head sagging, brain spinning, as the red stuff billowed through my guts at hurricane force. For a second I teetered close to vomiting, but the urge passed, and my belly gradually settled into sluggish acceptance of the awful glut.

I heard someone groaning nearby and snapped my head around to find him before realizing I was the guilty party. What a terrible sound it was, of pleasure and pain chasing each other in a tightening circle, neither one winning, neither one stopping, both leaving me exhausted and nerved up at the same time.

This, I told myself for the umpteenth time, was not good.

Down in a dark little cavity within, in a sad, chilly place I didn't like looking into but could never forget about, clanged the weary and terrifying alarm of what was happening.

The blood kept me alive.

And the blood was *killing* me.

4

NEON lights, streetlights, warm lights from house windows, cold lights hovering meekly in doorways, and no lights at all in some patches, Strome drove us past a myriad of such beacons of city life until we reached the fiery red diamond-shaped windows of Lady Crymsyn, my nightclub. As soon as we paused in front a man was there opening the car door for me. I stepped out, protected from a thin sleet by the entry's arched red canopy. I greeted the doorman, then bent for a last word to Strome.

"See how things are going with Hoyle and phone me. If I'm not in my office, ring the booth downstairs. I'll be here the rest of the night."

"You sure?"

"What d'you mean?"

"You don't look so good."

I didn't expect that. Not from him. "I'm fine."

Pushing away from the Caddy, I barely gave the doorman time to do the other half of his job. He moved quick, though, ushering me inside, then came in after. Some places insisted on having a guy stand his whole shift out in the cold, but I didn't see the point. Just as many customers would go out as came in, and so long as he did his job he could decide for himself where he wanted to be.

Wilton was busy at the lobby bar setting drinks before a newly arrived foursome, and nodded a greeting my way. There was a concerned look on his face, too. He'd been getting ready to open when Strome came to take me away.

I tossed the greeting back and asked how things were going so Wilton would know I was none the worse.

"Slow, but a good crowd for the weather," he replied.

"Any sign of Myrna?" Myrna used to be a bartender here long before I bought the place. Now she was a ghost. I didn't have anything to do with causing that.

"Not yet." Wilton was the only guy here who didn't mind working the front by himself. He liked Myrna even if she did switch the bottles around. "Whoops—spoke too soon."

"What d'ya mean?"

He pulled out a bowl of book matches and put it on the bar. Instead of being in orderly rows, neatly folded to show red covers with the club's name in silver letters, they were all opened wide and tossed every which way.

"Guess she got bored," he said, looking bemused.

"Ask her if she won't put 'em back right again."

"If she likes 'em that way, who am I to argue?"

The hatcheck girl came to take my things, but I waved her off, heading for the stairs and my office. I'd left a stack of work there a few ice ages ago.

From the short, curving passage that led into the main room came Bobbi's clear strong voice. She was doing a better job with "The Touch of Your Lips" than Bing Crosby could ever hope for. I paused next to the easel display for her. It held a large black velvet rectangle where her name glittered from silver cutout letters, surrounded by four stunning pictures of her, none of them doing her justice.

A second, similar display proclaimed the dancing talents of Faustine Petrova and Roland Lambert with an art poster of two stylized dancers locked together. It was surrounded by a half dozen stark black-and-white photos of them frozen in action. Classy stuff.

The third easel had a single dramatic portrait of Teddy Parris, a young guy Bobbi had discovered when he delivered a singing telegram to her. His long face and soft eyes were better suited to comedy, but he'd gone for a serious expression and gotten away with it. Silver stars fanned out around his picture, filling up the blank space since he could only afford to have the one photo done. Along with his name was an additional description identifying him as "Chicago's greatest new singing sensation!"

Well, most advertising exaggerated one way or another. He was good, though, or Bobbi wouldn't have given him a break.

Bobbi finished her set for the moment. She would wait backstage while Teddy came out to earn his keep, then join him in a duet they'd worked up.

I wasn't sure how much to tell her about why I'd missed the first show. Certainly I would let her know what had happened with Kroun, the question was just how detailed to get and if I should mention Hoyle and Ruzzo. Lately I'd been doing too much that I wasn't proud of; she understood that the rough stuff was often a necessary evil, but she didn't need to hear about everything.

She would know, though. If even Strome noticed how bad I looked, then Bobbi would see red flags and hear sirens.

I plodded upstairs.

The office lights were on, as they usually were, since they didn't always stay switched off. Myrna liked to play with them. She used to make me uneasy, but no longer. I had other spooks to wrestle with, truly scary ones. Like what I'd done to myself at the Stockyards. My body still hurt from the excess.

For all the vanishing activity in dealing with Hoyle I had not grown hungry, having fed only the night before. But I'd given in to I didn't know what demon and gorged myself to the point of sickness. In the hurried walk from Escott's street to the Stockyards I'd not thought to stop, turn aside, or even consider that feeding like that might be a really bad idea. I did it without thinking, the same as Hoyle when he shot at me. At some past point he must have known that killing me would bring down Gordy's full wrath, and yet he'd done it anyway.

So what horror would drop on me if I didn't shape up and get control of myself?

What if it dropped on someone else instead of me? If I . . .

Inside, the excess blood seemed to churn, thick and heavy.

The radio would help. I wanted other voices besides the nagging ones in my head. Turning the set on, I shed my overcoat, tossing it and the crumpled hat on the long sofa.

Then I paced, impatient for the tubes to warm up, for distraction to intervene. My skin felt like it was on inside out.

An unfortunate picture to conjure, the kind that bunched my shoulders up around my ears. I tried forcing them down. But the thought of blood and pain and screaming and a sadist's laughter—

Don't start. No more of this . . . no more . . .

I told myself not to listen to the echoes, to ignore, to hold on a little longer, and above all, not to scream. There was no actual pain, but the memory of the agony was enough to shred reason and sheet my eyes with blinding tears. Then I doubled over, hugging myself tight against a wave of uncontrolled shivering. It clamped around me like a giant's fist, shaking, shaking.

This time I was not cold. Far from it. The blood in me was fever-hot, and there was too much of it. My body seemed bloated to the point of bursting. Crashing just short of the sofa, I lay helpless and praying for the fit to pass, unable to control my limbs twitching and thumping against the floor. As before in the Stockyards I heard an alien noise; this time it was the sad keening whimper of a suffering animal.

And as before it was me, myself, and I.

Gulping air I didn't need, I wheezed and puffed like a living man and labored through the worst as it slowly passed. At least I'd not given in to the urge to scream. Knowing that there were people downstairs who could hear and come running might have tipped things. I must not be too crazy then, not wanting them to see me like this. Crazy enough, though.

Scared, too. Scared sick.

The radio had warmed up, and dance music filled the room. I didn't know the name of the song, but seized on it, listening closely to the melody, following the rise and fall of the notes. The knots in my muscles eased, and eventually I was able to pull together enough to stand up again as though nothing had happened.

Then I swiped at my damp eyes and came away bloody. *Damn.*

In the washroom across the hall I scrubbed off the red evidence of my latest fit, convulsion, seizure—I didn't know what to call it. Once it had a name it might gain more power. The one I'd had earlier at the Nightcrawler had been far more mild, but this kind of bloodshed . . .

There was too much in me. My eyes might still be flushed from feeding; maybe that's what Strome had noticed. Too much, and it had simply seeped out under the strain.

I took care not to look at the empty mirror over the sink. Since my big change well over a year ago, I had grown mostly used to not reflecting. This avoidance was in case I did see something. Me. Like when I'd really been out of my mind that night when everything changed. I'd seen me smiling ruefully and shaking my head over myself. Not anything I wanted to repeat. Too creepy.

Back in the office I ran a damp hand through my hair, grimacing to take the starch out of my too-tight jaw.

"So . . . when's this gonna stop?" I'd asked the general air, which never offered an answer.

But the lamp on my big desk abruptly dimmed out and came on again. It flared brighter than it should have for the wattage, then settled into normal.

I untensed from my initial startlement. "Hello, Myrna."

Of course, someone downstairs might have been working the light panel for the stage, and the load on the circuits could account for what had just occurred, but I knew better. The club's ghost was here somewhere, as invisible to me as I was to others after going incorporeal. Maybe she'd seen the whole sorry show.

I read that ghosts tend to haunt the places where they died. Myrna's regular stamping ground was behind the lobby bar. About five years back when the place was under different, much wilder, management the poor girl caught some grenade shrapnel in the throat and bled to death. The floor tiles there had a dark stain marking the spot. It was pointless trying to replace them, the new ones stained up just the same. Even in death, Myrna still seemed to like tending bar, frequently shifting bottles around for a joke. She also liked Wilton, but lately she preferred hanging around me. Maybe she knew what I'd been through and was worried, like my other friends. But I didn't feel as though I had to put up a front for Myrna.

The lamp flickered, almost too fast and subtle to notice.

"I really look that bad, honey?"

Steady burning.

"Yeah. It stinks, don't it—doesn't it? Aw, hell. Look what they're doing to me. I'm talking like 'em even on my own time."

She was on the ball tonight for responding. Usually she wasn't so overtly active. I took a breath to say something more, then forgot what it was. A strong scent of roses was suddenly in the air. Instant distraction.

For a second I thought it might be Bobbi's favorite perfume; she favored something like it, but this was different in a way I couldn't pin down. It also made gooseflesh flare over me like I'd not felt since I was a kid listening to ghost stories by a campfire. There was a reason for that feeling, and she was right here with me.

Roses. A message from the dead. I'd said things stank; she fixed it.

I rubbed my arms, working out the tightness. Who could be afraid of roses?

"Trying to tell me something, sweetheart?"

Silence, steady lights, the smell of roses in a room with no flowers.

Silence . . . ? But I'd turned the radio on, had been listening to the music. The volume was all the way down now. When had that happened?

I turned it up again, just enough to hear the chatter of a sales pitch for something I'd never buy.

Myrna was branching out. How far would that go? Hopefully she'd remain harmless. She'd always been a good egg, even helped me and Escott out of a jam once. I had nothing to worry about from Myrna. Myself was someone else again.

I stared without interest at the paper mess on the desk, the mechanical pencil for ledger entries right where I'd dropped it the night before. That stuff used to be important; Lady Crymsyn was my own business, a source of pleasure and pride. Now it all seemed so damned *futile*.

Pacing around once, I inspected the walls, then peered through the window blinds at the dark street below. Because of the thickness of the bulletproof glass, the world without had a sick green tint to it and was slightly warped. I had the feeling it would look like that to me no matter what window I might use, maybe with no windows at all.

Enough of that crap. I needed a change quick before I swamped myself in more of the same and brought on another paralyzing bout of bad memory. The radio wasn't enough.

Vanishing, I sank right into the floor. Not a particularly pleasant feeling; but it doesn't last, and I'd known worse. In a second or three I sensed myself clear of solid construction, flowing forward to and then through a wall. Though muffled, there was a change in the level of sound. Teddy Parris was singing. From the direction of his voice I was above him in the lighting grid over the stage. I went back to the wall again, following it until bumping into another wall, then eased straight down. It was just like swimming underwater with your eyes closed, and this pond was very familiar. I knew exactly how to get to my corner booth on the topmost tier of the main room.

But it was occupied, dammit. This seat was my usual spot to watch over things, and the staff always kept it reserved unless there was a really big crowd. No chance of that in midweek, so what was going on?

I brushed close to count how many. Just the one, but he was a paying customer and entitled. I guess. Nose out of joint, I'd just have to settle for the next booth over.

Then Charles Escott said, "Hello, Jack. Won't you sit down?"

The voice and precise British accent were unmistakable. If I'd had solidity, I might have snorted.

I lowered into the booth on the opposite side of the round table and slowly took on form. From the grayness emerged the soft light from the

table's tiny lamp. Its glow fell on the lean features of my sometime partner in business, strife, and well-intentioned crime. Shadows lent a sardonic cast to his expression, but they didn't have to work too hard to
bring it out. Escott's bony face and big beak of a nose were the kind that
could easily shape themselves into a villainous look. Years back when
he'd been on the stage in a Canadian repertory company, young as he'd
been, he was always given the lead in *Richard III*. I'd have paid money to
see that.

"How'd you know it was me and not Myrna?" I asked, once I could
draw air again. It was fragrant from his pipe smoke. Cigarettes were his
habit when on the move. Pipes were for his office or at home—unless he
had a problem that needed to be thought through. Instead of the usual
gin and tonic, there was a brandy in front of him. Must be one a hell of
a problem.

"I didn't, but the odds favored you." Escott had developed a wary
respect for Myrna. He'd annoyed her once, and she'd plunged the whole
club into darkness, then the room got arctic cold, but only for him. After
that he was always careful to be extra polite to her.

"She's in my office. Made my lamp flicker."

"I'd wondered where she'd gotten to," he said. "It's been quiet, no
lights playing up. How are you?"

Of course I was ready to attach all kinds of meanings to the innocuous
social inquiry. But if anyone had a right to be irrational . . . "I'm fine."

"Why the unseen arrival?"

"I didn't want to distract from Teddy's number." Nor did I want the
whole room to see me going up to my table. Some of the regular customers might follow and want to chat with the friendly owner, and I'd have
to pretend to be cheerful. Not in the mood for that just now.

The place was much less than half-full, not bad for the middle-of-the-
week slump with sleet coming down, but illogically discouraging. It was
the same as for any other club in town, and by Thursday things would
pick up again. Come the weekend we'd be packed. Business wasn't on its
last legs just because I'd not been at the front door as usual to greet people. Until a week ago I was always there, shaking hands, fixing my gaze
on customers, and *telling* them they would have a good time, and so they
did. But I couldn't trust myself yet to look happy and sincere, nor could I
trust the hypnosis to so casual a use if it meant an instant killer migraine.
Safer to keep a lid on it until I was in better shape.

A spotlight pinning him to the stage, Teddy sang smoothly through his number in good voice. I contrasted him with Alan Caine. Teddy didn't have Caine's onstage experience, but he sure beat him for offstage personality. Caine might draw in the patrons, but he wasn't worth the trouble. Gordy's outfit, being much larger and grander in scale than mine, could handle that kind of problem child.

"What happened earlier?" asked Escott. Though not on staff, he liked to come over and help out. Maybe it reminded him of his theater days. He'd been here since before opening tonight and must have seen my exit with Strome. "You've had adventures."

"What is it? My tie give it away?" I could feel it was on crooked.

"That and a few dozen other clues. Mr. Strome walking in and you two going missing for several hours led me to think that Dugan might have been found."

"No such luck."

While Teddy sang, I told Escott almost all of it, from the talk with Kroun to Hoyle's murder attempt, leaving out the falling-down nightmare of a headache, the Stockyard gorging, and its sequel in my office. He made no comment afterward, for by then Bobbi came shimmering onstage for the duet, and we watched her instead. She wore a glittery silver gown that clung tight till it reached her hips, then flared wide. She said it was perfect for dancing. Teddy took her hand, and they made a couple fast turns, enough to raise the hem daringly to her knees. Dandy view.

Seeing her, even at a distance, warmed me in a deep and gentle and basic way, like a flame on a cold night. She could make me forget, for a time, what it was like to be alone in the dark inside my head.

The band swung into the introduction for "The Way You Look Tonight," getting a smattering of anticipatory applause that faded when the singing started. She and Teddy sparked off each other in such a way that it seemed as though they'd fallen in love for real and hadn't quite figured it out yet. I knew better, but the audience ate it up. The applause came not only from the customers, but the waiters as well. They adored her.

Instead of taking their bows, she and Teddy remained onstage. For a second I wondered if anything had gone wrong with Roland and Faustine's exhibition dancing. Bobbi leaned toward the microphone and made an announcement, naming some couple celebrating their anniversary, so I eased back in my seat. One of the stage crew swooped the spotlight around until it rested on the right party, and everyone clapped. Bobbi and Teddy began a second duet, this time of "The Anniversary Song."

During an instrumental part Teddy squired her around the stage in a very staid waltz, looking so serious that it bordered on parody. The celebrants in the audience got teased from their chairs by friends and took to the dance floor. Before the end, it was filled with other sentimentally minded couples. In all, a very successful moment.

Bobbi left the stage, and Teddy continued with another of his love songs, which wasn't part of the regular program.

"Where's Roland and Faustine?" I asked. They'd arrived at their usual time. I'd unlocked the door for them myself before heading toward my office to work on the books. Then Strome came in and . . .

"Backstage, I believe," said Escott. "There's nothing amiss. They'll be waiting for the dancers to clear so they can start."

Teddy and the band gave out another three minutes of crooning, then ended with a big flourish, the lights coming up. Everyone looked pleased as they wandered to their tables and put the waiters to work. The musicians changed their sheet music during the pause. Waiters circulated, snagging empty glasses, replacing them with fresh drinks. All normal. I eased back again. For someone who seemed to think his business was damned futile I was showing too much nervous concern. Escott certainly must have picked up on it, but made no remark. He finished his pipe and tapped the bowl into the thick glass ashtray between us.

"Well. About Hoyle," he said. "That's a remarkably nasty business. Very sudden."

"Nah, he's been building up to it. I just wasn't paying attention. You ever deal with him?"

"Rather less than you. Strome will be your best source of information on him, should you need it. Or Gordy."

Who was on the bench for the moment. "I won't bother him with this. My job is to hold the fort and try not to break anything. God, I can't believe he turned up there tonight. He looked like hell."

"He must have been worried for you."

"He's worrying *me*. If he'd just rest up like he's told he'd be back in a week."

"I think you should inform him of tonight's near calamity."

"It's covered."

"Hoyle and five others made a sincere effort to kill you. You may well be nearly bulletproof, but it would be unwise to so lightly shrug off such an assault."

"I'm not. Hoyle's been seriously discouraged. He'll be too busy licking his wounds tonight to do anything else. If he's stupid and hangs around town, I'll have him brought in for a more severe talk to keep him out of trouble. I'll send him on a long vacation, maybe his whole crew."

"Havana again?"

"I don't feel that kindly." I quirked my mouth, remembering some of the words to "Minnie the Moocher." "What do you think of Sweden? Some place really cold so he can cool off."

"There's always the lake," he said casually. "Very cold down there."

Every once in a while Escott scared me. It wasn't a joke. He had a dark streak in him and definite opinions on what to do with troublemakers. But maybe there was more going on here. Maybe he wanted to see how I'd react. "I just want the guy away. When Gordy's back he can deal with this kind of bother. He's good at it. I'll turn the whole mess over to him and forget about it."

"One may hope for as much."

"What do you mean by that?"

"It's come to my attention through Bobbi that Gordy's lady friend is urging him to find another type of business."

If Gordy left, my temporary position could become permanent. My still very full belly tensed at that horror. I made myself ease down. Adelle Taylor had a lot of influence over Gordy, but not in certain areas. "Gordy won't leave. This kind of work is what he's all about."

Escott made a noncommittal grunt and sipped his brandy. "I wish you good luck then. None of this can be too terribly easy for you."

"Actually, it is. Derner does all the day-to-day stuff and keeps the Nightcrawler running smooth, Strome sees to the rest. Mostly I'm a convenient figurehead—or target—and now I've got Kroun's approval. Sort of. It would have been fine if Hoyle hadn't put his foot in. There won't be a repeat with him, but others might want to try."

"Hm." He managed to put a lot of meaning into that.

"You think I should have killed him to discourage future challenges."

"It's the way their world spins 'round. Do you see Gordy as some sort of gangland Robin Hood? That he never killed anyone to keep his position secure?"

"Of course not. I know the score with him. But there's guys out there lots worse than Gordy. You and I've both met 'em."

And I let it hang in the air. That was one Escott couldn't dispute.

The lights faded, and the general conversation noise died down. The band started in on a low, dramatic fanfare, growing louder as the darkness increased. The drums and horns came in strong like a thunderstorm.

For a few seconds the whole place went pitch-black, then *wham*, a spotlight picked out Roland and Faustine magically on the dance floor, still as statues, poised for their first step. Their timing was perfect as the music launched into a sultry tango, carrying them along. At first it seemed too dated, until the rhythm shifted to swing, but they went on with the South American–style dancing, holding eye to eye, body to body, and generally steaming up the place.

It shouldn't have worked, but it did. More than half the heat came from their own kind of electricity. They were recently married, and passions were high, but they'd already crashed into some rocks, one of them right here at the club. Roland loved Faustine, but had a hard time keeping his pants buttoned around other women, like Adelle Taylor. She was his ex-wife from a decade back. From what I'd heard through the walls of their impromptu backstage reunion, the renewed attraction was very mutual. But since Adelle was with Gordy, it was just a bad idea from every angle for her ever to be alone with Roland again.

Not wanting a future problem—like him ending up with broken legs—I'd had a talk with him, so he was behaving himself, and apparently Faustine was slowly and cautiously forgiving him. As long as they kept the fights away from the customers and did their act without any hitch, I was satisfied.

Then the music shifted to a darker, more intense mood, and the white spot flared red. Faustine's white gown took on that color, her skin, too; she looked like a diabolic temptress. Roland's black tuxedo blended with the background shadows and his white shirtfront, cuffs, and gloves also went blood red. It was a new addition in their routine, and the effect raised a collective gasp from the audience.

Faustine broke away from her partner and did graceful ballet-style spins, then he stepped in to support her through other classically inspired moves, finally lifting her high. Stretching her arms, she arched her back so much it looked close to breaking, but held firm as he carried her around, making it seem effortless before bringing her to earth again. The crowd was enthusiastically approving with their applause.

"So that's what they've been rehearsing," Escott muttered. "Bobbi said it would be a showstopper."

"Yeah, it's great." My voice didn't sound right to me. Too tight. Too fast.

Not again. Please . . .

"What's—" He turned.

Ham-fisted, I tried to switch off the little lamp and succeeded in knocking it over. The bulb shattered with a hollow pop, like a very small gun going off. It made me flinch.

"Jack . . . ?"

"Minute." I'd not wanted him or anyone else to see me doubling over. I resisted the urge to hug myself, holding tight to the edge of the table, fighting a flash of nausea and an involuntary shudder. Escott's eyes must have been used to the thick shadows. He watched with apprehensive concern as the fit peaked and finally passed. Thank God he was being sensible and not going agitated on me. I had enough of that on my own.

This seizure wasn't as bad as the last, but bad enough. I wanted to shrink away into a small hole.

"All right now?" he asked after a moment.

"No, goddammit." If I was alive in the normal sense, I'd have been panting like a dog. As it was, I barely drew in enough air for speech, so my reply came out a lot milder than I felt.

The lights on the dance floor rose a little, and Roland and Faustine enjoyed their extended bows, then broke apart to do the other half of their job. He picked out a lady from one of the closer tables and invited her to a fox-trot. Faustine simply stood in place and a couple of guys nearly broke their necks trying to be the first to get to her for a turn. The shorter and more nimble of the pair won, and she granted him the honor of her company. Within a minute the floor was half-full of other dancers.

Everything for everyone else was as normal as could be. I hung on by my fingernails and managed not to slip, convulsing, under the damn table.

Escott found the small switch for the broken lamp and made sure the juice was off. "I suppose this is an improvement over your pacing and the jumping up to stare out windows and not talking for hours on end. Any more left to go?"

"Donno. Just that red light caught me by surprise. It looked like . . . reminded me . . . you know."

"No need to go into it. Has this happened before?"

"No. Yes." Now why in hell had I said that aloud?

"Indeed?" He expected more information. Waited me out.

"W-when my guard's down. Or if I think too much. I don't dare relax."

"Understandable."

"Any blood around my eyes?"

He hesitated, probably working out why I'd asked, then said, "I can't really tell."

Just in case, I pulled out my handkerchief. It came away clean. Small favors. My hand trembled, though. Aftershocks from the earthquake. I stuffed the square of white silk back in my pocket.

"I knew a guy in the army," I said, staring at the dead lamp. "Shell shock. He just couldn't stop shaking. Any sudden noise would set him off even worse. It was hell during a thunderstorm. They had to dope him to the eyeballs with morphine to stop his screaming, and he'd lie there tied to his bed twitching like a fish."

"Well, you're not as badly off as that poor devil."

"Maybe. Guess this will take a while."

"More than just a couple of days, but you'll get through it. A bit more rest on your home earth—"

Had done me squat. "I should be through it now, Charles. It's finished. The bastard who worked me over is gone, he can't come at me again, it's never going to happen again . . ." But I got a flash in my mind of Hog Bristow's grinning face and his knife blade flashing, catching the light, and what came next, and another freezing wave churned my insides around so much I had to grip the table again, head bowed. "Oh, damn."

Almost as a physical effort I pushed the shuddering away, then dropped weakly back in the shadowed plush of the booth.

"Intellectually," Escott said, "you know the ordeal is over. But your body and, certainly, your subconscious mind do not understand that yet. Your reactions are to do with survival instinct, the overwhelming need to escape. It tends to hang about long after the threat is gone. The symptoms *will* subside, given time."

"I want it to stop now. I'll be fine, then right outta the blue it hammers me flat. Am I really nuts or just being self-indulgent and looking for sympathy?"

"The latter? Certainly not. You're nuts." He said the so-American colloquialism with such matter-of-fact conviction I came that close to taking him seriously. Then I wanted to sock him one. Then I wanted to laugh.

"Maybe I'm just half-nuts. Should I see a head doctor about this?"

"The best thing for you would be a vacation. That's nearly the same as escape and might fool your internal watchdog. Go off someplace where it's quiet."

"Then I think too much."

"Don't we all." He made it a statement, not a question, giving me a sideways look. He'd been through his own version of hell and survived. "That's why they invented this marvelous stuff." He lifted his brandy snifter. "Have you tried mixing alcohol with your preferred beverage? You might begin with a really good vodka. It will likely not alter the taste, only thin things a bit, and there's the added advantage of no telltale smell on your breath—when you bother to breathe, that is."

I'd already tried that ploy. It hadn't worked. "You wanna turn me into a drunkard?"

"If it will help, yes, of course, certainly."

What threatened to be another shudder turned into a half-assed chuckle. Not much of it, but better than screaming.

He lounged in his end of the half-circle booth, failing to keep a smug look in check. It was the first time in days he'd seen me give out with a smile. His pipe apparently finished, he tapped it empty in the ashtray and laid it aside to cool.

"I used to be a drunk," I said.

His smile faded. He'd been down that road, too, knew how rough it could be. I'd never before mentioned my own irregular trips. The new ground must have surprised him. "Indeed?"

"Back in New York, after Maureen disappeared. I could only manage to do it part-time. The newspaper job didn't pay enough to buy a lot of drinks, so I'd have to wait for my day off to get in one good binge a week. Now look at me: I got a bar full of booze, and it isn't doing me a damn bit of good."

"Quite ironic, that," he agreed. "But perhaps just as well. The consequences of too much of a good thing are not pleasant, and one tends to offend one's friends while under the influence. I had Shoe Coldfield around to bludgeon sense into me once he was sufficiently annoyed by my being a drunken fool. I doubt there's anyone about who could do the same favor for you."

"There's Barrett."

"True, but he's far off in his Long Island fastness, happy with his dear lady. You'd have to delve yourself into an incredibly deep crevasse to warrant my asking him to come all the way out here to bash you between the ears for the salvation of your soul and restoration of sanity."

"Donno. He'd probably enjoy it."

Jonathan Barrett and his reclusive girlfriend Emily were the only others like me that I knew of; we're a rare breed. He'd been the one who'd made Maureen, who, some decades later, made me before vanishing out of our lives forever. We'd both loved her. She was a sore spot between us, though that was gradually healing. Barrett had been around since before the Revolutionary War, giving him a longer perspective on life, and he wasn't above rubbing that in when he thought I needed reminding. Though our case with him was long over, I knew Escott kept in touch. Sometimes the mail would have an embossed envelope with Barrett's distinctive old-fashioned handwriting on it. The fancy calligraphy was always made by a modern fountain pen, though, not a quill. He wasn't the type to stand fixed in the past.

I should take a lesson from him on that. An idea glimmered in the back of my mind about running off and visiting him and Emily for a week or so. It faded pretty quick. Until Gordy was on his feet I was stuck in Chicago; besides, I couldn't leave Bobbi in the lurch to run Crymsyn by herself.

Escott righted the little lamp; shards of bulb glass dropped from its miniature shade. He used a napkin to sweep the pieces into the ashtray. "You will recover, Jack. Just not tonight."

"Tomorrow for sure, huh?"

"Of course."

It was one hell of a lie, but heartening. I wanted to get through the rest of the evening without any more shakes. Laughing *had* helped. The back alleys in my head knew that, which was why I had Strome tuning the car radio to comedies. Even when I couldn't summon the energy to laugh at the jokes, the desire was there. I wanted more. Unless I could pick up a second broadcast for the West Coast, it was past time to try finding other shows. The best stuff was usually on too early, since I was dead to the world until sunset. I wished there was a way of getting recordings of favorites so I could hear them later. Recording machines were pretty large and cost a fortune, but I did have space upstairs and money in the bank. It would be a legit business expense. Certainly Bobbi could find a use for it, maybe doing up sample records to send around to the local stations so they'd remember her name. The radio shows I wanted would use up a lot of record blanks, though, with only fifteen minutes for each side.

"And that's a lot of bucks to invest just so I can listen to *Fibber McGee and Molly.*"

Escott stared. "I beg your pardon?"

I realized he'd not been aboard my train of thought. "Nothing. I think I'm getting better."

"If you say so."

"You want another brandy? There should have been a waiter up here by now. We shorthanded?" I leaned forward for a look, but all the boys seemed to be at work.

"No, thank you. I told the fellow who tends this section that I did not want to be disturbed for the remainder of the evening unless I specifically signaled him. I had the idea that you might prefer some privacy once back from your errand with Strome. He was rather grim of visage when you two left."

"I didn't know that you'd seen us."

"Yes, I was just coming into the lobby as you went out the front door, and it took a great deal of restraint on my part not to dash after to find out what was afoot."

"Why didn't you?"

"You actually appeared to be concerned about something. I wasn't about to step into the middle of that. It was time you showed signs of life. Whatever the crisis, I thought it could only do you good to get out and deal with it. Perhaps slamming a few heads together would wake you up a bit."

"You knew it'd be like that?"

"Given Strome's place in the organization, he would only engage you in something really important, and given the nature of the organization itself, most crises tend to be of a violent nature. However, I would never have suspected Mr. Kroun's direct involvement. I understand he's rather high up in the ranks."

"You know anything about him? Just in case he's not sensible and tries to surprise me with a bullet."

Escott looked at his pipe as though considering another smoke. "But you hypnotized him."

"If he was really set on rubbing me out, he could start having second thoughts after a good sleep."

"Then you're the best judge of the chances. Weigh that against your perceptions of the man."

"Go with the gut, huh?"

"Yes."

I usually did, only lately I wasn't that trusting of my instincts. "I'm safe enough. I'm not too worried, just paranoid."

"Which is an excellent means for maintaining good health. As for Mr. Kroun, I am familiar with the name, which has occasionally appeared in the press. Even allowing for exaggeration, he is not a fellow one wishes to cross. There have been a number of New York mob deaths connected to him, but the links were so tenuous as to make prosecution impossible. By that we can infer he is clever at avoiding legal action and entirely capable of either ordering a murder or committing it himself."

"I can believe it. He knows how to get people to move without putting out much effort. To the right types he can be pretty intimidating. Had the damnedest eyes. Nightmare eyes."

"Didn't care for him?"

I shrugged. "Even Gordy said he was scary. I might think so, too, if I was still on that side of breathing, but I got him under control, and he agreed with me on the important stuff."

"You pique my interest. A man defined by such a word by a man like Gordy must be a rarity."

"I should hope so. We don't need more of 'em wandering around."

Down on the dance floor a new song started up, and this time a woman cut in to dance with Faustine, which startled her at first. She was gracious about it, though, and did her job. I wondered who would lead. Roland, with another lady, seemed amused. Would he have that grin if a man cut in on him for a turn? Show business was wonderfully educational.

"How'd you know I'd be here?" I asked, meaning this, my favorite booth.

"You may be in the throes of a difficult mending, but you are a man of habit. Sooner or later you'd show yourself in this haunted gallery. It struck me as the best place to waylay you for an account of your impromptu jaunt."

"Not my office?"

"No. You would logically go there first, but might not be in a receptive mood for talk. When you were ready to deal with people you'd emerge."

"Optimist. You hung around here all evening instead of going to see Vivian?"

"She's busy. A bridge gathering for one of her charity organizations. In between play they plot out fund-raising strategies."

"She's finally going out again?"

"It's at her home. She's not up to venturing forth just yet."

Vivian Gladwell had been his most recent client. During the two weeks when he helped her get through the kidnapping and recovery of her daughter they'd grown very close indeed. A rich society widow and a gumshoe calling himself a private agent—I'd seen worse mismatches going up the aisle and thriving. Besides, it was about time he settled down. Maybe he could sell me his house. I roomed in his basement and was kind of used to the place.

"A hen party," he said, staring down at the dancers, perhaps watching Faustine and her partner.

"Huh?"

"Vivian's bridge night. Ladies only. Otherwise, I might be there. It's important to her, her first social occasion since the notoriety of the kidnapping. She's been a bit nervous about it, hoping her friends will have ignored the yellow press headlines and turn up as usual."

"What's this? You feeling left out?"

"There's no room for me in what promises to be a gossipy gaggle of hats, gowns, cucumber sandwiches, and tea."

This didn't sound good. If I read him right, Escott was actually moping. "Tell you what. Ask Vivian out this Saturday. Bring her here. We'll give her a red-carpet good time. Find out her favorite songs, and I'll ask Bobbi and Teddy to sing 'em all."

"I could never persuade her to leave Sarah home alone. The poor child's still not over her ordeal."

I could fully sympathize and then some. Sarah was the daughter who'd been kidnapped. Sweet sixteen in body, only around nine or ten in mind and would remain that way for life. She'd survived the wringer, though, which made her a tough cookie in my book.

"Bring Sarah," I said. "After all they've been through I bet they could do with a night out."

"But the reporters . . ."

"Haven't come by as much, have they?" The kidnap case had been pretty sensational, but now it was the day before yesterday's news.

"Only a few of the more stubborn ones."

"I can shoo them else-place and no problem. What d'ya say? It'd help me, too. Get my mind off myself."

"Very well. But . . . I'll put it to Vivian as being your own special invitation."

"Why? Is she cooling off with you?"

"If I've interpreted that correctly, then I don't think so, but a nightclub like this is well outside their routine. The idea wants getting used to for them."

"You worry too much. They'll have a good time. I'll even have a birthday cake for Sarah."

"It won't be her birthday."

"What kid's gonna turn down a surprise party where she can make a wish and blow out candles? We'll have funny hats and horns and give her a rhinestone crown."

"Let's not overdo things." He looked alarmed.

"Okay, but at least cake and ice cream and a few balloons. We deserve a little celebration."

"Well . . . all right. Thank you." Under the reticence he seemed pleased.

I actually felt normal, even cheerful, for having a purpose in life again. One that didn't involve mayhem and killing. It lasted nearly a whole minute.

The layout of the club's main room was such that from most any point in the horseshoe-shaped tiers of tables, you could see the entry and thus anyone coming in. That's how I spotted Evie, the little dancer who was so inexplicably sweet on Alan Caine. One of the waiters came up to guide her to a table, but she started talking to him, looking upset even at this distance. She still wore her overcoat, gloves, and hat, and carried a big purse. Under all that I glimpsed spangles on her stockings and the flashy shoes she wore for her dance routine with Alan Caine.

"Now what?" I asked.

Escott followed my look. "Trouble?"

"I hope not. She's the chorus girl I told you about. The one that Hoyle was going to use for a football."

"Hm. Then it's likely trouble, else she'd be at the Nightcrawler doing her show. Let's hope he didn't return to finish what you interrupted."

"She seems to be okay."

The waiter gave in to whatever Evie wanted, leading her up the long, carpeted stairs. He couldn't have known I was here and must have decided to turn the problem over to Escott.

Who must have got that, too. "For what we are about to receive . . ." Escott muttered out the side of his mouth.

"May we be truly thankful," I also muttered, completing the blasphemous old battle prayer.

5

THE waiter reached the booth. "Uh, Mr. Escott, this lady wants to see—oh." He spotted me. "Didn't know you were here, Mr. Fleming."

Escott and I stood as the little lady trotted up the last steps.

Her big-eyed gaze fell on me. "Jack Fleming?"

"Yeah. Something wrong?" I signed for the waiter to retreat.

She waited until he was out of earshot, then nodded vigorously.

"What?"

"They're going to kill Alan Caine," she blurted in her Betty Boop voice. Apparently it wasn't an affectation after all.

"Who?"

"Those men."

"What, they're back?"

"Not yet, but they will be. His life is in danger!"

"As in later tonight, but not just this minute?"

"Please, this isn't a joke! He needs help!"

Escott cleared his throat, giving me a look, the kind with a raised eyebrow in it.

"Just checking the urgency of the situation," I told him, then turned back to her. "You're Evie . . . ah . . . ?"

"Montana. I'm Evie Montana, just like the state, it's my name."

"Charles Escott," he volunteered, taking her hand and adding in one of his polite little bows.

"Pleased, I'm sure," she said, cute as a Kewpie doll.

"If the emergency is not immediate, perhaps you will sit and tell us all about it," he suggested, motioning her into the booth.

She cocked her head. "You're English, aren't you, just like in England?"

"Once upon a time. Please . . . ?"

She took the hint and slipped in. Released from our gentlemanly duty, we sat opposite her. I leaned back in the middle of the half circle; Escott clasped his hands on the table in his best listening posture. "What is the problem, Miss Montana?"

"Well, Alan Caine is just the greatest singer ever, better than Caruso even, and he's just really too artistic and innocent and people take advantage of him and he gets into jams and he's in a jam now and these guys are gonna kill him if he doesn't pay what he owes and they really mean business."

"I see," he said. "And who are they exactly?"

"They're muscle for the Nightcrawler Club. They got gambling there and these cardsharps took advantage of Alan and he ran up a marker and they're gonna kill him if he doesn't pay off."

"The cardsharps?"

"No, the *muscle*. They want him to pay the club."

"So the money he owes is to the Nightcrawler, not Hoyle?" I asked.

"Who's Hoyle?" She turned her big eyes on me, blinking.

"That guy you jumped on earlier tonight."

"He's the *muscle* trying to collect the *marker*," she said, as though I should know already. "They got dozens of guys just like him, and they're all gonna kill Alan tonight if he doesn't pay off."

"I get that. You're sure he doesn't owe personally to Hoyle?"

"He owes the *club* and that goon is their *muscle* and—"

"Okay-okay. I get that, too. So why'd you come to me?"

"Because you helped us earlier and because some of the other girls said you were all right because you dated one of the singers there once and they said you were all right because she was all right."

"Not because you think I'm running things?"

"You're running things? What things? They said *this* was your club. If you're running things at the Nightcrawler . . ." She started to get up, but Escott caught her hand.

"It's all right," he assured. "I'm sure Mr. Fleming can sort this out for you."

I said, "Shouldn't be a problem. If he owes money, he has to pay the marker, but no one's going to kill him for it."

"But that big goon was *hitting* him!"

"The big goon won't be back. I'll make a call and put in the fix for you. If Caine's dead, he can't pay off his marker, so he's safe enough."

"It's not just them, it's that witch of an ex-wife, too. She keeps calling him and threatening him and it gets him all upset and then he goes into the casino to try to win what he owes her and then they take advantage of him and then—" Her voice rose shrill, threatening to compete with the band.

I put my hand up like a traffic cop. "Slow down, Evie."

She stopped altogether, looking like I'd just slapped her. She made a peculiar *sup-sup* noise, then her face suddenly screwed up. She plowed blindly in her handbag and pulled out a handkerchief just in time for the waterworks.

Escott was better at holding hands and saying "there-there" than I was, so I gritted my teeth and sat out the next few minutes until he got her calmed. Sympathy came easier to him; he'd never met Alan Caine.

"Don't you believe me?" she asked. "He's in real *danger*. I thought you might help. I thought you could make them leave him alone."

"I said I'd fix it."

"But I *heard* them and they were saying awful things about him and they got no right to do that. They're all just so *mean*."

Likely they were blowing off steam about Caine and his singular lack of personal charm. "I'll make a call and take care of it. Caine will be fine, just keep him sober and—"

"Oh, but he *never* drinks! He just gargles with a little brandy and hot water to keep his vocal cords loose."

From what he'd been breathing on me earlier tonight he kept them loose enough to flap on a windless day.

"It prevents colds, too," she brightly added.

"Aren't you supposed to be dancing in the show?"

"This was more *important*, because he doesn't know just how much danger he's in, and I could lose my job, but I thought you could help him because . . ."

After repeating everything in full she eventually ran down. No wonder Caine drank.

"I'll take care of it," I said. "You can go back to the club and don't worry about anything."

"You will? You really, really *will*?"

Escott stood so I could get out. "Babysit?" I muttered.

He gave a good-sport smile and nodded.

I made my way down, going to my office in the usual manner, no vanishing. A few regulars noticed and waved, inviting me over to their various tables. I smiled automatically, mimed a mock-helpless shrug to show I was busy, and moved on. Given a choice I would rather go with

Strome to face Kroun down again than pretend to be jovial to the customers.

A quick call to the Nightcrawler's office soon put me in touch with Derner.

"Back at the desk again?" I asked him.

"Pretty much. Anything wrong?" Derner was a man who expected phone calls to have trouble on the other end of the line.

I ascertained that Evie Montana had the basic facts correct and got how much Alan Caine owed the club. It was a lot, but nothing he couldn't afford on what they had to be paying him. I found out how much that was, too.

"Okay, ban him from the casino and let him know what he owes is coming out of his wages."

Derner laughed once. "He ain't gonna like that much."

"Tell him it's pay up this way or get another working-over."

"He won't like that much, either, but I'll make him listen."

"Who booked him in, anyway?"

"His agency. They never mentioned he was walking sandpaper, though. He's outta New York like Kroun."

"They hooked up in some way?"

"You kiddin'? Kroun wouldn't stand for that kinda crap. By the way, congrats on getting out alive."

"Thanks. Where's Kroun now?"

"He left not long back, with Strome driving. Gordy said treat him good, so he gets the fancy car till he goes home."

Having Strome playing chauffeur was also a good way to keep tabs on Kroun. "When will that be?"

There was a shrug in Derner's tone. "Who knows. He's the big boss. Comes and goes, it's his business an' no one else's. He can't stay away from New York for too long, though. Has to be busy like the rest of us."

"Did Strome tell you about our run-in with Hoyle?"

"Yeah. Congrats on that, too. None of those guys has showed here."

"If they do, they're on the outs. Especially Hoyle and Ruzzo."

"No loss with that bunch."

"Did Gordy go home, I hope?"

"Yeah. He left after he got word you were still walking. Lowrey took him home."

"Great. If he calls tomorrow, fill him in on Hoyle, but don't bother him tonight."

"No problem."

If it would only continue to be so, I thought, hanging up. The mob's idea of no problems and mine were usually two different animals.

And it looked like a new one just strolled in my front door. As I came down the stairs a threesome in dark overcoats entered the lobby. One of the men removed his hat and ran a hand through iron gray hair with a distinctive streak of silver-white on the left side.

Ah, shit. Now what?

Whitey Kroun spotted me almost in the same instant and sketched a wave and smile. Mitchell and Strome were with him but in an odd way were almost invisible. Kroun seemed to fill the room as though he was the only one with a right to be there and telegraphed it clear to the corners. Some of the people lingering at the bar for the next show glanced up from conversations as if he'd called them by name.

I wiped off what must have been a "Hell, what are they doing here?" look and assumed my friendly host face, coming the rest of the way down the stairs.

"Good evening again, Mr. Kroun." I managed to sound sincerely welcoming, but there was something about the man that set the skin to rippling on the back of my neck.

Kroun took in the chrome-trimmed, black-and-white marble lobby, impressed. "Fleming," he said as a greeting. "You look like hell. How's the damage?"

"My doc says I'm still healing."

"And after just a couple hours. That's pretty good."

Had he heard about my fun and games with Hoyle? I couldn't tell from Strome's expression whether or not he'd mentioned the incident. Not that any of it mattered, but Kroun's curiosity reminded me that I was supposed to be walking wounded. I'd better act accordingly.

"Quite a place you got here," Kroun said, very approving.

"Thank you." It could be a mixed blessing when a guy in the mobs liked something of yours. They were in a position to take it from you. "May I offer you a table?"

"Sure."

The hatcheck girl hovered within view, but none of them handed over their coats. Maybe they wouldn't stay long, then. So far the lights held steady, indication that Myrna—if she was around—didn't see trouble ahead. She messed with them when she got upset about something.

Mitchell did a double take on the display easel for Bobbi, fairly gaping. It hit me smack between the eyes that he'd remember her from when he worked for Morelli. I felt a cold twisting inside again. Bobbi did not need to stroll down memory lane to the bad old days without first getting a fair warning, but I didn't know how to tip her off without broadcasting it to these guys. Play it by ear and hope for the best, then.

I led the way through the short, curving passage to the main room and a second-tier table looked after by the most experienced waiter. He appeared out of nowhere, took orders, vanished, and returned with a trayful almost before my guests were settled in. He'd correctly read the discreet signal I'd given. There would be no check for this party.

Glancing up, I noticed Escott watching us with interest. He knew Strome and would identify Kroun easily enough. That white streak was hard to miss. But beyond that, Escott had a hell of a memory for names and faces, especially the ones in the mobs. I suspected there was more in his head about the Chicago wiseguys than the FBI files.

"Gentlemen," I said, "excuse me a sec—club business." I withdrew as the waiter handed out glasses, and went up to the third tier, remembering to move slow and stiff.

"Anything afoot?" Escott asked.

"I don't think so. Kroun probably just wants to check me out some more. We're friends now, after all." I was starting to regret that suggestion.

"Did ya put in the fix for Alan?" asked Evie, anxious. "Did ya?"

"All done. So long as Caine pays his marker, no one gets hurt."

She let out a little squeal and jumped up to hug me, planting a kiss on my jawline, which was as high as she could reach without a footstool and me helping. "Thank you! Thank you!"

Well, this was nice, but attracting attention. I was supposed to be feeling tender around the middle and with difficulty gradually unpeeled her. "Glad to help, but maybe you should get back to the Nightcrawler while you still have a job there."

"I won't make it in time for the second show. The El doesn't run—"

"You certainly will," said Escott. "I'll give you a lift."

I almost raised an eyebrow, but didn't quite have the trick of it the way he did.

He still caught it, though. "Just being polite, old man," he said dryly.

That was good to hear. After Vivian, Evie didn't seem to be his type, though she was cute. He guided her downstairs, and I went back to take a seat at Kroun's table, him on my left, Strome on my right, Mitchell opposite. The band went on break just then, marking the end of the first show. Some of the patrons got up to leave, a few new ones trickled in to replace them, and the rest stayed put, which was good.

I looked around for Bobbi, but when performing she tended to stay backstage even when on break, seeing to God-knows-what details and her own costume changes. I wanted her busy with that tonight.

Kroun had finished his small whiskey, Mitchell was still working on his, and Strome sipped a short beer.

"*Quite* a place," repeated Kroun. "What's she pull for you?"

There is a certain level of business where such inquiries are not considered offensive. "Last night, sixty-three dollars."

That got me a stony look, then comprehension as he realized I was talking net, not gross. "I mean outside of the booze sales."

"That's it."

"He don't have tables, Mr. Kroun," Strome explained.

"No tables? What about slots?"

"Nope."

"That's crazy." He turned on me. "You could pull in a hundred times that a night in a back room. You got the space for it."

"I do," I agreed. "But Gordy's better at keeping track of those kind of earnings than me. I thought it'd be best for everyone just not to compete."

Kroun's eyes narrowed with additional understanding. "Smart operator."

I didn't correct his assumption that I wanted to avoid cutting into Gordy's profits. It sounded better than the real reason, a desire to avoid legal trouble. To guys like Kroun the law was only a minor nuisance, not a major threat. He'd think I was chicken, too, but there is also a certain level and kind of business where such an assessment of character can contribute to one's survival. I'd gotten along pretty well in the past when people underestimated me.

Mitchell nodded toward the entry where Escott and Evie had gone. "Wasn't that the little trick you got in a fight over at the Nightcrawler?"

"I just kept her out of harm's way is all." A change of subject would be good about now. I decided to play the card Strome had given me earlier. "You used to work here in town, didn't you, Mitchell?"

His eyes hardly gave a flicker. "A while ago, yeah."

"Why'd you leave?"

"The weather stinks."

"Stinks just as bad in New York."

"Oh, yeah? I never noticed."

Kroun made a snorting noise. "Mitchell likes to work easy and get paid well for it. He found that in New York."

"Why you interested?" Mitchell asked.

I was chancing a fall on my face, but thought the risk would pay off. "Because you remember me from before you left."

He hooked a small smile. "Guess I do."

Bingo.

"What do you remember?" asked Kroun.

Mitchell's smile edged close to contempt. "That Fleming was some kind of half-assed threadbare reporter sniffing around Slick Morelli's operation, looking into stuff he shouldn't. Next thing you know Fred Sanderson's dead, Georgie Reamer's in jail for it, then Morelli's dead, Lebredo's dead, Frank Paco's in the booby hatch, Gordy's in charge— and *this* guy who was in the middle of it comes up smelling like a rose."

Kroun held silent for a moment. "That's pretty interesting. What about it, Fleming?"

I shook my head. "I don't know nothing about any of it. I was looking for a newspaper job here and heard there was some war brewing between those guys. Checked into it, thinking I could land a sweet place with the *Trib* if I wrote a good piece on it. That's how I met Gordy, but he steered me out of the way before it went rough. When things settled down after the ruckus I did a couple of favors to help Gordy, and that's all. We been friends since."

"Must have been some kind of favors to be able to afford this kind of club."

"I earned the club on my own. I got lucky at the track and hauled in a pile of cash. Gordy helped me with finding a good location and getting set up with suppliers, but that's all. He's been a good friend and stand-up. I'm returning the favor by helping him out now."

"And you don't expect anything out of it?"

"I'm getting plenty: a nice quiet town to run my business. We can all use some of that."

Kroun murmured agreement. "Quiet is what we want. Things are always changing, though."

"Oh yeah?"

"You gotta expect change. It's the way things are. Lot of the guys thought it was the end of the world when we had Repeal—Bristow was one of 'em—but it was just temporary. There's still plenty of tax-free booze being delivered. We're keeping an eye open all the time for new stuff to do. As soon as they make a vice illegal, we find a way to get rich by supplying it."

"Yeah, but those government guys are getting smarter at stopping up the chinks."

"It won't last. There's always a way to get around the rules. Like right now. Couple guys I know practically got the FBI in their pocket, or J. Edgar Hoover, anyway. They think they own the world, but it won't last."

"Why, is he onto 'em?"

"Nothing like that. He can't sneeze without they give him the say-so, and they think it's great, but they're going to have problems soon. The guy's forty-two, has ulcers, and is crazy-obsessed about commies. If the Russians don't bump him, he'll do himself in chasing his own tail and trying to nab headlines about it. I don't give him more than another year at the job before he drops stone dead. *Then* I'll start to worry. That damn FDR will put in some stand-up guy who knows what he's doing and can keep his nose clean. When that happens we'll have to start running for cover."

"How do they have Hoover in their pocket?"

Kroun shook his head, amused. "You don't wanna know. The key to owning anyone is knowing what a man wants most and knowing what he most wants to keep hidden. A man with small wants who doesn't give a damn what people think of him is usually free. Of course, that guy is not generally in a position where we need to own him, but there's a few out there. They're the ones to look out for."

And what secrets do you want most hidden? I thought. God knows I didn't want people hearing about mine, especially the current ones that were eating holes in my brain like acid.

"That canary out front in the pictures," said Mitchell, whose mind was clearly on other things, "when does she sing?"

"You mean Miss Smythe?" I asked.

"That's the one. Bobbi."

I didn't like the way he said her name. "Later. The second show."

"We're old friends. I'd like to go back and say hello to her."

He got a long look from me, and I didn't blink.

"What?" he asked, coming up with a puzzled front like he wasn't getting my message. "She don't take visitors?"

"That's right."

"C'mon, she won't mind a friend."

I didn't like the way he said that, either. Oily and unpleasant, yet with the smile. I wanted to knock it from his mug along with his front teeth. On this, I knew I could absolutely trust my instincts. "She'll mind."

"You go ask her, give her my name. She'll tell you different." He waited.

I still wasn't blinking. And had gone corpse-quiet.

He chose to ignore it. "What's *your* problem?"

"Mitch," said Kroun, who watched the exchange. "Lay off. She's just a skirt. There's plenty more back on Broadway you can say hello to instead."

Mitchell seemed to verge on a reply, thought better of it, and subsided. There was a "We'll see about this later" glint in his eye for me, though. I wasn't worried. They'd be on their way back to New York soon, end of problem. Maybe I wouldn't have to burden Bobbi with this ghost from her past.

Strome, who'd been silent all this time, let out a soft sigh that only I heard. I interpreted it as relief. I got the impression he was worried I'd do something stupid. It had been close. My second choice after punching Mitchell's face to pulp would have been hypnosis, but that would have risked another skull-splitter for me. After talking with Escott I'd gotten the firm idea that this suddenly excessive head pain was also connected to Bristow's torture, and it seemed pretty sound. I could hope the symptoms would go away after a while, but for now was stuck without one of my edges.

On the other hand, this was my club with my rules running. I had a right to refuse service to anyone, which included allowing undesirable types to bother my girlfriend.

When I started paying attention again, I noticed Kroun studying me, his own face unreadable. "Another drink, Mr. Kroun?"

He made no reply, just looked around again at the people, the band, even the lights above. "Quite a place." he echoed his comment yet again. "I like the chairs."

"Chairs?" I hoped he wasn't trying to drive a point home, because I was missing it.

"Yes. These are really nice chairs. Some places never get that right, but when it comes down to it, you have to offer people a place to park themselves. Really *nice* chairs. Nice. Chairs."

Maybe he was drunk. Mine might not be the first whiskey he'd had tonight. "Thanks. Took a lot of hard work to haul together."

Mitchell flashed an interesting expression. Made me think he thought his boss was being an idiot. It only lasted an instant.

"But all these chairs and no gaming tables," Kroun continued, unaware. "Seems like too much effort for no real payoff."

"It's plenty for me. I keep my vices simple."

"Like not drinking yourself?"

For social cover I had a glass of ice water in front of me, my usual, and all the waiters knew it. I'd not sipped any. "Well, you know how it is, the boss has gotta stay awake. You guys enjoy yourselves, though."

Mitchell smirked. "He wants to get us drunk like Gordy did with

Bristow. Thinks we'll talk." His tone was meant to bait. Kroun would know what he was up to and be watching my reaction.

Strome shifted in place, anticipating trouble.

I pretended amusement and confided to Kroun, "That's a cute kid you got there. Lemme know when he's outta short pants, and I'll find him a job."

Mitchell didn't take it well. If his boss hadn't laughed, he might have tried a swing at me. He'd get just the one shot.

"Relax, Mitch, we're off the clock," said Kroun. "Let the man run his bar. We'll be going now."

"But we ain't seen the show," said Mitchell.

"So?"

Under Kroun's dark stare, he subsided again, dropping into silence like it was a foxhole.

Doing a good impersonation of civilized gentlemen, we rose and strolled to the lobby. Kroun thanked me for my hospitality, and I walked them outside. We stood under the canopy while Strome went to get the Caddy. The sleet had stopped, but the streets were still wet, the wind bitter. For a moment it was eerily similar to the night of Gordy's shooting, and I couldn't help but look around, anticipating another hidden gunman.

"What is it?" Kroun asked, picking up on my nerves. His eyes were sharp. No sign of whiskey in them at all.

"Just feeling the cold."

He nodded, removing his hat to brush a hand through his hair. It seemed to be an unconscious gesture, always on the left side where that streak was. "Yeah, you'd think those bandages would keep you warmer."

He got a look from me. Was he playing games or just showing a weird sense of humor?

"Ease off on yourself, kid," he said sotto voce so Mitchell couldn't hear.

"What d'you mean?"

"I mean I know what kind of hell Bristow put you through."

"Oh, he skinned you alive, too?" I was jumpy enough to give him lip. Not smart. He just stared. Nothing hostile in it, but I wasn't about to ascribe anything like sympathy to the man. Guys like him were born without or had it burned from them early by life in general.

He leaned slightly, talking close to my ear. "I know what he was and what he could do."

"And you sent him."

"Yeah. I did that. It was supposed to be between him and Gordy alone, and somehow you got in the middle. But you survived. That makes you the stronger. Then you put Bristow exactly where he belongs."

"Yeah," I echoed. "I did that."

"So . . . ease off on yourself." He straightened and settled his hat firmly against the wind. "He was a bastard, but you beat him."

A pep talk from a killer? Some of it skated close to being almost apologetic. And how did he know about what was in my head?

On the other hand, he thought we were friends. Maybe this was how he was with them. He couldn't have had many the way he put my back hairs on high. I didn't get a chance to find out; Strome drove up, Kroun and Mitchell got in, doors slammed, and off they went.

Lady Crymsyn was officially closed for the night. Except for my Buick, the adjoining parking lot was empty, everyone gone home or off to unwind themselves at places that kept even later hours. The neon sign above the red street canopy was dark, but lights showed within. Of course, that didn't mean anything with Myrna in residence. Sometimes she'd have them blazing, including the neon; other nights she would only leave a small one on behind the lobby bar. She was the most consistent with it, wanting it lit nearly all the time.

I stood under the shadow of the canopy, not quite smoking a cigarette. My lungs refused to tolerate inhaling the stuff, so I puffed for something to do and watched the occasional car drive past. Chicago was too big to ever completely sleep. Someone was always up and around.

Humankind was roughly divided into daytime folk, night people, night owls, and the creeps of the deep night. Most of the latter, unless gainfully employed or with some other reasonable excuse for being out during the truly godforsaken hours, lived down to their name. If not for my job I could be counted as one of them—two jobs, to include the help I gave Escott when he needed it. Three, to include Gordy.

It was coming up on the beginning of the deep night. Lonely time for me since everyone was usually asleep. I was uncomfortable standing out here, not from the cold, but being by myself and out of range of some kind of distraction. No radio, no band playing loud, happy music, just the wind in my ears and the infrequent passing car. This was me testing the demons in my head; I was trying to get better at not thinking, not remembering.

By the time I finished my third smoke, Escott finally drove up, easing his big Nash right next to the front curb. It was a no-parking zone, but the doorman wasn't here to chase him off.

"You're in one piece," I observed brightly as he got out. "Congrats."

"Why should I not be?"

I shrugged. "This town."

"Where's Bobbi?"

"Upstairs counting receipts. You don't wanna disturb her."

"You're curious as to what transpired concerning Evie Montana."

"Well, yeah."

"A gentleman doesn't talk," he said, mock-lofty.

"Come on, you know what I mean."

"Inside, if you please. How can you not be cold?"

My overcoat was in the office. "Has to do with being dead, I guess. Sometimes I just don't feel it."

"I wonder why that is?"

"So we don't feel the chill of the grave after escaping it?"

"Possibly, but there may be some other reason for the peculiarity. After all, not every society buried their dead. The Romans were fond of cremation, and the ancients of my countrymen practiced open-air—well, I suppose you couldn't call it interment. Exterment? If there is such a word; I'll have to look it up. They left corpses in the open air until only bones were left, which would certainly have prevented any of your sort from returning from the dead." He drew breath to go on, but caught me looking at him. Just looking. "Ah. Well. Be that as it may . . ."

I opened the door for us, locked it behind, and felt better for it.

The deep-night world was shut outside and would require no more of my attention for a while. Escott unbuttoned his coat, dropping it and his Homburg hat on the marble-topped lobby bar, the whole time giving me one of his once-overs.

"What?" I asked.

"No holes in your clothing, no damage to the premises, and the lights are functioning. I take it your visit from Kroun ended amicably?"

"Yeah, but he gives me the creeps."

"Must be a novel experience for you."

I ignored that one. "Drink?"

"A very small brandy would be nice, thank you."

The liquor was locked up, but not for long. I couldn't find his favorite kind right away, though there was always a bottle on hand; it was a standing order. It finally turned up behind several similar-shaped bottles, the label facing the wall. Myrna must have been playing again, with him as the target.

The barstools were stacked to one side to be out of the way of the morning cleaners, so we went through to the main room. I forgot how dark it was to Escott until he bumped into a table that was slightly out of place. The insignificant amount of light coming from the small red windows above the third-tier booths was plenty for me. I turned on the little table lamp for him, reaching between a thicket of chair legs. The seats there had also been upended for the convenience of the morning's cleaning crew. I didn't care for the closed-up, dead look it gave to the club. Chairs were supposed to be sanely on the floor waiting for people to use them, not like this. I decisively moved two of them down for us, then the other two so I wouldn't get annoyed if I knocked elbows.

The place was very silent, very empty. A dust cloth was thrown over the piano, turning it into a large blocky ghost shape in the dimness. The stage gaped like an open mouth, needing to be filled with bright lights and people and music.

Listening hard for a moment I did hear music. Thin and distant.

"Something wrong?" asked Escott.

"The radio in my office is on."

"You can hear it?"

"Yeah."

"Your extranormal senses are quite amazing."

"Or I could just be crazy and hearing things."

"What song is playing?"

"Wayne King doing 'Mickey Mouse's Birthday Party.'"

"Ah. Then you are hearing things, and you are crazy. No one listens to that one anymore. It's all your imagination."

"Good, I'd rather be crazy than have it real. So? Evie Montana?"

He swirled brandy, letting it get used to the air. "I took her to the Nightcrawler. Since she chose to fill the drive with detailed and enthusiastic praise of Alan Caine's boundless talent, I was curious to see him and went in to catch the second show."

"And what'd you think?"

"That you met a completely different fellow."

"Huh?" I expected Escott to hate the guy on sight.

"He has an excellent voice, a commanding stage presence, and put across every song with an enlightened earnestness that was on a level with true genius.

"*Huh?*" I didn't want to hear this. "The guy's a jackass!"

"If so, then it's not when he's performing. He really should be singing opera, not wasting himself with popular songs in a club."

"What's with you? You gonna send him flowers next?"

He sipped the brandy, amused by my annoyance. "One can have an admiration for a performer's talent, if not for the performer himself. He's truly gifted."

"And a jackass."

"I'll believe that when I see it."

"Fine with me. Go by tomorrow before the show and watch him rehearsing."

"One only has to know how to deal with artistic temperament."

"Just don't go recommending him to Bobbi for this place. I'd end up strangling him."

"Or you could simply rearrange his mood for the duration."

I'd been known to do that with troublesome talents. Escott was unaware of my going temporarily on the wagon from whammy-work. No need for him to know, either. He'd just give me one of those worried looks I was sick of seeing.

"Mr. Derner came by my table. He had a message for you," he added.

"Oh, yeah?"

"A negative one. Some of the boys thought they'd found Dugan, but it turned out to be a false alarm. Not all of them were convinced, though, and might be coming 'round to claim the remainder of the bounty. Mr. Derner assured me he would take measures to prevent your being bothered by them."

I grunted and wished I could drink real booze again, even the cheap stuff, which was all I could afford back in my reporter days. "The guy they thought was Dugan—he okay?"

"So far as I know. He was dragged to the Nightcrawler, produced sufficient evidence to prove mistaken identity, was given a drink and an apology, and returned to wherever they found him."

"God, I'm gonna have to call it off. Those mugs are too stupid to be let loose."

"You don't think they'll find him, do you?"

"Dugan could be halfway to Hong Kong by now. I know I would be there if I had me after me."

Escott blinked a few times. "It's far too late for that to have made sense, and it did."

I glanced at my watch. The evening was getting into the deep-night hours. "Bobbi should be done with the receipts by now. I oughta get her home."

"Sounds to be an excellent idea for myself. That is, if you don't require me further?"

Escott really did like to help out at the club. "You've done above and beyond. Thanks."

He got up. "No problem."

His time in the States had corrupted him. He sounded just like Gordy.

In the lobby he boomed a loud good night toward the upstairs. Bobbi answered back, asking if I was around.

"Yes, he'll be up directly."

"Okay. Drive careful."

"Thank you, I will."

Theirs was a call and response thing like you hear in some church services. They'd done it several times now at closing, a comfortable form of reassurance. I hadn't been the only one left shaken by Bristow's work on me.

Escott let himself out using his own key. It would be a dark and chill ride home until his Nash warmed up again.

"Drive careful," I muttered, suddenly aware of the emptiness of the building. Were I here on my own, I'd have made like Myrna and turned on all the lights. Certainly I'd have gotten some music going to push back the silence. The stuff seeping thin through the walls from my office radio wasn't enough.

Thank you, Hog Bristow. Thank you so very much, you goddamned son of a bitch, and please, please do be screaming in a really deep, sulphur-stenched pit burning merrily away for the rest of eternity.

"Jack . . . ?" Bobbi's light voice jarred me.

"I'm here."

"Okay." She sounded like she was a few yards from the office door, ready to come down if invited.

"I'll be right up, honey, gotta make a phone call. Private." That was the word we used that meant I was busy with mob business. She knew it was a necessary task and to help Gordy, but preferred to ignore my moonlighting for the time being.

"Okay." Her tone was serene, almost singing, which meant I really should hurry. Her heels clacked down the hall, followed by the office door shutting.

I levered into the lobby phone booth, paid a nickel, and dialed very carefully so as not to wake up an honest citizen cursed with a number similar to Shoe Coldfield's nightclub. To my growing concern it rang nine times before someone came on halfway through the tenth.

"Coldfield, what is it?" he growled. Since it was his office, not his home, I knew I'd not wakened him, but phones going off at such hours never portend happy news.

"It's Jack. Charles said to say hello." I hoped in this way to tip him that all was well.

Didn't work. "Damn, kid, no one calls this late unless it's an emergency. You okay?" He traded the rough annoyance for rough concern.

A few days ago Escott had informed him about my recent experience; apparently the basic facts had been augmented with a mention of my problems recovering. "I'm fine." I tried to sound normal, whatever that was.

"Charles told me you were, and I quote—'a touch wobbly'—and you know how he understates things."

"Ah, he was just being optimistic."

"Well, you didn't call just to pass on a hello. What's up?"

"One of the New York bosses came to town. The one who arranged Hog Bristow's visit. A guy named Whitey Kroun. Know him?"

"With a name like that? You kidding?"

Coldfield, in addition to running his nightclub, some garages, and a few other businesses, also controlled one of the biggest gangs in the Bronze Belt. Unless it was assigned to him as a joke, any man nicknamed Whitey would not readily blend into the crowd.

"I'll take that to mean no. What about a soldier called Mitchell? He was in Morelli's gang about the time I first came to town."

"Nope, sorry. You know the colored and white mobs don't mix except when they can't help it."

"Yeah, but you generally know who's who."

"Only the local big boys, not the soldiers."

"Okay, one more item. A collector here named Hoyle is on the outs with me along with Ruzzo."

"Those bedbug-crazy brothers?"

"The same. You know Hoyle?"

"By sight. Tough guy, used to box. What happened?"

"He tried to play baseball, with me as the ball. I took his bat away and nearly made him eat it."

He wanted more details, so I gave them. Coldfield liked a good story. As before with Escott, I left out the ugly epilogue in the Stockyards. Even thinking about it threatened to make me queasy.

"You've had a busy night, kid," he said. He knew my real age, but couldn't be blamed for forgetting most of the time. Now and then I would shoot him a reminder, like mentioning something from twenty years back when I was in the War, and he'd throw an odd look my way for a few seconds.

"You don't know the half of it," I said.

"About this Kroun, I can ask around if you want."

"Nah, not that important. Charles can dig. He thinks it's fun."

"Kroun's not giving you any trouble is he?"

"Nothing like that, just me being curious. I figure he'll be going back to New York soon."

"Better hope so. No one likes when the boss drops in to nose around. Just ask my people."

Coldfield did run a tight ship, but I'd not heard of anyone trying to kill him lately. I thanked him; he told me to get some rest and hung up.

I remained in the booth, wanting a moment of quiet. The vast emptiness of the club was easier to handle in here. I liked having a place where I could put my back to a wall.

It couldn't last. I had to boost out and go upstairs, or Bobbi would come looking, and I'd have to assure her that my sitting shut into a phone booth without phoning was a perfectly reasonable occupation. Before my buckwheats session with Bristow she might have accepted it as absent-minded eccentricity. No more.

But I *did* seem to be better. The meeting with Kroun had gone very well. After that inner revelation, seeing those who would kill me as being no more than food, I'd been in control with not one wild, trembling muscle to mar the event. Maybe that's all I'd really needed to restore my confidence. Sure, I was still nervous about some stuff—like now—but there were lots of people who didn't like big empty, quiet, dark places.

So perhaps I should get off my duff and see my patient girlfriend. I'd been procrastinating with no good reason other than a vague and ridiculous trepidation that she would see all the stuff I wanted to keep hidden. Bobbi was closer to me and much more perceptive than anyone else I knew. She was the one person I couldn't lie to even when I successfully lied to myself.

Well, maybe she'd take a good look, and if she pronounced me miraculously cured of my waking nightmares, I could believe it.

I pushed the booth's folding doors open in time to hear a click, followed by several more, coming from the main room. A familiar sound, but out of place at this hour. Curious and cautious, I went through the curved passage.

All the little table lights were on. Spaced at regular intervals along the three wide horseshoe tiers, they made a grand sight even with the upside-down chairs, and I said as much out loud to Myrna.

"You're really getting good at that, babe," I added.

I half expected one or any of them to blink in reply, but they remained steady. There was no point asking her to shut them off. She would or wouldn't at her own whim. Besides, I could likely afford the electric bill; business had been pretty decent this month.

"See you upstairs. Maybe." Actually, I hoped not. Some instinct within told me I was not ready to actually *see* Myrna. She was disturbing enough just playing with lights.

Billie Holiday's version of "No Regrets" met me coming up the stairs. Bobbi hummed along to the radio, but stopped as I opened the door. She was busy at my desk, surrounded by empty tills, piles of wrapped cash, rolls of coins, a small stack of checks, the entry books, pencils, and the calculating machine. She'd traded her fancy spangly dancing gown for a dark dress and had a blue sweater around her shoulders. Her blond hair was pinned up out of the way. She punched keys on the machine, pulling the lever like it was a squatty one-armed bandit. When its brief, important, chattering died, she peered at the printed result.

"Hi, stranger," she said, raising her face my way for a hello. She'd gotten a ride in with Escott while the sun was still up, so this was the first chance for us to really be with each other tonight.

I kissed her on the lips, and instantly knew it was right, the way it was supposed to be, the way it had always been for us; everything was going to be fine now.

Which lasted for a few perfect, wonderful seconds.

Then I overthought it, and what began as a warm greeting went subtly and utterly wrong. The demons in my head tore gleefully at me, whispering doubts, magnifying fears, and pointing out the obvious fact that this recovery business was an impossibility, so I pulled back and smiled and tried to pretend everything was great, and the smile was so forced that my jaw hurt, and I turned away so she couldn't see how much it hurt.

Damnation.

Whatever had been repaired and rebuilt in me came apart so fast I wondered if it had been a sham to start with or if the sickness inside was simply overwhelming in its strength.

I didn't want that.

Thankfully, Bobbi did not ask me if I was okay. We'd had that conversation several times already and kept butting into the walls of assurances, protests, and denials I put up, which she would knock down with a word or three, then neither of us felt happy. We'd accepted the fact that this would take a while, and it would not be pleasant. It wasn't her fault that she terrified me. I was ashamed of it. On the other hand, if I avoided her or went on that vacation Escott had suggested, I'd go right off the deep end of the dock. She was my lifeline. I had to keep close to her.

"Ready to go home?" I asked. Her hat, gloves, and fur coat were ready on the couch. I sat next to them.

"Almost." She gave me a long, unreadable look, then peered at the latest printing from the machine, writing a number neatly in the account book with my mechanical pencil. "We had a pretty good night, all things considered."

"Oh, yeah?"

"You made fifty-two bucks and some change."

I looked at the stack of cash before her. "You've got more than that there."

"Subtract your overhead, salaries, and all the rest, and you have fifty-two bucks left over."

"Less than last night's take."

"Cheer up, there's not many guys who make that much in a month, let alone on a single less-than-perfect evening. It'll be better this weekend if the weather doesn't turn sleety again. What took you away? You were gone for so long."

"I had to talk with a gentleman from New York."

Bobbi understood the implications. "How did it go?"

"Good and bad. I'm still running things for Gordy."

"And what's the bad?"

"I called it right about why they sent Bristow. Kroun's on my side, now, so—"

"Whitey Kroun?"

"Yeah, the guy from the phone. You ever meet him?"

"No. Once in a while I'd hear Gordy mention him, but that's all. Just a name. I'll be glad when you're out of this, Jack."

"Same here." I took a deep breath and exhaled. I thought about asking if she remembered Mitchell, but held back. She didn't care to be reminded of the days when she'd been Slick Morelli's mistress. Gordy would be the best source for my idle curiosity when he was up to it.

Time for a subject change. "That was some nice act you had going with Teddy and the anniversary thing. It went over great."

"I thought it might. We'll make it a regular item if you clear it."

"It's cleared."

"I'll have to look up more wedding-type music or we're going to get really tired of 'The Anniversary Song.'"

"How about something from *The Merry Widow*? For the marriages that aren't going so well."

She rolled her eyes. "Don't be gruesome."

Some of our old comfortable banter had resurrected itself. All I had to do from now on was sit ten feet away from her. "I want to have something special ready for this Saturday, if it's not too short notice."

"Just no street parades, too cold. What is it?"

I told her about helping out Escott's suit with Vivian Gladwell by throwing a "birthday" party for Sarah. Bobbi was all for it.

"But don't go overboard," I cautioned. "You'll scare Charles."

"Don't worry. I've done enough singing at debutant balls to know what's right for that crowd. It'll be fun, but tasteful."

"You can tackle Charles tomorrow for details . . ."

The radio music died away, replaced by static as the station signed off. I reached for the dial.

"Wait a sec," she said, staring at it.

I withdrew my hand and waited, the static buzz making my eyeballs itch. "What?" I asked after a minute.

"Aw, I was hoping . . . I guess she won't do anything when people are watching."

"Myrna?"

"Yeah."

"What'd she do now?"

"I was working and some newsreader came on. I wasn't paying it much mind, and it switched to music right in the middle of a story. Gave me a turn until I realized she'd done it. I looked, and the pointer was on a different station than before. Isn't that something?"

"She didn't scare you?"

"Not really. She just surprised me. It must be boring for her to only play with the lights. Can't blame her for branching out. Maybe she's getting stronger the more we pay attention to her."

That disturbed me, but I kept it to myself, suspecting Myrna might cut the lights entirely in response. I didn't want dark.

Bobbi continued. "I like her company. The place doesn't feel so empty. Kind of friendly, you know? Like she's looking after us. So I talk to her. I think she likes it, must be lonesome, being a ghost."

"What do you talk about?"

She smirked. "You, of course. Women always end up talking to each other about their men sooner or later. Of course with Myrna I have to carry the conversation. Maybe we could get that record-cutting equipment up here and see if we can hear her talk back again."

"Maybe." I'd recently found it necessary to record a conversation and filled the office with hidden microphones. Much to my consternation a third voice, faint and strange, but definitely female, had also been on the wax disk, reacting to what was going on. Even thinking about attempting that once more made my neck hair rise. But . . . perhaps it could get a question or two answered, help us find out more about Myrna. "Wanna go home?"

Bobbi didn't think twice. "Yes. Please."

I put the cleaned-out tills on a table, ready for the next day while she scooped the counted cash into a bank envelope for the night deposit box. I put the change bags in the safe on top of the revolver I kept there, shut and locked, then helped Bobbi on with her coat.

As we started to leave, she swooped to one side and fiddled with the radio tuning until she found music.

"There," she said, as Tommy Dorsey's band came through. "I think this station plays all night. Myrna might end up with farm and weather reports in a couple hours, but it'll be company until then. You don't mind?"

"Nope. Leave the light on, too." I could sympathize all too well.

On the way out I checked the main room. The little table lamps were dark now. We left the one burning behind the lobby bar alone.

Bobbi shivered and went *brrrrrr* during the first ten minutes of our ride until the Buick's heater was warm enough to blow something other than arctic wind. I stopped briefly to drop the money into the bank's night deposit slot, then drove quickly through the near-empty streets to her hotel apartment. Drowsy, she leaned against me for the ride, and things felt normal again. I wanted to put my arm around her but had to have it free to change gears.

She woke up as I braked in the no-parking section in front of her building, got out, and came around to hold her door, leaving the motor running.

"Not coming up?" she asked.

"You're done in, honey, and I had a lot crashing into me tonight."

There must have been a dozen variations of protest hesitating on her lips, everything from "I could get untired in a hurry" to "That's all right, just let me know when you're ready, sweetheart," and she didn't say any of them, including the heartbreaking "Jack, I'm so sorry." It would have been too painful for both of us, so we accepted this nice, safe, not-quite-as-painful illusion.

I walked her through the hotel lobby to the elevator, and like well-rehearsed actors we said the familiar good-bye-until-tomorrow lines. They sounded hollow and sad compared to the cheerful call and response she'd traded with Escott earlier.

She broke, though, and stopped the automatic elevator doors from closing. "You're sure? Just for company?"

"The company is a rare and breathtaking creature of light and music and beauty who would make angels jealous, and I don't know what I did to deserve to be on the same planet with you."

She fairly gaped. I hardly ever talked like that to her.

"But—" I kissed her chastely on the forehead and left it at that.

Her hazel eyes were wide a moment, then she made a little dive at me, wrapping her arms tight around. We held close for a solid minute, and I felt my body responding to hers, felt the rush of warmth, the first build of pressure above my corner teeth, the desire to slowly remove all her clothes and settle in and come up with old and new ways of exhausting her and myself thoroughly before dawn swept my consciousness into its shallow grave.

Resisting while I still could, I gently pulled clear. "Get some sleep," I said softly, backing off. I turned away before seeing whatever look might have been on her face.

The doors knitted shut and took her up and away from me. I hurried to the car, hit the gears rough, and shot clear, taking corners too fast and abusing the gas pedal on the straights. Before I alarmed any cops, I found a space in front of a block of closed shops and pulled in, decisively cutting the motor.

Then I waited.

I'd *wanted* to go up with her, and not just for company. Still wanted. Ached for it. Was sick for it. Wanted to go back even now and surprise her, make love to her. I would hold her close and warm and bring her to the edge of that wonderful, feverish peak and oh-so-gently bite into her throat, and it would just *happen* and she wouldn't fight me, wouldn't even think to, and then it would be too late, and like a mindless, greedy animal I would gorge on her blood as I'd done on that cow, unable to stop . . .

The tremors began their fast rise from within, an icy tide come to drown me. I hugged my ribs and groaned like a dying thing and keeled over across the seat.

6

FULLY clothed, still in my overcoat, I lay flat on the army cot in my pseudotomb in Escott's cellar, waiting for the dawn.

It's really better than it sounds.

I had heat and light—always leaving the lamp on since I hate waking up in the dark—and it was profoundly quiet. My bricked-up alcove wasn't the overwhelming large space of the club, nor so cramped that I'd get claustrophobic, and I could put my back to a wall.

For now my spine was stretched tense on this cot, and between it and the canvas, protected by a layer of oilcloth, was a sufficient supply of my home earth to keep the daymares away. Without that piece of the grave with me I would spend the sunny hours being consumed by an endless pageant of inner horrors.

As though the ones I experienced while awake weren't enough. In the car I managed to cut short my latest bout into hell. I'd felt a scream beginning to rise, and before it went full force I denied it breath and a voice box by vanishing.

The awful cold shuddering melted into soothing grayness, and I let myself float like that for a very long time. To vanish meant to physically heal, and I'd hoped it would work again, with a different kind of healing. One for my soul.

But no such luck. I returned to solidity weak and drained and shivering.

And helpless and terrified, don't forget about those. My body and mind had both turned on me, and there wasn't a damned thing I could do about their betrayal.

I'd been so tired afterward I could not recall driving home, only coming back to myself while parked out front in my usual spot. While other guys could drop into bed and shut off their minds after something like that, there would be no sleep for me. Until the rising sun finally knocked me out I was in for a bout of Undead insomnia.

What I missed about being a normal man was the kind of sleep where you know that you *are* sleeping. When you drift through it, maybe skimming close to the surface of waking, then contentedly turning over to dive back in again. You have a sense of passing time, that you're getting actual *rest*. My daylight drop into death left me very rested, but it's not always satisfying.

Like now. I was still terrified, which would be exhausting to anyone, and the fear would be there when I woke again.

I lay on the cot. Waiting. Sensing the approach of the sun that would take my life away. Some part of me wanted utter oblivion, the kind from which you never awoke.

That would solve a whole lot of problems for me. All of them, in fact.

Out.

And return.

I'd felt it come and shut my eyes in time. They were open now. Another day had rushed over my unheeding head. The only way I could tell for sure was to glance at my watch. Yes, lots of hours were gone for good, with me not in any of them. Winding the watch, I made myself remember that the trembling fits were last night's old news. Hadn't Escott told me time would fix things? Time had passed, so I shut down the internal whining, then vanished and floated, rising through the floor to go solid in the dim, quiet kitchen. My hat was where I'd left it on the table so Escott would know I'd come home.

Damn, but I still felt cold despite the overcoat. "Charles?"

No reply, so he was probably already at the club. He was being a hell of a friend to look after his work and mine. I'd have to find some way to thank him. Bobbi would know what to recommend, besides putting him on the payroll. He was going to have a surprise pay packet come Friday. His own business might be suffering for all the time he'd been putting in helping with mine. He would help for free, but compensation was only being fair.

I went to bring in the mail, but the stack on the hall table told me Escott had been and gone. There was nothing for me, which was fine. I wasn't up to writing chatty correspondence.

Back in the kitchen, I phoned the Nightcrawler office and got Derner. "How'd things go today?"

"Pretty much normal, no problems."

"What about Kroun? He gone home yet?"

"Still in place."

The phrasing gave me the idea Kroun or Mitchell might be in the room with him. "You treating him right?"

"Red carpet all the way."

That was reassuring. "What about Hoyle? Any trouble?"

"Haven't heard from him. If he's gone, I donno where."

"Find out. Keep it low and easy." I wouldn't feel comfortable until I knew where he'd landed. "What about Ruzzo? They behaving?"

"They turned up looking like they had a gas attack to go with their shiners. One of the boys thought they were trying to find Hoyle, but not for sure. They know they're on the outs, but you want I should fire them, too? The hard way?"

That meant something fatal. Execution was the normal mob response for what Hoyle tried to do to me. "That'll be up to Gordy when he's back." He'd probably get rid of them, but I couldn't be bumping off all the guys in his gang who didn't like me. There wouldn't be a lot left.

I hung up and went to my second-floor room for a fast shower-bath and a change of clothes. Usually I preferred to sit and soak in a near-boiling tub, but didn't have the time. Too bad, it might have warmed me up. A hurried soaping with the water slopping past the cellophane curtain would have to do.

Shaving, as always, was a touch-and-nick adventure. I'd switched from a straight to a safety razor in the army, same as all the other guys, and once more blessed that change. If I still used the folding cut-throat device my older brothers had introduced me to, I'd probably have lopped my head off by now. Still, I made mistakes, but a quick vanishing fixed that.

What it did not fix were the long threads of scarring that covered what I could see of my chest and arms and certainly my back. I tried to avoid touching them; the white ridges along already pale skin always felt colder than the rest of my flesh. Those scars collected in my lifetime before my change had gradually gone away, even the one from the bullet that had killed me. But not these, no matter how many times I vanished. And I didn't know why.

Most of my physical healing from the damage had taken place that same night. To replace my lost blood I'd fed from Bristow. He'd been dying; my feast had simply hurried the process. I'd gorged—shameless, mindless, desperate.

And enjoyed it.

It hurt to heal then. I had been unable to vanish, and it hurt a lot. Left me shaking like an epileptic. Maybe that was the origin of my fits, just as my out-of-control draining of Bristow was similar to how I'd fed from that cow last night. Though the ordeal was past, some part of me kept me there, like replaying a record over and over but with the sound down low so you don't consciously notice that it's repeating and driving you crazy. I had to find some way to switch it off.

I'd reluctantly talked to Escott about going to a head doctor, but how in hell could any of them help me with this problem?

Hey, Doc, I get blindsided by these shivering fits and drink blood until I'm sick. You got a pill for that?

I didn't think so.

AND another less-than-perfect evening began with the discovery that the two street-side tires of my Buick were flat.

The problem didn't register at first. I walked around my car, unlocked the door, and was about to open it when the impression of what was wrong met up with the memory of what was supposed to be right. The car was lower than it should be. I backed off and stared and couldn't believe and stared and couldn't believe; and then I got pissed and wanted to hit something, only that would have left a dent in my blameless vehicle.

I was certain Hoyle or Ruzzo had done it. A kid's vicious prank.

It wasn't anything that could be proved. Not ordinarily. If I confronted Ruzzo about it, they'd happily lie in my face. I had my own way around that. Our next talk was going to be very unpleasant—for them. They would also be paying for the new tires. Four, so they'd all match.

Then I'd probably beat the hell out of Ruzzo. For some guys logic or threats never work. You have to kick their asses to get your message to sink in.

I called Derner again and explained the situation.

"We got garages, don't we?" I asked.

"Thirty-three, not counting the wrecking yards—"

"That's good. Find one close to my house and send someone over. I want the tires on my Buick changed out to four new ones." As long as the mob boys called me "boss" I might as well benefit from the position. "Have that done before tomorrow evening."

"Right, Boss."

"And I need a car until mine's fixed."

"No problem," said Derner. "You can use Gordy's. Strome'll drive you. He's away now, but can be there in an hour."

"Nah, I'll cab over and wait at the Nightcrawler. In the meantime I want Ruzzo. Both of 'em. Hoyle, too."

"I'll send out the hounds."

"They can cough up cash for replacement tires unless I take it out of their hides."

Derner's "yes" sounded oddly faint, and I wondered why before realizing my own poor choice of words. He'd seen me hanging skinned from that meat hook, after all.

Next I called the lobby phone of Lady Crymsyn. Wilton answered. I told him I'd be late on account of business and to open as usual. He said okay and no problem, unknowingly echoing Derner. At least some pieces of my life were still in place. Then I phoned for a cab.

I was still too mad to let the tire slashing go. Directing my driver to the Nightcrawler, I blew off steam to him. We both heartily agreed that crime was completely out of hand in this town and, united against the world by our mutual righteous outrage, were fast friends by the end of the ride. He got a dollar tip for my two-dollar ride, since by then I felt almost good. Maybe I didn't need a head doctor, just a lot more taxi trips.

The outer bar was open, but the Nightcrawler's main room was still being readied for the evening show. I sent someone up to tell Derner I was here, then settled in at one of the tables, breaking one of the rules for surviving in the mob: sitting with my back to the door. If I'd had vulnerable company along, I wouldn't have made such a slip, but while on my own I really didn't give a damn. The mugs watching the front were on my side. Sort of. They'd spot trouble and deal with it. I kept my coat and hat on. For some reason I just could not shake the cold tonight. All in my head, probably. Everything else was, so why not?

Without being asked, a girl brought a glass of water to me and inquired if I wanted anything stronger. I said no and shooed her off with a neutral smile. More waitresses in short spangly skirts hurried to and fro and traded talk loudly across the breadth of the room. I had waiters for my place. In the early days I hired on a few girls to come in on the busier nights. They had red velvet skirts to match the décor and were cute as bugs. Many of the male customers liked their looks as well, taking them to be part of the after-hours entertainment. Some of the girls followed through on it, and made a hell of a lot more money in the parking lot than they did collecting tips in the club.

On one hand I didn't mind, but out of self-preservation had to cut them loose. If something went wrong, it would reflect on the club and me. Gordy could take that sort of heat from the local vice squad; I just didn't want the grief. Bobbi was still trying to figure out what to do with the leftover costumes.

The Nightcrawler's talent trickled in. They weren't supposed to use the front, but did anyway, leggy dancers heading backstage, musicians setting up, everyone busier than me and consumed by their own concerns. I liked that.

Whitey Kroun walked in. People paused to look up; I felt the draw, which is why I turned to see who'd arrived. Even here he filled the place. Some types were like that: actors, singers, politicians. Bobbi had that electric quality, but she only threw the switch when working because it sometimes left her tired out afterward. Kroun's seemed to be going all the time, and if he was aware of it, he didn't let on.

He took off his hat, brushed a hand through his hair. He used the gesture as a means to look around, spotted me lounging, and sketched a casual wave. I returned it, half-expecting him to come over, but he continued on through the casino door. Only then did I notice Mitchell in his wake like a plain-Jane pilot fish.

He gave me a look.

Make that more of a glare.

It must have been inspired by my stay-away-from-Bobbi message of the night before. He seemed the type to stew about things. On one hand Mitchell was only doing his job. A good lieutenant is supposed to make life miserable for anyone who could potentially annoy his boss. But I was getting bored with this one. If he didn't leave for New York soon, I'd be inclined to inspire a sudden interest in ice fishing so he'd go away for the rest of the winter.

I just looked back, again not blinking, not giving a damn about his obvious dislike of me. He finally got bored and went elsewhere. I returned to watching the club's opening routine. It was much the same as my place, but with more money.

Jewel Caine, the obstreperous ex-wife of this week's star performer unexpectedly appeared, beelined to a booth with a view of the stage, and hunched down in its depths. Under her black coat, which she unbuttoned, she was all in blue from hat to stockings. It suited her better than the previous night's green. One of the casino bouncers passing through finally noticed her while she jerkily plucked off her gloves. It was no business of mine, but I signed for him to lay off.

She pulled out cigarettes and grimly smoked, watching the stage with needle-sharp eyes. A woman with a mission, I thought, trying unsuccessfully to read her mind. Sometimes you can tell what's in a person's head by his or her carriage. Now that she wasn't screaming threats she showed some good looks. Hoping she might be in a reasonable mood, I picked up my glass of water and ambled over. I was still boss. Maybe if I found out what her plan was, I could head off trouble, breakage, and hospital bills.

"Mrs. Caine?"

"Who wants to know?"

"My name's Jack Fleming."

"So how do you know me?"

"I'm associated with this club."

Her chin went up. "You gonna throw me out?"

"I hope not. All right if I sit with you?"

She thought it over, giving me a hard up and down, then nodded. "What do you mean by 'associated'?"

I took my hat off, put it to one side, and slipped in opposite. "I know the owner. I'm helping manage the place for the time being."

She made no reply but stubbed the old cigarette and went on to the next, her fingertips yellow from chain-smoking. There were matches on the table. I had one lighted by the time she needed it. She leaned forward and puffed her smoke to life. "So you manage the place. What do you want from me?"

"Nothing. I just noticed last evening you seemed to have a stack of grievances against your ex-husband—"

"More of a mountain. He owes me a lot of alimony, that's the main one. It's pulling teeth with tweezers to get him to cough up anything, but I really need it, the landlord's leaning on me, and I owe for groceries. It's not like I'm wasting anything . . ." She shut herself down, mouth twisted with disgust. "Christ, but don't I sound pathetic."

"If he's holding out, you've a right to be upset. What about getting him into court?"

"That costs money. I can't feed myself, much less some lawyer." She sucked in a draft from her cigarette and politely vented it to one side. "Look, kid, maybe you want to help, but I've been over all the angles, and unless Alan pays up, I'm on the street in the morning. But then he'd enjoy that, the son of a bitch."

I raised a hand and a waitress came over. They knew about my temporary rise in rank. Fast service for the boss was part of the job. "What will you have, Mrs. Caine?"

Surprisingly, she wanted only water and a twist of lemon. From her behavior last night I took her to be a hard drinker. The waitress came back quick with a glass and a bowl of peanuts. Jewel attacked them, but one at a time, yellow fingers delicate. I wondered if she'd eaten lately. She didn't look starved, but you didn't have to look it to be hungry. I was acquainted with that a little too well.

"Thanks, kid," she said, lifting her glass.

"Just call me Jack."

"Yeah. I've seen you around. Heard you run that red club with the funny name."

"Lady Crymsyn."

"Any jobs open? Or has Alan gotten to you, too?"

"What do you mean?"

"He's a big draw. Bigger than me, now. He won't sing at any club that's given me work. They always go with the money, and I get bupkis. He sees to it."

"What can you do?"

"Just about anything. I can sing, but I'll wait tables, clean the damn toilets if I have to."

"How good a singer are you?"

"I do all right with wistful throaty stuff, nothing fast." She tapped ash off. "These things spoiled my voice, put a limit on my range, but I can't seem to kick 'em. I've got plenty of songs I can get away with that aren't a strain on the cords, and I'm good with mood pieces. I can make a rock cry."

That told me she knew her stuff. "I'm booked for acts this week, but maybe can give you a short set to do."

Jewel stared, hovering between disbelief and hope. "You sure? For real?"

"That jackass is never gonna sing at my place. It's only a short set. It won't pay much."

"Kid, I'm making nothing now, I'll take it."

"Can you start tomorrow?"

"Yeah, but—"

"I'll notify my booking manager." I got my wallet and gave her a business card for the club. "Go over tomorrow around three with your music and work things out. You'll talk to Bobbi Smythe. You know her?"

"Yeah, but—"

"Your landlord? A loan, then." I had forty bucks and gave it to her. "Interest-free. You need more?"

"Christ, kid, that's two month's rent!"

"It's okay, I'll take it out of Caine's salary. He must owe you more than that, though."

"A few thousand."

"I'll set something up at this end. So long as he sings here, you'll get your alimony. It won't be permanent, all he has to do is leave for someplace else, but maybe you'll have enough to get on your feet?"

"Hell, yes." She seemed very taken aback. "Why you doin' this?"

I shrugged. "It gets my mind off my own troubles."

"Must be some troubles."

I didn't want to talk about what churned my guts. "How'd you two get together?"

She snorted. "Ten years back I was the big star and he was . . . well, you've seen him. He's a knockout. He still is."

"Not to me."

"Men." Jewel puffed, wearing her cig down half an inch in one draw. "He got to me with that big smile and those gorgeous eyes and sweet talk like it was going out of style. I went nuts over him. It's the only reason I can think of, that I was out of my mind. We got married, and it was good, and I got him singing lessons, then jobs. I wanted us to work up a duet routine, but he said he got more work as a single act. Eventually I figured out it meant he got more women that way. He was vile about it. Shoved it in my face like it was my fault."

I listened and nodded as she touched on the low points. She had a long list of bitter grievances, the usual for when life and love goes bad for a couple. Caine had gone out of his way to be a jerk, though. Jewel struck me as being able to give as good as she got, but he'd worn her down, then moved on.

She wore a kind of choker necklace made of blue beads, and when she held still the beads moved in time to her pulsing veins. I took a breath and caught the scent of blood under her sallow skin.

Not good. I shouldn't be noticing those kinds of things. I'd fed myself sick at the Stockyards, wasn't remotely hungry tonight, and human blood was off my menu, anyway. Didn't matter. I was wanting it the way I used to want a drink back when I lived in New York. Except for weekend binges when I could afford it, I had that under control. I did it then, I could do it now. Really.

"If you got any brains, you'll never have Alan perform at your place," Jewel concluded. She'd apparently forgotten what I'd said before. This sounded like something she repeated often to many people.

"I'll hire a special bouncer just to keep him out."

She broke into a smile and looked pretty for it. "You're all right, Jack."

Past her shoulder I caught sight of Mitchell, returned from someplace or other so he could watch me for some reason or other.

Jewel noticed and glanced where I was looking, snorting again. Her eyes sharpened into a glare, an odd look on her face, then she smiled again. This time it took away from her looks. "There's another one to keep clear of. Used to run with the Morelli gang before Gordy took over. You don't want to know why *he* had to leave town." She gave a short, unpleasant laugh.

"Of course I do. You can't do a fanfare like that and leave me hanging."

"No. It's vile, too, and I've had enough for one night. Besides, Alan just came in."

True. Alan Caine, with Evie Montana in close and adoring tow, sauntered in on the other side of the room, not noticing us. He did see Mitchell, though, and made a point of walking right by him. Caine gave him a big, disarming smile, and Mitchell went stony.

"You got a problem, Mitch?" Caine acted puzzled.

Mitchell kept shut, but clearly they had some kind of feud going, probably carried all the way from New York. Easy to understand, given their personalities. What was coming out from behind Mitchell's eyes would have melted steel. Evie noticed and tugged on Caine's arm to move on.

"I feel sorry for her," said Jewel. "There's no point trying to wise up her type about Alan, though. She'll have to learn the hard way."

"He's gonna break her heart?"

"Yeah, but only after he's gambled off all her money and hocked everything she's got, up to and including her step-ins."

Evie seemed to be a girl not too interested in wearing much in the way of underclothes. Her satin skirt was pretty tight, and I couldn't see lines showing through. Bobbi did the same thing herself a lot of the time.

And I didn't need to be thinking about . . . about anything.

Caine resisted Evie's efforts to move him, continuing to smirk. The idiot must have thought his talent made him bulletproof, but there is a certain kind of mug who doesn't worry about consequences. Mitchell might be one of them. If Caine wasn't careful, he could get a broken leg or worse. He could sing sitting down, but wouldn't be happy about it.

Not liking Caine, I wouldn't have minded letting matters take their natural course; but as caretaker for Gordy's investment, it was up to me to keep the peace. A week or so back I'd have involved myself, but didn't trust how I might react if either of them got stupid with me. Instead, I signaled to some of the club's muscle to make themselves visible to Mitchell.

He saw, if Caine didn't, and strolled off, Caine laughing at his back. Even from here I could pick up on the booze tone in his voice. This time Evie Montana succeeded in dragging him away.

"Men." Jewel gave a deep, derisive sigh. "Alan's a damn fool. Never does know when to quit. He's the kind of guy who drinks and pretends he doesn't."

"If he's too drunk, you could have a job here tonight," I said, half-joking.

"He's smart enough to never miss a cue. But I *should* have this job. Instead, I got bills and this." She lifted her glass of water. Sipped.

"That mean something?"

"Yeah. It was easier being married to him if I stayed drunk all the time. Trouble was, after the divorce I kept on being drunk. Thought I should warn you . . . in case you want your money back."

"You're having water now, though?"

"I'm on the wagon. You might as well know I'm going to Alcoholics Anonymous. Someone told me they can really help, and so far so good. I've been sober two weeks. Two weeks and six hours."

"Congratulations."

"Thanks. Though when I look in a mirror and see what the sauce has done to me I think maybe I should go back to it so I don't care anymore."

"You look just fine."

She smiled and patted my hand. "Sweet of you to say so, kid. I used to stop traffic in fog at midnight. Don't mind me. This is how I feel sorry for myself when I'm sober. It's better than when I'm drunk, though."

By this time she'd finished off the bowl of peanuts. "You hungry?" I asked. "The kitchen'll do you up a steak on the house."

She hesitated before giving an answer, but finally nodded and smiled. "Thanks. You're too decent a guy to be in this joint."

"No, I'm not. This is exactly where I'm supposed to be." I flagged a waitress, and she wrote down Jewel's order, then whisked off to the barely opened kitchen.

"You got a girl, don't you?" asked Jewel.

"How's that?"

"A guy as nice as you has a girl somewhere. Hope she's treating you right."

I felt myself going red. "Far better than I deserve."

Strome walked in the front, saving me from having to come up with another change of subject. I waved him over and explained about needing the car until mine was fixed.

"No problem," he said. "Except Kroun wants a ride back to his hotel when he's done here. I can get you another car."

"I'll wait." Strome might pick up things of interest from Kroun and Mitchell he could pass on. They'd likely be too smart to talk openly in front of him, but you never knew. "Why's Kroun still hanging around?"

"More business with Gordy. They're talking now."

What? "Gordy's *here*?"

"In the casino."

"He's supposed to be resting, dammit."

"Try telling him that. When the big boss says jump, you ask how high. That's how it works."

Hell. I got my hat and stood, excusing myself to Jewel, adding an apology.

She took it in stride. "Men," she said, lighting another cigarette.

I went into the not-quite-opened casino, but Gordy wasn't there after all.

Strome only shrugged. "Means they're up in the office. You might wanna steer clear."

"Why?"

"The more people in a room talking business, the longer it takes to finish."

That bordered on the genius. "Yeah, okay. But have someone tell me when they're done. I want a word with Gordy, too."

"Sure."

"Anything new on Hoyle?"

"He ain't left town yet. Donno why."

"Where is he?"

"Donno that, either. Dropped outta my sight, but some of the other boys have seen him."

"Doing what?"

He lifted his hands. "Sayin' good-bye?"

"See if you can find out more. I'm getting so I don't like that guy."

Strome's face almost twitched, and he moved on toward the back exit, presumably heading for the office to watch for the meeting to break up.

I found a phone and called Crymsyn's lobby to check in. Instead of Wilton, Bobbi answered. "You're not backstage?" I asked.

She sounded a little breathless. "I just came down with the cash tills. Something told me that was your ring. You need to put a phone behind the bar."

The place already had one official phone in my office; I didn't see why we needed more, but this wasn't the time to discuss it. "I should be there to help, but I got sidetracked."

"I know, 'business.' We're fine here, Jack, there's no need to worry. Take a vacation why don't you?"

"At another nightclub?"

"Sure, see different faces for a change. Charles is helping me open, everyone's in on time. We're *fine* here."

"Okay." I tried not to read anything into so much insistence. "Listen, you remember a mug in Gordy's mob named Hoyle? Used to be a boxer."

"I know him by sight. What's going on?"

"Just keep an eye out for him if you can. He's got a grudge on for me, and I don't want you or anyone else getting in the middle."

"How big a grudge?"

"Enough so I'm sending some muscle over to play bouncer in case he shows, but—"

"Jack . . . ?"

"*But*—I think I'm overdoing it. Look, I know I've been edgy lately and this will make me feel better. The muscle is only insurance; if they're there, chances are they won't be needed."

"For this I'll want to know the whole story."

"Right now?" Not something I wanted to talk about over the phone, especially with Nightcrawler staff within hearing. There were enough rumors about me floating around.

"You kidding? I've got a show to get ready for, you'll tell me later."

"Deal. And one more thing, totally different subject: you know a torch singer called Jewel Caine?"

"Sure, she's not been around much, though. Used to be good until the booze got to her. Why?"

"She needs a break. I told her to come by to see you tomorrow at three if that's okay. Can you work a short set for her into the show?"

"I think so, but are you sure?"

"She's trying to sober up and needs rent money."

"Oh, Jack." Her tone wasn't reproach for being a soft touch, quite the opposite. If Bobbi had been here, she'd have kissed me. I wanted that. Almost. Another part was glad she was miles away. I fought off a shiver inside my coat.

"What about a guy named Alan Caine?"

"That's Jewel's ex-husband. I don't like him, but he can sing. You going to hire him, too? He's trouble."

"I know. I met him last night, forgot to tell you."

"How'd you meet him?"

"He's working at Gordy's club." Though Bobbi usually kept up with who was playing where in Chicago, she'd lately not had much time to read papers or talk with others in the business. My fault.

"Poor Gordy," she said. "He's all grabbing hands—Alan Caine, that is. I've done some shows with him way back when. He's one of those jerks who thinks he owns a place, lock, stock, and chorus line. The awful thing is most of them go along with it because he's so handsome."

"Except you."

"Back then I was wi . . . well, never mind." Slick Morelli. I recognized the avoidance. That mention of him still made her uncomfortable after all this time told me I'd done the right thing not bringing up Mitchell's name. "But even before I wouldn't have gone near Caine. He's a big jackass, and—did you just laugh?"

I'd not been doing much of it lately. I had to be careful or my face would break. "Sounded like it. I think you must be psychic, Miss Smythe. I thought the same about him myself. He won't be playing at Crymsyn. He mouthed off to the wrong guy. Jewel seems okay, but she's had it rough from him. She's sober, but kinda fragile." I should talk.

"I'll look after her, don't worry. We're out of dressing rooms, though."

Huh? Oh. It took me a second to get it. Roland and Faustine weren't the top billing act—that was Bobbi's spot. But he'd had some minor leading-man work in Hollywood and British stage, and Faustine was a full-blown Russian-trained ballerina. The Depression and life in general had not been kind, but they were still higher up the status ladder than Bobbi. As a diplomatic gesture we assigned them side-by-side dressing rooms one and two. Besides, being a couple, they didn't mind sharing the shower and toilet in between. For some reason I'd not been able to figure out, Faustine's wardrobe filled up the whole space.

Bobbi had the number three dressing room; Teddy Parris had number four. I suggested bumping him out.

"Jewel deserves a higher number than four."

"This is nuts, you know."

"Well, I can't put her in the basement with the musicians."

Additional downstairs dressing areas had been roughed out months back, but so far there'd been little need to finish things. It resembled a locker room with coat hooks along one wall, a standing mirror, and a couple of long benches. I didn't go down there if I could help it. Some years back someone had died in that basement, and it would take more than a coat of paint and lights to blot out that horror.

"We can rig a curtain across one of the corners . . ."

"Impossible. I couldn't put her there no matter what."

"Hah?"

"Jack, she used to be a big star around here, it'd be terribly insulting to foist her off in a cellar like some has-been."

Showbiz. I was still getting used to the shifting rules of its pecking order. "Well, just don't use my office."

"Actually, that room next to your office will do for me. If she signs on, I'll move my stuff up there, and she can have my dressing room. There, that's all worked out."

Bobbi did have a flair for problem-solving. Concerning club stuff. Not for me so much. Which was no one's fault but my own.

"You know," she said thoughtfully, "maybe you should think about turning that upstairs washroom into a real bath. You could put in a shower easy enough."

"Hey, I'm still paying for the other ones. Let's turn some more profit first before redecorating."

"All right."

Sounding cheerful, she gave in a little too easy. I knew damn well now that she'd gotten the idea it would be executed into reality sooner or later.

And . . . I suddenly realized we were talking normally again. I even felt normal—until I realized it, and that spoiled the moment.

Damnation. If I could just quit when I was ahead and not overthink, I might have drawn that feeling out for whole minutes instead of just a few seconds.

"Jack?"

"Yeah?"

"I have to go get ready for the show. You okay?"

"I'm fine." God, I hated lying to her, but over the phone she might not be able to pick up on it. "I'll see you when I get there. Break a leg." I didn't know if civilians to the stage were allowed to wish good luck to the talent with that phrase, but what the hell. She thanked me and hung up. I stood very much by myself next to the casino bar and fought off another shiver. All the cold in the city was outside these fancy walls; why was it that *I* had to be picked out to carry a piece of it around in my flayed skin?

Distraction. I called over one of the bouncers and made arrangements with him to send some guys to watch things at Lady Crymsyn. They all had to know Hoyle, which wasn't a problem. The story about Hoyle's interrupted batting practice with me had gotten out and made the rounds. Surprisingly, his reputation was in a hole and mine was on the rise. Just when I was getting used to being unpopular. Everyone's favorite part was my breaking the revolver in his face. I hoped they wouldn't ask for an encore as a party trick.

No sign of Strome yet. Thinking I could fill the waiting time with a few hands of blackjack, I went through to the private area of the club where everyone in Chicago with money to lose was made welcome. I'd played more than a few hands here, picking up extra cash when I wanted. Thinking he might open early for me, I looked around for my favorite dealer, the one who always gave away when he had a good hand. Instead, I saw Adelle Taylor coming decisively toward me, threading between the tables. She showed off her elegant figure in a clingy dark dress with a matching hat and purse that were clearly worth more than a few months' rent in Jewel Caine's neighborhood. Adelle seemed to be a woman on a mission; she moved more quickly than usual, but didn't broadcast any sign that an emergency was on. However, her eyes were strangely fixed.

When Adelle got close enough, I saw how it was for her, figured what to do fast, and led her to one of the semiprivate gaming alcoves, one with a curtain. Soon as we were inside I swept the curtain shut then put my arms around her so she could collapse and soak my overcoat shoulder.

7

CRYING women are not my favorite thing, but sometimes you have to come through for them and weather it out. It's not too bad. Adelle wasn't one to casually lose control of herself, either, so it had to be something important to get her into this state. Most likely to do with Gordy.

She didn't make much noise, but it was a strong and violent crashing down of her protective walls. I'd never seen her like this. Adelle was always cool-headed and even in the face of surprise, quick to land on her feet. Like the night of the shooting. Once she got through the initial shock and terror of seeing Gordy drop, she'd pulled together to help out as though she'd trained on a battlefield.

That restraint was nearly gone; the only remnant was how hard she worked to smother her sobs. I could tell she really wanted to let go completely and howl. That would have drawn attention, maybe prompted the curious to come in and interrupt. She needed release, not talk, but a suppressed breakdown was better than none at all.

Adelle knew nothing about what I'd been through with Hog Bristow, and for some reason that helped me to be stronger for her. I felt better for the giving, like my old self, and it lasted longer than a few seconds. I held her tight and murmured the often useless but frequently comforting, "It's okay, everything's going to be all right" at the top of her head.

Damned if it didn't work. After a while, she pulled away. Makeup running, eyes puffed, her whole face seemed bruised. She sat on one of the cushioned chairs and scrounged in her purse for a handkerchief—no dinky lace thing, but a large practical one—and blew and dabbed and swiped. I sat across from her, waiting to listen. Damn, the things I do for friends.

"Most men," she said, her voice deeper, more husky than normal, "go into a dithering panic when a woman cries. They either want to run for the hills or instantly fix the problem so she stops. Or they try to kiss her or slap her. I'm glad you're the sensible type."

"Nah, I'm a fake. I couldn't make up my mind which would work."

She unexpectedly giggled while trying to blow her nose again and made a real mess of it, requiring another handkerchief.

I sat next to her. "If I ran, the mugs here would shoot me out of reflex. I can't fix the problem, not knowing what it is, so that wasn't the right road. If I tried kissing or hitting, I'd risk a sock in the chops from you, being shot by Gordy when he found out, being shot by Bobbi when she found out, or all three."

Adelle put a hand over her mouth to stifle the laugh. "God, I wish you could stay with us. I need the change."

"Maybe I can swing by later." Gordy had been staying at her place I'd heard.

"It's all right. I know you're busy with . . . the business. There's no one I can talk to. Gordy's men are polite, but they're not . . . well . . ."

"You can't let 'em see you cry."

"No. You're different from them. You've got a heart. To you I'm a friend, not just the boss's piece."

"Hey, you're not—"

She waved it away. "I overhear their talk, but it doesn't matter. They can only define me by the limits of their world."

"You lemme know which ones are being disrespectful, and I'll widen their experience. Now, what's the big problem?"

"Gordy."

"What? He not treating you right?" No way. For all his rough side with the mob, he was always a gentleman with her, emphasis on "gentle."

"It's not that. Oh, Jack, he's ill."

"Ill? Pneumonia? Measles? What?" God, if he caught anything while he was still shaky from the bullets . . .

"Not that kind. He's pushing himself and he's up too soon and he's exhausting everything in him and I can't make him *listen* to reason."

She'd work herself into another bout of tears in another second. I made calming motions. "Take it easy, I was going to talk to him about it anyway. Strome told me he was here tonight, and I couldn't believe he was outta bed again."

"Gordy thinks if he doesn't show a strong face, it'll undermine his authority over his men."

"He's got a point, but if he falls on his duff, it'll undermine worse."

"It's more than that. I'm afraid it's killing him. He's so gray, and he hides it, but I know he's weak. He barely made it from the car into here, then Kroun came in, and he went upstairs like nothing was wrong. It's all a front and—"

"I get the picture."

"You'll talk to him? Make him rest?"

"You bet your sweet . . . ah . . . tonsils I'll do that."

"He looked awful yesterday and worse today. That Kroun's got him all stirred up. Gordy doesn't let on to me, but I hear stuff when he's on the phone or talking with Lowrey."

"What stuff?"

"One of the things I heard . . . the boys here said Kroun was going to kill you." She whispered the last part.

I took her hand and gave it a squeeze. "That's *old* news. We're copacetic now."

"You're sure?"

"Yeah. Guaranteed. Everything's fine there, or I wouldn't be here." Not strictly true. If all the guys in the gang liked me, I wouldn't have had slashed tires. Then I wouldn't have been around to help Jewel and Adelle. Instead I'd have been in my upper-tier booth of my club hiding in its shadows and probably feeling very sorry for myself. Funny how things can turn out.

"I wish you could make that Kroun go back to wherever he came from."

"Same here." Maybe I could, if I felt up to it. "Do you need anything?"

She blew her nose. "A new head on my shoulders?"

"I'm fresh out. What's wrong with this one?"

"Gordy makes me crazy."

That was my second time tonight to hear the same tune from a woman. Adelle made me wonder if I was driving Bobbi crazy in some way. The odds favored it.

"It's the life he's got that's doing this to me," she said. "It forces things like that shooting to happen. I've been able to ignore it until now. At first dating a gangster seemed very thrilling, but suddenly it turned different. He's not some kind of a misunderstood hero with a dark side, he's a man with a lot of insane, vicious enemies who will cut him down at the first chance."

"The hard part for you is that Gordy accepts that."

"*One* of the hard parts. There are a hundred other things."

"More like a couple thousand."

"To him it's just part of the job. You prepare as much as you can, then go on like you think it won't happen. But it does and it did."

"He's still here, Adelle."

"And for how long? Oh—no, I'm sorry, that was a stupid, filthy thing to say."

"You're scared, honey. No one blames you for that. But the fact is, whether he's a gangster or a streetcar conductor, it's all the same. Any one of us can die at any time; we don't get to pick and choose when or where, it's out of our hands."

"I know that. But Gordy's in a business where the chances are higher against him. It's one thing to know you could get accidentally run over by a truck; it's quite another to keep standing in the middle of the road."

"Touché and no arguments. But if he did any other kind of work, he wouldn't be Gordy. Don't kid yourself that you can change him."

She made a "ha" sound. "I gave that illusion up when I was married to Roland."

This was the first time she'd ever referred to him with me.

"I tried and tried, but I could *not* change that man, even when it was to save his life from the booze. Gordy's the same. I'm hoping he'll change for himself and quit the mob, like Roland when he decided to stop drinking. So many never do change, though."

"Almost never." I'd certainly done it, involuntarily, doing things now I'd have never dreamed about two years ago. It was about then that I'd begun thinking about coming out to Chicago and starting my life over. My hope to find Maureen was nearly gone, and it seemed like every corner of New York reminded me of her. I did a lot of thinking and boozing and selling off or hocking stuff to save up the train fare. Hard to do when I kept drinking a substantial part of the gleanings. It took me all the way until August to finally save enough cash to leave New York . . . and find death in Chicago. A slow, hard, and ugly dying.

And if I had stayed in New York, what then? I'd be a thirty-seven-year-old reporter rapidly drinking my way to forty-seven, which was about when I could expect Bright's disease or some liver problem or a car crash to do me in, if not sooner.

Looking at it that way made it almost seem like I'd been a different man whose unfinished biography I had read a long time ago. A man who had indifferently squandered his all-too-finite life by spending it feeling sorry for himself.

"Jack?" Adelle touched my hand.

"Yeah?" I hauled myself back from the might-have-been wreckage.

"What is it?"

"I was thinking that once in a while life makes the change, not the man, but whether it's for good or bad is usually up to the man."

"Or woman."

"You got it. Listen, Angel: Gordy has to do the kind of tough dealings you never want to know about, but where you're concerned he's a good man and always will be."

"I've felt that. But I'm not enough. He's already talking about when he gets back to work, the things he's going to do. . . . They're apart from the business, though. He says he wants to set me up at his club like you have with Bobbi. A regular headliner, the big star, Chicago's favorite. I like the life, but I don't know if I like it as much as I used to."

"What, you planning to move to the country, maybe buy a chicken farm?"

She laughed a little. "That sounds pretty good about now. But it would drive me quite rollicking mad."

"So long as you know."

"But I do wish . . . I just want a world that doesn't have this in it." She made a sideways gesture as though to take in gangland and all its grief.

I could wish the same.

With more waiting to do for the both of us, we left the casino for the outer bar. Adelle looked like she could use something to steady her down. I could watch while she drank it.

Jewel Caine was gone by now. I checked with her waitress. The lady had engulfed her meal and departed backstage. I couldn't imagine why she'd talk to Caine unless she wanted to let him know part of his check would be going to her as alimony. Not smart. He'd raise a stink and could find a different club to sing in, cutting her off. I sent a bouncer to go find Jewel; he came back to say she was backstage visiting girlfriends in the chorus. She was nowhere near Caine, or there might have been a ruckus.

Adelle and I parked at the house's best table and watched the place gradually fill up. The band started earning their keep and couples made forays onto the dance floor. A few people came by to say hello, and a woman asked for Adelle's autograph, which lifted her mood.

Then Whitey Kroun emerged from the back, saw me, and came over. Mitchell was with him, still doing his glaring game. He would seriously bore me in a minute. Strome walked through, heading for the front entry. I wondered if he ever got tired of all the driving.

"You might want to leave," I told Adelle.

"Should I? This is my chance to meet the big boss."

"I thought you had."

"Gordy likes me gone when there's business to conduct."

"Why do you want to meet Kroun?"

"The face of the enemy," she murmured darkly. She was all charm when Kroun stopped at the table.

I stood up and started to introduce them, but Kroun beat me to it, taking her hand and looking deep into her eyes.

"Miss Adelle Taylor," he said, making a pleased announcement of it, as though to confirm it to himself. That personal wattage he had going went up a few thousand volts. Adelle actually blinked from his surprisingly warm smile. "This is an honor and a very great pleasure, Miss Taylor. I knew you were in Chicago, but never expected to meet you. Knock me over with a feather, I'm in heaven."

For a second I thought he'd kiss her hand, but he settled for holding it just long enough to make his first impression on her memorable, then released. Somehow, without being asked, he was sitting at our table. Thankfully, Mitchell remained standing, but on the other side. I wouldn't have wanted him looming over my shoulder.

"Mr. Kroun," Adelle said, in turn, graciously.

"Please, call me Whitey. You can see why." He brushed a hand through his hair, combining the gesture with an ironic but genial, invitation-to-intimacy smile. Special friends only.

She didn't fall for it, but did ask him about the white streak. "It's very striking."

"Well . . . I can't exactly take credit for it."

"Really? I thought it was natural."

"Anything but. I was shot there." His tone softened what should have been alarming news down to the level of amusing anecdote. "Some guy got too frisky and tried to take my head off, but he just missed. The bullet cut this into my thick skull. When the hair grew back . . . well, you can see what happened."

"How horrible for you."

"I didn't feel a thing."

"What happened to the man?"

"They're still trying to figure that one out," he said, which wasn't really an answer.

Adelle was savvy enough to know when to stop.

Kroun smoothly filled in the gap. "I just want to say I am a *great* admirer of yours. Soon as your movies hit town I'd watch three and four times in a row. Couldn't get enough of 'em. Why don't you make some more? You're terrific."

"Why, thank you!" She instantly warmed up. He'd struck one of her favorite chords. "Tell that to the producers in Hollywood. The casting is quite out of my hands."

"That's just not right. They should have you starring in all kinds of things. I've already said you're terrific, now I have to let you know you're wonderful."

Mitchell stopped glaring at me long enough to spare a look at his boss and did a restrained rolling of eyes. I might have done the same, but for picking up that Kroun's high regard for Adelle was absolutely sincere. He seemed to be utterly smitten, but not pushy about it. He held the personal charm note perfectly, drawing it out.

"I'll be around, Mr. Kroun," Mitchell said, and drifted away without waiting for a reply. Good thing, since he didn't get one.

Adelle agreed with Kroun about Hollywood's lack of judgment in regard to her career. They had plenty of common ground: his veneration for her and her agreeing with him about it. I wasn't going to leave her alone with him, but she turned her big eyes on me. "Jack, would you mind doing that little favor I asked?"

"You sure?" This didn't seem to be the best time, but Gordy would be free. She'd keep Kroun well distracted, too.

"Certainly."

I took that to mean she knew how to deal with him, and she had to like the flattery. Who wouldn't? "I'll be back shortly, then," I said, leaving. My money was on Adelle, that she'd learn more about Kroun in five minutes than I would in a week. I was glad she and I were on the same side.

Upstairs I bumped into Derner in the hall. "Gordy wants to see you," he said.

"Mutual, I'm sure." I went past him, not breaking stride. Evidently this would be a private meeting, since Derner went on to clatter down the stairs. Suited me. I pushed open the office door and found Gordy sitting the same as ever in his big chair at the desk. What was unusual was him apparently being asleep. His eyes were fast shut, his head down on his chest. He didn't look so good.

As I drew closer I chanced to take in a whiff of air. In this place with the familiar chrome furnishings and pastoral paintings I was startled to pick up a very out-of-place hospital taint. Heavy, sweet, but with an odd acidic tang to it. Certain smells will trigger memories. This one stripped away half a lifetime and hauled me back to the casualty wards from when I'd been in the War. I'd lost too many friends there.

My heart sank. Adelle's assessment about Gordy being bad off were all too right.

In addition to the sickroom miasma—it wasn't that strong, just enough that only I could have noticed—I picked up bloodsmell. His wounds must be seeping. If it triggered another damn bout of shaking . . . Gordy wasn't the only one who had to limit the number of people seeing him vulnerable. He didn't need my troubles on top of his own, either.

Going to a window, I eased it open, lifting high. The curtains immediately billowed as icy air swept in. We were high enough off the street for it to be fresh. After a minute the place was freezing, but much of the smell dissipated. Because I'd been chilled through since waking, this cold got to me more than it should. I fought off increasingly violent shivers until it hurt. Enough was too much. I lowered the window, leaving it short a couple inches, and turned toward the desk, trying to rub warmth into my arms. Wasn't working. That was for people with circulating blood, and mine . . . well, mine just didn't work that way.

"'Lo, Fleming."

If my ears hadn't been so sensitive, I might not have heard him.

Gordy's eyelids cracked, and he took a deep breath. "That's good. I tell 'em to leave a window open, but Derner's afraid of pneumonia." He sounded worse than last night and whatever rest he'd had failed to clear away the circles under his eyes and the weary droop around his mouth. He looked a lot older and more tired than he had any right to be. His large body took up just as much space, but seemed oddly hollow, as though all the strength had been scraped out.

My heart went into my throat, and I hoped Gordy didn't see the fear. I made a thumbs-up sign to him and felt like a complete ass for its inadequacy.

"You need anything?" I asked, taking a chair by him.

"Have it. Forgot what air's like. Adelle keeps me wrapped like a mummy when we go out."

"How you doing?"

Gordy shut his eyes and opened them, slow. He looked steadily at one of the landscapes on the opposite wall. It was a good one and must have been his favorite since it faced his desk. I wondered what he liked best about it. "Doc Clarson says the holes are healing clean. No fever. I'm fine. Getting better every day."

Yeah, sure you are. God, but he looked tired.

"He kept me pretty doped at first. I say I want to lay off except at night so I can sleep. I seen what too much of that stuff does to mugs. I'm better. Something wrong? Kroun givin' you grief?"

"Not really." Gordy was throwing out distractions. I knew all about that angle. "You're the problem. You've got Adelle scared half out of her mind."

"What d'ya mean?"

I tapped my shoulder where Adelle had cried. "This ain't rainwater making a damp spot on my coat. The woman's on the ragged edge because of you not taking care of yourself."

"I can do that after Kroun leaves town."

If you last that long. "Hey, you put me in charge, right? Let me do my job and run interference. You've impressed everyone already. Take some time off. Go home and rest."

"Can't. Kroun." He licked his lips, seemed about to say more, then clammed up again.

It hit me with a nauseating certainty that Gordy was *afraid* of Kroun. Impossible. Gordy was a rock. People were afraid of him, not the other way around. But Kroun had that personal electricity going, maybe it was enough to affect Gordy. "So what? I got him all behaved and put in the word for you while I was at it. This is still your organization when you're better, but first you have to *get* better. Even Kroun will see that."

"There's other things going on you don't know. Only I can deal with 'em."

"You worried about being a target to some up-and-comer if you don't keep showing yourself?" That was the way of the mobs, one sign of weakness, and you got cut down, quick as thought.

"Like Hoyle? Derner told me about your tires."

I made a brief scowl. "The guys are looking for him. Anything else happen?" Being out for the day, I could have missed all kinds of grief.

"Nope. He's no problem."

"All right, then. But for now, you need a quiet spot, away from the yapping dogs. Someplace outside your normal haunts."

"Maybe."

That's all I needed, a "maybe." It would slant things in my and—eventually—his favor. An opening.

Of course, this was smack in the middle of doing something for another guy's own good whether he liked it or not. I didn't have the right to impose this, the ultimate manipulation, on him. On the other hand I wasn't about to go back and look Adelle in the eye and tell her I turned chicken.

"Kroun and me did some talking. About you," he said.

"Oh, yeah?" I must have gone too far in giving Kroun the idea we were friends, should have told him to go back to New York instead. Kroun had had plenty of opportunity to talk with Gordy about all kinds of interesting details relating to myself and how things were running in Chicago. Not that I could blame him. If Kroun asked, Gordy would have to answer. Given the circumstances and the chance, I'd do the same. Knowledge is power, especially with this bunch.

"He wants to know if you'll be taking over for good."

"Of course not—"

"Lemme finish. Taking over . . . if I don't make it after all."

I couldn't believe he'd said that. Gordy dying was just not in the cards. He was my friend—in a very cockeyed way considering his work—and he *had* to go on breathing. "What the hell?"

"You have to think about these things," he continued. "If you don't want the operation, it goes to Mitchell."

"Screw that."

"It's him or you, kid."

I almost objected again, then shut it down. It would be less upsetting to him if I went along with this line of talk. He had to get it out of his system. I hated that he'd been mulling this stuff over.

"But you don't want it. Derner, then. With you helping him, like with me. Like you're doing now."

"Uh-uh, you got my exclusive. Nobody else. So you have to get better."

Before he could respond, I moved in, going as soft and easy as I'd ever done on anyone before with my evil eye. My head immediately began to hurt from even this minimal effort, but I continued, careful as a brain surgeon, speaking low and with infinite confidence. "You're going to heal up just fine, Gordy. You listen to me, you're going to fight this and get well. There's a pretty gal waiting for you. Can't disappoint her. You hear me?"

A low murmur. It sounded like a yes. Good thing he wasn't doped with painkillers just now. I could use some, though. I'd barely started when the thunderstorm behind my eyes began building at record speed. I pressed through it. In the War I'd seen a lot of guys talk themselves into a recovery while others just sat there and got worse. I had to get Gordy to talk himself into getting well.

"This is something that's just going to happen. You're going to listen to Adelle and listen to your doctor and to me and you *will* rest. That rest will make you stronger and better with each passing hour, with each day. You will get well."

The pain rolled in harsh as a fury; I winced and couldn't maintain eye contact, had to brace against the big desk to keep my balance.

"I-I want you to go stay with Shoe Coldfield. You two get along, and he won't mind doing you a favor. You're going stay with him in some nice, quiet place until you're well again. You understand?"

Couldn't hear any reply. The worst migraine in the world was pounding my brain to mush, which was trying to leak out through my ears. Had to ignore it. Gordy was more important than . . .

"You'll do this. You hear me? You'll *do* this and get well."

Too much. It sliced into my eyes like twin axe blades. For a second I thought someone actually had come up to slam razor edges squarely home into my skull. The rising agony shot to a screaming zenith.

I'd really done it. Overdone it. What was supposed to have been a light touch turned into a hammerblow that bounced back in my face. The cold that had bothered me all evening clawed and grabbed hard as death.

Lurching up, I tried to reach the couch, but banged solidly to the floor, doubling in, knees drawing to my chest, arms around my exploding head, trying to cushion the worst and failing.

So *cold*.

Trembling . . . limbs twitching . . . oh, God, not another one . . .

Before the seizure peaked I went invisible.

The grayness was peace and comfort *and free from pain*. No jittering spasms, no betrayal of mind and body or hidden terrors surfacing to rip me or anyone else apart.

What had set it off? I'd not been thinking of Bristow. Just trying to help Gordy. The hypnosis? Why was *that* hurting? It didn't use to, not this badly—

Stupid questions. I didn't want to think them up, didn't want to find the answers. If I could just *stay* like this. Without a solid body to feed and care for, I had no anchor to what had become an increasingly ugly world. So long as I was chained to flesh, I was stuck with its memories, disappointments, responsibilities, and pain. Lots of pain. I wanted to float in this sweet respite forever.

Floating. Invisible. Almost a ghost. But ghosts were sad, weren't they? Or angry or scared. I didn't want any feelings at all.

On the old home farm we had a big spring-fed stock pond, and one rare summer day I had it to myself. Without a mob of older brothers and sisters to spoil the stillness I'd stretched out in the middle, shut my eyes against the noon sun, spread my arms to embrace it, and let the water buoy me up. Baking heat above, chill water cooling below, I drifted, gently rising and falling, each intake of breath like a small tide, and thought it was the best thing ever. Until then I'd never realized how good it was to have that kind of absolute, yet utterly serene solitude.

Soon enough I grew bored and moved on, and I never got to swim there alone again. I should have stayed longer. When you're a kid you *know* things will always be there for you. Growing up teaches you different.

With twenty-five years between me and that perfect childhood moment I came back to solidity in Gordy's office, standing upright, shaken, but at least not shaking. An improvement. This fit hadn't lasted long; my muscles weren't twitching from exhaustion.

Still cold, though. I wanted to turn up the heat, but it wouldn't help. My usual immunity was gone. Perhaps at long last I was finally feeling the chill of the grave. Why, after this long a stretch since my death, was it trying to catch up with me?

What *had* triggered the fit? A run-of-the-mill suggestion, the kind I'd done hundreds of times before? It didn't seem possible that so ordinary a thing—for me—could be to blame. Maybe my subconscious had been saving this one up, waiting to drop it on me at the first opportunity.

The moment I'd let my guard down? I had to do that to focus on Gordy. And it left me vulnerable . . . to things in my head, buried things . . .

Great. If that was true, then to prevent further attacks I only had to go through the rest of life with my shoulders bunched around my ears and never look anyone in the eye ever again. Why hadn't I thought of that sooner?

I waited to be sure the attack was truly over, pacing the room a few times, and making a point *not* to look out the damn windows. Nothing untoward stirred within, so it seemed safe enough to wake Gordy. No more attempts to influence him or anyone else, at least for now.

Thankfully, I didn't have to try for a second whammy to do that part. Just a hand on his shoulder, an easy-does-it shake.

He must have nodded off for real. He woke with a start, one hand automatically reaching for the inside of his coat where he wore his gun.

"Fleming? Jack?" He never called me Jack. Always Fleming. God, but he sounded tired. About the same as I felt. "What's wrong?"

"Nothing. Ain't it time you took Adelle home?"

He thought it over. "I guess so. But not to her place. After Derner told me what Hoyle and Ruzzo pulled on you I should find some spot they won't look. Keep her clear of this."

"You're worried about them?"

"You should be, too. They might not be the only ones wanting to take over, given a chance. I know Hoyle. He'll spout that he's steady for me, but he'd as soon cut my throat if it could get him in charge. Derner's nervous, too."

This was interesting. "And here I thought I was his least favorite."

"You think Coldfield would mind helping me get scarce so I can rest?"

I smiled. The evil-eye whammy had dangled me headfirst in hell, but it had worked. One of its influences on others was making it seem to them that they'd thought up my suggestions on their own.

"I'll call him right now," I said. "Why don't you stretch out on the couch while I arrange it?"

"Good idea. I need the rest."

I stood by ready to help, but he left his chair unassisted and made the journey across the room. It hurt to look at him, because he was trying not to shuffle like an old man.

SHOE Coldfield was a little surprised by being asked to play host to Northside Gordy. He'd helped keep Gordy safe before, and didn't mind doing the favor again. Coldfield gave me an address and said he'd be there in person to look after things. I knew the street. It was one of the borderline areas. One side was Bronze Belt, the other side white. Gordy and Adelle showing up there wouldn't raise as much notice than if Shoe put them in the next block over. And day or night, it would certainly be the last place where mugs like Hoyle and Ruzzo would hang around.

Plans fixed, I made a sedate and slow trip downstairs, cautious about setting off another fit. The internal chill clung to me, not as bad as before, but noticeable.

Music played in the Nightcrawler's main room. That helped take my mind off the constant annoyance. Tonight's show had been going full swing for some while now. Alan Caine's voice rolled rich and strong even through the intervening walls. It was really too bad I'd met him, else I'd have enjoyed the sound. He was singing for free for the time being, since a large piece of his pay was going elsewhere. I'd have to ask Derner how that had gone over when he'd broken the news.

I found Strome just off the backstage area and told him he'd be driving Gordy and where to take him. Strome was evidently familiar with the street, too, since his distaste for the idea was obvious. He didn't like colored people, but happily for everyone he wouldn't have to remain there. His partner Lowrey had no such problems and would stay on to play watchdog as usual.

Adelle was at the same table, still holding her own with Kroun. During a pause in the music, I heard him talking, and almost didn't know his voice. It had gone low and pleasantly seductive. He said, "It's a great place, I can get you top billing and an unlimited run, and you can pick anything you want to do, singing, acting, dancing, radio, the works . . ."

"That's very kind of you, Whitey—"

I walked up just then, delaying her reply. "All done," I said. "Sweetheart, you get a vacation until *you* say different."

She immediately understood what that meant. Visibly relieved and beaming, she stood. I put my arms around her because she looked like she needed it, and just held her a minute. She sagged so mightily, I thought I was holding her whole weight, and for a second she seemed about to cut loose and sob, but being in public must have stopped that. But the holding seemed to help. Felt good to me, as well. At times that's what we need, a simple sharing of body presence, just that and no more, then you let go and move on. I patted her, told her everything was going to be fine, and when she seemed ready, stood her square again. She pulled a handkerchief from somewhere and blew her nose.

I looked her up and down. "Doll face, you're always tricked out better than a million bucks, but you should get some sleep tonight. You don't want to give the doctor a second patient, do you?"

"But I—"

Tapping my ear, I shook my head. "Oops, sorry, I suddenly can't hear anything. Happens at the darnedest times, but comes in handy. It means no one can argue with me and win."

That raised a crooked smile from her. "All right, Jack. I'll get him home and turn in. I feel like a zombie."

"Strange, you felt like all-girl to me."

"So that's why Bobbi keeps you around. Good night and *thank you*!" She pecked my cheek and shot away, perhaps worried that Gordy might change his mind if she didn't hurry. He would let her know where they were headed. I didn't think she'd care where they stayed so long as he got better.

Kroun stared after her, then at me, questions all over his craggy face. "What's the deal? Are you an' she . . . ?"

"We're just friends."

"Friends with a dame? You funny or something?"

I let that one pass, still feeling good about being helpful. That hug made all the pain worth it.

Watching her leave, Kroun sprouted a smile of unabashed pleasure that lingered while she was in sight. "I heard Gordy was dating a looker, but didn't know she was Adelle Taylor. What a woman. She just made this whole trip worth it."

We apparently had some things in common. Maybe I should be worried.

He suddenly snapped his fingers. "Damn! I shoulda got her autograph and had the camera girl here to take a picture. Think you could get her back?"

"She won't be in the mood for it. Another time."

"What a woman," he repeated, like a prayer. He leaned forward, arms crossed on the table. "Lissen, Fleming . . ."

I sat at the table the better to hear. He'd lowered his tone, and Caine and the band were going loud. "Yeah?"

"Seeing's how you're such good friends with her, you think . . . you think she'd go out with me if I asked? Asked nice?"

I pulled back, gaping, and was tempted to poke him one in the eye. Kroun held to an utterly serious face, waiting. Then he blinked, head cocked, eyebrows high and innocent, and I finally realized he was pulling my leg. An unexpected laugh popped out of me, lasting a whole two seconds. It sparked an equally brief one from him in turn.

"You're a pip," I said, thinking a little late that that might be getting too chummy with the big boss, but he didn't seem to mind. Against all sense and good judgment I was starting to like him. That suggestion I'd slapped on him about us being friends was working fine, but had it become a two-way street with me not knowing? With the nervy stuff going on inside my head, I could believe it.

"What was that about, anyway?" he asked. "Something with Gordy?"

"She said you were working him too much. I talked him into some time off."

Kroun shrugged. "I don't twist his arm about needing to do business, but it wouldn't hurt him if he hit the mattress."

There were two ways of taking that statement. When a gang war was on, the mob boys dragged their mattresses onto the floor to be out of the line of fire from through-the-window shooters. The other way meant just getting some sleep. Kroun's relaxed attitude led me to figure he meant the second definition.

Good. Real good. I had enough worries. "She hugged you pretty hard," he said. "Didn't that hurt?"

He was too observant for my own good. "I got a pain shot earlier."

"What kinda shot? Morphine?"

I was far too alert to be on morphine. Best to be vague. "Donno. Stuff works okay."

"It sure must." He held my gaze for a moment, his dark eyes nearly all pupil in the low light, then nodded at the stage. "You like this singer?"

Alan Caine had a spotlight song going. It made me wonder how Jewel Caine might have done the same number with her dark, husky voice.

"He sings okay. Don't like him much," I said.

"Not a lot of people do, only the ones who haven't met him."

"You met him?"

"I've managed to avoid the honor."

"Probably for the best. He's like sandpaper on a burn. Wouldn't know it to see him."

Caine, flashing perfect teeth, drifted along the edge of the dance floor, stirring up the women as he sang to them. He skillfully kept just out of reach while giving the impression he wanted to move closer. It was all a sham, but they ate it up and grinned for more.

"Quite a gift he's got," Kroun added. "Wish I could get women to fall on me like that. Well, actually they *do*, but only 'cause of who I am. Don't matter to them what a guy looks like if he's got money and power. I mean, look at Capone, for cryin' out loud. Face like a nightmare and built like a whale, but the women were all over him. You think it'd have been the same for him if he worked in a butcher shop like some regular guy? Not for a minute."

From the stories I got from Gordy and others, Capone actually had been something of a butcher, but he also knew how to have a good time. That wasn't an observation I felt like sharing, though. I wondered if Gordy was downstairs yet, on his way to Coldfield's neck of the woods. Coldfield was supposed to phone Crymsyn when his guests were settled. If Strome came right back to drive me over, there was a chance I could catch the call.

But . . . Escott or Bobbi or even Wilton could take care of that; I didn't *have* to be at Crymsyn. It just felt *odd* being someplace else.

"Don't you have a club to run?" Kroun asked, still watching Caine.

Damn, was he psychic or something? "Had to take a detour here. Car trouble. Strome's driving me over later."

A waitress came by. Kroun didn't want anything, still focused on the show. I waved her off and lighted a cigarette for something to do. Kroun glanced over.

"You smoke?" He seemed mildly surprised.

"Yeah. That a problem?" Everybody smoked. The club's air was thick from it. The spotlight on Caine fought through a slowly shifting blue haze.

"No. Just—"

"What?

He shook his head. "Nothing."

Maybe he was one of those fresh-air types. I could have told him that smoking actually exercised and strengthened the lungs. I'd read it in a magazine ad someplace. Of course I couldn't inhale, so none of that applied to me. Jewel Caine must have lungs stronger than Walter Winchell's.

Alan Caine's number ended on a big, heartbreaking, and beautifully clean note. I was no musician, but knew enough about how hard that was to pull off. No wonder Escott was impressed. The spot winked out, and the houselights came up. Caine had delivered; the audience wanted to let him know about it. His voice had filled the room, and in the wash of adulation for that talent he glowed. He graciously smiled and humbly bowed, and whatever magnetism he had going sent them wild. The women called his name over and over, blowing kisses, waving handkerchiefs. It was crazy. I'd seen something like it in a newsreel, but the film had been about Hitler. Just as well Caine wasn't in politics. We didn't need an American version of Germany's most famous house painter.

Caine made a last bow and dashed lightly off to get behind the curtains. They didn't quite close, and I saw him visibly shut down his performance personality the second he ducked backstage. He wouldn't need it until the next show. He had thirty minutes for a costume change, going from a black to an all-white tuxedo for the second set. Plenty of time to swap clothes, have a belt of booze. Or gargle. I glimpsed a flash of spangles beyond the curtain: Evie Montana trotting eagerly past to catch up with him. Yeah, there was time for her, too, if she didn't mind rushing things.

I suddenly shivered in my overcoat. Couldn't help it.

"You cold?" Kroun asked.

"Yeah. I must be in a draft."

"Or it's that medicine you take. I heard some of that stuff can do weird things."

"Or I'm catching cold."

Kroun's deadpan look returned. "A cold?"

I'd not been sick from an ordinary illness since my change. Didn't know if I *could* get sick in the ordinary way. For all I knew this could be the Undead version of the Spanish influenza.

"Maybe you should get more sun."

Most of the guys who worked these nightclub jobs were fish-belly pale. I fit right in. "Nah, I'm allergic to daylight."

"Ya think? Never heard that one before."

The band swung into dance music, and couples moved onto the floor for some fast fox-trotting. That was one way to work off the extra energy Caine had built up in them. The waitress came by again, got waved off again. After a few tune changes I checked my watch. Bobbi's first set was over, and Teddy Parris would be stepping from the wings. I could almost see and hear it in my mind. After his set and their duet, Roland and Faustine's red-washed dance—

Shut it down. Quick. Better to not make pictures of anything in my head. I might go fragile, which could get humiliating. Strome should have returned by now. Maybe he'd gotten sidetracked backstage. Plenty of cute girls there, and this was their break time.

Kroun's attention wandered around the club, then he looked at his watch.

"Expecting someone?" I asked.

"Mitchell. He said he was catching up with some friends here. You?"

"Strome's due. Maybe they're having drinks."

He snorted. "Not likely. Mitchell said friends. Those two are oil and water. They only mix when they have to."

"I can have the boys find him." I had an odd feeling about Mitchell. What if he'd decided to make a quick trip to Lady Crymsyn to see Bobbi? I stood to leave. "I'll check on 'em both."

Kroun flapped one nonchalant hand, apparently content to watch the dancers. The waitress, either determined to earn her keep or responding to his particular magnetism, came back with a glass of ice water for him. He smiled warmly up at her. She smiled back. He wouldn't be short of female attention tonight if I read her look correctly. Alan Caine had nothing on Kroun when it came to acquiring company.

There was a phone at the Nightcrawler's bar—the kind Bobbi wanted me to put in—and I used it to call Crymsyn's lobby booth. Several rings went by until a drunk guy answered. I'd expected Wilton, but he was probably busy.

The drunk guy was remarkably unentertaining, parroting my questions back at me and giggling. A woman's voice cut in, there were sounds of a wrestling match, a slap and a yelp from the guy, followed by more giggling. I wondered if I'd been that boring in the days when I'd been able to get properly drunk. One of them hung up the phone.

Hm. Bobbi's idea was looking better by the minute. Crymsyn was a swank place. Busy. No reason why I couldn't have *two* phones in it. I waited a minute, watching Kroun use his charm effectively on the waitress, then dialed again. This time Wilton answered. He sounded harried and said he'd get Escott.

Clunk, as he dropped the receiver onto the booth's small writing ledge. From the sounds filtering through there was a large, noisy crowd in the lobby. That was reassuring. I should be there to greet the customers as usual. A smile, a firm handshake, the suggestion they'd have a *great* time, hit home with a little eye whammy . . . well, maybe not that. Until the axe-blade migraines stopped I'd have to stay on the wagon from artificially winning friends and influencing people.

The waitress was now sitting with Kroun; but that was okay, everyone knew who he was, and none would nag her to get back to her job. In passing I noticed she was slim and dark-haired, very like Adelle Taylor but shorter. He must have liked that type. The waitress sure seemed to like him.

"Hallo?" Escott. Finally.

"It's Jack."

"You all right?"

"I'm dandy. Just checking on things. Remember Mitchell from last night? The mug who wasn't Strome and didn't have a streak of silver in his hair?"

"The ill-favored Casca of the trio?"

I recognized the theatrical tone and perfect inflection. Escott must have had a good dollop of brandy. It brought out the Shakespeare in him. I'd had to read some of the plays just to get his references at times. Looks like I'd have to put another one on the list. "I guess. He's not shown up there, has he?"

"Not that I've noticed. Is there a problem?"

"So long as he stays away. I sent some extra bouncers over. They doing their job?"

"Of looking formidable and threatening? Yes, they're covering that most excellently well. One of them said they were there to keep Hoyle and his cronies out."

"Yeah. It's probably nothing, but I don't wanna take chances. Tell them I said to add Mitchell to the list. I don't want him bothering Bobbi."

"Why would he do that?"

"He knows her from when she was with Morelli."

A pause. "Indeed. I take it you'd prefer she not be subjected to unpleasant reminders of that chapter of her life."

"Bull's-eye. If Mitchell shows, tell him his boss Kroun wants him back at the Nightcrawler, toot-sweet."

"I shall be pleased to do so."

"You seem to be in a good mood."

"Ah. Yes, well, I am, as it happens. Vivian was *delighted* at the idea of a party. Bobbi's setting it up for Saturday. My appreciation is *boundless*, old man."

"Uh, okay, likewise." Escott in love. What a picture. Color it pink. Lace it with brandy. "I'll be by later. I got business here still."

"Take your time, all's well."

I hung up. Next he'd be skipping in a meadow throwing flower petals around.

No he wouldn't. But still.

Kroun looked like he might not care to be disturbed. I left him to proceed with his conquest and went on to pass the word for the help to be looking for Mitchell. Let *him* interrupt his boss's canoodling.

Another shiver. Damn.

Since Strome was likely to come in by the alley door, I made my way to the rear of the club. The kitchen would be warmer than the rest of the place. I'd wait by a fired up stove and hope to thaw out. If that couldn't shake the chill, then I didn't know what else to do. Maybe retreat to my office and turn up the radiator and sit on it all night with a hot-water bottle. Come the daytime, and the cold wouldn't matter.

I didn't get as far as the kitchen. Strome was in the wide hall of the backstage area with Derner, and their heads were close together. Even at a distance I could see something off in their posture. They weren't the sort to broadcast much in the way of emotion, but I did pick up there was trouble of some kind going.

They spotted my approach at the same time, and each gave his own suppressed version of a guilty start.

"What is it?" I asked, my voice low. The lights were necessarily doused here to keep from showing on the stage area in front. Only thin threads seeped from under the dressing room doors. All but one: Alan Caine's.

"Got a problem, Boss," said Derner.

"We can take care of it," said Strome.

"What is it?" I suspected that Caine and Evie Montana were locked in, most likely involved in some very advanced canoodling. Not unheard of in a dressing room. Hell, Bobbi and I had . . .

The grim mugs in front of me said I was on the wrong track. I waited them out, just looking and frowning.

Derner broke first. "There's been an accident."

Strome winced at the word. That he reacted so strongly was more than enough to put my back hairs up. "Accident, my ass," he muttered.

He *was* upset. "Spit it out," I said.

Derner rubbed a hand over his face, a show of weariness and frustration in the gesture. Next he checked the wide hall, which was empty, which was not normal. There should have been chorus girls wandering about, the stage manager, stray waiters. All I saw were a couple of the muscle boys at the other end, waiting and watching . . . me. Derner opened Caine's dressing-room door. It creaked inward to silence.

No sounds of an interrupted tryst, no squawk of outrage, no movement at all.

Dark inside. The dim spill from the hall didn't penetrate far, even for me.

"What happened?" I asked. "He leave?"

"Caine's still here, Boss," said Strome.

And without going any farther, without any visible facts, I knew what was wrong.

8

OF course I'd have to *look*. I was the boss. It was my job to deal with this kind of disaster.

Disaster it was. An almighty ugly one.

With me on the threshold and using his body to block the view of anyone passing, Derner reached in and flicked the light switch.

Alan Caine had his back to me, slumped awkwardly over his dressing table. There was a big mirror above it, and I couldn't chance Derner noticing my lack of reflection.

"Gimme a minute," I said from the side of my mouth, then stepped in and shut the door on him before he saw. If only I could hypnotize without hurting myself, then I wouldn't have to be alone in a room with a fresh corpse.

I chanced to take in a whiff and got what I expected: talcum powder, grease paint, and sweat mixed with the stink of urine and crap. Death had been brutal to Caine, and once relaxed, his body had given way with everything. No sweet peace here.

Fists in my pockets, I kept my distance. Had to bend low to check his face. What I expected: bloated and purple, broken blood vessels in his bulging eyes, tongue sticking out as though to offer a final opinion to the world. Something that looked like a blue necktie but wasn't was wound tight around his throat, the middle part almost lost in the folds of violated skin. Whoever had done it hadn't wanted noise and was strong enough to make it quick. No signs of a struggle anywhere else; the only evidence of the violence was the body itself.

"Damn."

The guy had been abusive, obnoxious, and *alive* not too many min-

utes ago. I hadn't liked him, but to take the life out of another this swiftly
and easily was just wrong. Having killed as well as been killed, I understood how little effort was needed to do that which should be unthink-
able. We unite to build towers to the sky, make music and art to feed our
souls, can sacrifice selflessly to help others, yet cling with a lover's greedy
passion to the lowest and darkest of our emotions. Most of us don't act
upon that hate-driven force. We resist.

But for someone . . . not this time.

That blue thing on Caine's neck. Jewel had worn a blue dress. I didn't
want her to be involved. A quick check of the closet turned up nothing of
similar color.

Ah. Coatrack by the door. There was a blue satin smoking jacket
hanging from a peg. Same color as the tie. Empty loops on the garment.
Same material. Good. But Jewel wasn't off the hook entirely.

The killer must have stood *here*, watching Caine, maybe listening, but
looking for something to use against him. Something quiet. A .22 being
fired might not be heard, or the sound misinterpreted. Knock a wooden
chair over the right way and it makes more noise. But the killer might not
have known that or possessed so small a gun. Most of the guys in this
outfit never went with anything less that a .38.

Why not a knife, then? Plenty of them in the club's kitchen and simple
enough to boost one and walk out. Or bring your own.

They can take time to do the job, though. You have to know what
you're doing. Human skin is tougher than one would think, and dragging even a razor-sharp blade through a couple of inches of muscle and
cartilage of a throat takes effort. The victim doesn't die instantly. There
can be messy thrashing around; the killer can get splashed with telltale
blood.

But strangulation, it's very intimate. That's one way to feel the whole
progression of things shutting down as the life goes out of the body.
There's no doubt about death. If you have the strength and speed and cut
off the blood to the brain quick, a few moment's effort will do it. After
that, then only forty pounds of pressure to crush what needs to be
crushed, and it's over and done, make a quiet exit.

Freeing up one of my hands, I lifted one of Caine's by the shirt cuff
and checked his manicured fingernails. Small dark crescents were under
those nails, but not dirt—bloodsmell. He'd managed to dig in deep in his
last struggle and left marks someplace on his killer's body. The wrists . . .

Looked the rest of the small room over. No cover, no place to hide.
Just me and what Caine had left behind of himself.

Bobbi had also used this as a dressing room at one time. And Adelle Taylor. And lots of others I knew by name or in person. Their ghosts seemed to shift uneasily around me, disliking what had happened in their sanctuary. I stood and was dizzy from the shift, staggering a step. Waited, expecting another fit to sneak up from within, but it didn't happen. It was the air here. The presence of death. I didn't have to breathe to be overwhelmed.

I got on the other side of the door, met Derner's and Strome's gazes.

"Yeah," said Derner, apparently agreeing with whatever he saw on my face.

"Any ideas?" I asked.

"'Bout what?"

"Who did it."

He shrugged. "Try a phone book."

"Not good enough. Show me your hands, both of you. Push your sleeves up."

They were mystified. Good.

"We don't shoot dope, Boss," said Strome, misinterpreting.

Derner was clean. Strome's knuckles were banged up and raw, but that was from the fight last night with Hoyle. His arms were free of nail gouging and scratches. I needed these two to be in the clear. On the other hand, they might have ordered someone else to strangle Caine, though the why of it was a mystery. I could settle such questions easy enough, but at the cost of collapsing in agony at their feet. Bosses weren't supposed to do that in front of the hired help.

Until I knew better, I'd just have to keep shut. "Who knows about this? Who found him?"

"Stage manager, just a few minutes ago," said Strome.

"Did he see anyone else in or out?"

"Nope. I asked him special. He knocked on the door, it opened, and he saw, then locked up and went for me and Derner. He won't say nothing."

"We gotta get Caine out of here," Derner advised, casting a glance up and down the hall. "The next show starts soon, there's no backup act—"

"Where's Jewel Caine?" I asked.

"What? His ex? She's here?"

"She was when we opened. Came back here to talk with friends. See if she's in with the dancers."

He did so, banging once on their dressing room door and barging in. No one screamed a protest, and I heard their negative replies to his question.

"She left just a little bit ago," someone within volunteered. "What's the idea locking us up? Hey—"

He returned. "You think *she* did it?"

Strome nodded. "She was plenty burned with him last night."

"I don't know," I said. "We'll figure that later. Where's the stage manager?"

Derner got him, explained that Alan Caine had come over sick and had to leave. The manager nodded slowly, rightly taking this to be the blanket explanation he would pass to others. After that, we did some fast shuffling to fill out the second show for the evening. An apologetic announcement was to be given to the house. One of the dancers also sang, so she'd have to change to a gown and do some solo numbers to keep things going. The other dancers had a hoofing routine already worked up that would pad the bill. The manager went off to fix things.

"What if the audience wants a refund?" Derner asked me.

"Give 'em their money, we can afford it." We sure as hell wouldn't be paying the star. I turned to Strome. "Hoyle might have tried collecting markers again and got too rough. I want to see him before we call the cops."

They were shocked. "The *cops*?"

"You heard."

"But we can't," said Derner.

I almost demanded to know why not, then bit it off. The Nightcrawler was already a favorite target for easy headlines; a murder under its roof just couldn't happen. Too many of the people here had records, and I wasn't about to draw official attention to myself if I could help it.

The trump card against bringing in the law was Gordy. If I didn't clean up this mess, he could get hauled off by the cops. He was in no shape to deal with even routine questions.

I debated over which course to go with, and not for the first time settled things by thinking, "What would Gordy do?"

"All right," I said. "We take care of it ourselves."

"Take care of what?"

None of us were virgins when it came to dealing with death firsthand, but the three of us gave a collective jump at that mildly put question from an outside party.

Kroun stood rather close to our group, and no one had heard his approach. "Take care of what, Fleming?" he repeated.

Now I knew how Derner and Strome felt when I'd turned up. "We got a problem."

"What problem?" Kroun's tone indicated he would like a full and truthful answer.

I didn't want to say it out loud, so I opened the dressing-room door. The light was still on. Kroun looked in, but did not go in.

"That's a problem," he agreed. "What are you going to do about it?"

Strome said to me, "Boss, I can disappear him like the others and no one's the wiser."

"No," I snapped.

"The others?" asked Kroun.

"Like Bristow," I said, to explain. "We're not dumping this guy in pieces for fish food. He can't just mysteriously disappear, or we'd never hear the end of it. He's too famous."

Kroun gave me a long look and nodded in thoughtful agreement. "What, then?"

"We smuggle him out after closing. Put him in his own place without anyone seeing. He can't be found in the club. We just say he walked away and stick to that and not know anything else. The cops will come by and ask questions, but it won't be on the same level as it might if they knew he'd died here. Strome, you pick some guys who can keep their yaps shut, and I mean buttoned tight. They do the job, then forget they ever did it."

"Right, Boss."

"He was killed with something off his smoking jacket, make sure the jacket is taken to his place along with anything else he might normally have along with him. Make sure his wallet, keys, and stuff like that is on him. Take his hat and overcoat, and don't touch the tie around his neck. Don't just dump everything, make it look like he went home, and that's where he bought it. Everyone wears gloves."

"Right, Boss." He went inside the dressing room, shut the door, and from the sound of it, was preparing things for departure. He would have to work quick before the body stiffened up.

"Derner, find out where Caine hung his hat and case it. Figure the best time to get him inside. Arrange for a closed truck, something that won't stand out. No speeding, no busted lights, or whoever screws up will take the fall. Anyone too stupid or too nervous is on their own."

"Right, Boss."

"I want to know who was where from the moment Caine walked off the stage—wait—was Evie Montana in the dancers' dressing room?"

"I didn't notice."

"Find out. I saw her follow Caine when his act was over. Where is she now?"

Derner cut away to bang on the chorus dancers' door again and looked inside. He traded words, then withdrew, shaking his head at me. "None of the girls have seen her since the end of the first show. They said Jewel came by to shoot the breeze. She stepped outside to have a smoke. Not allowed to smoke backstage."

"See if she's still outside, then."

He tapped on Caine's door, and Strome emerged. If I expected him to be pale and shaken from his grim work, I was disappointed. This wasn't anything disturbing to him. Derner explained what was wanted, but Strome paused.

"Boss—there's something gone from there." He gestured back toward the room.

"Yeah?"

"I looked, but Caine's overcoat's gone."

I digested this a few seconds. "Maybe the killer took it."

"Ya think?" Kroun put in. "You're sure it's gone?"

Strome nodded. "Not that big a place, and it's a hard-to-miss coat. Tan-colored vicuna. Real flashy, expensive. Someone could get some money hocking or selling it."

"It'd be too hot an item. Why else would they take it?"

"'Cause it's cold?"

Kroun look at me. I shrugged. "As good a reason as any. It'll make a search easier. Strome, go check the alley for Jewel Caine and see if you spot anyone dumb enough to have that coat."

Strome shot off, moving casual, but not wasting time.

With this kind of distraction I'd forgotten about my internal cold. It flooded its way back, and I had to fight to keep from visibly shivering. Evie Montana and Jewel Caine were gone, and the man between them thoroughly dead. I didn't think either or even both working together would be strong enough to strangle him like that, so quickly. As for motive . . . well, Jewel had none to speak of; Caine alive meant money to her. Unless my loan of forty bucks had taken the pressure off, and she'd come back to have a gloat and one thing had led to another. If so, then why had Caine turned his back on her? He liked baiting people face-to-face to enjoy their reaction. Of course, he could have watched the reflection in the big mirror, but then he might have seen the attack coming and put up more of a fight.

Where had Evie gotten to, anyway? The way she dogged him, she might as well have been on a leash. Had she seen him killed and run? That was my main worry. If either of them saw something she shouldn't, she was dead, too.

Derner went off to arrange details, leaving me and Kroun in the hall.

"You handled that," he said, "like you had it written out on a chalkboard."

I shrugged. "Just trying to anticipate. If I left anything out, I wanna know."

We looked at each other a minute. I knew for sure that Kroun hadn't personally done it since he'd been in my sight all during the break in the show. But Mitchell could have managed, and he'd been missing for a long time.

"Where's your boy?" I asked.

"You think Mitchell pulled this?" Kroun didn't seem angered by the implied accusation, only curious.

"He and Caine had a history, what was it?"

"Damned if I know." The deadpan look moved back in. He should charge it rent.

"How can you not know?"

"Mitchell's job is to watch my back and run errands, I don't need his life story for that."

"He was throwing looks at Caine."

"He does that for everyone. You, too, I noticed."

"Yeah, but I'm not strangled yet."

Kroun pushed the dressing-room door open. "Is that how it happened? He was strangled?"

"Yeah. Quiet."

"Knives are quiet, too."

"No knife, or I'd have sme—seen the blood."

He backed out. "Look, Fleming, you got a half-assed reason against Mitchell, and I'll admit it's a possibility. Who else is on your shit list?"

"A guy named Hoyle. We'll find him before the night's out."

"There must be others. From what you've said there could be a hundred people all wanting Caine dead. You said he owed markers?"

"To this club, maybe others. The money was coming out of his pay. He was more valuable alive."

"Not to one person." From where he stood Kroun took another look at the room, a long one, then shut the door. "That's all it takes."

"Figure the cops are going to go in big on this," I said. "Caine was popular. Catch his killer fast, and they get approving headlines. We gotta hand them someone. Preferably the right someone."

"His ex-wife or girlfriend? There's usually a dame behind these things."

I told him why I didn't think they were likely prospects.

He was unimpressed. "Maybe you haven't seen how worked up a woman can get when she's mad enough. I have, and it's damned scary."

Actually I had seen a small woman take on two grown men and nearly win before the handcuffs were safely in place and we could call the cops on her. Escott still had the scars. Mine had healed. "I don't get that feeling here."

"Feeling. Uh-huh." Kroun clearly didn't think much of my instincts, and he was probably right. Just because I liked Jewel and thought Evie was cute was no reason to take them out of the running.

"Okay, they're on the list. Might as well add in the chorus girls and the band."

"The band was performing the whole time. Listen, let's just go find these two dames, have a talk, and settle it."

"Why are you so lathered to find the killer?" I asked.

More of the deadpan stare. "Why not?"

Couldn't think of a reply to that one. I'd rather have Kroun stay out of the way, but he was the big boss, and I still had to listen to him. It rankled not being able to influence him to my way of thinking. I'd gotten too used to the luxury of being able to order people around.

Derner came back to say arrangements were in hand, and he also had addresses for Jewel, Evie, and Hoyle. "I'm sending some of the boys for Hoyle. You want him alive?"

"Yes. Even if he didn't kill Caine, he owes me for those damn tires. What about Ruzzo?"

"They move around a lot. Landlords keep kicking them out."

"Lemme know when you bring 'em in. I need a car, too."

"Gordy's is back, but Strome took off to fix things. I can get another driver."

"I'll drive myself. You check everything on everyone who was backstage. Make up whatever story you need for cover and make it reasonable; don't leave them room to guess what really happened."

Derner nodded, then reached in again from the hall to shut the light off before locking up. Apparently he didn't like putting himself any closer to the dead man than the rest of us.

KROUN and I left by the club's back door. The outside cold abruptly and painfully meshed with my inside chill. Ganged up on me like that, I didn't stand a chance and nearly doubled over from the shivering that hit like a gut punch.

"You okay? What's the matter?" Kroun paused from opening the passenger side of the Caddy, looking over the roof at me, half-annoyed, half-concerned.

"Freezing my ass off," I muttered, and slammed in behind the wheel. The keys were in their slot. No need to worry about anyone thieving this car. I tried to control the shaking to get it going.

"Stop," Kroun said.

I wasn't used to being ordered, even when I knew it was part of the job. "What?"

He made no reply, just walked around and opened my door. "Move over, I'll drive."

"But—"

"Do it."

I did it.

Kroun gave me an irritated up-and-down. "You got a fever or what? Only time I saw a man in your kind of shape he had the DTs. You sick?"

"I donno. Don't feel sick." I hated that he was picking me apart.

"You don't look sick. Not much." He figured out the starter, put the car in gear, and we glided forward. "Which way?"

"Left at the corner, then right."

He drove as directed, throwing a glance my way now and then. The car was still warmed up from taking Gordy to the Bronze Belt. Kroun fiddled with the heater and opened the vents wide. Hot air breathed on my feet and legs. "Better?"

"A little."

He looked unconvinced but kept it to himself. "So what's really wrong with you?"

"Nothing."

"Fleming, you don't have DTs, St. Vitus Dance, or malaria, and that's the limit of my educated guessing. You know what's wrong."

"It's probably the shot I had."

He threw a hostile glare remarkably similar to Mitchell's. "Shot. There's no medicine makes a man cold like that. If it was the winter getting to you, then your teeth would be chattering, too. This has to do with what Bristow did to you."

I shook my head to mean I didn't want to talk about it.

"Yeah, and it's got you bad. I've seen guys just like you going right off the dock, but because they were in the War. It did that to them. You didn't have the War; you had Bristow. The son of a bitch is *dead*, he can't come at you again."

Which I knew very well. Funny, but Escott had been on this same trail the night before.

"I told you to ease off on yourself, so when's it going to commence?"

No answer to that one, since I sure as hell didn't know. "Let's stick to business, if you don't mind."

"Business. That's what we call it. It's what got you where you are. It's what killed that guy back there, sure as shit. Business." He sounded none too pleased with it.

What was this about? But he shut down.

The heater was a good one. Eventually the hot air blowing against my legs filled up the rest of the car, blunting the edge. The pain from the inner cold eased, whether from the warmth or Kroun trying to talk some sense into me, I couldn't tell.

He turned on the radio. "This okay with you?"

"Go ahead." I was surprised he'd bothered to ask.

We listened to Harry James. The music gave me something else to think about besides myself. I'd interrupt with directions now and then, as needed. Our route more or less followed the El line as we headed to Jewel Caine's home. It was the closest to the Nightcrawler.

The song ended, a grimly serious ad instructing everyone to use Bromo-Seltzer to fight off colds replaced it. Foiling the announcer, Kroun turned the sound down. "This is some car," he said. "Gotta plan ahead to make turns, but it's a smooth ride."

"It has truck shocks to take the extra load," I told him. So long as we kept the topic aimed away from me, I didn't mind socializing.

"That would be the armor plating making the weight?"

"Yeah. Top, bottom, and sides, with bulletproof window glass, special tires. This thing's built like a German tank. Gordy had it done by this guy in Cicero. I think he was the same one who fixed up Capone's car likewise. Did a better job for Gordy, though."

"He fix the motor up, too? She runs easy for this kind of load."

"Some other guy did that. I'm not sure exactly how, but she'll do one-twenty on the flat and not raise her voice."

"Sounds sweet. Real sweet."

I could agree with that.

"This the place?"

"Yeah."

He had to circle the block to find parking. The neighborhood was run-down, but not quite on the skids. Sad old piles of brick made up the better buildings, jaded clapboard was on the rest. Even when new, the area would have been depressing, and I speculated whether the architects had been solitary drinkers.

A three-story brick was our destination. It had once been a hotel, but was converted to flats. Nothing fancy. No doorman, no night man out front to watch things. We walked in unchallenged and went up to the second floor. No elevator.

I heard radios tuned to different shows as we walked down a dim, door-lined hall. Someone with a fussy baby walked the floor in there, a couple traded opening salvos in that one, somebody snoring just here—the usual. Down at the end a radio was turned up loud, but not too loud. It was in Jewel Caine's flat.

Kroun did the honors, banging on the door. "Mrs. Caine?"

I stepped close to call through the thickly painted wood. "Jewel? It's Jack Fleming from the club. Open up, would you?"

We waited and tried again.

"This doesn't look good," said Kroun. "Why turn the radio on and go out?"

Had I been alone, I could have answered that for myself by vanishing and sieving inside. Without hypnosis to make him forget, I was crippled on what I could do.

Kroun reached up, feeling along the trim above the door. "No key. I don't want to bother looking for anybody who has one, either. We'll do it the hard way."

He dropped to one knee and pulled out a small case. Picklocks. A very nice set. He used them. To him it was the hard way, to me it was expertly and quickly done, and I was accustomed to Escott's skills. Even he couldn't work with gloves on.

"Turn it," Kroun said, holding two of the picks in place.

I turned it; the door drifted open. He withdrew the picks and put his kit away.

Lights were on, and a single window overlooking the front of the building on the right had its shade drawn. Jewel had left after dark, then. Or come home and left again. I hoped so. The radio was in a corner, a table model. Kroun started over, a hand reaching to perhaps turn it off, then stopped. He put his hands in his pockets.

"What?" I asked quietly.

He shook his head and seemed to be listening, but I couldn't hear over the radio noise. I took in the rest of the place. Jewel was an indifferent housekeeper. The room was small, a kitchen and parlor in one, with only the barest necessities, cheap stuff. Mail, opened and not, was scattered on what served as a dining table. She had a fine collection of sleeping and some other kind of pills for her nerves which made me uneasy. I knew what too many of those in one dose could do. Most of the containers seemed to have stuff in them. The bad thing would have been finding them empty. I wish I'd not thought of that angle.

Kroun went into her bedroom. I followed.

Unmade bed, clothes piled up. I took a whiff and got stale cigarette smoke, very heavy, some kind of perfume vainly fighting it, and the scent of desperation. I couldn't explain the last one; the feeling just swelled up in me.

And one other . . . oh, *damn.*

I slumped. We were too late.

The bathroom. Pushed the door open. It wouldn't go all the way. Her body prevented that.

Didn't want to, but I had to look, to make sure.

The bloodsmell overwhelmed even the old cigarette reek. It looked like she'd stood in front of the mirror over the sink, put the gun to her head, and that was it. No doubt about her being dead. The white-painted walls were splattered with blood and . . . and other stuff.

"What?" asked Kroun. He had to pull me out to see for himself.

She still wore her coat. Was that normal? If there was a normal. Didn't suicides prepare themselves? Write notes or something . . . ?

Distraction. It wasn't working. I backed away, going to the small kitchen, stood by the sink there, and waited. I was hot and cold both together, feeling the sweats you get as your body works itself up to vomiting.

That didn't happen, though. The sick weight stayed bunched in my throat, twisting through my belly. I wanted to throw up just to get it over with.

The cold won out. I leaned forward and trembled from it. My knees started to go. Managed to fall onto one of the chairs by the dining table instead of the floor.

Kroun came out. Kept silent a while. I couldn't look at him. Too busy fighting off the shakes. I would *not* let myself give in to another damned fit with Kroun looking on.

"Wasn't anything you could have done," he said, after some moments.

"Gotten here sooner."

"I don't think so. Listen, someone makes up her mind to do that, she'll find a way no matter what."

I shook my head. Didn't quite know why.

"What is it?" he asked.

"She didn't kill herself."

"Looked pretty clear to me."

"Someone made it look that way." I sat up straight and did what I could to shove all the sick darkness within into a box and slam the lid. I needed to be thinking. "See if you can find her purse."

He moved around, turned up three purses. One was the same blue as her dress. I upended it on the table, amid the clutter of makeup, keys, tissues, matches, and crushed cigarettes—the twenty and two tens I'd handed over to help with the back rent.

"That's my loan to her." I gave him a short version of my talk with Jewel earlier. "The woman was cleaned up. There's no booze here, check and see. She was sober and had some hope back, had a job waiting. She wouldn't have shot herself."

"She would if she'd murdered Caine."

True. Jewel *could* have killed her ex, then in a fit of remorse came back here to escape earthly justice. But everything in me said it was wrong. "He meant money to her. She had no motive."

"You don't know that."

"I was with her, she was—"

"Wise up, Fleming. You talk to her for half an hour and think you know what's going on inside her head? You can know a person a lifetime, and he'll still surprise you in ugly ways."

"She was murdered."

"Give me a reason to believe it."

Hell, I had to give myself one, besides the churning in my guts. "That gun, what kind is it?"

He went to look and came back. "Long revolver. A forty-five."

"That's a lot of iron for a woman to carry."

"So she kept it under the bed to scare burglars."

"A woman's more likely to have a smaller gun."

"So she was a tougher girl than most. I've met more than one broad carting a cannon around and not thinking twice about it."

"Me, too, but Jewel—" This was getting nowhere. I'd thought of a new angle for him. "Look at these."

He looked. "Pills. The sleeping kind. Okay. What about 'em?"

I shook one of the bottles. There were enough to do the job. "Lemme put it this way: given a choice, wouldn't you rather just fall quietly asleep to do your dying? Why put a big, noisy gun to your head?"

Kroun unexpectedly went dead white, his skin almost matching the streak in his hair. Maybe I'd dredged up a bad memory for him, of when he'd been bullet-grazed. "She . . . might have been in a hurry."

That wasn't funny. "I think someone else must have been instead." Evie Montana? Hoyle? Mitchell? Why, though?

"Someone made her kill herself? How? Holding another gun on her? 'Shoot yourself before I do it for you'?"

"I donno. She could have been knocked out, he stands her up, puts the gun in her hand, and—"

He shifted. Frowned. He went back to the bathroom again. When he returned his color was no better, but something had changed. "Okay. I'm convinced."

"Where did I go right?"

"The gun. It's in her hand. Her hand's relaxed around it."

"So?"

"When a shooter that size goes off, it's gonna kick like an army mule. It should be lying anywhere else, but not where it is. Somebody set her up all right."

Her hands . . . he'd reminded me. Wearily, I went and looked for myself. I made my gaze skip over the blood and mess and focus only on her hands. Enough of the skin was visible. No finger marks, no crescent-shaped cuts from Caine's nails digging into her flesh. She'd not done it.

"C'mon, let's get going," said Kroun.

I blinked, my mind trying to shift gears to keep level. "What?"

"That other dame you wanted to see. Let's find out if she's still breathing."

"Shit."

He snagged up the money. Shoved it at me.

"Hey, I don't—"

"If you don't, someone else will. Use it to buy her flowers, but don't leave it for the damn vultures when they come."

We'd kept our gloves on, so wiping away prints wasn't a problem. We left, moving quiet, but it seemed a wasted precaution. If the tenants here had been able to ignore a gun noise like that, they wouldn't pay mind to much else, including the radio we'd left on.

Kroun drove, with me muttering directions and trying to feel the heater's warmth again. There might not have been anything I could have done to prevent Jewel's death, but part of me thought otherwise, and was beating me up about it.

"Hey." Kroun broke in on the internal pounding.

"What?"

"She was dead before we could have gotten there."

"How do you know?" And how was it this guy could read me so well? I might as well be wearing a sandwich sign.

"The way the blood was dried. I . . . got some experience about that."

I didn't care to ask for details. I had experience, too, and he was likely right, but her death hurt all the same.

"It's not fair," he said, as though agreeing to something I'd spoken aloud. "Not by one damn bit. We'll get the guy, though. Or girl. We will."

Cold comfort, Escott might have said. I wanted him here, but the less contact between him and my current business associates the better. I'd tell him about it later.

Evie's place was in another not-so-great neighborhood. Her flat was one of two above a street-level shoe store. Other small businesses filled out the block, each apparently with living quarters a mere stair climb away. Convenient. Kroun parked out front, and we hurried up to the tenant's entry. No need for picking the lock, the thing was open.

He banged on the flat's door, and I called Evie's name, a too-eerie reprise of what we'd done at Jewel's.

Thankfully I heard movement on the other side of the door. A groggy-sounding woman wanted to know what we wanted. I said I was Evie's boss and trying to find her.

"What's she done now?" the woman asked. Still through the door.

"She left without her pay."

The door was abruptly opened. A thin brunette, rumpled hair, no makeup, wrapped in a too-large flannel robe, peered out. She gave us the eye, a suspicious one. Kroun stepped diffidently back and looked surprisingly harmless and humble.

"Sorry to come by so late, Miss," he said, his smile matching his apology. "But we're trying to find Evie. It's important."

She blinked against the onslaught of charm, then shook it off. "What's that about her pay? She owes me back rent."

I pulled out one of the ten-dollar bills. "You know where she is?"

"At work, some club—if you're her boss, why don't you know?" She stared with unabashed fascination at the money.

"Evie left suddenly, before the show was over. We thought she might be ill or have an emergency. Is she here?"

"Of course she's not here, or she'd have answered the door. This is the middle of the night in case you haven't noticed."

"Yeah, sorry about that. Where would she go if she had a problem?"

"What kind of problem? If it's with a man, she moans to me about it. If it's about money, she moans to her boyfriend."

"The singer?"

"What singer? That creep Alan Caine? Not him. Her *other* boyfriend, the sailor."

What a surprise, but Kroun landed on his feet. "Is he that big blond Swede from Minnesota who stutters?"

The woman rolled her eyes. "She's got *another* one? The only guy I know is a bald Polack merchant sailor who talks smooth. He lives somewhere by the river—with his *wife*. Evie's got no more sense about men than—than I don't know what, but she's an idiot about anything in pants."

"So where do we find this Polack sailor?"

"Canada. He shipped out a week ago. He sent her a letter from some place. They were stuck in port because the weather delayed a shipment or something, and he said he'd be late getting back. He should be so considerate to his wife."

Probably wasn't, I thought. "You sure he's out of town?"

"Oh, yeah. Evie was in the dumps for a whole hour over it. I had to listen. Say, why are you so interested?"

"It's really important we find her. What other friends might she go to if she was in a jam?"

"That's it. She comes to me first, then her boyfriends. She's angling to be the next Mrs. Caine, you know. What a dope."

"You don't like him much?"

"He walks all over her and thinks it's funny. She doesn't want to see that, though. I don't care how handsome a fella is, if he doesn't treat you right, throw him back in the water, he's not worth the trouble. Is she in a jam?"

"We just have to find her."

"Then call the cops. If she's not here or with Caine or the Polack, then she's not anywhere. She's used up her favors with everyone else."

I pulled out a business card for Lady Crymsyn, penciled the lobby phone number and Escott's office number on the back, and handed it to her along with the ten-dollar bill. "If she comes home or calls, you ring any of these until you get an answer from someone."

She looked from the money to me like I'd just become her new best friend. "Well, *sure!*"

"And you don't have to say anyone was by looking for her."

"*Sure!*"

We said good night and started down the hall. When her door shut and the lock clicked in place Kroun signed for me to wait, then cat-footed back to listen, his ear to the keyhole. I should have thought of that. I'd have heard a lot more.

After a moment he returned, shaking his head. "I thought she might call someone, but no dice. I think she went back to bed. Any other ideas?"

"The Nightcrawler again. See if Derner came up with anything."

"There's another place to check . . ."

"Oh, yeah?"

"Alan Caine's."

Damn. I wish I'd thought of that, too. Evie might have taken refuge there given the chance. Strome and his men wouldn't get over for some hours yet. "I'll call Derner for the address."

9

ALAN Caine's rooms were at a good hotel, which meant Kroun and I had to get around the night man out front. It wasn't hard. From a drug-store phone booth I called the desk, said that I was Caine, gave the room number, and instructed him to let up two of my friends as soon as they came in.

"And show them respect," I imperiously added. "They're important." I was taking a chance the guy on the line knew Caine's voice. On the other hand, if I was bossy enough, he might fall for it. Must have worked; I got a weary "yes, Mr. Caine" in reply.

Kroun drove half a block and parked across the street. We walked into the lobby. "I'll handle it," he said, and veered away. He murmured to the clerk there, who eventually nodded and handed over a key.

"When the cops start investigating, he'll remember your face," I said.

"Yeah, but by then I'll probably be back in New York, won't I? Besides, I got one of those hard-to-remember mugs."

He had to be kidding. The clerk noticed us, noticed Kroun, the moment we came in. There was no dampening of his magnetism at all. On the other hand I was wallpaper by comparison and content to stay that way.

He continued, "Most people only see the white streak in my hair, and I kept my hat on. Let's go."

The elevator was one of those fancy push-button ones that didn't need an operator. Everything these days was going automatic, from gearshifts in cars to toasters. Looked like another job was being shut down in the name of progress.

We stopped on the fourth floor, doors magically heaving open on their own. I noticed the fire exit was close to Caine's room. That would be convenient for Strome when the time came.

Kroun unlocked, let the door swing open, and paused, listening. No radio going. In a place like this a loud radio would be investigated. So would gunshots. He went in, flipping on the light.

Yeah, Caine had done himself swell. His shades were up, the curtains wide. He had a wide slice of view of the street below. Nothing spectacular, but better than Jewel's or Evie's lot.

Evie didn't jump out at us. Neither did anyone else. We went through each room more thoroughly than they deserved.

Maid service had been in that day. The bed was in order, fresh towels in the bath, wastebaskets emptied. His clothes were hung up or in a hamper. In the living room was a studio piano parked against the outside wall, a stack of sheet music, and a well-stocked bar. He'd taken generous samples from all the bottles and had a preference for scotch to judge by the many brands.

The hotel's furnishings were in place but no pictures were on display except his own. Handsome portraits abounded. Caine had been a man thoroughly in love with himself.

"Ain't that cute?" Kroun pointed to a large, beautifully executed nude photo of Caine that had a place of honor hanging above the sofa.

Caine was posed full length, but sideways to the camera so nothing really showed, but there was no doubt he had a body to match his perfectly sculpted face. Every lean muscle showed in the play of shadow and light over his form. I knew a thing or two about photography from my days as a reporter, and understood the kind of work that had gone into making such a picture. You had to be able to get the whites white and the blacks black, yet preserve the countless shades of gray in between.

"That cost him a bundle," I said.

"Must have been stuck on himself real bad. Only guys I know who put up pictures of themselves are funny. I've never seen one go this far, though. Singers."

"Vanity's expensive, all right." I went to a desk and dug in, finding nothing as eye-catching as the portrait. Caine had bills, clothing receipts, old letters, and handwritten IOUs. Lots of those. Nothing for less than a hundred, and several for over a thousand. Trusting souls. They must have fallen for the pretty face and charm, too. The people he owed used nicknames mostly, but perhaps Derner might know some of them. Rather than mess up the investigation for the cops, I pulled out a hotel envelope from the stationery drawer and scribbled down those that were legible. One of them might have gotten fed up waiting to collect and decided to get fatal.

I found an address book and decided to take it along. Plenty of names—and nicknames—and numbers for both Chicago and New York exchanges to tell by the prefix letters. I could mail it to the cops later. Or not.

Kroun saw what I was doing, grunted approval, and went over the rest of the place again, poking in cupboards. He whistled once, having found a respectable cache of beer in the pantry, with an even larger number of empty bottles crated and ready to go back for the deposits. "Nothing," he announced when I was done copying. "No Evie, but some of her clothes are in his bureau. It's sweet stuff."

"Maybe he was going to pawn it," I said. I told him what Jewel had said about Caine hocking step-ins.

"You mean women buy stuff like that at a—" He shook his head. "You're kidding. I've never seen those at a pawn shop."

"Ah, Jewel was kidding. Maybe. My girlfriend doesn't tell me where she gets her scanties, and I don't say where I buy my drawers. I'm glad to leave it at that."

Kroun snorted a laugh. "That it for here?"

"Yeah."

I went down the fire escape to see where it came out, which was an alley. Strome could use it as a means of getting in the flat.

When I returned, Kroun considerately inquired after my health.

Damn. I should have tied a string to my finger so I could remember to act feeble.

"I'm fine," I said.

"Just watching out for you. That's what friends do." He smiled. It was ingenuous, almost too much so, like he had a private joke.

Was he remembering what I put in his mind the other night? The words were a close echo to what I'd given him. There'd be hell to pay if he shook off the suggestions and recalled my vanishing act. The hell would be in my head, since I'd have to put him under again. It could kill me.

We went out the front way, so the night clerk could see us leaving. He didn't ask for the key back, but considering the way Caine treated people, it was not surprising. The staff must have gone out of their way to avoid all unnecessary contact with their guest, and were willing to extend the policy to anyone associated with him.

Fine with me. We'd need that key for later.

Once outside, the cold returned to my bones. I'd almost been able to put it aside up in Caine's flat. It wasn't as bitter as before, but I would be glad when the night was over so I could lose myself in oblivion again. Even when unaware of the passing hours it was still a time of healing. I wanted it to heal me from this before it drove me crazy.

Crazi*er*.

WHEN we got back to Gordy's office Derner was at the big desk, up to his eyeballs in paperwork, phone calls, and loose cash from the casino. Another guy at a nearby table thundered away at a calculation machine, punching in numbers as fast as he could read from a clipboard and pulling the lever. Derner looked on my return with too much relief. I knew I was in for it.

Over on the couch, with two of the tougher lugs standing guard, lay a man, gagged, blindfolded, and hands bound behind him.

"What the *hell* is this?" I demanded, and only my surprise kept me from roaring the walls down.

"We found him for ya, Boss," said one of the lugs, grinning.

"Found who?"

Derner slammed the phone receiver and came around the desk. "These two brains ain't listening to me—"

"Found *who*?" The guy didn't look familiar.

"That kidnapper you want so bad, Boss," said the lug.

I stared at the figure on the couch. He wasn't moving much, but from what I could read off his posture he was scared shitless.

"The kidnapper?" said Kroun. Hands in pockets, he cocked his head, highly interested.

"Dugan?" I went closer. Gave what I could see of his face a good long look. Pulled the gag off. The mouth was all wrong, and so was the voice that went with it.

"PleaseforGodsakedontkillme! I don't know nothing about anything! I swear! I got a wife and kids an—"

"Shuddup!" I snarled.

He shut up.

"Hey!" I said to Derner.

He approached. Cautiously. "Yeah, Boss?"

"Get rid of adding boy there, he's giving me a headache."

He stopped the man from punching more buttons and told him to take a short hike. The guy went, shutting the door. Except for faint band music that I could hear even through the soundproofed walls, it was very quiet.

"Okay," I said, tiredly. "Let's keep it short. You with the blindfold. What's your name?"

"J-j-john C-c-c-oward, sir. I'm from W-waukegan and—"

"Stop."

He stopped.

I found his wallet. Showed the driving license to the lugs. "Gentlemen, may I introduce you to Mr. John Coward of Waukegan?"

"Naw, *he's* the guy! He's just like the picture in the papers!"

"Yeah-yeah, just like an apple looks like an orange. You got the wrong man."

"But—"

I didn't need the evil eye to freeze him, I was that mad. He rocked back and put up a protesting hand. It cut no ice with me. "Get out of here before I ventilate the both of you. And spread the word that the hunt for Dugan is *over*."

"But if you ain't caught him yet . . ."

"Doesn't matter," I said through my teeth. "It's over, called off, finished, *finito*, shelved in a box. Anything about that you didn't understand?"

They shook their heads.

"Get out."

They got.

"Derner?"

"Yeah, Boss?"

"Did you have any kind of a conversation with them or Mr. Coward?"

"Yeah, Boss. I *tried* to tell those two, but they wouldn't listen. They said you'd tell it straight, so they parked here. They found this guy in a craps game, made him to be Dugan, and been carting him all over Chicago trying to find you, first at your club, then your house, then that gumshoe's office . . ."

"Oh, my God." I rubbed a hand over my face. "They're dumber than Ruzzo."

"Well, they kept him in the car trunk so no one would see. Ruzzo wouldn't have done that . . ."

I snarled, and he corked it. Glanced at Kroun. He was doing his almighty best to not laugh. John Coward sat very still and trembled, his head high. He must have been able to see a little out the bottom of the blindfold. "Okay, I get the picture. Mr. Coward, I'm going to have someone take you back to wherever you belong."

"N-not gonna kill me?"

"Not going to kill you. They thought you were someone else, and I apologize for that. If you'd like to forget about this mistake, we will, too. I'll have to insist you keep the blindfold on for the time being. In this case what you don't know can't hurt you."

"Anything, whatever you want, anything, please! I won't say a word."

"That's good enough for me. I suggest you stay away from craps games in the future, hm?"

"Yes, whatever you want I'll do it!"

I went to the desk, shuffled together five hundred bucks, folding it into Coward's wallet. I put the wallet into his pocket. "Just remember: *none* of this happened."

"Nothing, not anything."

"If we see your face again, well, you wouldn't be happy. Now we'll get you back to the wife and kids where you belong. You just say where you want to go."

Derner took his arm and stood him up, walking him slowly toward the door like an invalid. I didn't relax until they were well down the hall.

"What a night." I groaned and eased onto the couch.

Kroun finally cut loose. He didn't quite bust a gut, that wasn't his style, but his laughter was catching. I succumbed in a much more moderate way. Oddly, the chill inside lessened. Yeah, I was onto something there in regards to a cure. It didn't last. It couldn't. Not with Caine's body still in the dressing room below and Jewel lying in her own blood and brains halfway across town. The cold came back, but I was able to ignore it better. Just had to stay busy, that's all.

Kroun found a chair, sat, and put his feet up on Gordy's desk. "You know what you should do?"

"Tell me."

"Find yourself a quiet shore on one of these lakes, settle in, and see what you can do about decimating the local fish population."

I'd have never suspected that he knew such big words. "I don't eat fish."

"That's not the *point*." He shook his head. "It's not about *eating* fish. It's about *fishing*. For fish. Just . . . just . . . *fish*."

He had an idea there. It was right up there with Escott thinking I should take a vacation. Kroun angled his hat over his face and clasped his hands over his stomach. I got the impression that was how he did his fishing.

Derner returned. "The guy's on his way home. Sorry about that, Boss."

"Never mind. The other boys know the hunt's canceled?"

"The word's getting spread now. No one's gonna be in a good mood over losing that ten Gs."

As though some of them could resent me even more. "They'll tough it out. You got the lowdown about the backstage people?"

"Yeah. A big fat nothing. They saw plenty of it."

"Good trick," said Kroun, from under his hat. "Seeing nothing."

"Who was backstage?" I asked.

Derner parked his duff on the desk and crossed his arms. "That I know of: the dancers, eight of them, the stage manager, Caine, and Mrs. Caine. Seven of the dancers were having a break while Caine did his solo. They said Evie left to hang around just offstage, waiting for him. She usually did."

"They all stayed in their dressing room?"

"Talking with Jewel Caine. She was happy about getting a job, wouldn't say where, and they was just gabbing. You know. Hen-talk."

"Yeah. I know." My mouth went dry.

"Just before Caine's number finished Jewel went out for a smoke. She said she didn't want to bump into him when he came backstage. With all this talking the girls was running late and stayed in the dressing room to get ready for the next show. Next thing they know the stage manager shoves his snoot in and tells 'em to stay put, then locks the door. They were still plenty mad about that, saying if there was a fire they'd be cooked, but—"

"Where was the stage manager all that time?"

"Well, after he found Caine he stayed in the hall to keep watch, so if there was a fire, he coulda let them out easy enough. He called one of the busboys over and sent him up to get me, then I ran into Strome on the way down. By then the manager got a couple more guys in to watch the other end of the hall. They didn't see anyone."

"What about before he found Caine?"

"He was up in the lighting booth. There was a problem with one of the spots, and he had to find a spare bulb. The lighting guy backed him. The manager didn't leave the booth until after Caine was offstage."

"So he had opportunity."

"But no reason. He's not big, either; you've seen him. Caine was near twice his size. He could have fought him off."

"Ya think?" asked Kroun. "If Caine was taken by surprise . . ."

Derner shrugged. "Yeah, maybe. The manager's been with us for years, and Caine was just another act to him. He cares more about this club's staging than anything else. Even if he had a reason to bump Caine, he'd have done it some other place. He's show people, and they're all crazy that way."

"Okay," I said. "He's off the suspect list until we get desperate. No one saw where Evie went?"

"The girls said she went with Caine into his dressing room. She was usually in there during his breaks. They thought they were being on the sly, but everyone knew."

"So maybe Evie did do it," said Kroun.

"When we find her we'll ask her," I said. "And Hoyle. And Ruzzo. And Mitchell." All I needed was to check hands and arms for scratches. I thought about sharing that detail with Kroun, but held back. Mitchell was still his boy. Under his protection.

"Mitchell?" Derner was surprised and glanced uneasily at Kroun for his reaction, only there was none.

"Just covering the bases," I added. "Mr. Kroun doesn't mind."

"It's business," Kroun put in with a snort. "Biz-iii-nessss."

I got Derner's attention back. "Have you seen Mitchell tonight?"

"Only earlier. I heard he left before the ruckus."

"Find out for sure. See to it the guys are looking for all five of them and it's only to *talk*. I want everyone alive and undamaged. Let the boys know when *I* say talk I mean only talk. No sparring sessions, no turkey shoots."

"What if the ones they're after shoot first?"

He got a look from me.

"Okay-okay!" He left to take care of things. After a minute of thinking about it, I moved to the desk and the phone there. Kroun still had his feet up on the edge.

"Nice shoes," I said.

"Thanks."

I dialed Lady Crymsyn's lobby phone.

Wilton answered pretty fast this time. "Yes, Mr. Fleming?"

"How di—ahh, never mind. Everything going okay there?"

"No problems. We had a good night. Good shows, lotta people. You want I should get Mr. Escott?"

"Nah. Just tell him or Bobbi that I won't be back, so they'll have to close. It's business." They'd both understand. Wilton said he'd pass the message, and I hung up.

"Biz-iii-nessss," Kroun drawled, then snorted again.

I checked the clock. "It's pretty late. If you're tired . . ."

"Just resting my eyes, kid. There's still one more errand to run tonight."

KROUN had surprised me about overseeing the transport job. I'd have thought he'd want to stay well clear of a potential disaster if anything went wrong. Instead, he sat in the front seat of Gordy's Caddy with me on the passenger side. We were parked just up the street from Caine's hotel. It was so late that only the deep-night creeps were out—which included us and a select few others.

A gray panel truck sat backed into the alley between the hotel and the next building over. I couldn't see what was going on. That was good. None of us wanted the activity there to be visible to passing cars. I was mostly worried about cops. They would be the only others out at this hour. A sharp one might wonder why laundry was being delivered at this time of the morning.

Strome was one of the laundrymen. He'd turned up at the Night-crawler with a couple of shut-mouthed goons, coverall uniforms, and the truck. An hour after the club was closed and the last straggling worker left, Strome helped the goons load in an exceptionally heavy laundry basket, then they drove off. Kroun and I followed at a distance.

Things went without a hitch. About five minutes after parking in the alley, Strome and his crew were out again and driving away. They must have used the service elevator instead of the fire escape stairs to get up to the right floor. No matter, so long as they weren't caught. Kroun had supplied the key. Wiped clean, it was to be dropped on the desk in the room, just like he told the clerk earlier.

There would be a hell of a stink over this tomorrow. I felt sorry for the poor maid, who'd likely be the one to find the body. I also hoped the night clerk would be unhelpful about descriptions of Kroun and me. When it came down to it, we had a pretty lousy cover. Two mystery men go up to Caine's room. Caine is found dead there the next day, but not seen to come in by the front entrance. Any halfway-good cop would tear into that pretty quick and backtrack to the Nightcrawler. The best I could expect from our interference was to confuse things, buy some time to find the killer. Then—if the hideous head pain would leave me alone for long enough—I could whammy him or her into marching into the D.A.'s office to dictate a complete confession. We'd all be off the hook.

Of course, that was the ideal way for this to turn out. I focused on thinking about it, rather than the countless ways it could go wrong.

Kroun had cut the motor for those five minutes. He started the car again, and the heater blasted air against my legs. I winced. "You still cold?" he asked.

"Yeah." I'd been fighting off shivering again, vowing to buy a heavier coat.

"Go home then. Get some sleep." He didn't look remotely tired himself.

"I need to see to things."

"What things? We're finished here. Even those guys are flying back to their roost." He gestured ahead, where the taillights of the panel truck made a turn and vanished. "Where's home?"

"Just take me to my club."

"You live there?"

"I flop in the office sometimes. When it's a late night."

"That's what we have here, ladies and gentlemen. A late night. Which way?"

As before, I gave directions, and he drove. He seemed to enjoy hauling the big car around corners.

* * *

KROUN dropped me at the front of Crymsyn, and said he knew how to get back to his hotel from there.

"Why are your lights still on?" he asked. "Someone inside?"

"We leave 'em on to scare off burglars." That was better than trying to explain about Myrna.

He tossed an easy good night at me and drove off, the well-tuned Caddy barely making a sound. I hurried to unlock Crymsyn's front doors.

Kroun was right about this chill not being related to winter. I shook from it, but my teeth weren't chattering.

Shut the door against the cold, cruel night, turned to check the lobby. The overhead lights glowed, as well as the one behind the bar, almost as though Myrna knew I'd be coming in and would need them.

I'd often been here before on my own, and each time noticed the silence. Of course, with my hearing I could pick up on every damn creak and pop, which was ignorable or twanged at my nerves depending on my mood. I was in a foul and fragile frame of mind for now. Something about Kroun bothered me. The way he'd been acting at some points was worry-making.

The uncomfortable suspicion rolled through my head that Kroun might be immune to my kind of hypnosis. If he was crazy and able to hide it, then just pretended to be under the other night . . . I didn't want to believe it.

Distracted as I had been with the pain, he'd remained dead-eyed and not reacting the whole time—even when I'd vanished. No one could be that good at faking.

Unless he'd met another like me and knew what to do, what to expect. That might explain it. I was one of a rare breed. If Kroun knew about vampires that would account for his changed manner. He might see me as a possible ally to cultivate. Make me a friend, then I cease to be a threat.

Or I was imagining stuff, and this was all a load of crap.

I could just about hear Escott agreeing with me, too. Whatever I was reading from Kroun was certainly colored by what I'd been through in the last week. There was no reason to trust any of it. I needed to take the advice I'd given to Gordy and get some rest.

Perhaps Kroun was just . . . I guess *relaxed* would be the word. He sure didn't match up with the ill-tempered man I'd first talked to on the phone or the commanding mob boss who could clear a room with just a look. Gordy said Kroun was scary. I wasn't seeing that anymore. Or feeling it. That must be what set off the doubts in my gut. Gordy wouldn't have used that word without good reason.

Capone was known to be as charming as all get out when he was in the mood for it. He was still a killer.

Maybe that was the scare about Kroun. Lull a person with the charm, then bang-bang-you're-dead.

Too late for me.

I went up to my office—lights were on there, too. The ledgers with Bobbi's neat entries were with that night's respectable take in the desk safe, meaning a bank run tomorrow. I put the money bag back, along with the .38 Detective Special I kept there. Sure, I was fairly bulletproof, but if I could head off trouble packing heat of my own, then why not?

Heat . . .

I turned up the radiator and hovered over it, hoping to thaw out.

It occurred to me that maybe I should have more blood inside my shuddering body.

Rotten thought.

I was *not* hungry, but the impulse strongly tugged to bring that living heat inside, to glut on it and drive away the death chill. In my mind I knew it would be futile, but the malicious darkness within urged otherwise.

Phone up a taxi, it said. There was time to squeeze in a trip to the Stockyards before dawn. Time to drink myself sick again.

I fought it off by telling myself it was too much trouble, would endanger me if I got caught by an early-morning yard worker. I ran through a few dozen other discouraging excuses of varying degrees of likelihood. All served to delay until the craving passed, and depression firmly took over, finally immobilizing me.

It's a sad thing when self-pity becomes a safe and welcome alternative for heading off self-destructive activities.

Left the office, went down to Bobbi's dressing room. I had some spare clothes shoved into the back of the closet there. No need to move her stuff out now that Jewel was dead.

Damnation.

Stripped and turned on the shower water as hot as possible, risking a scald to just stand with the spray square in my face. With no need to breathe I was there for a long while, the water hammering my eyelids. Lost track of how many times I soaped and scrubbed, soaped and scrubbed. I emptied the club's huge hot-water tank. Finally warm, or at least not cold, my skin was cherry red when I emerged.

Except for the long, thin, white scars.

I decided it was time to look at them. Adelle had said *the face of the enemy*. I should lose my fear of this, lose my hatred of them. On one hand the memory of getting them was as sharp as Bristow's knife, on the other, it was as though it had happened to a different man who had told me about a harrowing, but long-ago experience.

They still didn't seem to be fading. Was their trauma so great that they'd always be with me? How would Bobbi react to them?

If she saw them. If we ever made love again. Certainly never as long as I was unpredictable, out of control. I didn't dare touch her.

And it wasn't a big help standing here in her empty dressing room in front of an empty mirror.

I dressed quickly, went up to the office where the radio I'd not turned on now played. I didn't recognize the band or their song, must have been new, and sprawled on the sofa and stared at the ceiling and tried not to think of anything at all.

And, God, it *hurt*.

Too much.

This time I foiled the seizure by vanishing quick, before it could peak.

The floating helped. No heavy body to twitch and flop, no pathetic groaning. Instead, through my muffled hearing I picked up the radio's music. The song, whatever it was, helped steady me. I hovered over the couch. Its cushions each had a bag of my home earth sewn inside for those sleepover days. I didn't know if its proximity would help.

I held formless for a long time and thought about how I'd floated in the stock pond as a kid. This was very much like it, except back then I didn't have to shut out bad memories.

One other sense was left to me in this state: touch, and it was more muffled than my hearing. I could feel objects, get a general idea of something's shape, size, and the space around me. And people. I could touch them, leaving behind a profound cold.

I felt someone in the room with me. Couldn't think who it might be, but wasn't unduly alarmed. Escott and Bobbi had keys. Why would either of them come here at this late hour, though?

They wouldn't, not without making more noise. Bobbi usually said hello to Myrna. Escott would have called out to me by now.

So who was here? Kroun? He could have picked the lock to get in. I reached out, thinking whoever it was would soon have to move or complain about the cold, and I could identify the voice. Only that didn't happen. The person stayed put.

So *I* moved. I floated into the hall through the door and re-formed, then stepped back in the office again.

I fully expected to see someone *sitting* on that couch.

Nothing. I was seeing nothing. A lot of it.

But I had *sensed* . . . uh-oh. Mouth dry again. I cleared my throat. "Myrna?"

No reply. But I *knew*.

In taking a breath to speak I was overwhelmed by the scent of roses.

10

WOKE up on the dot of sunset, about one minute later than the previous evening. The year was turning, the days getting longer. Shorter nights. Lucky me. Less time to be in oblivion.

The rose scent was much faded by now. That had been . . . spooky. Okay, it had thrown me, but I could figure that Myrna had again been trying to give comfort, that's why I chose to remain on the office couch rather than retreat to my other bolt-hole under the tiers in the main room. How I'd actually been able to *feel* her as a physical presence was something else again. Maybe it was because I was on her side of the veil half the time. Dead.

I'd have given a shiver, but wasn't cold. Now *that* was good news. The radiator had been chugging away for hours; the place must be jungle-hot by now.

I got up to turn it back to normal and listened to familiar activity going on below. Lady Crymsyn was waking, too. She'd started the process earlier, but for her it took more time. A dame's privilege.

Someone had been and gone. Escott, probably. A stack of newspapers lay on the desk like a no-nonsense message. He'd have made a connection between my uncharacteristically spending all evening at another nightclub that was now violently minus its star act. Certainly he'd want to know the real story. The papers sure didn't have it.

The evening headlines were big and harsh, their theme murder-suicide. Apparently after Caine's body was found the cops went to question his ex-wife and in turn found her. Facts were thin, with no mention of Evie Montana or gambling debts. There was no official verdict yet, but Jewel was getting the blame for Caine's death.

My heart sank. Jewel deserved better than that. How the hell could they be so stupid? If Kroun and I could figure out she'd not killed herself—and how could they screw up so badly about the faked crime scene in Caine's flat? Was this some kind of misdirection to throw off the killer, make him think he was safe?

I phoned the Nightcrawler and got Derner. Mindful that the line could be wired, I was as vague as could be managed. "How did things go today?"

"A little rough, but it turned out all right," he cautiously told me. "Everything's fine here."

"What about our guest and his pal?"

"Haven't seen either of them today."

"What about that party I want found?"

"Nothing yet. They're being scarce."

Damn. "Is my car ready?"

"Not yet, Boss."

"What d'ya mean? It's just changing tires."

"Uhh, well, the tow truck guy didn't understand exactly and took your car to Cicero."

I considered that one a minute before asking, in what I was certain was a very reasonable tone: "Why?"

"Uhh, they're gonna fix it up for you."

"In what way?"

"Like the way the Caddy's fixed up."

"*What?*" I had visions of my humble Buick outfitted with steel armor, thick glass, and a motor that should be driving a battleship, not a car. "Call it off! I just want new tires!"

"They're doin' them, too, Boss."

"Don't give me a 'too,' just get my car ba—*what* are they doing?"

"Well, seein's how your tires were cut up like that, they're puttin' on the solid rubber kind. No more flats. You'll love 'em."

"Derner."

"Yeah, Boss?"

"Get my car *back*. No fancy stuff like the Caddy, nothing special. Just put on some *tires* and get it back to me."

He almost sounded hurt. "Okay . . . I'll talk to 'em."

"Good. If you need me over there tonight, you'll have to send a driver to pick me up."

"You mean you don't have the Caddy?" His voice went up a little.

"Our guest has it. Seems to like it a lot."

"Oh, well, that's okay, then. You still want some extra muscle for your place?"

"Yeah, send 'em over. Just find that other party." As soon as I cradled the receiver the phone rang.

"Fleming!" It was Kroun, sounding cheerful.

Now what? "Yeah?"

"You finally warmed up yet?"

"Mostly. What's going on?"

"Thought I'd come by your club, see if you turned up anything interesting on that business last night."

"Not really, no. Been sleeping all day."

"All day? You lazy bum! Your place open tonight?"

"Yeah, in about half an hour."

"Save me a good table, I'll be coming by sometime later."

"No problem. Have you seen Mitchell?"

"He's been out gallivanting with old friends. Still is."

Mitchell had friends? "Shouldn't he be watching your back?"

"I'm safe enough. Besides, he always turns up." Kroun rang off. Wonderful. Why come and hang around my club? I'd have to stop giving away booze.

As I walked downstairs Wilton was getting bowls of matches, ashtrays, and cocktail napkins ready on the lobby bar.

"Hey, Mr. Fleming. Come in early?"

"Yeah. You seen Bobbi or Charles?"

"They're both here. Main room."

"I'll bring the tills down in a minute."

"Sure, Boss."

Somehow, when he called me that, it was perfectly fine. "Myrna around?"

"Not that I've noticed."

I went into the main room. A few early-arrived waiters were there talking with the bartender. Everyone straightened and found something to do as soon as I showed. I liked that and continued on to the backstage area.

Someone banged loudly on the stage door that opened to the back alley. I unlocked and let in the first band members. Five of them barged past out of the cold, smoking like farm trucks and talking a mile a minute and paying me no mind, I was only the boss. I yelled at them to douse their cigarettes, and most of them heard, dropping the stubs into a sand-filled fire bucket hanging next to one of the many extinguishers.

From the corner of my eye I saw Bobbi flit from the number three dressing room, rushing toward the stage like she forgot something. She wore a long silk dressing gown that flapped alarmingly wide as she moved. I caught up with her at the master lighting box stage right.

"Anything wrong?" I asked.

"Hi, sweetheart! Just checking." She absently went tiptoe and pecked my cheek, as normal as could be. But then she didn't know about the fit I'd had in my car after leaving her the other evening or any of what I'd been into last night. That was good. We both had enough worries.

"I'll do this, you go finish getting ready."

"Okay-thanks." She shot off. Her feet were bare, and she scuffed along in quick little steps back to her dressing-room haven. She would be fully occupied putting herself together for the show, and I knew better than to follow after she slammed the door shut. The door didn't exactly slam so much as make a subdued *whump*; they were all fitted out with special rubber stripping on the inside edges to be less noisy. That had been Bobbi's idea when the place was being built. She maintained there was nothing more distracting for a performance than having unscheduled noises coming from backstage.

I looked over the settings for the light box and all seemed normal and unchanged. With Myrna around checking it was an ongoing chore we'd all learned to do. Of course, sometimes the lights played up while the switches were correctly in place, so we tried not to mind too much when that happened.

Roland and Faustine arrived next through the alley entry and seemed pleased with themselves. Maybe things were smoothing out in their marriage. He called a friendly hello; she gave me a regal nod, and said, "Zo pleeeezed" at me. At first I didn't think her Russian accent was real, but I'd come to change my mind. The way she looked she was a knockout in any language.

As the purposeful bustle seemed under control, I got out of the area so the showbiz juggernaut could continue bowling along without interruption from an outsider. The bartender and waiters were getting the main room ready. Most of the chairs were properly on the floor again, and the table lights on. Chatter was up, everyone anticipating a better night for tips since we were one day closer to the weekend.

I returned to the front lobby, half-expecting to see Kroun walk in early just to be annoying.

"Tills, Boss?" Wilton reminded.

"Getting them."

Everything was so *normal* it gave me the creeps, as though last night's deaths had not happened. The papers with their headlines hadn't changed, though, as I saw when I returned to my office.

Escott was seated at the desk, hunched over the phone. He glanced up, nodded at me, then refocused on listening. He seemed intent, but not in a bad way, so I walked around and swung open the false door front that hid the desk's safe. I had to try to ignore his conversation while spinning the combination, and it was hard. The guy was actually *chuckling* at something, and not the dry, sometimes ironic sound I was used to; this one was warm, sincere amusement. It matched his low tone of voice, which at one point dipped even lower into something like a purr.

He wound his call up as I pulled out the cash bag for making change and relocked the safe. "Well, Vivian's sure got your head turned."

"How did you—oh, never mind."

"Hey, you don't talk like that to our booze supplier. If you did, we might get it for free."

His ears went red. When it came to Vivian, he turned into a schoolboy. "Was your evening out as horrendous as these seem to indicate?" He gestured at the papers.

"Yeah, it was tough."

"You didn't call me?"

"I thought you should stay clear. Kroun was all over this one, and he doesn't need to know what you look like. We had to do stuff; none of it made the papers, though."

"And what is the real story?"

I sighed and sat on the couch. "Someone strangled Alan Caine backstage between shows. We had to hide it, then move him to his hotel to take the heat off the club."

"Was it a murder-suicide, as the papers said?"

"No." I gave Escott the short version of events, and it still was too much bad news.

"You and Mr. Kroun seem to be getting on, then."

"That or he's just responding extra well to my telling him we're friends. He's coming by here soon. I think he wants to talk about this mess. I don't trust him, though."

"Very wise. He could be protecting his man, Mitchell."

"Thought of that, though why Mitchell would want to bump Caine is anyone's guess. My money's on Hoyle. He's a guy who holds a grudge."

"You put him as being behind the flat tires, too?"

"Him or Ruzzo. It wasn't just about trying to make a flat; someone did a real Jack the Ripper job front and back. Rubber ribbons. Lot of anger there."

"Dear me. What about Ruzzo strangling Caine? A possibility?"

"Ruzzo don't have the brains to act on their own, though they might have been put up to it. They're good at anything to do with intimidation, have a natural instinct for it, but need direction and specific simple instructions. They could have gotten away clean on blind luck."

"And Miss Montana?"

"Have to find her." I shrugged. "Women. Who can figure?"

"Indeed. Well, Shoe called me today and passed on the news he was looking after Gordy at your instigation."

"Yeah, he'll kill himself if he doesn't get some rest. I figured Shoe was the right man to keep him safe for it. Any news?"

"Gordy was sleeping a lot. Dr. Clarson is supervising and seems to think that is quite the best thing."

What a relief. Something was going right.

"Was any undue influence applied to assure Gordy's cooperation?"

"It was only for his own best good, I swear."

"And how are you doing?" It wasn't a casual health query.

"No shakes tonight. So far."

Escott was giving me a look. One of *those* kind of looks.

"I'm *fine*!" For a while I'd almost felt like my regular self. I resented the reminder that he still saw me as ailing. It had the effect of dragging me back into the sickroom.

He made an innocent "hands off" gesture and quit the chair. "Shall we open, then?"

We divvied money up between the tills, ten bucks and change for each, more than enough for the night. We carried them down. Escott took one to the main room, I gave mine to Wilton. "Got what you need?" I asked.

"A little short on lemons. Hard to get this time of year."

"Then we do without. It's time."

The extra bouncers from the Nightcrawler were smoking in the lobby and greeted me with respectful nods. Derner must have handpicked them to avoid sending anyone who was personally hostile toward me. They knew who they were to look out for and would be hanging around front and back, two to a door, inside and out, eyes open for trouble.

My regular staff seemed a little walleyed about the tough newcomers, or so Wilton confided when he motioned me over to the side.

"Ain't the people we got enough?" he asked.

"You read the papers today?" I countered. "That club singer who got bumped?"

"Yeah . . ."

"These guys are to make sure that doesn't happen here."

He gave an exaggerated nod of understanding and flashed a welcoming smile toward the toughs. "Gentlemen! If you need coffee, just ask!"

That's what I liked to see. Cooperation. I ascertained that the doorman had his fancy red coat buttoned and that the hatcheck girl was ready for business, then turned on the open sign and the outside lights of the canopied entrance. No crowds were waiting to flood in just yet, but soon.

Before leaving I said, addressing them all, "There's a guy turning up later tonight, forties, lean, has a white streak of hair on one side—"

"That movie star?" chirped the girl, eyes bright. "He was *cute!*"

Not my word for Kroun, but she'd obviously responded to his brand of charm in a big way. "He's no movie star, but he is important. Give him the royal treatment when he shows and take him up to my table. He gets whatever he wants."

"And how!" she agreed. The men merely nodded, and I went on to the main room.

The band was running late, still more drifting in and tuning up. When the leader spotted me he snapped at the others to put some hustle in it, knowing we were officially open. Just over half came to attention and began playing at his signal. The music was thin at first, then gradually surged and filled out as more of the guys joined in on their usual warm-up number. By the time I was seated at my third tier table they were in full swing.

Opening was always a little sweat-making with them playing to an empty house. The worry was that it would remain empty for the evening, but usually within half an hour we'd have enough of a crowd to justify the endeavor. I sat well back in the shadows of my booth, watching, going over details in my head in case I missed anything.

Once I finally admitted to myself that all was well I started chewing over Jewel Caine's murder. Whatever reason someone had had to kill Alan Caine, I couldn't think why they'd go after Jewel, too.

Unless she'd seen them. She'd been smoking out in the alley. It was very possible. If the killer had left by that route—the fastest exit was the stage door—she could have been right there. She might have said or done something to set him off, or maybe it was enough for her to be in the wrong place just then. He'd have to shut her up as a witness; he lured or kidnapped her away, then staged the fake suicide. And as great good fortune would have it, the cops, or at least the papers, had fallen for the sham.

I wasn't going to leave it like that for her. The right person would take the rap for this. All I needed was five minutes with him.

But was I up to doing hypnosis yet or in for another crippling migraine leading to a seizure? The constant chill that had plagued me last night was somewhat mitigated. I wasn't shivering in my overcoat and hat. My day sleep had accomplished some healing after all, but did it extend that far? I wouldn't know for sure unless I tried, and I wasn't inclined to try.

Escott had been backstage and now emerged from the side exit door on the left. He had a word with the bartender, got a brandy, then began the climb up to my table. Several couples had come in, and the tables were gradually filling up. It was early, but looked like we'd have a good crowd.

"May I?" he asked, ever polite, even when there was no need.

I waved him in on the opposite side, and he took a load off. "Charles, I know you're curious about Kroun coming in, but you've been doing two jobs. It's okay if you head home and rest."

"Rest? My dear fellow, gadding about here *is* rest for me. I always look forward to abandoning my office to enjoy this glad escape." He lifted his snifter. "And a free drink."

"Okay, if you're sure." That was my way of being polite. "But where he's concerned I think you should be invisible."

"That shan't be a problem. I agree with you on the anonymity point. I'd rather not be anyone he knows."

"Did you look up more on him today?"

"Oh, absolutely."

"And . . . ?"

"There is a remarkable lack of material on him. Now and then his name popped up in the New York papers in connection to certain acts of violence, but he's avoided any arrest and prosecution. One day he's the focus of someone's official attention, the next they've never heard of him."

"He must bribe or threaten them away, then." Another half dozen customers came in. Good. Kroun wasn't one of them. Better.

"What's odd is that reporters seem to lose interest in him. Walter Winchell had the start of what promised to be a very juicy piece connecting him to a murder, then it simply never happened."

"You think he bribed *Winchell*? He'd have boasted about turning it down."

Escott shook his head. "You'd have to ask Winchell that. You're former colleagues. Write him a letter."

I almost laughed. Sure I'd been a reporter, but so far down the journalistic totem pole as not even to exist when compared to Winchell. "Why don't you write Helen Hayes, and ask if she'll put you in her next play?"

"Because I prefer Chicago over New York," he replied.

"Don't tell me you know . . ."

He bounced one eyebrow, very deadpan.

"Ah, never mind."

The band went into a fanfare, and Teddy Parris launched onto the stage, taking charge of it as easily as an experienced trouper twice his years. He introduced himself, welcomed everyone, and promised them all a great evening. It was almost how I glad-handed people in the lobby, but without the whammy-work.

He swung his way into "Christopher Columbus" with enthusiastic help from the band. It was a great song; people responded, clustering on the dance floor. During an instrumental interlude Teddy bounded from the stage, cut in on a couple in a comic way, and took the lady around some fast turns. He deftly handed her back to her date and continued to spin, making like he'd gone dizzy, artfully ending up at a table sitting on a guy's lap. Wide-eyed Teddy tickled the guy's chin, then mimed mortified horror and switched laps to flirt with the girlfriend instead. Fortunately they thought he was funny. I'd seen that gag not work in many a spectacular way.

He dropped to one knee, gave the lady the red carnation from his lapel, then made a fast exit, cartwheeling back to the dance floor, managing not to hit anyone. Up onstage again, he was in perfect time to resume singing, but breathless, so he made a business out of that, mopping his brow and purposely wheezing out the words. He miraculously recovered enough to deliver a strong finish. It went over well, with laughs and applause.

"You'll have to start paying him more if he keeps on like that," Escott observed.

"Don't give him ideas."

Teddy's set continued through several more lively songs, and he used his long, expressive face to play up the humorous delivery, sometimes adding in comments, but he included a plaintive love song to prove he had a voice. The women ate it up.

Escott pulled out his pipe and tobacco pouch and prepared a smoke. He didn't seem to be in a contemplative mood. It was strangely very much like any other evening.

"Thought you preferred cigarettes," I said.

"Used to. Vivian prefers the smell of pipe tobacco."

Ho-ho. "So how's the date for Saturday? You sounded pretty happy about it."

"Yes, Bobbi and I had an additional planning session when I drove her in tonight. All is progressing extremely well." Escott looked kind of odd. Pleased and bemused and nervous at the same time, but it didn't seem like a bad feeling to have. It cheered me up seeing him like that. "Vivian gladly accepted your invitation, and Sarah is looking forward to going out to a grown-ups' event. She doesn't know you're the one who actually rescued her, but has picked up from her mother that you're a cross between *The Lone Ranger* and *Gangbusters*. She may want your autograph."

"Son of a—" I broke off, almost laughing. "What a kid."

"You know she plays the piano?"

That hauled me short. "But I thought she wasn't . . ."

He shrugged. "Well, gifts of talent and intellectual development do not necessarily walk hand in hand. She doesn't read music, but she can play whatever she's heard. She's quite amazing."

"Huh. Who'd a thought it?"

"Actually, Vivian did. She read somewhere that doctors had determined Albert Einstein to be so backward that they recommend institutionalization. His parents got him a violin instead. Vivian encourages Sarah in a similar direction. Seems to give the girl comfort, too."

"Oh, yeah?"

He lifted a hand. "She has nightmares about her kidnapping. Has to have the lights on all the time. Doesn't like to be alone."

That sounded uncomfortably familiar.

"Vivian told her that day or night, whenever she felt frightened or sad, she was to go to the parlor and play the piano and she would feel better. It seems to work."

"You dropping a hint?"

"I believe you already understand the merits of music in healing a damaged spirit. You have the radio on nearly all the time."

"That's just to keep me from thinking too much."

"Exactly."

Teddy made his big finish and took his bows, then began Roland and Faustine's introduction. The tone of the band changed dramatically, the drums coming in strong.

"I can't make music," I said. "Can't carry a tune in a bag, and Ma gave up trying to teach me piano when the rest of the family said my practice would lead to a hanging."

"What do you mean?" His pipe went out. He gave it an irritated look.

"If I kept trying to play, one of them was going to kill me. That last lesson was a relief to everybody, especially myself."

"And here you sit, owner of a nightclub full of song."

The lights went out so Roland and Faustine could take their places. Clearly Bobbi had changed the ordering of the show again, leaving out the anniversary duet with Teddy. Perhaps none of the couples here tonight were celebrating. The music built upon itself, horns and drums filling the space right to the walls, thundering into the tango.

"I don't paint but can appreciate art. You saying I need to hang around here more?"

"Yes, of course. The rest of the time you could indulge in expanding your record collection. I would strongly suggest acquiring some of the pieces from the Baroque period. They have a most soothing effect on the nerves."

I knew that stuff; it all sounded alike to me. "Fats Waller is more my style."

He relit the pipe. "Whatever does the job."

We watched the dancers, though I was sure Escott was keeping at least one eye on me and my reaction to the show. He didn't have to; I was worried enough for both of us.

"Any new problems, past or pending?" He was talking about my fits again. Great timing. Keep me distracted as the music reached its apex and the lights changed for the bloodred finale.

Shutting my eyes, I leaned on the table, head low. Bracing. Just in case. "Not tonight. Knock wood."

"Hm. Sounds hopeful."

Closing my eyes made it work. Not long after, a roaring burst of applause told me it was safe to look again. I held up a nontrembling hand. "Maybe there's something to it."

"Then congratulations. Every step forward is for the better." He'd finished his smoke and tapped the dottle into the ashtray. Only then did I notice a shiny leather pouch that had his initials stamped on it in gold.

"That's new," I said.

He smiled a little self-consciously. "A gift from Vivian."

"Well-well, quite a girl you got there." I was going to razz him some more, but Teddy reappeared to introduce Bobbi. She took center stage and seemed to glow all on her own. It hurt to look at her.

Roland and Faustine melted into another exposition dance to complement her opening song. There was a spotlight on Bobbi and a traveling spot on them. The effect was great. While some club owners might object to Bobbi's constant changing of the bill, I welcomed it. She kept the place out of the doldrums of repetition. The regular customers liked it, and the performers stayed interested.

End of number, lights up, bows, plenty of applause, graceful shift as Roland and Faustine broke away to take new partners. This time an impatient guy, still in his hat and overcoat, got to Faustine first, and he wasn't half-bad squiring her around the floor.

Bobbi sang, others danced, and the rest were caught up in her voice as she did a plaintive but not overly sentimental version of "Pennies from Heaven." The arrangement had one of the trumpets doing something that sounded reminiscent of falling water, which was echoed in places by a clarinet. I'd not heard that part before. They must have come up with it during daytime rehearsal.

Faustine's partner maneuvered them close to the stage until they were just below Bobbi, then he held in place, not doing much of anything but looking up at her. Smiling.

What the hell . . . ?

I abruptly recognized Mitchell.

He was waiting for Bobbi to see him. The lights would be in her eyes; maybe there was still time to head him off. I suddenly vanished and shot right over the heads of everyone between, going solid just as suddenly on the dance floor only steps from Mitchell. I didn't care who saw.

But I was too late. Mitchell sidled close enough so she caught the movement and looked his way. Grinning, he waved up at her. She didn't react, singing on, then did a kind of slow double take and froze in sheer horror. I thought she would dislike a reminder of the bad old days, but didn't expect this. It required a hell of a lot to get Bobbi to miss a line, and she did just that, dropping several words and stumbling through the start of the chorus. She pretended to have a throat problem, pulling away from the microphone, hand to her mouth as though to cough. The band continued. Singers forgetting words were part of the job.

Mitchell just kept grinning.

I clapped a hand on his shoulder from behind, grabbed his right arm so he wouldn't go for his gun, and turned him before he quite knew what happened. His baffled surprise turned into a snarl when he saw my face, but I chivvied him along as quick as any of the bouncers. I'm a lot stronger than I look, and where the hell were they?

"Lay off, pretty boy!" Mitchell started.

I clocked him smartly, rapping his skull with my knuckles as though knocking to get in. As mad as I was the force was the same as if I'd black-jacked him. His legs ceased to hold him so well, and I had to take his weight to keep him moving.

By now we were a spectacle. The joker running the traveling spot picked us out from the crowd on the dance floor and followed, much to everyone's amusement. A few applauded, thinking this was part of the show. So far no one was screaming in reaction to my magical appearance out of thin air.

I veered to the right, going toward the door that led to the backstage area. It had the closest exit. I glanced over my shoulder at the stage.

Bobbi made it to the end of the chorus, but her tone was wrong for the mood she'd set, her face fixed, eyes staring at nothing, like a mannequin. She threw a jerky signal to the band leader, and he muttered a song title to his people. The music shifted and changed key. Out of sequence, Bobbi hastily introduced Teddy Parris, calling him up again. He must have been ready in the wings, for he bounced forward and took over as though this was business as usual. The spotlight shifted to him, so Bobbi's hasty departure went mostly unseen.

Mitchell and I blew through the door. Just within was a wide service area with the alley entry at the end and a smaller hall to the right leading to the dressing rooms. To the left were the basement stairs. I wanted to bounce Mitchell down them, but instead slammed him against the back-stage wall, my forearm under his chin, his feet dangling free. He recovered enough to put up some fight, so I rattled him again, taking a lot of satisfaction from the rotten-melon thump his head made on impact. The wall was brick.

Then Escott got between us and pushed me back, shouting my name. It was just enough to keep me from a third try, which would have probably killed Mitchell. He slithered to the floor. Escott shot me a loud "What the devil is going on?"

I wasn't in a mood to explain. "Go check on Bobbi. This creep . . ."

Escott instantly got the idea she'd been threatened in some way, but didn't leave. "Jack . . . ?"

"It'll be all right. I promise not to kill him." Not here, anyway.

"Who is he?"

"I'll tell ya later, go to Bobbi!"

He went.

Where were the damn bouncers? But they were on the lookout for mugs like Hoyle and Ruzzo, not Whitey Kroun's top lieutenant.

Mitchell had a thick skull and had roused himself back to alertness. The first thing he did was reach inside his coat for his gun.

Only I'd taken it off him. It weighed down my coat pocket.

Some guys can't handle being without their heat, but he wasn't one of them. He shot to his feet and went after me, fists flying. Very bad move. I got inside his first punch, taking it on the flank under my arm, and gave him two sharp ones in the breadbasket left and right. Mitchell gagged and dropped and spent the next few moments trying to get air back in his lungs.

He was vulnerable as he ever would be. I thought of hypnotizing him, my first choice for solving the problem he'd become. It wouldn't take much to give him both barrels in the face and see to it he forgot Bobbi ever existed. But even thinking about the attempt seemed to make a steel band tighten around my head. In my current state I'd either send him insane, send myself off into another damned fit, or both.

However, my second choice—beating the crap out of him—was entirely acceptable. I impatiently paced side to side, waiting for him to get up so I could knock him over again.

"What's your beef?" he gasped, staying down. "I only wanted to say hello."

"Try again, and you'll do it without teeth. She doesn't want to see you."

"Huh. Ask her, wise guy. Think she rolled and spread 'em just for you? She'll wanna—"

I hauled him up and threw him across the room.

He hit the brick wall on that side hard but didn't quite lose enough balance; he staggered and kept his feet. "You're gonna pay, you stupid—"

I was too fast for him to see the move and too angry to stop. Not knowing quite how, I got hold of one arm and yanked the wrong way. For that I had an earsplitting howl in response, followed by some truly foul cursing.

"Ya busted my arm!" he informed me.

"Dislocated," I said. I sounded calm as a doctor diagnosing a cold. How could I be this furious and speak so softly?

He tried another swing with his undamaged arm. I stepped back out of range plus a few steps. I'd promised Escott there'd be no killing. Mitchell was making it hard to remember.

That's when the alley door swung inward. One of the bouncers, I thought, finally reacting to the commotion inside.

Except he wasn't a bouncer. Rawboned and face red from the cold, Hoyle shouldered past Mitchell, raising the gun in his fist until the muzzle was level with my eyes. Hoyle's gleamed with unholy delight. He had me square.

"Kill 'im!" Mitchell yelled.

Hoyle seemed barely aware of him. "Payback," he said to me, grinning. He still looked worse for wear from the pounding I'd given him. "Outside, Fleming. Now."

Mitchell, apparently figuring to have a front row seat, darted clumsily through the door, holding his arm close. Were they working together, or was it just glad coincidence that put them on the same team tonight?

"Outside!" Hoyle repeated. "Or I'll drill you here, you—"

His gaze abruptly snapped to the side, toward the hall leading to the dressing rooms.

Faustine Petrova stood not ten feet away. She was out of her tango dance costume, wrapped in a blazing scarlet silk kimono, a look of fascination on her exotic face.

"You are hav-ink important beeznuss meet-ink, yesss?" she asked brightly.

My guts swooped. "Faustine! Get out of here!"

But she stood her ground staring intently at Hoyle. He glared back at her, and his gun muzzle wavered in her direction. Then his eyes went wide.

Faustine made a small, elegant shrugging motion, and the kimono suddenly fell from her shoulders. She was completely naked except for her lipstick. *"Daunce wit' me, beeg boy!"* she sang out, spreading her arms.

Holy mackerel.

Hoyle's eyes got even wider, and his jaw sagged. He had to have seen a naked woman before, but Faustine possessed a unique electricity, and it always turned heads.

Including his, for just long enough.

I launched a full-body tackle on him. Being stronger, I could cover more distance in a leap. I slammed into him, and down we went. Hoyle's reflexes were·too good, though. His time in the boxing ring made him quick to recover. He fired, and I felt the sear as the bullet grazed my side. It was a scratch, nothing to sweat over . . .

But Faustine dropped, giving a little cry.

11

WHILE I tried to take the gun away before it went off again Hoyle got in some double-quick punches. We rolled and grunted and kicked and suddenly he wasn't there anymore, and I found my feet, but he was outside and racing down the alley where a car waited at the far end. It was Ruzzo at the wheel. Didn't know which one. Hoyle made the running board, and they took off.

No sign of Mitchell.

Faustine.

I turned and choked, for she seemed to be huddled in a vast pool of blood until the mass of brilliant color resolved into being her kimono. Took a whiff. The only bloodsmell was my own.

Went to her quick. She stirred and cautiously opened an eye. "Es over, yesss?"

"You okay, doll?" At a loss to help I plucked at the kimono.

A smile. "Amer-i-kans, zo shy." She gracefully found her feet, slipping the silk wrap around her lithe body in one move. She was unhurt and beaming. "Es like Jeemmy Cagney seen-e-ma, yesss?"

About two inches from where her head had been was a bullet pock in the brick. "Oh, yeah."

"But Jek, you are heet?" She spotted the bloody graze in my side.

"Faustine!" Roland hurtled toward her from the hall and grabbed her up. "I heard shooting! Jack . . . ! My God, what's going on? Darling, are you all right?"

The last was aimed at his wife, who had a ready explanation, except it was in fast-flowing Russian, which he clearly didn't understand.

I went to the alley door, looking both ways as I emerged into the cold wind. All clear. No Mitchell, and no bouncers, either. I shoved the door shut, took a chair off a stacked column of spares in a corner, and angled it under the doorknob. Randomly, I thought I'd better get a new lock, the kind that only opens from the inside.

Faustine recovered enough English by then to provide Roland with the beginnings of a highly dramatic episode of how she'd saved my life. He seemed to be getting more upset by the second, so I skipped toward the main room. The second I was out of sight I vanished, not inclined to see anyone on my way to the lobby. I materialized in a blind spot in the curving hall leading to it and kept going.

All four bouncers were gone.

"Where are they?" I roared at Wilton. He looked ready to duck behind the bar, and the hatcheck girl went *"yeep!"* and did duck under her counter.

"The men's room," he said, astonished.

All of them? If they were having a craps game, I'd have their balls on a—

I pushed in, loaded for bear, and found them sprawled or heaped on the floor like so many bodies after a battle. I froze for a second, thinking the worst, but one of them groaned. To a man they'd been coshed. From the way they were lying, they must have been lined up and hit one at a time. Even Ruzzo could have done it with no trouble, one to hold them in place with a gun, the other to swing away like Babe Ruth on a Sunday.

Checked them quick. Alive. Fortunately. The man that groaned opened his eyes and squinted. "Boss? Wha' happened?"

Went to the door and yelled for Wilton. He came in and gaped. "Boss, what happened?"

"Look after them, make sure nobody dies."

As I left, the groaning guy made it to a urinal and began throwing up.

I returned to the backstage hall the same way, but going solid more slowly to make sure no one saw. No need to worry. Waiters clogged the place, all looking in the same direction. Faustine was apparently telling her story again, this time with sound effects and gestures. She pointed with finger and thumb, not needing the pistol Mitchell had left behind.

That lay forgotten on the floor where it had dropped in my fight with Hoyle. I quietly pocketed it again.

"'I vill keel you, you dirdy radt!' Zen *beng-beng-beng* off goes de gun, but Jek *leaps* on de bedt guy like de mad tiger! Ah! My heee-rrro!" Faustine beamed at me, parting their ranks as she flew through them to throw her arms around me. Suddenly she was kissing both my cheeks and planting more all over my face. Roland rushed over, too, and grabbed one of my flailing hands, pumping it.

"Grand work, sport!" he yelled, as though I'd gone deaf. "That will teach those rowdies! You saved her life! I can't thank you enough!"

Teach who? I wondered. *What* had she been telling them?

"Uh . . . well . . . yeah, okay, glad to have been of help." I managed to get out of Faustine's grip, firmly guiding her toward Roland's protective embrace. "C'mon, guys! Show's over, get back to work!"

"What happened, Boss?"

"Drunk customer. He's gone. Now, back out there while we still have others. If anyone asks, you don't know nuthin'."

"But we *don't* know nuthin'," one of them grumbled as they filed past, disappointed.

I leaned against the wall and rubbed my face. My hands came away red, but it was only Faustine's lip color. The vivid red spooked me for a second.

Roland gallantly gave me a clean handkerchief. "I'd like to talk when you're recovered."

He got a vague nod. Mopping the war paint, I looked past him and saw Escott frowning severely at me. I was everyone's favorite tonight. He waited until Roland and Faustine went by to get to their dressing rooms.

"That man was with Kroun the other night," he stated. "His lieutenant?" He said *lieutenant* like it had an "f" in it.

"Yeah. Mitchell."

"What has he done to upset Bobbi so much?"

"I donno, but he used to run with Slick Morelli's mob. He kept saying he and Bobbi were old friends. I warned him to keep clear, but he—"

"Indeed he did, and you nearly gave me heart failure with that vanishing business."

"It was dark, everyone's drinking, they're welcome to prove it. How's Bobbi?"

He frowned a bit more, which was going some. "She is in a 'state.' Extremely distressed."

I started past him, but he caught my arm. "Jack, make her cry, and I'll murder you."

And he knew how to do it, too.

I shot down the hall to the number three dressing room and very softly knocked. The show was still going on, with Teddy doing his best to fill in. Bobbi didn't reply, so I pushed the door open.

"Bobbi? Honey, you okay?"

From the bathroom came a long exhalation of breath. She emerged, wobbly, clutching a wad of tissue in one hand like a soggy bouquet. "No." Her voice was too high. She stared at the blood on my shirt. "Are you hurt? I heard a shot, but Charles made me stay."

"It's nothing, I'm all better, everything's fine. I took care of the guy. He's gone. He won't be back."

"You know who he is?"

"His name's Mitchell, and he's with a guy named Kroun outta New York. I heard he'd been with Morelli before that and didn't want him bothering you . . . I'm sorry."

She sat at her dressing table, back to the mirror. "You *knew* about Mitch?"

Mitch. She called him Mitch. Why was that? "Only that he left when Gordy took over. Strome told me."

Bobbi didn't exactly cry like Adelle, but expressed similar symptoms, subdued, but intense, right on the edge. "Did Strome tell you why Mitch left?"

"What is it? He hurt you?"

She shook her head. "No." She turned toward the mirror and dabbed her eyes. The damage wasn't too bad. I realized she could no longer look at me straight, though I could see her fine, front and back. Why wasn't she looking at me? That crap Mitchell said . . . "He told me Mitchell wouldn't play second fiddle under Gordy."

"Nothing more?"

"Listen, if you don't want to talk about it . . ." I wanted to hold her, but something told me not to try. I had the sudden feeling of treading on eggs.

"Oh, it's nothing horrible. He's—I'm acting stupidly about the whole thing. He just surprised me showing up so suddenly like that, and then you . . ." She dumped the wadded tissues in a basket and clawed more from a box on her vanity table. Blew her nose a lot. That seemed the end of it, but tears were leaking out now. She stood and made the limited rounds of the room, fiddling with stuff, trying very, very hard not to lose control. "Anyway, he's long gone, right? You made him leave, so everything's fine. You don't need to be worrying about . . . *oh, don't* LOOK *at me like that!*"

I backed off. I didn't know how I was looking at her. "*What?*"

Bobbi made a strange wailing noise and fled into the bathroom, slamming the door.

I called to her. All I got in return were the big, racking, moaning sobs of a full-blown breakdown. "Honey? What is it? Bobbi? Come on." I'd never seen her like this before, and it was scaring me. Somehow dealing with Adelle had been so simple, and this . . . wasn't.

Well, I'd been assured by Adelle that just holding her had been the right thing to do. This might get worse if I waited.

I vanished, sieved through, and re-formed. Bobbi was on the toilet lid with another bouquet of paper to sop up the outpour. My appearance startled her.

"Not fair!" she yelled. "No! Not fair! You leave! I don't wanna—"

I did what I did with Adelle, arms holding close and tight. Bobbi hiccuped and sobbed, stuttering, and finally broke into a steady shower and, oh, God, didn't I hate every minute of it.

After forever went by, she wound down to a slow finish, and was a dandy mess from the effort. Women never look good crying unless they're on a movie screen. That's how you can tell it's acting.

She blew her nose for the umpteenth time, but still sounded stuffy, and her voice was thick. "I'm sorry."

"Honey . . . whatever it is . . . it's okay." And I meant that. I didn't want her going off the deep end again, or I'd wind up in a booby hatch.

"It's about Mitch."

"I kinda figured that. Bobbi, whatever it is, it won't make me hate him any less."

"What does that mean?"

"I don't know, but please don't cry anymore. Say the word, and I'll make him disappear, but *please* . . ."

Sniff. "Okay, Jack."

"You want him gone?"

"Not the way you're thinking. I just don't *ever* want to see him again. That's all I want. He j-just brought all the bad stuff back, and I don't want to go through—"

"Okay! It's done. He won't get within a mile of you, I promise."

"Oooh, now my head hurts."

"Don't move, I'll get you something."

I backed from the room, watching her as though she might vanish like me. Halfway down the hall was Faustine, still in her kimono. Roland and Escott watched from the far end, hopefully out of earshot. They had worried faces and were smoking. They both knew better than to do that backstage, but it wasn't the time to play theater cop.

"Jek?" said Faustine, halting me.

"Yeah, not now, I gotta . . ."

She held a glass of water and a bottle of aspirin. "Heerrre. Take eet. Gif her thrree, make her drink whole glessfool."

"Uh . . ."

She arched both eyebrows. "Men! Zo 'fraid ov leetle tears. They are de rain ov lof. Now go beck, feex et. Don't come out until she lofs you again! Go!"

I went.

Bobbi settled down after the dosing. She apologized some more, and I told her it was all right and unnecessarily held my breath, but she didn't bust out afresh, so that was good.

"Can you tell me what's wrong?" I belatedly thought that I should have sent Faustine in to do this. Women were better at it.

"This was a couple years ago," Bobbi began.

I nodded.

"Back then it was like I knew everything, yet nothing at all. You know how that is?"

"Several times a night."

"Remember how it was with me and Slick? When we first started it was great, and then it got so he decided he owned me, and I couldn't get out of it. If I did, he'd mess things up for me in every club in Chicago. In order to sing I had to keep myself available and do what I was told."

I nodded some more. I also felt rotten to have to hear all this, knowing how much it tore her up.

"M-mitch was one of the boys there, and he liked me. A lot. For a while I thought he could help me. He said he could get me clear of Slick, and we'd go to Hollywood. We were so careful and it seemed safe and he was much nicer than Slick."

That side of Mitchell I couldn't begin to imagine.

"We planned out *everything*. I figured what to pack into two suitcases, and it was hard, because I was leaving so much behind, but it was worth it for being with him. Starting over. No mistakes this time . . . then Gordy showed up at my hotel flat.

"He knew Mitch and I were going to run away, when we planned to do it, the works; it was like having your mind turned inside out and read like a book. I denied it all, but he went real patient like he does and told me not to be a sap. Slick was beginning to suspect, and if he told Gordy to find out for sure, Gordy would have to tell him."

"Did Gordy talk to Mitchell?"

"No, not then he didn't. Only me. Gordy was nice about it, but he scared the hell out of me. He didn't threaten or anything like that, he just told the truth, very quietly. If I didn't cool things off with Mitch, I'd disappear. There was another guy there, Sanderson, and he did whatever Slick told him, even killing a woman if that's what Slick wanted."

"I remember him." It would probably be decades before the memory of how Sanderson died faded from my mind. Knowing that suddenly made carrying it a little easier.

"So Gordy broke me, not with threats, but with kindness. He said 'You're a good kid in a bad place, an' I don't wanna see you hurt.' He made me hungry for something I didn't have, and I thought maybe he wanted the same, that that's why he'd come, because he wanted me, too, but Gordy said no. I was cute, but it wouldn't work. Then I begged him to help me get out, and he said that wouldn't work, either. The only way I'd leave was when Slick got bored with me. It would take time, but would happen sooner or later. I'd have to accept that I was Slick Morelli's girl until he decided different."

I'd known some of the story. Didn't make it easier to take, though.

"So I got real busy with my work and rehearsals and couldn't sneak off with Mitch, and Gordy looked out for me and would come up with ways to keep him busy, sending him out of town to do stuff. That's how I finally figured out Mitch was only in it to have the boss's twist and a laugh on him. If he'd *really* loved me, he'd have found a way around all that and . . ." She drew and puffed out a deep breath. "And then . . . then one night *you* showed up."

"Well, we know what happened after that."

"Glory-hallelujah. When the dust settled and Gordy took over he sent Mitch to New York. He might have left anyway, but Gordy said Mitch had been bragging to the guys that with Morelli gone he'd be 'inheriting' me. That was the word he used."

"Nice guy."

"That's why I was thrown so hard when I saw him. The look on his face was so . . . so damned *smug*, and I *knew* what was going through his head. He thinks he can—"

"Not going to happen, lady. You tell me what you want, and it's there on a silver platter or heading east on the next train. Unless you want to tell him yourself." It was a genuine question, not a joke. Bobbi was sometimes touchy about her battles and tended to fight them herself.

She shook her head. "No! I don't want him anywhere *near* me. I wouldn't know what to say and he'd go all nasty and then I'd want to belt him and he'd hit back and . . ."

"Okay! It's solved. He's gone."

Bobbi gave me a look of pure and powerful love and launched up to hug me. It felt good. "Thank you. For this time, anyway. I've got to handle stuff like this better. Something else is bound to crop up—"

"No, it's not. Nothing's left in that barrel of woe. It's empty and dry, and we'll bust it up for kindling and roast hot dogs over the fire."

A strange light came to her face as she pulled back to look at me. "Oh, Jack, I do love you."

I almost froze up at that, but miracle of miracles, did not. No shakes, no chill, only warmth. From her and for her. The other night I'd been terrified about getting close. Tonight . . . not so much. I welcomed the familiar heat of her touch, and soon felt the pressure above my corner teeth that would cause them to descend . . .

And decisively extricated myself before anything bad happened. I didn't have the warning symptoms of an approaching seizure, but did recognize the roiling within that proceeded a bout of gluttony in the Stockyards. No matter how tender my feelings toward her, she was . . . was *food*.

God help me.

"Jack? What's wrong?"

"Nothing. There's stuff going on in the club because of that goon, and-and I gotta go . . . it's business."

I might as well have slapped her. She blinked, startled, then recovered, squared herself. "Okay," she whispered. I left before she started to cry again.

Faustine was still in the hall. "Vell?"

"She's better."

That got me a scowl. "Men!" She stalked toward the number three room, knocked, and went in. "Bob-bee, poor dar-link. Me you tell all about eet." The door shut with a muffled *whump*, the closest she could get to a slam.

Recognizing defeat, I fled to the end, where Roland now waited alone. "Where's Charles?"

"Something came up to call him away. How did it go?"

Shrugged. "Women."

"Ah. Yes. Wonderful, aren't they? Still, I wouldn't have them any other way or they'd be like us, and that wouldn't work at all. And we certainly can't be like them."

"Oh, yeah?"

"Absolutely, sport. We'd look ridiculous in their little jimjams, now wouldn't we? And I got the story of just *how* Faustine helped you with that crazed drunk with the gun. Now if I'd been there instead and done what she'd done, he'd have probably shot me on purpose. *That's* why we can't be like them."

Sounded right to me.

"I do need to talk with you about that . . ."

"I'm sorry, but I can't just now. Business." Like four groggy bouncers on the men's room floor.

He swallowed back whatever annoyance was brewing. "Later, then, sport," he promised.

There was no way of going invisible with him watching, so I had to use the door in the ordinary way and walk through the main room. Poor Teddy was still winging it, filling in for Bobbi's interrupted set. Jewel Caine should have been up there instead, reclaiming her career and going on to better things, sober and free of dragging anvils like her ex-husband. By God, if Hoyle was the one behind her death . . .

"Hey, Jack!"

Regulars hailed me from their tables. I dredged up a smile, waved, and kept going. No one remarked about my miraculous appearance on the dance floor, but I got stares. That's when I realized I was less than perfectly turned out. My clothes were messed around, suit scuffed and dirty from rolling on the floor, shirttails hanging, a bloody streak where I'd been grazed (now healed), tie crooked, buttons torn off. I continued on like the display was in their imagination.

The bouncers were gathered around the lobby bar, pale and holding ice-filled towels against their heads. Three had drinks, the fourth a Bromo-Seltzer, Wilton's brand of Red Cross aid. Escott was also looking after them, and had a special glare ready for me as I came in. Like any of this was my fault.

"They insist they will be all right," he said.

"But we're gonna kill Ruzzo," said Bromo-Seltzer. The others growled collective agreement.

"After you've seen a doctor," Escott added.

Less growling, more grumbling.

I got the story, and it was pretty much as I'd guessed. Ruzzo, both of them, had invaded, getting the drop on them all. Two men guarding the outside were marched in at gunpoint to join their pals, then the party was quietly moved to the men's room, where they were bashed from behind. It had been accomplished very slick and quiet since neither Wilton or the check girl had noticed anything. Hell, not even Myrna had flickered so much as a single bulb. Was everyone on sleeping pills?

"I'm not sure just when Mitchell made his entry," Escott concluded.

"And I donno if he's working with Hoyle and Ruzzo," I said. "It sure looked like it." I gave him details about the fight and the outcome, but nothing on the reason behind it.

"We'll keep in mind that an alliance has perhaps taken place between them, though God knows why or how, but it might well have been chance. Now I'm going to take these fine fellows off to make sure their brains are still in place. There's a doctor they know who—"

"Yeah, I think I know the one. Thanks."

"And about Bobbi . . ." He took me to one side, voice lowering.

"She's better," I said. "She tell you about Mitchell?"

"Not much. Too upset. I was the shoulder to cry on until you were free to take over. But I got that Mitchell was an extraordinarily bad memory from her past, and it was a terrible shock to see him again. Also, she was afraid it would in some way destroy your relationship."

"No! No, nothing like that. We're fine. I listened, she talked, it's fine, all fine now."

He seemed about to say something to the contrary.

"Faustine's with her, she'll be all right," I insisted.

"She can't be candid about everything. It's good she has another woman to confide to about you, but your condition is a significant influence on matters. Keeping *that* a secret rather precludes a full lifting of the burden."

"Oh." Not good. The way she looked when I walked out . . .

"But—" he continued. "You should know that she seems to think you're worth all the trouble and bother. There's no accounting for women and their taste in men."

Yeah, maybe. But Bobbi was miserable, and it really was all my fault.

ESCOTT took the four guys away in his Nash, and a few law-abiding citizens of Chicago still ignorant of Lady Crymsyn's unplanned renovation into a shooting gallery came in to enjoy themselves. By then I'd tucked my clothes more or less back into order, hiding rips and bloodstains by buttoning the coat. I glad-handed a few people, told them they'd have a great time—leaving out the whammy—and was about to go back to see Bobbi when another guest walked in.

Whitey Kroun took one gander at me and frowned. I returned the favor.

"What the hell happened to you?" he demanded. Nothing like an experienced eye to recognize the aftereffects of mayhem.

"That idiot lieutenant of yours," I snapped.

"Oh, yeah? Explain."

I threw a look past him to make sure Mitchell wasn't in his wake along with Hoyle and Ruzzo. No one like that, just a lot of women (and men) picking up on Kroun's magnetism and like the check girl perhaps mistaking him for a movie star. "My office. This way."

We climbed the stairs, I ushered him in. The radio was on, but low. By now I couldn't remember if I'd left it that way or not. Kroun took his hat off, brushing his hand over the streak in his hair, and sat on the couch. He pitched the hat by its brim toward the desk, and it landed square on top of the papers. "So what gives with Mitchell?"

"He came by tonight and bothered my girlfriend."

Kroun waited for more. "That's it?" he finally asked.

"It was enough. He pulled his little reunion stunt smack in the middle of a show, threw her into hysterics . . . I had to drag him backstage." I told the rest, sparing no punches, ending it by putting Mitchell's gun on the desk next to the hat. "If he comes back for this, I'll ram it down his throat."

"You think he's working with Hoyle?"

"I donno, but it was pretty damned coincidental of them showing up at the same time. Hoyle tried to kill me—with Mitchell urging him on— got within a breath of shooting an innocent lady, and his pals Ruzzo lambasted four of Gordy's best. If they are working together, then you should tell me why."

"You think I'd know that?"

"He's your boy. Where's he been all day?"

"Out." Kroun's eyes were hotting up.

"This isn't just me with a gripe. It's about Gordy, too, because of his men being here. If you know what Mitchell might be up to—"

"I don't know a damned thing!"

"Then you should find out. If he was doing a job for you or someone else or for himself, he's been made."

"What kind of job? Killing you? Hoyle tried to do that the other night all on his own, he doesn't need Mitchell."

"Then take me out of the picture. What else would he need Mitchell for? What else would Mitchell need Hoyle and Ruzzo for? The four of them wouldn't be hopping into the same bed just to knock *me* off. Something's brewing."

"Until tonight Mitchell had no reason to kill you. Now he might go with Hoyle just to help out."

"Not going to happen. They've crawled out of whatever hole they've been hiding in, and someone's gonna spot 'em and pass the word to me. You better hope Mitchell isn't there when I go in."

Kroun leaned forward. "You listen to me, kid, you don't take any action about Mitchell. He's my department. You got away with bumping Bristow because of special circumstances, but do anything to Mitchell, and nothing will save you. You will disappear the same as Bristow: dismembered and in the lake."

Well, that would do the trick of killing me for good. Death, the ultimate solver for all my problems. "Okay, I got that. But you get this—your boy was warned off from seeing my girl and came in regardless. He got his ass kicked because he deserved it. So long as he stays away from her I won't have to repeat the performance. That's all I'm concerned with. If Hoyle's a separate thing, then I'll take care of it separately. But if Mitchell's cooking up something *with* him—"

"You bring him to me, and *I* will deal with it."

The silence stretched. For a long moment I was tempted again to influence Kroun over to my side, find out for sure if he was truly ignorant about Mitchell's actions. Again, just thinking about it made me ache. I knew I didn't want to risk that stab-in-the-eye agony; I might not be able to vanish fast enough.

"Well?" he asked.

"No problem. In the meantime you might want to locate your boy and find out where he's been keeping himself."

Another silence. Kroun almost seemed to be waiting for something. Finally, he nodded. "Fair enough. You just remember we each have our own corners."

"I'll remember. How long's Mitchell been with you?"

"Couple years."

"You friends?"

"What's it to you?"

"I have friends. I look out for them."

"Like Gordy."

"Yeah."

Kroun grunted. "I need to talk with him. Face-to-face. Derner doesn't know where he is, hasn't got a number. Said you'd know."

"He's safe. Resting." And healing, I hoped.

"Take me to see him, then."

I was tired of getting the kid-brother treatment. "What's with Gordy that you can't settle it with me?"

"It's about you. You want more, you put me and Gordy in the same room."

That set up a whole new batch of speculations, most of which I was sure I wouldn't care to know anything about. I could guess it had to do with me taking over for Gordy permanently. Or not. "Not" was fine with me, so long as Gordy was the one back in charge.

I reached for the phone and dialed Coldfield's club office. It rang a lot, then someone picked up the receiver. "The boss there? It's Fleming."

COLDFIELD agreed to allow Kroun a visit, but not until tomorrow. Apparently Dr. Clarson put his foot down after seeing the condition of his overtired patient. He'd barred all visitors, and the phone was off the hook. I asked if Gordy was better, but Coldfield had no information, only that the patient was safe and quiet. I passed the meager news to Kroun. He nodded, but wasn't pleased by the delay.

"I'll be by tomorrow, then," he said.

"Come just after opening, and I'll get you there."

"Why not earlier?"

"Because it's what the doctor ordered." That lie came easy.

Kroun picked his hat up along with Mitchell's gun and walked out. It was only after he'd gone that I realized he'd made no comment at all about the Caine murders, and the papers were still on the desk, big as life with headlines and pictures. I thought Kroun had come over in the first place to talk about them. Mitchell's behavior could have knocked that out of his head, seeing's how it was closer to home. But Kroun might have turned up to see my reaction to Mitchell's threat and Hoyle's shooting.

Damn it all, I should have tried hypnosis no matter what it did to me. Too late now.

LADY Crymsyn's second show was nearly over by the time I worked up enough spirit to leave the office. I was drawn out by the sound of Bobbi's glad voice. She was back onstage, confidence firmly restored along with her smile as she belted her closing song. She was amazing. Not one sign of what she'd gone through showed. It was as though it had never happened, and that was unsettling.

I watched from the entry, just out of sight from the patrons in the main room, not wanting to distract her. The damage was covered up, I thought, and covered very well, but still there under the surface. Escott would say to be patient and let time do the healing, but I'd hurt her and would continue to hurt her. No way out of that.

Some small commotion in the lobby got my attention for a moment. By now the front entry was closed to new customers, but someone wanted in, banging on the door. I heard Escott's muffled voice and the doorman's response. I went back down the passage in time to see Escott hurry across the lobby toward the stairs, his arm around a huddled-over female in a too-large coat.

The female was Evie Montana.

12

EVEN after all this time, when I should have been used to it, Escott still had the ability to make my jaw drop. How he could have left with four of Gordy's goons and returned with Betty Boop I could not imagine.

He glanced over his shoulder as I dogged him to the office. "Oh, good," was all he said, and continued on. Evie wore her dancing shoes and spangled stockings from last night's show. Her long overcoat seemed several sizes too big until I realized it was a man's coat. Not only that, it was a tan-colored vicuna, and had belonged to Alan Caine.

Jeez, what now?

Escott guided her to the couch, made her sit, then went to the liquor cabinet, poured her something, and made her drink. I kicked the office door shut and stood in front of it.

"What gives?" I asked.

"She said she saw the murder."

"I didn't see! I *heard* it!" she choked out, then fell into tears.

I'd had enough of those for one night and left Escott to deal with the deluge. My only help was to go to the washroom across the hall and bring back a roll of toilet paper. She traded her drink for the roll and began pulling off yards at a time, blowing her nose between bouts of howling.

It took a while before she settled down enough to answer questions. Escott filled in things up to a point. Evie left the Nightcrawler Club in a hurry, rented a flop someplace, and hid there, trying to think what to do. Eventually she remembered Escott had been a nice man. She'd been hanging around outside Lady Crymsyn for hours hoping to spot him. When he'd returned from driving the muscle to the doctor's, she made her move.

"Poor child's half-frozen," he added. "I doubt she's had anything to eat, either."

"We'll get her an eight-course dinner with music if she'll just tell what happened."

Evie did more carrying on, but I figured out she was enjoying the attention and barked her name, loudly. That hauled her up short.

"What?" she asked, sounding hurt.

"You tell us. What did you see?"

"I didn't *see*. I *heard*."

"Okay, what did you hear?"

It came tumbling out almost too fast to follow. She'd gone with Alan Caine to his dressing room as she usually did between shows. They liked to spend time together . . . talking. They were shy about people knowing anything, though, so when someone knocked at the door, Caine bundled Evie into the closet. That always made her giggle, but she was real quiet when he called his visitor in. Caine pretended to be alone; it was their secret.

Caine said, "Hello, you. Come back for more? I think I can—"

Then he stopped talking and made a funny sound. Then there were some vague, thrashing noises. None went on for long, but they were odd. Evie couldn't see any of it since the closet was fast shut, and she knew how mad Caine would be if she left before he said so.

The dressing-room door opened and closed, so it was plain that the visitor was gone. Caine didn't call to her, though. Finally, after a long, long time, maybe a couple minutes, she ventured to peek out.

She didn't like what she saw. Nearly fainted from it. Survival instinct overcame her fond feelings for Caine, and she knew she'd have to leave and quick. Not knowing who had done the deed, she could trust no one. She didn't dare go back for her own coat, and lit out wearing Caine's instead, using the stage door and running as fast as she could in her dancing heels.

"Did you see anything in the alley?" I asked. "Anyone?"

"No."

"What about Jewel Caine?"

Evie seized on the name. "That *witch!* She did it. I know she did!"

"She didn't," I said.

"You don't *know* her! She *hates* him."

"She didn't do it."

"She *did!* I'll make her tell!"

"Fine, we'll go talk to her. Where does she live?"

"I don't know. You go do that, call the cops, I don't care, I just wanna get out of town and go home!"

Unless Evie was a remarkable natural actress, she truly was ignorant about Jewel. Escott signed to me to step into the hall for a conference.

"There's only one way to remove all doubt here," he said. "Will the drink she had unduly interfere with your work? I wasn't thinking when I gave that to her."

I quelled a sudden flare of nausea. "I . . . uh . . . I can't."

"What?"

"You heard. No hypnosis." Damnation. I'd hoped to somehow avoid having to say anything about this to him.

"Why ever not?"

I worked very hard not to yell. "Because I just can't. It hurts."

He paused, at a loss. "But . . . it's always hurt you to a greater or lesser degree."

"Not like this. Something's changed, gone wrong. I think if I tried again . . . it could kill me. The last time I tried, I thought my head would explode."

"You're serious." He seemed flabbergasted.

"Yeah, and it keeps getting *worse.* Maybe building up to—I don't know. But I don't dare try. It might even damage Evie." I was more worried about damaging myself, though. "I'm deadly serious, Charles. I can't help you."

"Well," he finally said. "That is a bundle of news. I'm sorry."

"Yeah, me, too." It got quiet, and I thought he might ask more questions than I wanted to hear, but he held off. I motioned toward the office. "What d'ya want to do with her?"

"Keep her out of sight, for one thing. Here should be safe enough until I can arrange for other digs. We can get her out before dawn."

"Why hide her if the killer doesn't know she was in the room?"

"Because you have half the city looking for whoever took that vicuna coat. The killer knows Evie's the only other person besides himself who had any close dealings with Caine. Even Ruzzo might work it out. She could be murdered for no more reason than that."

"Okay. But we get her safe, then what? I may personally think it was Hoyle, but there's no guarantee he's going to be found. And if I turn out to be wrong, then who knows if we'll ever find out who did it?"

"According to you all we need do is check the hands of anyone involved and look for scratches. Admittedly it's not too practical, and time will certainly heal the damage, but if—"

"I know. I've got Strome and Derner checking that angle. Everyone who went out the Nightcrawler's doors last night had to show their hands. They didn't know why, but it cleared them. I managed to keep from tipping Kroun off about that detail just in case his boy Mitchell was the one. He's missing, but he can be more missing if Kroun arranges it."

"Did he ever come in tonight?"

"Oh, yeah." I told about the deal I had with Kroun. "Damn, if I hadn't been wound so tight about what he did to Bobbi I could have had a look at Mitchell's hands then. Might have avoided some friction. Kroun's real touchy about his territory. If Mitchell pulled that hit on his own, I think Kroun might send him over, but I can't be sure. He could just as well send him back to New York."

"It would be a mistake on Kroun's part to keep a viper so close."

"People get stupid."

"Unfortunately, yes."

"I'm hungry!" Evie wailed.

"Oh, my God." He didn't quite roll his eyes. "There are few things more inconvenient than a witness who's not seen anything."

Actually I could think of worse stuff, but volunteered to remedy the food situation if he'd babysit.

"Only if I may avail myself of your alcoholic stores."

"Avail away."

DOWNSTAIRS I gave the doorman five bucks and asked him to run over to an all-night diner that everyone usually went to after work. I told him to bring back a half dozen sandwiches, a dozen donuts, some milk, and he could keep the change. His eyes popped at the windfall, and he hurried off.

Not inclined to hear more of Evie's tiny little voice, I filled in for him as customers finished their last drinks and sauntered out.

In the main room the band began "Goodnight, Sweetheart," and the trickle became an exodus. Too many of the regulars wanted to stop and chat with the friendly owner, and there wasn't anything to do but get through it until they said their piece and left. I used to enjoy that kind of stuff.

Going to the lighting panel, I switched off the outside sign and the canopy light. Lady Crymsyn was officially closed.

The main room was empty of customers, the band breaking up and packing away their instruments. The waiters were yanking tablecloths and flipping chairs onto the tables, in a hurry to leave. Stale cigarette smoke hung thick in the air along with the pungent cleaner stink. The bartender had already divided up the tips for them and handed me the till and clipboard. The liquor was locked away and the last glass wiped clean and stored. I wished a general good night to all.

Wilton was closed out; I collected his till and clipboard and carried them upstairs, putting them on the desk over the papers. Escott sat on the couch next to Evie, patting her hand in what I hoped was a big-brotherly way.

"I sent out for food. Should be here soon," I said.

"Excellent. Evie's remembered something more."

I waited. So did he. She looked bewildered.

"The smell?" he prompted.

"Oh!" She seemed surprised. "Cigarettes. He smoked. Alan doesn't smoke, says it's bad for his voice. Whoever was there, it was all over his clothes."

"It was a man? I thought you were after Jewel for this. She smokes."

"She coulda *made* a man do it for her. It was a man. There was sweat, too."

"Sweat?"

"I smelled sweat, and it was a man's sweat."

"Don't women sweat?"

"Not the same. The smell's different."

"Uh-huh."

Escott patted her hand again. "He's just getting used to the idea. Jack, I'm inclined to trust her senses on this one."

I read between the lines. Evie wasn't an intellectual giant, but knew how to survive and get on in the world. Her edge was more to do with intuition than anything else. Some part of that would be geared to knowing the difference between male and female sweat. "Okay."

"Am I gonna stay here?" she asked.

"For a few hours," Escott said. "You may nap right here on this nice comfy couch if you like. We'll watch over you." He sounded like he was addressing a ten-year-old, and Evie didn't seem to mind.

I was glad he limited it to a few hours. When it got past dawn, I would be hard to explain. Sure I had a bolt-hole under the tiers of seating, lockable and light-proofed, but I liked the couch for myself, dammit.

The doorman brought his delivery upstairs. I had the till money counted, ledgers updated, and everything sealed in the safe, so the desk was cleared for a feast.

"I can't eat all that!" Evie declared, eyes big.

No, but she'd likely pack away at least half of it. I knew dancers. "Charles will help you, won't you, Charles?" It was a long-running battle for me to make sure he ate if not well, then at least at regular intervals. He said he would be delighted to join her for dinner. I told him I needed to take Bobbi home and could I borrow his car?

"Of course," he said, handing over the keys to his Nash.

"What about a hiding place for Evie?"

"You've a phone and a phone book. I'll get on very well indeed finding something."

She cocked her head. "You're English, aren't you, just like in England?"

I had a moment of déjà vu. She'd said exactly the same thing in the same way the other night. Escott obviously recalled it, too, and shot me a thin smile. It was going to be a long night for him.

Wilton and the hatcheck girl left together. Usually he or the doorman would walk her to the El. Coat and hat on, I made a sweep through the main room. All was quiet, the bartender and waiters having departed by the backstage exit. I yelled down into the basement, rousting out a lagging horn player before dousing the light and locking that door.

All the dressing rooms but number three were closed and dark. I hesitated before knocking, unsure of my reception. Until that night Bobbi and I had never had any real fight. Not that that'd been a fight. It was more that I'd let her down in a big way and couldn't make it up to her.

But I still had to take her home. I tapped softly.

Bobbi welcomed me in, nearly finished with her change to ordinary clothes. She greeted me a little too brightly, acting as if all was well again between us. It was, so far as the business with Mitchell was concerned, but not the business with me.

"Are my seams straight?" she asked. She twisted around, trying to check them in a long mirror, the skirt of her dress raised high.

"Uhh—they look Jim Dandy to me."

"Yes, but are they straight?"

"I could get a ruler to make sure."

"You men . . ."

"Oh? You ask other guys for help with your stockings?"

"All the time."

The banter was there, but with an artificial note to it. I thought I should talk to her about things, but this just wasn't the time. "We're closed up, but Charles is staying on for a while. We've got a case going. I'll take you home, then have to come back here."

"What case?"

"It's to do with the Caine murders."

"I saw the papers. Poor Jewel. Are the stories true?"

"They're totally wrong in a big way. It's murder-murder, not murder-suicide."

"Does it have to do with Gordy?"

"I don't think so, but with Alan Caine having been employed at the Nightcrawler, I have to be around to keep the boat from rocking. That's why I had to leave earlier and . . . and I'm sorry about that."

"Okay." She looked like she might have more to say, but turned to straighten stuff on her dressing table. There seemed to be a lot of unsaids growing between us.

WHEN we reached her hotel, Bobbi leaned across the seat and kissed me good night. It was a nice, safe kiss, very sisterly.

"You wondering why not more?" she asked. She could always read me.

I didn't know how to answer that.

"There will be when it's the right time. You'll know when."

After she left the big car and was in the lobby waiting for the elevator to take her up I gave in to a long shudder. No doubling over, no groans about remembered pain, no needing to vanish to head off the screaming.

You could call it progress. But I hung on to the Nash's steering wheel so hard that it bent in my hands.

The fit gradually passed. I didn't hurt all over, just felt like I should.

Then I drove off quick. Headed for the Stockyards.

No hunger, yet I needed blood. Craved it. Had to have . . .

I'd stopped thinking and turned into an automaton.

When I came back to myself I was slumped against one of the high fences of a cattle pen, my arms looped over it, holding me up. Every part of my body was stretched and bloated. Even my eyelids felt swollen. It was hard work to blink.

I glanced at the pen's occupants, half-expecting to see a dead cow lying in the muck, but they were still on their feet.

Had I been careless coming in? This seemed to be the same spot from the night before. To cut down the odds of being seen I always went to different locations. This craziness was out of hand.

Despite the excess of blood—my face was smeared with it—I began shivering from cold.

It's fear, you idiot. This is fear. Get that through your thick skull.

"Okay, I get it," I said aloud to the head-demons. "Now lay off me."

The glut made it easy to vanish and soar above the crossword-puzzle pattern of fencing. I had to go high, partially materialize, and look around since I couldn't remember where I'd left the car.

Dimly I recalled trying to pull myself away from gorging, but at the time there didn't seem much point. I was well and truly started, why not keep going so long as I was there?

Winced at the memory.

God, yes, when I lost control like that I had every right to be scared. I had to keep myself away from Bobbi.

The Nash was parked close by under a streetlamp, something I'd never normally do. The keys were in the ignition. It was just my good luck no one else had been by to find such a choice offering. I got in and checked the wheel. The damage wasn't too bad, more of a bend like a warped phonograph record than anything else. It would need to be replaced, but was otherwise fine for driving.

Where to drive to . . . ?

Escott's office, to clean up. I'd not been careful during my binge.

It was only a few minutes away. This time I took the keys when I got out.

On the other side of his office door the place was much too quiet and dark. Though there was plenty of light filtering through the closed blinds—pitch-dark to anyone else—I wanted more and flipped switches on my way to the back.

Eerie feeling in the washroom as I bent over the sink and scrubbed my face with cold water. I'd come here after staggering away from the gory wreckage of Bristow's party. He'd been drunk, and his blood had turned me drunk and brainlessly foolish. That was the why behind my insanity then; what the hell was I doing to myself? That horror was *over*. If I kept up with this inner sickness, I'd only be finishing the job he'd started.

Sickness. I made myself use that word. It was the right one.

There wasn't a lot of difference between me and Alan Caine. For him it had been gambling. For me it was blood. And before that booze. Roland Lambert was the same. He'd traded his drinking for womanizing, which had hurt the one women he loved. If he went back to the bottle . . . a different kind of self-destruction.

But you could live without drinking, and if you absolutely had to, without women. There was no way I could live without blood.

Perhaps I could limit things and prevent myself from overdoing. I had lately begun siphoning it into bottles, keeping them in the icebox for emergencies. One a night was plenty. More than enough. I'd been able to dole things out like that before my change. A beer a day, then cut loose with a good rip on Saturday night, only I'd just not have any Saturday nights. I could do that.

Which still left the problem of Bobbi not being safe with me. In the throes of passion I could kill her.

And then Escott would have to kill me.

I'd make him promise to do it.

If not him, then Gordy. What are best friends for if not to trust them with the hardest favors for you?

Shaking cold water from my face, I dried off and told myself to shut the hell up before the dark possibilities chorusing through my head turned themselves into a grand opera.

I went back to the car, started it, and let it idle, not sure where to go. Escott liked driving his Nash around at night. For relaxation. Used to, anyway. His insomnia was pretty much gone now.

There were still some long, lonesome hours ahead, though. Before things had gone so far off course I'd either spend them with Bobbi or put in extra work at Crymsyn or pound on my typewriter or just read. Life had been so much simpler a week back. I'd had my share of horrors and grief, but could live with them. The good old days. Not nearly enough of those.

Kroun's advice to find a place in the middle of nowhere and do nothing but fish was very appealing. The wild temptation to take off this very moment was almost overwhelming. What tore it away were my countless obligations to everyone I knew. Between them and the drive to have my own business I'd cemented myself into the pavement in front of Lady Crymsyn and couldn't leave. It was better than swinging from a meat hook, but I was still stuck just as firmly in place.

I pulled into the alley behind the club rather than my special parking spot. If Escott wanted to get Evie away later without being seen, that was the place to do it. Ghosting out, I passed through the locked door and walked through the dark and silent club.

Very dark and silent. Myrna wasn't playing with the lights at all.

"Myrna? You there, baby?"

She must have tired herself out last night making that rose scent for me. It really had helped. For a time. I wanted to thank her, but how do you thank a ghost?

At least the lobby light was still on. She was very dependable about that one. Before going up to the office I got into the phone booth, dropped in a nickel, and dialed the Nightcrawler. Derner didn't answer, but someone got him for me.

"Yeah, Boss?"

"Have you heard about the trouble here tonight?"

"Yeah, the guys told me. They're mad as hell at Ruzzo—"

"That's great, but this snipe hunt for Ruzzo and Hoyle's been going on too damned long. Is *anyone* actually *looking*?"

He avoided sounding defensive. "They're doing what they can do. The boys are covering all the hotels, from flops to the fancy places, boardinghouses, bordellos, and rooms to let. There ain't a bed in this town they ain't looked into or under. If Ruzzo's in Chicago, we'll find 'em sooner or later. But if they've blown town or run off to the sticks . . . maybe not."

"I want them even if they are in the sticks. Where does Hoyle hang around?"

"Here, usually."

"Where else?"

"We looked in those places. He's letting himself be missing."

I gave out a disgusted sigh.

"We got the word out you only want to talk with him, but since he's trying to shoot you, I guess he misunderstood."

In some mobs "talk" meant beat a guy up, just not to the point of crippling him permanently. "Keep at it. Get me a location. We are not dealing with the Harvard debate team here."

"Who?"

"Never mind."

"Boss? That special guest we got was back here, looking hot under the collar. Anything I should know?" Derner was yet on guard against listening wires. Good man.

"He's lost his traveling friend."

"That's what he said in so many words. He's plenty bothered about something."

"Let him work it out. Help him however he wants, and tell me if anything screwy happens. I'll be at my club until morning."

"Got it. Any word on the other boss?" That would be Gordy.

"He's resting is all I know. They're taking care of him. Soft berth."

"Should I pass that on?"

"Yeah." It would be reassuring to a few that Gordy was still around. Certainly reassured me.

I rang off and was about to trudge up to the office when someone banged loud on Crymsyn's front door. What and who the hell now? Hoyle? But if it was a determined bad guy, he'd have shot the lock off, not knocked and given warning.

Standing to the side just in case, I yelled through the door, "We're closed!"

"Jack, it's me!"

Roland Lambert. He said he'd wanted to talk to me. Must be pretty damned important to get him back here at this hour in the cold. I unlocked and went outside rather than inviting him in. He didn't need to know Escott and I had company, and if we were both out in the wind, the business wouldn't take as long.

"What's the matter?" I asked. His green Hudson was parked right in front of the canopy. No passengers. "Is Faustine all right?"

"She's fine, probably asleep by now. I told her I'd forgotten something and had to come back. You often stay until very late, don't you?"

"Uhm . . ."

"Faustine's why I'm here, sport. It's about the shooting tonight."

"Roland, I'm sorry. That's never going to happen again, I promise. I'm getting special locks for the doors, and people are looking for that bum. He's not coming back."

"I'm delighted to hear it. Don't think I'm ungrateful the way you tackled him. It turned out well, and Faustine had a great time, but it was also terribly, terribly dangerous. She thinks it was a lark, something out of the movies."

"I got that from her."

"And we know better. Look, I've played my share of derring-do roles in films, and it is fun, but in real life, it's just *not* the done thing."

"You going to leave?" I didn't see how they could afford it. Faustine was not cheap to keep, and they were making steady money working for me.

"I'd really rather not. You're a grand fellow to work for, one of the best. It's just this is extremely disturbing to me."

"I don't blame you. If anything happened to Bobbi . . ." I didn't want to finish that thought.

"Then we understand one another."

"What do you want me to do?"

"Well, there's not much you *can* do beyond what you've already said. But—"

They were getting smarter, more crafty at it. Instead of a car roaring up the street to give warning to anyone paying attention, they'd all but coasted in.

Hoyle hung halfway out an open window; one Ruzzo drove, the other was busy keeping Hoyle from falling out. They drove up, sedate as any honest citizen, but when they crested the front of the club Hoyle cut loose with his semiauto.

I pushed Roland aside, but not quite in time. Bullets bit and banged around us. Roland caught one, yelped, and dropped like a stone.

13

A few seconds of mind-numbing panic, the taste of metal on my tongue, then I shoved the fear as far away as I could. As Ruzzo hit the gas to take them away I kicked open Crymsyn's door, grabbed Roland, and hauled him inside. His legs weren't working, and once on the black-and-white marble tiles he gasped out a sudden halt. Blood seemed to pour from him, the scent sharp and arresting.

Before I lost all sense I bellowed for Escott to get the hell down there and rushed to the bar for towels. I was in cold syrup; nothing I did seemed fast enough or smart enough or good enough. Escott was halfway down the stairs and stopped to gape for all of a second, then also rushed forward.

The lobby lights blazed on. I whirled; this was the perfect time for an ambush, but no one was there. Myrna, then. The lights went out, then on again. She'd done it for me once. Trying to help.

"Leave 'em on, goddammit!"

They stayed on.

"My God, how—?" Escott began.

"Hoyle. Trying for me again."

"Bloody bastard." He got Roland to lie flat while I ripped the man's trouser leg open to the knee and pressed a towel to the wound. The white cloth soon loaded up with blood despite the pressure I put on. God, if that was an artery . . .

"Hospital," I said. "Now."

"Is it safe outside?"

"Probably not." I turned pressure duty over to him and shot through the passage, the main room, the backstage, moving silent and fast. I'd traded solidity for speed and regained it in the alley after bulling right through the club's walls. The Nash was still warmed up and easily roared to life. I hurtled it around two corners and braked just short of ramming the parked Hudson. I'd have used Roland's car, but the Nash was bullet-proofed.

The street was empty of Hoyle and his crew, and just as well for Roland, or I might have gone after them. I bailed out, leaving the motor running.

Evie was in the lobby by then, visibly upset, asking questions in her little voice and not being too damned helpful. She was still in the vicuna coat. I told her to go out and open the back door of the brown car outside. If I'd said Nash, she might not have been able to pick it out.

"The brown car?"

"*Go!*"

She made a single yipping noise like a small pooch and fled outside.

"Roland?"

"Right here, sport. Remember my talk about doing this in films? Well, a make-believe bullet is much better." He forced out a ghastly grin.

Escott had cut Roland's suspenders off with a folding knife and improvised a tourniquet, which seemed to help, but the stack of blood-soaked towels had grown. "Come on, let's get him to the car."

"Yes, please hurry. This hurts like a bad review!"

I hoped joking meant he was going to be all right. When I'd been in the War—and this suddenly and unpleasantly reminded me of it—I'd seen guys cracking wise to the very end.

Opening a door on a brown car was evidently not one of Evie's talents. She'd overdone it and opened them all. What the hell, we could manage. I had Roland's shoulders, Escott his feet, and we somehow got him into the back. Escott slammed the door on his side, urged Evie into the passenger's, and came around to close mine on his way to the wheel.

"What the devil . . . ?" He stared at the warpage.

"Later," I said. "Get this bucket moving."

He got us moving.

Roland held on through the drive to the hospital, which was hair-raising enough to distract me from the fresh bloodsmell. I didn't think Escott planned it that way, he was just in an unholy hurry. He skidded to a halt, missed rear-ending an ambulance, and bolted inside the hospital. As a kid he'd worked at one or for a doctor, I couldn't recall which, and would be better at raising the troops. I told Evie twice to get out and open the door. She kept blinking and saying, "I don't like this, I don't *like* this."

Perhaps playing to the hilt the devil-may-care suave, Roland grinned,

"That's all right, my dear, you're in the *best* of company on that opinion."

"Huh?" She saw his smile and responded with a little laugh, the kind people with no sense of humor give when they know you've made a joke, but they don't get it, they're just being polite.

"Open the damn door!" I snapped at Evie, in no mood to be a gentleman. A couple of orderlies with a stretcher were on their way over, double-quick. She barely made it in time. Thankfully, Escott took her arm and kept her clear while I helped ease Roland out. The men took over, loaded up, and swept him toward the hospital's receiving area.

"I don't *like* this!" she cried.

THIS was the time for the deep-night predators to venture forth, but they would be elsewhere in the city, creeping through the cheap, run-down jungles where the desperation was greater, the victims more plentiful. I was where the victims ended up if they were lucky enough to survive. The waiting room was crowded.

I'd phoned Derner first and told him what happened and to send someone to Bobbi's hotel, then I phoned Bobbi to tell her what had happened. She was stunned for only a few moments, though.

"You need me to help with Faustine?" she asked.

"I was hoping."

"Of course I will. I'll be dressed again when you get here."

"I've already sent a car to pick you up. The driver will take you anyplace you want."

"One of Gordy's?" She sounded weary.

"'Fraid so. I have to be here. With a gunshot wound they bring the cops and . . . uhhh . . . I'm thinking you know all that."

"A lot too well. I'll get Faustine and be there as soon as we can."

"I'll see you then."

"Be safe, sweetheart."

None safer. From bullets. Insanity and rage and fear were other matters entirely.

About ten minutes later several large guys with big coats and mashed noses walked in and not for emergency treatment. They spotted me and came over. "Derner sent us," one of them told me.

"Thoughtful of him," murmured Escott. He sat with an arm around the supremely unhappy, but heavy-eyed Evie. She was tucked up on her chair, the tan coat covering her like a blanket with just part of her face showing. None of the mugs seemed to recognize her.

"Fine," I said. "Spread out, on your toes, and if you see Hoyle try to make it look like self-defense, there's cops here."

The man smiled. "Cops." Apparently he was unimpressed. Where had Derner found this bunch? They were tougher-looking than the bouncers had been, and came across as made men. No matter, so long as they were on my side.

"No shooting civilians," I added.

He grunted. Disappointed, maybe. He jerked his head at the other guys, and they trundled away. Everyone got out of their path except the nurses.

And a cop.

My favorite cop was Lieutenant Blair, but he must have had the night off. This new guy was Sergeant Something who flashed his badge too fast. Escott patted Evie's shoulder and spoke low to her. She didn't move. Asleep, I hoped.

The sergeant got a statement from me about the shooting. I used to be a lousy liar but had since improved my skills. I can lie to strangers better than to friends, and this guy heard one of my best efforts. He got the facts as I knew them, but I pretended ignorance of the identity of the shooters.

"You're pretty calm about it, Mr. Fleming," he noted.

"It's late, I'm tired, and I'm worried about my friend. Call it shell shock."

"Don't you want to get the guys that shot him? They could come after you next."

"I think they were after me in the first place, and Roland just happened to be in the way." There, an absolutely true statement.

"Why would anyone want to shoot you?"

"You know how this town is. I opened a great club, there's other guys jealous, they want to take me down a notch, even scare me out of business."

"Has it worked?"

"Hell, yes. I'm closing until further notice. Nobody else is gonna get hurt."

This last was caught by a guy whose job I recognized as easily as the mugs who'd walked in. I used to dress just like him. He scribbled in a notebook and threw a question at me, but the cop shooed him off like an out-of-season horsefly. I knew what that was like. No nostalgia stirred in me to go back to the simple life of being a reporter. You ask so many questions and then one day you get more answers than you really want.

The cop finished with me and skipped talking with Escott, who hadn't exactly put himself forward. I'd said Escott hadn't seen anything and had only helped with the wounded.

When the cop cleared off the reporter moved in.

"It's just a shooting," I said to him. "What's the big beef about it?"

"A shooting at Lady Crymsyn." He grinned. "You are headline material for me. After that 'Jane Poe' case—"

"That's yesterday's fish wrapper. This is nothing. I donno who did it. I just want my friend to be okay."

"Your friend being the famous Roland Lambert, star of stage and screen. Why's he tripping the floor in your place if he's such a big star?"

"He's just doing a favor for a pal. Thought it'd be a lark. He and his wife are cut-ups like that, always having fun." It was a better story than the truth about trying to make ends meet. I shoveled a lot of bull at the Fifth Estate and made Roland an altruistic hero who'd saved my life at the risk of his own. The reporter, apparently not good enough yet to have thought up the angle himself, went away happy. If he could write it fast enough, he might make the afternoon edition.

Bobbi and Faustine turned up next with their driver, who turned out to be Strome. He hung off to one side and smoked a cigar to fill the time while I did my best to calm Faustine down and give her the same story I'd passed to the cop.

I also advised her not to mention the shooting incident she'd been involved in earlier.

"Vhy ever nodt?" She was startled enough to stop demanding to see Roland.

"I'm shutting the club down for now, but if they catch wind of any more fishiness, they could keep it that way."

"Budt de show musst go on!"

"So we all keep quiet about it."

"About vhat, doll-ink? Poof! I forgedt whole tink. Now vhere iss my poor Roland? I musst see heem. I musst see dok-tor."

EVENTUALLY we all saw Roland, from a distance. His leg was bandaged and elevated in some kind of pulley contraption, and he was too groggy to say anything. Only Faustine was allowed in with him.

The doctor was optimistic. There was a lot of damage, and the bullet cracked, but hadn't broken, one of the leg bones, but if there was no infection, he would get well soon enough. I saw to it at least one of the mashed-nosed guys was to be within call at all times. Bobbi explained to Faustine that they were there to look after them and left it at that.

We were all told to go home, but Faustine refused to leave, and Bobbi said she'd stay to keep her company. I knew better than to talk her out of it.

She gave me a look, though. "Jack, I know this isn't your fault."

"Oh, yes it is."

"Shh! I just want to know when you get the guy who did it."

"So you can slug him, too?"

"So I know when it's safe to come back to the club."

"You'll be the first. I got eyes and ears out. We'll find him."

"*They'll* find him. You're not one of them, remember?"

"I'm trying, doll. I'm trying."

ESCOTT announced he was taking Evie somewhere safe. He'd found a suitable hotel to go to ground.

"You got proof you're a Mr. and Mrs.?" I asked.

"I fear none is required for this establishment. I only hope Vivian never opens an inquiry into this."

"It's in a good cause. Call at the club if you need anything."

"You'll be asleep."

"I meant the Nightcrawler. Derner knows who you are."

"Oh, dear God."

"What?"

"Does this mean I'm your gangland lieutenant?" He said it with an "f" again. Someday I'd ask him if that's how it was spelled in England.

"Let's just keep it 'babysitter to dancers' and leave it at that."

"And what happened to my steering wheel?"

"I . . . had another . . . another damned fit."

"A fit." He went still, waiting for more.

But I shut down, shaking my head. "I'll get you a new one."

"You bloody well better," he finally said, then went to rouse Evie from her nap. She protested but went along with him. I had two of the mugs follow to see them off.

AFTER a run by Crymsyn to check things (normal) and Escott's office (also normal) I had Strome drop me a block from Escott's house, telling him I'd walk from there, that I needed the fresh air to clear my head.

"Pick me up tomorrow around . . . oh, just come after dark." I couldn't remember the time for sunset. Dawn was my main concern. I kept track of that.

"It's freezing," he said. "You noticed? You shouldn't walk."

"Yeah, but I don't mind." The chill that had plagued me before was either gone or I'd just gotten used to it. Waiting until his taillights were a memory, I vanished, speeding along the sidewalk until I figured to be in sight of the house. I went solid and had a good look around the neighborhood, front and back.

Nothing. Dammit.

I'd been hoping, really, really *hoping* that since the club and the office came up empty, Hoyle would catch a case of the dumbs from Ruzzo and be lying in wait for me here.

Too bad. Pounding their heads together would have improved my mood a lot.

I ghosted inside the house, went through it for intruders (none), ran a bath, used it, shaved, put on fresh clothes for tomorrow, and dropped invisibly into my basement sanctuary.

The light was on, as I'd left it. The dim bulb didn't use much juice. It also didn't heat the place much, as in dry out the damp. Was I in for another broken pipe?

This spot used to be cozy and safe, and it was fireproof, but still . . . I wanted to *not* be home.

Maybe if I fixed up something better, larger, took over the whole basement.

Jonathan Barrett had a great place, lots of room, bookshelves, lots of lights, but then he was richer and had a rich girlfriend who didn't mind the improvements in the cellar of her Long Island palace.

Maybe I could get my own place.

Actually I already had one. Lady Crymsyn.

And I didn't feel safe there, either.

STROME was punctual. I was on the phone with Derner within minutes of rising to find out what had happened during the day when the doorbell rang. I let Strome in and went back to my call. Shouldn't have bothered. Nothing new on the hunt for Hoyle. He'd gone to ground again and had either found an exceptionally good place for it, or no one would admit to knowing where. With there still being a substantial number of men against my sitting in Gordy's chair, a stonewalling might be in progress. Paranoid of me, but I had a right to be so, and, without hypnosis to force things my way, I was stuck with the situation.

Speaking of stuck . . . "Is my car back yet?" I asked Derner.

"No, Boss. I got them to lay off and just do the tires, though."

Dammit. I could have gone to Detroit and back and had a whole new car made by now. I suppressed a growl, and asked, "Has Kroun been in?"

"Not today. If he was steamed last night, he's gonna be boiling to-night."

"Why?"

"The papers."

"What's in them?"

"They're screaming about a mob hit on Roland Lambert."

"*What?*"

"That's what they got. I didn't write it, that's what they got. Your club's all over it, your name, and they pulled out the Jane Poe case again."

Oh, hell. I shouldn't have talked to that reporter. I knew better. Give them one straw, and they'll spin a mountain of gold. I'd been known to do it myself. "Hoyle will know that he missed killing me again."

"Yeah, that's gonna piss him off."

"I'll send him flowers."

"Hey, Boss, it's the way it is."

"Yeah-yeah. Look, the guys who do know where he is ain't cooperat-ing, that's plain enough. You put the word out that his location is worth two grand to them."

He nearly choked. "But that-that's—"

Two years' income to most, a tip to others. "Take it out of petty cash. These bozos are gonna cost us five times that if they're left running loose. I'll be at Crymsyn if anything new comes in."

I hung up before the sputtering started. The phone rang as I shrugged into my coat. My hat was gone. I suspected I'd lost it in the Stockyards during my binge.

Escott was on the other end of the line. His tone was tense. "Good, I wanted to catch you before—"

"What's wrong?"

"Bloody Evie Montana. The little—she slipped her leash."

"Ah, jeez. How?"

"Oldest trick in the book, through the bathroom window and out."

"When?"

"This afternoon. I should have anticipated. She'd been harping all day about wanting to go home. I think the girl is rather backward—"

"Can it, Charles, we both know she's the original Dumb Dora."

"Yet she managed to outfox me. I'd tried to explain the situation to her, but she seemed to think—oh, bloody hell, she doesn't think. That's the problem."

Hanging around smart women like Vivian and Bobbi had gotten him spoiled. "Well, meet me at the club, and we'll try to hash out a way of finding her again."

"Right." He sounded tired. Apparently a day with Evie had not been a picnic.

With a twinge of guilt I realized I should call the hospital and ask after Roland. It wasn't his fault the papers were in a lather about the shooting. I had the operator connect me, not wanting to bother searching the phone book. Eventually I got through to the nurses' station on Roland's floor and was informed he was doing well, whatever that meant. When I asked for more details I was told when evening visiting hours were, then the line went dead. Standard replies to the standard questions. If something was truly wrong, the answers would have been different. Maybe.

"Two grand for Hoyle?" asked Strome on the way to his car.

"Yeah. You know where he is?"

He shook his head. "But I might know some guys who might know some guys who might. And they don't need to hear about the two grand."

"No, they don't." If Strome had been holding out on me . . . but I decided I didn't care. Whatever it took to get Hoyle in a box.

ROLAND's Hudson was still parked in front of Lady Crymsyn, along with another car. A hopeful reporter. Strome drove around back. I let us in that way, we walked through, then I unlocked the lobby door and let him out again. Less than a minute later the hopeful drove off at a good clip. Strome came in, his face bland. I didn't ask questions and went up to the office.

Lights *and* radio off. Myrna was being different tonight. I turned both on and rummaged in the desk, finding a piece of cardboard in a box of typing paper. I lettered an optimistic CLOSED, BUT BACK SOON! on it in black ink, then went down to tack it on the entry door.

The lobby phone rang, startling me. I was the one who usually called in on it. Strome kept his hands in his pockets, so I answered.

"Jack?" Bobbi's voice.

"Yeah, honey? You okay?"

"I'm fine, we're all fine. It's been rough, but I got some sleep. I was hoping to catch you. I already tried at Charles's."

"Oh, yeah?"

"I thought you should know I called everyone not to come in tonight." She just saved me a ton of effort. "You're an angel. How's Roland?"

"He's in better shape than me and Faustine put together. The papers have been all over him. He's enjoying every moment."

"Enjoying?"

"His name is in the news, people are wanting his autograph. This is the best thing that's happened to him in ages."

"Yeah, but will he dance again?" That was a huge nagging worry I'd tried not to think about.

"He seems to think so. I wouldn't put it past him to be up and rehearsing tomorrow. I told him you'd closed the club for the time being, though. He said to tell you not to do that. I couldn't really explain that there was more going on, mostly because I don't know anything."

"I'll tell you all about it whenever you want."

"When it's over, then."

Which could be never at this rate. "It's a deal." And I hoped she didn't pick up on the pain that lanced through me just then. The false front between us wasn't going to come down.

After last night's uncontrolled debauch I knew I'd have to get away, especially from Bobbi. The longer I stayed, the worse the hurt would be for us both. Club or no club, responsibilities aside, I had to get clear of this mess before I lost my head and killed her.

"Boss?" Strome called up.

Calling *up*? *What the . . . ?*

I looked around and had to steady myself. I was in my *office*. Didn't remember leaving the phone booth or climbing the stairs.

"Oh, God . . ." I sat on the couch, my knees gone weak.

No scent of roses for comfort. Just me alone and crazy in my own skull.

"Boss? Mr. Kroun's here."

I must be in hell, I thought. *Or a nearby neighborhood.*

"Be right down." My voice sounded frighteningly normal, like there were two of me. The man who worked the front and kept things moving and the guy in the back who was losing himself in wholesale lots to the darkness within.

Stood up, squared my shoulders, and started to shut down the radio before leaving, then changed my mind. Maybe Myrna would like to have a little music going.

"I'm off to see some bad guys, Myrna. Keep an eye on things, would you?"

I collected my coat, wrapping up and pulling on leather gloves.

That's when I noticed the gun on my desk.

For several mad seconds I froze completely. I could not think how it had gotten there. It was the same Colt Detective Special I'd acquired once upon a time. How in hell . . . ?

I picked it up, hefting the solid, otherwise reassuring weight and broke it open. Fully loaded, with the brand of bullets I favored, still smelling of its last cleaning, it was definitely the same gun. I went cold all over, put it down and backed away, the flesh on my nape going tight.

Had I somehow opened the safe, taken the gun out, placed it on the blotter, and totally forgotten? If that was true, then I really was crazy, and in a much more serious way than before.

A table lamp next to the couch went on and off suddenly. I twitched and whirled to face it.

Oh, jeez . . . what a time for . . .

"Myrna?" I whispered. "Was this your doing?"

No more light play, but I knew the answer, however impossible it seemed. She switched vodka and gin bottles around as a joke, and cut lemons up to help Wilton, but this was a first. A big first. Was she getting stronger? And how far was this kind of thing going to go?

"Thanks, honey," I said to the air.

I made myself relax and put the gun in my overcoat pocket. At least I'd not been the one who'd done it and forgotten, so I wasn't all that crazy. Just haunted.

"Look after the place, okay?"

No lights flickered in reply as I shut the door.

KROUN was in a shut-mouthed mood, which suited me just fine. He'd parked behind Strome's car, driver's side to the curb. When it was time to leave he slid across the seat. I didn't think he was tired of driving Gordy's car, but only I knew where we were going, and this way minimized conversation.

Strome said he was going to go someplace and see someone, and I hoped it meant turning up Hoyle.

I took a lot of unnecessary turns on the ride toward the Bronze Belt. Kroun would probably know where we were on arrival and could find his way back again, but this way I could tell Coldfield that I'd made an effort. I took one final corner onto a street lined with parked cars and spotted a single opening halfway down. It seemed suspiciously clear, and I expected to find a fireplug, but Isham, one of Coldfield's lieutenants, stepped from a little grocery store next to the space. I parked Gordy's tank and got out.

This was one of the border areas of the Bronze Belt, where the whites and coloreds had to intermingle as dictated by geography. Despite the presence of so many vehicles, it was a hard-knock area; the Caddy stood out.

Isham nodded at the car. "Shoe said there'd be you and Kroun. That him? Everything okay?"

"Pretty much."

"Where's your Klansman?"

He meant Strome, who did not behave well in mixed company. Isham had made a hobby of baiting him. "He wet the rug, so I tied him in the yard."

Isham chuckled, and I went back to the car. Kroun slid across the seat again to get out on the curb side. He tried his stare out on Isham. Isham looked past him in such a way that he had to eventually turn to see what was so interesting. There were suddenly a lot of guys visible that we hadn't noticed before. They were in doorways or coming out of other stores or the alleyways. They all had the look.

Kroun grunted, almost smiling. "Peachy."

We followed Isham into the store, which was a small-time husband-and-wife operation. The couple stood behind the counter, watching the parade with flinty faces. I'd been through there before on a case for Escott and politely saluted the lady since I was minus a hat. Neither of them reacted.

Isham took us out the back door, turning right down the rear alley, then went into another door, this one to an eatery. I got a partial whiff of grease and stale coffee, then made a determined effort not to inhale accidentally. Food smells made me nauseous, even the expensive stuff.

We didn't bother going to the front, but through an inside door to a small washroom. Isham opened a closet door, revealing a narrow space with a mop and bucket and shelves crowded with cleaning supplies and junk. He pulled on one of the shelves and the wall—rather a door fixed to look like a wall—swung out. A bare hall, badly lighted, lay within.

Kroun paused. "Jeez, what kinda place you got here?"

"The kind that's safe," said Isham. "Fleming knows the rest of the way."

"It's okay," I said, going in first. Kroun doubtfully followed. It was only twenty feet, not enough to make me nervous, and the opposite door also opened into a storage closet, this one full of bed linens and towels. I pulled on the light cord. The bare bulb above us went on, and I carefully shut up the passage behind. It clicked softly into place and once more resumed looking like a back wall supporting a couple coat hooks. A work apron dangled limp from one of them.

"Up and through," I said.

"Then what? Secret ladders?"

"Nah, just stairs."

Outside was a regular back hallway, no frills. Shiny linoleum, plain white walls, a hotel maids' cart shoved to one side. At the end were service stairs, and we went up two flights.

"Where the hell are we?" Kroun was puffing. You'd think a mobster would be in better shape.

"Somewhere in the next block from the car. You saw the neighborhood. It wouldn't do for a couple of white guys to be seen going in and out of a colored hotel."

"Why'd you bring Gordy here, then?"

"Is this where you'd ever look for him?"

"Huh. That's good. How'd you fix it?"

"Connections and a donation or two to a good cause."

Dr. Clarson and those of his colleagues who took care of Gordy were being well compensated, as was the owner of the hotel, but that we were here at all was Shoe Coldfield's doing. Without his blessing and help, Gordy might have been a sitting duck even in his own territory. Coldfield would have done it anyway as a favor to me and Escott, but he was also doing himself a favor. With someone like Gordy owing him in such a big way, a gang boss could get a lot of things done for his turf.

When we reached the right floor I knocked twice and pushed slowly on the service door. A guy a little shorter than Isham stood with a revolver in his fist. He knew me by sight but didn't put the gun away. I slowly emerged, my arms out a little. Kroun did the same.

One of Gordy's boys, Lowrey, came up and said we were okay. The other man nodded and retreated a few steps, watchful.

Lowrey and another trusted man had taken turns standing watch since all this began. Strome might have been here to help, but he wasn't much of a mixer with color. Lowrey didn't give a damn one way or another, it was just a job. Most of the real guardianship was done by Shoe Coldfield's people.

Lowrey took us along the length of the hotel hall and up another flight. This floor had rooms with open doors, plush carpeting, and people, but nothing noisy. It was almost like a library. So long as it didn't turn into a funeral parlor.

Adelle Taylor emerged from one of the rooms, apparently expecting us. She was soberly dressed, not in her usual film-actress style, but everything looked nice. She gave me a smile.

I bent a little and bussed her cheek, then gave her a good looking over. "Woman, you have him get on his feet pretty soon, or I'm gonna start asking you out."

She reacted well. "Is that a promise or a threat?"

"Both."

At the sight of her Kroun underwent an amazing transformation. He dropped the dour face and blazed out with his charm once more. "A pleasure again, Miss Taylor. You're looking very fine tonight."

"Thank you, Whitey. It's so much better here. Like a weight's been lifted."

"I'm glad to hear it. If you need anything, absolutely anything at all, I'll make sure you have it."

"You're very kind." She beamed, and I could tell that made Kroun's whole week.

I was on her side—whatever put him in a good humor was good in turn for her boyfriend.

"The doctor's with Gordy now," she said. "We can wait in the hall."

She led us a little farther, pausing just short of an open door halfway down. A table outside was stacked with medical-looking junk and a food tray. I ventured a whiff of air and got the unmistakable scent of chicken soup.

Within the room I heard Dr. Clarson asking a question, then responding to the murmured answer with a heavy sigh.

"Well, Gordy," he said sadly, "you're going to die. Just not today."

Adelle shifted next to me, gaze raised toward the ceiling. She was not an aficionada of the doc's sense of humor.

"Fine by me," came Gordy's reply. There was a hint that his usual low rumble was returning.

"And you don't go waking me up for the rest of the night. I've had a tough day like you wouldn't believe and need my sleep."

"No problem."

Clarson emerged, wearing the white coat of his craft, the sterile white in sharp contrast to his dark skin. A similarly clad and dark-toned nurse came out, carrying a tray that she put on the table. Clarson looked us over.

"You may have two minutes," he said. "I'll be out here with my watch."

"That'll be fine, Doc," I answered for Kroun. I put my head around the door. "Hi, Gordy."

He was in bed, propped up on a lot of pillows, with the sheet and blankets pulled high, almost to his chin. One bare arm was out, the other tucked under the coverings. He was pale, but that awful hollowness looked more filled out than before. "'Lo, Fleming."

"You better?"

"I'm better."

This time I believed him. "Mr. Kroun's here."

"Send 'm in."

Adelle moved off to another room, by now well schooled to be scarce when business was afoot. I would have liked to have heard what Kroun wanted to say to Gordy; but if it concerned me, I'd find out later, and if it didn't, then I didn't give a damn. Instead, I asked Clarson for a verdict on Gordy. He didn't want to get optimistic about his patient, having seen too many others carried off.

"He's much better, and that's as far as I'll say, 'cause I don't want to jinx him."

"If there's anything I can do . . ."

"Have that fine little lady of yours come up and visit Miss Taylor tomorrow. She'd do better for some company. Everyone else keep clear so Gordy can rest."

"I'll see to it."

"Then that's all right."

Something about the arrangement of the bed coverings nagged at me. A familiar outline . . .

"Doc? Is Gordy's sleeping with a .45 in his fist part of your remedy?"

He snorted. "Not really. He usually has it on the nightstand, but that company you brought in . . . he felt better having some heat close."

Hell of a world, I thought.

*   *   *

"OUT the way we came in," I told Kroun when he emerged two minutes later.

He hesitated, looking past me toward Adelle's room.

"What, you want her autograph?"

He continued to hesitate. "We can come back later, right?"

This guy was a pip. "When she's not as distracted."

We retraced our steps without escort, but in the alley between the buildings Kroun paused. "You know what that was about?"

"You'll tell me if I need to."

Kroun snorted. "Smart boy. I can see why Gordy likes you. He looked like hell. I thought he'd be better than he was."

"He'll be fine," I said.

"If he isn't, there's gonna be changes. He asked you to step in for him as a temporary thing. You say you don't want the job, which means somebody else takes over."

"Derner."

"Uh-uh, Mitchell."

A flare of real anger rose in me. "Mitchell?"

"If the worst happens, Mitchell's taking over. He knows the ropes. The boys won't object to him the way they've been doing with you."

"They won't, but I might. You pulling another Bristow here?"

For a second I thought he was going to slug me. His dark eyes blazed a moment. "Listen up, Fleming. You say you don't want to be boss, but you sure as hell don't mind throwing your weight around when it's convenient. You handled yourself okay dealing with that Alan Caine mess, and you got lucky surviving those hits from Hoyle; but when all that clears away and you're standing in the sweet spot, you still don't have what it takes to be a boss."

I kept my anger belted down tight. I had to hear him out. There had to be some way of getting Mitchell off the list of replacements. Gordy was improving, but next week he could be hit by a bus. "What am I missing?"

"The guts to kill and to order a killing. That's not in you. Mitchell can do a piece of work and not think twice about it—but you think too much. You're a stand-up guy, but not for this kind of job."

On one hand I agreed with him. I'd killed before, but I didn't like it. Some nights I carried those souls around on my shoulders like a flock of carrion crows. Kroun must have seen it. He was the kind to read people. "What about Derner? Why not him? He and Strome are both made."

"They follow. They don't lead. Not enough imagination."

"And Mitchell's got that?"

"You don't know him. If you're worried about him making trouble with your girl or you, I can get him to lay off, and that's a promise."

I didn't have much confidence that Mitchell would obey, though.

"He was supposed to have Chicago in the first place."

"That's what he told you when Morelli died?"

"Yeah. But Gordy moved in faster. He turned out to be good at the business, so we kept him."

"Mitchell didn't like that?"

"Nope."

"He got a grudge on?"

"Not that I've seen."

Hardly a reassuring answer. But I nodded like it meant something. "But all this is just so much eyewash. Gordy's better. You and Mitchell will eventually go home, and we all settle back to business as usual."

"Yeah. But if that changes . . ."

On our return the small grocer's was empty except for one very large man in a custom-tailored overcoat. He threw a dark, impersonal glance at me, then pretended to study a stack of canned goods. I walked outside with Kroun and Isham, getting partway to the car, then excusing myself.

"Just remembered I forgot something," I said, and motioned for Kroun to go on to the car. He shrugged and kept going, opening the front passenger door, but not getting in. He leaned against the body of the car and watched the guys in the street who were watching him.

I turned back to the shop, but Shoe Coldfield was already emerging, filling the doorway a moment. The building seemed smaller with him in front of it.

"So that's the man," he rumbled in his deep voice. "He ever on the stage?"

"Don't think so."

"It's a wonder he's doing what he does. It's too easy to pick someone like him from a lineup. Makes an impression."

"Unless you got a lot of intimidation going for you."

"That's true. I expect he's one of that type. Knew a few, but they were all onstage. Could play meek and mild, then open up and cut you in half with it. Good actors they were, the ones who knew how to control it."

"I don't think Kroun's in the meek-and-mild club."

"No he is not. I've done some checking around since getting his name, and he can be damn dangerous if you don't watch yourself."

"He's leashed." Sort of. I'd come to think the suggestion on friendship was wearing off faster than it should.

Coldfield approved. "You're just playing with him?"

"Not for long. I'm hoping he and his boy go back to New York tomorrow. Soon as I get them clear I've got other things to work on."

"Like that singer who got the noose?"

"Yeah."

"I'm sorry about that. I saw Caine perform once. Hell of a talent."

"It's less for him than for his ex-wife, Jewel. She's got the blame for his death, and she didn't do it. That's not right."

"Yeah, Charles filled me in today about all the trouble. Said you were looking dangerous."

"Only to the killer."

"That's what's bothering our mutual friend. You're planning to kill the killer."

"I haven't decided yet."

"Charles thinks you have. He's on your side for it."

"I thought he might be."

"Well, the fewer criminals walking around, the better is how he likes it. Of course, I'm the exception to the rule."

"I've wondered about that."

"So have I," he admitted.

"If Charles likes the idea, why's he bothered?"

"It's not over the killing, it's you. He's not been too happy about your state of mind. He's worried what it'll do to you. He doesn't say it like that. He dresses it up in a hell of a lot more words, but that's what it is boiled down."

Escott had a valid point. "I've been shoved against the wall on this kind of business before, and I've learned I can live with it."

"Uh-huh. But not too happily."

"Shoe, I know you want to help, but what's going to work best is for me to find the bastard who killed Jewel and make him pay for it. No, I won't be happy afterward, but it'll be better for me than if I did nothing at all."

"I know what that's like. On the other hand . . ."

"What?"

"Have I told you lately how I really *hate* scraping you off sidewalks?"

"I'm on the lookout. I know who I'm after, and so far they don't know I'm after them."

"Who would that be?"

"A troublemaker named Hoyle is the odds-on favorite, two idiots named Ruzzo—"

"Oh, God, *them*?"

"You've met 'em?"

"Yeah. Two brains and not a mind between them. They're stupid, but cunning and faster than rats when they need to be."

"I won't turn my back on any of them. Hoyle's the favorite for this job. I gotta find him, ask a few questions, then make a decision."

"As in just how to bump him?"

"You reading minds?"

He shrugged. "I've been doing this a while."

"With any luck I'll settle it tonight, then we can try and"—I almost said "forget it" but that wasn't going to happen—"get back to what passes for normal around here."

"Yeah, my guys are getting their noses out of joint for all the extra marching around in the weather."

"Listen, I don't want you putting yourself out—"

"Forget it, it's good for them. Walk some of the fat off their shanks. They're keeping a sharp watch on Gordy. There's no white people come within a hundred yards of this neighborhood we don't know about. He'll stay safe."

"I appreciate it, Shoe."

"It's good for business to look out for him," he said.

I didn't gainsay. If that's what Coldfield had to put about to seem to have a tough, practical front for his troops, then I was all for it.

"That movie star mutt of yours looks like he's tugging at the leash."

Kroun had begun to pace up and down a few times, looking my way impatiently.

"If he's cold, why doesn't he get in the damn car?" Coldfield asked.

"Probably thinks I'll forget him if he's out of sight. I better go."

"All right, but watch yourself. I'm fresh out of brooms and scrapers."

I walked toward the car, the wind picking up and pushing at my back. Kroun saw my approach, putting on an "it's about damn time" face. He dropped into the front seat and hauled the passenger door smartly shut.

It made a hell of a lot louder noise than it should have. Rather than a metallic bang, there was a deafening *krump*, then it was like the sound itself slammed me in the chest. I was hurled backward, right off my feet, not understanding why. I glimpsed smoke suddenly blacking the windows of the Caddy on the *inside* before I hit the pavement. Some instinct told me to keep rolling. Each time I saw the car a different view presented itself.

Smoke flooding from under it, thick and black.

Another explosion, the boom too loud to hear, only feel.

The rear end suspended five feet in the air and nothing holding it up.

The heavy body abruptly crashing down on all fours, flames engulfing the back.

The tires ablaze, adding smoke and stink to the picture.

Pieces of metal shooting by like hot hail.

A tumbling wall of fire and blackness roaring toward me like a train—

14

INSISTENT, annoying things plucked at me, at my clothes. I waved them off, but they made a solid grab, pulled strong, and dragged me over a rough, hard surface. A man yelled in my ear, but it was muffled, as though I'd vanished. He might have been cursing.

Fire rained down. It was almost leisurely. Fat drops floated confetti-like or struck the cement, bouncing to scatter yellow-and-blue flames. A second look, and they proved to be attached to dark bits of burning things. It seemed a good idea to get out of their way, so I got my feet under me and working together. Hours later we reached the cover of a building and ducked in. Someone had broken the front window, and the lights were out. When I chanced to breathe, the air reeked of gasoline, burned rubber, and hot metal.

Doubled over, coughed it clear. Two other men were with me, Coldfield and Isham, also coughing.

Eyes stinging, I looked through the window—the shattered glass had blown inside—and saw the big Cadillac's shell engulfed in a fast and furious inferno. Smoke roiled from its stricken, blackened carcass in a wide, twisting cloud that was fortunately blowing away from us. Even at this distance the heat warmed my face, but I couldn't hear anything from what should have been a blast-furnace bellow. Touched one ear. Came away blood. A lot of it. My face, too. Damn. Without thinking, I vanished and returned. My hearing popped back to normal and other hurts that were starting to make themselves felt ceased altogether.

"Jack?"

Turned. Coldfield stared at me, concerned. So did Isham, but with a different expression. He rubbed his watering eyes, shook his head, looking puzzled.

"Jack? You hear me?" Coldfield again.

"Yeah." What the hell had happened?

"You okay?"

"Think so."

"That makes one of you. Your friend out there's gone."

I didn't get him. "What? Something happen to Gordy?"

"The guy you came with. Kroun."

"What? No . . ." Looked again at the wreck. Too much smoke to see inside the car, but that was just as well. For some things you don't want details.

"There was no way to help him."

"Oh, goddamn."

"Yeah. This puts everybody up shit creek. Gonna be hell to pay." He wiped his streaming eyes with a handkerchief.

Someone touched my shoulder. The woman who always stood behind the counter offered me a damp towel. "You're hurt, Mister. Your face."

I accepted the gift and used it. My ears no longer streamed blood, but the leftover gore must have been an alarming sight. "Thank you."

"Come in back, we'll get you cleaned up."

Back, meaning a bathroom or kitchen, meaning mirrors at some point. I pulled enough of my scrambled thoughts together to thank her again. "This is more than enough."

"We gotta get him out of here," Coldfield told her. "We gotta all get moving."

"The hotel," said Isham.

"Farther than that."

"The club." He'd mean Coldfield's place, the Shoebox. But we had to check another place first.

"Call Lady Crymsyn," I said. "Charles is there by now. If there's other bombs . . ." It finally got through that I'd seen one going off.

"Jeez." Coldfield, moving with astonishing speed for his size, threaded past dark aisle displays toward a door, where presumably he would find a phone. I hoped Escott would answer.

"The lobby number," I called after. "Try that one. Let it ring."

The fire rain of blown-up car pieces had stopped, but not the smoke. The wreckage lay all over the street, shattered windows gaped, their stares blank and cold. Most were ground floor, though a few second-story ones were gone. I hoped to God no one had been in front of any of them.

Isham left the grocers for a look-see, keeping a healthy distance from the car and moving fast. I went as well, standing just clear of the door. No other casualties were in view, but people were cautiously emerging, Coldfield's soldiers. Isham talked to some of them, and they began to melt away from the attraction. By the time I heard the first fire-engine siren, the street was empty except for civilian types. Other cars rolled up, full of vultures who'd come to view the burning body. The smoke forced most of them upwind. A white man came over and asked if I was all right.

I swabbed the towel around, hoping to get the telltale blood off my face and neck. "Yeah, I'm fine, got cut by flying glass. Did you see what happened?"

"Was gonna ask you. Looks like the gas tank blew. Must have been a humdinger. Anyone in it?"

"I donno. Hope not."

"Anyone else see?" He pulled out a notebook and a chewed pencil, and I recognized yet another of my own kind. What used to be, anyway.

"I don't think so."

"Hey, I know you, don't I?" He gave me a squint. "You got that fancy nightclub. The one what had the body in the basement—"

"I gotta go." I retreated into the grocery. People on the sidewalk parted for me, but closed up for him. He shrugged and looked for other witnesses.

It hadn't really sunk in yet about Kroun. Hard to think beyond the burning car. The flames were less now, running out of fuel.

Coldfield returned. "Charles is fine. He'll keep his eyes open and not be driving. You and me, this way." He headed to the back.

He was in a hurry, but I paused long enough to leave the stained towel on the counter and fish out my wallet. I pressed five twenties into the woman's hand.

She backed a step. "No, we couldn't . . ."

"For the window."

"It's too much!"

"I'm apologizing, as well, ma'am."

I rushed after Coldfield, who had cut left down the alley and was waiting impatiently by a row of trash cans. As he turned I only then noticed his coat was smeared with street dirt. Apparently the blast had knocked him down, too. I'd been much closer. There was a singed patch on my jacket and holes torn in my shirt. It was black so no staining showed, but I could smell my own blood on the fabric, along with the smoke.

With me half a step behind him, he led us down a much more narrow alley that opened to the next street. Just as we emerged Isham pulled up in Coldfield's Nash, barely braking, and we dove into the back.

This car was also armored, for all the good it would do.

I looked when we had enough distance and saw the smoke rising over the buildings, thundering fast and black against what for me was pale gray sky.

"No one's gonna follow," said Coldfield, misinterpreting.

"Where we going?"

"My club."

"Drop me at the Nightcrawler."

"You joking?"

"I got things to do or there really will be hell to pay. Kroun comes to Chicago, gets killed, and, if I don't get the blame, it will drop like a ton of bricks on Gordy. I gotta steer that away."

"Seems to me you should be keeping your head a lot lower. I give you a talking-to, then *bang-boom*, there you are on the damn sidewalk being another damn mess."

"Thanks for pulling me clear."

"Thought you were a goner when that hit. Isham, who the hell got close enough to the car to rig that thing?"

"No one, Shoe. We watched it good."

"It didn't happen here," I said. "Someone had to have done it earlier. The guys know Gordy's car and that Kroun and I have been using it. Anyone could have wired it up at any time."

"Why didn't it go off sooner, then?"

"The trigger might have been on the passenger door. Kroun didn't get in on that side when we left. It was pure chance. It was supposed to take me and Kroun out together." I'd survived a hell of a lot, but being blown to pieces might have done the trick for real.

"So who did it?"

"Mitchell. Kroun's lieutenant."

"You sure?"

I spread my hands. "If that was meant just for me, then I'd have other names to give you. But if Kroun was supposed to go, too . . . the passenger door trigger changes things. A lot of people might know I'd be driving him and that he'd probably sit in the front. Mitchell's the only one I can think of who'd stand to gain by Kroun's death. He might be set to take over Kroun's job if anything happens to his boss. With Kroun getting killed here, the Chicago outfit gets the blame, and Mitchell is clear to walk in. He wouldn't be the first mug in the world trying to improve himself by knocking off his boss."

"It worked great for Cassius. Didn't last. He bought it later."

"Hah?"

"In *Julius Caesar*? Cassius got a bunch of other guys to go in with him for the hit on Caesar. Dropping you at the Nightcrawler strikes me as being a really stupid thing to do. You don't know who could be on Mitchell's side."

"I got an edge."

"Yeah. Sure was helpful against that bomb."

Actually it had kept me alive and had certainly cured a couple of busted eardrums if not more, but Coldfield needed to grouse and grumble and get it out of his system. He was shaken by the business, and this was his way of handling it.

When he ran down, I said, "I still have to go there and deal with him. I can't let Gordy catch hell for something I didn't do."

Coldfield managed not to heave a huge sigh, just most of one. "All right. Isham, drive this guy to the lion's den."

"Thanks," I said.

"Uh-uh, I'm not taking the responsibility."

"No problem."

"You're certain Mitchell's the guy?"

"At this point he's the likeliest, but there might be stuff going on I've missed or never knew about. I wasn't exactly tailor-made for these kinds of fun and games."

"The hell you're not." He gave me a look that was meant to include my supernatural condition.

"Maybe now, yeah, but I never wanted this job. That's why I don't get all the stuff happening. Too damned trusting. Soon as Gordy's better I step clear."

"Amen, brother. This shit's bad for business."

"The cops are going to be all over that wreck once it's cooled down. They'll eventually trace it to Gordy and want to question him. You got the name of his lawyer so he can run interference?"

"Yeah, Adelle's had to deal with him. That's covered."

"You sure about this trip to the den?"

"I'll go very carefully." I checked my watch, but the crystal was cracked right across, the time stopped at the moment I'd been flung backward. It could probably be fixed, even the damaged innards, but I would replace it, buy something with a different face to it so it wouldn't be constantly reminding me. "You wanna do me a real favor, you and Isham run over to Crymsyn and help Charles stay out of trouble. They might target there next."

"I told him to get out, go to my club, and I'd put him up, but he said he was staying put."

"Playing lieutenant," I said, saying it with an "f."

ISHAM dropped me a block from the Nightcrawler and drove off. I ghosted the rest of the way in, brushing quick between pedestrians on the walks, giving them a brief, intense chill that had nothing to do with the weather. When I encountered the uncompromising solidity of a building, I rose high, found a window shape, and sieved in. Men were in the room and a radio was on, tuned to some fights, but they didn't pay much attention, talking over the commentator. I identified a couple of the voices as being regulars who worked the gaming tables below. They were expecting some local politicos tonight, and the pickings would be good except for one guy who was to "win" his weekly payoff. There was a discussion going on over the best way to make it seem like a genuine game.

Shifted from that room to the hall and floated along, counting doors until reaching Gordy's office. I eased through to the other side and listened, handicapped by this form's cottonlike muffling. No one seemed to be in. That wasn't too likely. I pushed on, finally going solid in the bathroom. I kept quiet and waited. Derner was on the phone, and he was pissed.

"Oh, yeah? Well, you get your ass moving and *find* him! The boss is raising hell over this. If we don't find Hoyle tonight, tomorrow there's gonna be fresh food in the lake for the damn fish."

Since the phone was probably tapped I hoped he meant that threat for effect and wasn't planning to carry it through. On the other hand, the

FBI would like nothing better than for the wiseguys to knock each other off. Less work for them.

Derner hung up. I peered around the door. He was consulting a book for the next number. He dialed, let it ring a long time, then hung up in disgust. Before he could find another to try the phone rang.

"Yeah?" He sounded impatient. There was a glass of water on the desk and a toppled-over bottle of aspirin. He'd been busy. And frustrated.

Silence as he listened. So did I. I could almost make out the speaker's words on the other end of the line.

"What? What'd you say?" His voice lost its decisive force, like the air had been sucked right from his lungs.

The caller repeated, his tones emphatic.

"Th-that's impossible. I was just on the phone with him tonight. You sure?" Now he sounded uneasy. I could guess what the bad news must be. "*Both* of 'em? Where? You *sure*? Are you? Okay. Stick around, keep an eye on what the cops do. Call me again. I know it's been busy, you just keep calling!" He slammed the receiver down, staring at the opposite wall with its pastoral painting and probably not seeing it.

After a moment, with elbows on the desk, he slumped until his head was between the heels of his hands. He let out a long low groan, gently rubbing his temples.

"Ahh, jeez. This is too much," he whispered, eyes shut.

I went semitransparent, floating noiselessly over the floor. Stood right in front of him, going solid. Waited.

He must have had a really bad headache; he didn't look up. He gave a sluggish jump when the phone rang and muttered a curse.

Then he straightened to answer, saw me, and froze.

After the first yelp, no cursing, no nothing, just pure shock on his face. Couldn't tell if it was from dismay or guilt, then it slipped suddenly into genuine relief.

"You-you're okay!"

I nodded, keeping a sober and somber mask on. "What did you hear?"

"One of the boys . . . said a bomb, the car blew up. Took you and Kroun . . ." He looked around. "Where is . . . ?"

The phone continued ringing. "Get that," I said. "I'm still dead. Understand?"

He answered. It was someone else relaying the same bad news. He said he'd heard already and told them to leave the area, then hung up. "Was that what you want?"

"That's fine. Take the phone off the hook."

He did so.

"Kroun's dead. I was there."

"How'd you get away?"

"I wasn't in the car when it happened."

"But you—" He just now noticed my appearance.

"Stuff hit me. I'm not hurt much. Listen, I think Mitchell might have arranged it."

Derner seemed to hold his breath. He let it out, picked up his water glass, and finished what was left, not looking well.

"Who in this town knows how to rig a bomb?"

The man visibly winced.

"Well?"

"You ain't gonna like it."

"Aw, don't you be telling me—"

"'Fraid so, Boss. Hoyle."

I didn't quite hit the ceiling. "Oh, that's great! That's just *peachy*! I thought that son of a bitch was a boxer!"

"He was. But before that he did mining. Out West. He learned how to set charges as a kid. He learned boxing in the mining camp, and that was his ticket out."

"And in the good old days did he used to run around with Mitchell?"

He shrugged. "I donno. Could have."

"So how is it Mitchell's able to find Hoyle when no one else can?"

"Maybe Hoyle found him. It's no secret him and Kroun came to town. Coulda looked him up, they got to talkin' . . ."

"Yeah, then decide to kill two birds with one boom." Which didn't explain Alan Caine's death. Maybe he'd overheard something he shouldn't.

"He ain't getting out of Chicago alive." said Derner. "None of them."

"Make sure New York knows what really happened. I want them to hear it from you first, not Mitchell."

"Right." He reached for an index book with phone numbers, then slapped his hand on it. "Damn! I got some good news for you! Ruzzo—they been found. That two-grand reward tipped things. One of the guys phoned in with the name of a hotel and a room number. Not five minutes back. They probably been there under some other name this whole time. I can send some guys to get them now."

"No, I'll do it."

He looked me up and down. "But you need a doctor."

"The address."

He gave me what he'd scribbled on notepaper.

"I'm going now. You go on and do what you've been doing and play the angle that me and Kroun are *both* dead. You don't tell anyone different. Make sure New York understands they have to play along with the act, too, in case Mitchell calls them. If he comes in, pretend go along with whatever he says, find out all you can of what he's up to. Don't let him kill you, though."

"No, Boss."

"Protect yourself, but we need Mitchell alive to tell us what he's been doing." The last thing I wanted was Mitchell catching lead before I had the chance to take him apart myself.

"Right, Boss."

I hurried to a smaller room off that one. It had once been Bobbi's bedroom when she'd been with Slick. Completely redone, the stark white walls were partially hidden by gray metal file cabinets, a five-foot-tall map of Chicago, a large neon beer sign meant for outside display, and a desk too ugly for any place public. As depessing as an army barracks, no fond memory of our first encounter stirred in these surroundings.

It did have a fire escape, though. I opened the window and climbed out, thereby giving Derner a plausable explanation for how I'd gotten in in the first place.

Outside, I shut the window, vanished, and, holding close to the side of the building, slipped down to terra firma, then glided over the sidewalk until reasonably sure I was out of sight of the club.

The street where I materialized was busy with early-evening traffic. I walked quickly toward an intersection and waited, palming some dollar bills. I used those to hail a cab, figuring my now-scruffy clothes were not something to inspire trust in any driver. On the third try I got one to pull over and gave him the street for Ruzzo's hotel.

It was west of the Loop. A good place twenty years ago, less so now. They couldn't charge the pre-Crash fancy prices to travelers anymore, so they switched to bringing in long-term tenants who didn't mind that service wasn't what it used to be. I paid off the driver and sauntered in the opposite direction, circling the block to see what the back alley looked like.

Pretty much what I expected, but the loading-dock area was taking a laundry delivery and full of busy men in work clothes. I blended with them, waving a familiar and confident hello to complete strangers who nodded in return. You can get away with nearly everything doing that. Obligingly I shouldered two paper-wrapped bundles and took them in. I dropped them onto a flat trolley cart with other bundles and, without looking back, kept going down a short hall until I found the service elevator. There was no operator at the moment; he might have been on a coffee break or helping with the delivery. I stepped in and took myself up to the sixth floor.

The inside layout was in a squared off U-shape with the elevators in the middle. I went down the wrong branch, retraced, and found the right door. Ruzzo's room was at the very end, next to the window that opened to the metal framework of a fire escape. I wondered if they'd chosen it on purpose to have an extra exit or just naturally got lucky.

As I bent down for a look and listen at the keyhole the air in my dormant lungs shifted from the motion, and I got the first whiff of bloodsmell.

Quickly I backed from the door, hands out defensively.

As though the damn thing would break off from its hinges and jump me.

It didn't.

After a moment, I pulled together enough to think twice about entering. Both times the decision was to go; I just couldn't bring myself to move.

Never mind peering through the keyhole, just get it over with. Before I could think a third time, I vanished, streamed through the crack above the doorsill, and reformed just inside, but taking it easy.

No lights on, but the blinds were up on the window across the room; plenty of glow came in for me to use.

Nothing fancy about this place. A bathroom opened on my immediate left, an alcove served for a closet on the right, then the entry widened to a larger area with a sofa along the right-hand wall. Two beds were at the far end on either side of the window, and a couple chairs and a table, as normal as could be except for the bodies.

The Ruzzo brothers were collapsed, loose-boned in the chairs, having fallen forward across the table. Their heads were wrong, strangely misshapen. One had his face toward me, and his eyeballs were half out of their sockets, his tongue protruding, like a cartoon mocking surprise. The realization finally came that their heads had been bashed to pulp, and exactly in the middle of the table between them was a bloodied baseball bat.

The light changed, went suddenly gray, and I thought Myrna must have been acting up, only she wouldn't be here, she was at Lady Crymsyn.

I blinked, looking around. I was in the hall again, my back to the Ruzzo door, with my guts about to turn inside out.

Oh, hell, not now . . .

Drew a steadying breath. Wrong thing to do with bloodsmell filling every crevice of this place, and the scent of it and death hovering so close was too much, and it dropped fast and hard, and I doubled over, hitting the floor like I'd been shot.

My own blood seemed to hammer the top of my skull, and for a second it felt like I was once more swinging upside down in that meat locker, then I was creeping purposefully over the red-washed cement floor seeking life from another's death, and after all that I still thirsted for more human-red fire to pour down my throat . . .

The memory of pain and the nightmare of failure left me curled, stifling the urge to vomit, and clutching my sides where the cold, taut lines of the scars prickled along new-healed flesh. My eyes rolled up, and I shivered and held back the rising wail and hung on, hating, hating, *hating* this weakness and not wanting to give in to it. If I vanished, it would mean surrender. This stuff had power over me, and it had to stop. I had to *stop* it, I just didn't know how.

But gradually . . . gradually, the seizure passed.

Exhausted, I couldn't move for a while. No one came down the hall, and, even if someone had, I'd have not been able to do anything for myself. This was soul-weariness, and I couldn't control it.

When I thought I could start to trust my coordination, I pushed up, one stage at a time, eventually gaining my feet. The tension left over in my muscles was bad, but beginning to ease. I stretched cautiously, and you could have heard the pops and cracks at fifty feet.

I regarded the Ruzzos' door with bleak and chill thoughts. They were long dead, I was sure. Going in for a second look wouldn't change that or help me. I couldn't go in there. They were dead, and that's all there was to it, leave them and get out.

I was five steps toward the elevator, then turned around and went back and went in, because that was what bosses had to do.

THE second visit was less bad because I was careful to not breathe and not look at them, letting my gaze skip over the bits that threatened to add to my internal library of evil memories. With enough practice anyone can learn to create temporary blind spots in their sight.

The baseball bat placed so neatly in the center of the butcher's chaos could have been one from the party in the cornfield. I checked the alcove closet and found a cache of other bats standing in a corner, a bonanza for sandlot kids. Someone had reached in and lifted one away, then turned to where Ruzzo sat having a drink at the table—there were two unbroken glasses on it. He'd perhaps playfully hefted it, making a couple practice swings, having a laugh. Then the next two swings were utterly serious, and he'd kept on swinging, just to be sure.

No one would have heard any of it even through these walls. What were a couple of dull cracks, followed by meaty thumps to this place? Just another sound effect on a radio show and who wants to bother Ruzzo, anyway? Surly pair, just stay outta their way and hope they shut up. This wasn't the kind of place where people wanted to notice things, so I'd leave questioning the tenants and staff to others. As easily as I got in, the killer could have gotten out. Hell, he might have taken the fire escape stairs easy as pie or hijacked the freight elevator as I'd done.

Blood splatters generously freckled the walls and ceiling, long dried out. Several hours at least had passed since their creation. Ruzzo had been killed long before Kroun and I had driven away from the Nightcrawler.

Why, though?

If they were helping Mitchell, wouldn't he want to have them around? They might have been dumb, but extra muscle could be useful. Unless he couldn't trust them to keep their mouths shut. If they knew Hoyle had readied a bomb for Kroun, it wouldn't do having them running loose.

I went through the rest of the room, not touching anything, fists stuffed in my jacket pockets. Just looking was enough. They didn't have much: some clothes, a radio, old racing forms, a scatter of magazines you had to ask for special so the druggist would pull them from under the counter.

The two beds were unmade, and there was a tangle of blankets and a pillow discarded on the long sofa. I suspected that I'd at last found where Hoyle had been staying. Was he the killer here? With all three sharing a common hatred of me, they might have stuck together until Ruzzo became a liability.

If not himself the killer, Hoyle could well be a target, too. Only it didn't fit what I knew of the man.

A very quick sideways glance toward the table. It would take a hell of a lot of strength to do that kind of damage, and to be able to do it cold, without working yourself up into a muscle-charged rage. Hoyle was big enough for the work. The punches he'd landed on me in that snowy field were meant to disable and might have succeeded on anyone else. I'd felt killing force behind them, seen it in his face.

Last on my way out was the bathroom. Someone had rinsed off using the tub tap and slopped around, leaving diluted red stains all over. Those were also long dried. In the sink were two wallets, empty of cash. Well, the killer had been practical. When you're on the run you need money, and whatever had been there would serve to give the cops a motive, however flimsy, for the crime.

Nothing left to discover here, but I had more questions. I'd have to return to the Nightcrawler and wait for the answers to straggle in. Unless he was already on his way back to New York where I couldn't get to him right away, Mitchell would have to show himself sometime to put in his claim for the boss's chair. It would give him a chance to bitch at the locals for not having enough protection for Kroun. Of course, Mitchell could be blameless and been off having a fine time at another club while Kroun was blown to bits. The whole business with the passenger-door trigger could easily be a misinterpretation. Not my first one.

But first a stop at Lady Crymsyn. Escott should know this latest.

I ghosted through the door, materialized, and found myself staring Strome square in the face.

15

HE was surprised enough for three, rocking back on his heels with a sharp yelp. I almost did the same, but the door was directly behind and wouldn't allow the movement. Instinct took over. I struck out fast, popped him one, and he dropped.

I stared down at him, considering my situation.

Two dead guys in the room and an unconscious one out here in the hall.

Who had seen me appear out of thin air.

A simple problem to solve—if I could still hypnotize without risk of killing myself. No. Couldn't chance it.

Damnation.

Well, first I had to get Strome out of here, then I'd deal with what he'd seen. I hauled him up on one shoulder and took the freight elevator. The area below was clear, though there were three flat trolleys piled high with paper-wrapped goods parked along the hall. People were talking around a corner, coming our way. I hurried toward the exit and pushed awk-wardly through, Strome's weight throwing my balance off. The cold air didn't wake him.

We were in an unused part of a blind alley. Not much sun could get in between the buildings, so the last snowfall, glazed over by a layer of sleet, was still in thick drifts. I braced Strome against a wall, scooped up some mostly clean snow, and rubbed it in his face.

"Strome? Hey, c'mon!"

His eyes flickered, then he came shooting awake, staggering and star-ing around, his hand automatically going for the gun in his shoulder rig.

"What the . . . ?" He focused on me.

I glared right back. "Did you do it?"

Confusion. Just what I wanted. "Do what? Where am I?"

"Outside the Ruzzos' hotel. Did you kill them?"

"What? I—" He felt his jaw and froze. "Ruzzo's *dead*?"

"Since earlier today. Someone bashed their heads in Capone-style with a baseball bat. That's why I popped you one. Was it you?"

"No!" He was outraged and perhaps a little scared. I was scared my-self.

I was used to his stone face as the norm, but this reaction rang true. Besides, it took his mind off other matters. A clout strong enough to send you unconscious was usually enough to scramble your memory. You could lose the last half hour or the last month, or even the whole works of a lifetime. All I wanted gone were the last ten minutes. So far he wasn't asking inconvenient questions. That was *my* job.

"Why were you at the hotel then?" I asked.

"Looking for Ruzzo. I got a line they were hiding there. Thought they might be hiding Hoyle, too."

"Sure you didn't kill them?"

"Never! I never went near 'em! No!"

I took him off my suspect list for the moment; even if he'd changed clothes and washed, I'd have picked up the bloodsmell on him. Plenty of other crimes to check out, though. "Did you put a bomb in Gordy's car?"

His reaction to that one was also convincing. "A bomb? What the hell you talking about?"

I told him, and he didn't believe it. I stood back so he could get a look at me. "Believe it," I said. "Kroun's dead. I think Hoyle teamed with Mitchell, and I need to know which side of the fence you're on."

"With you and Gordy!"

"What about Mitchell?"

"I hate that weasel-eyed son of a bitch. He ain't stand-up. Never was."

"Do you know where he is?"

"No."

"What about Hoyle? You know where Hoyle is now?"

"Yeah . . . I got a line. Maybe."

"Maybe?"

"If he wasn't with Ruzzo, I was gonna check on it. Word's out on that reward, but the guy I talked to don't have the stones to go after him. I promised him a hundred for the news, but only if it was solid."

Interesting. "Why didn't you tell me that before?"

Strome looked at me like I was being unfair. Which was true. He'd hardly had time to work up to it. "Listen, I was gonna call Derner, get some boys, and go in. Hoyle ain't the sort to come quiet."

"Where is he, then?"

"The garage where he keeps his car."

That made sense. Wish I'd thought of it.

"You wanna check out Hoyle's garage, Boss?" he asked.

"Lead the way."

Strome was plenty shaken to judge by the backward glances coming my way as I followed him from the alley. I must have been giving him the creeps. Not my problem. He took us to where he'd parked his car, and we got in. I thought about phoning Lady Crymsyn. Escott would be in by now, but there was no telling how long Hoyle might stay in this garage or if he was even still around. If he had brains, he'd be putting distance between himself and the murders.

If he *really* had brains, he'd have never crossed me from the start.

"Ruzzo's murder," I said. "If Hoyle didn't do it, who else would?"

"Anybody who met them."

"Seriously. What about Mitchell?"

"Yeah, he could do it. Donno why he would. You just covering the bases, Boss?"

Considering how the murders had been accomplished, his choice of phrase was unfortunate. "Yeah. Can you think of any reason why Mitchell would want to kill me?" So far as I knew, Strome was unaware of the run-in I'd had with Mitchell at Crymsyn.

"He'd only do it if Kroun told him to."

"That's what I thought. Kroun must have been the real target from the first, but they rigged things to take me, too. The trigger was on the passenger door. It was meant to go off when he had company. Derner said Hoyle knows explosives."

"Yeah, learned 'em in a mining camp out West. So Mitchell got him to make one? But why should Mitchell kill his boss?"

"With Kroun gone, Mitchell moves into his spot with New York, while Chicago gets the blame for the death. He's keeping his own back-yard clean doing it here. Sound reasonable to you?"

"Yeah."

"Ruzzo becomes inconvenient to Hoyle for some reason, and they die. What you bet maybe Hoyle becomes inconvenient to Mitchell?"

"Because he don't want Hoyle to talk about the bomb?"

"All he has to do to get away with bumping Hoyle is say it was pay-back for Kroun's death."

"Smart stuff, Boss."

"Would it fool New York?"

He shrugged. "Depends whether they *want* to believe him or not. Could be Kroun's got pals back there who don't like him much, and they have Mitchell here to bump him. We get the blame. You will, anyway. Far as New York goes, they don't know you and don't want you."

"The feeling's mutual, I'm sure. We gotta find out one way or another from Hoyle."

"Not easy. I might have a chance to talk with him, but otherwise he'll start shooting. He's got a grudge on for you, and I never heard of him holding back ever on one of those."

"He'll just have to take his chances. I'm not feeling too damned kind-hearted toward him, either."

The area Strome drove to was one of those little pockets of the city where the deep-night creeps could make themselves very much at home. During the day it was a place of cheap shops and small factories with obscure names turning out God-knows-what for who-knows-why. The grimy building fronts indicated business wasn't good, but struggling along. At noon the workers could descend upon the corner bar at the end of the street for a quick beer, sop up the sports scores, and lay bets down for the next event with their friendly local bookie. It was very likely part of Gordy's operation, and if I troubled to walk down there and give my name, I'd have his same level of respect.

Or be shot at. Territorial concerns were ongoing and strong in this town.

Strome parked the car and pointed. At the other end of the block from the bar was a low, one-storied structure. It looked like it had started out to be one thing, then changed to another halfway through, then no one finished the job. Brick and mortar with blackened windows, the roof was sheet tin that cracked and rattled as the wind passed over it. Part of one wall had been cut wide enough for cars to roll inside. There was no real driveway into it, someone had simply smashed the curb down and hauled off the rubble, so the change from street level was fairly abrupt. A faded sign next to it offered rates and a number to call.

We crossed the street, looking both ways a lot.

No watchman seemed to be on duty; the place was purely to park a car under shelter and good luck to you if it was still there in the morning. Actually, they just might be very safe there. Organized thieves would know better than to go after anything belonging to the mobs, and wise-guy stink was all over this block.

Nothing much to see, about twenty cars parked nose to the wall, ten to a side, all berths full. No lights. There was a string of bulbs hanging from a wire running down the middle length of the building, but a thrifty landlord had switched off the juice.

The racket from the stage-thunder tin roof was first nerve-racking, then annoying. The pops and bangs were irregular, and if anything else made a noise, I might not hear it.

The far end wall had been likewise cut open for a wide entry, but one of the berths was empty. I thought that might have been Hoyle's space and he'd long cleared out, but there was his car right next to it. I remembered the color from when he'd run the shooting gallery in front of my club. Good news at last. I hoped he'd be close to his transportation.

Right against the wall next to the entry were cement stairs leading down. The steel door at the bottom had a serious-looking bolt-type lock. Strome said Hoyle might be hiding out down there. I don't know how Strome thought he'd be able to talk his way in. When I gently tried the knob, it turned, but the door remained fast shut.

Strome produced a skeleton key and got the lock open, then shot me a sideways look. "Better let me go in first."

"I'm boss. It's my job. You watch my back and come if I yell. Get up top and keep your eyes open, he might not be in, and I don't want him surprising me."

He didn't much like that, but went up the stairs. As soon as he was out of sight, so was I. The gap at the bottom of the door was more than wide enough, sparing me from having to sieve through the bricks. I hated that.

I very slowly re-formed on the other side.

The pessimist in me expected to find pitch-darkness, but light there was, electric, its source at the other end of a cellar that was as wide and long as the building above. It strongly reminded me of Lady Crymsyn's basement before we changed everything. This one didn't look like any amount of new paint and lights would ever chase away the shadows.

The rough ceiling was low and, from where I stood, only a bare inch above my head. A long passage flanked by walls and support columns led the way to what might be a partitioned-off room; there was a blanket hanging across the opening. I breathed to get a scent of the place; the thin vapor hung miserably in the air. Cozy. The smell was of damp cement, oil, gasoline, with a strong hint of urine and sewer stink.

No bloodsmell. Encouraging. Quite a huge relief, too. I'd been mentally sweating about what might be down there.

Breathe in, sort out the flavors . . .

And there . . . very faint . . . human sweat.

It acquires a truly distinctive tang after reaching a certain age. This sample wasn't quite to the level of workhouse bum, that would take another couple weeks; so someone else was using the place for shelter. A dump like this was for emergencies only. Hoyle's circumstances must have qualified.

I also picked up cigarette smoke and . . . perfume?

The crazy thought that Hoyle had gotten lonely and hired some company to help pass the time danced through my head. Then a far more insane idea cropped up: Evie Montana.

If he'd killed Alan Caine, too . . . oh, hell. Had to get down to the end, see if she was still alive.

I'd been right about the noisy tin ceiling; it almost covered a humming sound coming from the direction of the light. Partially transparent, I moved cautiously forward for several yards, floating silent over the uneven floor. Coming to rest just short of the source of the light, I went solid, hugging the wall, and listened.

And son of a bitch, he was *behind* me.

Began to turn, began going transparent again.

"Hold it!" Hoyle's voice boomed in the confined space.

I halted the turn and the change. If he shot me, it wouldn't kill, but it'd hurt like hell. Hoyle thought he was in charge, but that could be a valuable advantage.

Half-turned, I glimpsed his revolver aimed square on me, and the muzzle was for at least a .32. Of course, from my angle it gave the illusion of being much larger. He was ten or twelve feet away. He could hit me if he wanted to, and he was right on the edge for it.

"Hands up! Stay right like that."

No problem. I raised my arms up and out, mostly out.

"How the hell did you get in?" he asked.

I thought his first question would be how the hell had I made myself float around half-invisible. The light was pretty bad in the alcove, though. He'd seen me come in, but perhaps only as a shape in the darkness, and could have missed the real fun. He might not even know it was me. One way to find out.

"I bought tickets. There's a bunch more of us on the way to take in the show."

"*Fleming?*"

"Yeah." I went semi again, expecting him to shoot. Counted to five. Nothing. Wanted to see his face. Solidified, I turned a little more.

"I said hold still!"

I cooperated.

"Out there. March."

I assumed he meant go to the end of the line where the light was and ducked under the hanging blanket. Since he didn't fire when I did that, I must have called it right.

He had more space than my walled-up sanctuary, but that was all the nice you could say about it. A mechanic's light hung from a nail, casting harsh shadows. There were bits of debris on the floor, empty tin cans, a lot of beer bottles. In one far area were some relatively clean boxes with warning and danger signs painted all over them. Next to those, spools of wire and less identifiable things, and tools. I knew just enough about bomb-making to be uneasy.

More prosaically, a pile of blankets lay on an aged army cot, and close to it stood an electric heater, the source of the humming sound. Home sweet hideout. Evie Montana, still wearing Alan Caine's tan coat, was tied up on the cot, a rag stuffed in her mouth, a blindfold on. Her body was tensed head to toe, listening.

I paused in the middle, feeling the ceiling pressing hard, and started to face him.

"No, you stay just like that." Hoyle was close behind, but not too close. I could still spin and take the gun away much faster than he could react, but he'd talk more if he thought he was the boss.

"Okay, you got me. Gonna bash my brains in like you did for Ruzzo?" That was one danger that was real for me, I was exceptionally vulnerable to any weapon made from wood. So long as he had only a gun, I was fairly safe.

"What do you know about it?" he snarled.

"I found what you left of them not long back. Then I talked with some guys, and they said where you kept your heap. Just call me Sherlock Junior. Why'd you do it?"

"Maybe they had it coming."

"That's all?"

"An' they knew some things they shouldn't."

"Like about the bomb Mitchell had you put on Gordy's car?"

"Who told you that?"

"I figured it out. You're going to have to buy Gordy a new car, you know."

"Stupid punk. Think you're so damned funny, think the sun rises and sets on your ass?"

"Not quite." No point sharing the irony of that with him.

"Well, there's some of us who know how things really work around here, and punks like you don't know squat."

"Why don't you tell me, then?"

He fired the gun. The bang was deafening.

I flinched, but was unharmed. The bullet bit a hole in the wall in front of me, above and to the right. I'd fired three into the ground next to his head, this was just returning the favor. We were lucky the mortar was soft and the bricks crumbly. A ricochet would have made this room a hell of a lot smaller, fast.

"How do *you* like it?" he asked.

"I'm gonna faint in a few days if there's much more excitement."

Another shot. I'd expected it, so I didn't flinch as much. My ears rang. I swallowed, trying to clear them.

"And that?"

"Hoyle, this wall's getting pretty boring. Even looking at your mug would make a change." I started to turn, but he told me to stay put again, his voice going up. Bad sign. He was the boss of the room, but he was nervous. "What's the matter? You think I can still follow through on what I said about killing you the other night? *You've* got the gun."

"I know how you work. I heard the boys talk. They say you can just look at someone and get them to do what you want."

"That's right. That's how I grew up to be president of these United States. I talked everyone into voting for me."

"Shuddup!"

Quiet now. Creepy to hear his breathing so near. Surprising it was that I could hear anything after the gunfire boom. I waited until he seemed more settled. "You got me. Now what?"

"I kill you."

"Not a good idea. Gordy's on the mend—"

"Gordy's on the outs! You can't hide behind him no more."

"I never did. I was only saying that you bumping Ruzzo is one thing, but bumping me . . . very bad idea. Too many people will go after you for that one."

"Yeah, and if I don't take you out, you'll still be after me."

"Not necessarily. Depends on what information you can give about Mitchell's plans."

"I don't know nothing."

"He told you plenty. That's how he was able to talk you into the bomb. He wanted Kroun removed and thought you'd be the best bet. Am I right? Then he sees to it you're protected from payback . . ." A new thought popped into my head. "Of course this place ain't his idea—it's yours. You're hiding from him."

No response.

"An' the only reason you'd wanna hide from him is if *he'd* killed Ruzzo. It's a double cross. Am I right?"

"Maybe."

"Come on, help me out here and help yourself. What happened with Ruzzo?"

"I went there and found 'em like that. It wasn't me."

"But you emptied their wallets, didn't you?"

"What if I did? They weren't needin' it."

"You were hiding with them?"

"At first. Then Mitch came over, an' we got to talkin'. He knew me from when he worked for Morelli. I tol' him how you was screwing things up, so we went off private for a drink and made some plans."

The plans being to send Kroun and me in pieces to kingdom come. "You make your bomb here?"

"In his hotel room; I was hiding with him for a day. I'd moved outta Ruzzo's place, but left some things, an' when I went back . . ."

"Must have been a shock." From which he quickly recovered and was able to coolly pick their pockets for spare cash. Nice guy. "Where's Mitchell?"

Silence.

"Why have you got the girl here?"

"Why do you think?"

He was just egging me. There were still bullets left. I make a move and boom. He'd want that. "You got the girl because Mitchell wanted her. Now why in the middle of all this malarkey does he want a date?"

"You tell me."

I couldn't see Hoyle's hands, couldn't see if they were scratched up or not, but the fact that he'd not killed Evie sparked a new line of thought about Caine's and Jewel's murders. "Because she knows something she shouldn't. Because he's afraid of her."

"Mitchell afraid of a twist." Contempt in his tone.

"Because he thinks she saw him kill Alan Caine."

More silence.

"But you worked that out already, didn't you? So why did Mitchell kill Alan Caine?"

"Damn you . . ."

"Come on, Hoyle. Bump me, and Gordy feeds you to the fish. You can definitely count on Mitchell disappearing you—you know too much. But ease off, and you get out alive."

"Mitch won't kill me."

"The hell he won't. He has to give New York a corpse for killing Kroun, and you're it. But I've got people waiting to grab him. If we walk into Gordy's office and say the same thing, he's toast. You can say he asked you to make a bomb, only he didn't say for what. I *can* get you clear."

"Why should you?"

"Because I'm just really tired of people getting killed. Kroun took me down a notch tonight because of that. Almost the last thing he said was I didn't have it in me to order people killed, and he was right. I'll look after myself and my own, but I don't mark through names on a page."

"No guts."

"That's right. But I can get you clear. Evie can back us up, too."

"You kiddin'? She's an idiot. That's how I got her so easy. She was dumb enough to go back home to pick up an extra pair of socks, then take a ride from a stranger. But what a mouth for saying a whole lot of nothing."

I could imagine that's why he'd gagged her, so he wouldn't have to listen to her talk. He'd likely questioned her, though, and figured out why Mitchell wanted her. "You wanna get out of this breathing? What d'ya say?"

He didn't say anything while I stared at the wall.

"C'mon, Hoyle." I must have cut close to the bone, given him too much to think about. Counted a slow ten, then said, "If we don't do what Mitchell expects, don't kill each other . . . then we can both go after him. We win, he loses."

A very long silence. Cautiously, I tried turning again. He let me get all the way around.

He looked bad. Unsteady on his feet, having to brace with one hand on the ceiling, unshaved, and eyelids twitching. He was scared. Of me. I understood now. My threat to kill him, with or without eye whammy, was something he'd taken to heart.

"Where's Mitchell?" I gently asked.

"I donno. If I did, he'd be dead."

"We need him alive to take the whole blame."

"None of that matters," he said.

I recognized the finality of his tone. Scared or not, he'd made up his mind. "I get ya. It's how it's supposed to be. You can come clean with me, I won't be walking out with anything you say. Why did he kill Caine?"

Hoyle made a slow smile. On his broken, rawboned face it was a very unpleasant sight. "You'll never guess." He centered the aim of the gun. "And you'll never know . . ."

Even as I rushed forward and grabbed—

—another gun went off and Hoyle's right eye exploded in a puff of red that splattered hot on my face. Bone and brain hit a fraction behind that, and Hoyle dropped heavily on me.

I reeled under his sudden weight, dizzy from the abrupt change, struck the wall, and felt my legs go. Couldn't do anything but fall over with his body on me, my wet face against the freezing concrete floor, arms loose, hands spasming. Too much like that other place where Bristow had . . .

No . . . please, God, no not again . . .

The stuff within unsympathetically took over, set me to groaning and shivering as though from malaria. I was cold inside and out and empty and lost in the dark forever; it would never let go its grip. I might as well declare a surrender and vanish.

But I couldn't. A dim part of me was aware I had a witness who'd already seen too much.

"Boss? Hey, Boss? Fleming? What is it?" Strome's voice cut into my fog. There was a concern in his tone that told all I needed to know about what he saw at the freak show.

The weight lifted as he dragged Hoyle's body off me.

"You're okay," Strome insisted. "I got him. It's over! Hey! It's over!"

Oh, God . . .

I pulled my arms in tight, tried to suppress the shaking. Locked my jaw, refused to let any more sound escape.

Nothing to do but wait for it to fade. I hated him seeing me like this. God, I felt sick.

The humiliation finally played itself out.

Strome knelt on one knee next to me, gun in hand, his stone face showing worry. "Jeez, I dint know you were so bad off. Thought for a second he shot you. You okay, now? You need a doctor or somethin'?"

"I told you to say put," I rasped. A change of topic. Anything so long as it wasn't about me.

"Seemed like I waited there long enough. Thought I should check on you. Good thing you left that key in the lock on the outside. Heard you guys, saw he had the drop on you. Jeez, you ain't mad 'cause I killed him, are ya?"

Shook my head. I felt a lot of things, but mad wasn't one of them. I was too tired and ashamed of my weakness to feel anything else.

"I'll back up whatever you wanna say about this," Strome added.

"I don't wanna say squat. Ever. If we work this right, Mitchell gets the heat for it."

"Sounds good. You need help?"

I was making ready to stand, and let him take some of my weight as I struggled up.

"You find out where Mitchell is?" he asked.

"No." I paced a little to make sure my legs weren't just fooling, making a point not to look at Hoyle's long form huddled on the floor. My face was still wet with his blood. I went to the hanging blanket and tried to wipe away the evidence. It'd take an all-day dip in that damned lake to clean this kind of stuff from my soul.

"Who's the twist?" He noticed Evie Montana. She lay so still I thought she'd been shot, too, but it was an animal's defense. Stillness meant you could be overlooked.

I went to Evie and told her who I was and to relax, she was going home. I said this before removing her gag and blindfold. Her eyes were crazy; I thought she might be in shock. She wasn't talking any. I found my folding knife and cut off the bonds, massaging her wrists, told her everything was going to be all right.

She must have been chilled through, but her flesh felt very warm to me, very soft and warm. I liked the feel of it too much. She looked up into my eyes, blanched, and launched clumsily off the cot toward Strome. She fit right under one of his arms. He looked surprised that anyone would come to him for protection.

"Take her up to the car, drive her where she wants," I said.

"What about you?"

Ignored him. "Tell Derner everything. Mitchell killed Alan Caine and Jewel Caine, God knows why. He's running loose, I want him landed. I'll look through this mess in case there's a lead to him. Now get out."

He got out, taking the strangely silent Evie with him.

I waited until they were quite gone, until the only sounds were caused by the heater and the wind playing on the tin roof. I waited, and if my heart had been working, it would have been going faster than any drum.

My brain was frozen, but the rest of me moved just fine.

My hands shook as I turned Hoyle so he was faceup. I pulled on his coat and shirt, opening them, freeing his neck.

Hovered over him, wavering, feeling the press of appetite. A part of me that stood outside myself looked down at the dangerous, crazy man crouched on the floor next to a body so freshly dead it was still twitching. Hoyle was gone—there was nothing left in his eyes—but that shot in the brain hadn't stopped everything yet. I heard that after death the brain could still send out messages, and the flesh, not knowing the futility of it, would try to respond.

My corner teeth were out.

And here was my food.

I dug into his exposed neck with the same force I used on the Stock-yards cattle, ripping the skin to open the big vein. When I was with Bobbi I never went so deep. The smaller veins close to the surface were suffi-cient. If I went in like this, tearing into her carotid, she would die, bleed-ing to death in seconds.

Didn't have to worry about that with Hoyle.

I fastened my mouth on the flesh and drew on the blood. Even without a heart to pump there was plenty for me. Death was in that first taste, not life. Dark, heavy, fascinating, and final.

For everyone else.

The realization flared through me like a storm.

It was my nature to feed from this kind of destruction. I was immune, so my craving for death was a safe, fundamental thing, inherent to what I'd become. Really. It had been like that with Bristow as he hung upended like a slaughtered animal, his blood flooding me, bringing me back from the edge. I'd thought the shadow taint was from his booze, but now I knew it had been his dying.

Another long draft, then I made myself lift away, sat up, and let it work in me. The cattle blood was pure and filling sustenance, but human blood satisfied another kind of hunger.

Or rather appetite.

They're different.

The awful and eager thing within urged me to go back for more, to empty him, take everything he had to try to fill my own void.

He won't need it, and didn't the taste feel so good?

This was why I so freely drained it from the cattle, trying to capture the too-swift thrill of red life that can only come from humans. Living, dying, or already dead, it didn't matter.

Yes, it was good. Much too good. I liked this far too much.

That was ugly to know.

But I continued to drink from this broken vessel, not caring, not caring as my soul slipped away.

THE next time I noticed anything besides blood, I was on the street, walking hunched over, hands in my pockets. My face was very cold at first, especially around my mouth. That was where Hoyle's blood had smeared.

I found a drift of snow and scooped some to clean up a little. Left behind a lot of fresh red on the pavement. Kept walking. I wasn't sure where I was and didn't have the energy to worry about it. My mind was fogged in. I wanted to sleep, but that wasn't going to happen. It was almost like being drunk, except with the opposite effect on my senses. I heard and saw everything, only none of it was worth my attention.

So I walked and walked and hated what was in my head, hated what I had become. Now *I* was one of those deep-night predators. Always had been. It had just taken me longer to figure it out.

With a kind of internal "Huh, how about that?" I realized I'd walked all the way to Lady Crymsyn. The look of the street seemed changed, but that was my doing. I was changed, and my perceptions made the world different.

I had company. Coldfield's car was in Crymsyn's lot next to Escott's. I tried the front door. It was locked, but, no problem, just vanish.

Listened when I went solid again.

Radio music upstairs, low conversation from the main room. Light on behind the bar as usual.

I whispered. "Hi, Myrna, I'm back. How was your evening?"

Nothing blinked in response. Maybe she was enjoying the radio in my office.

Wandered into the main room. Escott, Coldfield, and Isham had taken over a large round table closest to the curving passage. Before them was a litter of glasses, full ashtrays, and cartons gutted of their Chinese food. The boys were playing cards and hailed me as I came in. I stood in the shadows of the curved entry.

"Something wrong?" asked Coldfield.

I shook my head.

"Jack!" said Escott. "Derner called to say that Evie Montana is alive and well and that the other problems have been solved, but he refused to go into detail on the phone."

I stepped clear of the shadows.

"My God, is that blood on you?"

I looked at their alarmed and questioning faces and realized this long night was about to drag on even longer.

God, I wanted a drink. The old-fashioned, alcoholic kind. It was safer than the other stuff.

TALKING about it made it real all over again. That's why I'd sent Strome to deal with Derner. I didn't like the remembering or the taste of the words. The bloodsmell clung to me; I seemed to notice it more here. I skipped the ugly business with Hoyle. Even I didn't want to know that part, but was stuck with it. When I finished, the atmosphere had turned irredeemably gloomy, and no one seemed to want to speak first.

"Everything was quiet here?" I asked after a moment.

Escott stirred slowly, as though reluctant to move.

He shot a look at Coldfield, who asked, "What about this Mitchell bird? Your guys covering places like the train station and the buses?"

I almost winced at his calling them "your guys." They weren't mine, just borrowed. "Mitchell probably won't leave until he's killed Hoyle. He doesn't know he's dead yet." The leftover smears of Hoyle's blood seemed to pull at my skin. I wanted to wash them off. "Mitchell's our proof. If we can bring him in alive and send him back to New York in one piece, that'll clear up the whole mess and keep Gordy from getting blamed for Kroun."

"But Kroun's death happened while you were on watch. Won't they be blaming you?"

"It'll still come back on Gordy because he put me in charge. My reputation's not hot with the big boys, but I can live with that."

"You sure?"

"I'm sure. No problem."

COLDFIELD, Isham, and Escott went off their separate ways. I told them I was tired and wanted to clean up. Escott gave me an odd look, but didn't say anything. I felt sorry for him.

Once I'd locked up I went to the basement, turning on all the lights. We had a small workshop there with tools and other equipment. I found what I needed and made what I wanted. It took about an hour to make and get the fit perfect. I'd only need one.

Then I went upstairs and showered. Emptied the hot-water tank again. No matter. It still didn't warm me. I was past shivering, though, cold and numb inside and out.

Up to my office. Bathed, shaved, fresh clothes. They used to improve my frame of mind. Not tonight. Fortunately, there wasn't much night left.

I found a box of stationery and used a few pages. In the end none of the pathetic scribbles seemed right, so I tossed them in the trash.

Dawn was a minute away when I stretched on the couch. I would fight off the temporary death to the last second so it would seize me faster, preventing the awful paralysis from taking over a slow inch at a time.

Only a few seconds to go, my body beginning to stiffen up, I lay flat and shut my eyes. I sensed the sun's approach and fought it, fought its weight on my bones, its freezing of my joints.

When I was utterly anchored in place, so solid that it would be impossible to vanish and heal, I knew it was time—and that I could do it.

Absolutely my last conscious act was to put my revolver's muzzle to my right temple and pull the trigger.

16

I hurtled awake shrieking, then vanished almost in the same instant. The agony abruptly ceased, and, floating in the grayness, my dazed mind slowly grasped the appalling truth that I'd failed.

Solid again. Lying as before on the office couch. Bloodsmell on my left. A spray of long-dried rust brown blood on the lighter brown leather by my head. Hole in the leather from my carefully crafted wooden bullet. It'd passed right through my skull.

I still lived. Would continue to live.

God *damn* it.

Then I noticed Escott standing over me.

I'd never seen such a look on his face. Infinite rage. Infinite pain. It was raw as an open wound and still bled, the pain carving deep lines into his gray flesh.

"You bastard," he whispered.

I made no response.

His eyes blazed, hot enough to scorch what was left of my soul. Why couldn't I have just stayed dead?

"You bastard. You idiotic, selfish *bastard*." There was enough venom in his voice to kill an elephant.

I stopped meeting his gaze. Maybe he would get fed up and leave, then I'd find some other place to be at dawn and try again. Next time, a shotgun. Wood pellets in the cartridges. Ugly. I'd have to blow my whole head off. So be it . . .

Anger like a living force rolled from Escott to smash against my body. For a second I thought he had hit me. His fists shook at his sides. He trembled all over. "You bloody *coward*! Did you even *think* how it would be for her walking upstairs, opening the door, and *finding* you?"

Bobbi. He was talking about Bobbi.

"How could you *do* that to her?"

I'd done it *for* her. He just didn't understand. "She saw?"

"No, thank God. Instead *I* came in first and found you."

I shrugged. Better him than Bobbi, I guess.

"I've waited all day to see if you'd bloody wake up. *All bloody day,* DAMN *you!*"

"And I woke up," I murmured to myself.

His lips twisted. Teeth showed. "How could you *do* this to—"

"Because I *hurt*, dammit!"

"And how do you think *she'd* have felt?"

"She'd get over it. She's better off without me. Everyone is."

I saw it coming and didn't duck. He hauled back and landed one square and hard, one of his best. It knocked me clean from the couch. He'd know I wouldn't feel much; this clobbering was about expressing anger, not to cause pain. I had plenty of that already.

"Get your head out of your backside and think of somebody else for a change—"

"*I was!* Don't you *see?* I'm no good to her or anyone like this. And I *hurt*!"

"We *all* hurt! But you *don't* inflict your pain on others by doing this!"

I dragged off the floor onto the couch again. "Yeah-yeah, well, too bad, I thought it over, and it's better for everyone if I'm gone."

He called me a bloody coward again and knocked me over again. Much harder. The second time made bruises.

Dammit. Why couldn't he just leave me alone? I started to get up . . .

He got a good one square on my nose. I heard and felt it break. While he rubbed his battered knuckles and glowered, I sat ass flat on the floor with blood slobbering down my chin.

"What the hell's with you?" I snarled, snuffling messily at the flow. "You *know* what I went through!"

"That's no excuse!"

"It *is*. I'm never gonna get better from it—"

"Not by killing yourself you won't!"

"*I can't live like this!* Every night it gets worse—"

"So you have a few bad memories, poor, poor fellow. It gave you a reaction you don't like. Very scary, I'm sure. You're going to let *that* destroy you? Destroy Bobbi—"

"It's not your business, Charles. This is *my* choice, only I know what it's like in my head, not you!"

"I know what it's doing to the people who care about you. Don't you give a tinker's damn what you're doing to Bobbi?"

"Since when do you have to butt in about her? I never asked."

"But *she* did! We're here to help, but you shut us out—especially Bobbi. You're ripping her apart."

"That's what I'm trying *not* to do! This is to save her, dammit!"

"How?" he demanded.

The words stuck in my throat.

"*How?*" he roared. He rose, loomed over me.

"Because . . ."

"What? Come on, tell me! Save her from what?"

I couldn't. It was too much. "Go to hell. Just goddamn get out and go to hell!"

"Tell me!"

I got up, grappled him, pulled him toward the door to throw him out before I lost myself. Bloodsmell clogged my nose, in another minute I'd fall into another damned fit. He could sell tickets to the freak show.

Then he got his arms up and twisted and somehow slipped my grip and threw another punch, this time driving deep into my gut. There was surprising force behind it, powered by adrenaline and sheer fury; I doubled over and dropped.

His face was so distorted I didn't know him. "Tell me! You don't *know*, do you?"

I spat blood. "Get out! It's none of your damn—"

Then he really started in. Brakes off. Down the mountain. Full tilt.

Escott was *always* in control of himself. That iron reserve had only ever slipped once. He'd been blind drunk, then. Now he'd gone lunatic. He got me up only to knock me over, and when I was down he slammed my head against the wood floor again and again, cursing me over and over under his ragged breath.

Wood damaged, could kill me—and he knew it.

I didn't fight, wanting him to cut loose. If he pounded me unconscious, that'd be one less night I'd have to suffer through. He pummeled until his sweat ran and his face went bloated and scarlet from the effort, until his breath sawed and he finally lost his balance and fell against the desk and ended on the floor, too, glaring at me. That look said I'd made the right choice about killing myself.

He hated me, they all did for what I was doing to them. I had to get myself away from it, spare them from the wreckage Bristow's torture had left. No one needed to see me like this. *I* didn't want to see me like this.

Neither of us moved for a time. I lay in the pain and stared at the ceiling and ignored Escott. My head thundered, and when I blinked the ceiling dipped and pulled a sick-making half spin. Shut my eyes, kept still. With no need to breathe it was as close to being dead as I could get at night. Not close enough, though.

I felt it come. The churning within, bursting outward from my battered guts, settling cold into my bones, hearing that pathetic whimper leaking between my clenched teeth as the shakes took me.

Escott suddenly within view, staring down. Yeah, look, get a good look at the crazy man.

"Jack . . . ?"

Tried to vanish. Nothing doing. No escape. Was stuck solid because of the wood. *Damn you, Charles . . .*

"Jack, stop it!"

"I . . . c-can't!"

"Oh, yes, you bloody *can*."

He hit me again, an open-handed crack across the mouth.

It didn't work, either. Another strike. Another.

I was kitten weak, limbs thrashing, no control, and he kept *hitting* me.

Damn you . . .

"Come *out* of it, damn your eyes!"

Crack.

"You're better than this!"

Tried to push him off. Swatted hard with one arm, caught him firm in the rib cage.

He grunted, but kept hitting, harder, more frenzied. His eyes . . . he was right-out-of-his-mind berserk.

Using me for a punching bag. Wouldn't let up. All that rage . . .

"Dammit, Charles!"

". . . *bastard* . . ." Hitting. *Hitting.*

I hit back. Full force.

WASN'T sure when I woke out of it. Gradual return of awareness, of senses.

Of pain. A lot of that. Body pain for a change, not soul pain. That was there someplace, though. Had to be.

Pain followed by perception, then growing horror.

Escott's body lay across the office on the floor under the windows. He faced away from me and was very, very still.

Could not move myself. Only stare.

Oh, God . . . no.

"Ch-charles?"

No response. Stillness.

"Charles!"

Nothing.

I crawled over to him, afraid to touch him, but I had to see.

A heartbeat in the silence.

His.

Damn near fainted from the relief. There was life in him, but . . . turned him, very carefully. He was a bloody mess in the literal sense. I checked his eyes, rolled up in their sockets. He was definitely out for the count.

Crawled to the desk, dragged down the phone, and called for an ambulance. I could barely see to do it, barely speak to the operator.

He groaned as I hung up. Went back to him.

"Charles?"

He took his time answering, seemed to have trouble breathing. I went to the liquor cabinet and got the brandy. Wet his split lips.

"You bastard," he finally said.

"I'm sorry, Charles. I'm so sorry."

"Good."

"Help's on the way, you just hang on."

"Oh, I'm not dying yet. I won't give you the satisfaction, you sorry bastard."

"Just don't move. Is your breathing okay? Your ribs? I could have broken some."

"Shut up, Jack. Check me, see for yourself."

I didn't understand him, but he clawed for one of my hands and pulled it onto his chest. Something hard beneath his coat.

"Think I'm a total idiot? That I'd pick a fight with you without preparation?"

He had on his bulletproof vest. There was steel plating under my hand.

"I will have some hellish bruises, but nothing permanent."

"Oh, God. I thought I'd killed you. I thought you were dead."

"And how did it feel?"

"How do you *think*?"

"I already know, you fool." He sounded tired, tired to death. "I went through it for most of the day looking at your corpse, wondering if you'd wake at sundown. Not knowing, not daring to hope. Hours of it. The whole time wondering what I'd done, what I'd not done, how I'd failed you. Reading over and over the unfinished notes you wrote. Wondering how I could ever break the news to Bobbi."

Stunned, I watched tears stream from his eyes. He seemed unaware of them.

"And I *hated* you, Jack. I hated you for giving up. For not talking to us, to anyone. You gave up. I can't forgive you for that."

I lurched away, tottering blindly to the washroom, made it to the basin just in time.

It was all red. What was left of Hoyle's blood flooded out of me in a vast body-shaking spasm. I came close to screaming again. Or weeping. I hurt too much to know the difference.

When the bout passed, I crept back to the office and sat on the floor. I didn't trust myself not to fall out of a chair. Escott had propped himself up a little against the wall. His puffed and bruised eyes were hot with fresh anger.

"How long did Bristow torture you?" he asked.

What?

"How long did it go on? Tell me."

"Too long."

"How long? An hour, two?"

"An hour, I guess." I wouldn't have had enough blood in me to last beyond that. "So what?"

"An hour. Think of it. One hour."

I didn't want to think of it. "What are you getting at?"

"One. Hour. Out of the *whole* of your life."

What the . . .

"How many hours have you lived, Jack?"

"How the hell should I know?"

"How many hours are ahead of you?"

"Charles—"

"An unlimited span if you're careful. Are you going to let all that's come before and all that can follow be utterly destroyed by *one* tiny increment stacked against the broader span of time? It's one hour of your life, Jack. Only one."

"The worst I ever had."

"There's worse to come if you don't do something about yourself. And I don't mean eating a bullet. You've been letting that single hour control you. Hog Bristow is still torturing you so long as *you* allow it."

"*Allow?* You think I *want* this?"

"You're stuck in that damned meat locker until you make up your mind to leave."

"You don't understand. I've done things."

"Then *cease* doing them, you fool!"

"I can't help it."

"Of course you *can*! You're the strongest man I know! It's sickening to hear you bleat on like that. While you're buried in your hole for the day, Bobbi and I have to wonder what it's going to be like when you wake up. We're walking on eggs the whole night catering to you, trying not to add to your pain. Do you think we can't *see* you *bleeding* inside?"

"She hates me."

"You wallowing idiot! She loves you! You're so turned in on yourself you can't see that. You'd rather sit there and whine than accept such a precious gift."

"I could hurt her, the way I hurt you. Worse."

"Bollocks! Ultimately, *you* are in control, you are responsible. You can cower and let your fear run rampant like an ill-mannered child, or *you* can be in charge. Don't tell me you can't. If I can do it, you can, too."

"What do you mean?"

His look was steady and burning. "After what happened to my friends in Canada, those murders . . . they were my whole *family* for God's sake! Dead in one night. I couldn't sleep for months. Kept waking up screaming. Drank myself unconscious, and I still kept waking up. Nothing I ever faced in the War was that awful. It was Shoe who finally helped me realize I had to get control of myself or . . ."

"What?"

"Or he'd beat the hell out of me again." He paused, his gaze inward for a moment. Then, "*I* had to climb out of that pit. You're stronger now than I ever was then. And you're not alone. You are still *needed* here. This isn't your time."

I wanted to believe him.

"And however you think you could hurt Bobbi, it couldn't possibly be worse than taking yourself away. Don't put her through that, Jack. You're her rock. Don't crumble under her."

"She's strong."

"Because *you're* here! Stay! Stay for her sake. Or I swear I *will* beat the hell out of you again."

THE white-jackets came with a stretcher and for a couple of guys who had to have seen everything, they gave us a double take.

"You can't ride in with us," one of them told me. I figured he wasn't chancing my taking another shot at Escott.

"I'll follow then."

He didn't seem to like that idea. They carted Escott downstairs and were gone in a minute. I looked for my coat, couldn't find it, and borrowed Escott's instead. A very neat and organized man, he'd left it lying on the floor like old laundry. Must have had it draped over one arm when he'd walked in and seen the inert, bloodied mess on the couch. He'd have stood frozen in the doorway a moment, the coat slipping away . . .

The office phone rang, jolting me.

It was Bobbi.

This wasn't a good time to talk, but Escott would kill me if I brushed her off. "Hello, sweetheart. How are you?" I hoped nothing to tip her off was in my voice.

"Just *fine*," she said, sounding very cheerful and awake. Quite a change from the last call. Certainly she was unaware of what I'd tried to do. "When you coming over, Sweetie?"

Huh? "I can't right away, I've got to—"

"Oh, *Jacky*, you've been busy *every* night this week." Her voice went sharp, shrewish, petulant.

What the hell . . . ? I went cold. Deathly cold. "Well, Roberta, I got things to do."

She was pouty now, and completely ignored my use of her given name. "Oh, come on. I'll make it worth your while. Come on, you can spare a girl ten lousy minutes. Just come over and *do* it."

Sickness bloomed in my gut. "Well, maybe I could . . ."

"When you see what I'm *not* wearing, you'll wanna stay longer." She giggled seductively.

"Okay, but I gotta to do something first. I'll call again in an hour and let you know if I can get away. You'll have to hold your horses until then."

"You'll call in an hour?"

"And you better answer, sweetheart, or just forget about having any fun tonight."

"I'll be here. Make it a *fast* hour." She hung up.

Before I was aware of having moved I was down the stairs, heart in my throat.

But an apparition stood square in the middle of the lobby, blocking my way. I was in such a panic that the out-of-place presence didn't register. I nearly collided, then halted at the last second, backing in confusion from a snub-nosed revolver shoved hard into my belly.

Looked down at the gun, bewildered, backed another step, then truly *focused* on the man holding it: *Whitey Kroun.*

He was worse for wear, eyebrows gone and some hair singed off. There were cuts on his burn-reddened face, and his left hand was crudely bandaged. His torn and bloodied clothes stank of smoke and sweat, but he was standing, solid, and very much alive.

"Surprised?" he asked, his voice whisper-hoarse.

My lack of reply was answer enough.

"Thought you'd be." His dark eyes blazed. "All right, you son-of-a-bitch punk, you tell me why you tried to kill me."

"*What?*" I didn't have time for this.

"You set me up, but for the life of me I can't think why you would. What's your game, Fleming?"

"No game. It wasn't me."

"I had the car, so I had to be the target. Was it some kind of deal with Gordy?"

"Kroun, listen to me—"

"*Why?*" His arm straightened to fire. He would shoot to wound. Killing would come later.

"It was *Mitchell*, dammit! I got half of Chicago looking for him!"

Kroun hesitated. "Mitchell. No . . . I don't think so."

"Why the hell not?"

He made no reply.

"Listen, dammit—he got with one of his old pals from here and *they* cooked up the bomb. I donno if he wants to take over your spot in New York or Gordy's spot here like he wanted before, but you gotta believe me, *he's* the one who did it! Now put that damn thing away—I know where he's hiding!"

"Uh-huh. The hell you do." He swung the muzzle up toward my chest.

I moved faster than he could fire. Snagged the gun from his hand and gave him a push. He spun around, but without his heater he was in no shape to take me. On second look he was banged up pretty bad. I couldn't see how he was able to walk. He should have been in the ambulance with Escott.

I started for the door, then thought better of it. "You're comin' with me," I told him.

"Where?"

"Mitchell's got my girlfriend. You want proof? Come on." I hauled him out the door, pulling it closed behind, and going left. "Into that Nash."

Kroun was limping, his left trouser leg was crusted brown from dried blood. He wheezed badly. I gunned the motor, shifted, and shot us away.

"What's with you?" I asked.

"Got some smoke. Coughed most of it out by now, but jeez."

"What else?"

"Some burns, the concussion from the boom was the worst. Like someone hit me all over with a building."

"How the hell did you survive?"

"Gordy's car."

"What about it?"

"The damned thing's built like a safe. There's so much metal in it I'm guessing most of the blast went down and sideways, not up and out. The bomb was bad, but not enough to get around all that armor. It bought me a few seconds. I didn't know what I was doing, only that I was doing it. The whole thing was smoke inside, and I couldn't see, but I found the door handle and rolled clear and kept rolling. My eyes were watering, but there was another boom, and I just kept going. There were some trash cans on the street, and I hid behind them. They were full and didn't go flying like everything else, so I stayed there."

"And you didn't show yourself thinking I'd done that?"

"I was too damned hurt to think much of anything. The whole street was fulla stinkin' smoke, so I just got out of there before something else dropped on me."

"Where did you go?"

"Found an empty building. Picked the lock, went in, and coughed my guts out for a few hours."

"You couldn't call anyone? Even New York?"

"I was thinking again by then, and it didn't seem like such a good idea. With my looks I'd be too easy to spot walking around, and I don't know who's who in this town, so I sat tight and rested up. I thought I'd give it a day, then go after you for answers, but your goddamned club was closed."

"Yet you came in."

"I saw you and the guys with the ambulance. What the hell was that?"

"Me being stupid. Forget about it."

"How do you know Mitch is with your girl?"

"I think he made her phone me to get me to her place."

"She that singer, the blond?"

"Yeah. She tipped me off something was wrong, but I gotta get there fast in case she didn't get away with it."

"God, I hate this business," said Kroun, between clenched teeth.

I parked on the side of the hotel opposite Bobbi's flat. Mitchell could be watching from her windows and even from that high up might recognize me walking in. If he saw Kroun, it would be a disaster.

We went in through a smaller entry that led to the lobby and the elevators. There was still an operator on duty; I gave him the floor just above Bobbi's. He stared at Kroun, got a red-eyed stare in return then focused on his job. When he opened the doors again I waited until he descended before heading for the stairs at the end of the hall.

"What's this?" Kroun asked. He was gray of face as we hurried along.

"I don't want Mitchell hearing the elevator stop on her floor." At the service door, I listened, then cautiously opened it. The hall, identical to the one we'd left, was empty. "Okay, here's the deal: There's a servants entrance to her flat, and I've got the key. I can sneak in that way, but I need you to knock on the front door to get his attention."

"Then what?"

"Just knock. He might think it's me, so do it from the side in case he shoots through the door."

"Yeah, okay. Hand me back my piece."

"You won't need it."

"I sure as hell will. Don't worry, I'll only shoot him, not your girl."

I didn't want to trust him on that.

"I get my gun or you get no help. Come on."

Dammit. I gave it over. "But no shooting. You won't need to, anyway. I just need you to distract his attention. Stay here, count to a hundred, then knock loud."

He went into "one, two, three, four," and I counted along with him to match his pace. Kept counting softly as I slipped out, vanished, and sped forward, going solid just long enough to find Bobbi's door. Gone again, I sieved under it and listened as best I could in the grayness.

No one talking. Damn.

Nineteen, twenty . . .

Made a sweep of the front room and didn't encounter anyone. Tried the small kitchen. No one here, either. Decided to risk going solid.

Lights out, except for some spill from the living room. More than enough to see by. Listened. Would have held my breath if I'd had any.

Twenty-nine, thirty . . .

It took a few seconds to get it, like tuning in to a hard-to-find radio station. Vague movements, a heartbeat. More than one . . .

Invisible again, I floated toward her bedroom. Very much on purpose I wasn't thinking about certain things. If he'd touched her I would rip him apart. Literally.

No sound in this room. My muffled hearing worked against me. Swept through, located one person sitting on the bed, the second in a chair next to the telephone table. Another extravagant convenience of her very modern apartment was having two phones, one in the living room, the other just steps away, next to the bed. She usually kept that one in the bath so she could talk while soaking in the tub. Were they waiting for my call? And who was who? I could tell general shapes in this form, but nothing more specific. If one of them would just make a noise, I'd know who to tackle.

I drifted close to the one on the bed, brushing as light as I dared.

Unbelievable relief when Bobbi shivered and went *brrrrr.*

"What's the matter?" Mitchell asked from his seat by the phone.

"I'm cold. Can't I turn up the heat?"

"No. Pull on a blanket. Why is it you dames are always so damn cold all the time?"

Apparently recognizing a rhetorical question, she didn't reply.

Where the hell was Kroun? He should be knocking by now. Had he mistakenly gone to the other end of the hall? I could go solid and jump Mitchell, but I wanted Bobbi in the clear. He'd be armed and too many things could go wrong. I wanted them both—especially her—alive and safe.

"I know a way to warm you up," he said. "We got time."

Of course, *he* didn't absolutely have to be undamaged.

"Oh, *puh-lease*." A tone of voice like that always went with a rolling of the eyes.

"You turned into a real snot, didn't you? Slick had the right idea keeping you on a leash. You weren't too good for me then. You were plenty hot for me. I remember."

"I'd have been hot for a baboon if he coulda gotten me out of there."

"Well, you got a close second with Fleming. When the hell did he get to be such a big noise?"

"Just happened."

"I'll bet. You smelled the money and—What's that clicking?" he snapped.

Clicking? Then I remembered Kroun was an expert with picklocks. He wasn't going to wait or follow instructions . . .

Mitchell left the room. I went solid.

Bobbi suppressed her gasp of surprise, but it was enough to alert the nervous Mitchell. He stood in the living room facing the front door, but swung his gun at me.

"Fleming?" He was flat-footed for only an instant, then squared up the gun. Bobbi came forward; I shoved her back hard so she fell across the bed, then I started toward him. "Freeze!" he yelled.

I froze in the bedroom doorway, arms out. The .45 he carried would put holes through walls, and Bobbi was very much still in range. No shooting. Please.

The front door swung open. Kroun didn't show himself.

"Who is it?" Mitchell asked me.

I was within tackling distance, but wanted him distracted from me. "Your boss. It's payback time."

"What d'ya mean?"

"You missed with the bomb. Kroun's alive."

Mitchell laughed once. "No way. He's dead meat. Hoyle said—"

"Yeah, he did. He's dead, too, by the way."

"You're lying."

"Thought you'd be happy about it. You bumped Ruzzo, so of course you had to bump Hoyle. Can't leave witnesses to screw up you taking over Kroun's spot. That's what you're after, right? With Gordy still alive, you might never get a chance at this town, but there's no reason why you can't take Kroun's job if he's gone—only he ain't."

"Kroun's dead."

"Not so much," said Kroun. He eased around the front doorway, gun in hand, aimed at Mitchell. "So what's the story, Mitch? Anything to it?"

Mitchell didn't know how to handle failure and just stood there blank-faced a moment. Then he slowly went a deep, ugly red. I didn't read that as shame for what he'd done; this was sheer humiliation for having gotten caught. "How could you have . . . Hoyle said he'd—"

"Said what? Is that how it ran? You boys bump me to move up?"

"No! Hoyle was on his own. I didn't have nothing to do with—" Mitchell choked. It had to be impossible for him to think straight with a dead man asking such questions.

"C'mon, Mitch. You can tell me." Kroun's eyes seemed darker than ever, bottomless and hell-black.

Mitchell shook his head, abruptly recovering his internal balance. He wouldn't have time to aim the gun at Kroun, so he held fast on me. "Stand still, or I kill him," he said.

Kroun shrugged. "Go ahead. He's just another mug."

"I thought he was your new best pal."

"You would."

Mitchell went dead white, then red again. "Shaddup."

"With this in the picture some other stuff's making sense."

"What stuff?" I asked, drawing attention back to me. If we could keep him distracted enough . . .

"Alan Caine's murder," said Kroun. "Check Mitch's hands."

I'd seen. Gouges and scratching from Caine's nails as he tried, in a very few seconds, to fight his killer off. "Heh. Guess you could call that 'the mark of Caine.'"

Kroun wheezed a short, unpleasant laugh. "Ya think?"

Mitchell told us to shut up, face getting redder.

I didn't listen. "So why did you do it? Did Caine overhear you and Hoyle? Did Jewel Caine see you running away?"

Sweat, lots of sweat pouring from him. The stink of cigarettes.

"I'll tell you why," Bobbi called. She'd rolled off the other side of the bed and was on the floor in the far corner against the wall. There was a full bookcase between her and harm. Sensible girl. "He had to shut Jewel up, too. Jewel would have guessed."

"Guessed what?" Kroun asked, his thick voice still fighting against the smoke damage.

"What Mitchell—"

"Shaddup!" Mitchell practically screamed it. "Shaddup or your boy-friend gets it!"

But Bobbi could count on me being mostly bulletproof. "Mitch and Alan Caine got drunk one night. *Real* drunk. I heard it from Jewel. Alan bragged about it to her to hurt her, the bastard."

"Shaddup, you lying bitch!"

"Alan liked women *and* men! Mitch was so drunk that—"

Mitchell fired through the wall, too high. I was on him, a full body tackle. He kept shooting.

Grabbed his gun hand and yanked at a bad angle for him. He yelped and bucked, trying to twist around, but kept a solid grip. He was mad out of his mind and stronger than he looked. I used my other hand to slam his head sharp against the floor and still he fought.

I tried to take the gun. Another shot. The bullet went through my palm, but I was too pissed to feel it. Gut-punched him, blood flying. He didn't notice. Had gone crazy. We rolled and kicked and hit, and he fired again. How many goddamn bullets were in this thing?

His hand over my face, fingers digging in my eyes, I turned away . . .

And glimpsed Kroun, his arm out, his own gun ready, coldly and carefully choosing his moment. His face was blank, eyes gone black with that hell-pit look; he seemed a different man altogether. Fast as things were moving, I still felt a swift, icy jolt of panic. When a man's soul isn't there, you know, you just *know* it, and you don't want to be anywhere near what it's left behind.

Mitchell saw it, too, his own damnation staring down. He wrenched his gun around and up with that strange, desperate strength.

Two shots. Close. Deafening.

And it was over. Mitchell went inert, his body collapsing on top of me in a horrible reprise of Hoyle's death. Bloodsmell, blood pouring onto me, warm and still vital . . .

I threw him violently off, scrabbled over the floor to get clear of the thing he'd become, terrified that another seizure would rip away what sanity remained in me.

Then Bobbi was there. I caught her up, maybe too hard, but she kept telling me everything would be all right, it was okay . . . *Jack, it's okay . . .*

I waited, fighting it, waited, forcing down the shudder that tried to rise.

Fighting.

Her voice helped. A soft, melodious, songlike droning as she held me, reassured me.

I allowed myself a single, choking sob. There was more in me, eager for its turn to emerge from the darkness. I couldn't think about it, about what it might do if it got out, what it might be. Another siezure, or would the mindless craving take me over? If that happened and I hurt Bobbi . . .

I made myself focus on her sweet voice, the feel of her arms around me. I held on to that distraction from the internal demons. She was real, but they were so . . .

You are in control, you are responsible. You're stronger now than I ever was then.

Hard to believe. But Escott had never lied to me. He was right. I had a choice about being in charge or not. Of giving up and—

And however you think you could hurt Bobbi, it couldn't possibly be worse than taking yourself away. Don't put her through that, Jack. You're her rock. Don't crumble under her.

No. I wouldn't do that to her. She deserved better. I had to *try,* to believe that I could beat this.

Don't tell me you can't. If I can do it, you can, too.

Hell of a tough act to follow.

Stay for her sake. Or I swear I will beat the hell out of you again.

Damn you, Escott . . .

Something brittle and sharp inside seemed to break up and fall away, suddenly allowing my soul to breathe again.

There were no words for what it was, I just understood that something had shifted and *it* was gone.

Over.

Past.

Done.

It had been heavy. So damned heavy. Only when the weight was no longer there did I understand how heavy it had been.

Then it was my turn to collapse. I sank to my knees, and Bobbi came with me, letting me lean on her. God, but I needed her.

And Escott said that I was *her* rock.

"Jack?"

After a moment, I dredged a smile for her. "Hey, baby. You okay?"

"How 'bout yourself?"

"Just peachy." It felt so good, her holding me, but the hurt on my hand . . . it was knitting up, but damn, that burned. "'Scuse me a sec."

I vanished, came back. Much better now. Much . . .

Kroun—he'd have seen—

Turned to look. He hadn't seen anything. He'd caught a bullet.

He sprawled flat, a hole in his chest that bubbled air every time he moved. The pain had him helpless and gasping, and blood ran from his mouth. I knew the signs, he didn't have a minute left.

I went to him. Knelt close.

"Fleming." My name made more blood come out of him. He coughed and tried to suck air past the stuff clogging his throat. The smell filled the room, but now I was able to ignore it.

"I'm here, what can I do?" Hell, what *can* you do for a dying man? He looked like himself again, though. Whatever he had for a soul was back again, struggling hard to stay, but losing as his body failed.

"Mitch. Dead?"

Had to look. "He's dead."

"'Fraid I'd missed. Your girl?"

"She's fine. You hold on, I'll get a doctor."

"Past that." Coughed. "Damn stuff. First I burn my lungs, now this. Life ain't fair."

"No, it ain't."

"Promise . . ."

"Anything."

"No fish food."

What?

"No lake. No chopping. No oil drums. You bury me proper. No cremat . . ."

"I promise. Kroun? I promise. You hear?"

Then the rattle. His last breath going out. The slack stillness that went on forever.

Oh, damn. Damn it all. He couldn't have known about my nature. If he'd just held off I could have . . .

Feeling very old, I stood. Went to Bobbi. Had to hold her again, hold her and get and give comfort, quick before dread practicalities rose up.

"Your neighbors . . . the shots . . ." I finally said.

"We'll bluff them out. I'll say I was rehearsing a radio skit, a-a-and the fake gun was louder than it should be. I'll make 'em believe it."

"Just don't let anyone in. You're not staying here tonight, either."

"Damn right I'm not."

"I'll get you over with Gordy and Adelle. Shoe can look out for you all until this is cleared."

"God, Jack, what will you do?" She looked at the bodies. Any other girl might have fainted. Instead, she held on to me.

"I gotta call Derner, get some boys over here to clean up."

"But how will you explain?"

"I'm not. I won't have to with them, but no cops. We can't. I'm not putting you through that kind of hell. Mitchell can be disappeared."

She went pale, knowing what that meant. "And the other man? Kroun?"

"I made him a promise. You make a promise, you gotta be stand-up about it. Derner and I will figure something out, do the right thing."

Bobbi nodded, held me again, then suddenly went rigid and shrieked.

With a groan, Kroun rolled on his side. There was pain all over his face, but he used one arm to push and was slowly sitting up.

I gasped. Had an insane thought that he'd worn a vest like Escott's, but the blood was real, his absolute stillness, the wound . . .

Was closing.

He pressed his fist against it, wincing. "Ah, *son of a bitch.* That *hurts!*"

I gaped and couldn't seem to come out of it.

He grunted, groaned, and snarled. Then glared at me. "What? You think you're the *only* one?"

"Oh, my God, he's like *you,*" Bobbi whispered.

Kroun's mouth twisted with disgust. "Ain't that the pip? And now you two know *everything.* I tried to not move, but *damn* . . ." He failed to suppress a cough.

I stared and recalled and wondered and realized. "You never told me," I said, voice faint.

"Why the hell should I? I didn't know you. You run with an outfit like Gordy's and think that's a good character reference?"

"But I hypnotized you."

"You *thought* you did. I was wondering, 'What the hell?' and then played along to see what you'd do. Ahh! *Damn!*"

He pulled himself toward Bobbi's couch and eased down with his back against it, long legs sprawled on the floor, arms tight around his chest, pressing hard, visibly hurting. Why was he putting himself through that? Why not vanish?

Bobbi broke away from me and into the kitchen, ran water, and returned with wet dish towels. She knelt and Kroun let her try to clean him up. He gave her a bemused look as she swabbed blood from his face.

"You're all right, kid," he concluded.

"Are *you*?" She made him move his arms and opened his shirt. "The hole's gone, but . . ."

"Just on the outside, cutie. Inside stuff . . . it takes longer. I need to rest a little. I'll get better." He winked the way you do to reassure someone, then made null of it when he began to cough. He grabbed one of the towels, hacking blood into it. The bullet must have gone through a lung.

She glanced at me, clearly thinking the same question. *Why wasn't he vanishing?*

When the fit eased, Kroun said, "You surprised me, Fleming. During the hypnosis when you were trying to get me to change things . . . I expected a left, and you went right."

"What did you do?" Bobbi asked. "Jack?"

I shook my head. "I just wanted him to keep Gordy in charge. That's all."

"It was enough," he said. "What you wanted told me a lot about you. You didn't order me around, you didn't do a lot of stuff that others might. Didn't ask for anything for yourself. All you did was look out for a friend."

"But you weren't under."

"I *played* along. You *get* that, yet? I faked being under to learn more. Then you went funny, had—whatever that was—some kind of fit, I don't know, you were bad off, then you just weren't there. And that clinched it for me on what you are, what I was dealing with. But just *try* to pretend to still be out of things when someone pulls that on you. I damn near lost it there."

"Well, you fooled me."

"You had other problems than just worrying about my taking you on a ride to the boneyard. I wanted to know about 'em. I figured it was to do with Bristow's work. What he did messed you up. With hypnotizing. That right?"

"I think so." I flinched inside. "Yes."

Bobbi looked at me. "What's he mean?"

She had to find out sometime. "I . . . I can't do that anymore. Whammying people. It's . . . like my head's exploding. I don't dare try it again. Maybe not ever. Bristow messed me up, all right."

Kroun snorted. "Face it, kid, what Bristow did left you crippled, the same as if he chopped off one of your legs. You'll just have to live without. The way you looked, it could kill you if nothing else can." He winced again, coughing more blood into the towel. "Damn, this hurts."

"Vanish, then. Heal up."

He gave a short laugh. Coughing. "Believe me, I'd like to."

"Why don't you?"

"You know why I was talking with Gordy so much? To hear about you. He's always a gold mine of news about all kinds of stuff, but this was the mother lode. He knew everything, including why you were hanging in the meat locker instead of kicking Bristow's ass. You had a piece of ice pick stuck in your back. The metal kept you solid."

"What? So you've got the same thing? Shrapnel or something?"

"Or something. Remember I told Adelle Taylor about a guy getting cute and grazing my skull?" Kroun brushed at the white streak on the side of his head. "It wasn't a graze. That was how I *died*."

"Oh, God," Bobbi's jaw dropped. She started to sway. Kroun shot a hand out and steadied her a moment.

"Sorry, cutie. You okay? Good girl. The bullet that killed me is still inside. I'm as crippled as you are, Fleming. Between us we make a whole vampire—ya think?"

"But your looks," said Bobbi. "When the change happens . . . you— you get younger. Don't you?"

He shrugged. "Far as I know I look the same as the day it happened. Maybe the bullet screws that up, too. I can't exactly go to a doctor and find out, can I?"

It made for a hell of a good cover. Now and then I'd look twice at some young mug in his twenties, thinking he might be a vampire. I hadn't once considered Kroun to be a member of the club. "Guess not," I said. "But what now?"

He waved a bloody hand. "Damned if I know. I can't kill you—not the state I'm in, anyway—and I can't make *you* forget, but I don't want anyone else knowing about me."

"We can keep shut. You got my word. Both of us."

Bobbi nodded.

Kroun gave us each a long look with those dark, remarkable eyes. I wondered if mine had that kind of power behind them. "I think I can believe you. There's just one thing . . . I really don't want to go back."

"Back to . . . ?"

"Back to the business. It stinks. You know how it stinks. I'm tired of it. Mitch trying to blow me up . . . that could be my ticket out. A blessing in disguise. A real, real *good* disguise."

"But there's no body in the car. The cops'll know that by now. That'll get public."

He pointed a finger toward his eyes. "There are ways around cop records. Maybe you can show me where to find them, then I do a little talking to the people who matter. Whitey Kroun can die in Chicago and stay here. Fake burial, the works. Shouldn't be too hard to fix." He cocked his head. "Do me a favor?"

"No problem. And then what?"

"And then . . . maybe . . . maybe I go fishing."

I called Derner, told him how things had fallen out with Mitchell and what had to be done. I said I'd get Bobbi someplace else, and he was to send a cleaning crew over, not just to disappear the body but to scrub the place better than any hospital.

That took a while to arrange. He wasn't a happy man.

I had spare clothes in her closet and put on fresh ones. Blood was on my overcoat, but the coat was dark, so nothing incriminating was visible. Bobbi also changed and packed some things together. There wasn't much we could do to clean up Kroun. When he was able to stand, he washed in the kitchen, coughing over the sink to get his lungs cleared of blood. That done, he went down to wait in the Nash, out of sight.

When Derner's crew arrived, Bobbi left with one of them, bound for Shoe Coldfield's special hotel in the Bronze Belt. The way things were going, Escott could wind up recuperating there as well.

If he was going to be all right. He'd been sitting up and talking, but I knew how that could turn around in an instant. Before the night was gone, I'd have to see him, make sure he was all right, try again to apologize for what I'd put him through.

I'd tell Bobbi later why he was in the hospital; I hadn't quite figured out just how much to say about what prompted two grown men to beat the hell out of each other. She really didn't need to know about me trying to kill myself.

As for Kroun . . . I got the impression that he'd been alone and on his own with this for a long time. It must have been a hell of a novelty to meet people who could deal with his big secret, though I was still digesting what to think about him.

We're a rare breed. Hard to make. He'd not said anything about his initiation and who was responsible, what had led up to his death, how he'd dealt with his first waking. We would have to talk. Hell, maybe I could go fishing with him.

Derner's people came, and I handed over the key to Bobbi's place and left.

Kroun was in the backseat of the Nash, still hurting from the gunshot.

"Is *that* bullet still in you?" I asked, getting behind the wheel.

"Nah. They tend to go right through."

"You've been shot other times?"

"Let's talk about something else, okay?"

"Like why you didn't just continue playing possum on the rug?"

"I couldn't help the coughing. Even without it you'd have tumbled soon enough. Besides, you told me what I needed to know. You made a promise about burying me and were going to keep it."

"That's it?"

"Hey, come on. It's easy to make a promise to a dying man. Just as easy to break. You're crazy, but you're a stand-up guy."

I grunted. "Not an easy job."

"Yeah. But you do okay."

"And that's it?" I repeated.

"There's one other thing . . ."

"Yeah?"

"Well, any guy who's that good of friends with Adelle Taylor can't be *all* bad."

DARK ROAD RISING

With thanks to Rox, Jackie,
and Lucienne

1

WHEN I set the brake and cut the motor, the dead man in the backseat of my Nash shifted, groaned, and straightened up to look around. He suppressed a cough, arms locked against his bloodstained chest as though to keep it from coming apart.

"You okay?" I asked.

"Peachy." His voice rasped hollow and hoarse. He was lying, but that's what you do when you feel like hell and don't want to give in to it.

His name was Whitey Kroun. He was a big bad gang boss out of New York who had come to town to oversee my execution.

That hadn't worked out very well.

He'd taken a bullet through the chest only a couple hours earlier and should be healing faster. He needed blood and a day's rest on his home earth, but that would have to wait; I had one more thing to do before either of us could have a break.

"What's this?" His dark eyes were bleary with fatigue and pain.

We were in a parking lot close to the hospital. "I gotta see a man about a dog."

He grunted and pushed up his coat sleeve to squint at his watch. The crystal was gone, and the exposed hands swung loose over the numbers. "Well, it's half past, better get a move on."

I slammed out of the car and hurried toward the hospital entrance.

The streets weren't awake yet. At this bleak hour they seemed too tired, unable to recover from the pains of an overlong night. The smack of predawn air felt good, though, and I consciously tried a lungful. Clinging to my overcoat was the smell of Kroun's blood. The scent had filled the car, but with no need to breathe I'd been remarkably successful at pushing away the distraction.

Dried stains smeared the front of the coat, but the material was dark, no one would notice. Even if someone did, I had more serious concerns. I needed to check on my partner. The phone calls made hours ago to the emergency room and later to the doctor in charge weren't enough, I had to see for myself.

After convincing a lone reception nurse that I was the patient's cousin she got my name and other necessary information before giving away Charles Escott's location. He was in the men's ward.

I made sure that would change. "He gets a private room," I said, pulling money from my wallet. From her shocked look the stack was more than she'd make in the next two months. "He gets whatever he needs before he needs it." I folded the cash into her hand.

She stared at the money, uncertain. "Mr. Fleming, I—"

"Consider it a personal thank-you. Do whatever you want with it so long as my friend gets first-class treatment. I have to see him now."

"He shouldn't have visitors."

"We're not gonna play cards. I just need to check on him. Please."

She read my mood right: determinedly polite but not leaving until I got what I wanted. She slipped the money into her clipboard, hugged it to her front, and led the way down the empty corridors herself. Maybe I couldn't hypnotize people anymore, but a goodwill gift in the right place can take you far in the world. It had worked well enough for Capone, up to a point.

The ward was clean, but still a ward: a high, dim room full of restive misery. Some of the bodies shrouded under their blankets were frozen in place by injury, others twitched, sleepless from pain or illness.

I had a brief flash of memory of a similar place in France back when I was a red-faced kid still awkward in my doughboy uniform. There, the ward had been full of nuns gliding back and forth between the wounded. Some of the guys played cards one-handed, getting used to the new amputations, some groaned despite their doses of morphine, some slept, some wept, and one poor bastard at the end was screaming too much and had to be taken to a different part of the building. After twenty years, the picture was still sharp, but I couldn't recall why I'd been there. Probably visiting someone, same as now.

Escott was second in from the door, lying slightly propped up on the narrow metal bed. His face was puffy and turning black from bruising, his ribs were taped, his hands bandaged like an outclassed boxer who'd unwisely stayed for the full twelve rounds. He seemed to be breathing okay, and when I listened, his heart thumped along steady and slow as he slept. But he looked so damned frail and crushed.

That was my doing. My fault.

He shouldn't be here. I'd been an incredible, unconscionable fool, and he was paying for my lapse with cracked, maybe broken bones, pulped flesh, and slow weeks of recovery. God help us both, I'd come within a thin hair of killing him. He still wasn't out of the woods. If I'd broken him up inside, he could bleed to death internally.

Not recognizing my own voice, I asked the nurse about that.

She consulted the chart at the foot of the bed. X-rays had been taken, though how anyone could make sense of a mass of indefinite shadows was beyond me. She told me what was wrong and, more importantly, what wasn't wrong. It was cold comfort. I'd only *half* killed my best friend.

I wanted to help him, to do more than what had already been done, but no action on my part could possibly make up for such stupidity. This was true helplessness, and I hated it. My hand went toward him on its own, but I made a sudden fist, shoving it into a pocket. The nurse read this mood as well.

"He'll be all right," she said. "It'll just take some time."

It could take years, and still wouldn't be all right.

One of his eyelids flickered. The other was fused fast shut from swelling.

Guilty at disturbing him, I started to back out of view, but it was too late. He was awake, if groggy, and fixed me in place with his cloudy gaze, not speaking.

When I couldn't take the silence anymore, I said, "Charles . . . y-you don't worry. They'll get you whatever you want. It's taken care of. You just say."

His eyelid slowly shut and opened again, and there was an audible thickening of the breath passing through his throat. I took that to mean he understood.

"I'm . . . I'm sorry as hell. I'm so sorry."

He continued to look at me.

"I'm sorry as hell, I—I—" I would not ask for forgiveness. I didn't deserve it and never would.

He shook his head and made a small sound of frustration.

I understood. He was afraid for me . . . afraid I'd try to hurt myself. That had been the cause of the fight. My face heated up from shame. "I'm sorry for that, too. It won't happen again. I swear. On Bobbi's life, I promise you. Never again."

The corner of his mouth curled in a ghost's smile. His lips moved in the softest of whispers. *"Jack."*

I leaned in. "Yeah?"

"About damn time, you bloody fool."

He lifted a bandaged hand toward my near arm, gave my shoulder a clumsy pat.

Sleep took him away.

Men aren't supposed to cry, but I came damn close just then.

WHITEY Kroun, the corpse I'd left waiting in the backseat of the Nash, now slumped on the front passenger side with the door open, feet on the running board. His left trouser leg was rusty with dried blood, and he cautiously unwound a similarly stained handkerchief from his left hand. He flexed his fingers, checking them. Whatever damage he'd gotten seemed to be gone. He threw the grubby cloth away, hauled his long legs in, and yanked the door shut. The effort made him grunt, and he went back to favoring his chest.

He didn't say if he wanted to be dropped anywhere, and I didn't inquire, just started the motor and pulled away, mindful of the shortening time until dawn. We'd have to go to ground soon.

Shadows caught, lingered, and slithered quick over his craggy features as we sped under streetlamps, his eyelids at half-mast from pain. In good light Kroun's eyes were dark brown with strangely dilated pupils; now all that showed were skull-deep voids, unreadable.

Life had gotten damned complicated lately. It happens sometimes; for me it started when I tried to be a nice guy and do a favor for a friend in need.

That favor, along with circumstances beyond my control, had put me in the short line for the gang version of the hot seat. Kroun's arrival in Chicago was to sort things out and put me to bed with a shovel. Or an anchor. Lake Michigan makes for a very big graveyard when you know the wrong people.

But after looking me over, Kroun decided against carrying out the death sentence.

Mighty generous of him, except at the time I didn't know the real reason behind his choice. Outwardly, I'm not special; I own a nightclub that does pretty well, have a wonderful girl, a few good friends—I'm worse than some, better than most. Average. Most of the time.

Not ten minutes after we met, Kroun figured out about my being a vampire—you heard it right—and in the nights to follow never once let slip that he was *also* a card-carrying member of the union. I'd been tied up too tight in my own problems to notice anything odd about him or even remotely suspect. It had been one pip of a surprise when the boom came.

I was still getting used to it, the topper of a very busy evening.

It began with one hell of a fistfight between me and Escott, which was what had landed him in the casualty ward. I'd done something really stupid and his attempt to knock some sense into me set me off. I hadn't meant to hurt him, but I woke out of my rage a little too late. Before I could follow his ambulance to the hospital, I'd been sidetracked by a phone call from my girlfriend, Bobbi. In so many words she let me know there was a man in her flat holding a gun to her head.

That confrontation had ended badly.

Bobbi was fine, thank God, but there'd been quite an ugly fracas before the dust settled. Kroun had been present, caught a stray bullet, and died.

Apparently.

The shooter was also dead, and I was left with a nasty mess: two corpses, a shot-up flat, and me desperately trying not to go over the cliff into the screaming hell of full-blown shell shock.

By the grace of God, Escott's right fist, and Bobbi holding on to me like there was no tomorrow, I did not fall in. It had been a near thing, though. I was still standing closer than was comfortable to the edge of that dark internal pit, but no longer wobbling. Given time I might even back away to safer ground.

As I'd sluggishly tried to work out the details of what to do next, Kroun picked that moment to stop playing possum. One minute he was flat on the floor with a thumb-sized hole in his chest, the next . . .

Well . . . it had been interesting.

It took hours to clear the chaos at Bobbi's. I saw to it she was driven to a safe place to stay, then arranged to disappear the dead gunman. For this, I got some reliable if wholly illegal help involving the kind of mugs who are really good at guaranteeing that inconvenient bodies are never found.

Before the cleaning crew arrived, Kroun made himself missing. Temporarily. He hid out in the back of the Nash until the fuss was over.

That I was no longer the only vampire (that I knew about) in Chicago hadn't really sunk in yet.

Since we each had secrets to keep, we'd formed an uneasy alliance out of mutual necessity, and there was no telling how long it might last. I had fish of my own to fry and didn't particularly want to be looking after him—but he needed a favor, and, God help me, I turned sucker yet again.

I didn't want to think just how badly *this* could end.

KROUN seemed to doze. He'd not asked about our destination. I took it for granted that he wanted a ride away from the trouble and a chance to get his second wind, figuratively speaking. He had some serious healing to do; it might as well be in the company of someone who understood what he was going through.

He took notice when I made a last turn and pulled into the alley behind the house. Escott and I hung our hats in an elderly three-story brick in a quiet, respectable neighborhood. Not the sort of place you'd expect a vampire to lurk, but I'm allergic to cemeteries.

"What's this?" asked Kroun, blinking as I eased the car into the garage.

"Home. I'm all in. You'll have to stay the day." Maybe he had plans, but I wanted ask a few hundred questions, but later, when my brain was more clear. Right now it felt like street sludge.

"There's no need. I found a bolt-hole for myself," he said. "I got time to get there if you call a cab."

"At this hour?" I set the brake, cut the motor, and yanked the key. The ring felt too light.

"Cabs run all the time now, Fleming. It's a big burg, all grown-up."

"That's just a rumor . . . ah . . . damn it." I searched my pockets.

"Something wrong?"

"The house key's back at my nightclub. Left so fast I grabbed the wrong bunch." The wrong coat, too. Along with the Nash—which was Escott's car—I'd borrowed his overcoat. He wouldn't thank me for the bloodstains.

I cracked the door, careful not to bang it against the wall of the narrow garage, and got out. Kroun did the same, moving more slowly. Something must have twinged inside, for he paused to catch his breath, which was an event to note. Like me, he wasn't one for regular breathing. His reaction had to do with pain.

He'd left a dark patch on the center back of the seat, a transfer from a much larger stain on the back of his coat. It'd been hours; his wounds would have closed by now. The blood he'd leaked should be dried. Must have been the damp. The heavy air smelled of snow, but not the clean kind out of the north. This had a sour, rotting tang, as though the clouds were gathering up stink from the city and would soon dump it back again.

Going easy on his left leg, Kroun limped across the patches of frozen mud and dingy snow that made up the small yard, then stalled halfway to the porch. He began to cough, a big deep, wet whooping that grew in force and doubled him over. It sounded like his lungs were coming out the hard way. I started toward him, but there's nothing you can do to help when a person's in that state. The fit comes on and passes only when it's good and ready to go. Spatters of blood suddenly bloomed on the untracked drift in front of him.

I couldn't help but stare at the stuff. The smell had filled the car, but I'd successfully shoved it aside. This was fresh, dark red, almost black against the snow. He wasn't the only one with a problem. Mine was less obvious. I waited, holding my breath, unable to look away.

Waited . . .

But—nothing.

Nothing for a good long minute.

Couldn't trust that, though.

Waited . . .

And finally took in a sip of air tainted with bloodsmell . . .

Dreading what must happen next . . .

But no roiling reaction twisted my guts.

No cold sweats.

Not even the shakes.

It was just blood. A necessity for survival, but nothing to get crazy over. No uncontrolled hunger blazed through my gut, not even the false starvation kind that scared me.

So far, so good.

I relaxed, just a little.

Cold, though . . . I was cold to the bone . . . but that was okay. It wasn't the unnerving chill that left me shivering in a warm room, but the ordinary sort that comes with winter. I'd thought I'd lost that feeling.

Kroun's internal earthquake climaxed, and he gagged and spat out a black clot the size of a half-dollar. He hung over the mess a moment, sucking air, and managed to keep his balance. My instinct was to lend him an arm to lean on while he recovered, but he wouldn't like it. I didn't know him well, but I knew that much.

He'd made a lot of noise, perhaps enough to wake a neighbor. I glanced at the surrounding houses, but no one peered from any of the upper windows. The show was over, anyway. Kroun gradually straightened, his face mottled red and gray. He kicked snow to hide the gore.

"You okay?" I asked. I'd have to stop that. It could get irritating.

"Still peachy," he wheezed. When he reached the back porch, he used the rail to pull himself along the steps. He looked like hell on a bad week. "No house key, huh?"

"Yeah, but—"

He fished a small, flat case from the inside pocket of his tattered, filthy overcoat. A couple of nights ago it had been new-looking, but an explosion and fire had turned it into something a skid-row bum would have tossed in the gutter. Kroun might well have been rolling in that gutter. His craggy features were gaunt now, his hair singed—except for a distinct silver-white streak on the side—and when I inhaled he still stank of smoke and burned rubber. He opened the case, revealing a collection of picklocks. "Lemme by."

"No need," I said—and vanished. Into thin air. I was good at it. Didn't think twice.

"*Shit!*" Kroun hadn't expected that.

His reaction was muffled to me. My senses in this state were limited, but it did have advantages, like getting me into otherwise inaccessible places. Damn, I felt smug.

"Fleming? You there?"

I'm busy. I pressed toward the door, sensing the long, thin crack at the threshold, and slipped in. Though I could have passed right through the wood, this path of least resistance was less unsettling. Going solid again on the other side, I unlocked and opened up, gesturing Kroun in.

He looked like he wanted to say a lot of things, but held back. I thought I understood his expression: an interesting combination of annoyance mixed with raw envy. It only flashed for a second, then he pocketed his case. "Nice trick."

"Just a way out of the cold. C'mon."

He stepped into the kitchen, and I locked the door again for all the good that would do. Even the dumbest of Chicago's countless thugs knew how to break and enter in the more conventional sense, though none of them had any reason to do so here. Quite the contrary. I'd gotten into the habit of thinking that way, though. Blame it on the scurvy company I kept.

"Phone?" he asked.

"The wall by the icebox." Actually, it was a streamlined electric refrigerator that looked out of place in the faded kitchen. I dropped my fedora on the table and shrugged from Escott's coat, folding it over the back of a chair. "But you can stay here. It's safe."

"I don't think so." Kroun wasn't being impolite, just preoccupied as he crossed the room, got the phone book from a shelf, and flipped through it looking for cab companies. He found a page, running a finger down the columns of fine print.

I flicked the light on. Habit. We could both see well enough in the dark.

He murmured an absent-sounding noise and stared at the listings. "How many of these companies have the mob on them?"

"They all pay dues. The hotels, too. Shocking, ain't it?"

"Cripes." He put the book back. "It's as bad as New York."

To his former associates in crime, along with everyone else, Whitey Kroun was supposed to be dead. Not Undead, which none would know about or believe in, but the regular kind of dead, and he wanted to keep it that way. He did not need a cabby remembering him and blabbing to the wrong ears. There were ways around that, but Kroun must have been considering the trouble and worth of it against the shrinking time before sunrise.

He was clearly exhausted. He'd barely survived getting blown up, gone into hiding God-knows-where for the day, and only hours before had taken a bullet square in the chest. The slug had passed right through, ripped up his dormant heart, maybe clipped one of his lungs before tearing out his back.

My last twenty-fours hours hadn't been even that good. We both needed a rest.

"Spare bedroom's up the stairs, third floor," I said. "All ready. Just walk in."

Kroun frowned. "Is it lightproof?"

"The window's covered. You'll be fine."

"Where do you sleep?"

"I have a place. In the basement."

He gave me a look. "What? A secret lair?"

That almost made me smile. "It's better than it sounds."

Not by much, but it sure as hell wasn't a claustrophobia-inducing coffin on the floor of a ratty crypt like in that Lugosi movie. Just thinking about a body box gave me the heebies. My bricked-up chamber below was a close twin to any ordinary bedroom, being clean and dry with space enough for a good arm stretch. I kept things simple: an army cot with a layer of my home earth under oilcloth, a lamp, a radio, books to fill in the time before sunrise, no lurking allowed.

"Room enough for a guest?"

"I can only get into it by vanishing." That was a lie. There was access by means of a trapdoor under the kitchen table, hidden by expert carpentry and a small rug. I just didn't want Kroun in my private den. Since he was unable to slip through cracks I was pleased to take advantage of his limitation. Just because we had vampirism in common didn't mean I should welcome him like a long-lost relative. He'd sure as hell not tipped his hand to me about his condition.

"You maybe got a broom closet?" he asked.

"Yeah, but you wouldn't like it."

"I could."

"C'mon, Whitey, no one knows you're here—"

"Gabe."

"Huh?"

"My real name's Gabe." His eyes were focused inward. "Mom's idea. Gabriel. Hell of a name to stick on a kid. Got me in a few fights."

Now why had he told me that?

He got a look on his face as though wondering the same thing. Maybe he was dealing with his own version of shell shock. Well, I wasn't walking on eggs for him. "Okay. Gabe. No one knows you're here, and no one's looking for you. The cops are still sifting through what's left of that car. By the time they don't find your body in the ashes, it'll be tomorrow night and you can start fresh."

He seemed to return from memory lane. "You get day visitors? Cleaning lady? Anyone like that?"

"Nobody."

"What about Gordy's boys? Strome and Derner?"

"They know not to bother me with anything until tomorrow night. No one's gonna find you." There was no point telling Kroun to lay off being paranoid; the kind of stuff he'd been through would leave anyone twitchy. I understood him all too well.

"That won't discourage my pals in New York. First Hog Bristow gets dead, then me."

"Chicago's rough," I admitted.

"They won't blame the city." Kroun frowned my way so I'd be clear on who would be held accountable. He had good reason. Bristow's death was the mug's own stupid fault, though at the end I'd done what I could to help him along. Anyone else would consider my actions to be self-defense, just not his business associates back East.

Whitey—or was I to call him Gabe now?—Kroun had been my ostensible guest and looking into the Bristow situation when another mobster tried to take him out with a bomb. Kroun's apparent, and very public, demise had happened right in front of me, on my watch, and that made me responsible. The big boys he'd worked with in New York were bound to get pissed and react in a way I wouldn't like. Maybe I should try faking my death, too.

"Will your pals be sending someone here to deal with me?" I asked.

"Count on it. Unless Derner or Gordy can head them off."

Derner was my temporary lieutenant when it came to the nuts-and-bolts operation of mob business. His boss, Gordy Weems—a friend of mine and the man usually running things in Chicago's North Side—was still recovering from some serious bullet wounds of his own. I'd been talked into filling his spot until he was back on his feet. He couldn't get well fast enough for me. I had to be the only guy west of the Atlantic who didn't want the job. "Gordy stays on vacation. Derner and I will look after things, no problem."

"If you say so, kid."

Kroun had a right to his doubts. Running a major branch of the mob was very different from bossing an ordinary business. For instance, firing people was murder. Literally.

Another coughing bout grabbed Kroun. He tried to suppress it, but his body wasn't cooperating. He made his way to the sink and doubled over, hacking and spitting. When it subsided, he ran the water to wash the blood away. There wasn't as much as before; he must be healing.

I inhaled, caught the bloodsmell . . . and again waited. Nothing happened, no tremors in my limbs, no urge to scream, no falling on the floor like a seizure victim.

Very encouraging, but instinct told me I was still rocky and not to get overconfident.

"Cripes, I hate getting shot," he muttered.

"It's hell," I agreed.

He cupped hands under the water stream and rubbed down his face. "You've been through this, too?"

"Not if I can help it. But whenever I catch one, I always vanish. When I come back, I'm tired, but usually everything's fixed."

"The hell you say."

"You didn't know?"

He gave no reply.

"Didn't the one who gave you the change tell you anything?" I was very curious as to who had traded blood with him, allowing him the chance to return from death. *When* had he died? How long ago? He'd dropped no clue as to how long he'd been night-walking. He could be decades older than me in this life or months younger.

That streak of silver-white hair on the left side of his head marked where he caught the bullet that had killed him. Who had shot him and why? How had he dealt with his dark resurrection? The lead slug was still lodged in his brain, and the presence of that small piece of metal was enough to short-circuit his ability to vanish. It also prevented rejuvenation, kept him looking the same age he was when it happened. Instead of seeming to be in his twenties like me, he outwardly remained in his forties.

But Kroun wasn't sharing confidences. Making no answer, he twisted the water tap off and dried with one of the neatly folded dish towels Escott kept next to the sink. In the harsh overhead light Kroun looked even more gaunt than a few minutes ago. The coughing fit had sapped him.

"You hungry?" I asked. He had to be. He'd lost plenty of blood tonight. It would put him on edge, maybe make him dangerous. That was what it did to me.

"A little, but I can hold out till tomorrow."

I went to the icebox. In the back were some beer bottles with the labels soaked off, topped with cork stoppers. The dark brown glass obscured what was inside. They represented an experiment that had worked out. I pulled a bottle and handed it over. "It's cold but drinkable."

He eyeballed it. "You're kidding. You *store* the stuff?"

"Only for a few days. It goes bad once the air hits. Like milk."

He took the cork out and sniffed it. "It's animal?"

"Yeah."

He shot me a look. Checking. Appraising. "Good."

Damn. *That* angle . . . and he'd thought of it first. "Hey, you don't think I'd . . ."

"What?"

The son of a bitch. "I don't take from people."

"Sure you do. Your girlfriend."

"She's not food." I felt myself going red.

"No. There have been others who were, though."

"Where the hell do you—" I nearly choked.

He tilted his head. "Yeah?"

I shut down, because I was within a hair of knocking his block off, and that wouldn't accomplish anything. He was guessing, goading me for information. And had gotten it. "How do you figure?"

"The other night . . . in Gordy's office."

When Kroun first clapped eyes on me. "But you didn't know about me right away."

"No, I didn't. There was a point in the proceedings, though. You put on a face I didn't understand at the time, but afterward I got it. You were looking at me, at the whole room, and realized you were in charge."

My nape prickled at his insight. I remembered that moment and wasn't proud of it, yet the idea had bolstered me when I was in need and gotten me out of a death sentence.

He went on. "You'd just figured out you were the big fish, and big fish feed on little fish. Only with us it's a literal thing. The question is, do you make a habit of feeding from people?"

"I goddamn don't."

He made a "no problem" gesture. "That's fine then, fine."

"And you?" I'd once encountered a vampire who took human blood—often and any way he liked. I saw to it he came to a bad end.

"I'm not in the habit, no."

"That's not an answer."

"It's the only one I got." He scowled when I didn't respond. "Get off your hind legs, Fleming, I'm no menace to society. I'm retired now."

Time will tell, I thought.

He waved the bottle under his nose again. "You get this stuff from the Stockyards?"

I nodded.

"Pretty smart. Good for emergencies, but someone could find it."

"Who looks twice at an old bottle? Nobody but my partner is ever here anyway, and he's wise."

"That would be the guy in the hospital? Charles Escott?"

"Yeah. This is his house." Kroun had never actually met him, but had gotten plenty of information about my life and hard times from long talks with Gordy, who was also wise. Escott knew Kroun by sight and reputation, the latter being very grim, indeed. Somehow the reputation didn't seem to match up with the guy in front of me. Lots of people were good at hiding their real sides, though. I was an expert.

"And he knows all about you?"

"Yeah. Everything."

"You *trust* him with this?" He lifted the bottle, not talking about blood, but rather the condition that required I drink it.

"Completely. He's been one hell of a friend."

Kroun shook his head. "You're nuts to leave yourself open like that."

"Guess I am."

"Well, I don't want him knowing about me."

"He doesn't. Last he heard you'd been blown up in the car. Killed."

"Keep it like that."

"No problem." Escott was in no shape to be told. I also wanted to have some space between him and potential trouble.

"That girlfriend of yours . . ."

"Won't talk." Some edge slipped into my tone. Kroun heard it and picked up the meaning. Bobbi was strictly hands-off. He got the message.

He had a sample sip from the brown bottle. From his grimace it wasn't perfect, but drinkable; the blood would cure his hunger quick enough and speed his healing. He suddenly tilted the bottle and finished it off in one quick, guzzling draft. The stuff must have charged through him like a bull elephant. Head bowed, he gave in to a long shudder as though it had been 180-proof booze and not cattle blood.

"Wow," he whispered, almost in awe.

I knew the feeling. Taken hot from a vein, the internal kick is astonishing. When cold from storage, the reaction isn't that strong unless you're on the verge of starvation. Kroun possessed one hell of a lot of self-control to be willing to stick it out going hungry. If I went too long between meals, I got crazy—tunnel vision, unable to think straight, a threat to people around me, nothing pleasant. I made sure to feed every other night, though lately I'd been overfeeding like a drunk on a binge. It was a considerable relief now not to have that tug of mindless appetite urging me to clean out the rest of the cache in the icebox.

"That hit the spot, thanks." Kroun handed the empty bottle over, and I rinsed it in the sink. He looked improved, even filled out a little. Blood works fast on our kind. The whites of his eyes were flushed dark red and would stay that way for a short time, iris and pupils lost to view. I tried not to stare.

"Another?"

"No thanks." He moved into what was originally meant to be a dining room, but Escott wasn't one for fancy eating, preferring the kitchen.

His old dining table was a huge work desk decked with orderly piles of books and papers. There was a big sideboard along one wall, but it served as a liquor cabinet and storage for odds and ends. Kroun paused and peered through the glass doors at all the bottles.

"Your partner a lush?"

Once upon a time. Back then a very good friend of his got tired of the drinking and tried to beat some sense into Escott about it. It'd worked. "He likes to be prepared for company."

The next room was the front parlor with a long sofa, my favorite chair, and the radio. I didn't bother switching on a lamp; the spill from the kitchen was enough for us. It also wouldn't reach the parlor window and give away that anyone was home.

Newspapers were stacked so precisely on the low table in the middle that you couldn't tell if they'd been read yet. They were yesterday's editions, and Escott would have gone through them, it just didn't show. He was that neat about things.

I grabbed the one on top, which bore a headline about the mysterious deaths of nightclub singer Alan Caine and his ex-wife Jewel.

Damn it all.

The story itself was thin on facts, padded to two columns by biographical sketches for them both. The police were investigating what appeared to be a murder-suicide. The estranged couple had been seen arguing in public and so on and so forth.

Damn again. Removing the accusation of murder and stigma of suicide from Jewel's name would be impossible. The killer was on his way to the bottom of the lake by now. He had no direct connection to either of them that could be proved. Any stepping forward on my part would be a futile gesture that would pin me square under the cops' spotlight.

I couldn't risk it and felt like a coward by giving in to common sense.

But still . . . maybe I could fix something up . . . get some of Derner's boys to phone an anonymous tip or three to the rags while the story was still newsworthy, sow some doubt. A double murder was a juicier story to sell than a murder-suicide.

I'd have to talk to Derner about funeral arrangements for poor Jewel. She hadn't had two dimes; I didn't want her going to the potter's field just because her ex hadn't kept up the alimony.

I'd get things moving and hope it wasn't already too late. The world spun on relentlessly. New disasters rose up to overshadow the old as I discovered when I quit the parlor for the entry hall and opened the front door. Several editions lay piled on the porch. I grabbed them up, kicked the door shut, and dropped them all on the parlor table. To judge by the headlines, the presses had been stopped in order to fit in something special.

They all had the same story.

The only event that could eclipse a nightclub headliner's murder was the shooting of a movie actor. It warranted larger, bolder type to convey the importance of a near-fatal assault on the life of Roland Lambert, onetime Hollywood matinee idol.

Roland would hate the "onetime" part, but ignore it with bemused grace. He and his ballerina wife, Faustine, did exhibition dancing at my club, working to raise grubstake money so he could go back to California in style for a return to films. Toward that end, he'd made the most of the free publicity, having apparently granted an exclusive interview to every reporter in the country.

Above the fold in one journal was a picture of Roland in his plain hospital whites, managing to look devil-handsome, gallant, brash, and charming, just like the sword-fighting heroes he'd played on-screen. Faustine sat bravely at his bedside, holding his hand, decked out in the best Paris could offer, exotic and erotic as always. He wouldn't be dancing much anymore, having been shot in the leg.

That was my fault. Sort of. Roland had been in the wrong place when a bad guy had cut loose with bullets meant for me. The shooter was dead now. Not my fault—for a change—and someone else had bumped him off in turn. Roland didn't know that part and never would.

He had quite another story to tell, though, and it was a pip.

He'd sold the reporters the malarkey that he had run afoul of some real Chicago mobsters, and the tale was developing a life of its own.

"SHERLOCK" LAMBERT TAKES ON THE GANGS!—no kidding, that was how they'd printed it—headed an overwritten four-column section of a sob sister's feature. It was long on emotion, purple prose, with damn few facts, but why let the truth get in the way of such thrilling entertainment?

According to that version of events, a mysterious underworld figure had imposed his unwanted attentions on an innocent bride—at this point it was noted that film legend Roland Lambert adoringly kissed the hand of his beautiful wife, the famous Russian ballerina Faustine Petrova. After a brisk bout of fisticuffs, the gangster had been sent off in round order by her valiant husband, but that wasn't to be the end of it. Strange threatening letters began to arrive, compelling Roland to investigate and deal with their source. He was making serious progress at tracking the bounder to his lair, which was too close for comfort for at least one of the miscreants, and resulted in the present small setback. Here Roland gestured ruefully at his dreadful wounding.

Oh, brother.

At the time of the shooting, I'd been in a blind panic that I'd gotten him killed. Nothing like a little rest and a lot of personal moxie to turn things on their head. With a trowel in each hand, he'd plastered it on thick. I had serious doubts that any of the mugs in the gangs even knew the meaning of *miscreant*, but had to admire him. Roland's eyewash was a great misdirection. He'd made himself into a crime-busting hero, and my name was never once mentioned. What a relief.

The sob sister went into grand and glorious detail about how Roland had rescued his lovely bride from conflict-torn Russia. Their daring escape culminated in the Lamberts' romantic shipboard wedding amid the threat of lurking German submarines. Somehow, routine lifeboat drills took on an ominous significance, and the fate of the *Lusitania* twenty years back was remembered as though it had occurred yesterday. If there was ever going to be another war in Europe, stories like this would be one of the causes.

The couple had actually met over cocktails at a cast party for one of Roland's London plays, but that didn't make nearly as exciting copy.

The next paper went one better and compared Roland and Faustine to Nick and Nora Charles, speculating that a movie of their real-life adventures should be filmed, something that would even top *The Thin Man* for popularity.

Sleuth away, old sport, I thought.

Below the fold were a few short paragraphs about the mystery explosion in Chicago's Bronze Belt. It was old news compared to the rest, but could still sell a paper. A stark photo showed a smoke-filled street and staring bystanders frozen in the moment, but the camera flash hadn't reached far enough to show what was burning. It was a good shot, though; the photographer must have arrived with the fire trucks.

"You see this?" I asked, showing the page.

My houseguest was also catching up on the news and shook his head. "Huh. Doesn't look like the same place."

"You saw it from a different angle."

"I didn't see much but smoke."

Kroun had hurtled from the bomb-gutted car and hidden behind some curbside trash cans before going to ground for the day, leading everyone to believe he'd been blown to hell and gone. Our kind is pretty damned tough, but there are limits. Kroun had only survived because of the car's armor plating and the devil's own luck. He'd gotten seriously hammered around and burned, though. It was really too bad he was unable to vanish and heal the way I could.

The story was little more than a thin rewrite of yesterday's edition, but this time had names. Someone had traced the car's owner. The police wanted to question underworld figure Gordy Weems about the incident. He'd love that.

Kroun read the piece through and snorted. "They don't know anything. This guy got it all wrong."

"It happens. For you it's better if they don't have the facts."

"You used to do that, didn't you? Reporting?"

"Yeah. About a thousand years ago." I dropped into my chair, putting my feet up on the table.

"I hope that's a joke."

It occurred to me that he didn't know my real age, either. I was thirty-seven, but looked a lot younger. I felt a brief, smug grin stretch my face.

"So how long have you been like this?"

Just the question I wanted to ask. "You first."

"Uh-uh. You." He went past me to peer out the front window, pulling the curtain open just a crack, perhaps checking for the first changes that marked the coming dawn. You couldn't always trust a clock.

"Happened a year ago last August," I said.

"When you came to Chicago?"

"Yeah. Slick Morelli and Frank Paco did the honors."

They'd murdered me—a slow, vicious process—but I'd gotten some payback in the end. Slick was dead and Paco raving in a nuthouse God knows where. There was a lesson in that mess someplace about picking your enemies carefully, but I didn't like thinking about it.

"Morelli *and* Paco?" Kroun sounded like he'd met them once upon a time. "What'd you do to get noticed by those two?"

"Nothing I want to talk about." And he would know it already. He'd spent time with Gordy, who knew all the dirt about my Undead condition and how it had happened. Kroun would have used hypnosis to pick Gordy's brain clean about my death, so what was his game asking me? Probably to see if the stories matched. Suspicious bastard. I could get annoyed, only in his place I'd have done the same. "What about yourself? How did you buy it?"

He didn't answer, closely watching something outside. The only reasonable activity at this hour might be someone leaving for an early job or the milkman making his round.

"What is it?" I asked.

"Car's stopped in front of the house."

Now what?

"You know a big colored guy? Well dressed? Drives a Nash?"

Oh, hell. "What about him?"

"He's coming up the walk. Looks pissed, too."

"Let him in."

"It's your door, and I'm no butler."

The man outside began ringing the bell and pounding. I tiredly boosted up.

Kroun stepped into the entry hall. "Oh, yeah. He's pissed. I'd stay to watch, but—"

"Upstairs. Third floor. Keep quiet."

He went quick despite the limp, not making a lot of noise, though I couldn't hear much over the racket. He ducked from view at the top landing, stifling a cough.

I got the door. "Hi, Shoe."

Shoe Coldfield filled a very large portion of the opening, his anger making him loom even larger. Before I could say anything else, a word of explanation, an invitation to come inside, he slammed a fist of iron into my gut.

2

He had an arm like a train. All the breath shot out of me. I folded and staggered and kept my feet only by grabbing the stair rail with one flailing hand. It wasn't as bad as it might have been for anyone else. I didn't want a second helping, though.

Coldfield's dark face was darker than normal, suffused with barely controlled rage. "You know why I'm here," he rumbled. Volcanoes reach that kind of deep pitch before they blow.

Took an experimental sip of air for speech. "Oh, yeah."

"Why the hell did you do that to him?"

"How'd you—"

"I got people who work at the hospital. One of them saw Charles brought in looking like he'd been worked over by a bulldozer and called me. They wouldn't let me see him. Took one look and knew I wasn't a relation. I tracked down the ambulance drivers and got them to talk. What the *hell* did you do?"

I'd grown a thick hide over my ability to feel guilt over some of the more objectionable things I'd done in life, but it was no protection now. I was in the wrong, and there were consequences to face.

"Charles and I had a fight—"

"The hell you did! What about?"

The words got stuck long before the halfway mark. The situation was edging close to being a reprise of my fight with Escott. Sweat popped out on my flanks.

"What?"

I shook my head. There was no way I could tell Coldfield what I'd done that had infuriated Escott enough to beat the crap out of me—and then my going bughouse-crazy out of control and returning the favor. All I could do was thank God that I'd stopped short of murder. I couldn't remember much about the fight, but the aftermath was clear and sharp, especially those frozen-in-lead moments when I thought Escott was dead.

"*What?*" Coldfield loomed again.

"Charles was pissed with me about something and we got into it. It's not important now." Favoring my middle, I straightened, knowing what was coming. No way out.

"Goddammit, you put him in the hospital!" Coldfield piled in a rain of gut-busters, grunting from the effort. He was in on my secret. Had been for a while. He also knew about the ugly business with Hog Bristow, what the bastard had done to me. For all that, Coldfield didn't pull a single punch.

And I took it.

He finally knocked me ass flat on the floor. I stayed there, not quite keeling over.

"*Talk* to me, you sonovabitch!"

He wasn't going away. Come sunrise he'd probably continue beating on my apparently dead body to make sure I had more damage than Escott.

I raised one hand in surrender. Seemed like too much trouble to stand.

He'd just put me back again. It hurt to draw breath to speak. Took a minute to get enough air inside to do the job. "Look . . . you once socked him for his own good . . . didn't you? You got fed up?"

Coldfield nodded slowly. "What about it?"

"This time it was my turn. He did his damnedest to pound some sense into me. Nearly took my block off."

"You don't look it."

"I heal fast, remember?"

"And then what?"

"I wouldn't listen. So Charles kept at me . . . until I hit him. That's where the ambulance came in. I'm sorry, Shoe. I didn't mean for it to go that way. I'd take it back if I could."

"You can't."

Bowed my head. "No. I can't."

He made no comment, but I could still feel his anger. He wanted to hurt me and make it last.

I used the stair rail to pull to my feet. Damn, but he'd caught me good and hard, without brass knuckles, either. If he was like that with bare fists . . .

He laid in again with enough force so I'd remember not to forget. I dropped all the way, curled, and stayed there, gasping. Pain. More than I expected. Wouldn't be surprised if he'd ruptured something. I wouldn't vanish to escape and heal, though. That'd be spitting in his face. I'd take what he dished out and like it.

He stooped into my view and his voice went low, and for a chilling instant I glimpsed what was inside him that made him the boss of one of the toughest mobs in the city. "You *ever* cut loose on Charles again, I will kill you." He knew exactly how to do it, too.

I believed him.

"We clear on that? You understand me?"

"Yeah," I said, talking sideways because my mouth was mashed against the floor. "Never again. Promise."

Coldfield left, slamming the door hard enough to shake the house. A moment later he gunned his car, shifted gears, and roared away.

Good thing he was a friend or we might have both been in trouble. I don't take this kind of crap from enemies.

Another moment or three passed, then the stairs creaked as Kroun came down. He squatted on his heels next to me, hands clasped loose in front of him, and tilted his head. "You okay?"

Now that was one goddamned stupid question. And he wasn't a stupid man. I eyed him. He was concerned, just not one for mother-henning. "I'm great. Tomorrow I sell tickets to the real show."

"Huh." He got the message. It was none of his beeswax, but he almost smiled. "And *he* knows about you, too?"

"Yeah."

"F'cryin' out loud, put it on a billboard, why don't ya?"

"Okay."

A moderately long look from him, followed by a dismissive head-shake. "I can't find soap."

Soap? While I got pulped he was looking for soap? What kind of a loon was he?

"Try the second-floor bath," I mumbled.

His eyes went wide. "You got *two* johns in this joint?" My getting a beating was nothing to sweat about, but a house with two toilets knocked him right over.

Actually there were three. Escott had put in a bath all to himself just off his bedroom, which was overdoing things, but it was his house, after all. I didn't say anything as Kroun was already impressed, and mention of more would be pretentious. As a kid back on the farm in Ohio, I'd been told not to brag about our three-seater outhouse lest the neighbors think the Flemings were getting high-hat above themselves with extrav-agance.

"What was his problem?" Kroun asked, rising as I slowly found my feet again.

I checked my middle. Carefully. Oh, yeah, that hurt. A lot. At least Coldfield hadn't used wood. A baseball bat would have done some truly life-threatening damage on me, but then I'd have fought back. "Nothing to worry about."

"I'm not, but why'd you let him do it?"

"He had to work off steam. And he had a point to make. That was my way of listening."

Kroun thought that over, looking at me the whole time. "You," he concluded, "are crazy."

No reason to deny it. Tonight I happened to agree with him.

"Who was he? Looked familiar."

"Shoe Coldfield. Heads the biggest gang in the Bronze Belt. He's best friends with Escott. He was in that grocery store we walked through to visit Gordy the other night. You may have seen him there."

"Gordy said Coldfield was looking out for him. What's the angle?"

"It never hurts to have someone like Gordy owe you a favor."

"So I've heard. Is that what this is about? You wanting me to owe you a favor?"

"Huh?"

He stared a second. "Ahh, never mind." He went upstairs, dodging into the hall bath long enough to grab soap from the sink, then continuing up to the third floor. Soon water was running in the pipes, making its long journey up from the basement heater tank.

When I felt like moving again, I checked my ribs, but Coldfield had focused on the softer target of my midsection. He'd inflicted ample bruising and spared his knuckles. The man was a smart thinker when it came to his brand of mayhem. Everything still hurt, and I stubbornly held on to it as though that would somehow help Escott.

I hobbled into the kitchen to blink at the clock. If he rushed things, Kroun could get cleaned up and make it to bed before dawn. I could take my time.

I made sure the front door was bolted, checked the back again just because, then vanished, sinking down through the kitchen floor. Once solid again in my hidden alcove the bruising and pain were magically gone, but I was tired, very tired.

The small table light next to my cot was on, so I didn't reappear in fumbling blackness. I'm a vampire who's gotten really allergic to the dark. I didn't used to be that way; but, after the crap I'd been through since my change, anyone would want to leave a lamp burning in the window.

No windows were in my artificial cave, but that was fine, what with my allergy to sunlight. Kroun had a right to be concerned about avoiding it, but he could manage. Things had to be a lot better for him in this place than wherever he'd hidden after the big boom. Did he have a supply of his home earth with him? I'd not thought to ask.

Damn, I didn't want to think about him and what to do with him and all the attendant complications concerning his apparent death. But the problem would be hanging around like an unpaid bill when I woke again, no way out of it. The mess Kroun had come to town to clear up was worse than before.

Derner—following my orders—had the right story to give to the New York mob bosses about Kroun's demise, but the details might not satisfy them. They were told that Kroun had been killed in the car explosion, then the man who rigged the bomb was in turn killed by me in a shoot-out. Very tidy. Too much so.

"They won't swallow that goldfish," I muttered, shrugging from my suit coat and prying off my shoes.

It would get out that there was no body in the destroyed car. The bomb had been big, but not so much as to wholly obliterate its intended target. Unless Kroun did something, New York would only send another man to find out why and then bump me. I'd gotten myself noticed by the wrong people one too many times. The idea of getting clear of town for a while was tempting, but that would leave Gordy holding the bag.

My other option was just to get it over with and let the mob do the hit. Let them think they'd executed me, then they could go home satisfied. Easy enough. I'd survived such attacks before. The problem with that was I'd not be able to go back to my business again. Just getting the legal papers to a new name forged would be a pain in the ass. I had friends, family, a club to run, things to do, and I needed to be able to do them as myself, Jack Fleming.

I stretched flat on the cot, loosening my belt, and felt gravity tug me toward the center of the planet. Illusion. The pull was really from the spread of earth under the protective oilcloth. This was my portion of the grave I'd never gone to, a tiny scrap of peace in the red chaos, protection from the insanity of my subconscious. My body seemed to weigh a ton; the feeling was surprisingly pleasant.

If I could hypnotize that next mobster into forgetting his job all would be well, but even thinking about using one of my evil-eye whammies made my head buzz like a too-crowded beehive. The last time I'd employed that talent had damn near exploded my brain. Deep-down instinct said another attempt would kill me. My nights of pretending to be Lamont Cranston and clouding men's minds like the Shadow were over.

Kroun was not crippled in that area, though. I could probably talk him into fixing things, especially if it meant his own safety. If I were him, I'd be cooperative and willing to try.

Only he wasn't me.

Who the hell is he? I wondered—my last thought as the rising sun swept me into the dreamless abyss for the day.

KROUN

GOD, *my chest hurts.*

Not as bad as before, but it was like a hangover that wouldn't quite give up and leave.

The through and through Gabriel had taken was healed; he could tell that much because the itching deep under his knitted skin had almost stopped. It still felt as though pieces of himself had torn loose and were wriggling their way back into place again. What wouldn't fit kept trying to migrate up his throat. If he was careful not to breathe or move fast, it wasn't too bad. But just when everything seemed settled, the internal prickling would rise, crest, and set him off hacking like a lunger on his last legs. Gabe was damned bored with it.

He climbed the stairs slowly, hoping there would be no more visitors to make things exciting. He went to what Fleming called the guest bath, twisted the sink's left-hand tap, waiting, waiting, waiting until the water ran hot.

Gabe stared at the mirror over the sink. His faded, near-transparent reflection stared back. The ones like Fleming had no reflection at all. How did he get by without being able to see himself? Shaving must be an ordeal.

On the other hand, he could disappear and get well again anytime he pleased. Gabe would have given much to have that; it would have saved him a lot of pain the last couple nights.

Leaning close, he checked his tongue and eyes, didn't find anything of interest, then scratched his chin and neck. Yeah, a shave would be good, but have to wait. No razor. Did he need a haircut? If he could grab his hair in the back then it was too long. Gabe ran a hand over his head. Yeah, half an inch there at least. Time for a trim, get rid of the singed areas.

The ridge was still there of course—the one in the bone on the left side of his skull. It marked where the bullet that originally killed him had gone in. And stayed. That small piece of metal allowed him to discern a remnant of his presence in mirrors.

His head hurt. Not like when it first happened, but bad enough, aggravated by the latest calamities. People had tried killing him yet again, and he didn't like the violent reminder that not so long ago someone had actually succeeded.

He also didn't like thinking about how many other people wanted him dead. One fewer to their numbers, but still—

I'd trusted him. *Goddamned Mitchell. Goddamned bastard. I should have seen that coming.*

It wasn't as though Mitchell had intentionally shot Gabe tonight at the girl's flat, but he *had* planned the bomb for the car. What a dirty way to kill a man.

Too bad only Fleming got to have all the fun of beating the hell out of—

Jack Fleming. Now *there* was one crazy noodle. One minute trying to be helpful, the next letting himself get pulped flat in his own house. What kind of a screwball was he? He seemed to know all the ropes about being a—Gabe stumbled over *vampire*.

Ugly word.

He'd read up on it, of course, and other details had just come to him from God knows where. Northside Gordy had filled in more blanks, but getting the firsthand knowledge from a guy who'd actually been through the same mill was much more useful. Getting it without raising too many questions was the problem. Fleming was curious and had only begun to start with the snooping.

Reporters. They're incurable.

Gabe was inclined to shed him fast then get lost, but Fleming might come looking, full of good intentions. With the whole of Gordy's organization on the hunt, Gabe wouldn't stay lost for long. He'd have to handle this carefully, keep the man on his side until a real exit could be managed.

He had been lucky at surviving until now, until they sent him to Chicago to take out the piss-and-vinegar punk who'd iced Hog Bristow.

Having other errands to see to, Gabe had gone, hoping to figure a way to avoid killing anyone. Fortunately, the punk had been smart enough to save himself.

Finding out that he was in the same bloodsuckers' club—well, that had been a real distraction.

But while the company was interesting, Jack Fleming was too reckless about who he let in on his secret; sooner or later, he'd tell others about the new guy in town. Though he seemed all right for the moment, he could turn on a thin dime.

The man was *nuts*.

That was plain from their first meeting. It'd been damned hair-raising when Fleming had gone into that fit. Gabe couldn't recall ever seeing anyone acting like that before, the sudden uncontrolled shivering, the eyes rolling up, then the poor bastard vanished into nothing. He said he was better now, but if he forgot himself and tried to hypnotize anyone again . . . apparently that was what set him off.

Gabe felt sorry for what had been done to Fleming. Torturing a bystander had never been part of the plan to get rid of Bristow, and it was just as well Fleming didn't hold a grudge. For now. The guy was trying hard to keep himself together, but he was still loopy as a bedbug, and that made him dangerous to be around. Soon as Gabe was on his feet and able to make a good job of disappearing, he'd get clear.

For that he would need a car and money.

Lots of money.

There were ways to get it, but later, when he wasn't wheezing like a bad engine.

Moving with great caution to keep from coughing, Gabe stripped to the waist and ran a hot, soapy washcloth over his face and neck, going easy over the fresh scar on his chest. There wasn't enough time for a shower-bath. He would only have to put on the same wrecked clothes again. It felt like he'd worn these for a week. If this was what being dead involved then he should have planned it better.

God, what have I let myself into? Is this going to work?

Gabriel Kroun wasn't a nobody who could leave the party without a ripple. He'd been through that before, the first time he died and found himself trapped in his previous life. Things *had* to run differently this time, and he had to work it better to avoid the same problems. The boys back home either liked and feared him or hated and feared him, and there was at least one who couldn't let his very public death slide without doing something.

Fleming didn't seem to be too worried about that, and he should be; he was either an idiot or counting on Gabe to step in and help.

I might. But not if it ended with old enemies finding out he was still walking around. Gabe had gone through too much to waste the opportunity to get away from the mob life.

Some of them were okay guys, but then Mitchell had seemed to be an okay guy. With a hypnotic nudge for insurance, the man was made incurious about where and how Gabe spent his days, and that had been enough. Not once had Gabe thought to add, *Oh, by the way, don't try killing me.*

On no account was he going to go back to that. Somebody up there had handed him a new start on a platter. He was certain he didn't deserve it, and suspicious that it might be yanked away.

Money and a car. Have to figure out something . . .

The guest room was clean, but basic. There was a wardrobe, no closet. None of the rooms on the floor had closets. Except for spare blankets, the wardrobe was empty and too small to hide in. He pulled all the blankets out and spread them on the bed. Damn, that looked vulnerable.

The room had one tall, narrow window with curtains and a pull-down shade that would dim the full daylight when it came. Easing it aside he peered at the street below and each house within view. A few lights showed in windows. Early risers were getting ready for work, their wives making coffee, eggs, hotcakes, bacon. He could remember eating those things, but not their taste. It had been good. He was sure of that.

Bacon . . . greasy, hot, crisp when fried right, but was it sweet, sour, bitter, or salty? He just didn't know.

He put the shade back and yanked the heavy curtains together. The predawn light was strong, leaving painful afterimages on his eyes. Damn, his head got worse because of it.

He shucked his shoes and trousers, folding himself into a clean, soft bed. Not bad. Damned good, in fact. The sheets seemed too short for his legs, so he messed them around until they were loose enough to pull over his head along with the extra blankets. Black as a mine now, dark enough for—

Just a few seconds to go.

His head pounded in weary anticipation. The left side. Always.

Gabe slipped into absolute immobility swiftly, managing to shut his eyes at the last instant. He'd forgotten once and spent the day with them open. When night came, they'd felt like razor-edged rocks.

Images flashed over the inside of his lids. His own little movie show. He got to relive Mitchell's shooting him all over again. Several times. Even once was too many. Then memory swept Gabe back to that damn car and the explosion. He stayed there in the searing heat for a long, long while, tasting the smoke, feeling the blind panic, the pain, tearing his hands as he slammed out the door and rolled clear before hell could suck him in for real and forever.

He was trapped in that bad spot much too long, going through it too many times. After a very long, long eternity, it finally lost strength, like a storm wearing itself out. The inner lightning and thunder ceased, leaving only the wind.

That was a good sound.

When the nightmares faded, he dreamed of wind whirring through pine needles. It was hollow and haunting, sad, cold music; he thought he should be afraid of it, but just never seemed to feel anything but comfort. He was safe there. At peace.

The sound gradually merged with shapes, pale light, and shadows. He lay on his back under a black sky shot with stars. Raw bare ground chilled his body, the scent of pines and the bruised smell of fresh-turned earth filled his head. A pine tree loomed tall over him. Its boughs waved in the wind, restless, singing to the night. Theirs was the sweetest, most calming song he'd ever heard. He had never before felt so relaxed and content.

It lasted until a heavy wedge of damp earth slapped over his face.

What are they doing? Why are they doing this to me?

His face was soon covered, his body frozen, his mind screaming and impotent. He couldn't see, only hear: the grunt of a man, breathing hoarse as he labored, the scrape of metal in the dirt—a shovel?—somewhere in the distance a woman sobbed. Hers was the anguish of the heartbroken. It hurt to listen to that kind of pain. He felt sorry for her, grieving for him so hard. If he could just wake up he could tell her it was all right. There'd been a mistake. He wasn't dead. He tried to remember her face . . .

But a fire-hot flare sizzled through his skull, obliterating everything. When that faded, it was too late for anything but blank terror. He was completely buried. Earth clogged his eyes and ears. No more singing from the wind, only silence like death, but worse because he was aware of it, of being dead.

Other, much more fragmented, scenes shot past. Some were good, most were not. They flashed and flitted too quick to grasp and study. Green land, deep water, a sky so solidly blue it hurt to look on; a room stinking of blood, his own laughter sounding too open and happy for that place; a tall man standing over him, swinging the buckle end of a belt, face blank, eyes crazy.

He taught me to kill. Why?

The horrors rose and ebbed, and, in the pauses between, the soft deep rush of wind through pine branches gradually returned, offering a temporary ease. That never lasted, and he wanted it to; but in the end, at the very end, he would begin to shift and struggle and push at the earth until it crumbled away from his face and harsh, cold air dragged him fully awake.

Gabe pitched off the smothering blankets, yelling. Without air in his lungs no sound came out. There was a moment's absolute certainty that he was still buried, and then he drew breath, abruptly aware he was in Fleming's guest room. Sunset had freed him from the steel grip of the monsters in his head.

Somewhat. They'd retreated only as far as the shadowed corners in his mind, grinning, waiting for their next chance to come at him again.

He leaned over the side of the bed and coughed. A glob of blood and tissue splattered the floor.

Damn it.

Another night to get through, alive or dead or whatever the hell it was for him now.

At least his head had stopped hurting.

FLEMING

I woke instantly, my mind sharper for being rested, the question about Kroun still there, if no closer to an answer. Pulling on last night's clothes, I vanished and floated, going solid in the kitchen. The house was quiet, though I could hear Kroun stirring upstairs. He gave a groan and coughed wetly. I felt sorry for him, for not being able to heal faster. We needed a trip to the Stockyards to get him some stuff fresh from a vein. That would help.

The phone rang. It was probably Derner, following orders. I'd told him to call me only after a certain hour, keeping any mention of *sunset* out of the conversation. He just might be imaginative enough to put two and three together about my condition and didn't need more clues than he already possessed. Like most of the mobsters I dealt with, he knew I was uncannily tough and had earned Gordy's friendship, which was usually enough to keep them from asking awkward questions. Now more than ever, since I couldn't hypnotize people anymore, I had to be careful.

I finally answered. "Yeah?"

"Boss?" Derner's voice. Terse. Tense. He could pack a lot into a single word.

"Yeah. How'd things go today?"

"No hitches at this end. Everything went smooth on that job."

I took him to mean the cleanup at Bobbi's flat. Derner and I were both wary that the phones might be tapped. It was illegal, but that detail was not something J. Edgar was too particular about. So long as his name didn't come into things, and his agents didn't get caught, he'd turn a blind eye if it got him good headlines as a gangbuster. Thus ran the scuttlebutt I'd heard from others, especially Gordy. I wondered how he'd come to learn it.

"Anything else?" I asked Derner.

"There's some guys here. They're upset about their friend having car trouble."

That would be muscle from Kroun's New York mob, pissed about the bombing. "How bad is it?"

"Real bad. I told them what you said and that you'd talk to them here, but they went looking for you."

New York would know about my nightclub, Lady Crymsyn. The muscle would be waiting there. The sign tacked on the front door with its TEMPORARILY CLOSED—BACK SOON! wouldn't discourage them. "I'll just talk to them and—"

"Those guys who blew in were hopping mad. They won't be talking. No chance. You gotta disappear yourself. This is serious."

"They serious about the big guy, too?" I meant Gordy.

"Just you for now. They heard he wasn't involved, but you have to get out of town. I told them who was really behind it; but you were the boss at the time, so you get the blame."

"That figures." Doesn't matter what kind of job you've got, doctor, lawyer, Indian chief, when a disaster happens while you're running the show, it's your fault.

Derner said, "I can get you a ride out of town, money, too."

"No need."

"But—"

"It's all right. I'll deal with them." There was the sound of footsteps from the hall; Kroun had come downstairs. If I explained the situation to him in the right way he might be open to helping me out of this jam. He couldn't vanish, but was still able to make people change their minds to his way of thinking. If he wanted to stay dead to them, he could arrange it. "When the coast is clear, I'll stop by and fill you in."

Silence from Derner's end. He must be getting used to how I worked. He'd been there the night I'd faced down Kroun and survived. Maybe he thought I could somehow talk my way out of this one as well.

"How many of them are there?" I asked.

"There's two of us, pal."

I jumped. The reply hadn't come from the phone, but from directly behind me. A stranger's soft voice. Something, probably a gun, prodded my lower spine, forestalling further motion on my part. People who interrupted calls in this manner always had guns. How long had he been here? Not long enough to have searched as far as the guest bedroom. Or maybe he had—and discovered what appeared to be Kroun's dead body. Oh, hell.

"Say you'll call him back." The man's tone was almost conversational and very confident.

"Boss . . . ?" Derner sounded odd. He must have heard.

"I'll call you back," I said and dropped the receiver onto its hook.

The man said, "Good boy. Put your hands on the wall. High up."

I did so, and he frisked me, making a fast, efficient job of it, finding nothing threatening. My gun was in the overcoat hanging over the kitchen chair, well out of reach.

"You Jack Fleming?" he asked.

"Yeah. You one of Whitey Kroun's people?"

"No. Whitey was one of *my* people."

Oh, hell, again. Kroun's boss. Not that this should be a surprise. He sounded calm, but I sensed otherwise. Some of them could do that, hold a relaxed front, yet be flushed with rage. I was better at dealing with the ones who lost control and gave in to their emotions. This steadier type was a lot more unpredictable.

He went on. "Mitchell was also one of my people. So was Hog Bristow. They're dead, and you're not. You understand why I'm here?"

"You gonna buckwheats me?" I asked. My mouth went dry, just like that, at the word.

It was how the mob dealt with some of their enemies. Buckwheats meant a slow, hideous death, lots of blood, lots of screaming. I'd been through it and would not suffer again. I would kill to avoid it, no matter the consequences. Despite this internal promise, cold sweat flared over my skin, over the lines of scars Bristow had carved into me. My gut gave the kind of fast light flutter that presages vomiting. I leaned hard on my hands and took a deep breath, trying to stifle the nausea.

"That was Bristow's hobby," said the man. "I heard he did some knife work on you."

"Yeah. He did." The long icy threads left by his blade pulled tight on my flesh.

"And somehow you're still walking? Whitey said as much, but I didn't believe him." The man spoke quickly yet with careful, educated articulation. He wasn't any jumped-up street mug.

"He told you right." God, I was sick. Dizzy sick. A wave of it went over me, cold as gutter slush. If I fell into one of those damned fits . . . no. Absolutely not. Too humiliating. Swallowing dry, I let out my breath and sucked air, tasting my fear. "Whitey decided I'd paid enough."

"I get that. It's paid. Whitey let you off for Bristow, but I can't let you off for Whitey. How did you arrange the bomb?"

"Not me. Mitchell. He was behind it."

"You got Mitchell to—"

"No, he was on his own!" My voice was high and harsh. I pulled it down, fighting my not-unreasonable panic. Jeez, when had I started trembling? "I didn't know or I'd have stopped him. He wanted Kroun's job. If it'd worked right, I'd have gone up as well. Mitchell got his for it."

"So you say." The pressure of the gun muzzle increased and I couldn't help but flinch. "All the same, Whitey got blown to hell, and you didn't, and that's what matters to me."

This bird had not searched the place thoroughly, else he'd have found Kroun upstairs, dead to the world, and this would be a different conversation. Where the hell was Kroun, anyway? If he'd just walk in . . . "You know I didn't kill him. It was—"

"Not my concern."

Screw it. I wasn't going to beg for a chance to explain.

"I came to do a job," he said. "That's all."

I stared hard at the black phone. "One thing," I said.

"Yeah?"

"Who else is on your list?"

"Why do you ask?"

"I don't want others to pay for what you think I've done." The muzzle shifted and now rested hard against the back of my head. It felt good. It's a bad night in hell when the prospect of a bullet in the skull seems to be the easy way to get clear of problems. No bullet, lead or even wood, could slow me for long, but I did think about that kind of total oblivion for a few seconds. I wouldn't go there, though. Not ever again. I'd play the cards I'd been dealt and see the game through . . . with a moderate amount of cheating. "So when you're finished here—"

"You're it, pal," said the man. "No one else."

But I couldn't trust him.

I let myself vanish. I'd been fighting the urge to do so, and now I went out like a light, but only for the barest second, long enough to shift and return with death's own grasp on his arm. The gun went off. Twice. Right next to my ear. I barely noticed, twisting and slugging hard, anger blurring my senses. He grunted and sagged but got a strong left in with his free hand. Tough guy. But my second punch took him out, and he suddenly weighed a ton. I let him drop, dragging the gun clear of his grip, and stifling the itch to kick him for good measure.

He said there were two of them. I vanished again before the second guy could come running. My hearing was diminished, but I'd know if anyone was close. Nothing stirred. I rushed through the downstairs quicker than wind—no one else around—then went solid to check on the fallen.

He was taller than average, with a hard-packed build under the expensive coat. Considering his high level of confidence, he was younger than I'd expected, not far into his thirties. Despite the winter, his skin was tanned and healthy, and he might have given Roland Lambert a good run for his money for film-star looks. Jobs in the gangs tended to age a man, but this bird seemed immune. Myself, I felt about a hundred years old, give or take a week.

The back door was unlocked. Damnation. I'd brick the thing over, but the bastards would probably just drop down the chimney like Santa. I turned the bolt (for all the good that would do) as Kroun came in, but I saw him as a corner-of-the-eye movement. I was startled enough to swing the gun on him.

He froze in place, genuinely alarmed, palms spread. "Easy there, it's me."

As if that was reassuring.

Kroun wore only socks, skivvies, and had dragged on his bloodied shirt in lieu of a bathrobe. He frowned at the man on the floor. "Cripes."

"Friend of yours?" I asked.

"Unfortunately for you, yes."

I put the gun on the table, within easy reach. "He was shooting up the place. I had to clock him."

Kroun took that in along with the holes in the wall. "Well, you both made a good job of it." There was no longer a rasp in his voice. The day's rest must have fixed that, but he didn't look happy. "Is he broken?"

"Not permanently. Now what?"

"'Now what' what?"

"He's after me because of you. I'd have to kill him to stop him and then someone else will follow and someone else, and I've got enough god-damned dead guys on my hands."

He gave me a funny look. "You all right?"

"No, I'm—" I shut down, getting control. I still felt the gun's muzzle kissing the back of my head and couldn't believe I'd found that a comforting thing, even for a second. Shoving away the memory, the anger at myself and the circumstances, and taking a breath, I began again. "I am not all right. I got mugs like him breaking into my place to kill me. There's at least one other waiting somewhere else for his chance, and I'm damned sick of it. If you've got any influence over these bastards, get rid of them. I want them off my back for good."

He just looked at me, pupils dilated and unreadable, but his mouth went tight. He didn't like being ordered around, but then who does? "I can't do that," he said.

"You're the only one who can."

"I—" He bit off the reply, then looked at the fallen man again. "If I do that, they'll know I'm alive. I don't want them to know I'm alive."

"Hypnotize them not to remember you."

"It won't last."

"Long enough to buy you a head start."

"Hell, kid, you're not asking much. You know what I went through to get dead?"

"Yeah, actually I *do*."

That got me a double take.

"Welcome to the club," I added.

"Cripes," he muttered again. "All that for nothing?"

"It's how the world works."

His next remark was back-alley foul.

"You'll be a hero for surviving it—and you can tell them who's really responsible. That lets Gordy off the hook."

"And you, too."

"What's the big deal? Fix this mess, then take a vacation. Retire if that's what you want."

Kroun stared like I'd gone around the bend. Retirement in his line of work nearly always involved a funeral.

"You'll have to do the fixing anyway," I went on. "Odds are they're already wise to there being no body in that car, and they've been asking questions. My way they go home alive. Your way, they either get killed or kill other people, making an even bigger mess, and—"

He held a hand up, forestalling further persuasion. "Yeah-yeah, okay, enough already. I'll put the fix in. But you are going to *owe* me."

I worked hard not to show too much relief. He'd made a choice I could live with. I'd worry about the debt later.

"But not like this," he added.

"Like what?"

He gestured at himself. "Looks are everything in this game."

What?

"You want me to play? Get me cleaned up first."

He had to be kidding.

"Use your noodle. I'm not going anywhere fast looking like a train wreck."

I got my mental gearbox shifted. Finally. He *did* look pretty ridiculous. He must have clothes back at his hotel or wherever he'd stayed before the explosion. We could go there and pick them up.

"What about him?" I pointed to Handsome Hank on the floor.

"You got rope, don't you?" Kroun turned and went upstairs.

3

I had rope, or rather Escott did, stowed in the basement. I helped myself to the whole coil and trussed up the guy after searching him. He had a wallet filled with twenties, a pocketknife, a fountain pen, three money clips holding wads of cash I didn't bother to count, wire-rimmed glasses in a hard leather case, keys, and a map of Chicago with the locations of this house and my club neatly circled. No identification, though, not surprising for his sort.

In another case, larger than the one for his glasses, I found a clean syringe and four small, unlabeled vials. Their dark amber glass effectively hid the color of the liquid contents.

I gave the guy a second glance. So, did he go in for morphine or cocaine? Maybe he had diabetes; he didn't look like a doper, but some people were good at hiding their secrets. I should know. The lack of a label on the vials gave me the idea that the stuff hadn't come from any corner drugstore.

Everything went on the kitchen table next to my hat. I blindfolded and gagged him with a couple of the dish towels and dragged him into the hall. In case he felt frisky when he woke, I tied him fast to the newel post at the foot of the stairs.

In the parlor, I edged open the front curtain and saw an unfamiliar Studebaker parked where I usually left my Buick. Some people have a lot of nerve.

The street seemed clear, but that didn't mean anything; might as well see if he'd brought friends. I unlocked the front and got the mail and papers, tossing things on the hall floor, then went outside to look at the car, offering an easily bushwhacked target. No one took the bait. Damn. I still had plenty of rope left, too.

The car's registration was to a rental garage by the train station. The paperwork bore an illegible signature. My prisoner and his absent pal must have been confident about getting in and out of town without trouble. Had they planned to disappear my body or just didn't think the cops were up to tracing a connection between us? Probably the latter. A lot of these guys were either stupid or brazen depending on how smart they thought they were. Unless someone in Gordy's mob squawked—and no one would—they'd do their job and walk away clean, simple as that. Maybe New York expected Gordy to do the mopping up for them. He'd have done so; those were the rules.

I phoned Derner, who picked up halfway through the first ring. He sounded a whole lot more tense.

"It's me," I said. "Everything's okay, and I'll be in later tonight."

"You sure? What's going on?"

Jeez, he was going to make me think he cared. Maybe he did. If I dropped out of sight, then he'd have to run things. "Expect me when you see me. Business as usual until then."

"Right, okay." Not a lot of confidence there, for which I couldn't blame him. "The cops have been by—it's about Alan Caine. They want to talk to you."

This was tricky. The lines were likely tapped, and Derner knew it. He was a smart man, so this could be a way of feeding the cops misleading information. Fine by me; I could play with the best of them. "They'll have to wait, I've got things to do tonight."

"They're wondering about Jewel Caine, too."

"What do you mean?"

"The way they were going on, she didn't kill herself like the papers said."

"She didn't?"

"Which means someone did her in as well."

"Maybe the same guy who bumped Caine?"

"Whoever that is," he said.

Oh, Derner was doing genius stuff tonight. "My money's on Hoyle. He's crazy. Didn't Caine owe him money?"

"I wouldn't know, but I wouldn't be surprised."

"Okay, see if any of the boys have seen Hoyle. I wanna know what he's been up to lately. If he's the one, we send him over. I don't want no trouble with the coppers."

"Right, Boss."

I hoped someone was listening in. "Another thing—see about making arrangements for Jewel Caine."

"What?" He sounded surprised.

"Arrangements—a funeral. Anyone claimed her? She got family?"

"Uh—"

"Look into it. She was a good egg, we can do right by her."

"Well . . . uh . . ." Derner hesitated. He'd be thinking about the money it would cost. The night's takings from just one of the slot machines in the Nightcrawler's back room would pay for a nice service. If necessary, I'd point that out to him. "What about Alan Caine?"

"See if he's got family, then ship him out. Jewel wouldn't want to share the billing."

I hung up, then dialed a number I'd scribbled in pencil on my shirt cuff the night before. There was a delay as I negotiated with a hotel switchboard operator, then Bobbi's voice came on.

"It's me," I said again, but my tone was a lot warmer. "You okay?"

"Are you?" she countered.

"I am now, sweetheart."

"Anything wrong?"

"All the time," I said cheerfully. "But I'm taking care of it."

Bobbi required a lot more convincing than Derner, and such convincing would require us to be in the same room so I could give her a hands-on demonstration. Hands, lips, skin to skin, I was more than ready to show her exactly how well I was doing. I was a little nervous about it, but it beat the previous mind-freezing terror I'd felt before. Escott's version of a pep talk had sorted out a lot of things.

I owed him, all right.

And . . . Bobbi didn't know about the fight yet, or she'd have—

"I'm glad you're better," she said shortly. "Now what the hell happened to Charles?"

Oh.

Damn.

Damn, damn, damn, *damn*.

Given a choice, I'd rather have Coldfield come back and make me into a sparring dummy for a few hours instead of trying to explain things to her. "Uh, we had a disagreement that got out of hand."

"*Disagreement?*" Bobbi rarely shouted. As a singer, she thought it might damage her vocal cords, but this was an unequivocal shriek.

I winced. "Look, it's just something we got into, and it's over now. We're friends again."

"*You put him in the HOSPITAL!*"

"I know that, but—"

"*You could have KILLED him!*"

"Yeah, but—"

Bobbi made more loud and shrill observations about Escott's condition and my responsibility for it. I tried a placating tone when I could get a word in, then noticed Kroun had put his head around the corner. He'd shaved and resumed his damaged clothes and had his palms over his ears, letting me know he could hear her end all too well. I refused to be embarrassed about it.

"Let-her-talk," he whispered, exaggerating each word so I could read his lips.

I didn't have any better ideas, and it was obvious that Bobbi had been boiling for some time, so I shut up. She was staying at the same hotel with Gordy and his girlfriend, being watched over by Shoe Coldfield. He must have let her know a thing or three.

As before, I stood there and took it, and in some ways it hurt more than a physical beating. When she asked for the why of the matter, I fell back on the disagreement excuse.

"Why won't you tell me?" she demanded.

"Because it's not important anymore, and I know that sounds like a load of bull, but it's over now, it really is. I've apologized to him, and we're copacetic again."

She made a low growling noise, thick with dissatisfaction. Her protective soft spot for Escott was the size of the Grand Canyon. Perhaps he could persuade her to calm down. It struck me then that everyone had assumed I was the bad guy in the matter. Granted, I was still on my feet and a lot faster and stronger than Escott, but he did throw the first punch. A lot of them. But I'd thrown the last and most effective, so I was the bully. Those were the hard-cheese rules; I'd just have to live with them.

Kroun moved to the table to check the stuff I'd taken off his friend. He opened the cases, didn't seem surprised by the syringe, looked in the wallet, and tossed it back. He went through the contents of the money clips. Each had five twenties on top, and the rest were fifties and C-notes. I lost track as he counted through them, but at least nine or ten grand was there. He pocketed the fortune without a blink.

"Listen, Bobbi," I said, "we'll talk to Charles, and he'll let you know he's all right. We can visit Roland at the same time—and how is he doing?"

That subject change got me another earful, but not nearly as harsh. She knew I wasn't to blame for Roland's wounding. Not too much, anyway.

Kroun picked up the car keys, tossing them high and catching them one-handed, showing impatience. Nice to know that he was so well recovered, but I still had more peacemaking to conduct with Bobbi and put my back to him. She'd cooled down somewhat, hopefully to the point where she wouldn't take my block off when we did get together. Kroun cleared his throat, coughed, and spat something into the sink. He ran water.

"What's that?" Bobbi asked.

"My guest from the party you threw last night."

"I thought he'd be gone."

"We still have some loose ends to tie up. It's going to take a while."

"The last visiting hour at the hospital starts at eight. I'll be there, then coming back to this hotel again."

"I'll go as fast as I can, but you know how it is."

"Yes, I certainly do." Dry tone from her, very dry. Ouch.

There was no way to end this one on her good side, so I offered a weak bye-I'll-see-you-soon and hung up. I waited to see if the phone rang with a fresh emergency, but it kept quiet.

"You ready?" Kroun asked. He'd wandered into the hall. He watched the prisoner, who still seemed to be out.

"Not yet. I need a new shirt."

"Make it quick, I need one more than you do."

A hot bath and shave would have been great, but the most I had time for was a fast swipe with a wet towel, then jump into a fresh suit. Not my best one, nor the worst, but it went with the thickening chin stubble. Maniac killers lurking in dark alleys might think twice about taking a swing at me; I was less sure about the mugs at the Nightcrawler Club.

When I came downstairs, the man was no longer tied to the banister post, and rope ends lay on the floor. What the . . . ?

Kroun was in the parlor, feet on the low table, reading a paper. "Don't worry," he said, not looking up. "I just put him in the car is all."

"You—?"

"Carried him out the door in front of God and everyone, yes, that's what I did. No one's made a commotion about it. You ready?"

I couldn't wait to get rid of him. Them.

I went to the hall closet, shrugged on one of my old overcoats, then to the kitchen to get my hat, a spare house key from one of the drawers, and the gun from Escott's coat. The roscoe the intruder brought was gone, so it figured that Kroun was armed, too. Double-armed, since he'd had a gun last night. He'd left the other effects on the table. I scooped them into a pocket, noting the bullet holes in the wall above the phone. Those would have to be patched before Escott came home.

It hardly seemed worth the effort to lock the house, but I went through the motions. Kroun handed over the car keys and got in on the passenger side. After the barest hesitation, he slammed the door shut. I slipped behind the wheel, adjusting the mirror.

"Where is he?" I asked. The backseat was empty of mobster.

"Trunk," said Kroun.

"He'll freeze."

"Only if we keep sitting here."

Taking the hint, I started the motor. I'd driven a Studebaker once before when working on a case, and afterward read magazine ads with close interest. The car was supposed to have a setup so that when stopped on a hill you didn't have to dance with the clutch, gas, and brake pedals to keep from rolling backward before it went into gear. As we were in a flat area, there was no opportunity to test things, but it was a sweet ride all the same. I hoped the guy in the trunk had air and not exhaust fumes to eat.

"Which hotel?" I asked Kroun.

"Hotel?"

"Where your stuff is."

"Skip that, take me to a men's store. A good one."

What the hell? "You're going buy stuff? It'll take all night."

"Not if it's a good store."

"Longer than getting the stuff at your hotel."

"Just find a place and give me ten minutes."

Son of a bitch. I wasn't interested in arguing, though, so I drove a few miles and pulled up to a clear stretch of curb. There were plenty to spare for a change since this part of the Loop didn't do much evening business.

Kroun got out, moving easily. During the day his bum leg had healed. He reached the store's door just as some guy inside locked it. Fine, like it or not, we would swing by his hotel instead.

When Kroun rapped the glass, the man shook his head and made an exaggerated shrug of apology. He probably didn't like the looks of this scruffy customer. He suddenly froze in place. For a second I thought Kroun had done an evil-eye whammy. The guy glanced over his shoulder then stared at Kroun or rather at something in his hand. Not a gun.

Kroun had pulled out one of the money clips and waved several of the C-notes temptingly back and forth. A second guy joined the first and also froze, but only for a moment. The power of raw cash galvanized them, God bless America.

The door magically unlocked, and Kroun walked in like he owned the place. For all intents and purposes, he did. I marked the time to see if he'd make his ten minutes, then quit the car, going around to the trunk. The other key on the ring opened it.

There weren't a lot of pedestrians, and they were in a hurry to get out of the cold wind whipping around the buildings. Privacy secured, I lifted the trunk lid to check on the guy. He was curled on his side facing away from me, hands tied behind him, not looking any too comfortable. He stirred a little, his movements groggy and uncertain.

I adjusted his gag so nothing covered his nose. He jerked at the touch. "Easy does it, pal. You breathing okay?"

He *mumph*ed something, pissed. Couldn't blame him.

"Glad to hear it. Want to tell me where your partner is?"

The next *mumph* I interpreted as cussing rather than anything cooperative.

"I'm betting he's at my nightclub. Want to put something on that?"

More cussing, and he started fighting against the ropes.

I slammed the lid quick as a group of office girls scurried past; a few of them giggled as I tipped my hat at them, nonchalant as Fred Astaire pretending to be a bum.

Someone had pulled the store's shades down for the night, but the lights remained on. I strolled slow up and down the walk to stay limber and kept my ears open for noises from the car trunk. If the guy drew attention, I'd have to clock him again. He didn't, so I walked and checked my watch.

This was ridiculous, of course. The other night I'd tried to make myself permanently dead, and when that hadn't worked out, I'd planned for a second, more extreme effort that would have succeeded. Right now I should have been on a slab in a morgue, not standing in freezing wind outside a store waiting while some lunatic bought himself a suit.

And yet, here I was . . . and, strangely, it was all right.

Which had to make *me* the lunatic.

I'd read stories about suicides, and knew of some who had gone through with it, and at the time the thought was *what a waste*, felt a little sadness, and that was pretty much it. Not until I saw the blind fury on Escott's face did I consider its harsh effect on other people concerned, the ones close to the victim. There was no understanding or forgiveness for my actions, no shred of sympathy, as I'd expected. He'd accused me of being a selfish bastard for doing that to Bobbi, to him, to everyone who gave a tinker's damn about me. He was right. It wasn't only about my pain. It was the pain my hurting myself would give them. Better to just spit in their eyes and walk away with no explanation. Only I hadn't had the guts to do that—or the guts to ask for help.

So, I had indeed been a selfish, cowardly bastard.

Wincing, I silently added in *stupid* at the beginning of the list. I should have it printed for a sign and nail it to the wall over my bed. The idea would be to do my best to disagree with it each night when I woke up.

Would Escott remember my hospital visit? Would he believe me when I told him I was better? What I'd done had left scars on us both. It had changed things. For good or for bad, the change would always be there.

We'd just have to deal with it. The deed was done, and I'd have to live with the consequences.

That—or spit in his eye.

I shook my head. No. I wouldn't be traveling that road. He'd once crawled out of his own private abyss. I could do the same.

In nine minutes, Kroun emerged, looking a new man entirely in a sharp dark suit and polished shoes. When I first met him, he had a way of filling a room all by himself. People noticed it; men stood up straighter, and women leaned closer when he walked past. It had faded with the explosion and shooting, but that quality was back in spades. The hired help must have responded, for he was getting royal treatment.

He buttoned up a heavy wool overcoat and pulled on leather gloves. One of the shop guys clipped the tag from a charcoal gray fedora and handed it over with a slight bow and broad smile. They moved out of the way for three guys rushing past with arms full of boxes. I obligingly held the car door as they took turns shoving everything into the backseat. Last to go in were two suitcases wedged on top, blocking the window.

Kroun politely thanked everyone, tipped them each a twenty, which was twice what they earned in a week, and got in the car. They enthusiastically thanked him, adding invitations to come back whenever he liked, day or night.

I got in and turned the motor over. He checked his new silver wristwatch. "Ten minutes, if this thing is right."

It looked too expensive ever to be wrong.

"Now *that's* how you buy stuff," he said, satisfied.

"Oh yeah?"

"Let them do the work. They know the territory."

"What about mirrors?" Those were the main reason I got clothes only after a store was closed. It was easier than hypnotizing the whole staff—which was no longer an option anyway. I just slipped in, picked what I wanted, and left money in the manager's office along with the tags. Unlawful entry I was good at, but I wasn't a thief.

"I just stripped and had them dress me from the skin out. Ben Franklins make it go fast. How do I look?"

He was in blacks and charcoals, with a faint pinstripe on the suit, his white shirt nearly glowing in contrast to a midnight blue silk tie. "Like a mob undertaker."

Kroun settled the fedora at a rakish angle. "Let's go arrange some services, then."

"The other guy's probably waiting at my club."

He gestured for me to proceed.

There was traffic, as always, so it took some time to get there. If the man in the trunk hadn't tried to knock me off, I'd have felt sorry for him.

Not long for him now, though. I circled Lady Crymsyn's block, alert to lurking toughs. Neither of us spotted the prisoner's buddy.

"Think he's inside?" I asked.

"Count on it," said Kroun.

No point in asking why his bunch was so allergic to an ordinary invited entry after a polite knock; he wouldn't understand the question.

I pulled into my reserved spot in the parking lot next to the club. Damn, this Studie drove smooth, but I wasn't ready to give up my Buick yet. It had gone into the shop for new tires, then some eager beaver decided to put in some extra work. I'd made it clear to Derner—who only thought he was doing me a favor—that I didn't want solid-rubber tires, armor plating, and bulletproof glass added on. It was a *Buick*, for God's sake.

Just as I set the hand brake another car suddenly bounced into the lot and stopped directly behind us, blocking our escape.

Kroun and I went alert at the same instant. I didn't want to be trapped and piled out on my side, turning to face the threat. Kroun mirrored me, hand dipping to his overcoat pocket. I resisted the urge to go for my own gun, having the luxury of vanishing if need be.

Then I saw the kind of antenna on the other car and recognized the driver. "Nothing to worry," I called across the car roof to Kroun. "It's just the cops. Relax."

He muttered so that only I'd be able to hear. "Relax? You kidding?"

"Nothing to worry," I repeated.

"Body in the trunk," he reminded.

"*Relax*, dammit."

I shut the door and sauntered toward the Studie's back fender. Watching, Kroun stayed put, but took his hand from his pocket. His shoulders eased down.

The two men got out of their unmarked car, standing in place long enough to give us plenty of time to recall and sweat over our most recent sins. Even an innocent person has that reaction when getting the eye from a cop. They do it to people on purpose. I've seen it. It goes together with the fact that a cop can say "come with me," and you have to go. I usually didn't have a problem with that so long as it wasn't aimed my way.

I remembered the driver from last night; he'd asked a lot of questions about Roland Lambert's shooting. Sergeant something-or-other. He must not have been happy with my distracted answers, and it was a cinch he didn't believe any of Roland's malarkey.

"Hello, Sergeant . . . uh . . ." I tried, but just couldn't pull his name from my mental hat. He was a tough-looking son of a bitch; I usually remembered that type out of self-preservation.

"Merrifield," he provided, apparently unoffended. "I'd like to talk to you, Mr. Fleming."

I rated a "mister"? Maybe that was to put me off guard, but the way they'd rolled in so fast was not reassuring. They must have been parked up the block on the lookout for any activity at the club. "No problem, what about?"

"How about we go inside?"

If there was a mug waiting to ambush me in the club, he might get nervous and shoot everyone. "Out here's fine."

Merrifield didn't like that answer but wasn't going to press. His partner eyeballed Kroun, who had somehow toned his personal magnetism down to show only a poker-bland face. "Who's your pal?"

"Old friend from out of town."

"What's his business?"

"Just visiting. What's it to you?"

"You got a lot of junk in the back, what is that stuff?"

"His luggage, see the suitcases? C'mon, Sergeant, what's the deal? You got some real questions, I'll be glad to answer 'em." I hoped he didn't want to look in the trunk. I doubly hoped the guy stashed there kept quiet. Maybe he'd heard me and knew there were cops at hand. In his line of work, they were the common enemy.

Merrifield wanted the story behind Roland Lambert's shooting. Again. I gave him everything I knew except the names of the shooters. "I didn't see them, they went by too fast."

"And why were they shooting at you?"

He got a reprise of last night's song and dance of useless information. "I wish I could help you, but that's all there is. I'm just glad nothing worse happened."

"Actually, it did."

I felt a sharp internal jab of fear, thinking some new catastrophe had surfaced, but Merrifield only wanted more about Alan Caine's murder. That was a relief, just not much of one. He knew I'd been at the Nightcrawler, where Caine was last seen alive. I confirmed that and again told him Caine had skipped out on the second show. The backstage talk was he'd claimed sickness and left, which I repeated.

"The guy was a real ass," I said. "Anyone could have gunned him down."

"He was strangled."

"Damn papers never get anything right." One of them had indeed swapped the facts, claiming Caine was shot and his ex-wife Jewel was strangled.

"Then what is the right story?"

"You're asking the wrong guy." I wanted to put him straight about Jewel's not killing herself, but you can't say something like that and not have to explain the why and how of it.

"Where were you when Northside Gordy's car blew up?" he asked.

"In my club minding my own business."

"What are you doing being such good pals with a mug like Gordy?"

"You know, my granny asks me that every Sunday after church. I'm still trying to figure it out."

Merrifield was the patient sort. Usually my lip would have me in more trouble by now. "We know you've been running the show for him lately. You were at the Nightcrawler for Caine's swan song, and you were sniffing around that little dancer he was cozy with. Then Gordy's car blows up, Lambert's shot, your limey Sherlock pal lands in the hospital, and two mugs associated with the Northside gang have their heads bashed in . . . shall I go on?"

"What mugs?" I thought I sounded convincing.

"You know them. We've talked to people, and the one connection they've given for all of it is *you*, Fleming . . . you're up to your eyebrows and sinking. Either you're doing this for Gordy or covering up for him while he does the dirty work. He'll hang you out to dry when he's done, too. Don't think he won't. Where is he?"

"Taking a vacation. I heard he's got a girlfriend keeping him busy."

"I'll bet he has. Why have you got a bounty out for Hurley Gilbert Dugan?"

He caught me by surprise. Only the guys in the mob were supposed to know about that. The cops had plenty of stoolies, though. "I was just doing my part as a concerned citizen by putting up a reward. Dugan kidnapped that poor girl, murdered those people—don't you think he should be off the street? Anyway, I withdrew it."

"Why? Is he dead?"

"Not that I know, but I wouldn't be sorry if he was."

"If he is, we'll talk to you about it first."

"I can't help you. He's probably dusted out of town for Timbuktu by now. Sweat those mugs who helped him out. They still locked up, or did a fancy lawyer spring them so they could disappear, too?"

Merrifield looked ready to shove my nose to a different part of my face. "Who's this bird again?" He jerked his chin in Kroun's direction.

"An old buddy from the army. We used to loaf in a bar and play footsie under the table, but don't tell his wife."

Kroun shrugged modestly at the other cop. "What can I say, he's crazy about me."

"Oh, yeah, real cute," said Merrifield. "I've had enough. Fleming, you and him get in the car. You can hold hands on the way to the station."

"You charging me with something?"

"No, I'm throwing a tea party so you can give me all the gossip. Come on." He took my arm, and I stifled the urge to pull away, or he'd say it was resisting arrest. I'd spend the night in the tank with the drunks. If I was lucky. "Garza . . ." he called to his partner.

But Garza was busy talking with Kroun. Listening, rather. Listening hard. Kroun had him fixed in place and was speaking low and intense. The wind carried away his words. Garza's face was blank, his jaw beginning to sag.

It was creepy seeing the process from the outside, and I wondered if I'd looked like that when doing my evil-eye parlor trick.

I had learned fast to rely on it, respect its power over others, and finally to fear it. Use it again, and the internal explosion would punch my ticket fast enough. But I'd gotten on without the talent for thirty-six years prior to my death and return; I could do all right in the future.

So long as I avoided situations like this, dammit.

"Garza!" snapped Merrifield. He still had my arm and drew me around as he turned.

Kroun kept up the patter for a few more words, probably telling Garza to stay put, then swung his gaze on Merrifield.

It was the reverse of a searchlight. Instead of a bright beam blinding you, it was like getting sucked into a hell pit of pure darkness. You were just as blind and falling, to boot.

I felt the dizzying tug like a physical force. That was wrong. I should have been immune to the influence of another vampire. If he'd thrown that directly at me, I'd have gone under the same as any human. I stepped back and to the side, as though to get clear of his range of fire.

Merrifield stopped in his tracks, not moving as Kroun stalked closer.

God, his eyes were unnerving. I'd seen them like that the night before when he'd taken aim at Mitchell, ready to kill. Kroun's soul was gone, well and truly gone.

In the vacated space I glimpsed something looking out from inside that made my flesh crawl. Sit in a pitch-black room, hear a noise, and ask "Who's there?" and of course there's no answer. What was behind Kroun's eyes was the thing that stands quiet and unseen just a few inches in front of you, aware of your growing fear, not answering your question.

Waiting.

It looked at me, blinked, and suddenly Kroun was back. Just that quick.

I'd not imagined it. I wanted to think so, but it *had* been there, and I was certain he was unaware of what was inside him.

Was it just him, or were we *all* like that?

Merrifield got back in his car, not saying anything or even seeming to notice me. Garza followed. The motor caught and rumbled, coughing when Merrifield shifted gears and backed out of the lot. Another metallic cough, and they drove off, blending with the rest of the traffic.

"Nice friends you've got," said Kroun.

"What'd you tell him?" I asked, voice faint.

"Didn't you hear?"

"Wind in my ears." Which was partly true. It had kicked up a lot and was colder than before. I'd been too spooked to hear. Was still spooked.

"I told him you couldn't help with his case, and he should go looking for a guy named Hoyle since he did all the killings. That was the one who helped Mitch, right?"

"Yeah." I didn't like thinking of Hoyle. I get that way about people who are shot right in front of me. The aftermath of his death had been even worse, and I wasn't going to think about that either.

Kroun lifted his hat and brushed a hand along the left side of his head, grimacing.

"You okay?" I said.

"Huh?"

"Does it give you a headache? What you did to them?"

"The eye-to-eye gag? As much as anything else. I can't take aspirin for it, either."

"Crush the pills up and mix them with blood."

"Really?" He seemed perfectly normal, wholly unaware of his quiet passenger. Not much I could do about it. He wouldn't believe me if I mentioned what I'd seen.

"Couldn't hurt to try."

He settled his hat into place. "C'mon, let's get this over with."

The front of the club was dark, but lights showed through the windows. My sign about being temporarily closed was still in place, barely. The wind and damp were having their way with the cardboard, and it would tear free before the night was out. Standing so I wouldn't be framed in the opening, I cautiously opened the door, letting it swing inward.

"Not too smart of him," Kroun observed. "He should have relocked it after breaking in."

"That's my doing. We left so fast the other night I forgot."

"Huh. Hope you said good-bye to all your booze, it'll be gone by now."

Maybe.

"Why would he put the lights on?" Kroun asked. "He might as well have a brass band announce he's here."

"That's Myrna."

"Who's she? Cleaning lady? You got someone in there?"

"No nothing like that." I doubted Kroun was ready to meet the club's resident ghost. Myrna had been a bartender killed during a gang war some years back. She liked to play with the lights. The fact that the place was blazing like New Year's Eve was meant as a warning to me.

"You first," said Kroun, gesturing, very polite.

"Why me?"

"You got the vanishing trick. Check the place out. Find him."

"You know who he is?"

"I think so. The guy in the trunk usually travels with a mug named Broder. Muscle. He's big and a lot faster than you'd think—"

"I'm glad to hear it, but I'm not going rounds with him."

"You might if you surprise him the wrong way."

"I'm not surprising him at all. The only reason they want to kill me is because they think you're dead. He knows you, just go in and tell him to lay off."

"Oh." He seemed nonplussed about the reminder. "Yeah. I'll do that then."

I held back, and he went first, calling Broder's name and identifying himself. After a few long minutes he returned.

"Copacetic."

"Sure?"

"Yeah."

I wasn't so confident, but followed him in.

Broder was damn near as big as Gordy and didn't look nearly as friendly and gregarious. I'd have tagged him for a wrestler, but he lacked the thick paunch around the middle most of them had. Football, then, and his teammates would nickname him "Bulldozer." He looked more maneuverable and a lot harder to knock over. He regarded me with hooded, unfriendly brown eyes.

"Broder," said Kroun, "this is Jack Fleming, the guy you're not going to kill after all."

Broder grunted; his voice box must have originally been dug out of the ground somewhere and replanted in him, the tone was that deep. He didn't offer to shake hands, and I was glad of it.

"Okay, that was nice," said Kroun, who could see this was as chummy as we'd ever get. "Fleming, if you'd bring in the last member of the party, we can finish this up."

At the mention of the other guy, I was sure Broder growled. It was so low it might have been the rumble of a diesel engine from two streets over.

The light behind the bar flickered. Myrna was letting me know she was on watch. Kroun and Broder both looked at it.

"You should change that bulb," Kroun said.

"I'll make a note," I said, and went outside.

The wind had a nasty bite. I rarely noticed the cold, which meant it must be a really bad night for regular folks. Because of it, I expected the man in the trunk to be half-frozen and in need of a blanket and something hot to drink.

I expected, but didn't count on it, and drew my gun as I lifted the lid.

Good thing, too. He came out swinging. He'd gotten free of the ropes and had a tire iron in one hand and a long screwdriver in the other. I jumped back as he lashed hard with the iron in a lethal backhand. He missed breaking my knee by a gnat's whisker.

"Hey!" I yelled, which didn't do a damn bit of good. He boiled out, staggered for balance, then went for me, mad as spit. I moved a lot faster to get clear. He was too far gone to notice the gun. When he did see it, he made a determined swipe with the screwdriver.

Damn. I couldn't tell if he was nuts for real or gambling I wouldn't shoot. A gun's only good if you intend to use it.

He had me there. Time to cheat. I pocketed the revolver, ducked around the bulk of the car, and vanished. Almost immediately I reversed, knowing he'd been right after me.

Yeah. He was just *there*, probably realizing I wasn't where I should have been. He hesitated a second, which was all I needed to get behind him. Reappearing, I put him in a full nelson. He was no shrimp, but I had a supernatural edge in strength. I aimed sideways toward the building and launched us against it—only I vanished an instant before impact. Momentum did the rest.

He hit it pretty hard, to judge by the thump and grunt. I went solid. He'd lost the screwdriver and was wheezing, having had his breath knocked out. I dipped in before he could recover and plucked the tire iron away. He started for me again, but his energy was gone. I sidestepped like a matador and grabbed the back of his coat collar as he passed, hauling him around so he fell forward across the hood of the car.

"Settle down, pal, we're just going to talk," I said, catching and twisting one arm behind him.

"Go to hell," he puffed, struggling.

I pushed until his face was mashed against the metal and lifted his arm a few notches. Any more would break or dislocate it depending on where I put the pressure. He still struggled. "I've already been there, thanks to you and Hog Bristow."

At that name, and the emphasis I placed on it, he paused.

"We *talk*," I said quietly. "And maybe have a drink. You wanna get out of the cold?"

He thought it over, then nodded. I let him up easy, ready for another round. He rubbed his arm instead, his gaze sharp. "This is your club."

That was a quick recovery. He knew how to land on his feet. "Broder's waiting for you."

His eyes flickered. How did I know the name? Then he figured it out. "Where is he?"

"In the bar. Great guy. I want him to meet my sister."

That got me the kind of glare I was used to; nobody likes a wiseacre. "Is he all right?"

"Just peachy," I said, mimicking Kroun. "C'mon and see for yourself."

I tossed the iron and screwdriver in the trunk, slammed the lid, and walked toward the front of the club. The man followed, alert to trouble. His hand went to the inside of his coat, a familiar gesture for those used to a shoulder rig. He'd certainly know his gun was gone; it was an unconscious habit, like looking at your wrist whether the watch is there or not.

I opened the door to Lady Crymsyn and motioned him in. He gave me a fierce once-over. In the brighter light, his eyes were a very startling blue, like honest-to-God sapphires. I'd have to keep him away from Bobbi. She had a weakness for blue-eyed guys. Those peepers and the film-star looks could keel her over.

He stepped in and halted. The club's décor was impressive: black and white marble, chrome trim, a high ceiling, and enough red to justify the name. Over the entry to the main room hung the larger-than-life portrait of Lady Crymsyn herself. She didn't really exist, but a lot of men wanted her phone number all the same.

My new guest was focused elsewhere, gaping and suddenly white-faced at the sight of a nonchalant Kroun standing next to the bar. "Gabriel," he whispered. "Son of a bitch."

"You keep my mother out of this, Michael," said Kroun, without humor.

I glanced speculatively at Broder. If his first name was Raphael, we could move this to a church soup kitchen and have a quick prayer service.

He glared back, and I thought better about asking.

THIS bunch did not indulge in a tearful reunion over Kroun's miraculous return from the grave. Not that I expected anything in even distant view of the maudlin, but maybe at least a handshake traded between acquaintances. Michael had been willing to kill me over Kroun, after all, but that business must have been more to do with restoration of mob honor than revenge for the mobster himself.

Michael got over enough of his shock to speak. "What the hell happened to you?"

Kroun leaned against one end of the lobby bar, Broder anchored himself solidly at the other, and Michael stood slightly distanced, able to see them both. Occasionally, his gaze cut to me, but without hostility, just including me in the proceedings. He didn't have to bother; this was their business, not mine.

While Kroun related his escape from the jaws of death, I eased past Broder and checked behind the bar. Everything was normal, not a bottle out of place. Despite the unlocked front door, no one had burgled the joint, and I didn't think it was just good luck. Maybe I needed to thank Myrna for looking after things. She was quite a good guardian angel.

I noticed I stood on the permanently stained tile that marked the spot where she'd bled to death. No matter that the tile had been replaced several times, the stain just kept reappearing. I moved off it.

Broder watched me as though I might plan to slip arsenic into the gin and offer him the bottle.

"Like anything?" I asked.

"No."

That earthquake-deep growl would take getting used to, and I'd had more than my share of experience at dealing with intimidating types. He shifted his attention back to Kroun, and though his face was impassive, Broder's body was tense. From the look in his eyes, I got the idea that he actively hated the man.

"*Mitch?*" said Michael, all stunned disbelief. His reaction looked and sounded sincere, which meant he'd not believed anything I'd said back at the house. "But Mitch was—why the hell would he take the chance?"

Kroun did more explaining about his homicidal henchman. I wondered when he'd get around to hypnotizing them so they'd go on their merry way. I had to get to the hospital before visiting hours ended.

"Why didn't you call me, send a telegram?" Michael wanted to know.

Kroun explained that as well. He'd shrugged from his coat, placing it and the new fedora carefully on the bar, and eased onto one of the stools as though we had all night. I concentrated on being invisible without actually disappearing. The other two remained in place, sponging up his every word. He made it sound plausible. Hell, I knew the real story, and he had me believing the eyewash.

But Michael didn't like what he heard. "We came all the way out here, nearly killed *him*"—he jerked a thumb at me—"and that's *it*?"

"It's enough," said Kroun. "Don't go blaming Fleming, either. I told him to keep shut until I knew the score."

Told, I thought. Nicely chosen, having it seem like I was one of the boys following orders the same as any other soldier in their line of work. Fine, whatever it took to get rid of these two.

Counting Kroun, make that three.

He continued. "Fleming's off the hook for my murder and whatever else you can think up. Call Derner, tell him everything's squared, and take the next train back, we're done."

"They still made a try for you. I can't let that pass."

"There is no 'they.' Mitch was my man, and Hoyle was already on the outs here. No one else is responsible for their shenanigans. I know that, the question is why you can't get it through your thick skull."

Michael's eyes sparked and narrowed. Broder shifted.

Kroun didn't seem to notice. "C'mon, Mike. If it'll make you feel better, sock Fleming in the jaw a few times, call it payback, and have done already."

It wouldn't have hurt me much, but that wasn't going to happen this side of hell. Michael didn't bother looking my way, just shook his head at Kroun.

"Okay," he said. "I get it. Mitch was a bad apple, he's gone—and you're ready to forgive and forget?"

"Yeah."

"That's not like you."

"What can I say? People change."

"Sure they do. See it all the time."

I'd long picked up on a deeper tension between them. Though Kroun was one of Michael's people, he behaved like the man in control. Michael made him work for it, though. Come to think of it, Michael could have been disappointed about Kroun's surviving.

"Maybe good old Mitch was acting on *his* orders," I said to Kroun. Not smart of me to provoke a fight, but I wanted him to start convincing these guys to leave.

He turned my way. "Ya think? What about it, Michael? You want my job?"

"Go to hell." Michael's reaction was instant, right on the surface. He made no effort to mask his disgust.

Kroun's relaxed expression remained the same, but he went utterly still. His friend had crossed a line. Maybe they both had. Oh, crap. Kroun was armed. If his eyes got empty again, I'd have to try and stop him. This was my place, and it had seen enough blood.

Myrna must have agreed. All the lights suddenly flickered, dimming, but not quite going out. This went on for maybe ten long seconds, then they steadied up normal again. It successfully broke the mood, creating a new one.

Michael snapped around at me, suspicious.

"Electrical short," I explained.

"Who else is here?"

"Nobody but us chickens."

He didn't believe me. "Broder."

Broder nodded, pulled out a revolver big enough to stop a charging rhino with one shot, and headed toward the main room. The curving hall leading into it was dark.

"Wait," I said.

He paused.

"You might need this." I tossed him a flashlight. There were a dozen of them scattered throughout the club, Myrna was that playful. He caught it one-handed, neat and solid. "But it's just a short. Electric panel's over there." I pointed to a spot on the wall next to the lobby phone booth. The utility was hidden by a red velvet curtain. Michael crossed to check on it, then motioned for Broder to continue. His footsteps faded.

It got quiet enough that I could hear Michael's heartbeat. A little fast. He shouldn't be so nervous.

"Drink?" I suggested.

"No, thank you."

"At least a short beer." I drew one and put it on the bar. "You gotta be thirsty after that trunk business, which I'm sorry about, by the way."

His focus shifted from Kroun, finally, and he came over for the beer. "You got some nerve."

"That part was my doing," said Kroun.

Damn. I wanted him to shut up so I could keep his pal's attention divided. Kroun seemed hell-bent on thinking up new ways to be fatally irritating.

Michael downed half the beer. Booze would have been better for such a cold night, but he didn't strike me as one who went for the hard stuff. I'd hung out in my share of dives and had learned a little about other drinkers.

"I got your stuff," I said. I pulled out the spoils I'd taken from him, spreading them on the counter.

He went first for the glasses case, opened it, and put them on. The gold wire-rims reflected the lights, making it harder to see his eyes. He looked less like a film star and more like the kind of brainy guy who lived in the college library. Neither image was in keeping with the reality that he was a big wheel in the New York mob.

He checked the wallet, put it away, then gave me a hard stare, mitigated quite a lot by the specs. It was difficult to take him seriously while he had those on.

"What?" I asked.

"The money," he said with a pronounced frown.

Money? Oh.

"I've got it," said Kroun, casually. He was messing with his handkerchief, his attention wholly on it. He shook open and refolded it so four points spilled over the top of his breast pocket like a tired flower.

"Hand it back," said Michael.

"Hm . . ." Kroun pretended to think, then shook his head. "No."

"That's my money, dammit."

"You found where I hid it in my hotel room. I recognize the clips. Next time I'll trust it to a safe."

"I thought you were—"

"Dead? That's a good reason to take it. I forgive you."

"One of those is mine."

"Huh. You're right." Kroun searched, produced the cash, and removed the money, tossing the empty clip to Michael.

He caught it reflexively, scowling. "Funny."

"You can spare it. You must own a bank or three by now. I bet you've made more in the last ten minutes than most guys see in a lifetime."

Glowering, Michael finished his beer and turned down my offer for a second. I washed the mug, stacking it with the others under the counter, just your friendly neighborhood barkeep.

We all jumped when something big crashed in the next room. I recognized the sound: chairs clattering, hitting the floor, lots of them. Kroun's hand went to his pocket, but he glanced at me. I shook my head to signal "don't worry" and he eased off, doubtful.

Michael was just to the curved entry hall when Broder appeared, nearly running into him. For a big guy he had speed, but he hauled up short, as though he'd been caught in an embarrassing act.

"What is it?" Michael demanded.

Broder scowled. He was good at that. "Nothing."

No one bought it.

"The lights were out," he went on. "I bumped a table in the dark. Knocked things over. The batteries are dead." He threw the flashlight. I caught it less neatly than he had earlier but spared the bottles behind me from breakage.

Under the counter, I clicked the light's button. The thing worked just fine now. It would be unwise to point that out to anyone, so I quietly put it away. Myrna was expanding her activities. What a gal.

"Find anything?" asked Michael.

Broder holstered his cannon. "A lot of dark. Heat's off back there. Cold as hell." For all that, he was sweating, a sheen covered his broad face, and beads gathered at his temples. The heating was the same throughout the building. I'd not turned it down. He had a tan similar to Michael's, but under it, his skin had gone muddy. When he approached the bar, I tried catching a whiff of his scent and was rewarded with the unmistakable tang of fear.

Looked like Myrna had found a new playmate for the evening. What had she done? Maybe it was better not to know. I poured Broder a whiskey without being asked, and this time he accepted, downing it quick.

"You okay?" I asked.

That got me a suspicious look; he knew I knew something about what had spooked him. "I am fine."

"Are we done here?" Kroun asked.

"Yes," Michael said shortly. "There's a late train back to New York tonight—"

"Enjoy the trip."

Michael visibly steamed. "You're coming, too."

"Uh-uh. I've got unfinished business."

What the hell? The three of us glared at him, waiting for the rest. Kroun spread the handkerchief out flat, refolded it, and tucked it back so two neat triangles showed over the pocket.

"Which one's better?" he asked. "This or the other way?"

"Like that," I said. "What unfinished business?"

"Don't get your feelings hurt, but I had other things to do out here besides bumping you off." He flicked at his pocket with one finger. "You sure? I liked the other way."

"So do floorwalkers. What other things?"

"A floorwalker? Nah . . . not in *this* suit."

"Whitey," said Michael. "We're going back to New York. You don't have any more business here."

"Actually, I do. It's none of *your* business, and it's going to take a while, so don't expect me back any too soon."

Michael's tanned face went muddy like Broder's. "No. We're all leaving. Don't cross me on this."

"Come on, Mike. I nearly got blown to perdition and back, then had to put Mitch down like a rabid dog. I'm taking a rest. You've got guys who can fill in for me."

"No."

"I'll hang around here, see a few shows, maybe do some fishing—"

"*No!*" There was angry force behind that, far more than the situation warranted. Not knowing Michael, I couldn't tell for sure, but his anger was covering up something else.

It was . . . fear. No such vulnerability showed on his face, but I could smell it. I remembered a moment when, with no small shock, I realized that Gordy was afraid of Kroun. Gordy didn't know about the vampire angle; it had been fear of the man himself. He and Michael had that in common. So, why were they afraid of him, and should I be worried?

Kroun's eyes were darker than before. His voice remained low and level and deadly patient. This was Whitey Kroun, not the more affable Gabe. "I'm not getting on that train. If I go back to New York, who's to say the next guy I run into won't try to finish what Mitch started? No, thanks. I'm staying here until you've done some housecleaning."

Michael recovered his self-control. Quickly. Throwing his weight around wouldn't work. His tone shifted, became the reasonable one of a man willing to compromise. "Okay . . . come and help me, then. Only you know who you've pissed off lately."

Kroun barked a short laugh. "That would be everyone."

"I'll make sure you're protected. No one's getting another chance at you. I guarantee that."

"Thanks very much, but I'm staying—until further notice."

Michael's hand twitched, reminding me of the gun no longer under his coat. Broder didn't make a move, just watched and listened. Apparently he'd seen this kind of thing before. I tried to read him for a clue as to how it might end, but would have had better luck with a brick wall.

"It's the old bastard, isn't it?" Michael asked. "You're here to see him."

"Yeah," Kroun admitted, after a moment.

"It's no good, he's crazy, you'll only stir him up. Stay away from him."

Kroun made no reply. Making an effort, I kept my yap shut, wanting to know more.

Michael glanced at Broder, who did not react.

Kroun poked at the handkerchief, pulling it out again. A quick refold and he put it back, this time showing a razor-thin edge of white. He looked at me for an opinion. I gave a thumbs-up.

"I'm gonna look up an old friend or two," he said. "No one you'd know."

"And do what?"

"None of your damn business, kid. I'm not repeating myself."

"Whitey—"

"Mike." Kroun raised one hand in a sharp "back off" gesture and met his gaze square and granite-hard. "Enough."

Silence stretched, but not to a breaking point, and the lights remained steady. Michael continued, body tense, but his voice was calm. "All right, fine. But since you're worried about people taking potshots, you'll have to have a bodyguard. Someone who will be the first person I hold responsible if anything goes wrong."

"Not him," Kroun nodded at Broder, who again did not react.

"No problem." Michael looked at me. "He'll do."

"Forget it," I said instantly.

"I can take care of myself," Kroun said.

Michael's mouth tightened, not in a smile. "You've got a point about being a target. Anything happens to you again, and I break this town like an egg—and Fleming knows it. You've vouched for him plenty tonight. He'll bust heads to keep you safe."

I'd also be motivated to get Kroun to leave as soon as possible. That might not be in keeping with his plan to retire from the business. I threw him an expectant look. Now was the time to put them both under and make them leave.

"Cripes," Kroun muttered.

"It's him, or Broder and I tag along."

"Go ahead," I put in. "I don't want the job."

"Gee, thanks," said Kroun.

"You can get out of this," I reminded him, knowing he'd catch the meaning.

He shook his head once, surprising me.

"Come on . . ."

"No. Drop it."

Damn him. The crazy son of a gun wasn't going to do it. I snorted, turning to Michael, framing an appeal. "Look—"

Kroun broke in. "Won't work, Fleming. He's made up his mind. I know what that means, you might as well learn it now."

I already did and didn't like it. He *could* force a change in Michael's views, but it wouldn't stick. Depending on how strongly a person felt, the hypnosis might last for weeks or just a day or so. It was worth the effort to me, though. However difficult to influence, once Michael and Broder were on their way out of town, they might think twice about coming back again.

Yeah, sure.

I'm often a victim of my own optimism.

"It's just for a couple days," Kroun went on. To him I was hands down the lesser of two evils, giving him good reason to cave in so fast. "This place is closed, what else have you got to do?"

"Plenty," I said.

If I'd been *asked* instead of appointed, it would have been different. I'd been my own boss too long to go back to being pushed around by a bunch of murdering bastards. Yes, I was one myself by now, but . . . they all looked at me, hostility, assured expectation, and cynical resignation parceled out between them.

Oh, what the hell. I wanted to keep an eye on Kroun anyway.

He read my face easily enough. "That's settled. When's that train leaving?"

"Never mind the train." Michael held his glasses up to the light. He rubbed at a lens with the end of his tie. "Broder and I are staying in town."

"Why?"

"None of *your* damn business."

"You want to see how it turns out with the old bastard."

"Among other things."

God, were they going to start up all over again?

"Fleming watches you, Broder and I watch Fleming. Everyone's happy."

Except Fleming, I thought.

"You—" Michael pointed at me, then gestured me over to the side.

I hated being ordered around by anyone, especially in my own place, but put up with it in the interest of getting them out more quickly. From the signs, Michael wanted an off-the-record talk. He couldn't know that Kroun would be able to hear it from across the room.

"Yeah?" I said.

He put the glasses in their case and looked me up and down. "You understand how we do things?"

"I'm wise."

"We'll see. You look after Whitey, and when I ask about what he does, you will tell me."

"No problem." *Look after?* That was a funny way of saying it, like Kroun needed a keeper.

"Lie or leave anything out, I'll know about it."

Threats were easy to drop, but I had the feeling he was giving me a legitimate warning. "Okay. But tell me why you're so anxious to know what he's up to."

"You like him? Think he's a friend?"

"I like him. The jury's still out on the other." I didn't mind Kroun knowing that.

"Smart of you. It's okay to like him, but don't trust him even if he tells you the Pope's Catholic."

"Why?"

"He came here to kill you, and you have to ask?"

Good point.

"It takes a certain kind of man for such work. He's one of them."

"You, too. You were ready to pull the trigger on me."

"Yes, that's true." He tilted his head. "But I would have felt really, really bad about it."

"You'd have felt bad?"

"For a long time. Yeah."

He'd had me fooled.

"Whitey doesn't have a conscience, he never did. He's amusing, can be very charming in fact, but killing is no more to him than driving a car is to you."

"You're worried he'll kill someone while he's here?"

"I don't want him stirring up trouble."

"Who's he after?"

"I wouldn't know. You get a hint of it, you call me."

If he knew, he'd probably tell me, and my job would be easier, but that wasn't going to happen. Admitting his ignorance would be weakness, and he'd never show that to the hired help. I hated games. "Where you staying?"

"Whitey's hotel. Derner has the number. This is important, Mr. Fleming. Important." He looked almost comically intense.

Kroun had him on edge, and it would be stupid to dismiss that. I nodded.

"What I hear from the crowd at the Nightcrawler is you have scruples," he said. "You don't like it when people die."

"I'm old-fashioned that way."

"Good. You watch him, keep him out of trouble, keep him from *making* trouble. Do whatever it takes."

"What do you mean by that?"

"That—despite what I said about you being the first to get the blame—I guarantee there will be no reprisals."

What the hell? I went cold inside. "Oh, now, just a damn minute—"

"You don't know him or you wouldn't balk." Michael sent me a long, level stare. He was smart enough to see past my third-best clothes and chin stubble, reading that I was a cut above the usual mugs in his line. For all that, he'd still misjudged me, and I resented it.

This smelled to high heaven. It could well be another version of what I'd just avoided: Kroun gets bumped—preferably by someone expendable like myself—then they bump me. "Fill me in."

"Get him to tell you. He seems to like you. He just might. As I said, do whatever it takes to keep him in line. If his stay here is quiet, you won't have to do a thing. When he's ready to leave, Broder and I will go with him."

Sounded great, except for going against Kroun's plan to retire. If he wanted Michael to know, he'd have mentioned it by now. It wasn't my place to bring it up.

"This is business, Mr. Fleming," Michael added, with a meaning to the phrase that was familiar.

I'd heard it from Gordy enough times to get the message loud and clear. Great, someone else to be on guard against. What the hell, it couldn't hurt to pretend to go along with him.

Well. Actually, it could.

"We're done," Michael pronounced. He should have told me not to repeat this conversation to Kroun, but hadn't. Did that mean he trusted me to keep shut, or he didn't care if Kroun knew?

Damn, I hate games.

Kroun snorted, eased off the barstool, and pulled on his new coat and hat.

"What the hell is that?" asked Mike, gaze fixed on the fedora.

Kroun took it off, checking it carefully. "Looks like a hat. What are you seeing?"

"It's black."

"Charcoal gray," Kroun corrected, putting it on.

"You always get white."

"People change. I have mentioned that, I know I just did." He must have noticed my expression. "Right?"

I shrugged, wanting to stay clear. "Who wears white in the winter?"

Mike seemed puzzled. "Whitey does, always has. It's how he got the nickname."

"I thought it was from the—uh—" I made a vague gesture on the side of my head.

"A white hat," said Mike. "Always. Since he was a kid."

How far did these two go back?

"It's the end of an era," Kroun pronounced. "C'mon, Fleming, close the store."

The clothing talk reminded me of something. "Minute. I'll be right back." I started toward the curving hall.

Broder got in my way.

I looked at Michael.

"What is it?" he asked.

It is infuriating to have to get permission to walk around in one's own place. I really missed my hypnosis, for then I'd have had the two of them out in the street dancing a fox-trot till dawn.

Pain like red hot railroad spikes in both eyes, followed by my brain exploding . . . but maybe worth it.

"Business," I said, deadpan.

Michael waved dismissively, and Broder made a slow nod. He wasn't moving, so I had to go around him.

In his low rumble—not directed at me—he said, "He'll be fine."

It's amazing what you can infer when your mind's working right. Michael must have signaled to him to follow me, and Broder had refused. He wasn't about to take a second trip into the main room. It was creepily dark in there. I'd not bothered with the lights, nor taken a flashlight, and couldn't blame him for hanging back.

There was enough glow coming from the high, diamond-shaped windows for my eyes. One thing I noticed right away: every chair and table was in place. There was no sign of what caused the big crashing noise that had chased Broder out.

"Myrna . . . you're the pip," I said at a conversational level.

No response. Maybe she was tuckered out from all the fun.

I crossed the dance floor, hopped onto the stage, and passed through the wings to the dressing area. There I did flip a light switch, as it was quite black with no windows, and went into one of the rooms.

Some of my clothes lay on the floor where I'd dropped them. That night, the damage Bristow had done to me wasn't healing and seemed to be getting worse. I'd come here hurting and afraid and had tried to wash it off my soul in one of the showers. When that hadn't worked, I'd tried to kill myself.

I snagged things up quick and piled them on a chair. Bloodsmell floated up, rusty and stale. That came mostly from my overcoat. It would need a good cleaning—if I could bring myself to wear—

No, definitely not. A dead man's blood was all over it, invisible against the dark fabric. I'd not killed him, but had drunk deeply from his twitching corpse.

Yeah. I'd done that.

Not something one can forget, not anything I wanted to remember, but there it was: insanity.

I was ashamed. Ashamed I'd lost control, crossed a line. If I was lucky, I would wince over that one for decades to come and learn from it.

If unlucky, I might do it again.

Face flaming, I rifled the pockets and found an address book, a plain thing in thin brown leather. It had belonged to the late Alan Caine. I'd taken it from his hotel apartment on the night of his murder on the off chance that it might prove useful in finding his killer. The problem had resolved itself, but now I had an idea for using the book to get the cops out of my hair. Derner could help, and it wouldn't cost a nickel in bribes.

Halting in midturn for the door, I realized I couldn't leave this stuff. If the cops ever decided to search the place . . . no . . . such complications I did *not* need. I spread the overcoat flat, threw all of the clothing on it, then rolled it into a bundle, ready for dumping.

I hurried out, bundle under one arm and the book in my pocket.

"What have you got there?" Michael wanted to know.

"Laundry."

"*That* was your business?"

"Yeah. I'm short on clean shirts."

He snorted. "Let's get out of here."

"Car keys," Broder said, his hooded gaze traveling between me and Kroun, not knowing which of us had chauffeured.

I handed them over. It never occurred to me to argue about who was to drive. He stood by the front door, making it plain we were all to exit first.

The leather case with the syringe remained on the bar. I got it and quietly passed it to Michael. He shot me a sharp look, but I wore my blandest "I don't give a damn" face. He shoved the case deep in his coat pocket and moved on. If Kroun noticed, he didn't show it.

I locked the front door. As we walked toward the parking lot, the outside lights winked on and off. The others saw and looked back; I kept going.

"It's just a short," I said to no one in particular.

At the Studebaker, Michael turned and smiled. "It's been a pleasure meeting you, Mr. Fleming. I'm very happy I didn't have to kill you. Tonight."

Some guys enjoy being cute. Michael and Broder quickly got in the car first, locking the doors. They moved fast, as though rehearsed.

"What's this?" Kroun asked, pitching his voice to go through the rolled-up windows.

One hand cupped to his ear, Michael mouthed an unconvincing "*What?*" and met our irritation with a good-natured, innocent smile. Broder started the motor, shifted, and backed out.

"He's stranding us?" I stared as Michael did the kind of playful bye-bye wave usually reserved for small kids.

"That's what it looks like." Kroun just shook his head. "Payback for the money I took off him. Michael's a big one for payback."

"I'll remember that."

"Huh. He's got my new stuff," he added.

"He said he was at your hotel."

"I heard. I'll pick it up later. Where to now? This hospital?"

"Yeah. There's an el stop just up the street. It'll take us. Cabs don't like this area much when the club's closed."

I turned, walking into the wind. My hat tried to fly off, so I carried it. Kroun jammed his on tight and kept his head down. He muttered unkindly about the cold and folded his coat lapels over his chest, turning up the collar. Maybe he felt it more than I. That slug in his brain might make a lot of things different for him.

"So," I said, "*is* the Pope Catholic?"

"Mike doesn't know things have changed. I'm not the man I was. He wouldn't understand that, even if I gave him the whole story—which I'm not."

"Doesn't anyone know about you?"

"Hell, no. Just you and your girl. There's no need for it to go any further. I survived the car exploding. The exact how of it stays with us."

"What about the other stuff? You heard everything. Michael as much as said I should kill you if you got out of line."

"You can try."

"Don't give me that. He was serious."

"Yeah. He was."

"Well? Why?"

Kroun shrugged. "I couldn't say."

"You could have asked. And gotten an answer. Why didn't you?"

"Because I learned more by letting him run off at the lip. If Michael makes a real nuisance of himself, I'll deal with him. You stay out of it."

What constituted being a real nuisance? Apparently the threat of getting killed wasn't enough for Kroun. Of course, he was already dead—Undead—and it might have changed his perspective on that point. Mine had certainly shifted considerably since my demise.

I tried another angle. "Who's this guy you want to see?"

"The old bastard," he said, with a finality that meant there would be no further elaboration.

"Where is he?"

"Not far away. It's my private business. I don't want you along."

"My hands are tied. I keep tabs on you or get in a bad spot."

"Yeah-yeah."

Kroun could give me the slip easy enough, which we both knew. He seemed disinclined to run off just yet, though.

There was a drugstore open near the el platform. He turned into it. I followed to get out of the wind. We must have looked like suspicious characters, what with Kroun being dressed so sharp and me so ratty. The clerk behind the cash register straightened, his hand going out of sight under the counter.

Kroun ignored his apprehension and pointed to the goods behind the glass. "Cigars, please," he said. He pulled a ten from one of the money clips. "The del Mundos will do. The whole box. Thanks. Keep the change."

He put the box under one arm, leaving the guy to gape after him.

"A seven-dollar tip?" I asked as we took the stairs up to the platform.

"I can afford it."

"Thought you didn't smoke." The other night he'd expressed surprise that I indulged. My habit was infrequent and mostly for show; I could only puff, not inhale. Maybe I should try cigars.

"I don't. They're a gift. You'll find out soon enough. Now when's the next damn train due?"

*   *   *

THE hospital was busier than the previous night, though things were slowing down. A different nurse was on duty at the front, and she gave me directions to Escott's room, along with that of Roland Lambert.

Her eyes sparkled at the mention of his name. "You're his friend?"

"One of them."

"Are you in the movies, too?"

Behind me Kroun stifled a snort, turning it into a throat-clearing noise.

"Only when I buy a ticket."

"I got his autograph," she said. "He was so *nice* about it."

"Yeah, he's a smooth one." In another day he'd be running the place. I led off down a hall, then toward an elevator. The lights were brighter here; I crushed my bundled clothes into a smaller wad.

"Laundry, huh?" said Kroun. "Like hell. I can smell the blood. Whose is it?"

"Hoyle's. I was standing too close when he bought it."

"Ain't life sweet? You're not sentimentally attached to that stuff, are you?"

The elevator doors parted, we got in, and I asked the operator where the hospital's incinerator might be. He didn't like my looks and wanted to know why.

"My cousin's got mumps, and I'm supposed to burn his clothes." I offered the bundle to him.

He dropped back against the wall and held his breath. No grown man wants to deal with mumps. He kept his distance and took us to the basement, no stops.

Kroun grunted amused approval when the doors slid shut behind us, then got distracted by our surroundings. He looked around the nondescript area as though we were in an art museum and not some man-made concrete cave. Further directions from a passing janitor got me to where I needed to be.

Hospital incinerators are pretty impressive in terms of size and noise, but the door was oddly small. I had to use a long steel poker to push my bundle through the little opening, shoving the clothes deep into the roaring fire. I watched, fixed in place as the blaze attacked and began to eat the fragile fabric, then I slammed the door shut.

Until then I'd no idea just how heavy the bundle had been. I instantly felt better.

"You did more than just burn evidence," Kroun said when we were back up in the hospital's public area looking for the right corridor.

"Getting rid of a bad memory."

"That easy, huh? What do you do about keeping the good ones?"

I shrugged. "Pictures, I guess. Keep a diary."

"What about regaining good ones you've forgotten?"

This was a screwy subject, but I was getting used to his being screwy. His fussing with that handkerchief while important stuff was being discussed was a good dodge to gain thinking time. Only I had the suspicion his main concern had indeed been the handkerchief. "Talk over old times with family."

"Huh." He gave that one more consideration than it deserved, keeping quiet for the trip up to Escott's floor.

His room was at the opposite end of the hall from some kind of commotion. A lot of people were gathered around one of the doors: doctors, nurses, curious visitors carrying flowers and candy boxes. There was a party mood in the air, and I was sure it had to do with Roland. For a man who'd come close to bleeding to death, he knew how to land on his feet.

The atmosphere was considerably more subdued at the other end. The only activity was one old bushy-haired janitor arthritically pushing a mop around. He wore a hearing aid that must have been switched off and paid no mind as we approached Escott's door, but someone else was alert. Bobbi was just within the room, keeping an eye on the hall. She spotted me and came hurtling. I almost braced for a well-deserved smack from her purse, but instead she nearly knocked me over with a hug.

That was nice, really nice. Then she pulled abruptly away, her face like a thunderstorm. "You—you . . ."

I put my hands up, offering full and humble surrender.

"You . . ."

Damn, she had a cute scowl. Even when really serious, she was stunning with her big hazel eyes, platinum blond hair, and a face that always made my stilled heart leap. By some strange miracle, she loved me. How had I forgotten that? My death *would* have ripped her apart. Escott had called me a selfish, unthinking bastard. Guilty as charged. Again.

I still couldn't tell her what had been behind the fight.

"Jack?" Her storm clouds wavered. Maybe she'd expected more from me than hangdog silence.

"I'm sorry, baby. I mean that. It's my fault he's here, and I'm sorry as hell. Won't happen again." I was sincere. She had my number and could always see right through me. Anything less than total honesty she'd throw right back.

"I don't have to yell at you any more about this?" she asked.

"Not about this. Anything else, I'll take my licks."

She nodded, still looking at me with wary deliberation, hopefully getting over being mad.

Without thinking, I raised one hand and gently brushed the side of her face, half caress, half reassurance. Suddenly I wanted to tell her I loved her, but you don't say such things in public. Touching her like this was the closest I could come.

Damned if she didn't get it. Her eyes blazed up, and I felt like she'd just kissed me.

My little corner of the world shifted an inch in a direction with no name, settled into place, and suddenly felt *right* again. How long that would last I didn't know, but I'd try to keep it that way come hell or high water.

"How are you?" she asked. There was a lot more to the words than their surface meaning.

"I'm fine, sweetheart. Believe it."

She got that as well.

"And I'm fine, too," put in Kroun, who had a ringside to our interplay.

Bobbi turned and smiled, which was usually enough to knock most men off their feet. "Aren't you trying to be dead?"

His expression warmed as he flipped his charm switch on. "It turned out to be impractical."

"Why are you here, Mr. Kroun?"

"Call me Gabe. Please."

"I thought it was Whitey."

"Not for ladies who try to stop my bleeding all over their floor. I'm just along for the ride. Your boyfriend needs a keeper."

He should talk.

"Keeper?" she asked me.

"It's business."

That was the wrong thing to say, and I'd said it one time too many. Her lips tightened; the storm gathered again, frighteningly fast. Her voice was low, but every word had the force of a thunderclap. "I've had enough, Jack."

I couldn't pretend not to know what she was talking about. No placation I could think of would make things better. Not after the horrors of last night. She was the toughest woman I'd ever met, but had limits. "I know. And it's over. I'm winding this circus up."

"What do you mean?"

"I'm turning the show over to Derner until Gordy's on his feet. Tonight. After I leave here, we're going to the Nightcrawler to fix things. Gabe said he'd help." I shot him a look.

He kept his face on straight and shrugged agreement. "Figured I owed him."

"No more 'business'?" she asked.

"Just Lady Crymsyn, nothing else," I said. "I'm a tavern keeper, not Al Capone." I meant that as well.

"And if trouble comes up again?"

That was the tricky part. "If it's to do with me and mine, I take care of it, but anything else can take a hike."

She knew how the world worked and that I might not be able to prevent mob business from horning in on my life. But she also knew I'd give it my best to steer clear. To my vast relief, that turned out to be sufficient. She smiled. Not a big one, not the kind that was like a sunrise in my heart, but it did the job.

"You're really okay?" she asked, one hand brushing my coat lapels and thus my scarred chest.

I had her meaning. After Bristow's handiwork, I'd not gone near her out of fear of losing control and hurting, even killing her. He'd given me something far worse than a few surface scars. The damage inside my head, my soul . . .

Was *healing.*

In reply, I pulled her close and held her tight. She didn't need to know why I'd been distant, only that it was past. "Yeah, baby," I whispered. "I'm really okay."

She abruptly relaxed and melted against me. It was a perfect moment, and those never last long enough. Had we been alone, it might have progressed to something even more perfect, but we were limited to a long hug in a hallway.

With people watching. I became aware of Kroun and the old janitor looking on. The latter sociably blew his nose, wiped his house-sized mustache, and adjusted thick glasses. Kroun wore an "ain't that cute" smirk on his lean face.

Just inside Escott's room stood Shoe Coldfield. He was scowling and stepped forward. The janitor quickly went back to his mop work.

Bobbi picked up on my shift of attention and self-consciously pulled away, patting her hair and smiling.

"Visiting hour's about over," growled Coldfield. He filled most of the doorway. I wouldn't be getting through unless he allowed it. Then he noticed Kroun. "What the . . ."

"Shoe Coldfield, meet Gabriel Kroun," I said.

Coldfield didn't move. "The guy in Gordy's car. The car that blew to hell and gone."

Kroun shrugged. "Hell doesn't want me yet."

They cautiously shook hands. I was glad for the distraction, not putting it past Coldfield to bust me one again just to make sure I knew my place. He stood aside to allow me in, then fixed his attention back on Kroun. Clearly he wanted more details, and Kroun would give him the same eyewash he spilled earlier. I passed up a second helping and went into Escott's room, halting short just inside.

Damnation, he looked *worse*. He'd been bad last night, but this . . .

His bruises had had all day to mature. The idea of beating someone black-and-blue was no abstract concept on him. Much of his face was nearly as dark as Coldfield's and the rest was a gray tone that put my hackles up. His eye was still sealed shut, but the open one blinked sluggishly at me.

"How are you?" he asked, barely above a whisper.

What the hell? "Charles, I—"

"No more bloody apologies."

"What?" Was he drugged? Feverish?

"You've done that already. Accepted. Now—how are you?"

"You remembered last night?"

"This morning. You were inconsiderately early. How are—"

"I'm fine, just fine."

"No more thoughts about pistols at dawn?"

I got his meaning. He was still worried that I'd try shooting myself again. I checked behind to make sure no one was hearing this and stepped closer. "No, Charles. No more. Word of honor, hand on my heart, I promise. On Bobbi's life, I promise."

He made no reply, and with his face so banged up I couldn't tell what he was thinking. He grunted. "Some water, please?"

A tumbler with a glass straw was on the bedside table. His private accommodation came with a tiny washroom with a shower. I made use of its sink for fresh water, then held the tumbler for him until he drained most of it. This close it was too easy to pick up the sickroom smell. He wouldn't be coming home anytime soon. "How are you?"

"Bloody awful. Can't sleep in this place. I want my own bed. And a beer. Something dark and a little sweet. Cool, not cold."

"Maybe Shoe can smuggle in a bucket for you."

"He won't. Stickler for hospital rules. I may have talked him into rye bread, though."

"Rye bread?"

"I don't understand why, but I've developed a craving for some. Fresh. A very thick slice. With lots of salted butter. But it's no good without the beer."

Okay, that was odd, but a hospital stay can make you crazy for the damnedest things.

"Jack . . . about Shoe . . ."

"We're okay," I said quickly, not wanting to talk about it.

"I don't believe that."

You couldn't get anything by Escott, even when he was doped and wrapped like a mummy. "He's a little sore at me. He wants to know why this happened. I can't . . . I just can't tell him."

"Yes. It's private. I've said it's been resolved. He's not one to back down."

"I'll stay out of his way."

"Most wise."

"Has Vivian been in?" I'd expected to see Escott's girlfriend here. After we'd saved her daughter from some brutal kidnappers, he'd gotten very close with the widowed Vivian Gladwell. Because of her, he'd lately drifted into the state of wearing a sappy smile for no good reason.

"I've not told her."

I was surprised at that. "You should."

"Why?"

He had me there. "Don't want to worry her, huh?"

"Precisely. And it would upset young Sarah to see me like this."

Sarah was in her teens, but mentally would always be a child. Escott had come to dote on her as had most of the people who'd met her, me included. She was a sweet thing, forever unspoiled by the adversities of growing up.

"Did you at least phone them?"

"Yes. Said I'd be out of town for a few days on a case."

It would take longer than that for his bruises to fade. I hoped there'd be no scarring under his bandages. My face went red again, and I had to work to keep from bumbling out with another inadequate apology.

He spared us both with a question. "Who's that with you? I heard another voice."

"Whitey Kroun."

Escott gave me a good long stare with his working eye.

"He survived that bomb."

More staring.

"Yeah. Surprised the hell out of me, too."

"Would you mind very much catching me up on events?" He still whispered, yet managed to pack in an acerbic tone.

"Didn't Bobbi say anything?"

"No."

To be fair, Kroun had asked her to keep shut about himself. "Well, it went like this . . ."

I was hampered, since Kroun didn't want others to know about the vampirism part. I had to respect that, even with Escott. In this case what he didn't know wouldn't hurt him. Leaving it out and keeping things simple, I told him what had happened to Mitchell, how Kroun had helped, and that a couple of his friends were champing to hustle him back to New York.

"Why does he not leave?" Escott asked.

"Says he's still got business here. I'm supposed to keep an eye on him till he's done."

"Then perhaps you should encourage him to waste no time concluding his errand. By all accounts, the man is dangerous."

"I'll do what I can. He's got his own mind." And more. I'd glimpsed Kroun's dark side and didn't like it. Other than that, he seemed friendly, but why take chances?

"A small favor?" said Escott.

"Name it."

"Please get everyone to go home. I think they may stay the whole hour, but this is as long as I can—"

"It's done. Go to sleep."

"Thank you." He relaxed into his pillows, looking completely exhausted and a lot older than his years. It struck me afresh just how awful he looked.

My fault. And he'd wanted to know how *I* had been.

I resisted the urge to ask if he needed anything. He'd have mentioned it already, like the beer and rye bread. I backed out, shutting the door.

"What's the matter?" Coldfield demanded. No doubt about it, I was on his shit list until further notice.

"He's tired. He asked for us to go home. He needs rest."

Bobbi touched Coldfield's arm before he could object. "Jack's right.

Charles will be better tomorrow. You saw how he was fighting so hard to keep awake for us. We can come back in the morning."

Her magic worked. Coldfield unbent for her and agreed to leave, but muttered about returning later. If he wanted to keep an eye on Escott through the night, he'd damn well do it, everyone out of the way, especially me.

Saying good-bye to Bobbi provided an excellent reason to kiss her, and I made the most of it. My God, but it felt good.

More than good. It felt *right* again.

"Will you be by the hotel later?" she asked. She was staying at one of Coldfield's business investments while her flat was being scoured clean of violent death.

"Not tonight. I have to—"

"Tomorrow then." That was final.

"I'll have bells on."

She started to say something, then shook her head. Kroun was within earshot. She gave me a last peck on the cheek, squeezed my hand, then went off with Coldfield, who had driven her over.

Kroun and I still didn't have a car to get to the Nightcrawler. It seemed wise for the moment not to ask Coldfield for a lift. A cab then, unless . . .

The ongoing commotion outside Roland's room brought something to mind. I'd called in mob muscle to bodyguard him; chances were someone would still be on duty. I wanted to look in anyway.

"Gabe? One more stop."

"The movie star?"

"Five minutes. Gonna rustle us a car."

He liked that idea and found a wall to hold up. He still had the box of cigars tucked under one arm. Gift, huh? Not for Gordy; they weren't his brand.

Roland Lambert was a popular man tonight. I recognized newspapermen from their pencils and steno pads. Photographers also stood by, ready to record anything that a headline could make important. They glanced my way, took in my clothes and hobo beard, and dismissed me just that fast. Men who looked like me really were a dime a dozen in the street; I was just taller than most.

I'd spotted one of the bodyguards, didn't remember his name, but knew his face, and he knew mine. I waved him over. He pushed through with no real effort.

"Yeah, Boss?"

"I'm calling off the watch on the actor."

"You sure?" He looked troubled.

"Yeah, what's the problem?"

He shrugged. "It's just he's a regular guy, y'know? Treats me like I'm some kind of big shot. And that Russian doll, what a lady . . ."

If I left him here any longer, he'd be ironing their sheets. "You get his autograph?"

"First thing. He was great about it, even thanked me for askin'. What a guy."

"He's a sweetheart, but I need you to—"

"*Jek Flem-ink! My heeeeeerrrrrrrro!*"

No mistaking that accent. The crowd parted, and Faustine Petrova enthusiastically flung herself at me.

I love Bobbi, but there's much to enjoy about a jubilant Russian ballerina jumping on you and using her lips all over your face like a machine gun.

5

To keep from toppling, I had to grab Faustine bodily. Staggering back, I hit a wall, but she didn't seem to notice, rattling on in Russian between the loud wet smooches she planted all over. I found out firsthand why the front of one's head is called a kisser.

Wow. Something began coming loose inside. I had no need to breathe, yet desperately sucked air, but it wouldn't stay in. For a second I didn't understand what was going on. I thought it was a bad cough or some strange hiccups, then it was both at once. The strangest damned choking noise clawed its way out of my throat.

Laughter. I was laughing.

Hadn't done that in a while.

Faustine laughed as well, a very full one, happy.

I couldn't stop. It felt good.

We were lunatics, much too loud for a hospital, but for a few moments we just had to cut loose. I hugged her, and I laughed.

Making a *mwah-mwah* noise she kissed each of my stubbled cheeks in turn then yelled, *"Godt blezz Am-er-i-ka!"*

Flashbulbs exploded, blinding, disorienting. Faustine posed with both arms around me, a big smile showing all her white teeth, except when she planted another kiss. Right on my mouth. My lucky night. This inspired hoots of encouragement from the audience and some applause.

In the back of my mind, I knew the cameras could have mirrors in their works, which meant no catching of my image on film. That could be trouble somewhere down the line, but I couldn't bring myself to worry about it. It just wasn't important right now.

She pressed me forward into the crowd. It was easier not to resist. A few strangers thumped me on the back, others shook my hand, an eager young nurse tried kissing me, too, and managed to bruise my ear in passing. Apparently they were willing to ignore my scruffy exterior so long as Faustine liked me.

What the hell had they been told?

Just inside the room stood a tall, round-bodied guy in a pale blue tropical suit and a melon orange shirt that had to have been custom-made because I'd never seen anything like it before. He grinned and grabbed my hand, pumping away as though I'd just flown over the South Pole.

"Hiya, hiya, name's Lenny Larsen! I wanna talk with you about a movie script!"

"Sure, first thing tomorrow!" I said, matching his hearty good cheer. It worked, and I got my hand back, albeit with his business card pressed to my palm. Faustine pushed us farther into the so-called sick room.

Roland looked just like his pictures in the paper, but more so. Cameras loved his handsome face, and he was sharply turned out despite the pajamas and hospital trappings. His thickly bandaged leg was elevated by a sling, wires, and a pulley device, the rest of him lounged comfortably against half a dozen pillows. Along with more well-wishers he was surrounded by a greenhouse of flowers and a shop's worth of fancy chocolates in ribboned boxes. Except for the pale cast to his skin, he seemed to be having a great time and smiled broadly.

"Jack! Welcome to the party. Toss me my wife back, would you?"

At no urging from me, Faustine flew to his side, managing to make it look effortless despite the people in the way. The Lamberts had already suffered some rough patches in their new marriage, but all seemed forgotten. She leaned in and kissed his forehead, then thoughtfully brushed at the red lip color she'd left behind. "My poor da'link," she murmured. "Doz et hurt steel?"

"Just a twinge when I laugh, m'dear."

The members of the press made notes.

I knew what was coming; there was no stopping it. Better to play along, then get out.

Roland introduced me as the man who'd saved his life.

More pictures. I wished them luck in the darkroom.

Floods of questions. They wanted to know who was gunning for Roland Lambert, did I have any leads, had the cops caught the shooters, was I in the mob . . . that one made me twitch.

I held my hand up, mouth open to make a statement, which brought a temporary hush. "Sorry, folks, I am just as puzzled as you, but I know that Chicago's finest—" Some goof in the back, who probably covered local crime, snorted loudly. "That Chicago's *finest* are on the job and will no doubt make an arrest."

That was the kind of statement I'd heard often enough while on their side of the fence. We all knew what it meant. I got hit with more questions but shook my head and waved them off. "I'm just glad Roland's going to be fine." So I assumed from the circus; I'd had no chance to ask.

"Is it true you've sold your nightclub to the mob?"

That was a new one. "No. It's just closed until my star act is back."

Taking the cue, the Lamberts beamed. More flashbulbs died.

"What about your gangster friends?" asked another wiseacre.

"Don't have any, sorry to disappoint you. Why don't you come by the club when it's open and see for yourself—first round's on the house!"

That turned the tide. There's nothing like an offer of free booze for distracting the Fourth Estate from the scent of a story. Faustine, a most canny woman, passed a big box of chocolates around the room, further distracting them and at the same time drawing attention back to herself.

"Jek iz Am-er-i-kan he-rrro, joost like my da'link huz-bendt. Jek doez not like the geng-sterz, they do not like heem. When they shoot, my brafe Rrrolandt throwz heemself een way! He savez Jek's life, Jek rrrushes heem to hoz-peetle."

Pencils scribbled more slowly than usual as their owners dug their way past Faustine's accent. It seemed heavier tonight, whether from the excitement or by design. Faustine glowed as they peppered her with more questions.

"Yez, I am Amer-i-kan by the marry-ink of Rrrolandt, but I vish to be *more* Amer-i-kan and take tezt for eet. I *loff* thees con-drrry!"

That went over well.

The guy in the orange shirt loomed next to me, big teeth in a tanned face. "That's right folks, you can call Faustine Petrova our own little Miss Russian America! You never saw a more patriotic dancer, and you'll see more of them both when we make the movie! The name's L-A-R-S-E-N, Lenny Larsen!" He passed out more cards. I pocketed mine and hoped never to see him again.

Faustine and Roland were clearly in on the details. I went along with them, figuring it had to do with Roland's Hollywood comeback. He'd left some years ago—too much drinking got in the way of his career—but he was on the wagon and might be worth something at the box office again after this debacle.

I waved to let him know I was leaving, eased into the hall, and found myself next to a doctor. I asked him about Roland's health.

"He'll be able to go home in a few days," he said. "We took out the slug. It's just a question of watching for infection. So far, he's clean."

That was good. When I'd been in the army, more often than not it was the blood poisoning that took a man, not the bullet.

The bodyguard didn't want to meet my eye. He looked forlorn. "You sure they're safe, Boss? I mean, ya never know."

"You're right. Stick around, then. I want you to keep an eye on Charles Escott, too."

"Who?"

"The guy in 305. He's with Gordy's outfit." Damn, but I really was getting better at lying, and the name-dropping tipped things. "Look in on him, make sure things are copacetic, send up a flag if they ain't. But I need your car."

"Sure! No problem!" Happy as a puppy with a new bone, he dug out a key, told me what kind of car and where he was parked. I said I'd be at the Nightcrawler Club, then got clear.

Kroun was still holding up the wall and shook his head. "That's quite a rash you got there."

"What?"

"The crazy dame who jumped on you. You're smeared with more war paint than she is."

I got my handkerchief and rubbed my face. It came away covered with Faustine's deep red lip color. "Jeez."

"You said it. So . . . how do I get your job?"

THE only parking at the Nightcrawler was in the alley behind the club. There was a guy hanging around to shoo away anyone who didn't belong.

I eased into a spot. There wasn't a lot of space; Kroun had to slide across to the driver's side to get out, grimacing more than the effort required. After what he'd been through, I gave him credit for just being able to get into a car, period.

The man on watch at the back door nearly swallowed his cigarette when we climbed the steps. He'd apparently heard the news about Kroun's demise. I asked if Derner was in, knowing he would be; he was always in. This was my way of letting the guard know it was business as usual.

Don't think he bought it.

The kitchen staff was too busy to pay notice, but a couple of mugs in the rear hall exchanged looks and quickly got out of the way.

Kroun grunted, putting in a note of disgust. Coming back from the dead clearly annoyed him.

We got a similar reception walking into Gordy's office upstairs, but more of it. Derner was on one of three phones now on the big desk. He glanced over, then did one hell of a double take.

"I'll call you back," he said into the blower then hung up, missing the first attempt, knocking the phone over on the second. He stood up, eyes big as he threw me a "what the hell?" look. "Boss . . . ?"

"Good news. Mr. Kroun's back," I announced cheerfully.

Kroun snorted and went past to drop himself into a deep, overstuffed leather couch. He kept his coat and hat on, cigar box balanced on one knee, telegraphing that this better not take long.

"Gee, that's great," said Derner, his voice faint. "What's goin' on?"

I gave him as much explanation as he needed to pull himself together, then tossed the ball to Kroun. Leaning back, ankles crossed and feet on a table, he issued a number of succinct orders, most of them to do with taking me off everyone's execution list and putting forward Mitchell as the ringleader of all the trouble. Derner had gotten that from me the night before, so it was no surprise, but he wanted to know why.

"Tried to give himself a raise the hard way," said Kroun. "He's in the lake, right?"

"Yeah, sir. Couple of the boys took him over to the meat packers and—"

Kroun raised a hand. "No details."

Couldn't blame him for that. I didn't like thinking what the cleaning crew had to do to distribute a man's body into several fifty-gallon drums along with enough cement to keep it all on the lake bed.

"Get New York on the phone, and I'll put the fix in," he said. "This should be Mike's job," he added, aiming that at me.

"I think people are more scared of you," I said.

He gave a grunt. "Good point."

In ten minutes, regardless of whether the lines might be tapped, Kroun got me cleared of trouble with everyone else who mattered. He shot me a look as though to say, "Happy now?"

Relieved was the word.

Kroun got up, went to the desk, and just stood, looking down. Derner quickly relinquished the chair to him. Kroun switched on the desk radio, searched the phone book, and made a call. He kept his voice lower than the music and scribbled something on the inside of a matchbook. Derner and I exchanged looks; neither of us knew what was going on. I could figure it had to do with the kind of stuff Michael wanted to know about.

Hanging up, Kroun arranged to have someone pick up his carload of new clothes. He informed Derner that Broder and Michael would be staying on for a few more days and might be dropping in. Derner took it in stride. Entertaining the big bosses was easy enough. Booze, girls, gambling, and more booze usually did the job.

"We still got a problem about Alan Caine," he said. "Should they know about it?"

"No," said Kroun, moving back to the couch. "I'll handle them."

Caine's murder had had the cops sniffing around the club. The latest news reported that Jewel Caine's death had not been suicide after all. Small comfort to her family, if she'd had any. Derner had found out she didn't.

"Okay," I said. "Get something organized on services for her. She was friends with the girls here, make sure they show up and give her a good send-off. Tip the papers. Find people to say nice things about her."

"The cops will want to know why we're paying."

"An anonymous cash donation to the funeral home. I'm sure you can find one that understands what's expected."

He started with another objection. Kroun cleared his throat. Loudly. Derner nodded and went back to the desk to make phone calls.

"That's the only good part of this job," Kroun muttered. "I say frog, and they have to jump."

"Thanks," I said.

"Why do you let him argue like that?"

"He brings up things I need to remember." I had more to do before calling it quits for the night and told him as much.

"What else is there?"

I showed the leather address book, not quite taking it from my pocket. "This belonged to Alan Caine, I have to leave it in a spot where the cops can find it and solidly link Hoyle and Mitchell to the murders. Should take the heat off the club and send it Mitchell's way. We can put a rumor out that he ran off to Havana after killing Hoyle—"

"Who?"

"The guy who rigged the bomb. The clothes I burned . . . that was his blood . . . remember?"

"Who killed him?" he asked.

"Doesn't matter, I just make sure the cops blame Mitchell. He'd have bumped Hoyle anyway to cut a loose end about the car bombing. No one's found the body yet, but it's only a matter of time. This book on him might suggest to the cops that Hoyle killed Caine for gambling debts." It was thin at best, but better than nothing.

"Did you kill Hoyle?" Kroun's voice was conversational.

"No." I had the impression he wouldn't care if I had, he just wanted the facts straight.

"And this Hoyle *is* dead?"

"Yeah." Thoroughly. What was bothering Kroun? Did he have any reason to doubt my word on it?

"He's not going to surprise you the way I did?"

That was straight out of left field and right between the eyes. "Uh."

"You never know," he said, matter-of-factly.

Damn. The possibility never occurred to me. There had been no blood exchange, no chance that he'd rise again. I'd drunk from Hoyle only after he was dead. There was also *no* way that Kroun could know what I had done. Even Escott didn't know, no one ever would.

For a bare instant I'd been thrown off-balance, but decided Kroun was just stirring things up for the hell of it. He was damned good at that. He had a point, though.

"What do you know?" I asked.

"Enough to not take anything for granted."

"But what do you know?"

"I'm only trying to get you to think, kid. You've been lucky and done okay for yourself, but one of these nights it'll catch up to you."

I thought of Bristow. "It already has."

"If we're here, there can be others." He cast a glance at Derner. The radio was still on, masking our low voices. "You think you'd have run into more like us by now? Not if they're more careful than you. You didn't get my score because you weren't even looking."

Another good point, but I couldn't agree with him on the rest. I'd always kept my eyes open at the Stockyards on the chance of spotting another member of the club. Nothing had come of it yet. "Why think that about Hoyle?"

"Why not?"

No arguing with that. "Okay, I'll be more paranoid."

"The only way to live," he said. He went on. "So how does that book connect Hoyle to Mitchell?"

"Mostly it connects Hoyle to Alan Caine, who owed money to Mitchell. The cops can ask stoolies all over town and get the same story of Hoyle and Mitchell having a falling-out over who knows what. Derner will see to it."

He shook his head. "Needs more. Gotta cover the 'who knows what' part."

"I'm listening."

"Caine gambled. You need markers. With the right dates. Mitchell's name on some, Hoyle's name on others, and Caine's signature on them all to clinch it."

I got him. "Plant 'em where they'll be found."

"So the cops figure Hoyle killed the Caines, one for not paying his debts, the other to shut up a witness. This shorts Mitchell out of his marker money. Mitchell kills Hoyle for shorting him. It's not what happened, but it's reasonable. Cops like reasonable, don't they?"

"Son of a bitch."

"Glad you agree."

Derner earned his keep that night. He contacted a specialist and had the guy in the office thirty minutes later. Samples of Caine's writing came from the address book, and we kept it simple. On various types of plain paper and using different pens the forger wrote several IOUs, signed Caine's name, collected a fee, and left. I don't think he said ten words and never once asked a question, the perfect mob employee.

Hat over his face, Kroun stretched on the couch and pretended to nap until it was done. "Ready to go?" he asked, standing.

I'd hoped he would stay at the club waiting for his clothes to arrive while I finished things. Despite orders to babysit him, I didn't want company. "This won't take long," I said.

"Good."

He left the cigars on the table and strode out. I had to follow.

DERNER had called in additional help for this last errand. As I rolled to a slow stop up the street from a battered parking garage, another car turned the corner and pulled in behind me. Kroun went alert, maybe thinking it was cops again, but I told him it was okay, and we got out into the icy air.

Strome, the stone-faced guy who'd been my lieutenant since I'd taken over for Gordy, got out and stood ghost-quiet. He had shot Hoyle the night before, thinking to save my life, and I couldn't fault him for that. Of course, given the right circumstances, he'd shoot me without a second thought; it was just another job to him.

He glanced once at Kroun and left it at that; apparently Derner had filled him in. Strome gave me a hard look, though. "You okay, Boss?"

That surprised me. "Yeah."

He nodded, just the once. Granted, the last time he'd seen me—sprayed with Hoyle's blood and brains—I'd fallen into a seizure, and it had left one hell of an impression.

Best to change the subject. "That girl who was down there . . ." Hoyle had kidnapped a little cutie who had been in the wrong place at the wrong time during a murder. She'd been in need of a rescue. It was just her hard luck Strome and I were the ones to do it. "Did he hurt her?"

Strome understood what I meant. "She didn't say, but I don't think so."

"How is she?"

He considered, then shrugged. "Blubbed a little, then made me buy her supper and take her home. Guess she's okay. Dames." Clearly he found women to be a vast, if not-too-troubling, mystery.

"Let's wind this up," I said, taking the lead.

The garage had a tin roof that bucked and banged in the wind. The place was mob-owned; chances favored the vehicles inside were, too. Hoyle had chosen it as an emergency bolt-hole to hide from the world, and it had almost worked. The whole area was empty of foot traffic, and cars passed it by. The surrounding small factories and shops were closed tight. Every city had deserted pockets like this. They look dangerous and lonely after dark, but are often safer than a bank vault simply because no one's around to make trouble.

We crowded down a short flight of concrete steps to the basement entry, and Strome handed me a set of keys. On our last visit he'd picked the lock to get in.

From the doorway you could see a light on at the far end of an other-wise black basement. I'd not expected that. It was as though Hoyle were waiting for me to return.

Strome hung back to watch the street. I was highly aware of the bloodsmell tainting the freezing air and tried not to take any in as I entered. There was decay in it and the strong odor of something else unpleasant. Kroun followed, looking around and frowning. He'd caught the scent, too.

Ducking to avoid the low ceiling, I trudged the length of the basement to the curtained-off room at the end. Harsh illumination came from a mechanic's light hung on a nail. The too-bright bulb hurt my eyes and made the shadows just that much blacker. I cast around, trying not to be nervous about it, but no one was hiding anywhere. It felt like we had company, Hoyle's ghost perhaps. If that was the case, he wouldn't be a nice one like Myrna.

I told myself to shut the hell up.

One of the mystery smells was from an electric heater I'd left running. It had burned itself out. The rest was from Hoyle when his bowels and bladder had given way in death. He wouldn't be coming back. The smell of his advancing decay confirmed it. He lay facedown, a hole in the back of his skull. There should have been more blood, but I'd—

"You waiting to sell tickets?" Kroun asked. The top of his hat brushed the low ceiling. He hunched to avoid problems.

There was an old cot against one wall. I shoved the book under the thin pillow.

"Fingerprints," said Kroun.

Damn. He was right. I'd been careful about wearing gloves so only Alan Caine's prints were on the brown leather, but it wouldn't sit right if Hoyle's were absent.

Hoyle's left arm was flung wide. It'd have to do.

Even with gloves on I didn't want to touch him, but it was unavoidable. His arm was heavy and stiff as I lifted it. Rigor would have worn off by now; this was a result of the cold seeping down from outside. If he stayed here, he could freeze right through.

I pressed his fingers to the book and the IOUs, hoping something would stick. He'd not washed since going on the run. I got a few greasy smears no one could miss. Good enough. I left the book on the floor, dropping it so the papers would spill out, sufficiently obvious to catch attention.

Then I backed away, grateful Hoyle's face had been hidden. Dying was bad enough, but to peg out in a dank, deserted basement where only your killer knew where to find you . . .

"C'mon, Jack." Kroun's voice jarred the silence. His tone was different. Was this his version of concern?

"Yeah, okay." I followed him out, leaving the light on. No need to look back; that tableau would be in my head for a long, long time.

Strome would make a phone call to the cops sometime in the morning. He'd ask if they wanted to know where Mitchell stashed Hoyle's body. The question would make sense to Merrifield and Garza.

Soon after, the cops would give the place a good going-over, find what I wanted them to find and more that I didn't. Along with the bullet entry and exit holes, the coroner would certainly note the ripped flesh on Hoyle's throat and wonder at the lack of blood in the corpse. I'd been clumsy and crazy with hunger, but if the guy was good at his job, he might determine the damage had been caused by something akin to human teeth. There was nothing I could do about it. Hoyle's body was needed to set up a false trail to Mitchell, and that was more important. The authorities would be more inclined to think "mad-dog cannibal killer" than "vampire." When working as a reporter, I'd seen stranger things while covering the crime beat.

I emerged into the fresh air, thankful to be clear of that claustrophobic tomb. What I'd done there was shameful and would always be with me, but I had gotten good at distracting myself from the darker memories swarming in my skull. In time, the worst of them would fade.

That was what I told myself.

KROUN and I headed back to the Nightcrawler. Strome went off to God knows where to do God knows what. I did not care to inquire.

I drove slowly, certain that Derner would have more minutiae requiring a decision from me. When I'd taken over this branch of the mob, the arrangement was for me to be just a figurehead until Gordy got better, but somehow it had turned into real work. I figured I should get paid for services rendered, and the sum should be offensively high. Derner would squawk, but that was chump change compared to what the Nightcrawler raked in from the gambling in the private club. Gordy would shrug it off and call it a bargain.

Once I had the cash in hand I'd turn the reins over to Derner. Bobbi would be happy. That was all I wanted.

Derner, again on a phone, hung up when we came in. His hands weren't shaking this time so his aim was better.

"Your car's back from the shop," he told me. "It's parked out front."

That was good news. I'd had it towed to get new tires and some eager beaver decided it needed to be fancied up. I tossed the keys to my borrowed ride on the desk. "Have someone get these back to the guy on watch at the hospital. I got another car to fix." I told him about the bloodstains on the upholstery in Escott's Nash that needed to be cleaned off. No need to explain to him how they got there; this was a messy trade.

"They'll just replace everything, it'll be easier," Derner said. "Like another color?"

"Just match what's there and have them put on a new steering wheel. The old one's bent."

He did not ask how it had come to be damaged either, only made a note. "Your girl's hotel flat is clean. She can go back tonight."

Somehow I didn't think Bobbi would want to do that just yet. "Thanks. I'll let her know." I'd tackle the details about my getting paid when Kroun wasn't around. He might not care, but then again, he might. "Anything else?"

"Everything's copacetic." That meant all other business was under control, no immediate problems, but Derner glanced at Kroun as though expecting a cue, mindful there could be more. Kroun just stood in place and looked back steadily, which was confusing until I caught on. He was doing the same thing that the cops had done to us earlier. Stare long enough, and you'll get the other guy feeling guilty about something.

"My new clothes?" Kroun prompted.

Derner looked relieved. "Yes, sir, got 'em downstairs in a dressing room. The costume lady's in tonight, I told her to get the stuff packed for you—if that's okay?"

"Sure, fine. Which dressing room?"

"Uh, not that one." He meant where Caine had been strangled.

"Good. When she's done, have a guy put them in Mr. Fleming's car."

My, weren't we formal? On the other hand, he'd just let Derner know I was back up on my rung of the ladder. However temporary, I was to get respect, same as Gordy.

Remembering something I should have asked Bobbi hours ago, I gave an internal wince. "How's Gordy doing? Any news?"

Derner's usually gloomy face brightened a little. "I talked with him on the phone for a minute today. He sounded good."

"You sure?" I knew Gordy could put up a front. There wasn't a poker player born who could beat him at a bald-faced bluff.

"Yeah, Boss. His girlfriend said he'd be resting for another couple weeks, maybe more, but he was feeling a lot better."

Okay, Gordy could lie, but Adelle would not. "That's great." I'd risked myself, pushing right to the edge to impart one last hypnotic suggestion to Gordy so he'd stay in bed until fully recovered. I'd come that close to blowing up my brain from the inside out, but it was worth it if it kept him alive.

"We're done, let's go," Kroun announced. He'd reclaimed the box of cigars—no one had dared touch them—and resettled his hat.

Fine with me.

OUTWARDLY, my Buick looked exactly the same, just cleaner. The paint and chrome gleamed as though fresh from the factory. There wasn't a scratch or dent to be found, and I knew there'd been more than a few scars in place the last time I'd seen her. The windows were different, the glass thicker, but that was the only other sign of the special tinkering.

Kroun's suitcases were on the backseat, and the keys were in the ignition. Just like the cigars, no one had dared touch the car, not while it was under the eye of the club bouncers.

We got in, I tried the starter, and damned if the motor wasn't running more smoothly than before, and the gas tank was full. I could get used to being the boss with stuff like this as part of the job.

Shifting gears, it took a firmer foot on the accelerator to get her to move the extra weight. Just how much armor plating had they put in? She rode heavy; I had to haul the wheel to make the corners and put the brakes on sooner with more force. The solid-rubber tires gave off a different sound against the pavement, and despite the special shocks, I could feel the change in how they handled the bumps. No improvement there.

I'd just have to get used to things unless I wanted to buy a new ride. That Studebaker came to mind, but there were still plenty of miles left in the Buick. It didn't make sense to spend the money.

"Wanna stop at the Stockyards?" I asked. If Kroun had further business tonight, he'd made no mention of it.

"Why? You hungry?"

"I could be. You have to be."

He appeared to think about it. "Guess so. But find a butcher shop instead."

"Risky."

"How so?"

"There's only so many times you can tell the counter guy your wife's making blood pudding."

"Huh." That amused him. "I'll take the chance."

"It won't be fresh."

"Fresh enough."

"But—"

"I just got these clothes, and I'll be damned if I'm going to slog through a stinking stock pen just to get a meal. I'll make the counter guy forget."

All right, put it that way.

Only I wasn't sure where to find a shop. I knew every angle about getting in and out of the Stockyards, but not much about where to buy their end products. "There's a place near the house. Charles goes there when he wants to cook something." Which was almost never. The butcher's was next door to a Chinese restaurant, and Escott was their chief source of income. He loved his chow mein.

Behind us, a car horn blared. I checked the mirror. The vehicle's headlights flicked on and off. The driver hammered the horn again, rapidly.

"What the . . . ?" If it was a hit, they'd have pulled up even to us without warning. I slowed and stopped at the next corner.

Kroun shifted slightly. The cigar box was on the floor, and he had a gun in hand instead.

"I think I know 'em," I said.

"Make sure."

If there was a problem, I did not want to be trapped behind the wheel. I put the car in neutral, pulled the brake, and got out.

The other driver did the same, trotting quick to meet me. He was one of the bouncers from the Nightcrawler. "Derner sent me," he called.

"What's wrong?" Something like this could only mean trouble.

The man's face screwed up with thought, apparently recalling specific instructions. "He said to say your girlfriend said to come to the hospital right away."

"What's wrong?" I repeated, my gut going hollow.

"She said to say your partner's gotten worse, and you're supposed to—"

I dove back into the Buick.

KROUN at my heels, I charged past the hospital's main reception. When the elevator didn't open fast enough, I tore up the stairs to the third landing, finding the right hallway in the maze.

Bobbi stood a few steps from Escott's door, her posture tense, arms tightly crossed as though to hold herself in one piece. Coldfield had his back to the wall opposite. There was no anger in him. Anger would have been normal, welcome. Instead, he seemed lost, punch-drunk. More than anything, that scared me.

Bobbi turned, tears brimming in her eyes. She didn't move, just waited for me to come up and took my hand in both of hers. I couldn't speak. The look on her face . . .

"What's happened?" Kroun asked.

"They won't say," she whispered. "Relatives only."

That said just how bad it was.

A nurse inside the room heard and came out. "Are you the family?"

I remembered putting myself down on paper as being Escott's cousin. "Me. It's me. Is he okay?" It was a damned stupid question, but the kind that pops out when you desperately want a positive answer. Of course he wasn't okay, not with so many people in white uniforms milling around in there. They were busy, which was hopeful. It was when they stopped work and didn't meet your eye that—"What's going on?"

"The doctor will tell you." She went back in.

I could feel it swelling, a mix of rage and terror growing too quick and too strong. I flinched when a hand dropped on my shoulder.

Kroun. He shook his head once. That was all. Then he took his hand away.

It was enough.

One instant I was ready to hit the roof, and the next a chill calm replaced the anger. I still wanted to punch through walls, but that wouldn't help. That was why Bobbi and Coldfield were so pulled in on themselves. They had to be, to keep control. Kroun, on the outside of things, took up a post next to Coldfield.

"Tell me?" he asked softly.

Coldfield blinked. "It . . . uh . . . it was Gordy's man, the one watching the actor. He checked on Charles, didn't like what he saw, got the nurse, started things moving. When they couldn't find Fleming, they knew to call my place. Bobbi called the Nightcrawler, and we drove . . ."

The guard himself came up. "Boss?"

"What'd you see?" He didn't hear me the first time; I had to say it again.

"I looked in like you asked. His color wasn't so good, and he was breathing funny, sweatin' bad."

But Escott was all right. Just hours ago he had been weak, bruised, and tired, but otherwise all right. *A good night's sleep and he'd be better in the morning . . .*

"I seen it before," the man went on, shaking his head, not meeting my eye.

"Seen what?"

"Mr. Fleming?" This from a doctor. He looked—I didn't want him to look like that.

"Yeah, what's going on?"

I didn't want him to say what he said: his words came out in a low sympathetic tone, words that said my friend was dying.

The words washed past. I just stood there. It was someone else doing the listening. Some other guy was going through this, not me.

"Can't you do anything?" Bobbi asked the doctor.

"We're doing what we can."

"But he was *fine* earlier."

"I'm afraid septicemia can work very fast. Once an infection's passed into the bloodstream . . ." He went on, not pulling punches. The odds were against Escott. Six out of ten people died from blood poisoning, died quick and ugly. I grabbed at the hope that he might get lucky and be among those who threw it off and recovered.

They finally allowed me in to see him.

One look.

I knew he wouldn't make it.

But I wasn't a doctor. I could be wrong, desperately wanted to be wrong. I found myself in a chair by the bedside, looking at Escott's face. His skin had a blue cast; he was sheeted with sweat yet shivering, jaw clenched, his breath coming fast and shallow, eyes sealed shut. He didn't react when I said his name. I got a whiff of his sweat when I spoke, and that took me back twenty years to some nameless hospital in France where young men who had survived gas and bullets and shelling and disease succumbed to infections just like this one.

The stink was the same, exactly the same. My friends had died then, and my friend was dying now.

I'd put him here. I'd killed him.

Bobbi slipped up next to me. "He's going to be all right, Jack."

"They're gonna do something?" Maybe they had better medicine now. Twenty years was a good long time. Someone must have figured out how to cure this.

She made no answer.

"We just need get his fever down," said Coldfield, who seemed to be talking to himself. He'd come in to stand on the other side of the bed. His sister was a nurse; he might know more. But all he did was put a damp cloth on Escott's forehead. "We need some ice in here, that's all. A little ice."

The doctor was out in the hall talking to Kroun. I didn't bother listening. Only one nurse remained; the others had vanished. The old janitor from earlier worked his way slowly past, pushing his mop around an already clean floor.

"Some ice, please?" Coldfield said, his voice mild. He used another cloth to dab at Escott's face and neck.

The nurse nodded and left, not hurrying, and she should have. If Escott had had any kind of chance, she'd have moved faster.

Eventually she returned with a bowl of ice and a full ice bag. Coldfield took them both and thanked her. She backed off to stand by the door.

It was my fault. I did this.

Coldfield shot me a murderous look, and that was when I realized I'd spoken out loud. "You're goddamn right on that," he whispered. "And you know what's going to happen next."

Coldfield would kill me.

I didn't care.

"Stop. Both of you," said Bobbi. Her fingers dug into my shoulder. She was trying to keep her balance. Tears spilled steadily from her eyes. She couldn't have been able to see through them.

I got up and made her sit. She gently took Escott's near hand and bowed over it, bowed until her cheek lay on it, her face turned away from me.

That smell again, the rapid rasp of his breath, his shivering—he wasn't going to wake up. They wouldn't even try to wake him. Better that he just slip away in his sleep, that was what they'd say.

The room went blurry.

My hands closed hard on the cold, white-painted iron of the bedstead, and I held tight to keep on my feet. Something was wrong with my knees; I couldn't feel them or anything else except the nausea slithering in my gut. A knot of it clogged my throat, high enough to choke on, but too low to swallow.

I couldn't take this. I couldn't stay here and watch.

But I'd have to. Somehow.

He'd stay for me.

6

As the night crept by, the nurse periodically checked Escott, making notes on a clipboard for whatever good that would do. Coldfield kept up with the compresses. The doctor came again, but didn't have anything new to say, just looked tired.

Escott got worse, sinking as we stood by. The sound of his fast, shallow breathing filled the little room. It was the only sound in the world. I hated it, and I didn't want it to stop.

I thought about calling Vivian Gladwell. Escott hadn't wanted her to know he was in the hospital. Would he want her here now? Would it help? I couldn't work it out, couldn't decide, couldn't do anything.

Faustine came in. Gordy's man had gone off, maybe to get her. She'd shed the reporters. I hardly noticed when she hugged me, then moved on to speak to Bobbi. Couldn't hear what she said, but after a minute the two of them left. Bobbi held herself together until they were in the hall. Soon as she was out of my sight, she broke down sobbing. I went to the door. Bobbi wept and clung hard to Faustine, who slowly took her toward Roland's room, speaking in Russian. The words didn't matter; the soft, caring tone in them did.

Kroun was still out there holding up the wall, hat in hand, overcoat draped over one arm. He watched Bobbi, frowning.

"Hitting her pretty hard," he observed. "Must really like him."

"They're close friends, yeah."

"Friends with a dame. How 'bout that?"

I'd heard him say it before. "It can happen. Like me and Adelle Taylor."

The mention of her name caused Kroun to crack a brief, pleased smile. When it came to Adelle, he was starstruck. "She's friends with your pal in there?"

"Yeah. She is. Listen, you don't have to stay."

He shrugged. "When you gonna do something?"

I shook my head. "They can't do anything."

"Yeah, I got that from the doc. What about you?"

"I can't—I . . . what?"

"Give him some blood."

Must have misheard him. "What?"

"You know what I mean."

I did. I'd thought of it. A lot. But I couldn't decide; I just didn't know what Escott would want. "It might not work. He might not change. It hardly ever—"

Kroun gave me an odd look, then went in the room. The nurse was writing a new entry on the clipboard. He walked around her to the bedside. Coldfield straightened to glare first at him then me.

"He looks like hell," said Kroun, his attention on Escott. "Why haven't you done anything yet?" This was directed my way. He dropped his coat and hat on the chair.

"Done what?" Coldfield rumbled.

"He wants me to do an exchange on Charles." There was only so much I could say with the nurse present. I closed the door to keep things private.

"An exchange?"

"The kind that made me . . . like I am."

"Like you?" That shook him. "He *knows*?" Coldfield straightened to face Kroun.

"Yeah. He's in the same club."

"*What?*"

"Hey!" Kroun hadn't wanted that news spread.

"What's it matter?" I said.

Coldfield pointed at Kroun. "He's like *you*?"

"That a problem?" Kroun asked.

"I donno yet."

"An exchange," I said again with enough emphasis so the meaning was clear. "You know Charles best, what would he want?"

Coldfield visibly fought to focus. He must have gotten details from Escott at some time or other about how vampires are made. I take in blood, let it work through me, then give it back again. After death, Escott might return, but it rarely worked, or there'd be a lot more vampires in the world. He might not come back as I had done. "It would make him like you?"

"It probably won't work. Long odds, Shoe. Real long. Against."

It was a lot to take in, a lot to think about. He looked at Escott, then at me.

"What would Charles want?" I asked.

"To *live*, goddammit! What the hell you waiting for?"

"I can try, but you've got to understand that—"

"Cripes," said Kroun, disgusted. "Stop wasting time and just give him blood before it's too late."

The nurse had picked up that something out of the ordinary was afoot. "A transfusion?" she said.

"Yeah, sweetheart, one of those."

"Let me get the doctor." She sidled toward the door.

"Ahhh, *cripes*." Kroun slipped his suit coat off and unbuttoned one shirt cuff, rolling it up.

"Sir, you can't just—"

He ignored her. The tumbler with its glass straw was still on the bed-side table. He took the straw and snapped it in half, then dumped the leftover water on the floor and put the tumbler back but nearer the edge.

"Sir? What are . . . *stop!*" Her voice shot up.

Kroun let out a few ripe words as he swiped the jagged end of the straw hard across his exposed wrist. Blood suddenly flooded out. He held his wrist over the glass to catch the flow.

We stood rooted—me, Coldfield, and the nurse—too shocked to move or speak while Kroun freely bled.

He grimaced and cursed some more and finally grabbed up a discarded compress. Shaking it open he wrapped it tight on the cut. The bloodsmell hit me hard.

"Gabe . . . ?"

"Not now." Kroun tapped Escott's face with the back of his hand. "Hey. Hey, pal. Wake up. Come on!" He hit harder, once, twice, and Escott's eyelids fluttered. He made a protesting moan. He wasn't awake, but could respond a little. Kroun held the glass to Escott's lips and tilted it.

The nurse screamed and surged forward. I caught her and kept her back. I didn't see what good this might do, but Kroun seemed to know his business.

"Come on . . . drink up, pal," he murmured. "That's it."

Some of the blood trickled down one side of Escott's mouth. The rest made it in past his clenched teeth.

Coldfield gaped at me, out of his depth. I shook my head.

The nurse got to be too much of a struggling handful, so I swung her toward the door. She pushed it violently open and kept going, shouting for help.

"Gabe?"

"He got most of it," said Kroun, putting the glass on the table. "Didn't choke." He went into the washroom. He twisted the sink spigot and carefully undid the cloth, holding his cut under the stream of water. "Damn, that stings."

He'd heal quick enough, but Escott . . .

Bobbi rushed in. "Jack?" She froze, seeing the blood that smeared Escott's face and pillow. "My God, *what are you DOING?*"

The doctor, arriving with what seemed like half the hospital, asked the same thing and almost as loudly. While he checked Escott, he also instructed several heavyweight orderlies to escort us from the building. Things might have devolved to a fight, but Kroun caught the doctor's eye for a moment. I was too busy to hear, but the eviction was abruptly canceled, and the orderlies and everyone else were kicked out of the room instead. Confused, they hung close, peering in with other bystanders attracted by the commotion.

I shut the door on them, leaving me, Bobbi, Coldfield, and Kroun inside with the oblivious, hypnotically whammied doctor.

Kroun sat the man down and told him to take a catnap. Things fell quiet except for the fast, labored saw of Escott's breathing. He was fully out again.

Bobbi started up. "What did you do to Charles?" She'd aimed both barrels in my direction.

"It was me," Kroun muttered. "Just trying to help." His bleeding had stopped, leaving a hell of a red welt on his wrist. He frowned at it.

She put that together with the blood on Escott. "How? How does that help?"

He didn't answer, just shook his sleeve down, buttoning the cuff.

I stumbled out with a half-assed account of what he'd done.

Bobbi looked at Escott, then at us. "*Will* it help him?"

Kroun shrugged. "Maybe. Left it late. Have to wait and see."

"Jack, will this turn Charles into—"

"I don't know. Gabe?"

He shrugged again, pulled on his coat, buttoned it, checked his handkerchief. If he started fiddling with it again, I'd knock his block off.

"C'mon . . . talk to us. How did you know to do that? I never heard of it."

"Well, it's a big world, you learn something new every day."

"Not something like this!"

"Hey! Sickroom! Pipe down!" Hat on, he slung his overcoat over his good arm and started for the door.

"You gotta talk, dammit."

He paused, back to us, head half-turned, considering. Then, "No. I don't."

He went out.

"Son of a bitch," rumbled Coldfield. "The son of a bitch is crazy as a bedbug."

"You're all crazy," said Bobbi. She went to Escott, found a clean, damp cloth, and dabbed at the blood. It took her a while; her tears were back.

I went to her, but she didn't want to be held.

Someone ventured to open the door. It was Faustine.

"Things go-ink how?" she asked, gently easing inside. A damn good question. "Bob-beee, poor da'link. You let me help, yesss?"

"I'll be all right, I need to stay."

Faustine looked hard at the doctor, who was still out for the count. "Zen I find coffee. Yesss?"

No one turned her down. She swept out. I heard her dealing with the crowd in the hall, telling them to leave, all was well, all was fine. I recognized the nurse's voice raised in challenge, but Faustine wouldn't let her by and kept asking about coffee.

Hours of hell later I went looking for Kroun.

He was in a dark waiting room at the far end of the hall, feet up, nose in a magazine. The glowing spill from the corridor was more than enough for our kind to read by, but it looked odd. I turned the light on.

He squinted. "Ow. Too bright."

"Too bad."

"How's your friend?"

It was hard to speak. Almost too hard. I had to swallow, and my mouth was cotton dry. "His . . . his fever's down. He's breathing better."

"That's good."

"Is he going to need a second dose?"

"Nope." Kroun turned a page.

"The doctor woke up."

"He remember much?"

"Not a lot."

"That's good, too."

"He checked Charles out, took a blood sample, did some other stuff.

The infection's . . . Charles seems to be throwing it off. The doc said it's a goddamn miracle."

Kroun shrugged. "Maybe it is. Thanks for telling your big friend about me. Next time use a megaphone."

"He had to know."

"No, he didn't."

"Coldfield won't say anything. Who'd believe him?"

"That's not the point—"

"Where'd you learn *that* angle on the blood? Who told you?"

"Doesn't matter." He continued to read.

"The hell it does. The one who made me didn't know, and neither did the one who made her. Who did your initiation?"

"Drop it, kid."

Was he ashamed? Granted, such things could get embarrassing. "You don't have to go into detail."

"I'm not going into it at all."

"Where'd you meet her? When?"

"You deaf? I'm not—"

"Or was it a man?"

That netted me a beaut of a "what the hell did you just say?" expression.

It lasted about two seconds.

I blinked at dark green linoleum, disoriented. I was facedown on the floor with no understanding of how I'd gotten there. My jaw hurt and hurt bad. I tried moving it, and some dim insight—along with a sudden burst of agony and the taste of my own blood—told me it was broken. Shattered maybe. In several places. The rest of me wanted to vanish, and I didn't fight the urge.

When I resumed solidity, everything was in working order again, though I still drew a blank on what had happened. I found my feet, taking it slow.

Kroun sat in his chair as before, but leaning forward, rubbing the knuckles of his right hand. They were raw and red. His expression was calm. "Are you anywhere near the point of backing off, or do you want your face rearranged more permanently?"

I stared at him, wiping leftover blood from my mouth with the back of one hand.

"Well?"

"I'm thinking."

He snorted and picked the magazine up from the floor. "And the man said *I* was crazy. I heard him." He flipped pages filled with pictures about hunting and fishing. "I need to get out of this town."

"Thought you still had business."

"I do. Tomorrow night. Till then, I got nothing else."

"No need to hang around here."

"Some babysitter you are. Forget about Michael and Broder already?"

"You could say."

"Word of warning: don't. Mike looks nice, but he isn't. Broder looks dangerous, and he is."

I'd figured that out already; Kroun just wanted a change of subject. "I'll keep that in mind."

"Smart boy. I'll need a ride tomorrow night."

"No problem." I could guess that it had to do with those cigars. It seemed a good idea to not try any more questions. I'd goaded him enough for one night. "Lemme tie things up here then we'll go. Thank you."

"Mm?"

"Thanks for what you did for Charles. I owe you."

He grunted again and found a page to read.

BOBBI looked up when I came in. She smiled—a small, sleepy one—but my world tilted another notch back toward its proper place once more. I could deal with anything so long as she smiled like that.

"Faustine's left?" I asked.

"She's bunking in Roland's room," she said. "If there's more excitement she doesn't want to miss it. You got more waiting in the wings?"

"Not that I know of."

I checked Escott over again for the umpteenth time, looking for changes. His heartbeat was strong and steady, no longer racing fit to tear itself apart.

"It's getting late for you," she said.

"You, too."

"I'll be fine. Shoe and I are staying."

Coldfield didn't speak, but his expression was eloquent. Yes, Escott seemed to be safe now, but that did not mitigate the fact that I'd nearly killed him. If not for Gabriel Kroun and the devil's own luck, Escott would almost certainly be dead by now. However matters had turned out, I had been stupid, and Coldfield did not forgive stupidity.

We were very much alike on that point.

The blue tinge to Escott's skin had faded. His color was nearly normal except for the bruises, and he looked to be in a natural sleep instead of deeply unconscious. That death smell was still present, but it was old air not yet cleared by the ventilation. What I got from him now was ordinary sweat, and that more than anything reassured me that he was truly recovering.

It'd happened extremely fast. In a tiny span of hours he'd drifted back from the brink. I'd *watched* the process and hardly dared to hope. The doctor had muttered about a miracle and recorded it on the clipboard. The nurses would glance at me and whisper to others, and on down the ladder went the story. Even the deaf old janitor must have gotten word; he kept his back to the commotion, clearly not wanting any part of it.

What the consequences might be later for Escott I couldn't begin to guess. Bobbi—all of us—wanted to know if it would change him in some other way.

I only knew of one means to turn a person into a vampire and just how rarely it worked. A blood exchange takes place, but with a normal human donating first, *then* taking in the vampire's blood; *that* was how it was done.

Kroun's variation was new to me, only he wasn't talking, which was nuts. What harm was there in telling?

Would Escott recall anything about drinking Kroun's blood? Perhaps as a fever-induced dream?

Coldfield might tell him. I wouldn't know where to start.

Bobbi promised to phone me at sunset tomorrow. I kissed her good-bye, nodded at Coldfield, who did not react, and left.

I drove to the Stockyards.

Snow sifted down, cheerful as Christmas. It was pretty until the window wipers began to clog. The milk trucks were out, as were the newspaper trucks, not a lot of cars. We made good time.

Kroun was pale as paint, though he wouldn't admit to being hungry. I was, mildly. Before Hog Bristow put me through hell, I'd gotten into the habit of never letting my hunger go beyond the mild stage. I found a place to park under a broken streetlamp and we got out.

"Cripes, what a stink," he complained.

"Don't breathe."

"Huh."

A high fence separated us from the source of the stink. Not a problem for me, but he'd have to climb get in. He studied the fence and shook his head, apparently mindful of his new clothes.

"It's not that bad," I said.

"Yes. It is. You have more of those bottles in your icebox?"

"Yeah, but—"

"I know. Not fresh. I'll get by. Hurry it up before we're under a drift. I'll be in the car."

He had a hell of a lot more self-control than I did. By now I'd have been crazy-starved, shaking, and suffering tunnel vision. Maybe the bullet in his skull had something to do with it. Kroun sauntered back to the Buick and shut himself in.

I vanished, passed through the fence, and re-formed on the other side.

After my resurrection, it'd taken months for me to get used to my new diet. The profound physical satisfaction I got was one thing; it was the part about biting into a living animal's vein and feeding from it that had bothered me for a long time. The benefits outweighed the unpleasant details, though, and eventually I reached the point of not thinking much on them.

Getting blood while it was still flowing and hot might not have the same importance to Kroun. Some people demanded bread straight from the baker's oven while others were happy enough with two-day-old leftovers. Others wouldn't even notice a difference. Maybe he was like that.

These nights I had to be cautious about choosing a four-footed victim. My hypnosis had been handy for soothing skittish animals; now I had to find ones that were already calm. Not easy. Cattle could be deceptive: one second lethargic, the next trying to trample you. Horses were easier prey; they were used to being handled. The shorter hair on their hides was a bonus.

Three tries to find an animal that allowed me to do what I had to, then I rushed the process. Things were getting damned cold. The snow swirled and fell more thickly, caking on my shoulders. Kroun's idea of going to a butcher shop was looking better by the minute.

The cattle in the next pen over abruptly stirred, restless and noisily fretting. They might have smelled their impending death on the freezing air, but if not, then something else had bothered them. Kroun's advice about being more careful was still fresh in my mind.

You can't be paranoid if someone really is after you.

I broke off feeding and looked around, listening hard, but I heard only lowing and the wind. Sight was limited because of the falling snow. The cattle could have been reacting to the weather or one of the yard workers. I'd learned to avoid them, but sometimes got spotted. Usually a man would shout, which was my cue to vanish, leaving him with a mystery. I was sure stories were circulating about a dark-clad specter haunting the stock pens.

Had it been a worker, he'd have yelled by now. My neck prickled the way it does when you think you're being watched. Most of the time we're wrong, and no one is around, but I paid attention to such warnings. The instinct is there for a reason. The last time I'd felt it, Hurley Gilbert Dugan had stepped out of the cold shadows and shot me.

He didn't seem to be around, which was just as well for us both. I'd have killed him on sight. Not a lot of people inspired that kind of reaction in me, and I wasn't proud of it. On the other hand, given the opportunity to bury *him* in the lake, I'd do it and no second thoughts.

I had come a long way down my private road to damnation.

Sparing my shoes further damage, I vanished and floated out, not re-forming until I was close to the Buick. If anyone saw, then their view would be as impaired by the snowfall as mine.

I took a last gander at what I could see of the empty street, got in, and wasted no time flooring it.

"What?" Kroun asked. "Something wrong?"

"Not much. It's been a hell of a night."

No disagreement from him on that.

THE house had been broken into, again.

Any other time, I'd have gotten somewhere a few miles beyond mere anger, but it was late, and I was tired. I should have a revolving door installed so the next wave of housebreakers would have an easier time of it.

Instead of picking a door lock, someone had let himself in the hall window at the back with a brick, smashing out the glass near the top so he could twist the catch, lift, and climb in. The front door looked straight down the hall, and right away I noticed the curtains fluttering. The window was wide open, and glass shards gleamed from the melted snow that had blown in. It overlooked the alley behind the house. The neighbors had missed the noise, else the cops would be waiting.

"Your friends were here again," I said, disgusted.

Suitcases full of his new clothes in hand, Kroun put them down by the stairs, balancing the box of del Mundo cigars on top of one. He walked to the window and studied smears left by the intruder's wet shoes. "Don't think so. Michael can open any door, and Broder would just kick it in. They're not this sloppy."

Yeah, maybe. I did a quick search of all three floors, attic, and the basement, but no big bosses from New York lurked in the shadows. Sweeping outside, I looked in the garage, but Escott's Nash was safe. I found footprints in the snow by the house, but the fresh fall had nearly filled them in—not that I was an expert tracker. The intruder had pushed a garbage can under the window and used it to boost himself up; ignoring the locked doors, he'd left the same way. His prints led toward the alley entry and the street beyond.

"Michael's got no reason to return," Kroun said when I came back. "If he wants to know more about you, there's other ways for him, like talking to Gordy."

"What if they were here for you?"

"Then they were disappointed, but this doesn't smell like either of them."

"They're trying to shake me up."

"Why should they bother?" He shut the front door, cutting down on the cold cross draft from the broken window. "Anything missing?"

"Don't know." I made a second search of the place. Escott and I didn't have much in the way of valuables. He had an old gold pocket watch, but kept it in a safe hidden under the basement stairs along with his petty cash. I had a few cigar boxes stuffed with money there, too. Neither of us trusted banks much. The safe hadn't been broken into, but throughout the house someone had rummaged around in the drawers and closets. Nothing seemed to be gone, though.

"Not a burglar," said Kroun. "A reporter after dirt? There were plenty of them around when that Russian dame was all over you."

"Maybe. Faustine wasn't shy about naming names. But if anyone wanted to know about me, he could ask for an interview. No need to do this."

"What about the FBI?"

I didn't like that one. "I'm not important enough for them to bother with."

"Don't be so sure. That Hoover is crazy. He tells his boys to do something, and they do it, whether it's a good idea or not. Like me with Gordy's bunch."

"But—" I broke off.

"You think of something?"

"It's nuts."

"But worth considering?"

"Gilbert Dugan—that society bum behind the kidnapping I worked on? He was going to send anonymous letters off to a lot of places, the cops, the FBI, the tax people, to let them know that I was a suspicious character they should investigate. I got rid of those letters, but he might have written more."

"They'd pay attention to mail from some lunatic?"

"Probably not, but it'd only take one guy having a slow day to set a ball rolling. Maybe the G-men would burgle a joint, but this doesn't make sense. They'd pick me up for questioning first."

"Who else has it in for you?"

"Hand me a phone book."

"Don't stay here then. I'm not." He went into the kitchen and opened the icebox. He pulled out a brown bottle and yanked the cork. I'd seen drunks guzzle a beer that fast, but not often. As before, it hit him like a jolt of hard booze. "Wow. That's good stuff you keep there. Thanks for the hospitality." He left the empty in the sink and went toward the front hall. He looked at his suitcases a moment, shook his head, and walked out the front door without them.

"Hey, I'm supposed to keep an eye on you," I called from the porch.

"I'll stay out of trouble, I promise."

"Where you going?"

"Don't know yet. Safer that way."

"You need a ride there?"

"Nope."

"You coming back?"

"Tomorrow night, first thing. Still need to wind up some business." He moved briskly down the sidewalk, ignoring the snow.

No point asking what the business might be. He would return, if only to get his clothes.

I shut the door and muttered unkind things about the ass who'd broken the window. The place wasn't secure for me, not during the day.

My secret room under the kitchen . . . well, someone had found it.

The heavy kitchen table and the rug under it were slightly out of place. Escott was meticulous about keeping one of the table legs squarely over a small cigarette burn he'd made on the floor. He'd put it there on purpose, claiming it was a kind of burglar alarm, and damned if it hadn't worked. The burn was visible now. I was seriously spooked.

The intruder had not made it down into the room. A normal human could drop in but needed a ladder to get out. I had a folding one kept out of sight under my cot, and it was still out of sight, unused.

The intruder chose to avoid getting trapped in my basement lair, but he'd still seen it. What had he made of it? I didn't keep any secret diary or important papers there, just my attempts at writing lurid fiction for dime magazines. One close look, and he'd probably laugh himself silly.

A sense of violation, shaken confidence, and rage—I had the whole list of what it feels like when an unknown threat invades one's supposedly safe castle. This was far from the first time I'd been through the experience, but you never get used to it. If I found the guy . . . he wouldn't be happy. With both arms broken, it's hard to climb into people's houses.

I scavenged scrap boards in the basement that were long enough and got the hammer and nails. Fastening the boarding to the sash, I stuffed layers of newspapers in the gap between them and the remaining glass. If anyone wanted to get in again, he could do it; this was just to keep the weather out. As a repair it stank, but I felt better for the effort.

It was too dangerous to sleep the day here, and there wasn't time to drive to Lady Crymsyn and hide out in its hidden sanctuary—if it was indeed still hidden. The bad guys might have found it as well. I thought of calling the Nightcrawler and having a couple of the bouncers come over to watch the house, but for all I knew they might be in on it. Maybe it had been an overeager reporter looking for dirt. Maybe it had been those two cops, Merrifield and Garza.

Locking the front and back doors—including shoving a chair under each knob—I inspected all the windows, pulling shades, seeing to it the catches caught. It was more habit than expectation of keeping anyone out. I worked my way upstairs.

The clock on my dresser showed I had enough time to take care of some much-needed details so long as I was quick. One scalding-hot shower and a close shave later put me in an improved state of mind. I dressed to be ready for tomorrow night, intending to waste no time getting back to the hospital to see Escott. Yes, he was better, but a relapse could happen. Hope and worry chased themselves around inside my skull, each feeding and exhausting the other turn on turn, no end in sight to their insane race.

Grabbing two spare blankets from a cupboard and an oilcloth packet of my home earth, I went up to the attic.

A determined break-in artist could still get in despite a heavy trunk I'd dragged over the trapdoor, but I wouldn't be sleeping there. Stooping to avoid rafters, I walked to the far end of the narrow space where a small window with cloudy glass peered at a similar window across the alley. Vanishing, I sieved through, floated over, and re-formed in the neighbor's attic.

I got my bearings, went semitransparent, and drifted to a dark corner behind some junk that hadn't been moved in years. Solid again and moving quietly, I put one blanket on the dusty floor, lay down, and wrapped up in the other. Very cozy. I'd done this before for a little peace of mind. The packet of earth was snug under the small of my back. It was cold, but nothing I couldn't handle. I'd rest well for the day, as safe as could be improvised, and not too worried the neighbors would find me. Spring cleaning was weeks away.

What arrangements would Kroun make? Perhaps something similar. With those picklocks he could walk through most any door. He could also hypnotize people into forgetting his presence. He'd look after himself well enough, hopefully without hurting anyone along the way.

That gave my conscience a pang. He was supposed to be a bad guy, same as his friends. Michael had specifically warned me to beware of him. But Kroun's reputation wasn't matching up to the side he'd shown tonight. If he was that bad, then why had he saved Escott? So that I'd owe him twice over? Maybe, but he had looked genuinely concerned at the time.

Why wouldn't he talk?

Wh—

Sunrise.

KROUN

COLD *town. Damn cold town.*

Gabriel felt a lot better with a bellyful of blood, but even that wasn't enough to take away the heavy weariness that had crept up on him over the last few hours.

He needed rest, the kind he only ever got from sleeping on soil, but that was a luxury he'd just have to put off. Leaving himself open to having the dreams, nightmares, night terrors in the day, whatever they were, was more important.

Mixed in with their horrors was information . . . memories.

Bad ones, like the bomb ripping through the car, but if they also led to something useful—like how he'd known his blood would help that man—then Gabe would take the bad with the good and get through it.

Fleming was getting too pushy with his questions.

Gabe hadn't enjoyed busting the kid, but sometimes you have to make a point when the other guy's playing dumb. Fleming wasn't dumb, not for damn sure, but he had a hell of an instinct for getting under the skin. No wonder Hog Bristow had . . .

Gabe's shoulders jerked. No, better not to be thinking about *that* mistake just before bedtime. The memories he courted had to be his own, not imaginings about another man's run of bad luck. He did not need to dream about being skinned alive. How the hell had Fleming survived the ordeal? Even Gordy didn't have those particulars.

Looking over his shoulder more than a few times, Gabe checked to see if anyone followed. Whoever had gotten into Fleming's house might have been watching from a distance, waiting to come after one or the other of them.

No one showed himself on foot or in a car; what could be seen of the street through the thick snowfall was clear. Fleming was the target, then. Presumably he would find a safer haven for the day than that drafty brick barn.

Not my problem.

Long strides eating up the pavement and the snow filling in his tracks, Gabe left the rows of houses, entering the beginnings of a business area. This was where the neighborhood wives bought their groceries, where their husbands worked, where their kids ran errands. A good life when you could find it. Gabe's life before his change had not been so tranquil, he was certain of that.

He found the shop he wanted, one that Fleming had driven past on the way back to the house. On second look it still seemed suitable. The dingy window fronting the street was obscured with sheets of yellowed newspaper to discourage the curious from peering in, and a faded CLOSED sign hung crookedly on the door. The alcove entry was littered with minor trash, indication that no one had been there for months. Make that years. The papers dated from '33.

Good enough.

The picklocks got him inside.

It might have been some kind of store before things went bust on Wall Street. There were a few long tables, shelving, and a single counter for the clerk and cash register, but no other indication of its history. The dust was thick and the stale air cold, but Gabe had known worse places to spend the day.

He found a small storage closet in the back. Solid door, no windows.

Good. No room to lie down . . . not so good, but he'd live with it. He scrounged around the shop and found a spindly wooden stool that would serve. A few swipes with a forgotten rag cleaned the dirt off the seat. Gabe took it in the closet and positioned it just right. He sat, back against the closed door, legs braced so he wouldn't fall over. No one could sleep like that, but then his bout of daylight immobility couldn't really be called sleep. Better this than sitting on the floor in his new clothes.

Gabe let his head droop forward, shut his eyes, and waited for the sun to smother his conscious mind for the day.

The dreams did not disappoint.

THE monsters that had retreated into the shadows hurtled free again. There was no losing them, not when they called the inside of his head home.

His trip through hell began with the exploding car. He felt the fire, the ripping within his chest as the smoke seared him from the inside out. Close, too close. He could have died there. Died again. The changes in his body prevented that, but the awful recovery . . .

He was swept farther back and heard the wind threading through the pine needles again. How he loved that sound. Peace, pure peace. It did not last. The soothing music cut off as earth, wet and icy cold, was heaped over his inert body.

Yes, it was bad. One of the really bad memories.

He'd been buried and would stay there, deep in his grave.

No ending to this one. Death was like that. It was forever. He was dead and aware of every grinding moment, every second passing him by.

Aware of the loneliness.

Never mind the soul-killing panic, the weight crushing his chest, the dirt clogging his mouth, nose, and ears, the absolute paralysis, the cold; he was completely *alone* in the blackness. No angelic choir, no hell's chorus, no afterlife at all, only infinite, unrelieved isolation. He'd go mad from it; anyone would.

No. Not for me.

He had to get free, somehow.

The earth was heavy, but he could shift it if he tried. Maybe.

Some shred of will returned to what was left of his consciousness and transferred to his dead limbs, generating feeble movement.

He struggled and squirmed, gradually working upward. He hoped it was up. There had been stars framed by pine branches above him before that first shovelful hit his face. He just had to dig toward them.

Hard going, though. The hardest thing he'd ever done. Had they heaped rocks atop his body? He pushed at whatever it was, shoving it to one side rather than lifting—

His frozen hands clawed air.

More effort, and he worked his torso free, then his legs, boosting himself upright but dizzily swaying. He grabbed at a tree trunk and held on, spitting dirt, blinking.

Woods. Darkness. A small cabin not fifty feet away through the trees. No lights. No sound but the wind and the soft lap of water. A lake . . . no, a river. He came here to do his fishing. That, and . . . and . . . what was it?

He was filthy, and he stank. Smells were painfully sharp: the clean cold wind, the scent from the pine trees, the muddy earth, the blood. His clothes were soaked with it.

And God in heaven, his head *hurt*. He pressed palms to his temples and tried not to whimper like a sick dog. Take a lifetime of headaches all at once, triple their pain, and it might come close to what he felt. It rushed over him like a lightning storm.

It hurt the most . . . there . . . some kind of bump . . . no, a ridge, right in the bone. As he touched it, the pain exploded. He dropped in his tracks, unable to bite off the scream. He writhed on the broken earth of his grave and shrieked until his air was gone. Not replacing it seemed to help. Strange as it was to go without breathing, he understood it was all right. He was dead, and things were different now.

Dead. Just not a ghost. Something else.

He'd remember when the agony eased.

Only it didn't.

After a long, long time he realized it wasn't going away.

He swiped dirt from his eyes. His vision blurred and failed for a few moments, then returned. *Blinding* pain: he had the firsthand meaning of that now. He'd just have to get through it. He was in danger from . . . something . . . the sun. It would rise soon. He had to find a place to hide from it.

Back under the earth?

His grave? No. Not there again. Not ever.

Besides, there was . . . no, that couldn't be right. For a tiny instant he forgot his pain, trading it for curiosity.

Gabe touched an oddly familiar shape half-submerged under the loose clods and rust brown pine needles.

His numbed fingers slid over a layer of grit, brushing it off.

When he realized what it was, he yanked his hand back as though from a fire.

GABRIEL shot awake, one hand twitching up to the left side of his head as though to keep his brain from bursting through the bone.

He had no comparable pain, but remembered what he'd felt then. How the hell had he gotten through it?

Where was that place? Not near Chicago. It was . . . the cabin . . . and it was . . .

Gone now. The sunset took it from him, damn it.

The thing he'd found . . . *what* was it? He could almost feel it again under his fingertips . . .

The sunset took that as well.

Damn.

His raised hand was a fist now, and he considered punching a hole in the wall, then thought better of it. This deserted and forlorn old shop wasn't his property to damage. He made himself relax and stretched out of his braced posture.

Not too bad, just a little stiff. He'd lose that on the walk back to Fleming's house. Gabe wasn't fully rested, but he would make up for it later.

Patience. Another day's worth of dreaming might get him everything.

In the meantime he'd talk to the old bastard and see if that would help.

7

FLEMING

THE neighbor's attic had some heat seeping up from the lower floors, but it was still cold. It took a few minutes to get myself moving again. My usual sanctuary was fairly close to the basement furnace, and I missed its comfort.

After floating back to the house, I made sure that no one had moved the trunk from the trapdoor, then descended through the floor and down the stairwell to the front hall. The kitchen phone was ringing as I materialized.

It was Bobbi, calling as she'd promised.

"How's Charles?" I asked.

"He's fine, sweetheart, just *fine*. It's a miracle." The jubilation in her voice flowed through me, warm and reassuring, and I sagged as the worry fell away. I knew she was smiling, and the spark would be back in her eyes.

"I'll be right over."

"Don't go to the hospital. He left."

I thought I'd not heard her right. "Come again?"

"He was well enough to check out this afternoon. The doctor wanted him to stay, but Charles insisted on leaving."

"What the hell? But last night—"

"He's *better*, I'm telling you."

Miracle, indeed. This I had to see.

"Shoe brought him to the hotel. The one I'm at."

"I'll be right over."

She made no reply.

"Bobbi?"

"You should wait awhile, Jack."

"But—" Oh.

"Shoe's still upset by what happened."

"You are, too."

"Darling, I know that Charles getting blood poisoning wasn't your fault, but Shoe doesn't see it that way."

"He's right. It was my fault. If I'd . . . oh, never mind."

"What did you two fight about? Shoe won't tell me."

"He might not know. It was between me and Charles, and it's over now. Please, believe that." My tone begged her to drop it.

She grumbled something away from the receiver that I didn't catch, but it did not sound kind. Time to change the subject. I asked after Roland and Faustine. They were both fine and making plans to leave for Hollywood as soon as Roland was on his feet again. Things were happening, it seemed.

"Does it have to do with that guy who was there?" I asked. "The fast talker in the funny shirt?"

"Lenny Larsen? Yes, he's got a deal for them. A real movie deal!"

"He's crazy."

She went indignant. "For getting them work?"

"No, he's just a crazy guy. He's too slick by half."

"Jack, you only saw him for a minute."

"It was enough. Don't you let him spin you around, okay?"

"What do you mean spin me around?"

"Con you. The guy's got to be a con man."

"Well, of course he is. They're like that in Hollywood. You just have to make sure he's working for *you* when he's giving others the business."

Oh, God. She sounded as though she knew what she was talking about.

"What was that?" she asked.

"Nothing. Look, I've got to see Charles. I could find a way in if you tell me which room, which floor."

"The same floor as mine and Gordy's—he's better, too, by the way. He found it's easier to just rest than to argue with Adelle."

"That's good. I'll want to see him."

"Am I on your list?"

"You're first up, baby."

"That was the right answer."

I told her Derner's news about her apartment being clean and ready for her. She didn't exactly turn handsprings. "I'll go with you if you like," I added.

"You certainly will. I'm not sure I want to see the place yet. I'd like to stay another night here."

"At a noisy hotel?"

"It's about the same as my place, only I know everyone. I feel safer here with them around. How nuts is that?"

After what she'd been through in the last few days, it sounded perfectly sane to me. "It's a vacation. Not nuts at all."

"There's more."

"Oh, yeah?"

"It can wait. When do you plan to sneak in?"

"Uh."

"Thought so. You've got business, right?"

"Has to do with Gabriel Kroun." I braced for a touchy reaction.

"Oh. That's okay, then."

What the hell? "Hey, you're not—"

"Mad? Jack, he saved Charles's life. If it wouldn't make you jealous, I'd give him one lollapalooza of a big kiss."

"Uh . . . um . . . uh."

"Oh, relax. He's safe. I'll just shake hands."

"Uh-nuh . . . um." I cleared my throat next. It seemed the best response. "Well, uh, if you really want to thank him—"

"Yes?"

"He likes Adelle, seen all her movies. Maybe she could autograph a picture, put his name on it so it's specially for him?"

Bobbi thought that was a great idea. She wanted to know more about Kroun, but I didn't have much to say since I didn't know much. Telling her about the run-in with the cops, with Michael and Broder, the burgling of the house would just throw a cold, wet blanket on her high spirits.

We moved on to other topics, such as when Lady Crymsyn might open again and how to replace Roland and Faustine's big dance number. As always, I thought Bobbi should do the whole show, but her instincts were better on what to put on a nightclub stage. While I never got tired of hearing her sing, the customers might have other ideas.

Someone knocked on the front door, loudly rapping out "shave-and-a-haircut" but skipping the "two bits."

Bobbi heard the noise. "That your friend?"

"Not exactly friend, but I think so."

"Bring him over. Shoe won't have a problem with you if he's along."

Optimistic of her. "Maybe. I gotta go, don't know how long it'll take. Expect me when you see me?"

"Don't I always?"

We hung up.

I moved a chair from under the doorknob and let Kroun in. He had a few smears of dust on his new overcoat and declined to say where he'd spent his day.

"What put you in such a good mood?" he asked after giving me a once-over.

"My girlfriend."

He glanced around. "She's here?"

"She phoned." I told him about Escott's recovery. "He's at Coldfield's hotel—the one where Adelle Taylor is staying with Gordy." As I'd hoped, the mention of her got Kroun's attention.

"Maybe we should go over, say hello," he said. "Ya think?"

"You got anything else to do?"

He grimaced. "Unfortunately, yes. I've an appointment and need a ride."

"Where? For what?"

"Later. I need a shave first."

He took one suitcase upstairs to the guest room and soon had water running in the bathtub. He might be a while.

With little to do but kick my heels, I gathered up the day's papers from the porch and brought in the mail. Nothing in the latter was for me, but the papers were full of reworked angles on Roland Lambert's escapades as Chicago's newest gangbuster. Fresh pictures of him grinning or looking devotedly at Faustine were below the fold but still on the front page. Speculation was again raised about Hollywood doing a movie based on their exploits. No pictures of yours truly being affectionately assaulted by Faustine were there, though a couple papers mentioned me as a nightclub owner involved with the mobs. In one they called me "Jim Flemming." I was almost used to people spelling the last name wrong, but they could at least get my given one right.

The Alan Caine murder had moved to page two, small photo, with the cops apparently following a new lead. There were hints they had a suspect and were close to capturing him. Hoyle had been found. On page four was a two-paragraph filler about a man's body in a basement under a garage, foul play was suspected. No name, no mention of the address book I'd planted, no connection to the Alan Caine investigation. The cops were playing it close to the vest there.

Back on page two the header on another column read, SINGER'S SUICIDE WAS MURDER! with a quote from the coroner about Jewel Caine's autopsy proving she had not taken her own life. Cold comfort. Very cold. For a few seconds I wished Mitchell alive again so I could kill him, then discarded it. If I had a wish, then better to use it to bring back poor Jewel instead.

Though the cops were still on the hunt, tomorrow the story would be considered a dry well by most editors and passed over for other news. There might be something in the obituaries about Jewel's funeral, but no more, a sad and unfair end to a tough life. What was the point in trying if this was all a person had to show for it: a few lines in a paper and a headstone no one would visit. Some people didn't get even that much.

I tried to shake it off, as this was just the kind of thinking that would annoy Escott. Better come up with a distraction . . . like the damned broken window at the end of the hall. Despite my makeshift patch, there was quite a draft blowing through.

Taking advantage of being the boss once more, I called Derner. He knew someone who knew someone who could fix the glass after hours.

"I'll be by the club later," I said, "to drop off the house key."

"He won't need no key, Boss," he assured me.

The surprise was that I wasn't surprised.

By the time I'd worked through the rest of the papers, Kroun came downstairs, ready to leave. His singed hair and eyebrows had filled out sometime during his day sleep, and he looked better for a shave and a fresh shirt.

"Where to?" I asked, resigned to playing chauffeur for the time being.

He gave me a matchbook from the Nightcrawler. There'd been some scattered on the office's big desk. This was the one he'd scribbled on during his one private call.

I opened the matchbook. An address was written inside. I knew the street, but not the number. "What's this?"

"Let's go see."

We didn't have much to talk about on the drive over, so I switched the radio on and listened to a comedy show to fill the time. It had me chuckling in the right places, and Kroun snorted now and then. He wasn't the type to go in for a full belly laugh, though he clearly had a sense of humor. When the show was over, he turned the sound low and asked how long I'd known Adelle Taylor. I filled him in and told some harmless tales about her work at the Nightcrawler.

"She's a real humdinger," he said, drawing the word out, looking content.

I grunted agreement and pulled my heavy Buick to the curb, having found the address. It was some sort of a rest home and private hospital in one, to judge by the discreet sign attached to the iron driveway gate. An eight-foot-high brick wall with another foot of iron trim on top ran around the entire block. The trim ended in sharp spearpoints poking up through the latest layer of snow, giving me an idea of just what kind of patients were inside.

Kroun had his box of cigars in hand. He tucked it under one arm and led off.

The gate was locked, and a sign posted visiting hours with a warning no one would be admitted without an appointment. Kroun pressed an intercom buzzer, gave his name, and the gate rolled open along some tracks as though pulled by an invisible servant. It ground shut once we were inside. I thought they only had stuff like that in the movies.

A paved walkway that someone had shoveled clean wound to the main building. It was red brick like the wall, three stories, and on the plain side. The fresh drifts of snow softened its lines, but it didn't seem too friendly. Most of the windows were dark, with their shades drawn.

A large man in an orderly's white shirt and pants unlocked the door for us, locking up again. He gestured toward a reception desk in a small lobby where a nurse sat. She was busy with a stack of papers, but left them to deal with Kroun. He took off his hat, switched on his formidable personal charm, aimed it right at her, and damned if it didn't work. She warmed up, acting like he was an old friend she'd not seen lately, and conducted us down a hall and up some stairs to one of the rooms. The big orderly followed.

He had the keys and opened doors along the way.

It was that kind of hospital, all right, where the patients are shut inside for their own good and everyone else's. Who the hell did Kroun know here?

I kept my yap shut.

The orderly unlocked the last door and stood back.

The nurse gave Kroun a sympathetic smile, told him to check in at the desk before leaving, then went off.

Kroun cut the charm soon as she was gone. Face grim, he put his fedora on a small table just outside the door. He paused—hesitated more like—before reaching for the handle. I'd never seen him unsure of himself.

"Be careful," said the orderly.

"Hm?" Kroun looked at him.

"We cut his nails today. They're gonna have sharp edges."

Kroun nodded, then went in. He didn't tell me to stay out, so I followed. Quietly. The orderly hung by the open door.

Pale green paint on the brick walls, a cage over the overhead light, and the tile floor was layered with newspapers. Most lay open with uneven holes torn from the middle of their pages as though someone wanted to save an article. The biggest thing in the room was a hospital bed. It had thick leather restraint cuffs at the corners. Next to it was a reading chair, which looked out of place, so it must have belonged to the room's occupant, who was in it.

He was a big-boned, lean old devil, seemed to be in his eighties, and ignored us as we came in. He had a newspaper spread over his knees, peering at it through double-thick horn-rimmed glasses. The lenses must not have been strong enough; he hunched low to read. He had things open to a department store's full-page advertisement for an undergarments sale. Drawings of female figures in girdles and brassieres had his full attention. Carefully, he worked a hole into the sheet, his ink-stained fingertips and recently cut nails outlining an illustration.

On the bed next to him were a number of torn-out pictures, some like the one he was working on, others were photographs. All women. No portraits, he preferred them full length, matrons at charity events, debutantes, mannequins modeling the latest fashions. Painstakingly trimmed of their backgrounds, they lay in uneven piles, limp and ragged paper dolls.

Kroun took it in, his expression unreadable. "Hello, Sonny."

The old man grunted and continued his task. When he had the drawing torn free, he studied it under the harsh overhead light, then added it to one of the stacks on the bed. He had large hands, once powerful, but his fingers were twisted with arthritis, reduced to knobby joints and tendons. He had to work slowly to get them to do the job.

"Sonny."

He looked up. His mouth was a wide straight cut with hardly any lip, and he had the big nose and ears that come with age. His skin was flushed a patchy red, mottled by liver spots. White hair on the sides, a shock of gray on top, it needed cutting.

The glasses magnified his blue eyes to larger than normal. They were blank for several moments, then sharpened as an ugly smile gradually surfaced.

Something inside me writhed; it was the kind of instinctive warning that says run like hell even when you don't see the threat. This old man couldn't possibly hurt me, but the feeling was there and damned strong.

"What d'you want?" he asked Kroun in a gravelly voice full of venom.

Kroun pulled an institutional wood chair—sturdy with a lot of dents—from a corner and sat almost knee to knee with him. He held up the box of cigars.

"Give," said the man, quickly shoving papers from his lap. He was in faded striped pajamas and shapeless slippers.

Kroun opened the box. "They're all for you, Sonny."

"My birt'day or som'tin'?"

"You want a smoke or not?"

Sonny grabbed a cigar, biting one end off, spitting it to one side. "You forget a light? G'damn jackets here won' lemme have no matches."

Kroun produced a lighter, a new silver one he must have gotten when he bought his clothes. He helped Sonny get the cigar going. I was glad I didn't have to breathe.

"Now that's a smoke." Sonny puffed, eyes narrowed to slits by satisfaction. "Who're you again?"

Kroun didn't show it, but he seemed thrown by the question. "Don't you remember?"

"I see lots of people. Which one are you?"

"Look at me. You'll know."

Sonny puffed and stared, but no recognition sparked in his distorted eyes. "What's wit' the hair?" He pointed the cigar at Kroun's white streak.

"Accident at my job, nothing much."

He nodded my way. "Who's the creep inna corner?"

"Just my driver."

"Fancy-schmancy, you gettin' all the drivers in town. Come here to high-hat me?"

"Thought I'd see how you were doing."

Sonny snorted and blew smoke into Kroun's face. "*That's* how I'm doin', you g'damn bastard. Locked in like a dead dog waitin' to be shoveled inna ground. You know how they treat me? No respect! You get me outta here!"

"I'll see what I can do."

"Liar. Everyone lies to me here."

"When you get out, where would you go?"

A slow, evil grin spread over Sonny's face. "*You* know."

"The fishing cabin?"

Sonny chuckled. At length. He sat back in the chair, his spine not quite straightening. The hunched-over posture was permanent. "Yeah . . . fishin'. I had some good times there. When you listened to me, you had a good time. You goin' up?"

"I don't know how to get there."

A scowl replaced the grin. "You're *stupid*, you know that? G'damn *stupid*. The g'damn place is still in g'damn 'Sconsin 'less some g'damn bastard moved it."

"Probably not," Kroun allowed. "I'm just not sure where in Wisconsin."

"Jus' over the state line, y'stupid dummy."

"And then where?"

"Hah?"

"It was a long while ago, Sonny."

"You're g'damn stupid. They got me shut in, treat me like shit, but I know how *long*, so don' go pissin' on me wit' that. You was here two mont's back—"

"No, I wasn't."

"You *was*! Lying li'l shit! Sat right *there* jus' like now, an' y' had 'nother bastard like him out inna hall an' you had *her* over where *that* bastard's standin'. Nice li'l twist, but you can afford 'em to be nice, can't ya? Brought her in, then went off and never come back. You were gonna come back and you din'. 'Stead you show up two mont's late in a fancy coat and nothin' to say but a lotta g'damn *lies*!"

Kroun held himself still as a statue as Sonny's voice beat against the painted brick walls. "Guess I lost track of things at that."

"Puh!" Sonny drew on his cigar, threw me a murderous glare, then seemed to relax. "So . . . how'd it go wit' her?"

"How do you think?"

The ugly snigger was back. "I bet. Picked a good 'un. She was a real humdinger." He drew out the word.

Kroun went dead white.

Sonny leaned forward. "Well? How'd it go? Tell me, g'dammit!"

Kroun swallowed and continued to hold very still. His tone was conversational but tighter than before. "Remind me how to get there, and I'll show you. I'll spring you from this dump, and we can both go fishing again."

Sonny laughed out loud, then stopped, his gears abruptly shifting. "You liar. No sharin' wit' you. Y' too good to have me along. Too good! Now y' won' even tell me nuthin'."

"Wouldn't you rather I show you?"

"Puh! Teach yer granny to suck eggs, g'damn li'l bastard. There's still things I can show *you*."

"Sounds good. I want that, Sonny. We can do it again. Wouldn't you like one more trip?"

The old man's eyes blazed. One of his big hands dropped to his crotch. He chuckled and rubbed himself. "I still got juice in me. What d'you think?"

Kroun nodded. "Yeah, sounds real good. You tell my driver how to get there. We'll sit in the backseat and smoke cigars like a couple of big shots while he does the work."

Sonny abruptly rattled off directions fast as a machine gun. Belatedly I found a pencil and scribbled on my shirt cuff. He thought that was funny and took pains to repeat everything. His cigar died. Kroun got the lighter working and held it out again.

His hand shook.

Sonny noticed. He relit the cigar, puffed blue smoke in the air, and smirked. "Got you excited, huh? Jus' thinkin' about it?"

"Yeah, Sonny. Just thinking about it." Kroun snapped the lighter shut and pocketed it. He rested his trembling hand on one knee. His other hand gripped the chair arm hard, his knuckles white.

Then Sonny shifted gears again and glared. "You ain't springin' me! I see that. You 'n' your fancy ways. Think you're too good, huh?"

Quick as a striking snake, Sonny threw an open-handed slap at Kroun's face. The impact of palm on flesh cracked loud. Another crack— Sonny connected again, backhanded.

Kroun didn't try to duck or block, just sat there and took it.

Sonny's mouth worked, and he spat. It hit Kroun's chin, then dripped to his coat.

Kroun still didn't move. He stared at Sonny. Stared long enough that Sonny's gears shifted once more. He pressed back in the chair and showed teeth. "You stay away from me. The jacket out there ain't gonna let you touch me, tha's his job, so you get out."

When Kroun stood and turned my way, I understood the old man's reaction. Kroun's eyes had gone blank, all pupil and no iris. Hell pits. When they leveled in my direction, I again felt like running, but he blinked and was himself. I was no more superstitious than the next guy, but this . . . it made my skin crawl.

The normal-seeming man that I now saw jerked his head toward the hall. Time to leave.

I got out. Sonny's curses and threats poisoned the air until the orderly closed and locked the door. It did a lot to mitigate the noise.

"You okay?" he asked Kroun. "He nick you?"

Kroun felt his cheek, checking for blood. "I'm fine." He got his hand-kerchief and wiped spittle from his chin and coat, then collected his hat, putting it on. He wasn't shaking as badly as before but was still ghost white. "The nurse wanted to see me." His voice was calm, soft.

We followed the orderly downstairs. Kroun had to deal with some paperwork, sign a couple of things. I stood by the exit next to the orderly, ready to leave as soon as possible.

"Crazy old guy," I muttered.

"Yeah," the big man agreed. "Those cigars helped. Got him in a good mood. He's usually a lot worse with visitors. Not that he gets any."

"No one else comes?"

He shrugged. "Just two guys that I know of. Haven't seen the other for a long time, but I'm night shift."

"What's he look like?"

"Like a doctor. The bills get paid."

"Know anything about this fishing cabin?"

"If I listened to their baloney, I'd be locked in one of those rooms myself, so no I don't. That bird's right out of his head most of the time. Nothing he says is gonna be up-front. You point at a horse, he'll call it a dog."

Kroun put the charm on again with the nurse, but from my vantage it seemed brittle. He glanced my way once, indicating he'd heard my questions and the orderly's replies. The somber and sympathetic nurse pointed at something on a clipboard, and Kroun signed it.

When the time came, the orderly let us out of the booby hatch. The clean, cold winter air was sweet. Kroun and I breathed deeply, then headed for the electric gate. Someone must have been on the lookout; it opened as we approached.

Kroun paused on the sidewalk, watching the gate roll shut as though to make sure it locked properly. Only then did some of the tension leach from the set of his shoulders.

"You got those directions clear?" he asked.

"Yeah."

"I remember most of it, but put 'em on paper for me, would ya?"

"No problem." What did he want with that fishing cabin? I had an idea and it wasn't pleasant.

"Leave it with Derner. I'll be by the Nightcrawler tonight."

"Where you going?"

"Gotta take a walk, clear my head. I'll cab over later."

"Gabe, I'm supposed to stick with you. If that guy was the old bastard that Michael—"

"Yes. Yes, he was. You heard some stuff."

"And I'm wondering why I heard it. You didn't have me in there just to take down directions."

"Actually, I did. But I figured if I had you wait in the car, you'd go invisible and sneak in anyway to listen."

"You figured right. What was he talking about?"

Kroun closed his eyes briefly and shoved his hands in his overcoat pockets. "Nothing I want to discuss. He's nuts. Didn't know me, my name. Lot of stuff comes from him that doesn't make sense."

"Made sense to you."

He turned away. "I'm going to get some air and think."

"Gabe—"

He snapped around. "And forget the goddamned watchdogging for a couple hours! If Michael calls you on it, say I gave you the slip. He'll believe it."

"Okay, but—"

"*What?*"

"Who's the crazy guy?"

That got me a scorching glare. "Mike will tell you."

"Uh-uh. You."

More glaring, then his anger suddenly faded. His shoulders didn't ease down so much as shrink. He seemed older. He took the handkerchief from his pocket where he'd absently stuffed it after wiping off the spit. Kroun studied the crumpled fabric a moment, then threw it away. The wind caught the white square, swept it a few yards, then it nose-dived into a snow-clogged gutter, merging with the trash already there.

"Gabe?"

"Yeah, sure. Why not?" He lifted his fedora, rubbed a palm along his streak of white hair, then resettled the hat again. "The son of a bitch is my father. Now ain't that a kick in the head?"

He walked away, moving fast.

KROUN had his thinking to do, and so did I, but mulling things on my own wouldn't do the job this time; I needed to see Gordy. Working hard to avoid going over what I'd seen and learned, I drove straight to the Bronze Belt, not quite crossing into the territory, and parked a couple blocks away. It didn't take long to leg the remaining distance to the residence hotel where Shoe Coldfield had obligingly given safe shelter to Gordy and just about everyone else I knew.

I took it for granted that one of the countless lookouts in the area had spotted me, but with my collar up and hat low, they might not know me from any other lost white guy. Soon as I had the building in view, I vanished and floated the last hundred yards—not easy with the wind—and sieved through an upstairs window.

Damned if I didn't get it right the first time. I partially materialized on the third floor, or so the door numbers declared once I was solid enough to see. The place was pretty active; I went invisible again and bumbled down the hall, careful not to brush close to anyone. Coldfield knew that an inexplicable chill might mean I was hanging around.

I passed rooms where people talked and radios played. Gordy was somewhere halfway down on the left, so I drifted from door to door, hoping to hear his voice. No such luck, but I did catch one that surprised me. I slipped under the threshold crack and hovered out of the way in a ceiling corner.

Michael, and presumably his tough friend Broder, were there.

"I don't like this guy you picked," Michael said. "He doesn't have what it takes."

It was Gordy's room, and his response sounded confident. "He does when it's needed. The boys are used to him. The trouble's over. I'll be back soon enough."

If I'd had ears, they'd have been burning.

"There shouldn't have been trouble in the first place. Your kid put his foot right into it with Bristow."

"That was me. I'm the one who took Bristow to the kid's club. It wasn't his fault Hog didn't like his face and decided to go buckwheats on him. That was out of my hands. Besides, Hog jumped the gun. He put me here. And that's your fault. You're the one who sent him."

I could almost hear the steam coming out of Michael's ears.

Gordy continued, "But the trouble's over. The kid's got things running smooth. That's all that matters."

Michael gave him the point. "All right. I get you. If he screws up again, it's on you both. You got that?"

"Yeah. No problem."

"We'll see. Next is Whitey. I want him on a train back to New York."

"He's your man. You make him leave."

This resulted in a long silence. It was Michael's night to paint himself into a corner. "You know he could be more trouble."

"It's part of the business. You said you got Fleming watching him. Nothing's going to happen."

"You sound very certain about that, why?"

"The kid has a way with people."

"Like he did with Bristow?"

"Bristow was nuts. If you're saying that Whitey would—"

"No, not the same thing. But he's dangerous."

Gordy sighed. "Still your problem. You ordered him home, and he wouldn't listen. Right?"

Michael made no reply.

"If he won't listen to you, what chance have I got? I'm thinking he'll leave when he's good and ready. You want him out faster, offer to help him do what he wants done."

Another long silence. Then, "C'mon, Broder."

Footsteps passed close below me, then the door shut. I waited. If anyone else was in the room with Gordy, they would say something, but it continued quiet. Drifting down, I slowly took on form.

Gordy was propped up in bed, and his eyes went wide. He was wise to my peculiar talents, but it didn't make them any less alarming to witness. "That's some cute gag you got, Fleming."

"It's handy. How are you?"

"Better. A lot better."

He looked it. His color had improved since my last visit. The sickroom smell was gone. One of the windows was open an inch. He'd apparently convinced someone of the benefits of fresh air.

"Was Michael here for long? I just caught the tail end of things."

"Couple minutes. He ain't one to socialize with the help. You heard he don't like you much?"

"I'm used to it. He's right. I don't have what it takes, but I'll keep swinging at the ball until you say different."

"Good enough. Have a seat."

I pulled up a chair and took off my hat. "Where's Bobbi and Adelle?"

"Down having supper. They'll be a while. Dames. Always talking. Coldfield's been looking after 'em good. Lookin' after us all. I owe him."

"Is he here?"

"Went off with Escott. Donno where. Heard your pal had a close one."

"Yeah. He did."

"Bobbi told me. What had you and him fighting?"

"Nothing important. But Coldfield's blaming me for nearly killing Charles."

"Bobbi told me that, too. She told me everything." He let that hang. My mouth dried out.

"Think Michael knows about Kroun being like you?" he asked.

Oh, crap. "Gordy, you're not supposed to know that."

He waved a large hand. "I'm not supposed to know a lot of things, but I do anyway. If Kroun's got a problem with that, he can make me forget, can't he?"

"He'll have a problem with it all right. Bobbi shouldn't have told you."

"It wasn't only her. Coldfield put in a few words."

"Jeez, at this rate the whole city'll have the headlines in the morning, and Kroun's gonna blame me."

"Nah. It stops here."

"What about Adelle?"

"I won't tell her if you won't."

"Deal." I sat back in the chair but didn't relax. Some part of me was alert for trouble. I heard the doorknob being worked. It was enough warning; I instantly vanished.

Hinges creaked. "You okay, Gordy?" It was one of the guards belonging to Coldfield's hotel fortress.

After a pause Gordy said he was fine. My disappearance must have startled him.

A scraping sound as the man moved the chair. "Those two guys are gone. Didn't say where."

"No big deal. I'm gonna take a nap now."

"Sure. Lights out?"

"Leave that one in the corner on."

"Sure."

A click, steps, then the door was closed.

I went solid. The room was much dimmer than before.

Gordy's eyes remained wide. "Real good trick, kid," he said, his voice low. "You don't want no one knowin' you're here?"

"Coldfield's that sore with me. It's better I keep my head down for a while. You serious about that nap?"

"Nah. Siddown."

I gently returned the chair to the bedside. "I won't be long, just a couple questions. On Kroun."

He nodded as though he'd expected as much. "You didn't answer— does Michael know about him being like you?"

"Kroun said no, and he wants to keep it that way. Take that how you like. Whether he's wise or not, Michael's got a hell of a worry going about him."

"Must have a reason."

"Yeah. I may have the why behind that."

I told about the visit to the nuthouse and Kroun's talk with Sonny. I told about the newspapers and how Sonny tore out pictures of women from them. I told about the hospital bed and its heavy cuff restraints. I told about the things Sonny said and Kroun's reaction to them.

Gordy didn't reply, just looked at me a long while. I'd given him something he hadn't known before. Something pretty big.

"Is that crazy old man really his father?" I asked, to break the silence.

"I can check into it and find out."

"Without anyone else catching wind?"

"No. If I was on my feet, maybe. Not now."

"Hold off then. I don't want Kroun to know I've talked to you."

"He'll figure you will."

"Yeah, and he won't like it. Why did he let me in on it, though?"

"Donno." Gordy's face was always hard to read, but I could tell this had thrown him.

"What do you know about this cabin? The other night Michael pitched a fit when Kroun said he might do some fishing. Putting that with what the old man said . . ."

"Don't sound so good, no. Sounds like he takes girls up there, gives 'em a rough time."

"Maybe worse?"

He shrugged.

"You never heard anything?"

"If there was anything to hear, I'd have gotten it. Whitey comes over from New York now and then, does whatever business needs doing, has himself some fun, but I never got nothing on him visiting any old man, nothing on that cabin."

"What do you know about Kroun's past? Where's he from?"

"He came out of nowhere, worked his way up in New York. Only got to be a big noise in the last few years. Lotta boys are like that. Nothing on them their whole life, then suddenly they're running things. Happened to me."

That happened because Gordy's boss had been killed. Promotion in the mob was often the result of inheritance. "He knock off his boss to move up?"

"The guy before him was skimming off the top, then—for a guy who didn't hunt—he went on a hunting trip and never came back. That's the story I got. Whitey was in the right place at the right time and slipped into the empty spot. No one argued with him."

They probably didn't dare. "What about Michael?"

"He's the one who figured out the skim. He's got schooling, but keeps out of sight. He looks after the books, squares the deals, does the thinking. He runs stuff, keeps the money moving, but Whitey sometimes has the last word. For some it *is* the last word."

I asked more questions and got everything Gordy had stored in his file cabinet of a brain. Such history was not easy to hear.

Kroun had ordered at least a dozen executions over the last few years;

those did not count however many he'd personally carried out himself on the side. Gordy had been present at three, twice as a witness, once as a participant.

About two years ago, when Slick Morelli had been the big boss, Gordy had helped get a man down into the Nightcrawler's basement on a pretext, then held him in place. Kroun put a gun muzzle in the man's mouth and took the top of his head off just that quick. The thick walls and the club band playing upstairs covered the noise. The whole process had taken less than half a minute. Kroun hadn't cracked a sweat, hadn't even blinked. Right afterward, he'd gone up to the club and danced with the chorus girls as though nothing had happened.

No, not good to hear at all.

I considered Gordy a friend, but that dark side of him was part of the package. When it was necessary, he could kill and not think anything of it. He didn't like the killing, but he'd still do it.

I found myself squirming inside, knowing I'd gotten that way myself, it just bothered me more. How long would that last if I stayed on this road?

"What had the man done?" I asked.

"Kroun never said. Just gave the orders, and we did what we did. He's good at that kind of job. Those mugs never knew from Adam when their number was up. He pals with 'em until it's time, does the job, then goes back and pals with their friends a few minutes later. Not a lot of guys are able to pull that off."

Michael had warned me. He'd said Kroun had no conscience. I'd met a few similar types, and you can usually tell there's something wrong with them even if you don't know exactly what it is. It's enough to make you cautious. Being able to hide it so well made Kroun different from them, and a hell of a lot more dangerous.

Gordy added, "When he came to town for you, I figured he'd do the same as always. Instead, he has you up to the office to hear you out. That never happened before."

"He always been called Whitey?"

"Yeah. Used to wear a white hat, winter and summer. The streak of white hair is new. Says he got skull-creased by a jealous husband who was a bad shot."

"Where'd that happen?"

He shook his head. "I heard it was in New York. But maybe that cabin?"

"And what happened to the husband? To the wife?"

A shrug. "You'd have to ask Kroun."

"I doubt he'd say."

"To you he might."

"Oh, yeah?"

"You got plenty in common. He didn't try to keep you out when he talked with the crazy guy. If Kroun didn't want you to know this stuff, you wouldn't."

"Carelessness in his old age?"

"Don't count on it. He'll have a reason. And don't trust him."

No. I would not do that. "But how did he get to be like me? You'd think he'd tell me of all people."

But Gordy had no answer to that, either. Instead, "Derner phoned today. Said you did a good job dousing the fire on Alan Caine and the rest of it."

I shrugged. I'd done what was needed but wasn't proud of it. "That fire won't be out until they find Mitchell, only they never will. Someone could still get burned."

"It's the best you can expect, kid. The heat's off our bunch, that's what matters. Derner told me you didn't like the fix job on your car."

I managed a short grin. "It's okay. If I'm being the boss, I might as well have an armored car. The wheels—I just wanted them changed, not swapped for solid rubber."

"Rough ride?"

"My eyeballs bounce so much I can't see the road."

That amused him.

"I'll swap for pneumatics once Kroun's gone home."

If he went home. He struck me as being sincere about getting away from the mobs. How would he do it, though? Fake his death again? That hadn't worked too well for him.

"Any idea where Coldfield went with Charles?" I asked.

"Said something about checking his mail."

"Then they'll be at Charles's office. I'll drive over and see. Maybe if Charles plays referee, he can calm Shoe down."

"Don't count on it," Gordy repeated.

8

KROUN

THAT sick bastard should have kicked off years ago.

Gabriel walked quickly despite the snowdrifts on the sidewalks, despite the ice hiding underneath. He wanted distance between himself and the venom-spitting monster locked away in that nuthouse.

And Fleming with his damned questions.

I should have had him wait in the car.

Too late, he knew the worst of it now.

"Not the worst," Gabe muttered aloud.

He missed a step, skidding on one heel before gaining his balance. Where had *that* come from? He glanced around, but the street was empty. No one had heard him. God, he should not be talking to himself, even when he was alone; he couldn't take that chance. Only crazy people did that, and he wasn't going to end up like Sonny.

Before that happened . . . well, he didn't know.

Maybe I should back off on this.

Tempting. He had money, easy enough to buy a cheap car and get clear of Chicago. He could disappear himself in Minnesota or Canada, find a place to live and . . . do what?

He didn't know that, either. But it would probably take care of itself.

Fishing would be good, but after what Sonny had said . . . there was now a taint on that pleasure.

Gabe couldn't kid himself, he had to find the cabin and get things settled. The last time he'd been there—wherever it was—he'd gone up with a driver and some woman. Had she been the one weeping over his death? His driver back in November had been a mug named Ramsey, who'd dropped out of sight. If he'd been the one to put a bullet in Gabe's skull, then making himself missing was the smartest thing to do.

What had happened there? Even if Gabe found the cabin, he had no guarantee it would convey anything useful. Backing off now would leave him with unanswered questions, but he could live with those . . .

No, he would not. Good or bad, bad or worse, he had to find out.

The goings-on Sonny had implied made Gabe's stomach turn. Those pictures so carefully torn from the papers . . . disgusting, sick. How could they allow that?

The old bastard's crazy, that's why he's locked up.

One of the reasons why, anyway. Gabe didn't want to think about the others and kept walking.

The street, a nice one with big trees on either side, opened to a wider road with businesses and more traffic. A hotel took up a sizable portion of a block on his side. There were a couple cabs out front. He opened the door of the nearest and got in, giving the driver an address. The phone work he'd done in the Nightcrawler's office had paid off, giving him two leads to check out. This second one promised to be considerably different.

The driver was apparently familiar with the number. He smirked when Gabe paid him off.

Gabe went up the steps of a large, prosperous-looking brick house similar to the other two-story houses along the street. Each had a small yard, some protected by iron-barred fences or painted wood pickets. Driveways had cars in them, walks were shoveled. The Depression seemed to have passed this area by, which could mean that mob money was all over the block. The big shots didn't always hang out at the bars and pool parlors. Even Capone had parked his family in that sweet place over on South Prairie.

No need to ring the bell. A bouncer on duty opened the door. His eyes flashed wide in recognition, then he shifted from surprise to stone-faced neutrality. His body tensed.

Gabe was almost used to it. He took his hat off and waited with the bouncer in the small entry until a pleasant-faced woman wearing a soft print dress and a long rope of pearls came. She also underwent a not-so-subtle transformation of expression, going on guard.

"Hello, Mr. Kroun," she said.

"You have anything for me?" he asked, radiating affability. He couldn't remember her name, but so far as memory served, most madams were alike. He thought she'd been pretty once, but life had a way of eroding one's assets.

She hesitated. "We're very busy tonight. It will be hours before anyone's available."

He looked past her into the parlor beyond where a radio played dance music. "Seems to be plenty available."

"I mean anyone suitable for *you*."

He was in strange waters now. Gabe knew in this area his appetite—there was a word as loaded as a set of crooked dice—had undergone a major change. He'd not availed himself of the services of the houses in New York, playing things safe. Out here in Chicago he felt better about indulging himself—except for the madam's manner with him.

He put on one of his best smiles. "Let me be the judge of that."

He started in, but she halted him with a hand on his arm. "Listen, Mr. Kroun, I got a business to run. You hurt my girls, and they can't work, then you gotta pay extra."

Gabe didn't know how to react to that so he went stone-faced, too. It clearly frightened the woman, but she stood solid. He put his hand over hers, patting lightly. "I'm not here to hurt anyone. Let's go in." He kept hold, taking her along.

Several young women sat around the parlor, some in oriental-style silk robes, others in evening dress, one in a pale blue slip and nothing under it. They looked good; the place was high-class enough to have very presentable merchandise for the clients. None seemed too enthusiastic, though. A couple of the girls clearly recognized him. They whispered to the uninformed, who avoided his eye.

The madam pulled free and pointed to a thin, angular girl by the radio. "That one," she said. "She doesn't mind your games."

He managed to not inquire just what those games might be and focused on the girl. Nice, but with an edge that had nothing to do with her lean frame. He'd slice himself up on those bones and suspected she used morphine. She wasn't his type. He wasn't sure what his type was, but she wasn't it. He checked out the rest. A shorter, more rounded one caught his eye. She wore her dark hair almost like Adelle Taylor, though the face and figure were different. She'd been one of the girls who recognized him.

He smiled and nodded. "She'll do."

The madam opened her mouth, but he looked at her. No need to put any special weight behind it. Early on he'd come to understand that people were afraid of him. He made use of it. She backed down from voicing whatever objection she had.

The girl flinched when called over and avoided his eye. He could get around that. What he could see of her arms showed clean of needle pocks. Good, he didn't want a doper. He couldn't understand why people did that to themselves. It had to hurt.

However fancy the place, it was payment in advance. He settled with the madam, then went upstairs with the girl.

Her room was much as he expected: a big bed, satin pillows, a few bottles of booze on the dresser, a curtain partway open to a closet full of clothes, heavy curtains over the window so she could sleep during the day. A small sink was in one corner, a lamp with a red silk scarf over it stood in another, imparting a rosy glow to things. She had a radio and a record player. Not too bad. The mirror on the dresser was thankfully tilted away from him.

Soon as he shut the door she dropped to her knees and started unbuttoning his pants. Her hands shook.

"Hey, slow down, sweetheart," he said, catching her wrists. She flinched again, going pale. He drew her upright. "What's the rush?"

"No rush, but the others said you was a busy man."

Probably said a few more things besides. "Not that busy. How about we have a drink first?"

"I'm not allowed. Mrs. Temple marks the bottles. It's only for guests." She stumbled over the word. He thought she'd nearly said "customers."

"How about you have one and I'll say it was for me?"

She thought a moment, then nodded. "Vodka. Straight."

A good choice, it wouldn't leave much of a smell on her breath. He went to the dresser, poured a double. The damn stuff was strong, nearly made his eyes water. He took it over to her, but didn't release the glass as she reached for it.

"Look at me, honey," he said.

They were close, she had to raise her head up quite a bit.

"Well, don't you have beautiful eyes? How do you like mine?"

She gave no opinion, but he had her full attention now.

"What's your name, honey?"

"Lettie."

"Okay, Lettie, I don't know what you've heard about me, but I'm not going to hurt you. I want you to relax and"—he recalled one of Fleming's quirks—"just pretend we're old friends. You like me a lot, and we're going to have a good time, got that?"

She nodded.

He shut it off and gave her the drink. Her manner changed just that quick. She was suddenly at ease and even dug out a smile for him, a sweet one. Then again, he'd paid well for it.

He looked at the bed, but wasn't quite ready to start. It reminded him of the one in Sonny's room. Fine thing to think of now.

A soft creak from the hall froze him. Someone was coming up to their door, being stealthy, but like a herd of elephants to Gabe's hearing. Either the madam or the bouncer was checking on things. What the hell had happened on his last visit?

He opened the door. The bouncer loomed tall, solid, unapologetic.

"We're okay here," said Gabe.

The man remained.

Goddammit, I can't do anything with him listening. Gabe focused on him. "I said we're okay. Go downstairs and don't bother us again. Everything's fine."

That worked. The man left. Gabe shut the door.

"Lettie?"

She'd quickly finished the vodka and even washed the glass in the little sink. She came up to him and put both hands on his waist in the front, fingers slipping inside his pants. Very friendly. Her robe was open. Under it she wore red satin step-ins with lace around the legs. Nothing else. Her breasts were nicely rounded, more than enough for . . .

He cleared his throat, backed off a step, and put his hat on the dresser. His overcoat went on a chair next to it. The gun he'd taken from Michael weighed heavy in one of its pockets. He took care to not let it bump anything. "Uh, tell me, you know anything about cutting hair?"

Her smile faltered. "W-what?"

"Can you give me a haircut?" He rubbed a hand over his head so she'd know just where he wanted the trim.

"You serious?"

"Yes, I am. Another day, and I'm gonna look like one of those English sheepdogs. If not you, then one of the other girls . . . ?"

She laughed, a small one. "I used to cut my brother's hair. He didn't like it much, though."

"Hey, brothers are put on this earth to not like things." He took off his suit coat, watchful for her reaction to the gun he wore in a shoulder rig. She made no comment, didn't even seem to notice it. He slipped free of the leather straps, flexing his shoulders. "I bet you did a good job."

"You sure?"

He undid his tie, then the buttons of his shirt collar. "Yeah. Where do you want me?"

Bemused by now, Lettie took charge. She moved his overcoat to the bed, put some newspapers on the floor and the chair over the papers. Again, a reminder of Sonny's room. That had to stop, or he wouldn't enjoy any of this. He took his shirt and undershirt off next, but was strangely shy about his trousers. Damn fool way to be at his age, but he couldn't help it.

"Come on," she said. "You don't want to get hair on them; they'll itch."

He let her talk him out of his pants, socks, and shoes, then sat, feeling vulnerable in just his skin and skivvies. The room was warm, but goose bumps whispered down his arms as she pushed his head forward and started work on the back of his neck with scissors.

"You really needed a cut," she said. *Snip-snip-snip.* "I'll try to get it even, but you should have a barber with one of those electric-shaver things for this."

"Lettie, when I have a choice between you and some guy talking base-ball, you'll get the job every time."

She snickered. "Short back and sides?"

"Yes, please, and some off the top."

"Yeah, I know how to do that. I never had anyone want a haircut, lemme tell you. The others'll think you're crazy."

"You girls talk about us?"

"Sure, not much else to do."

"Remember the last time I was here?" The snipping ceased, and he was acutely aware of a stranger standing behind him with something sharp in hand. He hoped his suggestion about being old friends was still strong. "It's okay, Lettie. I want you to tell me everything. Who did I see then?"

"Nelly Cabot."

He held off on further questions, letting the name sink in, waiting for something to come to him. Nothing. "She have dark hair like you?"

"I guess. She went blond though. They get picked more often. She went blond. You know. *All* over. The men really like that."

Not the kind of information he sought, but interesting nonetheless. "And I liked it, too?"

"You liked the things she . . . didn't mind doing."

Gabe wasn't ready to go into that just yet.

Lettie resumed trimming. He kept quiet while she navigated the criti-cal areas around his ears, then started working the top. She used a comb in some way that yanked at his scalp. No wonder her brother had com-plained. "What's this white patch?" she asked. "You didn't have it last time."

"Accident at my job, nothing much. Did I take Nelly out?"

"Don't you know?"

"I tied one on that night. It's fuzzy. I thought we went out."

"Yeah, you did. For the weekend. You made a deal with Mrs. Temple. Nelly put on her best dress, got a bag, and you went off in a big car."

"I had a driver?" Ramsey, perhaps?

"Sure did. Other girls was jealous, but Mrs. Temple said to shut up and not talk about it."

"I made her nervous?"

"She didn't let on, but we could tell she was scared."

Yes. He did that to people. Some of them. "And then what?"

"I donno."

"Yes, you do. Tell me, Lettie." He stared straight ahead and would have held his breath had he a need to breathe.

"Next morning Nelly showed up real early. Woke the whole house, carried on like it was the end of the world, screaming and crying. Scared me good."

"What had happened to her?"

"Donno. All she had in one piece was her coat. Her dress was all tore up and bloody, and she was black-and-blue and . . . and tore up. You know. Down there. Called a doctor for her, and Mrs. Temple sent her off again. She never come back. Not here, anyway."

He couldn't speak for a long time.

Lettie finished, got a damp towel, and brushed at his shoulders to clean off the clippings. "I'm done, Mister."

He shut his eyes. After a few minutes, the bedsprings squeaked.

"Mister?"

"Gabe," he whispered. "Gabriel."

"You want to do anything?"

He blinked clear of the empty dark. She sat on one corner of the bed, bare feet dangling, the robe hanging loose and open. "Where did Nelly go?"

Lettie shrugged. "One of the girls said she went back to her mother. They brought in a new girl and told us to keep quiet. It was like Nelly was never here to start with. Mrs. Temple won't let us talk about her, gets mad if anyone says her name."

"But she's all right?"

"I guess. You'd have to ask Mrs. Temple."

Indeed he would, but not until the cold, sick roiling in his gut eased. A drink would help, but he couldn't touch the stuff on the dresser. As for the stuff in the girl's veins . . . he was sure he could not touch that, either.

Lettie slipped off the bed. "You wanna see how I did?" She picked up a hand mirror and offered it to him. "I think it's okay, but it's your hair."

He held the mirror and checked the faded image in it. The features were vaguely familiar, but he didn't know the man wearing them. "Best I ever had."

That he could remember. He gave back the mirror.

She was pleased by the praise, and he knew he had to get away from her. Lettie was pretty, and he'd wanted her, but that wasn't going to happen. He would talk with Mrs. Temple, find out what she knew about Nelly Cabot, and get the hell out.

He stood and reached for his pants. There, that hadn't changed, one leg at a time, pull them up, button the buttons.

"You leaving?"

"Yeah."

"But . . . did I do something wrong?"

No, but I might have. "Nope."

"You can't. I mean . . . Mrs. Temple will—"

"I'll fix it with her, don't worry."

"At least stay a little longer. They're gonna think I didn't do a good job for you."

He touched her cheek briefly. "I'll say you were terrific . . ." Her confusion got to him. Love was all she had to offer, paid for or not, and rejection hurt. She'd recover. He found his wallet and pulled out a century note. He folded it into her hand.

She gaped. "But I—but . . ."

"Call it a tip," he said. "For the barbering." He pulled his undershirt on, tucked it in. His feet were cold, in more ways than one. He sat on the chair and snagged his socks. When he straightened, Lettie suddenly crowded close and parked her duff on his leg, arms around his neck to keep from falling off.

"Hey!"

She wouldn't get up. "Hey, yourself. You wanna pay for nothing, that's your business, but I gotta do at least this much."

"Or what?"

"I donno. C'mon. We're friends, ain't we?"

Well, he'd been the one to put the idea in her head. Must have been one hell of a strong suggestion.

She squirmed, and he had to bring his legs together to balance her, dropping the socks. Her robe was wide open, and everything was close and smelled good. He didn't know what to do with his hands, finally giving up and letting them hang at his sides.

"You're not making this easy," he said.

She giggled. Damn, she was cute. She squirmed some more and gave him a closed-mouth kiss. That was first-class. Yes, he'd have some of her lip color on him, more than enough proof that they'd . . .

Lettie wriggled off his lap, turned, and straddled him. Her arms went around his neck again, but now they were face-to-face. "You're a good-looking man," she told him.

She was paid to flatter, but he liked hearing it. "Lettie, I—"

Another kiss, warmer, softer, her mouth opening just a little. She pressed close, but he cringed away. He couldn't do this.

"It's all right," she said. She stood, backing off him, her hands running the length of his arms. She tugged on his wrists until he stood as well. "C'mon."

"I can't."

"What, you're sick or something?" One of her hands dipped to his crotch, lingering. "You feel fine to me."

This time she was much slower unbuttoning his pants. They slid to the floor, and he stepped clear of them, getting just that much closer to the bed. She helped with the undershirt, too. The gooseflesh returned to his arms and thighs as she dragged his underwear off.

"That's better. Right over here."

Yes. The bed. It hadn't moved an inch.

She pushed him onto it.

Any protest at this point would be ridiculous. He made room for her, and she climbed in next to him.

"You like anything special?"

"Just you," he heard himself saying. He pulled her onto him, full length. The step-ins were in the way. She wiggled around and got rid of them. No bleach job that he could see. She was soft there, very soft; his tentative caress made her smile.

"You're beautiful, Lettie."

She didn't disagree with him.

He wanted to touch every inch of her. He could not remember how he'd been with women before his change but appreciated that he was different now. What his mind could not recall, his body did. His big hands slid over her smooth, smooth skin, and he found himself kissing her shoulders and breasts, going lower and lower. He finally rolled atop her and tasted that musky softness between her black curls. She writhed under him, and he held on to her hips.

How quiet she was, but her breath came fast, and her heart beat faster. He lifted enough to kiss the insides of her thighs. One of her hands was on the back of his head and pressed him down low again. She'd liked what he'd been doing there. He took his time, until the musk turned sweet and silky in his mouth.

She abruptly shuddered under him, which startled him until he realized what was going on. Well, anything to please a lady. He continued until she settled a little, then moved his way up, going slow.

Her eyelids were half-closed, a dreamy expression on her face. He nuzzled her breasts, then her throat. Yes, the big vein there, easy to find, too easy to damage. Just a little ways past it, then.

But first . . . there. He slipped right into her as though they truly were longtime lovers. Yes, that felt good, damn good. Her legs wrapped around his, hips moving for him.

Lettie did not quite match his rhythm, just enough out of sync to press herself against him. Her breath shortened again. Damn, the girl was going for a second helping.

He slowed, smiling when she made a somewhat frustrated moan.

"More, baby," she whispered. "Just a little harder."

His open mouth ranged over her throat, seeking that one spot. Yes . . . his corner teeth were out and had been for some time. His own throat ached. How he wanted her.

Her palms pressed against his backside. "Just a little more . . . please."

He obliged.

She arched under him again, trying to hold in her cry.

Now or never. He bit into her, not deeply, but enough. Her blood was better than the sweetness between her legs, and he drew strongly on it, tasting her climax as it whipped through her. An overwhelming release surged through his body in that moment, and he was able to draw it out in a way wholly new to him. Another taste, another crash of ecstasy for them both, over and over and over. She moved under him, hands clutching and beating against the mattress.

He held on, making it last, pushing gently inside her, drinking from her. He needed it to last, because to his wonderment he was able, for just a little while, to forget the pain of not remembering who he'd been.

In this room, and for this here and now, it was all about who he was learning to be.

* * *

GABRIEL drowsed, arms around Lettie as she lay on him. She didn't mind being held. She was solid but soft weight, and he liked the feeling of her heartbeat against his chest. He'd not realized how much he missed that sensation. From now on he'd have to borrow from others. Hell of a life, but better than that grave in the woods.

A clock ticked somewhere, other people in nearby rooms laughed, murmured, or grunted with sweating effort, beds squeaking under the pressure. Sometimes he wished his hearing wasn't so sharp. He wanted to come back to this place again, but with more privacy and less distraction.

Maybe that was what had happened with Nelly Cabot. He'd wanted to take her to a better, quieter spot, had arranged for a weekend out . . . then something had gone wrong. But it couldn't have been his fault. Mrs. Temple had to be mistaken about him. He could never hurt a woman, it just wasn't in him.

The driver . . . Ramsey. Gabe couldn't remember the man's face, just the name, and then only because he'd asked others. The people who knew him didn't know that much. Even with hypnosis to push things, Gabe got nothing more than that Ramsey was a tough son of a bitch who knew guns, cars, and kept his mouth shut. Indispensable traits for a mob bodyguard and probably why Gabe had chosen him. Certainly it meant the Gabriel Kroun of that time had secrets to hide. Ugly ones, if Sonny's ravings had any truth in them.

Why would I bring the girl to the sanitarium?

Showing her off to Sonny? Checking his reaction to her? Or had she been there for Sonny to play with? No . . . not that, or the old bastard would have bragged about it and demanded more.

I have to finish this.

Which meant speaking with Mrs. Temple.

Gabe checked his watch. He'd been here long enough to ensure Lettie's reputation in the house was secure. He unwillingly quit the bed and dressed. His movements woke Lettie. She got out on her side and pulled on her silk robe but not the step-ins. God knows where those had ended up.

He adjusted his tie by touch, but Lettie came over to make some small change for him. He caressed the side of her throat, close to the marks he'd left. They'd soon heal, but for the present looked alarming.

"You have anything to cover that?" he asked. "Beads or a collar or . . . ?" Damn, what kinds of stuff did women wear?

She went to the dresser mirror, checking. "It's not so bad. I've had worse."

He fixed her with a look. "Forget that I made them."

Her eyes clouded for a moment, then cleared. "You ever come back, ask for me, okay?"

He couldn't think of anything to say to that. Maybe she liked him, or his money, or it had to do with that suggestion about being friends, but it was nice to hear.

He bent and gently engulfed her in a bear hug. He held her tight for a long, sweet, contented moment, then reluctantly eased away and departed.

The bouncer was at the foot of the stairs when Gabe came down. The man threw him a quick glare and went up, probably to check on Lettie. The madam hurried out of a back room, her face taut with a frown.

"Mrs. Temple?"

She lifted her chin.

"Got a private place to talk?"

She went pale.

Not his easiest interview. Mrs. Temple had imbibed earlier, and it was hard to get past the booze; the effort made his head ache. Gabe got the name of Nelly Cabot's mother and that she ran a diner someplace, but no address. He also got the name of the doctor and where he might be found. As for what had happened that night, Mrs. Temple simply did not know, nor had she the curiosity to find out. The hysterical girl had been turned over to the doctor, and that was the extent of Mrs. Temple's responsibility. Asking questions about the private habits of the big bosses could make you dead.

The doctor, annoyingly, had since moved to another state. She didn't know which.

Gabe persuaded the bouncer to drive him to the Nightcrawler Club. The man hadn't known anything useful, so the trip was utterly silent. Plenty of time to think.

None of the previous goings-on at the brothel had gotten back to Gordy, or Gabe would have already found out from him. But Michael knew more than a little, though. He'd been in a lather to turn Gabe away from that cabin and from Sonny. Was that from having a guilty conscience? Might *he* have been involved and have something to hide?

I should have thought to ask Sonny, dammit.

But just looking at the old bastard made Gabriel's guts spin like a mill wheel. It'd taken everything he had not to puke all over those torn-up newspapers. He'd been playing that talk wholly by ear, improvising to get any information Sonny might have. Then came a point where Gabe couldn't stand to hear another word.

The easiest path would be to talk with Michael and get his end of it.

Which would mean coming clean with him. About everything.

Gabe wasn't ready to take that road yet. It would leave him too vulnerable. The less Michael knew about the whole blood-drinking angle, the better. Anyway, he would simply discount it and believe that Gabe had gone dangerously insane like Sonny and had to be put down. There would be no lingering in a loony bin.

I could disappear myself, but sooner or later he'd find me, and he'd kill me.

Yes, that was a given.

Mike would feel really, really bad about it—

But do it all the same.

9

FLEMING

On the way over to Escott's office, I stopped at a couple places and bought a couple things. I was unsure if they'd do much good, but what the hell, why not?

Not knowing what lay ahead, I approached the block slowly, on the lookout for Coldfield's Nash. It was a newer version of the one Escott drove, armored, of course . . . and parked right in front of the outside stairs leading up to the office.

I cruised past, circled the block, and stopped to wait far down at the end behind another car.

Yes, I was being chicken. Coldfield had already clobbered me this week, and I was in no mood to risk more of the same or worse. Not so long ago I'd have tried an eye-whammy to cool him down, but I couldn't play that card again; I'd just have to tough things out. Besides, Escott might get in the middle and he had to have enough on his mind already.

Just as I set the brake and cut the motor, Coldfield came downstairs onto the sidewalk. He looked both ways but didn't see me, got in the Nash, and drove off, alone.

Lights remained on in the office.

Not knowing how long that would last, I grabbed my parcels and moved quick.

I clumped up the stairs to the door with THE ESCOTT AGENCY painted on its pebbled-glass window. He'd have heard me, but I knocked twice before trying the knob. The door swung open easily with a soft creak.

Escott sat at his desk in the small, plain room, pipe in hand, stacks of mail in front of him, business as usual. I damn near choked at the normalcy.

"Busy?" I asked, keeping on my side of the threshold. I couldn't help but recall the first time standing there, pretending to need an invitation to enter, while he gave me a good long look to figure out if I was friend or foe.

He gave me another good long look, his lean face just as wary. By God, his bruises were gone. He looked the same as ever . . . but things were changed. Break a leg, and the bone could heal straight, and you might not even limp, but you'll still feel it, you'll always feel it.

What I'd broken was the trust we'd had.

"Were you waiting long for Shoe to leave?" he asked.

That was normal, too, him figuring things out so quick. "Just parked. You send him away?"

"I needed an uninterrupted hour to myself. Business." He indicated the mail.

"Oh. Okay."

"Jack."

I halted my turning to leave. Looked back. With the pipe he gestured at one of the empty chairs before the desk.

"Come on, old man," he said, not unkindly. "Let's get it over with."

I shoved the door shut with one foot and sat facing him. Things got quiet, and I didn't know where to look.

"Well. This is bloody awkward, isn't it?"

"Oh, yeah." I checked over the small office, avoiding his eye.

"What have you there?" he asked.

The parcels. I put them on the desk. "Peace offerings."

He pulled the paper from one, which uncovered a bottle of dark beer, cool, not cold. The others held a fresh loaf of rye bread and a quarter pound of salted butter.

His eyes went wide. "What the devil . . . ?"

"You asked for them the other night."

"I did?"

"Before the fever really took hold."

"They had me doped with some awful stuff. I don't remember."

Just as well. "You hungry?"

"As it happens, I am. This is perfect." He had a flat sharp letter opener handy and used that to cut the bread and spread on the butter.

I didn't much care for the food smells, but he was eating . . . and drinking. He knocked the bottle top off using the edge of the desk and washed down the bread with a healthy swig.

He noticed me watching. "Worried that I picked up one of your habits?"

"Huh?"

"Swilling blood instead of this excellent brew?" He tilted the bottle.

"Shoe told you what happened?"

"In rare detail. I missed the show, but he was highly impressed."

"Kroun laid us in the aisles all right. How are you?"

"Remarkably well, thank you." He brushed two fingers along the side of his face. Last night his eye had been swollen shut, his face more black than blue; not a trace of injury remained. "All better."

Jeez. I was used to that sort of thing for myself, but not for others. This spooked me. "You remember anything about that part? Drinking the—"

"Thankfully, I do not. Shoe's description was vivid, and I shall do my level best to forget even that much." He slapped on more butter.

The food smells didn't agree with me, but thank God he was eating. He was alive to do it.

Another slug of beer, and he set down the brown bottle, politely suppressing a belch. "Who would have thought such blood to be a curative? It's like some patent concoction from the back page of a dime magazine, only it clearly works."

"And Kroun knew about it. I tried to find out more from him, but he wouldn't talk."

"Doubtless he has a reason."

"We have to know if it's going to have a permanent effect on you."

Escott seemed to be at a loss there. "Hopefully, your friend might be persuaded to part with information on that point. I am understandably curious."

"You sure you feel okay?"

"Never better. Which disturbs me because I recall feeling damned rotten the last time I took stock."

"Anything else?"

He caught my meaning. "Ah. Well. I've not exhibited any extranormal strength, my vision at night hasn't improved, nor have I experienced any sanguinary cravings. My canines are their usual length, and mirrors still work for me."

I was relieved. "That covers it."

"Of course there was an alarming moment when I woke from a nap and found myself floating just a few inches short of the ceiling . . ."

"Tell me that's a joke."

"A poor one, to judge by the look on your face. Sorry."

Some of the starch went out of my spine. Then I couldn't say anything, just sit in my cold sweat feeling sick and helpless. This was how I'd been before, and it had led me to put a gun to my head. I didn't want to be like this.

"What?" he asked, his gaze sharpening with concern.

His trust in me was broken, maybe never to mend. He would *always* wonder if I'd do something stupid again. "I . . . I waited too long."

"For what?"

"I didn't know what you'd want. I couldn't think."

"In regard to . . . ?"

"Trying to save you. Whether I should have tried a blood exchange so you might have a chance—"

"Ah. Shoe told me about that as well, along with your reluctance to act."

"That's what he saw."

"You made your point that it had only a slim chance of success. We all know that."

"I wasn't sure he understood. And I couldn't make the choice for you; he did."

"But Mr. Kroun stepped in."

"Yeah. A good thing. We might not be here."

That hung in the air for a moment. Escott had more beer, looking patient.

"But I waited too long."

"Because you did not know my preference in regard to a choice between being dead or Undead?"

"God forbid this ever happens again, but what do you want?"

For the second time that night I saw a man suddenly unsure of himself, hesitating. "I have thought about it," he finally admitted. "And thought and thought. I honestly don't know."

"How can you not know?"

"Some days it seems a good idea; youth, long life, strength, all the other advantages, those balanced by certain disadvantages to which one must adjust. But other days . . . it seems like the worst thing in the world. *Your* decision was originally based on wanting to be with the woman you loved."

And lost. Yes.

"My circumstances are different. Whether I returned or not, either outcome would effectively remove me from my life as I know it now."

"You're thinking of Vivian?" If she was a part of the decision, then he'd gotten pretty serious about her.

"She's a very intelligent, knowledgeable woman, but I shall risk underestimating her and judge that she would not be at ease knowing of such matters."

"That's not fair to either of you. Just talk to her."

"Have you spoken to anyone in your family about *your* change?"

He stumped me on that one. "They wouldn't understand."

"My point exactly."

"You can't make a choice based on how another might react to it."

"Of course I can. It's done every day. Sometimes one stumbles in the process."

He was referring to my attempt at suicide. I'd gone into that with no regard for the harm it would bring to anyone else.

"Things might change in the future," he said. "For now, I just don't know. If—God forbid—another similar situation falls upon you, all I can say is use your best common sense in regard to whatever circumstance you find yourself."

"That's only if I have time to decide. What if you get hit by a truck or something?"

"Then it is my fate to be hit by a truck. But in the meantime, I shall endeavor to avoid wandering into the street."

"And if the truck jumps up on the sidewalk?"

Escott opened his mouth but hesitated again. He could read me easy, and saw that I was serious. An odd smile came and went on him, and he shifted a little. "All right, I'll tell you this and you can believe it or not. The other night some part of me was aware of what was happening. I recall that much."

"Aware of . . . ?"

"That I was dying."

Oh, God.

"Jack, let me assure you . . . it was all right. It really was."

This had to be a leftover from that time in Canada when all his friends had been murdered. Surviving that horror had changed him, made him careless about his own life in the years that followed. I'd thought he'd gotten over it, though. "There's nothing all right about wanting to die."

"I'm so glad to hear you say that."

"It's not about me."

"Nor is it about my wanting to die. *Wanting* was not a factor. I was simply aware that I was dying, and it did not trouble me. It was . . . not being forced upon me by the ill will of another, but just something that had come to happen."

"But my fault," I said. "I'm the one who—"

"Oh, don't start, you sound just like Shoe."

"He's right."

"No, he's not. You and I sorted our credentials, and that's the end of the matter. My going septic afterward was just bad luck. That sort of thing could happen anytime and come from a paper cut. I wish to hear no more about the business. Please."

"Okay," I muttered.

"Thank you. What I'm trying to say is that if you find yourself unable to offer your unique help to me, don't be troubled too very much. I'm refusing to worry about it, though I will give more thought to the matter. For now—again—I just don't know."

"You sure? That you're not sure?"

He shrugged. "Should I make a determination one way or another, I will tell you. I promise."

The way he said it told me the discussion was closed and only he could open it again.

"Besides, Mr. Kroun's unexpected hand in my recovery may have resolved things already. We need to question him. I thought he'd be along with you. Shoe had the idea you were looking after him."

"Kroun went for a walk. He's not exactly leash-trained. I put him up at the house at first, but last night he disappeared into some bolt-hole of his own."

"Not in the literal sense?"

"Hm?"

"Bobbi mentioned his inability to vanish." Escott raised a hand. "Please, she didn't purposely break her silence about him. After Shoe told me what happened, I asked her to fill in the gaps."

"Kroun's gonna love that."

"Secretive, is he?"

"Like a safe."

"Well, he is among strangers, all of whom know how to remove him. When one is wholly helpless during the daylight hours, one must be careful."

"Yes, one must."

"I would like to meet Mr. Kroun and thank him. Is that likely to come about?"

"Oh, yeah, I just don't know when. He's up to something I can't figure, and it's got a stink to it."

"Indeed?"

It was enough of an opening. Something shifted in the air between us, and we were suddenly back on another case again, same as ever. It was a conscious thing, and if a little forced for the effort, reassuring for being familiar.

I told him everything I'd told Gordy, then what Gordy had given to me about Kroun. It didn't take long, though it felt like hours before I ran out of words.

Escott finished his bread and beer, digesting both along with my information. "That business with Sonny is something I can look into."

"You stay clear of it. Kroun wasn't happy telling me the guy was his father."

"Yet he did. Why?"

"Moment of weakness?"

"I doubt that. It's odd. No idea where he went afterward?"

I shook my head. "He was plenty upset. Maybe he did just want to walk it off."

"His friends from New York will be less than pleased with you for not keeping track of him."

"They can take a flying leap, I've got my own row to hoe."

"Tomorrow I'll see what I can turn up on them, especially Sonny."

"Charles . . ."

"Be assured I shall be most circumspect. A phone call to the sanatarium while impersonating a physician should be enough, then I won't have to go near the place."

"Good. You don't want Kroun hearing you've been nosing around. He's going to figure I talked to you anyway, but . . ."

"Yes, yes, caution, absolutely. The directions to that cabin might prove helpful."

"He's going to be touchy about it. Don't go looking for trouble, okay?"

"Very well."

"You're not driving up there without me."

"Wouldn't dream of it. Word of honor."

While Escott sorted through his stack of mail, I transcribed the smudged shorthand on my shirt cuff to notepaper, making three copies. Kroun would want one.

"Now, about the Alan Caine case—"

"It's over," I said. "There is no case. I left a false lead for the cops, and they're off and running."

"Something went wrong for you on it. It had to do with Hoyle's death."

Escott was too sharp by half.

"What went wrong doesn't matter now," I said. "I wasn't thinking straight and wound up being stupid. You showed me just how stupid, and I nearly killed you. I can't apologize enough for that."

"You don't have to, old man. It's past, my number was not called that night. I've miles to go before I sleep."

My gut gave a twist at that thought. He'd come *too* close.

"Keep whatever it is to yourself if you must, I understand that. But I am still angry with you on Bobbi's behalf."

I felt myself go red. It was shame. Out-and-out shame. It blazed through me, intense as fire. It was worse than when I'd shot myself. "I get you," I whispered. "Never again. I swear on Bobbi's life."

He grunted.

"You gonna clobber me again?"

"If I have to."

"You won't have to."

"Are you going to tell her what you did?"

I gaped in shock. "Hell, no!"

He relaxed a bit. "I'm most relieved to hear it."

"She's asked why we fought . . . I can't tell her. She'd never be able to trust me again."

"Good instinct. It would only adversely taint her affection. What she doesn't know won't be a constant reproach to you and worry for her."

That told me how he was thinking. This was going to be a long road. "She's going to keep asking, you know that."

"Tell her that *I* made you promise. Pretend I was the one in the wrong about something and began the fight. You're only protecting my good reputation with her."

That was one hell of a favor. Too much of one. He'd done enough. "She'd never buy it. I can't—"

"You most certainly can and will. It worked tolerably well on Shoe."

The implications of that sank slowly into my thick skull. He'd put one over on Coldfield? I couldn't see how Escott had gotten away with it, but if anyone could . . . "Really?"

"Best to agree before I change my mind."

"Okay, okay!" I put my hands up, surrendering. "Is Shoe going to ease off being pissed at me?"

Escott went somber. "I doubt it. Not for a long, long while. Whatever the circumstances that led up to this near disaster, and whatever the miraculous cure that averted it, he's not going to cease blaming you."

I didn't expect otherwise. But, damn, it was tough. I valued Coldfield's friendship.

"Just give him time, Jack."

"Yeah, sure."

He glanced at his watch, shuffled the mail and food leavings to one side, and tapped his pipe empty. "Well, nothing here that cannot wait until the morrow. I'll be glad to sleep in my own bed tonight."

"Uh—there's one thing . . ." I told him about the break-in at the house. "It could be Kroun's two buddies messing around. Until I know what's going on, you should stay at Shoe's hotel."

"Bloody hell. I don't want some unknown thug dictating where I sleep."

"Me neither, but you're settled in already, aren't you?"

"At Shoe's quite forceful insistence."

"Go along with him. There's no harm in it. He'll feel better."

"Where will you doss down?"

"I'll be at Lady Crymsyn. If it looks safe. For all we know, it was just a regular burglar."

"You don't believe that."

"Not these nights, no. Another thing—your Nash might not be home for a couple days. I'm having the steering wheel fixed." I thought he'd be happier not knowing about the bloodstained upholstery. "You can call Derner at the Nightcrawler about it."

"Why, thank you. I'd not given it any thought."

Well, he had been sidetracked.

A car door slammed down in the street. "I think Shoe's back."

"Somewhat early. He's giving me a ride over to see Vivian."

It occurred to me that Escott could stay with her for the night, but I kept quiet. How he conducted his big romance was his own beeswax. "You going to tell her any of what's happened?"

He gaped in shock. "Hell, no!"

WHILE I stood quiet in the office's back room, Escott locked up and went off with Coldfield. The lights were out, but enough glow came through the blinds to allow me to dial the Nightcrawler.

Derner picked up on the first ring. "Yeah, what is it?"

He must have been having a full evening, too. I let him know it was me and asked how things were going. Michael and Broder had come by and were down in the club. They wanted a word with me—or Kroun, who was keeping his head low in the office. Derner gave the phone to him.

"Thought you'd be here by now. What's the holdup?"

"I had things to do. I still have things to do."

"You can kiss your girlfriend later. Come over. Quick. I'll meet you on the street in the back."

It didn't sound like an emergency, more like impatience. If so, then why wait for me? He could get a car and go off on his own easy enough. He damned well better not want to make an expedition up to that cabin. It was distant enough that we couldn't manage a round-trip in one night, and I was not leaving town without seeing Bobbi again.

GOOD thing Kroun waited outside, there was no parking anywhere close, including the alley behind the club. A delivery truck blocked the entry. Several large guys in dark coats (and probably up to no good) glared my way as I rolled by at a snail's pace. Stuff was being dropped off or picked up—bodies or booze, I couldn't tell what—business as usual for the Nightcrawler Club.

Kroun emerged from a shadow, stepped up on my running board, and opened the passenger door.

"Keep moving," he said before I could hit the brake.

I kept moving, feeding more gas once he was inside and had pulled the door shut. Even he had to work hauling it to, because of the armor and thick glass. "What's the deal?"

"Just head west and watch the mirror."

"What's got you spooked?"

"Broder. I think he saw me. I ducked and got scarce, but you never know with him."

"Why not just hypnotize him?"

Kroun didn't answer.

"Or maybe you tried once, and it didn't work? Crazy people are immune. Is he crazy?"

He thought that one over. "Single-minded. He's Michael's watchdog. Won't work for anyone else."

"Nice pals you got. Just talk for a minute and get 'em off your back."

"I have nothing new to say and better things to do. Michael will see it differently and waste time for everyone."

Sounded reasonable. "Why am I here?"

"I need you to drive while I figure the roads."

"Where're we going?"

"That mirror clear?"

"Seems so."

"Make sure."

I made sure. Broder was the kind of mug one should always avoid.

Kroun twisted around to watch for tails. His mood was considerably improved and more energetic, and I wondered why until an intake of breath tipped me to a faint trace of perfume clinging to his clothes.

I got uncomfortable pretty fast and opened my mouth without thinking. "Is she all right?"

"What?"

"The girl you were just with. Is she all right?"

"You followed me?" He was more surprised than anything.

"I can smell her on you. Is she—"

"She's *fine*. Cripes, can't a man have some privacy?"

"How much did you take from her?"

He didn't reply, apparently overcome by sheer disbelief for the question. "What the hell—?"

"Figure it out. The things Sonny said, the hints Michael dropped about you making trouble, and the other night you were harping at *me* about feeding from—"

Kroun cut me off with one burst of gutter language and slammed the back of his hand against the door in frustration. I kept driving, ready to hit the brake in case he took a swing. Instead, he steamed a while, shaking his head, then barked a short laugh.

"Fleming, it is no goddamned wonder that people want to kill you."

"Just doing my job."

"Now you start," he muttered. "Okay, fine. I understand. I've got a bad reputation, so I'll let this pass. On the level—the lady is just peachy. But don't take my word for it, find a phone, pull over. I'll even give you a nickel to call the joint."

He named one of the more expensive brothels under Gordy's supervision, the name of the madam, and the girl in question. A phone call wouldn't take long. My eating crow was preferable to letting him get away with something ugly. Of course, Kroun could have hypnotically primed everyone with a story.

His reaction was not that of a guilty man, but then Michael had mentioned Kroun's lack of a conscience. Gordy's accounts of cold executions backed it up. Sonny's obscene ravings—none of it seemed to fit the man on the passenger side of my car. I measured that against Kroun's saving Escott's life, getting me off the death list, and his behavior in general.

But some people were very good at hiding the dark inside.

I glanced at him. He was angry, but there was no sign of that hell-pit emptiness in his eyes. For all I knew, the same thing showed in me when I went off my rocker. Maybe it was part of our shared condition.

"I'll check on it later," I finally said.

"Lemme know what you find out."

"I have to do this. It's not connected to Michael's orders."

He thought that one through. "Yeah. I see that. You're a stand-up guy, you can't help it."

I didn't expect that response.

"But you know," he continued, "you could try, just *try* not to be such a pain in the ass while you're at it."

That was more like it. "Just part of my charm."

A few miles of twisting and turning around the Loop convinced him we were in the clear. He gave me a direction.

"West," I said. "Not Wisconsin." And I'd been braced for a fresh new brawl for refusing to head north.

"Nope. I want what you wrote down on getting to the cabin, though." He had a pencil and another Nightcrawler matchbook.

Rather than drive while reading from my shirt cuff, I passed him the copy I'd made.

He grunted a thanks, then checked the paper. "This is word for word."

"Just a knack. Again—where are we going? And how long will it take?"

"Can't say. I don't know the area." He folded the paper into the matchbook, shoving both in a pocket, brought out a map, and wrestled it open. A black circle around a thread-thin line of country road marked our general destination.

Closer than Wisconsin, but not all that close, and I'd planned to see Bobbi tonight. I pressed hard on the gas. "You need a chauffeur, not me," I grumbled.

"I'm keeping you clear of Michael."

"So he doesn't know about your visit to Sonny."

"He'll find that out on his own. This is just to keep the peace."

"How?"

"You're both used to being in charge, and neither of you likes to be bossed. He pushes people, that's how he operates. If he pushes you the wrong way, then Broder has to step in; someone could lose an eye."

"You don't trust me with your friends?"

Kroun didn't laugh but was mightily amused. "You trust me with yours?"

"I didn't have a choice. What's going to happen to Charles?"

"He's better?"

"Like he was never sick. And he's asking questions. Is he gonna become like us?"

"Why should he?"

"Because our kind of blood is different. It changes things."

He stopped smiling. "Sure as hell does."

"You knew it would help him, but how's it gonna be for him later?"

"Damned if I know."

"You *don't know*?"

"Yes, I said that. I really did. You wanna figure it out, read a book."

"There aren't any. I've read everything on what we are, and nothing mentions a word about what you did. All I've got is you."

"Then you're out of luck, because I don't know. I'll say it again if that hasn't sunk in."

That exasperated me, and I let him see it.

"I don't," he repeated. "Really."

"And why is that?"

He shook his head.

What the hell? But more questions wouldn't work; he'd pulled on his poker face. Escott might have better luck getting an answer.

Maybe—and I was disinclined to believe it—Kroun was giving me the straight dope after all.

I'd suffered a blackout about my death. I'd lost days of time, though most of the memories had eventually come back. Perhaps he had that, too, and didn't want to admit the weakness. It would explain a lot. The bullet in his skull might make his case worse, blotting out who had made his change, how he knew certain things.

I opened my mouth to throw that at him, then caught a glimpse of his profile. His head was pressed against the window so he could gape up at the buildings as we rolled along State Street. His grimness was gone, and he suddenly looked like a farm kid marveling at the wonders. Everything would seem different because of the internal changes. Those towers would be new, shining and miraculous under a night sky that wasn't dark anymore.

No need to interrupt that. I turned on the radio and found some music to distract me.

Go far enough away from Chicago, and eventually you run out of city. It trails off grudgingly. In the last ten years a million people had moved in—I was one of them—and while most clustered in close to the lake, there were plenty spread around the outer areas. Instead of tall buildings full of flats, you saw individual houses that gave way to fields and trees with no sidewalks running under them, no fences cutting between.

The roads turned rough, the solid-rubber tires made them bumpy as hell, and most corners lacked a signpost. If you didn't know where you were, tough luck. There hadn't been much traffic to break up the last snowfall, so I had to go slow in spots. The heavy car skidded uneasily when the solid tires weren't trying to rattle our teeth loose. It got too noisy to hear the radio. I shut it off to focus on driving.

Kroun scowled at his map and didn't answer questions. Annoying, but nothing new. I played chauffeur and paid attention to the route to remember it later.

"Pull in there," said Kroun after half an hour.

Suspecting he'd lost his bearings, I did, braking near some gas pumps standing sentinel before a run-down white building. Dropped onto a wide patch in the road, it was shaped like a shoe box with square windows cut into the long sides. Faded signs informed drivers that they could buy gas, hamburgers, and hot coffee, the latter two emphasized by bold, inexpert artwork.

The place was open; a lone light, the only one in view, shone over the screen door. Even in the most isolated spots out in farming country you can nearly always spy a light in the far distance and know that people might be there or had once been there. This would be the joint shining that light. Nothing else but trees and wind and loneliness lay beyond in all directions. When I cut the motor, the silence crowded in like an unwelcome witness.

The muddy slush between the building and the gas pumps indicated customers had been by that day, but no sign of them now. Kroun got out and looked around, his manner telling me that this was his intended destination. Who the hell did he know here? Another crazy like Sonny?

He struck off, heading for the door. I followed, and we went inside.

Like any hunter I scented the air: the stink of old cooking grease, onions, and stale coffee dominated. I'd eaten in countless diners just like this during my newspaper days. For twenty-five cents you could get a filling meal that sometimes digested without incident and flirt with the waitress if she was in the mood for it. This country-cousin version inspired the kind of nostalgic pang that made me glad I was now drinking blood.

The woman behind the counter looked to have had a hard life, but a lot of that was going around. Her black-and-gray hair was pulled back and pinned tight, her face amiable enough despite the lines. She had to get all types in, but nothing recent that looked like us. We got the quick assessing stare reserved for newcomers, and she asked if we needed gas, food, or both.

Kroun took his hat off. "No, ma'am, thank you. I'm looking for Mrs. Cabot."

"Who wants her?"

"I'm supposed to deliver something."

"You're no mailman. What is it?"

He hesitated, then pulled out a letter-sized envelope, holding it up. "Not sure. Looks like money. They don't pay me to be curious."

"Money for what?"

"I don't know. Are you Mrs. Cabot, Nelly's mother?"

She went dead still, her eyes going flat. "What about Nelly?"

"I'm here to make sure she's all right. If I could talk to her a minute . . ."

The woman pointed toward the door. "Get out, the two of you. Now."

"Mrs. Cabot—"

"*OUT!*" she bellowed.

He moved closer instead, but she was faster. Before he could even begin to give her the evil eye she pulled a Colt six-shot from under the counter, leveling the muzzle square on his chest.

"Our mistake," I said, and backed toward the door. I caught Kroun's arm and tugged. He retreated a few steps, reluctant.

"Please, ma'am, I only want to talk, there's no need—"

"*OUT!*" Her eyes blazed wild.

"C'mon, Kroun." I pulled harder. "Haul it."

She gave a double take. "Y-you're Kroun?"

He offered a hopeful smile. "Yes, ma'am. If you'd put that d—"

The barrel roared fire, short, ugly, and deafening in the confined space.

Kroun had hellishly good reflexes and ducked a bare instant ahead of the shot. I vanished entirely, came back, and grabbed him while the smoke still billowed.

The next second we were out the door in craven retreat for the car. Mrs. Cabot was right behind, taking aim, one-handed. Shaking and cursing as she was, she missed. Kroun slammed the passenger door shut in time to stop the third round. The thick glass chipped and went opaque right where his head was; he flinched back in the seat, and in a strange, strained voice told me to get us moving.

Good idea, but under certain circumstances it takes a damned long time to start a car and work the gas and clutch just right. I managed. In the meanwhile, she slammed two more shots into his window, each making progress toward shattering it completely.

We were suddenly bouncing onto the road, the motor howl drowning out any more gunfire though I was sure something pinged off the back. I didn't slow until a sharp turn half a mile down made it a necessity.

"Pull over," said Kroun.

"No, thanks." Just because I was more bulletproof than when I'd been alive didn't mean I enjoyed getting shot.

I put another mile between us and Mrs. Cabot, and he repeated himself. I'd gotten my own shaking under control by then and obliged. An

unpaved lane leading into trees opened on the left. I went far enough in
so we were hidden, cut the motor, got out, and went still.

Kroun got out on his side. "What is it?"

Held my hand up. "Listen."

He did, then shrugged. "Nothing. Just wind."

"Yeah, no siren. She should have called the cops by now. Even the
ones in the sticks have radio cars."

"Maybe Sheriff Hickory is on the other end of the county ticketing
cows without a license."

Good point. "What did you do to that woman?"

"Nothing. I wanted to talk to her daughter if she was there."

"About what?"

But he wasn't sharing. The wind threw itself through bare tree limbs
and brush, which always made me nervous. It sounded like a ghost army
was prowling around us. I was born on a farm but preferred the city. The
sharp angles made it easier to pick out people when they came at you.

"Back in," I said.

"What?"

"We gits while the gittin's good, before the law comes."

"We're staying."

"So they can find us? They know these back roads and can figure
where we might hide. I'd rather be a moving target. We leave now, and
we might slip clear."

"Jack, calm down. I can handle any cop who comes by."

"Like you handled her? No thanks, I've had enough." I got in, and so
did Kroun, but he yanked the keys out.

"We're waiting," he said.

Goddammit. A flash of anger went through me, and I understood
that woman's urge to shoot him. "Just tell me what you're trying to do!"

To give him credit, he thought about it. I could see wheels spinning
and gears grinding behind his dark eyes, and for one naked moment
glimpsed painful indecision there. Then he shut it down. He shook his
head, pressing his palm against that white streak as though it hurt.
"Can't."

I thought about slamming his forehead into the dashboard a few times
but decided it wasn't worth the effort. By tomorrow Escott might have
the whole story. "Okay. Why are we waiting?"

"For her to settle down."

"That could take a few years."

"You see her nose?"

"Not really." All I could see was the Colt swinging my way.

"Veins."

"Veins?"

"A nose like that means she has a bottle. She'll lock up, reload, have a drink or three, and fall asleep. We go back on the quiet, get inside, then I talk to her."

"Get inside? She's going to hear you sneaking up, I don't care how asleep she is."

He nodded. "I got that. The sneaking up is your job."

"The hell it is."

"All you have to do is hold her until I can put her under. I'll calm her down, make her forget everything."

Since Escott took me on as a silent partner in his business, I'd slipped into more than one place on the sly, but always in a good cause. Trying the same gag on Mrs. Cabot . . . no. Not without an explanation. "You tell me why, first."

Kroun gave a frustrated snarl, but cut it off. "I said I can't. I'm only here to find out if her daughter is all right and where she is. That's all. Don't ask who her daughter is. I can't tell you that, either."

He made it sound as though he was working under duress for someone else, but I wasn't buying. He'd ask the lady a lot more than just two questions. From those I'd learn more about what was going on with him. I'd pass what I knew to Escott, maybe Gordy, and they might be able to fill in the picture.

"We wait an hour," I said. "That's my limit."

He scowled, then gave a nod, handing over the keys.

THAT was one damned slow hour. I couldn't play the radio in case it ran the battery down, and neither of us was in a mood for conversation. For something to do I turned the car around so it faced toward the road. That filled up a whole minute.

The rest of the time it was dead quiet inside except for the wind outside and the tick of our respective watches. I'd gotten used to hearing breathing and a heartbeat with other people. Kroun had neither. Now and then I'd check to make sure he was still there, just my bad luck that he was.

It got cold, too. Even for me.

I wondered about Mrs. Cabot and her daughter Nelly and what either of them had to do with Kroun. My half-formed speculations were on the dark side.

Five minutes short, he had enough. "Let's get this over with."

Finally. I returned to the main road, keeping the speed sedate, slowing as we approached the diner. The CLOSED sign was up, every light was on, and a car was parked in front, partially obscured by the gas pumps.

"She called someone to come sit with her," I said. "No deal. Try again tomorrow."

"Just as easy to hold two down as one," he said.

"No, it isn't. She could have her whole family in there waiting with shotguns. Tomorrow." Before he could object I hit the gas.

We sailed by. Kroun grumbled to himself, looking back. "He's following."

I checked the mirror. The other car had pulled onto the road, headlights off. Anyone else would have missed him, but Kroun and I had the advantage at night. I picked up speed; the other guy matched me.

"Cops?" I asked. "Unmarked car?"

"I don't see any radio antenna. Some friend, maybe."

"We'll lose him in the city. Not much I can do out here. What'd you do to piss them off?"

But he didn't answer and continued to watch the other guy. "He's catching up."

I fed more gas, but didn't gain speed. Derner's garage pals might have tuned the motor, but they couldn't make it produce more power to compensate for the weight of the armor. My once fleet and sweet Buick was now a turtle.

Our shadow's windows reflected the surrounding snow, so neither of us could see inside. All I saw of the driver was a hunched form with his hat pulled low. The other car—it looked like a Caddy—came up fast.

He bumped hard into us, and I automatically hit the brake. He wouldn't slow, and on the slick road he was able to push and keep pushing. I floored my gas pedal, but it wasn't enough to get ahead until we started down a long slope. We gained a whole inch on him.

Crump, as he bumped again, much harder.

I fought to keep control. He hit the horn, which was supposed to unnerve me, and made a pretty good job of it.

Kroun rolled down his fractured window. He had his gun in hand.

"No shooting!" I yelped.

He looked pained. "Just going to discourage him. Drive."

Dammit.

The Caddy slewed toward the left as Kroun's first shot made a hole in the passenger-side windshield. Was his eye that good or had he gotten lucky? Before he could aim again, the other car hit the gas in earnest and plowed into my left back bumper. I nearly tore the wheel off keeping us straight and yelled at Kroun to get himself inside. He was half-out the window.

"What'd you say?" he asked, sliding back down.

"Stop shooting, you just made him mad."

"Chicken."

Hell, yes.

CRUMP.

It was a bigger and uglier sound than before, and the shock of impact went through the whole car. The Caddy had darted forward and slammed us broadside. I had the weight to resist, but no purchase with those damned solid-rubber tires.

We shot off the road.

10

FLYING is better when you don't have a body to deal with the inevitable hard landing.

But instead of sensibly vanishing, I held on to the wheel and stuck it out.

We were in the air for maybe three seconds, it seemed longer, then *wham*, we hit the snowy ground at about fifty, bounding quick and rough down an incline toward some trees. They would stop us, oh, hell, how they would stop us. I pumped the brakes (not working too well), kept the wheel straight, which was pointless since the car's momentum was in charge. We hit something, and the Buick slewed majestically, rear wheels coming to the front, the landscape rushing by sideways and far too fast.

A terrible low hammering noise, an abrupt and sickening twist—the big metal body tipped and tumbled like a kid's toy.

I was thrown around for one brutal, bruising, and frightening turn before winking out like a bad light. The steel bulk of the car pummeled my invisible form, but I'd be spared a maiming or worse. Dimly, I heard Kroun curse amid the tin-can noises as we rolled.

Then it stopped, just that quick.

Re-forming, I found myself lying faceup on the ceiling. The car was upside down, a fact that was slow to creep into my rattled brain. I understood it would be a good idea to get clear—especially when I smelled gas.

Kroun was curled awkwardly on his side, still clutching his gun. He looked dead, but was more likely just stunned.

I kicked at a window to break it—forgetting it was too thick for that kind of easy escape.

The effort made me grunt. I could almost taste the gas in the air.

Squirming and in a hellish hurry, I aimed myself feetfirst toward Kroun's open window, went nearly transparent, and slipped out backward, belly down. Solid again, I got purchase with my knees braced against the outside frame, grabbed his shoulders, and pulled. He weighed more than I expected. The bad angle wrenched my back, but I pulled again. Once my shoulders were clear, I was able to get a better grip. I dragged him free and didn't stop until we were twenty yards away behind a thick pine trunk.

Then I collapsed. Some nerve in my spine went off like an electric shock and had me close to screaming, but another quick vanish and return took care of it. I didn't bother getting up. Sprawling exhausted in churned snow in the woods was all I wanted to do for the next few weeks.

Kroun shifted and groaned. Yeah, things were bad all over. He sat up, wobbly, staring around.

"Over here," I said, raising one hand.

His stare concentrated full on me. It took a second before I realized something was off. His eyes had gone funny, dilated to the point of being all black with no pupil. That *thing* so carefully hidden behind them was back.

"Gabe?"

It didn't recognize me. We were complete strangers.

"Whitey?"

It still had the gun and swung the muzzle around.

Oh, shit.

I got out of there, invisibly, and not an instant too soon. I felt the bullet punch through the space I'd occupied.

No second shot, but I heard him moving, standing up. I shifted quick, trying to get behind him, but he'd backed against the pine trunk. He was silent, making no unnecessary moves.

He fired again, accurately. Unlike other people, he was able to see my amorphous form floating around.

I could wait until he ran out of bullets, but this crazy change in him sparked a matching fury in me. Hit me for no reason, and I'll hit back twice as hard; that's how it works.

He got off a shot as I rushed him, but no more when I went solid, grabbed his arms, and slammed him into the trunk. He ducked his head forward, twisted, and suddenly I was the one about to collide with the tree.

I faded, shifted, went solid, and hit him in the gut. He doubled over, but brought the gun up again. I stepped into his reach, knocking his arm wide, backhanding his jaw on the return with my fist.

He should have dropped, damn it. I'd gotten too used to dealing with regular guys. Kroun was a match for my own strength and speed and also knew how to fight dirty. He swiped his gun hand quick as lightning toward the side of my head. I had to fade again, coming up behind, but he was ready for that, so I wasn't solid for long. A glimpse of his face threw me; cool, purposeful rage distorted his features into that of a wholly different man. What in God's name had come over him?

He wasn't anyone I wanted to meet in the dark woods at night. I floated back some yards, hoping he'd waste bullets, but he wouldn't take the bait. Going solid, I cast around for something useful. The ground snow hid any rocks the right size for throwing. Tree limbs? Nope, those were hidden or still attached. I had my own gun in a coat pocket, but hadn't reached the point where shooting him was a prudent option. I was mad, but not that mad. He, on the other hand, looked—

Shot.

That one missed my nose by a fraction. I disappeared and rushed upward. Much as I hated heights, that was my best place to get a weapon. The plan was to break off a dead limb for a club, except this time of year they all looked dead. I shifted to another tree, going higher. Soon as I judged the branches thick enough to take my weight, I had a quick look, made a grab at one that might work, and yanked hard. It snapped off with a crack as loud as a gunshot—which I heard a second later. I made myself missing, dropping the branch. It was too big to vanish with me.

Moving to another tree, I skimmed down on the side away from Kroun, going solid just enough to get my bearings.

We were about twenty feet apart. He stood over the fallen branch, looking right at me as I held to a semitransparent state. I couldn't talk;

there wasn't enough of me formed up yet to push air. He kept his gun aimed point-blank at my chest. From his coat pocket he drew out another gun, the one he'd taken from Michael the other night.

Kroun—or whatever it was that was running him—pointed the second muzzle my way. He seemed ready to hold out all night like that.

We traded glares, catching our mental breath since neither of us had a need for the other kind.

He held himself tense, but his features began to gradually relax. That crazy blank-eyed rage ebbed, replaced by wary puzzlement.

He tilted his head, eyes going narrow. "What the hell are you doing? What's going on?" he asked, sounding annoyed. He looked like himself again.

But I wasn't taking chances. He had a beaut of a stare as I floated across the space between, going solid at the last second.

I busted him as hard as I could.

Damn, that hurt my fist. But this time he dropped and stayed down. I pocketed his guns, then leaned against the tree. The woods got quiet again.

WE were miles from anyplace except the diner. I'd had my fill of Mrs. Cabot's country hospitality and figured to take a stab at hitchhiking back to town.

Provided the road was clear of the guy who'd rammed us.

Of course my efforts were bound to be hampered by Kroun's unconscious body slung over my shoulder. He was goddamned heavy to haul uphill, too. I took it at a long easy angle almost parallel to the road, but the vanishings had tired me out. Halfway along I gave up, put him on the ground, and grabbed a handful of snow, mashing it against his face.

He came awake, snarling and struggling. Since I'd tied his arms together with his coat belt, I was in a better position to keep him from doing much damage.

"*What the hell is this?*" His outraged roar echoed through the trees.

"You're *nuts*, that's what it is," I said in a calm voice, which was surprising. Part of me wanted to bust him again.

Other guys might have done a lot more yelling, but he clammed up, giving me a second look and maybe a second thought to my statement. He could see neither of us was in a neatly groomed state. "What happened?"

Since he asked in a civil tone, I obliged with an answer in kind, filling him in.

The last thing he remembered was the car going off the road. He unexpectedly thanked me for pulling him clear, but shook his head over the rest, not believing it. "Why would I want to kill you?"

"Bad driving?"

That netted me a "go to hell" glower.

"Why do you think you wanted to kill me?" I asked.

He shrugged as best he could with his arms restricted. "Undo this, would you?"

"You going to go crazy again?"

"I've had two bad turns in cars in less than a week, how the hell am I supposed to know? C'mon, my head's killing me."

He did look bad, but his eyes were as normal as they could get—for him. I began to work the knot from the belt . . . and heard something.

Kroun caught it, too, and tried to stand. I shoved him back, signed that I'd check things, then moved toward the sound's source. Someone was working through the broken brush of the slope, following the trail my Buick had plowed. He was a distance away; only my hearing and the wind being in the right direction scotched his chance of going undetected.

The trees prevented me from seeing him. Between the trunks I caught a blur of a shadow heading toward my wrecked car. An innocent Samaritan might have seen the skirmish on the road and be checking for survivors, but my money was on its being the maniac from the diner come to finish us off. I was in a mood for dealing with the latter and crept closer. A little mayhem, followed by robbery, would suit me fine. Thump the guy to a pulp and take his car, yeah, that sounded good. Maybe I could persuade him to tell me why Mrs. Cabot had a grudge against Kroun.

The shadow far ahead was not careful about keeping quiet. The wind still restlessly stirred things around. He might have been counting on that to cover his own noise.

I could be absolutely silent, though. It just required going invisible.

Which I did, after fixing a direction in my mind and holding to it. I'd get to the car ahead of him, pop out of nowhere . . . yeah, a good old-fashioned bushwhack.

I streamed down the slope, flowing between trees, compensating for the push of the wind, going at a good clip. A partial re-forming showed that I was only five yards off course. I checked toward the road, hoping to spot him.

Lot of trees, black trunks stark against unbroken drifts of snow except for the wide gash the car had carved. My poor Buick was banged up, but not nearly as crumpled as it should have been. The armoring had held the frame intact, preventing it from pulping Kroun during the fall. He'd have probably survived, but he wouldn't have been happy.

Footsteps . . . up there. The man was too far away to see. Just another black shape concealed by the woods. Damn, but I preferred the straight lines of the city.

He paused a moment, probably checking things out. He might have smelled gas and was keeping a prudent distance. The wind was wrong for that, but the stuff was all over.

Something as big as a goose egg arced through the air. I could only track the movement and general size for a split second, then instinct took hold, and I vanished completely.

Damned smart of me. I'd have probably survived, but I wouldn't have been happy.

HE'D lobbed a grenade at the car.

I figured that out afterward.

The explosion—despite my muffled hearing—was impressive. Shrapnel and God knows what else tore into the space I'd occupied, violently and quick as thought. I felt each one, but had no real physical reaction. Stuff like that and bullets pass right through, disrupting a relatively small area.

Wind, on the other hand, can throw me around like a son of a bitch.

The grenade combined with the gasoline displaced a hellish amount of air in very short order. I didn't know what was going on, but the hurricane lasted entirely too long and was a few notches past unnerving. Abruptly going solid, I rolled downhill, no breath left in me but cursing a blue streak even when I picked up a mouthful of snow. I spat and rolled and cursed and vanished again, then popped back solid before coming to a halt.

It was another damned tree that did the halting. My upper legs banged against it, my body folded, and I finished up wrapped around the base of the trunk like a damp sheet of newspaper.

After all that I didn't feel like moving for a good long while. Except for a terrible roaring somewhere upslope, my world was fine just like this. I was tired. A nap would be nice. I couldn't have one, but it would have been nice.

The roar died, and the red lights dancing on the other side of my eyelids faded. By then I'd worked out what the goose-egg object had been and what the consequences of dropping one of those things close to a ruptured gas tank were, and that I'd gotten lucky.

Footsteps slogged my way.

Odds were the Caddy driver would miss me in the dark. He'd thrown his toy at the car, not me, probably unaware I was so close. I lay still and . . . well, it's not called waiting when you don't give a damn about what comes next.

The steps got closer, walked wide around the tree, then slowly approached.

Kroun crouched on his heels and squinted into my face. "Hey. You in there?"

He looked normal and had somehow recovered his hat. Mine was gone and my head was cold. I hated that he had a hat and I didn't. "Go 'way."

"Love to, but someone blew up your car, then lammed it. I might have stopped him from leaving if you hadn't trussed me like a turkey."

Yeah, I'll keep that in mind the next time you go nuts and start shooting at anything that moves. I wanted to say it, but all that came out was something sounding like, "Rrrer-nugh."

Kroun straightened, hands unencumbered by the belt that I'd tied tight enough to keep him out of trouble. He rethreaded it through the loops on his overcoat then bent again to peel me away from the tree.

That hurt, and I got even colder rolled out flat in the snow.

"You're a mess," he said, taking back the two guns I'd taken from him. He checked each for bullets and put them away. "Looks like you were right. I must have blacked out or something. Sorry."

"You do that a lot? Blacking out?"

"I wouldn't know now, would I?"

Good point.

"Come on, let's get clear before someone spots the smoke."

Oh, jeez. My car. I boosted up in stages after finding out just how dizzy my downslope tumble had made me, using the tree for support. I hung on to it like a drunk and gaped at what was left of my Buick. She lay belly-up, dead and strangely poignant. The gas had burned away; smoke from the still-burning seat covers and smoldering tires rose high into the night, making a terrible stink. The fire hadn't spread. The recent snowfall had discouraged that, thankfully.

Eventually I got close enough to throw snow on the tires to kill the smoke. It was a lot like dropping clods on a coffin after it was in the ground. She wasn't my first car, but had been the first one I'd paid for without help, even if I had taken the money from a gangster; I had a right to mourn.

"So . . ." said Kroun. "You got insurance?"

HITCHHIKING at night in the winter on a country road without your hat is terrifically boring. I don't recommend it, especially when you have to duck from sight to avoid grenade-throwing maniacs. Every time we spotted headlights, we dodged clear, so we weren't exactly hitching. My shoes and socks started out soaked through and icy and never improved despite the exercise.

Neither of us talked much. I was mad, and Kroun again mentioned that his head hurt, then shut down. At one point he made a snowball and held it against the white streak on the side of his skull, and apparently that helped. Sometime later he threw what was left of the ball at a fence post ten yards away, hitting it square. He grinned briefly and kept walking, taking on a cheerful gait. The way he could shift moods was both annoying and disturbing, and I wondered if that was a personal quirk or something to do with the bullet he carried.

We progressed a couple miles toward the city glow far ahead before hearing the low grumble of a truck motor coming east and decided to chance it. I stuck out a thumb; Kroun held up a ten-dollar bill.

The truck, a big one with a covered load caked with snow, slowed and stopped, the driver bawled down at us. "I'm goin' to Detroit. You?"

"Chicago," Kroun yelled back over the diesel noise. "Buy you gas to get there?"

"That's enough to pay for my whole trip. Climb in!"

I didn't get his name, but he and Kroun had a fine old chat about the weather, bad roads, lousy drivers, and who did what for a living. Kroun and I were stranded insurance salesmen whose car had died in a lonely and inconvenient spot. The driver was hauling machine parts and usually drove at night because there was less traffic.

The night-driving business bothered me, and I wondered if he was in the club, too. But he took a swig of coffee from a Thermos jug, and it smelled like coffee, not blood. He offered us some, which we turned down, and Kroun asked him about trucking jobs since it seemed a good way to make a living. That set me to wondering if he was just passing the time or really interested in the work. Though monotonous, it was one way to earn money without having someone looking over your shoulder.

"Your friend okay?" the trucker asked.

"He's just tired."

Nail on the head for that. I wanted to stretch out in a warm bed and ask Bobbi to rub the sore spots even if I didn't have any. If I turned up this late in her room, she was more likely to bounce a lamp off my noggin.

The driver was agreeable enough from the talk and the money to take a route through Chicago's North Side, dropping us at a hotel two blocks from the Nightcrawler Club. Kroun added another ten to the first, pumped the delighted man's hand, and wished him good luck on his haul. He sounded absolutely sincere, as though he'd made a new friend. When the truck was gone, he turned to look at me, his smile amiable. If he felt good, then the whole world should feel it, too.

"What?" he asked, when I just shook my head. "Is it the car?"

"You could say."

"I guess that was sort of my fault. We should have taken one of Gordy's. Tell you what, pick whatever you like, and I'll have Derner put your name on it."

"I don't want one of Gordy's cars."

"You're right. You should have something new." He pulled out one of the wads he'd taken from Michael and counted off a grand in hundreds. "This should set you up."

I took the money. The car was Kroun's fault, and that much cold cash did ease the sting. I was still mad and shaken that he'd shot at me, though there wasn't much I could do about it. As for what led to it . . . "Someone wants you dead and anyone with you. Why?"

That took his smile away.

"Nobody followed us out there. Your Mrs. Cabot called for help, and it came fast and packed grenades. Not a lot of farmers keep that kind of stuff in the toolshed. I wanna know what's going on. Everything."

Again, visible indecision as his mental gears spun and finally stopped. "Not now. I don't know when, but later."

"Why?"

"You'll know when I tell you."

It would be bad news, not that I expected any different, but he had a reason for having me along, and it wasn't just so I could tell tales to Michael.

With the wind freezing my ears and the street slush soaking my already wet shoes, I was in no mood to walk. The hotel had a taxi stand. I crossed to the first cab and got in. Kroun followed, and I gave directions. We got out again behind the Nightcrawler, and I tipped well since the drive was so short.

The delivery truck and mugs who had been in the alley were gone, but other mugs stood in their place. Soon as one of them saw us, he hurried inside.

"We're expected," said Kroun. He ran a hand over the white patch of hair and settled his hat in place. "Dammit."

Before we reached the back steps to the kitchen, Michael slammed the door open and came down. He was hatless, with no overcoat, evidently impatient.

"Where the hell have you been?" he demanded. He stopped and pushed his glasses up, giving us a once-over. "And what happened?"

"You tell me." Kroun put his hands in his pockets, apparently ready to stand outside all night and discuss it. "Where's Broder?"

"Back at the hotel. Why?"

"You sure he's at the hotel?"

Michael looked at me. "What's happened?"

I shifted in my soggy shoes. My feet were damned cold. "Somebody ran us off the road, then blew up the car. Does it bother you we got clear?"

He digested the news pretty quick. Smart guy, unless he'd known already. "You think it was Broder?"

"Unless it was you." I checked his shoes and pant cuffs—dry—but he'd had plenty of time to change from walking in knee-deep snow. "Give me proof to think otherwise."

"You—" Michael shut himself down. "Inside. We'll talk there."

"Mike," said Kroun. "Did you send Broder after us?"

He glared at me—I had the same idea, and it showed on my face—then he turned to Kroun. "No, I didn't."

"And you think he's at your hotel?"

"That's what he told me."

"Did you come after us?"

Michael shook his head. "I've been here all night waiting for you to turn up. Derner and half the dancers will tell you—"

"Only half?

"Never mind. Are you okay? You look like hell."

"I'm just peachy. Word to the wise, Mike: if it was Broder, you keep him out of my way. If it was some other mutt you let loose, you keep *him* out of my way."

"Are you done?" The wind was getting to Michael. He'd hunched in his suit coat, fighting off an initial bout of shivering.

"I'll tell you when I'm done."

"What'd the old bastard say to you?"

If the question was meant to surprise him, it didn't. Kroun took a moment, apparently considering his answer. "Not a damn thing. He's crazy, you know that?"

I got the sense that Michael was being careful not to look at me. He'd want to hear my version of tonight's fun and maybe hope Kroun wouldn't figure it out. I was tempted to vanish and let the wind carry me clear, but had a more prosaic option to take. "I'm leaving. See ya tomorrow."

"Not yet, you stay put," said Michael.

"I've punched my card for the night, I'm going home."

"And I need to talk to Derner," Kroun said. He stepped around Michael and went up the stairs, banging the door shut.

Michael started after him, then turned back to me. I picked up that he was worried, grimly worried.

"If you'd tell me what the problem is . . ." I said, slowly and calmly, though inside I was kicking myself. This was officially sticking my neck out. Or putting my foot in, I wasn't sure.

"Whitey didn't?"

I missed my hypnosis gag. It made many, many things a lot easier. "I think he means to."

"What happened with the old man? You were there, right?"

Kroun had allowed me into the small room with that two-legged snake, knowing I'd talk to Michael. Maybe it was why I'd been there. "The old man's crazy."

"Yes. But what did he say?"

"Whitey tried to get him to talk about that cabin, going up there for the fishing. The old guy seemed to think that would be a lot of fun. The rest of the time he was cussing us out or tearing pictures of women from a newspaper." I threw out the last bit to get Michael's reaction.

He pulled in on himself just that much more, nothing to do with the cold.

"That's why he's in the booby hatch, because of how he treats women?"

He kept his gaze fixed, unreadable.

It had long past come to me that if I showed too much interest, then dire consequences could follow. It might already be too late.

He gave me a long, assessing look. "About this car trouble—what exactly happened?"

"We were taking a drive in the country . . ." I made out that Kroun hadn't told me our destination, gotten us lost, and when we finally turned back to Chicago, the guy in the Caddy tried to kill us. It was a risk. If the guy was Broder, then Michael would learn his end of it and know I was lying for Kroun.

I wasn't exactly siding with him, but I did owe him for saving Escott's life. Besides, it might goad Michael into telling me something useful about whatever feud he had going. "If your boy Broder's behind this—"

"He won't be," Michael said quickly.

"You don't know that. He could have his own operation running, like the late, unlamented Mitchell. If that's the case, you may need a friend."

"You?"

"Uh-uh. Derner." I let that sink in. "I'm just a saloonkeeper. Soon as you guys leave town, I'm going back to my bar and keeping my nose clean. That's all I've ever wanted, it's no secret. For now I'm getting out of the cold, that was a hell of a long walk."

I turned to look for another cab, but he caught my arm. "Your car's wrecked?"

"Grenade, tank of gas—what do you think?"

"Here . . ." Damned if he didn't dig out a wad of cash and peel off ten portraits of Ben Franklin. "Get another on me."

He shoved the bills into my hand, then hurried back to the club, hunching low against the cold.

"Thanks!" I called after him. He raised one hand to show he'd heard, shot up the steps, and hustled inside.

I looked at the money. It was real. I would keep it. That Kroun had already bought me a replacement didn't matter. After tonight's excitement, I deserved a tip.

KROUN

GABE took the stairs to Gordy's office one at a time, but quick-stepping it. He wouldn't have much of a respite before Michael finished with Fleming and followed.

Derner didn't stare too much. "Have some trouble, Mr. Kroun?"

"You could say. I need a car. A good one, gassed up and with some heavy blankets in the back. No one's to know about it. Especially Michael."

"Uh . . . okay. Now?"

"Sooner."

That done, he crossed to the bathroom and shook out of his once-new coat. It wasn't a total loss, but the slush and mud stains annoyed him. No time to have it cleaned or get another.

He checked his faint reflection in the mirror and scrubbed the scrapes and dirt from his face. The hot water warmed his hands. He'd not realized how cold they'd been. Aware of the problem, he checked his shoes. Yeah, soaked and freezing, no wonder Fleming looked so miserable.

Gabriel gingerly touched the ridge in his skull, bracing for pain, but nothing blazed up. Holding that snowball against the damage had killed it. He'd have to buy an ice bag sometime.

He emerged, coat over one arm and a pistol in each hand. Derner was on the phone giving orders about the car and only looked a little curious when Gabe dumped the coat and put the guns on the desk. Gabe opened each, removing the empty cartridges from the revolver and checking how many bullets were left in the semiauto. He opened his hand in a "gimme" gesture. Derner pointed to a chrome-trimmed liquor cabinet against one wall and mimed opening a drawer.

The second drawer held boxes of ammunition of various types. Kroun found what he needed in the jumble and loaded his guns. He thought about packing extra bullets, deciding against it. If he couldn't turn a problem in his favor with the loads he had, then it was unturnable.

It griped that he'd had no chance to resolve matters with Mrs. Cabot, but the woman had surprised the hell out of him. Fleming should have done something then, damn him. He could have gone invisible and gotten the drop on her while they were there.

Instead, he hauls me clear.

But to be fair, Gabe hadn't argued the point. Though more or less bulletproof, he had no desire to go through another night coughing his lungs out and feeling that burning inside as he healed. But what was Fleming's excuse? On the other hand, any man with sense would have run from Mrs. Cabot and her six-shooter. The look she wore could scare granite.

What the hell had happened to her daughter in that cabin?

And was it my fault?

He felt cold sweat along his flanks, his usual reaction to the not-knowing.

"Got your car, Mr. Kroun," said Derner. "It'll be out back in five minutes with a driver."

"I won't need the driver."

"Oh. Okay."

"You remember my last visit here? When was that?"

"Uh, yeah. August."

"August. Not December?"

"No, sir. I had to get you tickets for Wrigley Field, and it was hotter 'n hell you said."

Gabe put his fists on the desk and leaned in; Derner blinked under the pressure but filled out the details. He had no idea who Ramsey was or where he might be. He did not know anything about a girl named Nelly Cabot or her mother. Gabe told him to forget and eased back.

A couple nights ago, Gordy had given the same story about Ramsey, didn't know about Kroun's December visit, and chances were he was ignorant of the Cabots. Whatever business had brought Gabe to Chicago two months ago had been very much under the table.

"Gabriel," said Michael from the doorway. He always used that tone and that name when he thought things were truly serious.

He turned, on guard as always with Mike, which was a shame. He wanted to like the guy. He *did* like the guy, but couldn't trust him. "You look cold. Why don't you get one of those chorus girls to fix that?"

Michael scowled and couldn't suppress a shiver, and it clearly irritated him. "Where did you go tonight?"

"You already know."

"Besides seeing *him*."

"I got a haircut."

"A haircut?"

Gabe brushed the side of his head and put on his hat. "I got 'em all cut for that matter. The barber talked boxing, and I didn't listen." Gabe pulled on his damp overcoat and slipped the semiauto in the shoulder holster. As he reached for the revolver, Michael beat him to it.

"That's mine," he said. The gun rested lightly in his grip, not pointing at anyone, but ready for use. He had long strong fingers, and they reminded Gabe of Sonny's hands.

"It's reloaded," he said cheerfully.

"Who did you shoot?" Michael's tone matched the cheer.

"Doesn't matter. I missed."

"You?"

"It was a new gun."

"Who'd you shoot?"

"Black Cadillac, last year's model. It'll have a damaged front bumper, a lot of scrapes along the passenger side, and a bullet hole in the windshield. Ask Broder. Let him explain."

Derner, who had gone very quiet as soon as Michael walked in, made a soft sound from the back of his throat. It had to be involuntary, the man was trying his best to be invisible.

"What do you know?" Michael asked him.

"Uh, I got a call about that. One of the club Caddies was stolen earlier. The boys were hopping mad about it. No one saw anything. They figured some kids hot-wired it and drove off. Anyone else wouldn't dare. We don't know where it is."

"Have them look within walking distance of Mike's hotel," Kroun suggested. "Was it stolen at about the time Broder left here? No, don't tell me, Mike will deal with it. I have to go." He pushed past, aiming for the door and hoping things were off-balance enough for him to make a clean getaway.

"Where?" Michael demanded.

"Wrigley Field. I heard it's an ice rink now."

Mike didn't follow. Gabe had raised enough doubts to make him think twice about Broder.

Seems pretty obvious.

Gabe hadn't been a hundred percent on it, but the timing worked out right.

Mrs. Cabot had called for help, and while he and Fleming waited in the woods, Broder came rolling up in his stolen car. He had no reluctance about running them off the road and dropping a grenade on the wreck. He was not concerned about consequences. That was Broder all over.

Was he on his own or working for Michael? How did the woman even know to call Broder? Or had she wanted Michael, and Broder answered instead? She'd have had to call New York first. No one there would have given up the name of Michael's hotel, but they'd have passed on the message. How did she rate that kind of service?

Or had it been Ramsey? Maybe he's still involved.

Michael wouldn't lie to him, but neither would he tell him everything. Gabe was tempted to go back, put the eye on Mike, open up his head, and find out what lay inside.

Not here.

Not at the Nightcrawler. He'd need someplace more private. He needed better questions to ask, too. Gabriel didn't *know* enough yet to ask the right ones.

The car was a new Hudson, painted a snappy green. It was warmed up, the tank full, and four thick wool blankets lay neatly folded on the backseat. What had Derner made of that request? Probably something to do with body disposal. He wouldn't be too far off.

The waiting driver was a young, friendly, chatty sort, with a mouthful of chewing gum. Gabe thanked him and got rid of him quick.

Once behind the wheel, Gabe went easy for a block to get the feel of the gears, then headed toward Fleming's house. He still had his crumpled and damp Chicago map in one pocket and only had to pull over once to get his bearings.

The lights were on, but no one answered the bell. He let himself in and listened. The house was empty, the only noise coming from the electric icebox. Good, else he'd have to put up with a bunch of questions from Fleming.

Gabe thought about tracking down the doctor who had treated Nelly Cabot. The man would have questioned Nelly and very probably called someone else for help with the problem. Not anyone in Chicago, or Gordy would have heard something. The disappeared doctor had apparently been high enough in the pecking order to have a number direct to New York. If so, then some word of what had happened must have reached Michael.

Who doesn't want me anywhere near that cabin.

That is, if Mike and Broder had been there . . . or had it been only Ramsey's doing?

The lack of memory was a different sort of pain than the physical kind that often hammered at Gabe's skull, but just as intense.

Gabe cracked open one of the suitcases and pulled on fresh clothes. The dry socks were the best improvement; he wore three pair since they were the fancy silk kind and thin. Wool would have been better for this trip. He wanted woodsmen boots, too, but had only the one pair of shoes. Wet, of course. None of the clothes he'd bought during that ten-minute shopping jaunt were suitable, but he'd survive. He left his discards draped on the stair rail for Fleming to marvel over and snapped the suitcase shut. He thought of taking it, but decided against. Better to travel light and make everyone think he'd be back for his stuff.

He *planned* to return, after all.

Thoughtfully, he relocked the door when he left.

The Hudson ran a little rough, but he got used to it. He checked his map again, compared its routes to the directions Fleming had so accurately copied down. It seemed simple enough: get out of Chicago, head north, follow this line, then that one.

Depending on the roads, he could make pretty good time before dawn.

11

FLEMING

I got one of the friendlier mugs at the Nightcrawler to give me a lift home and to take the long way so I could hear the club gossip. He filled me in, carefully not inquiring about my own state of scruffiness. Things in the trenches were copacetic, considering. Some of the guys were edgy about the Alan Caine murder, but only because the cops had hauled a few in for questioning. Chicago's finest were looking for Mitchell, but they'd have to hold a séance to get him now. He'd had a summons to a higher court, and good riddance to the bastard.

When I asked about my called-off hunt for Gilbert Dugan, the mug didn't have anything that could be called cheerful. Half the guys who'd wanted the reward money felt cheated, and the other half thought I'd just blown smoke to make myself look important. I shrugged it off as booze talk. Some of the boys were smart, like Derner and Strome, the rest couldn't beat a monkey at checkers.

Our ramble around the Loop turned up an unexpected bonus: a butcher shop that was open. Lights were on, and they seemed to be taking a delivery via the side alley door. Open late or up early, it would save me a trip to the Stockyards. My last meal had been interrupted, and tonight's exertions left me tired and in want of fuel, fresh or not. What they had couldn't be worse than the stuff I stored at home. I had the guy pull over.

My order got me a predictably fishy look from the hired help. He couldn't have had many customers stopping in at this hour in need of a pint of beef blood, but the crisp dollar bill I put on the counter must have reminded him the customer was always right. He put the stuff in a thick cardboard container, passed it across, and I told him to keep the change. He told me to come back soon, adding a smile that looked genuine.

I emerged, signed for my driver to wait, strode purposely off to the next alley, turning into its shadowed cover. Human eyes had no chance in this darkness, so I eased the top from the container and sniffed the contents. Not fresh, but better than anticipated. One sip, then another. Not bad. Though cold, it raised a nice heat in my belly that spread to my limbs. I'd taken a lot of abuse; it was good to feel warm again.

Only after I'd eagerly and with much relish drained off the last ounce did I realize I was not in the throes of frenzied compulsion. I'd taken in enough and was satisfied. The thought of going back to the shop for more raised no impulse within to do so. I gave it a few minutes just to be sure, then got bored with the waiting. Tossing the cardboard into a dented trash can, I left, revived and hopeful about . . . well, everything.

I took care not to look at my driver, knowing my blood-flushed eyes were something he wouldn't want to see. He asked no questions about our stop, seemed utterly incurious about it, and I liked that. Strome would have also not asked questions, but he'd have wondered.

My driver dropped me at the front door of my home and settled in to wait again. Apparently he didn't know I lived in the old pile. I tipped him a magnanimous five and told him to spend it in one place. He told me I was a card and rumbled away.

I unlocked the door and listened, but the house was quiet. A quick check proved that I was alone. The only intruder must have been Kroun, to judge by the discarded clothing thrown over the stair rail. His suitcases were here, so he'd return.

Maybe. He'd be off making another try at seeing Mrs. Cabot, I was sure of it, and if he wasn't quick enough, she'd put a second bullet in his skull. He could do his own damned sneaking around, though, I'd had enough. Michael could find someone else to babysit.

Upstairs I washed and changed into dry clothes, which improved my mood. I hid the two grand inside a hollowed-out book in my room and felt even better. That much money could buy a lot of car with plenty of change left over.

For insurance. Yeah. This time I would get insurance.

I phoned for a taxi, scrounged a dry overcoat from the hall closet, and had sorted through the day's mail just as my ride pulled up. A lot of them had radios just like the cops, and it made things faster. I gave the driver directions rather than say outright the address. Some guys were reluctant to go to the Bronze Belt, daylight or dark.

I spared this one and paid him off in front of a drugstore in a border area, going inside to phone Bobbi. She sounded awake and yes, she still wanted me to come over. Just as I'd done earlier, I walked within sight of Coldfield's hotel, then vanished, skimming the rest of the way unseen, eventually slipping inside. It took a few minutes to find Bobbi's door, but I figured it out.

When I was solid again, it was in a room very similar to Gordy's. Just one light by the bed was on. Newspapers and a couple of magazines lay on the floor by a reading chair. The radio played softly. I heard water running in her bathroom. She finished brushing her teeth and came out, stopping short with surprise.

"Wow, that was quick," she said.

"You complaining?"

"Nope."

The next little while was very pleasant for us.

It had been an ice age since I'd last held her, and this time it wasn't about hanging on to life and sanity or shared grief for a dying friend. If she sensed that, it didn't show. Tonight was about us being together.

I wasn't sure how things would go. If I felt the onset of a seizure, I'd have to leave, whatever the consequences. Better that I hurt her feelings than do something much, much worse.

When those fits began ambushing me, I'd not dared to go near Bobbi. While feeding at the Stockyards, I'd taken in more than was needed or wanted by my body. I'd fed until it was agony, then fed some more. Now I understood it was connected to how starved I'd been for blood when Hog Bristow had been carving on me. Some part of my mind was trying to take back that lost blood, unable to accept that the crisis was past.

The gorging had terrified me. If it took over at the wrong time, I could kill Bobbi.

My taking from her when we made love was a very delicate process; I *had* to be in control. Too deep a bite, too great a flow, too long a drink, and she could die.

Since the fight with Escott, though . . . I felt different. Much had changed that night and since.

"I talked with Charles," I said. "We're still friends."

"He told me when he came back. He's in his room if you want to see him again."

"No, thanks." She had to be kidding. I wasn't about to leave. However things went, I just wanted to be with her.

So far as I could tell through the smooth fabric of her silk robe, she didn't have anything on under it. I breathed in the scent of her hair while kissing her temple and tried holding her even closer. My body reacted to this in an entirely normal manner, which was damned reassuring.

"Ho-ho," she said, pressing against me down there. "Isn't this nice?"

"Oh, yeah." I felt my corner teeth budding—from arousal, not hunger. There's a big difference between the two.

But she pulled back a little. "Are you all right, Jack? I mean it. You've been—"

"I know what I've been, baby. And I'm sorry. I didn't . . . I wasn't ready."

"You sure you are now?"

"Pretty sure. Be gentle with me?"

She snickered, pressing close again. "The walls here . . . I'll have to be quiet."

"Both of us." After a moment, I took off my overcoat and suit coat, just to start things.

She liked to undress me and began with my tie, working her way down. In short order my tie was off and shirt open, and she stopped, stopped cold.

"Oh, Jack . . . oh, my God, sweetheart . . . I didn't *know*."

Oh, *hell*.

I'd forgotten the scars. A wave of mortification started up from God knows where, but I smothered it, quick and with absolute finality. They weren't my fault. I had nothing to be ashamed of; she'd have to see them sooner or later. "It's all right. They don't hurt."

Bobbi was a woman who didn't cry much, hated to cry, but she gave in to it now, silently, tears brimming, then streaming from her eyes. "I'm sorry," she whispered.

I couldn't think of anything to say. Might as well get it over with and let her have the worst of it. I removed my shirt and turned slowly so she could see them all, see every last square inch of Bristow's brutal handiwork—chest, arms, and back covered with thin white threads where he'd stripped away the skin with his knife. Ugly.

But I'd survived. I'd earned them.

She rushed back to the bathroom, shut the door, and sobbed.

I waited her out. When she was ready, she'd emerge again. It was how we did things. While I was prepared to offer her a shoulder to soak, that wasn't what she wanted this time.

The wait was hard, but I felt strangely patient. I thought about putting the shirt on again, but decided against.

Bobbi blew her nose, splashed water, and returned. She'd smoothed her expression out, but I didn't think she was finished with the high emotions just yet.

"They don't hurt," I gently repeated.

"Why don't they heal? When you vanish, shouldn't they—"

I shrugged. "I don't know." Maybe the damage had been too great or I'd come too close to death or bled too much or it was all in my head. Pick one, pick them all. "They might fade with time. Just have to wait and see."

"Is it all right if I . . ." She faltered, staring.

I took her hand in both of mine. "You don't have to. We can wait."

"What?" She broke off her stare. "Wait? What are you talking about?"

"Uh . . ."

"You think I don't want to be with you because of this?"

"I'll understand if you—"

The blazing glare she shot shut me right up. "Jack Fleming, stop being an ass."

"Yes, ma'am."

We didn't say anything for a while. She looked at my scars; I didn't know where to look. The mood was shattered. We'd been together long enough to not try forcing things back into place. It was there, or it wasn't.

She tentatively put her hand on my chest. "Is that okay?"

"Yes." I was not going to push her. She had a lot to absorb, and it could take days, weeks. However long, I would wait.

"You're so cold."

I didn't feel it. "How 'bout you?"

She made no reply, still getting acquainted with the changes, touching me. "I'm fine. I'm so sorry."

"It's all right." I wasn't sure what she was sorry about, that I'd suffered so much or that she'd not fully understood the extent of it. It was pointless to dwell, though.

She took my hand, tugging just a little. "Come on."

"Wha . . . ?"

"Let's just take this slow. Get to know each other again." She backed toward the bed.

"You sure?"

No reply, unless unbuttoning my trousers counted.

She tenderly stripped me, shed her robe, and we slipped between the clean white sheets. Kissing, lots of kissing. I'd missed that.

"We can shut the light off if you want," I suggested when she paused for breath.

"You'll still be able to see me. I want to be able to see you."

"So I really should stop being an ass?"

"Uh-huh."

She rolled on top, straddling me. I sprawled, arms up, fingers grasping the head rail of the bed. She moved over me, scarred skin and all, and at some point murmured that I was feeling warmer. Then she was too busy to talk, her beautiful mouth doing other things.

I didn't usually breathe, but could certainly gasp and call on God when inspired to do so.

Bobbi threw me a quick smile at my reaction and went back to driving me crazy. I remembered to keep quiet, but there was no helping the squeaking bedsprings as we rolled around, and I turned the tables. With my confidence restored, I pushed her legs apart and gave as good as I got. She stuffed a corner of a pillow in her mouth and bit hard on it as I kissed and teased and tasted.

"Jack." She had the softest whisper. That tone meant she was close to a release. I pulled away and moved up.

"You bastard," she said, grinning, reaching. I didn't move and let her play some more, but there was only so much I could take.

Rolling again until she was on top, she guided me in. She eased forward, her neck taut, brushing against my lips. I didn't take the invitation, though my teeth were out.

"Soon," I said.

She rode me, and I looked on her face in delight, wonderment, and awe as she climaxed. It was as intense as hell but all too brief, and she did not quite succeed at keeping quiet. As the last of it passed, she slumped forward, and I caught her shoulders, easing her on her side, then her back. I was still erect and hard and in need of my own release. I'd seen where she'd gone, my turn to take her there again . . . for a longer visit.

The vein in her neck pulsed, her heart pumping strongly, her blood rushing swift. I kissed her there for a long moment, this time teasing myself. She pressed the back of my head, urging.

But I moved down, nuzzling her breasts for some while before going lower, pausing at the velvet-smooth skin just below her navel, then biting just deep enough and no more. A very tiny flow beaded up, just enough to taste and trigger my own climax. Her response was immediate and strong, and she smothered her cry with one hand. I drew hard, seeming to feed as much from her reaction as from the small wounds in her sweet flesh. Her pleasure was mine, while it lasted. This was no slow rise and fast fall of sensation; I had us both at a peak and could keep us there for hours.

We had the time.

As requested, I took it slow.

SHE slept in my arms for a long while afterward. I kept still and held her until my muscles burned, and I was thankful for it. A sweet feeling that I eventually recognized as absolute contentment saturated me through and through. We had no past or future, the present was everything and more than enough. Those moments never last, of course, but while this one was upon me I would enjoy it. I wanted to sleep as well, but the closest I could get was this sense-swamped doze.

However thin the walls, no one had bothered to investigate the noise we'd made. This was a real hotel, and doubtless others were here tonight who had indulged themselves in a similar manner. Eyes half-closed, I drowsily regarded the shadows on the ceiling, and even at this late hour heard activity in the various rooms. Snoring was the main sound, distant, originating from several individuals on this and the other floors. A night owl's radio played far down the hall. The one in our room was tuned to a station that had signed off for the night a while ago; only low static came through the speaker. I pretended it was rain. In a few more weeks, if we were lucky, the first spring rains would fall and eat away the snow. That would be good.

Bobbi stirred, murmured something, and left our bed. She went to the bathroom still half-asleep, but returned woken up again.

Those moments . . . never long enough.

She turned the bedside light out and snuggled close for warmth. "Can we talk?"

Women. Always talking. Gordy had that right. "Aren't you tired?"

"Wonderfully tired."

"But things have been happening?"

"A lot of things."

"What's the matter?"

"You are such a pessimist."

"Which is how I can always be pleasantly surprised. On the phone you said there's more. This is the more?"

"A big bunch of more." Her tone indicated it could be a good thing.

"I'm not going anywhere."

She held her breath, then let it out. "It's to do with Roland and Faustine and Lenny Larsen going out to Hollywood."

"Yeah, he fixed them up with a movie you said."

"Not all of it. They want me to come out, too. Lenny can get me a screen test."

At that I went very, very still. With no breath or heartbeat, it's easy.

"Jack . . . ?"

"You serious?"

"Yes. This is what—"

"I know what it is."

She'd been working, dreaming, and praying for this. She had the talent and at long, long last the door had opened for her. I'd known that it would happen sooner or later, but had hoped for later.

"Jack?"

"Well, this is great." I tried to sound happy for her, but it didn't work. It failed miserably.

"You hate it."

"No, baby. I'm . . . getting used to the idea." I couldn't let her see that she'd pushed me off a cliff. Good thing the light was out. If she saw my face, she might start crying again. "When?"

"Not right away. Roland's in no shape to travel."

We had a couple weeks then. Plenty of time for me to get used to things. Maybe.

"Look, this might not work out. I could take the test, and they might not want me."

"Of course they will. They're not dopes."

"Jack—I want you to come with us."

We'd discussed this angle before. We knew it by heart. I didn't want to go to sunny California. My job was in Chicago, my friends, everything. I wouldn't know what to do with myself surrounded by movie people and orange groves. The one thing I could not do at this moment was to give her a blunt *no* or the coward's no of a weak and limping *I'll think about it.*

"Will you think about it?" she asked, and I wondered for the umpteenth time if she could read minds.

"Of course. This is a lot." Like getting gut-punched, only I couldn't vanish and heal from it.

"Your nightclub. I know what it means to you."

And I knew what this meant to her. The one sure way to lose her forever would be to try holding her back. She'd had this dream long before we'd met. She loved me but wouldn't put up with me being an unreasonable, selfish ass.

I thought of another angle that we'd never discussed. I had one hell of a lot of time ahead of me, decades, centuries of it. Bobbi had only a short span, and not just her lifetime. She had precious few years left of still being young enough for the merciless cameras to find her interesting.

"I'll think about it, baby," I heard myself saying, but it sounded sincere. "I mean that."

Dammit. She started crying again.

And kissing me.

Okay, I liked that part.

I left well before dawn and walked in the cold for a while, head down, trying to think.

Solutions to my problems came easily to me during that walk—what I wanted was some way to quash them.

Yes, I could hire a general manager to look after Lady Crymsyn. Gordy could help there and keep things aboveboard, no gambling, good acts, plenty of business, and someone mailing me a check each week. Hire the right people, and the place could run itself.

But I didn't want that easy a fix. I wanted a way to stop it, stop her, and it just wasn't coming to me.

There was no reason why I shouldn't go with Bobbi and the others when the time came. None at all.

So why did this feel like the end of the world?

That sweet contentment was gone. In its place ... yeah, something familiar and dark had flooded in.

When Maureen—my lover, the woman who gave me her blood, who changed me forever—when she vanished with no word, no explanation, that was a world-ender for me.

She'd never returned.

That too-familiar dark was the fear that I would lose Bobbi, too. Not in the same way, but just as permanently.

Damned stupid to feel like that, but there it was.

It had been a hell of a night. I needed a day's rest and would figure things out later. The situation would be there when I woke, but my mind would be clear. I'd think of something brilliant then.

Making my way to an el platform, I waited for one of the early trains. It took me to the stop close to Lady Crymsyn. I passed the drugstore where Kroun had bought the cigars. He was a problem that could wait as well.

The club's outside lights were off. I let myself in and locked up behind.

"Hello, Myrna," I said to the empty lobby. The light behind the bar remained steady. I listened, but the place was eerily quiet. That was wrong. It should be full of people and music, with Bobbi on the stage singing under the spotlights. Why couldn't that be enough for her?

I climbed the stairs. My office was dark, the radio off. I changed that, wanting sound and illumination, if only in this small space.

While the radio warmed up, I dropped in the chair behind my desk and had an unsettled moment noticing that things had been changed around. The mail wasn't in its usual spot, items were lined up, pencils sharpened. In the middle of the blotter was a thin stack of writing paper. The sheets had been crumpled, then spread flat. They bore my handwriting. My hand was usually hard to read—the years in journalism had degraded it—but the lines I'd put down were strangely neat, almost mechanical. In them I had tried to explain the inexplicable. I'd given up and left them unfinished.

Escott had spent hours sitting here. He'd walked in, found me on the couch with a hole blown through my skull, seen the gun, and in the trash found the notes I'd attempted. He'd have read them, over and over.

I couldn't imagine what he'd gone through in those hours before sunset waiting to see if I would wake up. For distraction he'd cleaned things, made order from the chaos, enforced some form of control in the room despite the cold presence of my corpse. He had sat in my chair, thought God knows what thoughts, and . . .

How could I have done that to him?

And how had he ever been able to forgive me?

Feeling sick, my face hot with fresh shame, I crumpled the papers again, took a big glass ashtray from a table, and burned them in it. The fire flared and died, the smoke lingered a bit longer. I used the blunt end of a pencil to crush what was left to gray powder. No one else would ever know about this.

The radio now played dance music, but when an announcer came on he was replaced in midword by a polka tune. Myrna was up and about. Of course I'd missed seeing the radio dial move. The polka ended, and some guy spoke enthusiastically in German or Polish. Another polka started. Who on God's green earth would be in need of such music at this hour in the morning?

"Hi, Myrna," I said again. "I've had a rough night."

Maybe I could tell her about it, but where to begin?

The less sprightly dance music returned. I didn't see the dialing knob move then, either.

"I'm spending the day here, if you don't mind."

I stared at the long leather couch against the wall opposite my desk. I'd planned to lock the door and sleep the day through on that couch, having done it many times before.

Not tonight. I couldn't go near the thing now.

At the far end was a hole in the leather back, and a messy spray of dried blood, visible evidence of my attempt to kill myself. The wooden slug I'd carved was probably embedded in the stuffing someplace.

It seemed like some other man had gone through that horror, suffered with and then caved in to despair. How could I have been that man?

I wasn't.

He'd been Hog Bristow's awful creation. Some portion of him was still inside, but no longer able to influence me. Maybe with time he would fade completely. I wanted that.

I should leave the couch there as a reminder never to be stupid again, but Bobbi would see the damage and ask questions. She wouldn't be fobbed off with a lie, and knowing me as well as she did, might even figure things out.

That couch was the scene of an attempted murder. Looking at the bullet hole and stains made me feel like I was my own ghost. No way in hell was I going to keep that hunk of furniture here one more minute. It had to go.

After removing several oilcloth packets of my home earth from under the cushions, I considered how to move it out. It was too big to push through the window. While I had the strength to lift it easily, I was short on space and leverage. The thing was almost too wide to get through the door and had to go in stages, pushed through until it wedged against the wall opposite. I had to crawl over to pull, then crawl back to push, and was sweating by the time I got the awkward bastard clear. How anyone had gotten it into the office in the first place was beyond me.

I manhandled it down the hall and regarded the stairs with aggravation. Certainly I could pitch the whole thing down, not caring if it broke apart, but the marble-tile floors below were of some concern. I didn't know how much abuse they could take before shattering.

In the end I took the hard road and worked the couch gradually down the steps into the lobby and outside. Once there I carried it toward the parking lot, placing it on the edge of the curb, where it would not block foot traffic. I had every confidence that some scavenger would take it away before the day had passed. The bloodstains and that hole might make someone wonder . . .

To hell with it. I couldn't be bothered with "what ifs" and went inside, locking the front doors with a sense of relief.

My office looked considerably larger now. Perhaps I could leave it this way with no couch, bringing in a couple of chairs instead. But the old caveman inside reminded me that sometimes Bobbi and I found a couch to be a very convenient and comfortable place for reclining.

I'd get a new one—but what was the point if she was leaving for Hollywood?

I sat behind the desk and scowled at its tidiness. There was always something that needed to be done, my club kept me damned busy. I always had paperwork, mail to answer, supplies to order; even with the place closed there was work needing attention, and I *liked* that work. But tonight I had absolutely nothing to keep me from thinking about Bobbi leaving.

Damn it.

Getting hot under the collar, pacing, grumbling about how unfair the world was, eventually speaking aloud, eventually shouting, it came rushing out, all the stuff I couldn't say to her face.

Just as some tiny bit of normality began to creep back to my life, *this* had to happen. I didn't want it. I wanted Bobbi to stay here and for things to be like they'd been. My job was to run a fancy nightclub, glad-hand happy customers, and her job was to be onstage singing to them. Her job was to be my girl, not go running off to be a movie star.

I got louder as what churned through my head got worse. The depth of anger surprised me, and I gave in to it. By God, she wasn't going to do this to me. How dare she? After all the crap I'd been through, I needed her *here*. I'd put my foot down—

The glass ashtray flew off the desk. The damn thing *launched* itself, crashing against a wall, landing hard on the wood floor, scattering ash from the burned notes, making a hell of a noise—yet not breaking.

I yelped and jumped about two miles.

As I stared at the ashtray, it slid half a yard toward me. It was as though someone had kicked it along. The glass grated loud over the wood. It moved again, half as far, then stopped. The place was silent. Even the radio was turned down. I seemed to feel a kind of pressure around me, like a pending storm.

Myrna.

She'd scared the hell out of me. All the anger, too. I would never have cut loose like that had anyone been here, but had forgotten about her. She must have gotten fed up. Dames. Always sticking together.

"Sorry," I said.

The lights remained steady. The radio music came up. Dance music. She was getting stronger, I thought.

In a much calmer tone—and feeling like a fool for talking to what might well be an empty room—I told Myrna what was going on and the problems it had brought and the fears I had. Whether she hung around to listen was unimportant, I let it pour out until nothing remained.

The room was quiet, but it was different from that earlier angry silence. At some point the radio had switched off again. The only sound was the desk clock ticking and the distant hiss of traffic in the waking streets below.

I'd not made a decision, nor did I feel any better, but the worst was past. Thankfully, Bobbi would never hear any of it.

Maybe things would be more clear tomorrow.

A glance at the clock told me to get moving if I wanted to beat the dawn.

I went downstairs into darkness. The light behind the bar was off. Myrna always liked having it on. Maybe the bulb had burned out again; it often did. No time to check and change it. I continued through to the main room, crossing to the larger bar at the far end.

The three tiers of platforms for tables and booths arranged in an ascending horseshoe shape created a lot of dead space below, but it wasn't wasted. A small access door led under the seating, and we used the area for storage. Usually I spent the day up in the office when I didn't feel like driving home, but this bolt-hole was more secure. I'd taken pains over it.

The storage section was sizable, stacked with bar supplies and extra chairs, with an unremarkable plywood wall that blocked access to the rest of the dead space. The wall looked solid, but with Escott's help I'd put in a hidden door. You had to know it was there, and even then you had to look hard for the trigger to get it open. The door was partially blocked by boxes; I usually entered by sieving through. Inside was a sliding bolt lock so I could seal myself in. I wouldn't have bothered with a door at all, but Escott pointed out that sometime or other I might have need of one should there be an emergency. The only drawback was that the place wasn't fireproof.

I vanished and went inside.

The concealed area was roomy, plenty of space for an army cot with a layer of my earth under an oilcloth sheet, a box, and a lamp on the box. It was a near duplication of the basement sanctuary at home. I re-formed in darkness and fumbled quickly to switch the lamp on. Nothing had changed since my last visit, just a little more dust than before. On the cot were several spare oilcloth packets of my home earth and a months-old *Adventure Tales* I'd forgotten. Well, something to read before the day took me. I had been thinking of writing a story for . . . maybe I could get back to that. In California, with no nightclub to distract me, I'd have plenty of time to write.

I snarled again. That was too much like giving in.

The cot-side lamp flickered.

"Not now, Myrna. I'm too tired, and it's too late."

It went out completely.

Damn her. What was her problem? Probably still mad about me yelling to myself up in the office.

I hated the dark, but had come prepared. On the way down, I'd pocketed one of the many flashlights scattered throughout the building. I took it out, snicking it on.

"So there." I slid the bolt, officially shutting myself away from the rest of the world for the next several hours.

Stretched on the cot, I opened the magazine and its half-remembered stories, flipping to an editorial page. Nothing like out-of-date opinions for numbing the mind.

The lamp came on again, very bright. I cut the flash and checked my watch. Not long now. No more than a few seconds. I felt the sluggishness sweep over me. It was a sweet lethargy. Things would look after themselves while I got a good day's rest. I fell gently toward that stupor, carefully not thinking about Bobbi leaving me.

The lamp went off-on-off-on.

Oh, hell.

Something was *wrong*. My internal alarm finally got the message and shrieked a belated warning. I struggled to stay awake, but was too far over the edge.

At the very last instant before slipping away, I heard the destructive crash as the hidden door was forced open, lock and all, then a shadow blocked the lamp's light from my now-sealed eyelids.

Too late. Much too late.

I'd made a terrible, terrible mistake—

12

KROUN

THE lines on the map and the written directions bore no resemblance to the actual lay of the road, Gabe decided.

He'd planned to be patient, aware he was exploring unknown territory, knowing it might take a while to find the right turnoff, but after a futile hour of cruising up and down, backtracking, and finding one dead end after another, he was justifiably irritated.

Somewhere he'd missed something. That, or Fleming had written things down wrong.

Or Sonny had given the wrong—

Gabe allowed himself a snarl of disgust, then hauled the wheel around in yet another U-turn. He went back three long miles in the country darkness to the last intersection, where a crooked sign pointed the way to the nearest town. The name held no meaning for him; it was ten miles distant and not on the route.

He stopped the Hudson, letting it idle, and got out to look at the sign.

As he thought, it was loose in the ground. Some fool had knocked it over and put it back, pointing in the wrong direction. A swell joke to play on a nonlocal, yessiree, that's a real knee-slapper.

Gabe slammed the wooden post into the ground so the sign was parallel with the road, then checked the written directions against the map.

Okay, *that* made sense.

Back in the car, he turned left from the intersection and covered five empty miles, counting them off and slowing. The trees were thick and grew close to the road, their black branches arching over and meeting high above, making a skeletal tunnel. Snow, unbroken except for animal tracks, lay heavy over humped shapes that marked brush and stumps. Plenty of deer were about; he'd seen a few dead ones on the way up. No roadside bodies mangled by hurtling machines were here, though. If Farmer Jones hit one with the old truck, then it would be fresh venison for supper that night. Country folk knew better than to high-hat a free meal.

The tires crunched a new path through the snow. No one had been up this way at least since the last fall, however long ago that had been.

Some flash of memory had him hitting the brake without benefit of thought, and the Hudson slewed and skidded to a reluctant halt.

He stared at three oak trees on the left, each more than a foot thick and planted so close that the trunks were fused together for about fifteen feet before separating into different directions. Some of their upper branches had twined as well in the struggle to obtain more sunlight. The thing was one huge, ungainly knot. The ground was distorted on one side where the roots were exposed, poking up from the snow in a black tangle, their fight continuing on under the earth. Rot had set in on one of the trees, and in the course of time it would spread and kill the others. Though not in the directions, this was a landmark he recognized; he could not recall details, only that it was important.

Just past the oaks was a break in the woods lining the road, no more than eight feet wide and overgrown, very easy to miss. The snow looked deep, and not even animal tracks crossed it. This was the turn he wanted, the one that would lead to the cabin.

He worked gears, fed the car gas, and urged it in. The Hudson rocked and slid over ruts hidden by the snow until it bumped something that scraped alarmingly along the undercarriage. It pressed gamely on, but Gabe judged that was far enough; no point in breaking an axle. He was well out of sight from the road. Anyone driving past might notice the tire tracks, but he doubted there was much traffic at this time of year. This area was disturbingly isolated.

He cut the motor and got out, feet sinking deep into a drift. There was less snow under the trees, so he floundered toward their cover, then threaded cautiously forward. Ahead, he heard the murmur of flowing water, lots of it.

The cabin was a few hundred yards in and dark. He expected as much, but studied the area carefully, looking for fresh prints in the snow as he made a wide circle. No recent visitors. Good.

The structure was about twenty feet to a side, with a stovepipe piercing a roof that extended out over a porch that ran the width of the front. Its one door faced a gradual downward slope that led to a wide black river. The far bank was a thin gray line covered with unbroken pine and beeches.

Gabriel couldn't remember its name but knew that he had fished there, his legs hanging over the edge of a boat dock, bare feet in the water, a blue, blue sky above, and sweet summer sun pleasantly baking the top of his head. In the mornings and late afternoons, the sun would spark on the water, the reflected light dazzling him.

Very unexpectedly he choked and felt chill, wet trails from his eyes. He swiped at them, embarrassed, ashamed . . . and suddenly afraid. Men don't cry. Especially if . . . but he couldn't carry the thought further than that; his memory failed yet again.

He'd fished in that river, but not here. No dock was in sight, nor the remains of one. The solitary picture from a long-ago summer vanished from his mind's eye.

When Gabe refocused, he took in the cabin and grounds in more detail, hoping the sight would kindle some other recollection to explain his bad dreams.

Nothing was familiar. The old wooden building had been constructed God knows how long ago. It needed paint but seemed sturdy, the walls and roof solid. A pump stood in the middle of what served as a front yard, and about a hundred feet to the right, downstream and built out over the river, was an outhouse, the door hanging open. No prints marred the snow between it and the cabin.

The wind kicked up. The place had been silent except for the river and his footfalls. Now he heard the soft whirring song that only pine trees sang, sounding exactly as it did in the dreams—only this time there was no peace to it. He thought of graveyards and ghosts. He didn't think he believed in ghosts, but if he did, then that was the kind of noise they'd make. Gooseflesh shot up his arms, spread over his spine, and down his legs. He wanted to put his back to something, anything, and had to quell the urge to pull out his gun.

When no invisible beast from the beyond leapt out, Gabe shook off the fit, if not his apprehension. He was sensibly afraid of what he might find here.

And more afraid that he might not find it.

He had to know what had happened in December, the why behind his very quiet trip to this lonely place, what had happened to the girl, what had happened to his driver . . .

And who put the bullet in my head.

He trudged toward the cabin, mounting an ice-coated wood step to the shallow porch. A small, uncurtained window on one side of the door gave a limited view of the interior. Nothing fancy, plank floor, some basic furnishings, no electricity or plumbing, but once upon a time it might have been someone's idea of a good place to live.

Gabe pushed the door open. It had no lock, just an old metal latch to hold the panel shut. After a moment, he went in.

His night vision was such that the ambient glow from outside was enough to see by. Even so, he made use of a candle stub shoved in a holder on a shelf across from the door, using his new silver lighter to bring it to life. The action reminded him of lighting Sonny's cigar, leaning in to the old bastard's ravaged face, smelling his breath, and hearing the creak of his finger joints. Gabriel had felt uncomfortable being so physically close, but he'd taken care not to show it.

He pushed away the memory and turned his attention on the rest of the cabin. It was depressingly plain. A sagging bed leaned in a corner next to a rusting potbellied stove, a narrow table, and two simple benches made from planks took up space under the front window. More planking formed a waist-high shelf that held battered cooking gear—and a dusty white fedora.

He looked it over carefully before picking it up. It was his size, and the label matched that of identical ones in his closet back in New York. No doubt of it now, Whitey Kroun had been here. This was the source of his nickname and a damn-fool thing to wear at any time of the year. The bold white made him a walking target in a crowd. Maybe that was part of his bravado: Whitey Kroun, afraid of nothing and nobody, just try starting something.

Clearly someone had, or the hat wouldn't still be here. He put it back.

I must have been an idiot. He touched the dark brim of his new hat, reassuring himself that he'd grown more sensible in the last couple months.

Shelves above the counter had a store of canned goods so old the labels had faded gray. Below was a stash of wood for the stove and several booze bottles, empty or nearly so.

All very innocuous—except for the splashes of dried blood on the floor by the bed. A rumpled and moldy blanket on top was also stained with the stuff.

He first took it for black paint that some vandal had splattered there; breathing in, he caught the thick, rusty scent.

After a long, long time of staring, he realized the stains were also from his bad dreams. In the dreams the stuff was fresh, red, and he'd been laughing for some insane reason.

He felt his throat tighten again.

Was that his blood? His head wound would have bled . . .

He felt physically sick as possibilities slithered through his mind. He'd seen blood before, damn it. He *drank* the stuff, for God's sake.

He still wanted to vomit.

Or had it come from the girl? What had happened to her?

The left side of his head throbbed wearily. He swept off his fedora and gently touched the ridge in his skull. The nascent pain bloomed into something truly awful, as though his brain had swollen too large for the surrounding bone.

Gabriel stumbled outside, slipping on the steps, grabbing at a support post to stop his fall. He forced his legs not to buckle.

He clawed for a handful of snow and pressed it against his scalp, biting off a cry. The agony was so bad that for a long, terrible moment he couldn't see. He held hard to the post and waited for the torture either to fade on its own or kill him.

Such vulnerability was foreign to him. He shouldn't be like this. It wasn't going to happen. He wouldn't allow it. He blinked until the black veil dissipated.

The compress of snow helped, really helped, but it was slow. Minutes crawled by, then bit by bit the pain reluctantly ebbed.

Breathing in icy river-tainted air helped, too. He made his lungs pump until his guts settled. It took longer for his brain to clear. Speculation about what had happened in the cabin could wait until he was calmer. He shut that part away for the moment, like closing a door. Out of sight, out of mind; he was good at forgetting, after all.

Gabe straightened, brushing snow from his hand. His fingers looked blue, but didn't feel cold. He cautiously put on his hat. No internal explosions sparked. He should have bought earmuffs at that store; fedoras weren't right for woodland expeditions.

Once he was sure his legs could manage the labor, he made another slow circuit of the area, this time facing outward.

He struck off, moving away from the river. No conscious memory prompted him, only some wisp of dream that made him think the area was familiar. The snow confused and concealed things, though. The place would look very different after the thaw in a couple months; he should come back then . . .

Like hell. He couldn't live with the not-knowing for that long. He *had* to get this over with—

The wind started up again, making the surrounding pines sing louder. He paused and knew he was close to something important. Looking back, he judged himself to be about fifty feet from the cabin. The candle glow through a side window seemed about right. Oh, yeah. Very close.

The glow flared and died, and he had to work to keep from twitching.

The nearly spent stub had finally guttered, that was all. No one had blown it out. He'd have heard company long before seeing them.

Unless Fleming followed me.

Not likely, but not impossible. The loon might have somehow managed to tag along; his ability to vanish was damned handy. He could have hidden in the trunk and—

Gabe held still and waited, but no ghostly gray shapeless *thing* floated between the trees. That was how Fleming looked while in that form, though Gabe had the understanding that regular humans couldn't see it. Just as well, too; it was hellishly creepy.

He wondered what it felt like: being bodiless, able to go through walls, instantly heal. Damned useful, all of it.

The snow layer thinned. The pine branches above had prevented serious drifts from forming. He picked out animal tracks: deer and rabbit, and several kinds of paw prints. He couldn't tell wildcat from wolf, but took for granted that four-footed observers might be lurking in the silent woods. Those he didn't mind so much.

An unevenness of the ground, a mound hidden by the snow, nearly tripped him. He backed off and studied things. The snow lay smooth, softening the irregular surface beneath. He crouched and brushed until reaching old leaves and earth. Nothing to get excited about, probably just a covered-over garbage pit dug for whatever wasn't burned or tossed in the river.

But the mound was grave-shaped.

And leaning against a pine trunk, only a few paces away, was a shovel.

Its wood handle was aging fast in the weather, the metal rusted. Someone had left it there, but had he simply forgotten it, or was it to mark a special place?

Gabe's hands closed on it, and *that* felt familiar. He dragged it free and used the blade to clear the snow away.

The pine tree . . . he looked up, hoping for a clue, but nothing came to him. Still, this had to be the place. The wind in the branches sounded the same.

He began to dig.

The frozen ground was not as solid as it should have been, but he had to work at it. His improved strength was a great help, though a few times he had to go easy as the handle threatened to break if he applied too much pressure. He slammed the blade in, cut deep, loosened, then cleared, his movements machinelike, giving him to understand that he was used to such labor. He felt like he was accomplishing something.

About three feet down, the shovel hit something that was not dirt, and he stopped.

By now he was sure of what would be there. The scent of the turned earth had done the trick, had merged what lay before him with what he'd dreamed.

He hated it, but continued, slowly.

The stink of decay rose and mixed with the pine, snow, and river air.

Soon he uncovered the man's face. There was enough left to recognize features, but Gabe's patchy memory failed him again. He had to dig farther to reach the rest of the body to check the pockets, finding a wallet. It held a few hundred in twenties, the tough paper still intact as legal tender. A New York state driving license was readable, identifying one Henry Ramsey, born July 15, 1912. Date of death? Sometime in December, 1937. Just a kid. His friends probably called him Hank.

Cause of death? Less certain, though Gabe thought the damage and stains on the front of the clothes might have been caused by bullets. There was a leather shoulder rig similar to his own on the body, but no gun in it. That lay in what remained of the corpse's right hand, fingers curled around the grip, index finger against the trigger. It was a .32 revolver, rusted and caked with dirt.

Gabe carefully worked it clear of the dead man's grasp. Four bullets were still in the cylinder. He wondered if one of the two missing slugs was lodged in his brain. Where had the other gone? Since Ramsey was holding a gun, chances were good he'd not been caught unawares. He might have gotten one shot off before dropping. Then what? The killer had dug a long hole and rolled him in?

The grave was too shallow. Come the spring thaw, animals would find, dig up, and scavenge the remains for food. Sooner or later a passing hunter, curious about the cabin, might discover it. It was a miracle that hadn't already happened. Was the hole deeper . . . yes . . . someone had dug a much deeper grave.

Mine.

Instinct, not memory, provided that conclusion.

With a bullet in his skull and all signs of life gone, someone had buried Gabriel Kroun a few yards from the foot of the pine. The first shovelful of wet earth had covered his face and, quickly after, the rest of him.

And at some point along the way, Ramsey had been dropped in as well.

Did we die together? Or was I first, then Ramsey?

In the dream-memory, Gabe had clawed his way toward the sky, pushing aside some heavy obstacle that lay on him. The rounded thing he'd touched, recognized, and recoiled from had been Ramsey's head. What happened afterward Gabe could not recall. His resurrection was a hazy, disjointed, painful event. The agony in his skull from the bullet wound had kept him thoroughly distracted. After dragging free from the grave, he must have reburied Ramsey before moving on. That didn't seem too likely, though.

Gabe straightened, the wallet and its contents in hand. He put the license back and, after a moment, the cash as well. It made little sense not to keep and use the money, but with some surprise he discovered within a profound loathing for robbing the dead. He returned the wallet to its pocket and went to work with the shovel, burying the man again.

The sky had changed by the time Gabe finished. He'd not be able to make it to that town before the dawn overtook him but had allowed for the possibility.

He was exhausted and half-frozen when he returned to the car and folded himself into the backseat. The four heavy blankets wrapped around him would block the weak winter sun and keep in his remaining body warmth. He chose not to worry about anyone finding him during the day. No one had been out to the cabin in months, after all.

He lay still, eyes closed, listening to the wind beyond the rolled-up windows. It whirred between the pine needles and hissed through the bare branches of other trees. Rather than being at peace, he felt lonely . . . and afraid.

Gabe sensed the sun, the change it forced upon his body, the slowing of his perceptions and thought as conscious control slipped away. This day's bout of dream torture might be the worst yet. He'd have to get through it somehow; he had to *know*.

He shifted to a more comfortable position, arms and shoulders stiff from the recent exercise. It didn't work. He'd be creaking around like an old man when he woke. He should have ordered up a small panel truck. He could have stretched out in the back . . .

Why hadn't he dropped off yet?

He should be out by now, not grousing to himself for picking the wrong kind of vehicle. What the hell . . . ?

He sat up, pushing off the blankets.

Yes, he was sore and cold and creaked, his muscles cramped from staying in one position for far too long—the whole damned day as it happened. One sniff of the damp air, one glance at the painfully bright sky with its last gilding of sunset, and he understood he'd slept right through the day, no dreams, no memories at all.

He'd been *cheated*.

He *needed* that internal hell. With the things he'd just learned, he had to dream again to find out what had happened. Awful as they were—

Damn it. God *damn* it.

He pitched from the car, looking around as though to find someone to blame. The woods were as empty as before and silent; the wind had died.

How was it that, after all this time, he'd finally—

Gabe looked down. His shoes and pant legs were caked with dried-out mud from his grave, enough to do the job. He knew from his talks with Gordy that Fleming kept packets of his home earth in his sleeping areas. He even carried some in a money belt should he get caught away from those shelters. Until now Gabe had been dubious about the idea of the stuff providing true rest during the day. It struck him as just being another kind of superstition associated with his condition. The sight of a cross and the touch of holy water didn't bother him, so why should grave dirt have such an effect? What a damned stupid thing *that* was. It had robbed him of that day's progress toward what had gotten him killed in the first place.

He grumbled and stretched out the kinks, which weren't too bad, considering. He *did* feel rested, far more energetic than he'd been in weeks. Okay, there was a good side to his mistake.

Gabe followed his tracks back to the cabin, wanting another, much more thorough search before leaving.

The dried blood still very much in place, he lit another candle and checked every corner, every stick of furniture, tapped each board, looking for anything resembling an explanation.

He soon found a six-shot .22 revolver, bullets spent, blood-smeared, rust creeping over its surface. It was behind one of the benches, not hidden, just not in plain sight. Perhaps the shooter had dropped or thrown it there. The numbers were filed away, and it had the kind of checkerboard grip that didn't hold fingerprints. A feeble weapon for some, but mob soldiers who favored the caliber liked the gun's small size and low level of noise. Fold a pillow around it or hold it directly against a target and it sounded like a balloon popping, if that much.

Gabe didn't know how he knew that, but was not surprised such details lurked in his mind.

Maybe Nelly had brought the gun, unless a fourth person had crashed the party.

Complications, he thought. They annoyed the hell out of him, but Gabe had to keep them in mind.

He left the bed for last. Gingerly, with thumb and forefinger, he pulled the top blanket off and spread it out on the floor. There was no pattern to the bloodstains; it was a mess. Someone had bled there.

A mildew-eaten gray sheet beneath was also bloody, most of it in the middle. He recalled what Lettie had said about Nelly Cabot's injuries and fought past a bout of nausea. He lifted the sheet to reveal an ancient stained mattress that also stank of mildew. The stuff was all over, dormant from the cold, but still disgusting. Touching as little as possible, he dragged the mattress away from the bed, which was made from simple planks nailed across a box frame, nothing store-bought about that operation.

In the spaces between the planks, the floor beneath was visible, and something shiny caught the light.

He tore a plank away and got it. Got *them.*

Should have looked there first.

He closely examined a small, empty amber vial and a syringe. Whatever had been inside them was long dried and gone.

Michael.

The fourth person.

A complication. A damned big one.

Maybe *he'd* hurt the girl.

And maybe he killed me. Or had Ramsey do it, then killed him to keep him quiet. But when I came back Mike thought the job had been botched and that I didn't suspect him. No wonder he didn't want me up here.

Upon his return to New York, Gabe had been very careful not to let on about his loss of memory. It was easier to do than he'd hoped. He was in a position where no one questioned him. You could get away with a lot using a stern look and not saying much.

Michael had been out of the country at the time, or so he said. Distracted by his own problems, Gabe hadn't thought to check.

He peered through the side window into a very silent night. The woman weeping in his dream-memory—had it been from terror instead of grief? While Ramsey filled in the grave, Mike could have been in the cabin with her, doing God knows what to ensure she would keep quiet.

Then I get the blame since she was last seen with me.

He put away the items. They clinked against the rusted revolver. He shifted the gun to a different pocket and found that his hands were shaking.

Rage. Yeah, he had plenty of that.

Soon as I see Mike again . . .

He pinched out the candle flame.

Grabbing the white fedora, he let the latch fall on the door and walked to the pump. Its works were frozen for the winter. The bucket next to it meant to hold priming water was topped with snow. He went down to the riverbank, loaded the inside of the hat with a few rocks, using a hand-kerchief to tie the brim tightly over them to keep them in place. He flung the hat far out over the water. It splashed once and vanished in the black flow.

Next he scooped sand and icy water and scrubbed his hands until the mildew smell went away, all the time regarding the dark cabin and what was inside.

He wanted to burn it.

Tempting, but a bad idea. However secluded, flames and smoke could draw the wrong kind of attention to this place. Someone might feel bound to track down the property owner . . . Gabe realized *he* could be the owner. He just didn't know.

Better to leave it for now. He could always return with a few gallons of kerosene.

That would cleanse the place . . . every square inch of it.

THE miles back to Chicago seemed to have stretched themselves. He had too much to think about and wished for company. Even Fleming, with his endless questions, would have been welcome. Gabe turned on the car's radio, and the noise of a comedy show helped.

Michael would not be in a good mood tonight; he was probably making Derner's life miserable. Half of the muscle at the Nightcrawler was probably out looking for the green Hudson and its missing driver. Fine. Let 'em earn their keep.

Gabe took a wrong turn, tried correcting at the next street, got lost, and pulled over to study the map. He wondered if getting lost was part of his lack of memory or if he'd always been like that.

His clearest postdeath recollection was waking in a cold barn loft where he'd hidden from the sun behind stacks of hay bales. From there he'd gone groggily down, washed off blood and grave dirt in an ice-crusted water trough, and taken his first feeding from one of the milk cows. That had awakened him fully, though the agony in his head kept him from indulging much in the way of thinking. He seemed well able to look after basics like getting food, to know how to deal with his change if not the how or why of it.

The circumstances—his blood-drinking, the bad dreams during his daylight sleep, lack of memory of how he'd gotten into such a spot, and all that came before—didn't really bother him. It seemed normal to be different. Not knowing himself was just how the world ran, and his instincts told him he'd be fine, just fine. He had a wallet with a driving license that provided a name to use, an address to go to, and more than enough money to get there.

A few nights later, first hitchhiking on country roads, then taking a train, then a taxi, he used a key from that wallet to get into a hotel flat in New York. Though he couldn't remember it, he assumed it to be his. Old mail scattered over a desk bore the name on the license. The flat was nice, and the clothes there fit. He moved into a stranger's life.

Pretty soon friends turned up.

Well, acquaintances.

They showed him respect and something he later came to recognize as fear. A very few asked about the white streak in his hair. He found a smirk and a shake of the head to be sufficient reply.

Mike had walked into the flat as though he'd been there many times before, looking uncomfortable and on guard. In retrospect could it have been guilt? He was the only one who met Gabe's eye and stood up to him like an equal, though.

They had a business meeting, which required going to a bar and sitting in a booth across from a tough-looking man. Michael talked a lot of business that didn't make sense. The man challenged him on a point. Mike looked at Gabe. At a loss for what to do, Gabe looked at the man, who abruptly backed down, agreed to something, then left, sweating. Mike said *thanks* in a flat voice and departed as well.

From that point Gabriel decided he'd better learn what the hell kind of job he had.

It didn't take long. He killed people. He was good at the work.

He wasn't sure how he felt about that. Not then. Later, he decided that cold murder wasn't something he wanted to do to anyone.

The roughhouse when he and Fleming had taken on Mitchell didn't really count. Heat-of-the-moment shooting was one thing, but to walk up and coolly put a bullet into a stranger . . . that was just wrong.

There had been a couple of times when he'd felt angry enough to do violence, such as when he'd thought Fleming responsible for blowing up the car. But Gabe had wanted to punch him in the nose more than anything else. The gun had been a tool, little more than window dressing to get attention.

On the other hand, Fleming had been pretty clear about what had happened after the car crash last night. Gabe couldn't remember anything after their car left the road, but *something* had upset the kid. The lapse was disturbing, but there was damn all to be done about it.

In that first month in New York, Gabe worked out how to hypnotize people. They told him a lot he didn't like and much he didn't believe. He decided the whole crowd, including Michael, were considerably crazier than he and far more dangerous. The only way to keep from being consumed by them was to maintain the long-established outward front.

Strangely, no one noticed anything different about him. They all had certain expectations as to how he should behave, and, when he drifted outside those expectations, the mugs simply stretched their limits to accommodate. It was their fear of him. They put on their own fronts, acted friendly, shook his hand, laughed at his jokes, but were still pissing-in-their-pants terrified of him.

Yeah, crazy.

Gabe observed carefully and from them learned how to impersonate the man he'd been. It wasn't perfect; he'd sometimes surprise an odd look from Mike, but the guy never said anything.

Down deep he had to be terrified of Whitey Kroun, too.

That covered *who* he had been, next came the *what* he had become.

He eventually went to the big library with the lions out front and looked up stuff about vampires. It was crazy as well, but since some of it seemed to apply to him, he shrugged, accepted, and moved on, keeping his lip shut.

Gabe had yet to find out exactly how he'd come by the condition.

Somewhere out there a woman—he was sure it was a woman, Fleming's reckless dig notwithstanding—had done something quite out of the ordinary to Gabe. The details were lost, taken away when the bullet had ripped into his brain.

Very damned annoying, that.

Once the dust was settled on his current problem, he might have to try finding her.

GABRIEL navigated the gradually thinning traffic, pulling up in front of Fleming's brick house a little after midnight. No lights showed, just like the cabin. He pushed the thought away, strode up the walk, and used his picklocks to get in.

That was also a skill he could not recall learning. Useful, though.

He listened before shutting the door, noticing that the broken window at the far end of the hall had been replaced. Hand it to Gordy, he ran a tight ship.

The place was empty, but Gabriel checked through it before turning on any lights. He didn't need them, but they'd let Fleming know company was present should he return. If the kid had any sense, he'd be cheering up that sweet blond girlfriend of his. Bobbi. Funny name for a dame, but it suited her.

Gabe got both suitcases and went up to the third-floor guest room. The rumpled bed was as he'd left it, and it almost looked like the one in the cabin, but without the blood.

I gotta stop that kind of thinking.

He straightened the top spread, opened the cases, found a crisp new shirt and the second suit he'd bought. It was identical to the one he had on, black with a charcoal pinstripe, very sharp. He didn't like to fuss over clothes, just pick good quality and forget about it.

Stripping and taking a shower-bath was a little piece of heaven. He stayed in until the hot water ran out, but emerged clean, shaved . . . and still feeling well rested. That grave dirt . . . well, clearly it worked. He'd have to start sleeping with a bag of it in the bed. What a luxury to be dream-free once this was over.

He thought he should save the residue on his discarded clothes and bundled them into a pillowcase and put it in the small wardrobe. Was it too close to the bed?

Only if he slept here for the day. He would use that abandoned store again. Broder and Michael didn't know about it.

Gabe dressed slowly, liking the feel of new clothes. Fresh and ready for anything, he went downstairs to phone the Nightcrawler.

Derner sounded harried. "Mike's on the warpath and wants to talk to y—"

"Give him a Bromo-Seltzer and a blonde."

"I would, I really would, but he's in Cicero."

"Well, that's his hard luck. What's he doing in—no, forget it." It would be business. With Mike it was always business. He could do half a dozen things at once and give each his full attention. Smart guy. Very smart. "Where's Broder?"

"With Mike."

Interesting. Broder must have spun one hell of a story to get himself off the hook for the grenade job—unless Mike had lied and faked his surprised reaction. If Broder's task had been to kill Gabe, then it made sense for Mike to keep him around.

But why does Mike want to kill me? Was it on general principles or for a specific reason? Why wait two months for another try?

"When will they be back?"

"Didn't say, but I've got a number you're to call."

Gabe wrote it down on a notepad by the phone. Cicero wasn't that far. He was reasonably sure he could find it, but a local guide would be better to have along. "Has Fleming turned up tonight?"

"Huh? Uh—no. Probably at his club. He usually calls in before now. You gonna talk to Mike?" Derner seemed worried. More so than usual, that is.

"In about two minutes." He pressed the hook long enough for the connection to break, then tried the new number. It turned out to belong to a hotel. He asked for Mike and got put right through.

He picked up on the first ring.

"Hello, Michael." Gabe used a friendly, cheerful tone, intending to be as irritating as hell. "Problem?"

"Where have you been?"

"Are you going to tell me to go back to New York again? Because the answer's no. Now that that's settled, how long will you be in Cicero?"

Mike made some strange choking noises. "A couple of days."

What the hell . . . ? Gabe continued the good cheer. "Fine. I'll keep busy. The old bastard wanted to get some air. I thought I'd take him fishing in the morning. It'd do him good to get out, have a little fun."

Dead silence. Lots of it.

Well, I wanted to stir things up.

"Whitey . . . please."

Pleading? That was a surprise, though Gabe wanted him off-balance and scared. "I've been to the cabin. The place looks great. You should see it."

"What have you done?"

"Nothing yet. You think I should do something?"

"No games . . . let's talk first."

"Sounds good."

"When can you get here?"

"I've had enough driving. We'll meet at Gordy's club." Mike would think twice about getting frisky in front of witnesses and be more likely to keep Broder in line as well.

"Okay. I'll get there soon as I—a couple hours."

"Why so long?"

"Business."

Gabe snorted and hung up. *Must be some business.* From keeping company with a girl to calling in extra muscle. Or arranging an exit.

For himself or for me?

Mike had agreed too readily. That could mean a lot of things. Gabe started to list the possibilities and how to counter them, then abruptly let it go. He'd find out soon enough and deal with it then.

Broder would be along, somewhere in the background, watching. Gabe knew how to keep his back to a wall, but Broder was nearly a ghost himself. He moved fast, quiet, and was a dead shot. If Fleming could be talked into helping out . . . but did he really need to know all this?

Yes. Better to have him as a friend than not. He'd want an explanation for the sickening things Sonny had said.

Both of us want that.

WAITING around the Nightcrawler held no appeal. Derner would be trying too hard not to ask questions. Gabe wanted a couple hours of not being watched like a zoo animal. He looked up the number for Fleming's club but got no answer. He would wait there; Broder and Michael wouldn't expect him to go to a closed club, and maybe Fleming would show. It would also be quiet. You could hear if someone tried to sneak in.

He snagged a newspaper from the pile on the front porch, kicked the rest inside, and relocked the door, then drove to Lady Crymsyn. Funny name for a club. Maybe Fleming had gotten the idea from his girl and her funny name. He could have spelled "crimson" right, though.

Gabe recognized enough landmarks on the trip to avoid getting lost. The club's inside lights were on, including the one in the upstairs office. A little glow escaped around the drawn curtains. Fleming must not be answering the phone or had just arrived himself. The parking lot was empty. He'd have walked or cabbed over, what with his car being all blown up and burned.

The street was clear of stray cops; Merrifield and Garza apparently had other duties tonight, leaving no one to watch as Gabe let himself in the front. He left things unlocked. It was always a good idea to have an escape route ready.

The light behind the lobby bar was on, and something was odd about the bar itself. As he drew closer he saw that dozens of matchbooks with the club's name on them had been propped open and set on end. Little red inverted Vs marched every which way, covering the whole length of the bar. What the hell . . . ? If Fleming had been here, he had some pretty odd ideas about how to fill the time.

The bar light flickered, not quite going out.

Gabriel stared, then called Fleming's name loud enough to reach upstairs.

No one replied. Why had he left all the lights on? Spendthrift.

The building was empty and dead silent. And big. Big, silent, and . . .

The light steadied.

Then the lobby phone rang. Louder than should be normal.

He didn't jump, but jerked around, stopping in midreach for his gun. He debated whether to answer or not.

The ringing was continuous, and then trailed off as though the bell had exhausted itself from the effort.

He waited, but no second ring came. Wrong number or a phone company hitch.

The bar light flickered again. Fleming had said there was a short.

His problem, not mine.

Gabe went upstairs to the deserted office. It wasn't as fancy and large as the Nightcrawler's but had the usual stuff except for a gaping space opposite the desk. From the dust pattern on the floor some large piece of furniture had been removed from the spot. A couch, maybe.

On the desk were several oilcloth packets. They were heavy and smelled of earth.

Well. Damn. What was Fleming doing? Moving house?

He checked the lock on the door. It was a particularly sturdy model: wood panels over thick metal. The windows—bulletproofed, with heavy curtains—confirmed that this was one of Fleming's daylight bolt-holes. Not bad. He did all right for himself.

Gabe shed his coat and hat and sat behind the desk. The chair was comfortable; you could tilt back and put your feet up. Not bad at all. He dropped the packets out of the way into one of the drawers, opened his paper, and settled in to read. It had been a busy day. New pieces had effectively edged out further mention of the car explosion in the Bronze Belt, the Alan Caine murders, and even that movie actor and his flashy foreign wife.

Those were all that interested him; the rest just didn't mean anything. He looked for and found the funnies. Hey, a crossword puzzle—he liked those.

The radio came on. All by itself.

He looked at it for a good long while, considering a variety of causes. The elusive electrical short seemed the most likely. Someone leaves the radio on, when the power returns, it warms up, then surprise: dance music.

He didn't mind, but wouldn't be able to hear anyone coming in. He shut the radio off.

While he was trying to work out if the clue to seven down was "gable" or "table," the front door downstairs opened and closed. Gabe listened, following the progress of the ensuing footsteps . . . a man's shoes by the sound. He got partway across the lobby and paused.

Bet he's wondering about the matchbooks, too.

The newcomer started up the stairs. "Jack?" he called.

Gabe didn't know the voice. He shifted his gun from its holster to the desk, slipping it under the paper.

The visitor pushed in and froze at the halfway point, his body partially shielded by the door. He was surprised for a moment at seeing Gabe, but clearly recognized him. The man was tall, lean, and angular. His face was all angles, too, with bony cheeks, a big blade of a nose, and needle-sharp eyes. He looked familiar . . . the dying man from the hospital. Gabe's last recollection had him flat on his back, unconscious, black-and-blue, and with a death stink rising from his skin. He'd been in bad shape then, the worst.

"Hey, pal, you're looking better," Gabe said.

"Thanks to you, Mr. Kroun."

English accent. Fleming hadn't mentioned his partner was from that far out of town. The way he spoke, this bird apparently knew everything. Until he had come to Chicago *no one* had known about Gabe being a vampire. Fleming might as well be broadcasting on the radio.

The man continued. "I'm very grateful for what you did. It can't have been easy. Thank you for saving my life."

"So long as it worked."

"Was there any doubt?"

He didn't know how to answer that one. "It's Escott, right?"

"Yes. Charles Escott. Jack said you were staying at the house."

"Only part-time." Why didn't he come the rest of the way in? Why the stony expression? Usually people relaxed after introductions. *He probably knows my reputation.* "I'll be leaving soon."

"Indeed?"

"I can leave tonight if you want."

"No need to trouble yourself." He took a quick look around the room, his gaze pausing on the empty space on the floor. "Why are you here?"

The man's tone was off. He had things on his mind. "Catching up on my reading. Yourself?"

Escott made no reply, but glanced at the paper on the desk and must have made a fast guess about what lay beneath the pages. He moved, smoothly, with much confidence. He'd been hiding one hell of a big damn revolver behind the door. He aimed it at Gabe's chest. "Raise your hands. Now."

"Hey, just hold on a minute . . ."

"*Now.*"

Gabe hesitated, throwing an involuntarily glare. He didn't know what he looked like, but the outward change always took the starch out of the toughest mugs in New York.

Escott, however, seemed immune. "I know how fast you are, but I *can* get one clear shot. It may not kill, but it will hurt. As you cannot vanish, you will require time to heal, during which interval I can inflict a great deal more damage."

Gabe assessed his options and reluctantly concluded the man was right. And certainly insane. He was breathing a little too slow for the situation, and he looked ready to follow through on his threat. Did his gun also have a hair trigger? "Come on—this is a new suit."

"Don't give me cause to ruin it."

Gabe slowly raised his hands. "What's this about?"

"Jack Fleming." Escott watched him, not blinking, holding the gun dead center and rock-steady.

He finally shook his head. "Still don't understand."

Apparently that wasn't the right answer. Escott cocked the gun.

Gabe felt a small jolt in his chest in response, as though his dormant heart tried to jump out of the way. "Hey! Slow down, pal, I'll help if I can. What do you *want*?"

"Jack Fleming," Escott repeated through clenched teeth. His eyes were the same color as steel and not nearly as soft. "Where the hell is he?"

Gabe thought his first reply—along the lines of *How the hell should I know?*—would get him shot. His second—*What? You lost him?*—was idiotic and would also result in gunfire. He did his best to read the stranger before him and decided that now would be a good time to cease being Whitey Kroun.

"Tell me what's happened," said Gabe.

"It's about what has not happened."

"Okay . . . tell me that, then."

Escott continued to study, probably trying to read him right back. Something changed behind those hard eyes. He took the revolver off cock, but otherwise kept it ready and centered. "Every night, without fail, as soon as he's awake, Jack calls his girlfriend or she calls him. That may seem trivial to you, but it is not. For him it is cast-iron habit. Also, without fail, he contacts a certain Mr. Derner at the Nightcrawler Club—"

"Yeah, he stays in touch 'cause of the business. So he's late on a couple calls, that's enough for you to want to shoot me?"

"A few minutes late, even an hour is acceptable, but not *eight* hours. That's much too long. Something's happened to him."

"And you've tried to find hi—"

"Of *course!* I've called everyone and been everywhere. The previous evening he went to visit Miss Smythe, and no one's seen or heard from him since. That is highly atypical behavior. He is not to be found. His car wasn't here, but I saw the lights on and hoped—"

"You talk to Derner?" Now was not the best time to let the man know the fate of Fleming's car.

"He wasn't forthcoming with information. He did admit that Jack had not checked in tonight."

"How about I call and straighten this out? Will that make you put the gun down?"

No reply.

"Look, I don't know where he is, either. Last I saw he was behind the Nightcrawler talking to one of the guys; after that, I couldn't say."

"Aside from myself and Miss Smythe, the only person he's spent any time with has been *you*. Mr. Derner did impart that you and Jack went on an errand for several hours last night."

"We did, but came back to the club, and I don't see how it could have to do with him taking off tonight. A man's got a right to keep to himself if he wants t—"

"No. There's something wrong. Seriously wrong."

That was uncompromising. "You know him better than I do. You say he's missing, okay, I'll help you find him. Lemme use the phone. I'll see what I can get from Derner."

Escott nodded, just the once.

It took Gabe a moment to remember the number for the Nightcrawler's office phone. Having a cannon aimed at his chest made him that nervous. You learned something new every night.

The connection went through. "Yeah, what is it?"

"This is—" Damn, what was he calling himself to this guy? "Whitey." Derner got more respectful. "Yessir."

"What's going on with Fleming? Where is he?"

"He hasn't checked in is all I know. Did you call Mike?"

"Yes, but forget that—I need to speak to Fleming. Now."

"Bu—"

"Hang up, make calls, find someone who knows where he is. Five minutes, then you ring me back here." Gabe read the number off the dial and dropped the receiver back on the hook.

"You enjoyed that," Escott observed. He seemed slightly less on the edge—by at least a quarter inch.

"It's good to be top dog, yeah." He'd bought five minutes, but didn't know what to do with them. Trying to sit still with a crazy man ready to shoot if he heard the wrong word was not a good way to fill the time. He gave Escott a serious appraisal and thought about hypnotizing him. That would bring on a headache; Gabe couldn't risk a reprise of the blinding skull-breaker he'd had at the cabin. "Look, I've been on the road since I left him in the alley last night, you can believe that or not. He could have had a fight with his girl, gone to a movie, be holed up in a pool hall. That guy Coldfield is pissed with him, maybe—"

"I've asked. He's not seen Jack. He's angry, but he'd tell me . . ." Escott paused, assessing. "You've been up to that cabin." Statement, not a question.

His mouth went dry. "What?"

"You heard. What did you find there?"

"Nothing I want to talk about." Gabe wasn't sure that was his voice.

"Something important, then." Escott showed a tiny glint of satisfaction.

How did he even know about . . . oh. Yeah. "Your partner talks too damn much."

"He was only expressing his concern about certain aspects of your visit to the sanitarium. He could not understand why you allowed him along on so private an interview. Perhaps he heard things he should not have known, thus giving you a reason to keep him quiet."

"In which case I'd have knocked him off after we left."

"And you would certainly know how to do that."

Gabe held his most intimidating gaze on Escott, who failed to react at all, much less show fear. The man knew how to focus. "Only I didn't."

"Your original purpose for coming to Chicago was to kill him."

"Funny, but that didn't happen either. I've got no motive."

"Then perhaps someone with you does. This Michael or Mr. Broder."

"I'm gonna do you a favor and ask—I just said *ask*—you to back away. If they're involved, I'll handle 'em. The worst thing you can do is let them know you exist."

"The best thing you can do is tell me the why of it."

Gabriel considered, then shook his head. "I'll pass. What's going on with them has nothing to do with Fleming."

"Michael sent him to watch you. That, sir, is not to be ignored."

He had a point. Maybe Fleming hadn't delivered enough details to satisfy. Michael could have gotten fed up and finally turned Broder loose to do something. Broder might well have turned himself loose without telling Mike. That would be bad for everyone.

The phone rang. Before Derner could speak, Gabe interrupted. "Hold on a minute. Whatever you have on Fleming, I want you to say it to this guy first." He held the receiver out.

Escott reached to take it, still keeping the gun level. "Yes?" Apparently Derner did not have good news. Escott fired off questions, but the replies were clearly not to his liking. He said thank you and hung up. "Very well, no one at the Nightcrawler has seen or heard from him. That leaves you."

"Only I wasn't around to do anything." He'd finally got that the man with the gun was deeply afraid and only barely able to keep himself from flying apart.

"Yes. You were at the cabin. What did—"

"It's a fishing cabin. I went up there to fish."

"In the dead of winter?"

"I never said I was good at it."

Escott wasn't amused. "That . . . that is the most bloody stupid thing I've ever heard."

Gabe shrugged. "The night ain't over, pal."

Another change—lightning fast—shifted everything behind those steel gray eyes. They somehow got harder and abruptly blazed with a lunatic fury. He raised the gun until Gabe found himself looking right down the barrel.

No . . .

Gabe tore his gaze from the gun and stared at Escott. No chance of hypnosis pushing through those emotions. He was too far gone.

Escott's heart pounded loud in the silent room, and now his hand shook. But at this distance he wouldn't miss.

"Why?" Gabriel blurted out the word.

Escott blinked once. Better than shooting.

"*Why?*"

He trembled all over, visibly slipping.

"Tell me, dammit!"

A thin crack in the man's intent. He blinked rapidly now, like a sleeper waking. "W-what?"

"You're not mad at *me*—who then? Why?"

The crack widened, and the moment stretched, and gradually Escott's pounding heart slowed. The gun lowered by an inch. Then another. It was a long progression, but Escott finally sagged and put the cannon away in a shoulder holster.

Gabe felt like falling over, but resisted.

"Mr. Kroun, I apologize for this." He spoke in a strangely neutral tone that sure as hell didn't sound right for the situation. "I shall not waste any more of your time." Escott turned and left, just like that.

It took a few seconds for Gabe to find his feet and lurch from behind the desk. Escott was halfway down the stairs.

"Hey! Stop!"

Amazingly, he did.

"Get up here."

Escott wavered, then turned and trudged back. He walked past Gabe, not meeting his eye, and on into the office. He went to the window, standing before the closed curtains, hands at his sides, shoulders down.

Gabe came around and peered at his face. There was a lost soul if he ever saw one. He went to the liquor cabinet, picked something strong at random, and poured. He had to fit the glass into Escott's hand and lift it to get him started. He drank without reaction, and the glass slipped from his fingers. Gabe caught it, not spilling a drop, and guided him toward a leather chair in a corner, making him sit.

The radio blared on, the volume all the way to the top.

This time Gabe jumped. He crossed the room in two strides and shut the damned thing off again. When he looked back, Escott was slumped forward in the chair with one hand over his face.

"Oh, Myrna, what's happened?" he whispered, very, very softly.

Myrna again. Who the hell is Myrna? "What do you think has happened?" Gabe asked aloud.

Escott glanced up, surprised, perhaps, that he'd been heard. He shook his head.

"You've got an idea, or you wouldn't be like this. So give."

He opened his mouth, but nothing came out. Gabe put the glass in his hand again. Escott eventually finished the rest of the drink. He still looked lost.

"You're scared," Gabe said. "But Fleming's a tough bastard and can take care of himself. Why are you so worried?"

"Things." Escott cleared his throat. He sounded like a strangling victim. "Things have been . . . difficult, because of what he went through with Bristow."

Gabe frowned. "Yeah. Go on."

The man stared at the empty space on the floor where the furniture piece had stood and didn't speak for a long time. Then, "Here the other night . . . Jack tried to kill himself."

"What?"

"And . . ." Escott's face worked as he fought to keep control. "And I'm afraid he might have tried again . . . and succeeded."

13

FLEMING

MY first moments at waking were the worst I'd ever had in a long parade of bad times, and it went downhill from there, headlong into hell.

The trip was in stages, like Dante's ten-cent tour, and not nearly as nice.

It began with a bewildering dream.

I became dimly aware of being dragged, carried, and awkwardly shoved into a cramped space. My eyes shut, my brain gathered information but was unable to take meaning from it. A single question floated through the shadows—*Where's my earth?*—then drifted out again, getting no answer.

After that, the space was in motion, bumping and roaring over pavement for an unguessable time.

Another bout of being carried and set down. I was dead, my body not responding to anything, unable to move. My limbs were arranged flat on something, not a bed. My arms were stretched wide, palms up, knuckles hanging.

Then my earth must have been returned, for the dream ceased.

Sunset.

Eyes wide, internal alarm bells on full, I shot awake in absolute darkness. I *hated* the dark. After my change, my eyes could make use of the least little sliver of light—if it was there to be used.

This kind of dark was cold, damp, and rock solid. I tried to reach for the cot-side lamp, but something kept my arm from moving, and at the same time hot, sickening agony shot from a spot below my elbow and straight into my brain like a spear. It was so intense that I yelled, tried to pull away, and that made it ten times worse—for both arms.

Things went cloudy for a long, terrible stretch as my body fought against whatever held it. The more it fought, the greater the pain, until I howled nonstop like a trapped animal.

When exhaustion set in, it was a blessing. The pain remained, but did not increase so long as I kept still.

When I was able to think—and that was a struggle—I wondered why I'd not vanished away from the pain. Even as the thought came I tried slipping into the gray oblivion that had always healed me.

But *nothing* happened. I remained anchored in flesh, and the effort exhausted me fast, like racing a car in neutral.

Panicking did no good. I knew that, but still failed to stop a choking wave from sweeping over me. I heard myself bellowing God knows what until the fit passed.

This wasn't like the seizures. I could escape them by vanishing, and that had been unaccountably made impossible.

I forced myself quiet, pushing the fear to one side, trying to find out . . . anything.

Flat on my back on something hard, arms spread wide, and hellish

pain if I moved either of them, yes, that was pretty damned bad. Whatever rope or chain bound me in place was too tight, and gouging into me
in a way I couldn't figure out.

The hard surface ran out a few inches from my wrists. My hands were
over free space. I could move them, but it hurt.

The room, cave, whatever, was empty and silent, but . . . someone was
nearby . . . in another room. There was a little distance and a wall or
floor between, but I heard a heartbeat and the quick saw of breath and
imagined him listening in turn.

Of course I yelled for help, but none came, and no one replied. Was he
in the same boat? Was he the one who'd brought me here?

My next wave of panic was more subtle, not as noisy, but there was
no coherent thought going on. I struggled, fresh agony stabbed through
my arms, and soon the physical pain pulled me clear of the fit.

Eventually I lay quiet, and again tried to work out what was around
me. My other senses failed to provide much help. Arms held in place,
pain if I moved them, and the sharp smell of my own blood and terror.
Whatever was wrong with my arms . . . dammit, they were *bleeding*. A
lot, enough to flow over the edge of something and drip to the floor. I
heard the soft regular patter as it hit a hard surface, sounding like a faucet leak you can't shut off. Oh, hell. Too much, and it would kill me.

I held perfectly still. I had fed well last night but could not afford to
lose any of it. Couldn't tell how much I'd already lost, only feel it as a
cooling wetness beneath my forearms.

They began to itch. Annoying, but a good sign, it meant healing.
Whatever wounds were there would seal up quickly enough, even without vanishing. Let them be and . . .

I was hungry again. God, it *hurt*. Not as bad as my arms, but given time
and no replenishment it would worsen. I never allowed myself to get so
starved. Too dangerous. The last time . . . yeah . . . the damned meat locker.

Okay, one thing at a time: what the hell had happened?

I was no longer on the cot under the seating tiers at Lady Crymsyn.
Someone had invaded that sanctuary and taken me elsewhere. Poor
Myrna had tried to warn me.

He'd come softly and cut the timing fine. Had he been in the building
earlier, I'd have heard him. In those last moments before sunrise, he must
have crept in, and only Myrna had known.

I had a choice of suspects: Kroun—or rather his cronies, Michael or
Broder—near the top of the list. He could hypnotically control them into
doing whatever he wanted. The *why* of it . . . I couldn't guess. Maybe he

wanted to be the king vampire of Chicago. Great, fine, he could have the job, I'd leave, no fuss.

Next up was Strome. He'd seen me walking around just fine after having much of my skin stripped off and might have gotten curious over that improbability. Just a couple nights back he'd seen me appear out of thin air, which surprised the hell out of us both. I'd popped him unconscious and been fairly sure he'd not remembered the Houdini act, but he could have faked it. With his stone face, he was the perfect liar. Again, the *why* escaped me.

Number one choice—and I hated it: Shoe Coldfield.

I didn't want to believe it. The idea made me sick, but he'd shown his violent side by pounding me flat the other night. Standing over Escott's dying body, he'd promised to kill me. Escott's recovery might not have been enough to change Coldfield's mind.

He had a serious grudge on and knew my weaknesses.

He was more than capable, but—and I grabbed hard onto this one—it wasn't how he worked. Coldfield would look me in the eye and slam me through a wall, but hold me prisoner?

I went back to Kroun again. When he fell into those blackouts where his eyes went strange . . . but that was also direct and short-lived. *Why* would he do this? Had he gone back on his decision not to execute me for Bristow's death?

There was a long list of mob guys I'd annoyed. While some might take a shot if they thought they could get away with it, none would know how pointless it would be. Whoever had done this knew how to deal with me.

Back to Strome . . . but I just couldn't see it. Back to . . .

What if Michael and Broder were acting independently of Kroun? Michael might have made a guess about my nature. Hell, he could know all about Kroun as well. There was no guarantee that he'd been able to keep his big secret. Michael could learn that I survived Bristow and a lot more besides—it was cheap talk at the Nightcrawler's bar; if you knew what clues to look for . . .

But I couldn't see the why of it, either—unless he was keeping me on ice in order to gain some kind of control over Kroun. Of course it would only work if Kroun was concerned about my welfare. I had no confidence in that.

However bad the thoughts, the thinking steadied me. I noticed more about my surroundings and myself. I lay on, perhaps, a long and very sturdy table. It had held out against my struggles without shifting. Maybe it was bolted to the floor or just exceptionally heavy.

I was dressed, so far as I could tell, in the same clothes, but the lower part of the sleeves were gone on my coat and shirt, cut away. What remained covered my chest; even the tie was in place. I longed to loosen it and undo the collar button. My legs seemed to be tied down to something. The restraints there gave a little and could be rope rather than chain. Strong, though. I wasn't moving, no leverage. I was under a heavy blanket or tarp, implying someone was either concerned for my comfort or wanted to be able to conceal me if needed.

The air was chill, but not freezing; there was an earthy scent to it, and my voice had bounced off hard surfaces. I heard no traffic or other outside noises. My best guess for location was a cellar with no ground-level windows. The utter silence—except for the heavy breather keeping his distance—indicated a deep and private hole.

Which was strangely familiar.

And threatened to bring on another wave of panic.

I crushed it. Quick. Giving in to more mindless fear was not going to help. I had to stay in control. Whoever had done this had kept me alive, had gone to considerable effort over it. He wanted something from me or would use me to get something. Maybe he was just waiting until I calmed down.

Okay. Why the hell not?

"Ready to talk now?" I bellowed. I sounded a lot braver and more confident than I felt. "Let's start the lodge meeting!"

No reply.

I chose to think he was mulling things over. I chose to think that I was not down here to starve to death in the dark.

"Hello!"

No reply. I waited a good long time.

I did hear something during the wait. Footsteps from the floor immediately above as someone paced around, unhurried. He was free to stroll, not tied up.

"Hey!"

The steps halted, probably in reaction to my yell. Good. I needed a way to get his attention.

A lunatic part of me with nothing to lose took over. I started singing "Happy Days Are Here Again" in an offensively loud bawl.

I have no vocal talent and limit my musical outbursts to the car or the shower when I'm alone. What isn't flat is off-key, or my voice just doesn't reach certain notes or cracks like an egg. It's a shame, because I like music.

In this case I hoped the racket would prompt a reaction. Even if all he did was come down to gag me, I'd at least get a look at him.

Nothing on the first chorus. I didn't know the other words, so I repeated it, putting in a remarkable amount of cheer and gusto. Maybe he'd think I'd gone nuts. Whatever it took.

Halfway through a third repeat a light came on.

The brilliance was too much after the darkness, lancing into my eyes. My lids hammered shut on their own, but I stubbornly kept singing. I tried to force them open and couldn't. I wanted to rub them—they were dry. After a bit I was able to squint past a veil of red and black sparklers and take in quick glimpses of the place.

Basement, as I'd guessed, gray concrete walls, low ceiling with dusty support beams for the floor above.

I was indeed on a table, broad, long, and sturdy, a Victorian behemoth built to withstand anything except modern times. Someone had shunted it down to the basement to age in solitude . . . until someone else came along and tied me to it.

My legs, not moving at all. I was bound like a mummy.

My arms—what the . . . ? No, that couldn't be right.

I blinked, desperate and disbelieving. The song died on my lips.

Both arms—no—that was goddamned *impossible*.

My fingers twitched when asked, but it hurt. There was something between them and my order-giving brain, something that went miles past mere horror and straight into stomach-turning grotesque.

I couldn't see for a moment; a gray mist settled on my eyes. I thought I was at last vanishing, but my body held solid. My mind simply didn't want to accept the straightforward cruelty of it.

Vision clearing . . . cleared . . . and the awfulness was still there.

My arms stretched out—and midway along below the elbows was a vertical piece of threaded metal rod.

The steel was half an inch thick and *in my flesh*, piercing right through, passing between the two bones of my lower arms.

The tops of the rods were at a right angle like the flat handle of a walking stick. If I pulled my arms straight up the L-shape of the angle would stop them. Presumably the rest of the length went through the table. I was held fast. I'd seen miniature versions of this used to pin insects to display boards.

It was too much. I couldn't help but struggle. This wasn't happening to me. The panic flooded back, full force.

Flailing against the immobile steel was useless, but I couldn't stop, not until exhaustion overtook me again. I finally collapsed, shivering from head to toe.

You're not supposed to be able to faint lying down, but I went black-out dizzy, and my guts wanted to turn themselves out. There was no waking from this nightmare.

"It's just going to get worse."

I looked around for the source of that voice. He sounded familiar.

Oh. It was me.

I was standing right over myself: cleaned up and in a sharp new suit, I looked sympathetic, but clearly unable to offer more than an opinion.

That other me usually turned up when I was right out of my mind.

Good timing.

Still, I was company of sorts. However crazy I got, I didn't have to be alone in the pit.

"Any ideas?" I asked in a shaky whisper.

"Try singing some more."

What the hell, why not?

Couldn't bring myself to do it just yet. No energy. My struggles had me bleeding again, and every drop falling to the floor weakened me. I'd lost a lot, and the hunger would continue to grow. My corner teeth were out, I was in all kinds of pain, hallucinating, and there wasn't a damned thing I could do.

Helplessness. I'd been here before, hanging in a meat locker, convulsing in the throes of a seizure, standing at the foot of Escott's hospital bed while he lay dying . . .

I imagined him rising to look at me, his face distorted by the bruises I'd put there, but still recognizable, wearing a sardonic expression.

"You're the strongest man I know," he told me.

I didn't feel it, but he was a good judge of character. I could put up a front, fake a courage I did not possess. If some bastard wanted me to die like this, then I'd go with a little pride.

Howling a fourth chorus, I sounded absolutely insane, even to me. That was scary, but I kept going.

"I know you can hear me," I called. "I can do this all night."

The me in the new suit smiled and nodded, giving a thumbs-up, and looked across the room.

A door opened. I couldn't see it but heard the drawing of a bolt and creak of hinges. Footsteps on wood stairs, descending, one-two-three-four . . . I counted sixteen steps, storing the information.

He crossed into my field of view. He was also in a nice suit and also smiled, though that was the natural expression of his pale face. It was how his mouth was shaped, giving him an air of smug perpetual amusement. He held a .45 revolver in one hand and seemed very confident.

My short list of suspects failed to include this man. The familiarity of a basement prison had been a clue from a hidden corner of my mind. Not so very long ago I'd chained Hurley Gilbert Dugan to a wall in a very similar place.

He'd gone me one better with this variation.

I stared, and Dugan smiled back, and damn, but he was enjoying the situation.

No reason why I shouldn't as well. I began to laugh again. The laughter was odd; I'd never laughed like that in my life. The me standing opposite Dugan approved, grinning as well. This was goddamned funny. It really was.

And it spoiled Dugan's moment.

He must have anticipated some other reaction from me, anger or fear, cursing or begging, but not this. His intentional smile soured, replaced by a flash of irritation. The man had no sense of humor, not the normal kind. He liked feeling superior to others and relished a good gloat, but take it away, laugh at *him*—he hated that.

I was in no position to be antagonizing, but there was little he could do to me that Hog Bristow hadn't done first. If Dugan found a way to improve on *that*, well, I'd die a little bit quicker.

And I would die.

I wasn't getting out of this one. I saw it in his eyes, knew in my heart that for him it was a practical necessity. This was where it would happen, no coming back from this lonely grave.

But if there was *any* way I could take him with me . . .

In the short time since my change, I'd killed. I was a murderer. There were deaths I'd caused indirectly and others that were without question my own doing. To one degree or another each had a measure of regret attached, not that I would have changed things in a couple cases, but taking a life lessens your own. It leaves a wound on your soul that never quite heals.

But sometimes . . . it's worth it.

Hog Bristow, yeah, I'd kill him again and no problem. There would be a certain physical disgust for the act itself, like stepping on a poisonous spider and leaving a mess. But you do it anyway.

Hurley Gilbert Dugan was different. I would take a great deal of pleasure in the act of killing him. I might even prolong it to give him a taste of the terror he'd given to others. As a kid he was probably responsible for at least two deaths: a governess and another kid. As an adult he was the brains behind a girl's kidnapping and the murder of a harmless old couple whose isolated farmhouse he wanted for a hideout.

There might be more, and I wondered about the fate of the owner of this place. Dugan lied, manipulated people for fun, and wrote countless essays arguing the merit of executing those he thought to be inferior specimens of humanity. He was genuinely puzzled when anyone disagreed with him. Clearly they were just the sort of shortsighted fools he would have culled from the herd.

He'd been in that meat locker, too, running loose in the background, not important enough for Bristow to bother with, and witnessed my torture. It had made him sick. He had no belly then for violence, not when he could get someone else to do the work. But he'd learned much in that hour. He knew things about me that I didn't want to know myself; for that alone I wanted him dead.

He would be dead if not for the rods holding my arms. That was why he'd not been present at my waking. He wanted to be sure I was safely pinned in place. Everything in me wanted to tear loose and rip him in two. But if I'd been unable to get free by now, then it wasn't going to happen. I was just too weak.

That was a hell of a lot of frustration, more than enough to make a man crazy.

So I laughed in his endlessly smiling face and sang off-key and laughed some more.

Until he gently pressed the muzzle of that revolver against my temple.

I trailed off but kept grinning. If he shot me in the head under these circumstances, it just might do the trick. I'd be dead without finding out what he wanted, though. If he'd simply meant to kill me, that would have happened back in the nightclub. He'd gone to a lot of trouble to get me here.

Dugan examined the threaded rod on his side, poking at the area where the metal went in. It hurt when he did that. From what I could see from my angle, the skin was healed tight around the metal, red and puffy, like an infection swelling around a splinter.

He abruptly grabbed the handle part of the rod and gave it a full twist all the way around. My skin parted from the metal, blood welled, and I couldn't stifle a gasp. When a small portion of the red-hot haze in my brain receded, he twisted the thing back again. I was almost prepared for it, but not really. I squirmed in vain to get free.

He watched with a calm detachment.

Well dressed, well fed, and yes, that complacent expression was starting to return. But I'd seen him puking and terrified. That gave me one up on him. Anything to boost my morale.

He'd made his point, though: this was his show.

He reached out of my view and drew up a chair, settling in. He seemed to be ready to spend a good long time with me.

God, what had I done to deserve this?

"I've been following you," he said.

No greeting, no preamble, he spoke as though continuing a conversation begun hours ago. Some people do that, usually the most self-absorbed.

"You never once looked over your shoulder. You made it easy."

I felt no need to reply, resigned to what promised to be a lengthy recitation of his life and hard times since our escape from the meat locker. He loved himself more than anyone I'd ever met, and he assumed others also found him fascinating.

He'd taken ten grand from a misguided lady friend and disappeared himself, a difficult task what with every mobster in Chicago looking for him on my say-so. I'd tentatively concluded that he'd left the city and hoped he'd departed from the country altogether.

Optimism can be a very, very evil thing.

Dugan must have been preparing his little speech for some while—there was a rehearsed quality to it as he told his story. I didn't give a tinker's damn how clever he'd been at watching me from afar. Nor could I work up any interest for his account of how he'd learned to use firearms. The .45 made him dangerous, not tough.

It was clear he cherished the sound of his own voice, and it was a nice voice: educated, articulate. He reminded me of Michael that way, but Michael was someone I could deal with; Dugan was not.

"Every night I've kept a close eye on you, Fleming," he said. "You never knew."

"You need a better hobby."

"Watching and studying and learning exactly how you waste your abilities."

"Should've gone to the movies. They have cartoons."

Dugan was very proud about how he'd broken the window and gotten into the house. He thought himself to be very slick, indeed. He'd found my basement shelter eventually, for he had reasoned I must have something like that.

Only my own caution had spared me from being kidnapped that night. He'd returned during the day, intent on hauling me out, but I'd slept safe in the neighbor's attic. Had I done so again instead of staying at the club, I'd still be free.

Dugan broke into Crymsyn that day, covering his tracks better, and scoured it for hidden sanctuaries. I'd been smart to have one someplace other than the basement; but being such a genius, it was inevitable he would discover it.

He'd been watching from afar when Kroun and I had gone to the Stockyards the other night. Good thing Kroun hadn't left the car. Dugan gave no hint of knowing there was another bloodsucker in town. He complimented me for later buying blood at a butcher shop, and it was unsettling to learn he'd been so close behind. How could I have not noticed?

I was sick of him. "You want applause? Undo my arms."

"Please, I went to too much trouble setting this up. I remembered what you told me when that two-legged animal had you hanging from the ceiling. You couldn't escape because a piece of metal lodged in your body prevented you from vanishing. That's fascinating. I'm delighted that my experiment to keep you here was so successful."

Some experiment. But I had to admit, it worked like a son of a bitch.

Dugan twisted the rod again, so the healing skin parted from the metal and fresh blood appeared. The sight of it and my pain didn't bother him tonight.

In one of those infrequent flashes that usually occur just a little too late to do any good, I began to get a glimmer of what this was about, and the bottom dropped out of my belly.

I could not show fear, hell, I couldn't even tremble. I was absolutely petrified.

He saw that, and it pleased him.

He rose from the chair, going around and behind the head of my bed, out of sight. I heard odd noises, a rustle and slither like stiff fabric shifting, a metallic click, his step as he returned.

He'd put on a butcher's apron. It covered the whole of his front.

And he'd traded the revolver for a scalpel.

My thinking he'd go one better than Bristow and kill me that much faster . . . I'd been crazy. Even if death was at the other end, I couldn't go through it again. I just couldn't.

I closed my eyes. In a safe and well-sheltered part of my mind there was a single perfect hour from a perfect summer day. I'd floated alone in the cool water of a stock tank, master of the world and content. In memory, I breathed sweet, hot air, felt the still water holding me up, and the lazy wind whispering over my skin.

It was fragile protection against what was to come. Far stronger was the memory of Bristow stripping my skin off. I'd done all I could to blot that out, but Dugan brought it hurtling back.

Unable to run, I trembled, head to toe.

My scars began to burn.

If he wanted me to beg, I would.

I'd do anything, say anything.

I had no pride, no courage.

He owned me.

14

KROUN

Gabe went to the desk, reached for the phone, changed his mind. Derner wouldn't know any more about Fleming's whereabouts than he had a few minutes ago.

The number for Michael . . . well, he was on his way in. Gabe would grill him then.

He checked Escott, who had not moved from the chair, though he'd straightened a little. He looked sick, but in a different way than the other night in the hospital. He continued to stare at the empty space on the floor.

"Hey," Gabe said. "Let's go."

It took a moment, but Escott found his feet. "Where?" His voice was flat, drained.

"Outside. I want air."

If Escott appreciated the irony of that, he gave no sign. Gabe pulled on his overcoat and hat and made sure Escott didn't fall down the stairs as they descended. They paused in the lobby; something had changed on the bar.

"Were those all propped on end when you came in?" Gabe asked. The dozens of matchbooks scattered about were flat now, the covers neatly tucked back into place.

"Yes. They were." Escott's eyes flickered.

"Who else is here?"

"That would be Myrna. She's a ghost," he said, deadpan as hell.

Gabe considered the circumstances and Escott's state of mind. He was crazy, but not that crazy. "Ghost. You got ghosts?"

"Just the one. She plays with the lights. I wish to God she could tell me what's happened."

The lobby phone rang. The bell went on for far longer than normal, then faded. Escott broke away and picked up the earpiece, listening, but apparently nothing came through. He returned it, disappointed. "She's never played with the phone before." He stayed put, apparently prepared to wait for it to ring again.

"Air," said Gabe. "Now." He wasn't afraid; it was just damned weird, and he didn't want to think about stuff like that tonight.

Freezing and windy, nothing new about the weather, though he hoped the shock might clear Escott's head. Gabe paced up and down the front a few times, the exercise working off adrenaline generated by having a gun pointed his way. He also checked the area for anything that shouldn't be there, like Broder or Michael. Nothing caught his attention; and no one shot at him, so far so good.

Huddled under the canopy of the club's entrance Escott tried to light a cigarette, but the wind kept blowing out his match. Gabe offered his lighter, noticing that Escott had gotten his shakes under control.

As good a time as any.

"So . . . what did Jack do? Jump off a building?"

Escott threw him a short glare, then looked away. He smoked the cigarette halfway down before replying. "He made a wooden slug, fitted it to a cartridge, then shot himself in the head."

Gabe winced, experiencing an uneasy sympathy mixed with disbelief. "Cripes. And he survived that?"

"At sunset he vanished and healed. I didn't know if he would, I—"

"What, you found him?"

He nodded. "On the couch in his office."

"What couch?"

"The one that's not there. I suppose he got rid of it. There was blood . . ."

No kidding.

"He'd survived, but I was so damned angry with him. That's why we got into a fight. It got out of hand, went too far . . . but he promised . . . he swore on Bobbi's life he'd never hurt himself again."

"Does he keep his promises?"

"I thought he did. He always has."

"Then lay off the worrying."

"What do you mean?"

"Ever think that something *else* happened to make him take off?"

"He'd phone—"

"Unless he's tied up somewhere against his will."

Escott snorted. "That's impossible. He'd just vanish and leave."

"Listen, the other night the cops tried to hustle us right over there in the parking lot. I made them forget, but they could have shaken it off and grabbed your pal. If they're throwing him a blackjack party in some station house, he wouldn't dare vanish, and he couldn't make a phone call. He can't hypnotize people anymore, right?"

"But they—"

"Please, tell me every cop in this town follows the rules, and I will personally apologize to each one and his dog."

With new hope on his face, Escott threw away his smoke, went into the club, and beelined for the lobby phone. He pushed nickels into the slot, making one call after another. Gabe stood by the bar and watched the scattered matchbooks. Not one of them moved.

Emerging from the booth, Escott shook his head. "I've contacted everyone who would hear if Jack had been picked up."

"Things like that can be kept quiet."

"Of that I am aware. It could even be the FBI taking an interest."

"Why would they do that?"

"Why not?"

Damned if I know. Gabe had mulled over the possibility that Michael or Broder might have stepped in. Fleming might be tied up somewhere in Cicero, getting questioned. He might put up with it, but not indefinitely. "You know how to get to the Nightcrawler Club from here?"

"Of course."

He handed over the keys to the Hudson. "C'mon. Maybe Derner can work faster if I'm looking over his shoulder."

*   *   *

THE suicide attempt had surprised the hell out of him. Fleming had given no sign—but then Gabe didn't know him. That twitching fit at their first meeting . . . Fleming had been in bad shape then, but he'd pulled out of it. A couple of times he'd acted odd, though: down in that garage basement and in the hospital, but anyone would be upset. He'd steadied up.

But shooting himself?

Damn.

No wonder Escott had been nuts enough to pull a gun. Gabe wasn't sure he should overlook that. On the other hand, the man had apologized. That was nuts, too.

Aren't there any sane people in this town?

Long odds against that. Just have to make the best of things. Find Fleming, deal with Michael, then what? Go fishing? Maybe not.

Escott parked the Hudson on one side of the building rather than in the back alley of the Nightcrawler. It was too soon yet for Michael to show up, but Gabe didn't mind waiting now that he had something to do and other things to think about than his own problems.

The mugs on watch got scarce soon as they saw him getting out. Apparently his reputation was as bad here as in New York, and he was not above exploiting it. That was how he'd survived those early days without people noticing anything was wrong.

He used it now, leading the way up to the office, aiming a grim face at Derner, who was at the desk.

"Haven't found him yet, Mr. Kroun, sorry," he said, correctly interpreting the reason behind the personal appearance.

Gabe stood over him. "Don't give up on that, okay?"

"No, sir." Derner spared a quick, curious glance at Escott and grabbed the phone. "Heard you were sick, Mr. Escott."

"I was. Much better now, thank you."

"Cops," said Gabe. "See if he's been picked up by any of 'em."

Derner winced. "Uh . . . there could be . . ."

"What?"

"Oh, you know—guys listening in. Some of those G-men . . ."

"So? You're just looking for a missing friend who might have been taken in by mistake. Nothing wrong in that."

Derner didn't seem too convinced on the point but went back to dialing.

Gabe gave Escott a critical once-over. The man was ragged at the edges. He must have been running without stop all night.

"You look like hell," Gabe observed. "Eat anything lately?"

Escott shook his head and sank into one of the overstuffed chairs facing Derner.

Dropping his coat and hat on another chair, Gabe went to the door and gave orders to one of the mugs loafing in the hall, who hurried off. In a wonderfully brief time, two of the club's waitresses—very cute in their short, spangled skirts—came in with covered trays. Gabe pointed them at Escott.

"Really, now . . ." Escott began, startled as they swooped on him.

"You need your strength," said Gabe. "Girls—give 'im the works."

He retired to a couch opposite the main desk, partly to watch Derner and partly to remove himself from the heavy smell of the steak-and-potatoes meal. Gabe found entertainment in the show, though. A clearly nonplussed Escott enduring the torture of two cooing, smiling Kewpie dolls cutting his food and hand-feeding him one bite at a time . . . the club photographer should be up to take a picture.

Gabe's smirk lasted until he saw Derner's face. The man had gone dead white as he stared at the fun. Gabe went to the desk, leaning in close. "What's wrong?"

"Nothing, Mr. Kroun," he said, voice very low. "It's your business."

He'd stepped in something, he just wasn't sure what. "Look at me."

Derner reluctantly did so.

It was risking another headache, but he had to know and pressed in. "Have I done this before?"

"Yessir."

"What happens next?"

"You take 'em down to the basement. They don't come back."

Oh, hell. He had no memory for any of that, but the stories . . .

He'd not understood what had suddenly prompted him to look after a guest; it just seemed like the right thing to do. This macabre twisting of hospitality was yet another ugly remnant of the man he had been. The more he found out about himself, the less he liked.

His head hurt now, a hot drill was burrowing into the bone. He frowned as he leaned over Derner again. "This isn't a last meal. We clear?"

"Yessir."

"This guy is our friend. From now on he gets treated with the same respect as I do."

"Yessir."

"Back to work."

Derner obeyed, no questions, no comment, just the way Gabe liked it.

In the last two months he had made a few such unpleasant discoveries. He'd do or say something innocuous and find a nasty surprise attached. More than once he caught himself questioning an impulse that came out of nowhere.

But second-guessing everything was no way to live. Better to keep his eyes open and catch the reaction of others, as he'd done with Derner. It had worked well enough so far.

Gabe went into the bathroom, wet a folded washcloth through, and pressed it to the knot of hot pain under the white streak. He peered at his ghostly image in the mirror but found no clue to that earlier life.

"Damn . . . you must have been one hell of a crazy bastard," he muttered.

THE arrowhead-tipped hands of a black-and-chrome wall clock made their slow circuit into the next hour, and there was still no news of Fleming. Gabe wasn't worried, but Escott took Derner's place at the desk and used the phone, rechecking with various people. Things got sticky when he called Fleming's girlfriend. She'd not seen or heard from him, and Escott had to do some quick talking so she wouldn't worry. With a fine disregard for the truth, he told her that Kroun was likely responsible for keeping their friend busy. She bent Escott's ear for a time, and whatever she said had his full attention.

"Oh . . . I didn't know that," he said. "Congratulations. Really. I'm delighted for you. Overdue and much deserved. Well, yes, I suppose he might not be too pleased, but he'll get over it, not to worry. Yes, of course I'll tell him to call you."

Escott hung up, looking flummoxed.

"What?" Gabe prompted from the couch. He'd stretched out to work on a more difficult crossword puzzle from a different newspaper.

"Miss Smythe informed me that she's soon to leave for Hollywood to take a screen test."

That explained the congratulations, though his delivery had been lukewarm. "Sounds good. A pippin like her should be out there. Better weather."

"Yes, well, Jack won't think so. They've had some considerable discussion on that topic. He wouldn't stop her, but neither is he willing to go with her. His job is here."

"He's choosing a nightclub over his girl?"

"Perhaps."

"He's nuts. You can open a club anywhere and make good, but a dame like her is once in a lifetime."

Escott shot him an appraising look. "Mr. Kroun, I think you should repeat that within Jack's hearing. It might sort him out. Miss Smythe imparted the news to him last night, and he did not take it with any great enthusiasm. It could explain his dropping out of sight."

"His girlfriend's leaving town so he goes off to sulk? Does that sound like something he'd do?"

"The more I think about it . . . yes, it does. He can get himself fairly deep into the dumps, though his club kept him happy until . . ." Escott didn't finish.

"Hog Bristow. Yeah. My fault. I know. None of that was supposed to happen."

"Yet it did."

Gabe felt himself get warm in the face. Shame was an unfamiliar feeling. He didn't like it much. "Where does he go to sulk?"

"No place special. His club, but I've been all through it, been to my office and—oh, hell." He grabbed the phone and dialed again, giving his name to someone on the other end. He scribbled on a pad, then stopped, his eyes going sharp as he listened. He gave a terse thank you, slammed the receiver down, got up and paced, looking exasperated.

"Yes?" Gabe asked after a suitable pause.

"Bloody idiot," Escott snapped.

"Him or me?"

"Neither. This is my doing—bloody *hell*!"

"What?"

"I never once thought to check my own answering service. He left a message earlier tonight."

Gabe put down the paper and sat up, the better to enjoy things. "A message?"

"To quote: 'I need to do some thinking, don't worry, be back soon.' Bloody hell, I'll flatten his skull for this."

"For what—leaving a message you didn't check?"

Escott responded with a few ripe and expressive words. For all that, he looked hugely relieved. He dropped into his chair, rubbing the back of his neck. "Once again I apologize, Mr. Kroun."

"Remind me—is that still for nearly blowing a hole in me after I saved your life? Think nothing of it. Could happen to anyone."

"You're too kind." Escott met the sarcasm with a dry tone, but evidently got the point. His ears had turned red.

Oh, yeah, it'll be a while before he lives that one down.

"This is being unconscionably inconsiderate to Miss Smythe. He could have phoned her. He could have phoned me. Why leave a message?"

"Probably just didn't want to talk." Gabe started to pick up the crossword again, but the office door banged open, startling Derner. Escott twitched, going alert.

Michael was early.

He wore his best poker face. The glasses helped. They reflected the lights, concealing half his expression.

Gabe remained seated and smiled just enough to annoy Mike. Strangely, he didn't react, just stood there.

Waiting.

Mike glanced at Derner, then Escott, and apparently dismissed him as one of the club's many hangers-on. "We'll talk in the car. Private."

"And cold."

"You can take it. Come on."

This was a new side. Maybe he'd learned something about Broder that had gotten him thinking. Reaching for his coat and hat, Gabe shot a surreptitious look at Escott, who seemed incurious and inclined to stay put. Smart of him.

The club's last show was in full swing out front, but the kitchen staff was gone, and most of the lights were off. The alley was also dark and empty except for Mike's Studebaker. Gabe emerged cautiously. Broder could be just around the corner at either end or even on one of the surrounding roofs, biding his time to take a shot.

Keeping his back to the club's wall, Gabe went down the stairs and did not cross to the car. Mike seemed to expect that and turned to face him midway between, hands in his pockets.

"It's safe," he said.

The wind was still up, masking sound. Gabe didn't like it; but if there was a bushwhacking in his near future, his reactions were a lot faster than before.

He looked at the man standing solid before him and once more tried to see something in his face that would spark a memory.

Mike was a familiar stranger, hostile, wary, more so tonight than before. Had he always been that grim? Had they ever been friends? Gabe had not seen a hint of that so far, but it must have been there once.

Of course there was the eight-year age difference. Growing up, Gabe might have been too busy to bother with a little brother, especially a half brother. He knew that some could end up hating each other, but at some point in their childhood, he and Michael must have played together, looked out for each other.

Gabriel had no memory of any of it, and no one he'd spoken to from the old neighborhood could tell him what had gone on behind the closed doors of the Kroun family flat.

Michael knew though.

Gabe had been tempted many times to pull the facts out of him hypnotically but never acted upon it.

For one thing, you just don't do that to family.

For another, he was afraid of what he might learn. The little that he had already gleaned was ugly.

Even without the slug in his brain, Gabe would not have remembered his own mother; she'd died a few months after his birth. He'd looked it up in the court records. Sonny had come home drunk one night. He claimed that beating his wife to death had been an accident. Since he worked for a neighborhood boss, a big shot who had influence with a judge, Sonny got sent up for manslaughter instead of murder.

Gabe went to a state orphanage, but no one adopted him. Eight years later his supposedly reformed father came to claim him, a second wife and a baby named Michael in tow.

What had that been like? An orphan all his life and suddenly young Gabriel gets a family. Had a brutal father like Sonny been better than no father at all?

Whatever had happened during his upbringing had turned Gabe into a killer. Chances were good that lightning had struck twice, doing the same for Mike, twisting him a little differently.

Until now there hadn't been a good enough reason to make him talk. The evidence up at the cabin changed that.

"So . . . how's Cicero these days?"

"Shut up, Whitey." Mike looked ready to burst, there was so much inside him wanting to get out. Give him time . . .

But the minutes went by. Nothing. Michael's hands worked inside his coat pockets, making fists, forcing his hands open. It was a mannerism he only ever fell into when they were alone.

He thinks he's still dealing with the son of a bitch he's always known. Not me. Who do I need to be to get answers?

"Where's Broder?" Gabe asked, checking both ends of the alley again.

"Maybe he's pounding the bullet dents out of that car he took the other night."

That was unexpected. "He told you."

"Yeah. He told me."

"After he drove us off the road things got a little hazy. What'd he say?"

But Mike clammed up.

"Oh, come on. What kind of arrangement have you got that someone like Momma Cabot can call Broder whenever she wants?"

"You stay away from her."

"Why?"

Mike shook his head.

"Is that why you gave Fleming the green light to keep me in line and no reprisals?"

"He told you that?" He stopped making fists and took his hands from his pockets.

"Your voice carries. Why do you want to kill me, Mike?"

No reflections on the glasses now, Michael's blue eyes were wide open and for an instant showed a mix of anguish and guilt. He shut it down. "I don't want to."

"But you wouldn't much mind if someone else did the dirty work. What problem gets solved if I'm gone?"

Michael shook his head again.

"I know it has to do with that damned cabin. You were there."

"I was never there," he stated, voice like a razor.

Gabe had hit the nerve he'd wanted. "I went up. I saw the blood, and I found Ramsey's body." He searched for further reaction, but Mike had turned to stone. "I'd like to hear your side."

He was taking a different kind of risk now. The man Gabe had been before his death would never have said anything like that.

"My side?"

"What happened there." Gabe pulled out the .22, holding it flat on his palm so it wouldn't be mistaken for a threat. "Is this yours? Or Ramsey's?"

"What is it?"

He can't see in the dark. Gabe crossed now, opened the driver's door, and put the headlamps on. Mike followed him to the front of the car, staring down at the rusted weapon in the harsh glare. They made fine targets, the pair of them.

"Not mine," he said. "That's your kind of gun."

He was probably right. There was every chance that Gabe had been in the habit of carrying a small-caliber shooter with the numbers filed off. He could throw it away after a kill. Okay, that just meant someone had taken it from him.

"And this?" He drew the amber vial out next, holding it between thumb and index finger.

Mike looked and dismissed it. "What do you want from me?"

This wasn't going the way it should. What had been conclusive up in the woods seemed ridiculous here. Michael should be angry and defensive for being caught out, not like this. Unless . . .

"Then it was Broder. He'd planted stuff. What was his angle? Kill me and Ramsey, then move up the ladder? Is that where that bastard Mitchell got the idea? Or did you order it from the start?"

Mike showed his lower teeth, eyes blazing. He raised one hand, fingers skyward as though to grab something. His fist finally closed on air.

"Well?"

"I'm sorry, Whitey. I promised Ma I'd look after you, but it's too much now. I can't do it anymore."

In the last two months, Mike had never spoken of his mother. All Gabe knew about his stepmother was her name and the official records concerning her death. Sonny had made such a vicious job of his second wife's murder that they'd thrown him into an insane asylum instead of hanging him.

Mike had been fifteen at the time; Gabe had become his legal guardian. Why was it that—

"No more," Mike whispered. Hands in pockets again, briefly. He pulled a gun out, the one Gabe had reloaded himself the previous night.

"Hey, wait!" Gabe backed clear of the lamp glare. He didn't know his brother that well, but this was completely wrong for him.

Mike fired. His aim was off, and Gabe dodged. The bullet noisily took a chunk from the wall behind him.

Instinct said to run, but insanity took over. Gabe dove forward and tackled him before he could get in a second shot. They hit the pavement and rolled in wet filth. Mike fought to win, was quick as a snake, not pulling a single dirty punch.

But the fight was finished in seconds. He just didn't have the same speed and strength. Gabe made his one hit count, and that was all she wrote.

He pushed himself off the dazed Mike, cursing a blue streak for the situation. He'd had enough. It was time to haul the kid into the club, put a light in his face, and bust his brain open.

He heard someone grunt, and after a moment realized he was on the ground again, facedown. What the hell—?

Gabe tried to get up and the movement set off a fireball in his head. Hideous blinding agony struck him flat.

Dimly he heard heavy footsteps, Broder's deep voice asking a question, and Michael's faint and groggy reply. Scraping sounds, a groan, the slam of a car door.

More steps. This time Gabe heeded instinct and went perfectly still. Not difficult; the pain had paralyzed everything but the urge to scream. He choked it off.

Pressure on his throat. Broder was feeling for a pulse. Getting none, he pushed up the back of Gabe's overcoat and suit coat, grabbing his belt. One-handed, he lifted and pulled Gabe's limp body along like a heavy suitcase, the man was that strong.

A gun went off. It made quite a roar within the confines of the alley. Three shots at least, so close together that they could have been from a machine gun.

Broder dropped his burden. Gabe forced his eyes open. Filling his view was one wheel of the Studebaker, inches from his face.

Another shot.

Broder was in the car, gunning it to life. The wheel slipped, grabbed, and spun away. The Studie departed, its open trunk lid bouncing, then slamming into place as the car screeched out of the alley.

Gabe dragged himself upright. He hurt too much to be doing anything so stupid, but anger was running the show by then. He staggered, using a wall for support, working his way toward the street. If they knew he was alive, they'd come back. He wanted a shot at Broder.

Behind him a car horn honked an irritable warning.

Now what?

He pressed out of the way as the Hudson tore past in pursuit. Escott was at the wheel. Eyes wide and blazing, he glanced once at Gabe, showing the mirthless grin of a crazy man, and kept going.

15

FLEMING

DUGAN held the shiny-clean scalpel rock steady between his fingers, looking down with that damned permanent smile that had never before reached his eyes. They glinted now. He was a truly happy man.

"You know what comes next," he stated.

I had no way to brace against it. I'd been to the brink and over. I couldn't go there again.

Eyes shut, I gave up.

My mind slipped away and hid in that perfect summer hour, adding more detail. The cool water contrasting with the hot breeze, shade tree overhead, sunbeams streaming through the leaves, birdsong . . . good, good, but I needed company.

Leaning against the tree was Escott, coatless, shirtsleeves rolled up, waistcoat unbuttoned, no tie. He sipped lemonade from a tall glass, his attention on the green fields around us. He looked surprisingly at peace.

Bobbi was in the stock tank. She held me, kept me from sinking. She wore a skin-hugging swimsuit . . . I couldn't fix on the color. It kept shifting from red to blue to yellow, sometimes black. None of them seemed right on her, but this was the first time I'd ever seen her in sunlight. It made her blond hair glow and set off the green sparks in her eyes.

She smiled like it was the world's first day and bent to kiss me. I felt her lips and knew if she stayed with me I would be all right.

Something stung my left wrist, kept on stinging, harsh as a wasp.

I held fast to my illusion for a few more precious seconds, then had to see what hurt.

It was and was not what I'd expected.

My wrist hung out past the edge of the table, and Dugan had sliced into it, but not to strip away flesh. He was hunched over holding a glass under the wound, collecting the blood.

My initial shock and disgust were overwhelmed by elation. He wasn't going to skin me, just drain me dry. That wasn't as painful. In the end I'd just fall asleep.

As deaths went, it was the best I could expect.

I smothered my relief, but while one part of me celebrated an easier passing, another part seethed with blind fury for what he was doing. I tried to pull away, but of course the metal held. The hot shock was more remote this time. My body was slowing down in reaction to the blood loss. I could feel my strength literally rushing out.

Dugan's smile was genuinely warm. "Things got so very interesting the other night, didn't they? The hospital. Your friend was so sick. I was there."

How . . . ? One of the reporters? But they'd left. The only other one . . .

"You are quite the catalyst for calamity, aren't you, Fleming? First that actor shot, then your partner hurt. What a terrible beating he had. I troubled to get close to your little group, and it was just too easy. You're all so tidily wrapped up in your concerns. You looked right at me once, but didn't really see. No one notices a humble janitor with his bucket and mop."

He had that right. Too late now to feel stupid over it. The wig, thick glasses, and a big mustache to hide his distinctive mouth had done the trick.

"Such a *remarkable* event transpired that night. The whole hospital was gossiping about the dying patient who was made to drink blood, then had a miraculous recovery."

The cut inside my wrist healed shut, leaving a welt that would fade if I lived long enough. The glass he held was a laboratory beaker with measurement lines up the sides. He'd drawn off at least a cup of my blood. Much more than that had dripped to the floor when I fought to get free. I was dizzy from the loss.

He straightened, sniffing the contents of the beaker.

"How generous you were to save his life—and letting me know for certain how to change mine for the better."

I wanted to smash his smile to the other side of his head. Underestimating him . . . not smart . . . damned stupid in fact.

His self-absorbed ramblings . . . I'd not paid them the proper attention. Now they made sense; he hadn't been lecturing just to hear his own voice. I understood now.

He wanted to turn himself into a vampire.

Dugan correctly interpreted my revulsion. He leaned in close. "Remember when we first spoke in your office? I told you then I wanted you for a very simple experiment—nothing that would offend your sense of morality. You should have listened." He thumped a finger sharply against the rod. It made my arm twitch, tearing the skin again, and more of my life leaked away. "All I wanted *then* was for you to get into one of the larger banks for a modest withdrawal. They wouldn't have missed it, and it would have been of considerable help to me. But you had to be difficult."

God, I was so hungry. Bloodsmell was everywhere, and I couldn't touch it. I had to fight to stay focused.

"I realized there would be no effective way to control you; therefore, my best course of action was to acquire your abilities myself. I did a bit of research, but there is appallingly little information available, and much of it is suspect. However, your friend's misfortune gave me all I really needed." He lifted the beaker. "I'm estimating that it will take three nights to effect the full transformation. The folklore is in general agreement on that point, though it's mixed up with religious nonsense. Now you know how long you'll be here. Once I'm like you, I will let you go—I know you don't believe that. You dealt me some very shabby treatment, but really, I was never your enemy."

I'll carve that on your gravestone.

"Be assured, I'll have a long head start before you're set free. I know you won't be persuaded to a sensible neutrality toward me, but I truly have nothing against you. You're no different from any other animal succumbing to instinct. You lack the capacity for—"

"Ya want in the union?" I asked. My voice had turned reedy. It was hard to draw in enough air to speak. "Why dint ya say so? I'da put th' word in."

"You waste yourself."

No doubt. I needed him to underestimate me.

"And you can't even see it. But you have my word: three nights, and I'll let you go. Oh—your friends won't miss you. I repaired the damage made when I broke into your little lair. I also left a suitably misleading message with that detective fellow's answering service. They're under the impression that you've gone off to do a bit of thinking. Exasperating, perhaps, but they won't look for you."

Would Escott question that? Or Bobbi? The way I'd been acting lately . . .

"This won't be pleasant for either of us, but I will be civil to you for the duration. Once this is over, you'll never see me again, and that should be some consolation."

Dugan raised the beaker to his lips and took his first taste. It must not have been to his liking, to judge by his expression. He had to force himself.

He drank all of it, which was more than was needed. A sip would do the job—if it worked. I stared the way you do at a car accident. It's bad, but you can't stop until you see the worst. What would it be, a dead body or a dying one? I was the one dying, though. I'd lost so much life, and he was drinking away the rest.

Yet as I lay there, weak and starving, I began to laugh, very softly.

He's got it wrong.

I used up what little strength remained, laughing.

If he thought me insane, well and good.

His eyes were strange, very bright. It would be hard getting him to think I was crazy. He was so far gone himself.

"What is it?" he asked. Suspicion from him now. I had to be more careful.

"You . . ."

"What?"

Huh. Had to finish it, give him a reply. Something to mislead. "You . . . look funny, Gurley Hilbert." I trailed off drowsily. Not an act—I was shutting down the same as I did at dawn.

He disliked the distortion of his name, but his smug smile returned. I hoped that meant he thought himself to still be fully in control of this two-legged animal. Hell, he *was* in control, but it wouldn't last. He'd made a big mistake letting me get so weak.

"That pettiness doesn't matter to me. You don't see that I . . . I don't—"

Then he abruptly broke off, falling from the chair, whooping and gagging.

Drinking blood is not something people just *do*. There's only so much an ordinary human can take before getting sick. Even with my change making the stuff taste good, it had taken months before my mind got used to the idea itself and accepted it. How much worse was it for this fastidious, fancy-pants society swan. You can't think too much on the process, and Dugan was obsessed with his intellectual superiority. Whatever was going through his mind . . . he'd have to quash it thoroughly. Odds were he'd find it impossible. Minds like his had no off switch.

But was his reaction a result from taking blood in general or *my* blood in particular?

Until that miracle in Escott's hospital room, I'd have bet on the former. Not so sure anymore. A vampire's blood had saved a sick man from dying, but what would it do to a well man? Make him healthier?

No matter. The bastard's got it wrong.

This had happened to me before, but the woman who'd forced me to change her had gotten the ordering right. If Dugan had somehow made me drink his blood *first*, and then taken from me, I'd have been worried. He'd left out that step. We were both in strange waters with this variation.

I wasn't going to tell him about it, either.

Pyrrhic victory to Jack Fleming, maybe.

He moaned, but it sounded more like ordinary disgust than physical pain. Escott hadn't reacted, but he'd been unconscious.

If I could just lift up a bit to see what was—

Then my eyelids suddenly closed on their own.

Death's own silent chill seized my body.

A relentless progress, feet, legs, trunk, it was like being buried in snow, very snug, very final. I'd been through this before, too. Didn't like it, but better than getting skinned.

I'd expected this, but still felt a hurt surprise.

My death would mess up Dugan's plans. Cold comfort, but serve him right. He didn't understand how vulnerable I was to blood loss. He'd ignored things while I bled. He had literally talked me to death.

I sought that summer day, and it flooded around me, sweet and warm. Bobbi held me safe until it was time to drift free.

It was very like those moments when I went invisible, but even that formless state had weight, keeping me bound to a physical world. Now I shrugged it off, lifting above myself, wonderfully light.

The clay I'd left behind was in poor shape. The face had gone terribly gaunt, fingers curled into grasping claws, outstretched arms so desiccated that the shape of the bones showed through the gray flesh. He'd been through much pain, but that was finished now. No more suffering for him, the poor bastard. The me that floated above him was unsure of what to do next now that having a body was of no further importance.

The other man in the room finally got off the floor and went to check on the remains. No amount of shouting or slapping of the face would animate that corpse.

The man rushed out of my field of view. I kept staring at me, reluctant to say good-bye. Once I left, that would be the end of it. No more ties to this world. No more . . .

Bobbi—she won't know what's happened.

That wasn't anything I could fix. What was done was done. I had to go soon.

I can't just leave her.

I hesitated. And thought. And thought some more.

And came to see what lay ahead.

What she'd go through—I couldn't do that to her. I'd carry the remorse with me forever. But weren't you supposed to shed that at death? Apparently not. I could deal with my private failures and mistakes, but not the wrongs I'd inflicted on others. Added up, they were worse than my time in hell hanging from the meat hook.

But this was out of my hands. Someone had taken my life and all chance to make things right with anyone. Bobbi would never . . .

The helplessness returned again. My regret had weight like a thousand anvils, and it dragged me toward the empty shell below. I hovered close to what had been familiar features. His mouth sagged, and his eyelids were at half-mast over dulling orbs. That was a dead man's face. I didn't want to sink into it and pushed away, just a tiny distance.

Bobbi will look for you and cry and wonder and worry and never *know . . .*

She deserved better than that. I couldn't let her go through what I had endured when my lover, Maureen, had disappeared. For years I'd searched, always wondering; the grief and anger and the not-knowing had eaten me hollow.

I brushed against the cold, leaden husk and recoiled. How could I possibly take up its burden again?

I couldn't. That wasn't for me anymore.

It was over; I had to leave.

At the end of the day, at the end of life, it's the same for us all. We get the answers we've always sought. Things are finally clear. Everything would turn out all right. Bobbi would go through a bad stretch but get past it. Decades from now, at some decisive future point, her time would come, and she would hover like this over her body. I'd be there waiting for her—

Unless she made the change and became Undead.

A small chance, but possible.

Then she would live on and always wonder and never know and perhaps blame herself, just as I had. Only she'd never find me. She would *never* find me.

I couldn't allow that.

I had to get *back* to her.

Desire and will added weight, and I sank lower. There was an invisible barrier between me and my cooling flesh. It seemed permeable, but I sensed that would not last long, growing thicker and more difficult to breach the longer I delayed.

With hard effort, I pushed past it and instantly felt the awful press of gravity dragging me into agony and blackness.

RELUCTANTLY I came to, the taste of cold animal blood on my tongue and clogging my throat. I gave in to a convulsive choking swallow and got most of it down. Whatever reviving magic it possessed began spreading through my starved body. Everything woke up at once: the constant pain, the helplessness, the rage, and especially the hunger. That hurt the worst.

Someone held my head at an awkward angle and had a cup to my lips. He cursed as the stuff sloshed past my mouth. I got another gulp down and another, and then it was gone. I still hurt, still needed—

"More," I whispered.

Dugan stared. There was a smear of my blood on his cheek. "It's disgusting."

"You're the one . . . who wants this."

He didn't move. He seemed to be having second thoughts.

"More . . . or I die."

"You won't. You're immortal."

There's no arguing with an idiot. My eyes shut again, and I didn't respond when he slapped me.

That worked. He hurried away and returned with more blood. I didn't want to gorge, but couldn't stop. My previous out-of-control overfeedings had been to sate an addiction; this was pure survival. That was what I told myself, and from the way the stuff gusted through me, sweetly filling out the corners, it was the truth. I'd come that close.

After several trips upstairs and back, Dugan must have run out of stock; he stood over me for a time, watching and asking variations of "Are you all right?" at intervals until I mumbled at him to shut up.

That seemed to reassure him. He went up and didn't return. He left the basement light on. An oversight, perhaps. What had happened must have spooked him badly.

That made two of us.

I kept still, resting, recovering, thinking of ways to kill him. None seemed a brutal or painful enough payback.

My brain cleared; I listened to his movements, heard the splash of water. Yeah, things had gotten very messy; he'd want to clean up. Wish I could. This place had running water, electricity, I'd not yet heard a phone. It was information, perhaps useful, perhaps not.

Then he paced. Restlessly, uneven, up and back in a not-very-large room, to judge by the number of steps he took.

Then things went quiet. I thought he'd fallen asleep until a very faint scratching sound came through the floor to me . . . a pen on paper. The son of a bitch was writing.

What would it be? A harrowing and heroic account of his first feeding? Perhaps another essay arguing the social practicality of killing off inferiors or maybe a scientific record of his reaction to my blood. How about a grocery list? *Memo to self, stop at butcher shop for another gallon* . . .

I'd recovered enough to laugh again, softly.

The other me turned up again at last, walking into view the same as a real person. He looked sad now. He was right, I'd had my opening to escape and chose to return. Neither of us had reason to believe Dugan's promise about freedom on the third night. He would kill me and put what was left where it would never be found. Bobbi would still never know . . . *No, dammit. Stop thinking like that.*

I would figure out something. I would get back to her.

Things had improved, such as they were. I'd taken in enough blood to ease my belly pain and allow me to think. I didn't feel very smart at the moment and looked to my benign doppelgänger for suggestions.

He shrugged. "What would Kroun do?"

That one was easy: not get caught in the first place.

His extra caution, not letting even me in on where he spent his days, had worked well. Of course, Dugan didn't know the man was a vampire, having assumed I'd been the one who saved Escott.

Unless Dugan *wanted* me to think that. No, let's keep this simple. He would have said or asked something by now. He had a trapped audience; there was no way he could resist crowing about his cleverness.

Had Kroun been here, he'd probably have tried hypnosis. It wouldn't have worked. Hurley Gilbert should be locked in the booby hatch down the hall from Sonny. Even if I'd been free and clear of giving myself a fatal headache from the attempt, the old evil-eye whammy didn't impress members of their club.

"Anything else?" I muttered, confident that the other me had the benefit of my internal reply.

"What about Escott? How would he get out of this?"

He'd be dead if his arms looked like mine did now. Otherwise, he would listen, learn, and use any little shred of information to his advantage.

Dugan's pen scratched away, fast and without pause. He was just bursting with thoughts tonight. He liked dark green ink on thick notepaper. When done writing, he used his handiness with origami to fold the paper into whatever shape he wanted, which was a very unique way to file things. Was the upstairs of this place filled with little paper sculptures, each one bearing his thoughts? He could make cranes, giraffes, boats, and once left a small paper coffin where I would find it. He'd not written on it, but I got the message that he would be back. Too bad for me I'd let other concerns crowd it out.

"How about Dugan himself?" asked the walking-around me. "What would he do?"

Manipulation. That was his specialty: getting people to go along with him against their better judgment. No one even thought to disbelieve him, such was the effect of his brand of charm. He exploited their weak points. He had plenty of his own I could use against him, but he would be suspicious of anything I said.

On the other hand he knew he was a genius, while I was little more than a talking animal. I'd already played on that. Giving him what he expected shouldn't be hard.

I winced. I wasn't good at that kind of thing.

"Better learn quick, then," said my friend who wasn't there.

16

KROUN

GABRIEL blundered his way clear of the alley before the nightclub's muscle turned up to deal with the noise. He ducked behind a parked car for cover and kept going until his legs decided they'd had enough. He ended up sitting on a curb, holding his head, in too much pain to even groan.

It was almost as bad as his first waking. The main improvement was that he wasn't covered with earth, blood, and Ramsey's body.

Broder must have used a blackjack, not that his fist would have caused less damage. He'd hit the perfect spot on the left-hand side.

Gabe found a patch of mostly clean snow, balled some up, and pressed it to his skull. That helped, but he felt sick throughout his body, not just his head. He wanted to hole up somewhere and, if not die, then sweat through this agony undisturbed until he healed.

After the snowball melted to nothing, he was able to stand without wobbling too much.

The next street over had a few other night owls prowling about, but no cabs in sight. He dug out another ten-dollar bill, stood under a street-light, and held it up at passing cars. As it represented over a week's wage for the lucky ones with jobs, it didn't take long for someone to pull over. The risk for this kind of hitchhiking was being found by a mug looking to take the rest of the money. Gabe was in no mood for games.

The man at the wheel checked him over. "You inna fight?"

Perceptive of him. "Yeah, can you get me out of here? My wife's on the warpath and—"

"Hop in!"

The driver was cheerfully drunk, in a let's be pals mood, and happy to commiserate about matrimonial tribulations. Gabe turned down an offer to share booze from a pocket flask and talked him into driving clear of the Loop, all the way to Fleming's house.

"Sure about this?" asked the man when they got there. "Won't she be waitin' for you?"

"Home's the last place she'll look," he assured his bleary Samaritan, who thought that to be extremely funny. He drove off laughing, ten bucks richer.

Gabe had trouble with the picklocks. He couldn't get his fingers to work together. It took nearly a minute to break in. He was well aware that he wasn't thinking too clearly, but willing to risk that Mike wouldn't come nosing around. He had a pounding to recover from himself, and Broder might still think his assault had been fatal.

As for Escott, well, he was supposed to be smart and good at his job, but his choice to follow them . . .

"Nuts. Everyone in this town is goddamned *nuts*," Gabe muttered to the empty house as he trudged upstairs in the dark.

He made his way by the faint glow coming in around the window curtains. It was brighter than before, too early for dawn, he thought, until checking his new watch. Damn. How long had he been sitting on that curb? It had seemed only minutes. Maybe he'd blacked out. He'd lost time after the car crash. Wouldn't that just be the pip if Fleming turned out to be right?

Gabe dug his earth-crusted clothes from the bottom of the wardrobe, grabbed blankets from the bed, and went hunting for the attic.

Behind a hall door he found a narrow stairs that ended in a ceiling trap, which at first seemed to be locked, though there was no mechanism, just a handle. He gave a hard push and the door lifted when something heavy fell away on the other side.

Somehow a trunk had been left on top of the trap. How the hell . . . ?

Oh. Fleming's disappearing trick. He'd pushed the trunk on the door, then slipped down past it. He probably used the attic for refuge, and this was how he locked himself in.

Gabe shoved the trunk back and cast around for a place to flop. There was a dusty window at one end; he found a spot far from it and curled up around the wad of clothes, covering himself completely with the blankets.

Just in time. His adrenaline gave out. He couldn't move another inch. Even fresh blood wouldn't have helped. He needed absolute rest to heal, and the earth would give him that. He cushioned his head on one arm, gritting his teeth until the rising sun brought oblivion.

No dreaming today, but this time he didn't mind.

He was only aware that he'd slept by the fact his pain vanished between one blink and the next.

Damn. That was . . . good.

And disorienting. One second it's dawn and the next full night. He didn't like that. Unpleasant or not, the dreams gave some sense of passing time. Without them, Gabe felt as though those hours had been stolen from him.

Michael would have had a whole day to get himself out of town to—where? He had friends in Havana . . . . but why should he leave if he thought Broder had—

Take it slow and in order. Mike tried to kill me. He managed to miss. On purpose?

Probably not. That he'd botched it said something for his ultimate reluctance, but he had been serious. The look on his face . . . that was real. He'd attempted the murder of his brother.

He'd have felt bad afterward, though.

Mike then lost the fistfight, Broder stepped in with his cosh, then gunfire from a third party cleared the playing field. Chances were good that lunatic Escott was behind the noisy interruption. Who asked him to horn in?

Maybe Fleming was back by now. He sure picked a rotten time to run off and sulk about his girlfriend—or else was showing sense by keeping himself clear of the mess. There was a first time for everything.

Gabe pushed upright in stages, cautious about sparking another fire-ball behind his eyes. He was rumpled and stiff, but otherwise felt fine. He checked his head and so far so good.

Someone was moving around below. Gabe froze. The sounds, muffled by the floors between, were too indistinct to follow. Perhaps the burglar who'd broken the window had returned.

Hell, it's probably Fleming.

But there was no harm in being careful. Gabe left his makeshift bed, quietly moved the trunk off the trap, and edged his way downstairs.

His gun was still in his overcoat pocket. He pulled it out on the second-floor landing. The other person was in the front room playing with the radio. Static and music, then it steadied on Bergen and McCarthy trading quips. Trusting that the program would cover the sound of his footsteps, Gabe made it to the ground floor and looked in.

Strome was comfortably ensconced in a chair that faced the hall. His feet were up on the low table before the sofa, and he was just raising a beer bottle to his lips. He noticed Gabe right away, nodded a greeting, and drank deep.

Thankfully it was real beer.

"What's up?" Gabe asked, not putting his gun away.

Unconcerned, Strome reached over to turn the radio down, cutting Charlie McCarthy off in mid wisecrack. "I was told to wait here in case you showed."

"Why?"

"That English guy asked Derner, Derner told me. If you showed, I was to drive you over to Fleming's club."

"You sure it was Escott?"

Strome shrugged. "I'm goin' by what Derner said."

"Is Fleming back?"

"Didn't know he was gone."

"What do you know?"

"Nothing, Mr. Kroun. Not one thing."

"Good way to get along."

"Yessir." He drank more beer.

As Strome didn't seem to be in a hurry, Gabe went back up to change his shirt and shave and felt better for it. He was out of suits; the one he was wearing would have to do, though it was creased, and the knees were muddy. The overcoat was past salvage, but Fleming wouldn't mind loaning him another. The one left folded over a chair in the kitchen was still there; Gabe pulled it on, and the fit was pretty good. He thought he could ignore the bloodsmell since it was his own.

Strome had nothing to say on the trip to Lady Crymsyn. He wouldn't know anything useful, so it was pointless to ask him stuff like "Does Michael know I'm alive?"

Once again, Gabe pushed away the urge to plan against the unknown. He might have done that in the past, but at the moment it seemed a waste of time. Actuality was always different from one's expectations. Better to see what's there, then figure out how to deal with it.

If Escott had arranged this trip over, it meant he'd have news.

If Michael was behind it, then Gabe wouldn't have to spend the night hunting him down.

The green Hudson was the only car in the Crymsyn parking lot. Gabe had Strome circle the block, but there was no sign of the Studebaker. Strome stopped at the canopied entry, leaving the motor running. Gabe got out and looked things over, ready to duck, if need be.

Escott opened the front door. Lights were on in the lobby behind him. "Ah. Very good. Thank you, Mr. Strome."

Strome lifted one hand to sketch a salute, shifted into gear, and rolled away.

Escott frowned. "That's my coat."

"Mine needs a clean. Why'd you want me here?"

"In the event that Jack turns up. When he does, it will be here, my office, the Nightcrawler, or with Miss Smythe. If he knows what's good for him, he will have an apology ready for her."

"What if he turns up at the house?"

"Mr. Strome left a note where it would be found." He stepped back inside, and Gabe followed, checking the room. They seemed to be alone.

Escott went to the lobby phone booth, thumbed in a nickel, and dialed. "Mr. Derner? The prodigal's returned, all's well. Mr. Strome is on the way back. Thank you so much for the help." He hung up. "Excellent fellow. Very well organized."

"I noticed that, too. You answered why you're here, not why I'm here."

"Sorry, I've rather a lot on my mind. I thought you'd want to know what's happened since we parted company. You're much improved from last night's misadventure. I thought that large fellow had split your skull open for sure."

"Me, too." Gabe removed his hat, brushing one hand over the white patch. "When did you get to the party?"

"Just in time, apparently."

"What did you hear?"

"I was too distant to follow your conversation. When things went against you, I decided to make a nuisance of myself."

"Are you a bad shot?"

"Not at all, but causing injury to your attacker was not needed. Do sit down." He nodded toward the bar, which was clear of matchbooks. There was no telling if Escott or the supposed ghost had cleared them away. Myrna. What kind of a name was that for a spook?

A light was on behind the bar. It went out while he was looking at it. There was no popping noise from an expired filament; it dimmed and went dark just like the ones in theaters.

Escott was nowhere near a wall switch. He saw it, too. "Myrna? Perhaps you would rather wait in the office with the radio on. If Jack returns, he will go there first." Again, he spoke with a completely straight face as though someone was there to hear him.

Wary, Gabe put his hat down and eased onto one of the stools, angling so he had the lobby door in sight. He decided to ignore Escott's digression. "What the hell were you thinking taking off after them like that?"

"I wanted to see where they went."

"Could have told you."

"They might have changed their locale. As it was, I enjoyed a drive to an unremarkable hotel in Cicero."

"Broder didn't spot you?"

"Right away, as it happened—traffic was very light at that hour. I let him lose me, then resumed tailing at a more prudent distance. He's a relative stranger here, whereas I know the streets quite well."

"Good for you."

"They seemed to settle themselves in for the night. I returned to find you long gone and the staff at the Nightcrawler considerably mystified about the contretemps in the alley."

"You always talk like that?"

"Like what?"

"Never mind, go on."

"I drove around and found you only a block away sitting on a curb like a vagrant. I tried to get you in the car, but you took a swing at me, used some foul language, then sat down again."

Impossible.

Escott searched his face. "You don't remember. Not any of it."

"Because it didn't happen."

"Of course it did. One can hardly blame you for wishing it to not be so. It's terribly disturbing to have a lapse like that."

Much too disturbing, Gabe didn't want to accept it. "What did Fleming tell you?"

"I've not heard from him since that message. What would he add, were he present?"

"He—" Gabe bit it off. No need to get started about the car wreck. He couldn't deny that he'd lost some time afterward, same as last night. "You left me there?"

"You were in no temper to be helped. On my second attempt you drew a gun, threatened to shoot my nose off, made a crude observation about its size, damned me to hell, and sat down again to hold a snowball to your head." He paused as though waiting for a reaction, then went on. "You did not recognize me at all."

What's he want, an apology?

"You have a serious problem, Mr. Kroun. It is most certainly to do with the bullet in your brain."

"Ya think?" Gabe thought hypnotizing Escott into a lapse of his own might be worth the headache. But the man knew where Mike was staying and had a car.

On the other hand he doesn't need to know about my business to play chauffeur.

Escott went behind the bar and built himself a short gin and tonic, heavy on the tonic. "Let's put that aside for now. You've recovered and seem to be yourself again. Perhaps if you simply avoid further injury— especially to your head—you can get by without threatening bodily harm to others."

Or shooting people in the woods. *One minute the car's leaving the road, the next I'm tied up and Fleming's talking crazy.* Gabe's face felt warm.

"In regard to your visit to the sanitarium . . ." Escott paused again, but Gabe remained silent. "Why did you let Jack come along? You must have known there was a possibility he would learn things you would prefer to keep private."

"It just happened. I'm not happy about it."

"Please, Mr. Kroun, I respect your intelligence. If you needed to exclude him, you'd have found a way of doing so. You wanted someone to hear your father. Certain details about your previous visit—"

"The old man is nuts. It doesn't matter what he says or who hears him."

"Indeed? Then what occurred at that cabin two months ago?"

Good question. "I hired a girl to keep me company up there, that's all. She was in the wrong place at the wrong time. I'm just trying to find out if she's okay."

"Then let me alleviate your worry. She's well enough."

"How do you know? Where is she?"

"I spent a portion of the day finding out things."

"Such as?"

"The reason why Michael wants you dead." Escott drank half the gin and tonic, then hauled his cannon of a revolver from its shoulder rig and aimed it at Gabe. "And I agree with him."

Gabe took in the gun and the gray ice of Escott's gaze and whatever expectations he might have planned against would never have included this. "Why is it you keep pulling a gun on me?"

"The first time was a mistake on my part."

"So's the second."

"Be so kind as to remove my overcoat."

"Don't want bullet holes in it?"

"Certainly not, but I'd rather the weapon you have in the right-hand pocket remained in place. If I asked you to surrender it, you'd be fast enough to risk a shot at me. Neither of us would be pleased with the outcome. It's best if you just put the coat on the bar."

Gabe undid the buttons and shed the coat. He thought about throwing it as a distraction, but Escott would be wise to that one and shoot first. "What's your game?"

"Justice, whenever possible. In this instance, justice for a young woman named Nelly Cabot."

There was only one way he could know that name. "You talked to Michael."

"Not easy, but I managed."

Gabe snorted. "What'd he tell you?"

"Many things. Now I want to hear your version of events at the cabin."

Well . . . he was the one with the gun, why not? "It's just over the state line. I went up for a look the other night. There was blood and the body of a man named Ramsey, who'd been my driver."

"That's what you found. What happened?"

"Someone shot us both and buried us in the woods. Only I didn't stay dead."

Escott had a good poker face, but his eyes widened at that news. "So that's when . . . you are new at this, aren't you? Who shot you?"

He shook his head. "Ramsey, I think."

"Don't remember? Jack had a similar problem. Bit of amnesia about his death, but the memory came back after a week or so."

Yes, Gordy had mentioned that. Fleming had thrown his weight around in a big way trying to find his killers. Not smart, but effective.

"Miss Cabot was the girl you hired?"

"Yeah. I think Ramsey was supposed to kill me, and she witnessed it." Gabe's mouth was dry.

"That sounds reasonable."

"I'm sure Mike was at the cabin, too, but last night he started shooting before I could get him to talk."

"He was in a calmer frame of mind today—as you will shortly see."

Cripes. He palmed the ace right in front of me. "That call wasn't to the Nightcrawler. Okay, I get it, fine."

"He'll be here soon."

"Good." It was last night all over again. Escott had his facts wrong and needed proof from a third party to straighten him out. Before it had only taken a call from Derner. This time . . . "Look, you want the truth here, the real truth, right? I can get it for you."

"Via hypnosis?"

Sharp guy. "If you let me."

"What do you propose?"

"I put Mike under, and you do the talking. Keep the gun on me the whole time and ask him anything you like."

"I expect Mr. Broder will be along."

"You can tell Mike to order him to go outside. You'll be in control. I won't do anything."

"That sounds . . . reasonable as well."

"This is too easy," Gabe muttered.

"It's an excellent idea, Mr. Kroun. We'll see how it works out. Before he arrives, perhaps you can clarify a point or two. If Mike was at the cabin, why did he allow Miss Cabot to leave?"

"He's soft on dames."

"And why was he not surprised to see you alive later?"

"He thought I'd gotten away."

"But this was a clandestine excursion. How did he even know you were there?"

"Broder can track anyone, anything, without getting noticed."

"Why would Mike want you dead?"

"You tell me." Gabe nodded at the gun. "You said you agreed with him."

Escott's mouth thinned. "Yes. I do."

"What'd he tell you?"

Outside, a car pulled up, the motor cut, and doors slammed. Gabe turned from Escott and toward the entry.

Broder barged in first, his gun out. He was hard to read at the best of times, but tonight was different. He looked ready to kill. Though used to Broder and his ways, a jolt of pure terror lanced through Gabe like an electric shock, leaving his fingers suddenly numb. Until now he'd always felt himself unquestioningly in control of everything. The look on Broder's face told him otherwise.

So did the look on Mike's face when he came in. The usual impatience, frustration, anger, apprehension, and all the shadings in between were gone, replaced by straightforward disgust. He stopped just inside, holding the door open.

A woman in a dark winter coat, a thick headscarf tied under her chin, reluctantly came in. Mrs. Cabot glared at Gabe with undiluted loathing.

"It's okay," she said. "They got him covered. He ain't movin'."

A younger, prettier version of her crept forward and paused on the threshold. She was paler than paint and visibly trembling head to toe. When she saw Gabe, she jerked and looked ready to run out again.

Can't blame her, seeing a dead man back on his feet would shake anyone.

"Nelly?" said Gabe.

She made a little choking noise and tottered into her mother's arms. She began sobbing.

Gabe closed his eyes. For an instant he was in his grave again, drifting in that brief moment of absolute peace and calm despite the sound of a woman weeping her heart out. He listened to the echoes in his tattered memory and matched them exactly to what he heard now.

"It's all right," he whispered. "It's all right."

When he opened his eyes, they all stared at him as though expecting him to say more.

Except Nelly, who continued to cry. Her mother opened a big black purse on her arm and groped for a wad of tissues. The girl soaked them through.

No one moved. Taking it slow, he reached toward his breast pocket for the silk handkerchief there. He held it out. The mother hissed and pulled back, dragging Nelly along.

"You don't touch her!" she snarled.

"I'm just trying—"

"Shuddup!" Mike got between them and suddenly plowed in with a vicious sucker punch. Gabe caught it under the ribs and dropped back, surprised as hell. Mike loomed over him a moment, then turned away, angry, but keeping himself in check.

For once, Gabe decided to listen and made no comment. He glanced at Escott for some clue, but the man was coldly hostile.

Whatever it was had them acting crazy. Gabe wasn't running things now, couldn't order them to tell him what was going on. If he waited long enough, one of them might talk; but the tangible fury hanging in the air was just short of catching on fire.

Mike was the key. Gabe focused on him, putting effort into it to get him under, make him calm.

"Mike, I need you to listen to me . . ." Usually that was enough. Catch their attention, throw a hard look, and they got cooperative.

Instead, Mike faced the Cabot women. "You don't talk, Whitey. Not another word."

Gabe next tried Broder, who was staring right at him. It should have been easy, but nothing got through. As he suspected, the man was too focused, and that was better than armor.

As for Escott? No point in trying; he was little better than a bystander now.

"I didn't think you'd bring the ladies along," said Escott.

Mike gave a small shrug.

"My girl should see him," Mrs. Cabot said. She made Nelly straighten up. "You look at him. You look at that son of a bitch and see how afraid he is."

Gabe went still. He was indeed afraid. He'd stepped in something again, and there was no bluffing his way clear. He looked at the girl, but absolutely nothing sparked in his memory about her. Her face and form were unfamiliar, though he liked what he saw. She was dark-haired with a soft, rounded figure . . . but Lettie had described her as being blond. A trip to the beauty parlor would change her quick enough.

Lettie had mentioned other things, but Gabe had dismissed them.

She's wrong. She has to be.

Only one person could set things straight.

He focused on Nelly, and it was nothing to break through to her. She was too vulnerable. She ceased crying and stared blankly back. Once he was sure she was hooked, he shot a glance at Escott.

"Ask her," he said. "You want to know what happened, *ask* her."

Escott looked startled.

"He's already heard," said Mike.

"Well, I haven't. Nelly—tell them what happened at the cabin."

Despite his influence, she was slow to speak. Mrs. Cabot stepped into the gap.

"No! You don't put her through that again!"

Gabe moved forward, stopping when Broder shifted his bulk in the way. "Let her talk, dammit!"

"Mr. Kroun," said Escott, "do not continue with this. She's been through enough."

"I got a right to hear what you have against me."

The sound of his voice startled Nelly awake. She scrabbled one-handed at the black purse. Instead of tissues, she pulled out a revolver, the same one her mother had used the other night, swinging it around.

Gabe made himself a moving target, but there wasn't space for it. He threw himself to the side away from Escott just as the gun roared. Something kicked his left arm, hard. His legs went out from under him, and he smashed back-first against the tile floor. Rattled, he tried to roll and get upright, but Nelly stood over him, the gun's muzzle right in his face. She was shaking and crying too much to hold it steady.

He was fast enough to grab it away, but unable to move. The rage in her face stopped him.

What did I do to you?

The answer was there, and he could not accept it. It was impossible.

I'm not like that!

Not now, but two months ago he'd been a murdering bastard capable of doing anything. And what he'd done to Nelly . . .

No. That was wrong. That kind of horror just wasn't inside him.

Broder yanked the gun from Nelly's hand and bodily pushed her toward Mrs. Cabot. The woman grabbed her daughter, her own anger shifting to fear.

"You can't hold that against her!" she yelled. "You know what he did!"

Michael went to her, and they held a short, intense exchange, which Gabe was too distracted to follow.

He was bleeding. It wasn't like that chest wound, but by God it hurt, and he couldn't afford the blood loss.

The bullet had torn a chunk from high in his left arm and out again, and even as he pressed a hand over the wound, it began to burn with hell's own fire. He snarled and cursed and couldn't see straight. The pain didn't fade so much as he made himself ignore it. He forced himself to his feet, trying to get a look at Nelly, but Mrs. Cabot put herself in the way, protecting her.

Escott was still behind the bar. He seemed unfazed by the gunfire. He found a towel and slid it over to Gabe. "Put some pressure on it."

Nodding a silent thanks, Gabe did so. The least movement made it burn worse. His blood was all over the place. It was stupid, but he found himself annoyed about his ruined suit. That lasted two seconds, then Broder was dragging him over to a chair and shoving him down. His big paws lay heavy on top of Gabe's shoulders, holding him in place.

Mike went from Mrs. Cabot to talk with Escott. "We have to keep this quiet."

"I am no representative for the police in this. Punish him as you see fit, but take him elsewhere when you're done. Mr. Fleming will be none too pleased to have his club so ill-used. I'll clean up."

"And keep quiet?"

"So far as I am concerned, this is a family matter between you and your half brother and none of my business. Once you leave, I shall do my best to forget this entire day."

"What about Fleming? He was supposed to keep an eye on things."

"As I said, he had some personal affairs to look after, but be assured, he will say nothing."

"Gordy said he was stand-up."

"You may have complete confidence in that assessment. What about the ladies?"

"The old girl said she wants to see it through. Thinks Nelly will sleep better at night, but there's some things you just can't make up for."

"Indeed not."

Mike came to stand before Gabe. "I didn't think I could hate anyone as much as the old bastard, but you . . . you're sick-crazy like him, and your kind of sick doesn't get better. You've gone too far."

"Doing what?" Gabe asked. "Say it."

"You're not worth the breath." Mike reached into his overcoat's inside pocket for a leather case, not the one he used for his glasses. He opened it, revealing a clean glass syringe and compact amber vials within, setting them out on a table.

What the hell? "Escott?"

But Escott put his back to him. He began cleaning blood from the bar top.

Mike loaded the syringe with the contents of all the vials.

"That's too much," said Gabe. "You'll kill yourself."

Mike ignored him. "Broder?"

Broder ripped away the towel and smashed his fist against Gabe's wound three times with bone-breaking force. Blood went everywhere. The pain exploded into a white-hot firestorm, unbearable. He tried to bite off the scream and failed. He dropped from the chair, consumed by it, unable to move. Someone grabbed his right arm and pushed the sleeve up. He didn't feel the sting as the needle went in; the other agony simply blotted it out.

"I don't know how you got through the day without this stuff," said Mike from somewhere above him.

No, this is wrong, it's not me, no, no, no . . .

Gabe felt the poison go up his arm, spreading throughout his body. It was a delicious cold balm to his wound. One second the pain's so bad you want to die, then the next it's gone. A dark miracle, almost like sleeping on his earth.

The chill slithered through him, curling around his brain, pressing against the spot on his skull and winding down to his feet. They lost feeling immediately, as though they'd somehow detached themselves and drifted from his body.

The cold flooded and filled him, and for a few moments he saw everything with bewildering clarity . . .

And it was beautiful.

The people stared at him with such unconditional hatred, but he couldn't hate them back. They were too wonderful. Every detail of their faces, the depth in their eyes, how they stood, each little movement— they had no idea just how *perfect* they were.

The room with its clean lines and stark colors was only the antechamber to a wider space of concrete and starlight and motion and more and more perfect people. There were so many to see and meet and cherish, so many bright marvels waited for him beyond these walls.

He loved them, loved it all; the whole goddamned world was his, and he loved it passionately.

A stranger used his voice to laugh for him.

Not a stranger.

It was one of the monsters that hid in the shadows of his mind, only emerging during his day sleep. One of the countless tormentors within that knew the truth but refused to make it clear was now awake, aware of him, and amused.

Looks just like me.

The poison inside lit it up like an actor onstage. It was handsome and confident, though possessing no substance, no more solid than the shadows it hid in.

But it was in charge now.

17

FLEMING

HOURS later the scratching of Dugan's pen finally stopped, springs squeaked, and shortly after he was snoring.

I was grateful, spared from listening to his voice, able to rest and think, though neither moved me closer to a way out.

I bled as I lay there. Even when trying to be motionless, you can't help but move. The muscles in my arms cramped around the rods and twitched involuntarily, opening the wounds again. Other times I just shivered, though still covered by the blanket. My bound legs ached, giving off sharp twinges when I flexed them, the long muscles cramping.

Despite the influx of blood, I was exhausted. My body was constantly trying to make itself vanish clear of the pain. Race a motor long enough without going anywhere, and it eventually burns out.

I tried to remember exactly what I'd seen while hovering over myself, but the impressions were general and fuzzy, no more than what I already knew. Nothing else had been important to me then.

The little I could see was of no help: low ceiling and off to the right a stairway of sixteen steps leading up to what? A house, barn, warehouse? The cement walls were bare of any clue, though Dugan would probably prefer a house. I couldn't turn enough to see what was behind me but guessed there might be another table for holding a scalpel and the .45.

When I tried to rise, nothing shifted but my flesh, and that made more pain. Everything was too secure, given my weakened state. Perhaps I could marshal enough strength to rip free, tearing muscle, breaking bone—but my bones were different since the change, denser, heavier. They would prevent such an escape.

Dozing, never quite going to sleep, I let myself drift into summer again. Bobbi and Escott weren't there this time. My arms were stretched wide, mirroring my current posture. Though free of the rods, there were holes in my flesh, and they bled into the stock tank's water.

A wasp sting on my right wrist startled me. I snarled, tried to jerk away.

Dugan was back and held the beaker to collect the blood flow.

It was a physical effort to shove my rage down, and when I collapsed, it was not pretense. I'd never been this tired or hopeless. Now I understood why an animal will chew off its own limb to escape.

How much time had passed? Was this the second night already? "Sprout fangs yet?" I asked.

He shook his head. He seemed very intent on the job, frowning.

There was damn little to read from his face. He seemed to be in the same clothes, minus the butcher's apron, and his skin was shiny as though from fever. I could smell his sweat. There was a taint to it I couldn't place, but it lacked the rankness that comes with time. Same night then, he'd just come down for a second helping. Crazy bastard.

The slash he made with the scalpel healed. He cut another, holding the beaker until he'd collected a cup's worth of red. Then he pressed a handkerchief to the wound, applying pressure. How thoughtful.

"I know this isn't terribly nice for you." He was not apologetic, just stating a fact.

"It's killing me, you son of a bitch."

"You recover quickly enough. I've made a note to lay in a fresh replacement supply. It ran short tonight, but there will be no repetition."

He took my blood in three big drafts, like a thirsty farmer downing a beer. This time he did not gag and collapse. Only when finished did he give in to a deep involuntary shuddering that was slow to pass. That reaction was too similar to my own after a feeding. Something was definitely happening to him, then. Maybe the ordering was not as crucial as I'd thought. Maybe the change was taking him regardless. There was too much I did not know about my own condition.

When he recovered, he smiled at me.

I wanted to pull his face off. "I'll bleed to death before the next sunset."

"I won't allow that to happen."

"Going to anyway."

"If you've a way to hasten the transformation process, I will release you that much sooner."

"The metal has to come out, at least during the day when I'm dead. You can put them back in before I wake at sunset."

He thought that one over, then shook his head. "I'd rather not take the chance. You lost more than this in the meat locker and survived, but you've given me an idea. I'll make sure to catch the lost blood, and either take it myself or give it back to you. A very practical symmetry."

I held off from telling him what to do with his symmetry.

His reaction informed me that the rods could be removed. He'd used the threaded kind for a reason. Perhaps twist them enough by the handles, and they'd come right up and out.

I didn't want to be awake for that.

He pulled the blanket down and lifted a packet of my home soil into view. It had been on the table next to my waist. "What significance does this have for you?"

"Read *Dracula*, figure it out."

"Actually, I saw the play in New York some years ago. Such a ridiculous melodrama. It makes no sense to keep earth about one or sleep in a coffin. It's superstition, nothing more."

"You'll find out different."

"There must be some scientific reason behind it. Have you given it no thought at all?"

Plenty, and I didn't give a damn. I felt myself slipping away. The sun was rising. Did he sense it, too? I ignored him until my eyelids were too heavy to hold up, then froze for the day.

He said my name several times, tried to wake me, but got no response.

I was aware that he stabbed my wrist again. The pain was a distant thing compared to the horrors just beginning to march before my mind's eye. I was back in the meat locker again, hanging upside down, but instead of Hog Bristow, it was Dugan skinning me alive.

* * *

He must have put my home earth back against my body, for I was suddenly fully conscious and blinking in the dark. The small packet had abrogated the whole of the day to an instant; I was wide-awake and still in hell.

And weaker than ever.

And hungry.

It hurt. The hunger goddamned *hurt*.

Where was Dugan? I hated being dependent on him, but that was how things were, and I'd just have to find a way to use it.

Pushing aside the initial wave of distracting pain, I listened and heard him stirring on the floor above. Springs squeaked, and he cleared his throat several times. Had he been sleeping, too? What was my blood doing to him?

Dugan took his time coming downstairs, his steps heavy. When he flicked the light switch, I shut my eyes and only sluggishly responded when he lifted my head, holding a glass to my lips.

I drank, of course. Cow's blood. Cold, but easing the pain in my gut. He'd gone out during the day to get more then. Hopefully, he'd brought back enough to keep me alive.

When finished and full, I continued with the listlessness act and didn't so much as flinch when he cut into my wrist, though I watched, hoping my eyes looked dull and vague.

He was focused on the task, paying no attention to me.

His hand shook as he held the beaker. A lot.

What did that mean?

He drank his dose straight down, then came that long, shuddering reaction.

He seemed to *enjoy* the blood now. Christ in heaven, that could not be a good thing.

When the last tremor passed, his eyes were bright, the pupils dilated like Kroun's. His heart thumped strong and too fast, as though he'd been running.

"Was this how it began for you?" he whispered.

I did not reply. I had to appear lethargic, and it was hard going because this new turn was scaring the hell out of me.

"I feel so alive. Your friend reacted very rapidly to your blood; no wonder he got well again so quickly."

If Escott were here he'd open your skull with a dull spoon.

My well-dressed twin leaned into view. "You're not going to get free without help," he said.

He was right. I was sure I could get Dugan to bring Escott here, but chances were one of them would get killed in the process—most likely Dugan. Escott had his own scores to settle and would shoot him on sight, which would leave me stuck here to starve to death. I went down the short list of people able to help me, but was not willing to risk their lives to save mine.

Not yet. Time and desperation could change that.

"Will he become like us?" asked Dugan. "Fleming? Answer me. Will your friend—"

"You won't make it," I mumbled.

"What do you mean?"

"Takes longer than three days. I'll be dead before then."

"How long does it take?"

"Weeks."

"I don't believe you."

"You'll see."

"Why so long?"

"Body has to adjust. Took me two weeks."

"The books said three days."

"Books . . ." That disturbing laughter bubbled on my lips again. "You're an idiot, Gurley Hilbert."

"I'll simply feed more often . . ."

"I'll be gone. You won't change." I let myself relax, eyes closed.

That shook him. He went upstairs and returned with more blood. I drank all that was offered and continued with the dying act. It didn't require much acting on my part.

"You've taken in more than you've lost," he told me. "You should be better."

"Dead blood," I whispered. "Not as good."

"That's what you drink. You buy it at the butcher's. I saw you."

"Can't live on it. Not for long."

"What do you mean?"

"'S gotta come from a living body, heart still beating."

"Don't be ridiculous."

"'S why we got the fangs."

His mental wheels were visibly turning. I couldn't explain my need to

have soil by me during the day, but the extra-long teeth . . . Animal predators had big canines to grasp and hold struggling prey. Since he seemed
to think people were another kind of animal, Mr. Genius just might
make the right kind of connection.

"You expect me to free you for a trip to some farm?"

That's it, figure it out. "Living blood . . . human. Keeps me alive."

"You can't expect me to donate."

"Your blood's poison to me now. Won't work."

"Poison? What do you mean?" He sounded alarmed.

"'S no good to me . . ." I wanted to remove the risk of taking any of
his in. Otherwise, his harebrained plan might have a chance of working.

"Why is that?" When I didn't answer, he shook me.

"Human. Best."

"Why?"

"Donno."

"I suppose I could find one of your friends . . ."

He was fishing for a reaction with that threat. I gave none. "No good.
Poison, too. Can't touch 'em."

"Well, then, who hasn't tasted your blood?" Skeptical, but he'd asked
the right question.

I mumbled something and seemed to drift off. It took him longer to
wake me. I made him work for it. That told me he was buying at least
some small part of the bullshit I was dishing. My hovering twin seemed
hopeful, nodding encouragement.

"Who?"

"Whitey," I finally whispered. "They won't miss 'im."

"Who's that?"

"From hospital."

"The man with the patch of white hair?"

"Healthy. Clean blood." I closed my eyes, relaxing into stillness again.
Dugan made no attempt to wake me now, probably thinking.

Kroun was the best choice. If Dugan got the drop on him, Kroun
would want to know the reason why and play along. He might even recognize him as the janitor. Though Dugan was immune to being hypnotized, he was laughably vulnerable to an old-fashioned strong-arming. It
wouldn't take much for Kroun to break him.

That was my *hope* on how things could go. Kroun could fall into one
of his black fits and kill him.

Just have to chance it.

Out of nowhere my body began shivering, violently. No act, I was really that cold.

"Fleming? What is it?" Dugan backed away, startled.

The shaking made things bad for my arms; I didn't fight it, knowing it looked damned ugly. I wanted him scared and off-balance.

The fit passed, leaving me exhausted and bleeding, but the involuntary dramatics had done some good: he brought me more to drink, and I took every drop. It gave me a stockpile of strength to fight the constant reflexive effort of trying to vanish.

"Your color is better. You're not dying just yet, Mr. Fleming."

"Ever eat paper?" I whispered.

"What?"

"Fills you, but you can't live on it."

Dugan thought that over, apparently, since it shut him up for a good long time. I listened to his heartbeat, which was still too fast.

Lying there and resting, my belly full, I noticed my skin had not knitted itself to the rods again and I wasn't bleeding as much.

Maybe my body was actually getting used to the torture. Dear God.

He finally gave a small grunt and stood. "In three days—well, two now—I'll know whether you're telling the truth. Should that be the case, then I'm sure I can arrange to bring you what you need. A healthy human is not that difficult to find in a city of this size."

He went upstairs, my heart dropping a mile for every step he took.

Damnation, I should have seen that. Why try for Kroun when Dugan could pluck just anyone off the street? Chances were too good that he'd grab someone more easily managed, someone he'd see as expendable, a woman, or God help us, even a kid.

Once the door closed, I checked over my situation once more, desperate to find a weakness.

The L-shaped ends of the rods were at right angles to my arms, each pointing toward the wall behind the table. It was effective for holding me, but it would have been better to have them parallel, the ends toward my hands.

But that would have interfered with his being able to easily cut my wrists, though. If the ends were swung toward my head, I might be able to get free by pulling my arms inward. This was as good as it would ever get.

Before I could think about it first, I jerked my right arm up along the rod, twisting.

Flesh tore and I swallowed, literally swallowed my scream. It burrowed into my gut and tried to claw another way out. My body bucked, and my legs tried to kick, and some of whatever bound them came a little bit loose.

Collapsing flat again, I sucked air with my mouth and throat wide open to keep from howling.

Then I couldn't move for a long while. My arm burned so badly I kept looking to see if it had actually caught fire. The skin around the rod was cherry red under the seeping blood. Not much feeling in my hand; both were looking clawlike again.

The burning got worse. In weak moments I whimpered like a dog, and tears seeped from my eyes. Neither made the pain go away. The more I worked to ignore it, the worse it got, until I started moaning. I shut it off quick because it was too close to how things had been in that meat locker.

Dugan came down hours later, hurrying, clutching a milk bottle full of blood. He poured some into a glass, then lifted and held my head up so I could drink. I eventually drained the bottle. He was sweating, and I picked up that strange taint again, stronger now, acidic, like rotting fruit.

"You never had this much while I was following you," he said, sitting.

"I wasn't pinned to a table and bleeding, idiot." I hoped he wouldn't notice the fresh damage. He'd not cleaned me up; new blood was well mingled with the old.

"I'll get you more then, but it won't be human, not for a few days, yet. Such an expedition will require careful preparation on my part."

That was something. He liked to plan things out in detail. "Go to the Stockyards."

"But the butchers . . ."

I had to keep up the lies, hope to waste his time, and buy myself more. "Fresh stuff will keep me alive longer."

He didn't want to hear that but offered no argument. "I suppose I'll have to learn how sooner or later. It's the price one must pay."

I gave in to maniac giggles, the sound eerie as it bounced off the cement walls. Was his hair going up on the back of his neck? Mine was.

I laughed until he jabbed the scalpel into my wrist.

18

KROUN

WHITEY felt himself relaxing for the first time in what seemed like months. It was as though he'd been holding his breath and could finally let it out.

He laughed. God, he felt great.

Sprawled on the floor, he grinned up at Michael, who looked sick. Stick-in-the-mud Mike had no time for real fun. This kind of euphoria would be wasted on him. Broder? Forget it. What about that skinny bartender?

"Hey, you, c'mere." He tried to wave him over. "Set 'em up . . . drinks are on me."

The man only stared. He must be able to see the monster, and it scared him.

That was damned funny. Whitey tried to explain it to him, but the words tumbled out too fast, slurring and blending into each other. There were so many words in his head that he couldn't say them all. That many crowding in there would make his brain explode. He kept talking to get them out.

And his head was . . . not hurting, but something was muddled within, verging on dizziness. A thousand bees buzzed behind his ears, swarming and spinning, banging against the inside of his skull, trying to escape. Noisy bastards.

He tried to get up, but Broder slammed him flat. Must have forgotten who was boss here. Whitey suddenly rolled clear and stood, rounding on him, still grinning. The man seemed surprised, but pulled out his gun.

That was funny, too.

"You should go on the radio," Whitey told him. He swatted at the gun, slapping it from Broder's grip; it spun across the room, cracking heavily on the marble tile.

"Whitey?"

He pointed at Mike. "You, too." He aimed himself at the bar and somehow his feet got him there. "Set 'em up. Beer for everyone." He fumbled for money, fingers clumsy. He snapped the money clip like a dry twig. Fifties and hundreds exploded across the bar top.

The bartender seemed not to notice the expensive mess. His mouth shaped itself into a brittle smile. "Mr. Kroun, your table is ready. Please take a seat, and I'll bring you your drink."

Whitey liked this one. "You've earned your tip, boy. Where izzit?"

"Just over there, sir." He pointed to a chair.

"Don't like it. Too far away from company. Serve 'em up here." He slapped the bar with the flat of his hand. Look at all the money. "You play poker?"

"Yes, sir. Would you like me to arrange a game?"

He took in the others. "We got enough players . . . but I want some fun first. Li'l dancing, some laughs, where's my damn drink?"

The man hastily drew a beer.

"Escott," said Mike, addressing the 'tender, "what the hell are you doing?"

"Humoring him. Please stay back."

Whitey wrapped both hands around the glass. He couldn't feel them, had to look to be sure they closed. He downed half his drink. It was cold, but the taste . . . he doubled over, retching.

"What kind of rat piss you serving here?" he demanded after spitting out the last disgusting drop. He threw the glass, but Escott ducked. The shelving behind him shattered as though struck by a bullet.

Someone grabbed Whitey from behind. Broder again, but he seemed to be moving in syrup. Whitey avoided his fist, and gave him payback with interest. Broder staggered drunkenly and toppled.

How about that? Barely tapped him.

"Mike, you need to hire a better class of—"

Escott quit the bar, going to the two women behind Mike. Whitey hadn't noticed them, they'd been so quiet. One of them was pretty. A real humdinger. Escott seemed hell-bent on hustling them out the door.

"No need to get greedy. There's plenty to go around," Whitey told him, and suddenly he was between them and the exit. Now they all seemed to be suspended in syrup, moving so slowly—that was funny, too. The looks they had . . . Escott had gone dead white, and Mike was outright dumbfounded.

The girl, well, she needed cheering up. Her face was blotchy, tears brimming and falling from red, swollen eyes, but still a humdinger of a twist. You didn't need to look at what was on top to enjoy the rest.

"C'mere, cutie. Let's go someplace else, we can have a good time."

Mike had *his* gun out, sighting down the barrel at him.

"No need to be like that. C'mon, Mikey. *Look* at me." Whitey spread his arms, smiling at his too-serious little brother. "Put that away."

Very strangely, Mike did just as he was told. His blue eyes were wide open, yet at the same time he looked asleep on his feet.

Whitey glanced at Escott, but he was busy hauling the women backward, urging them on. He sure was intent on getting them into the main room of the club—and the place wasn't even open.

Whitey put himself in their way again, gave Escott and the old bat a shove, cutting the little cutie out of the herd. She screeched, but a hand over her mouth shut that off quick enough. He hauled her easily along the curving hall into the dark, where they could have some privacy. The others were moving so slow it'd take them hours to catch up.

No more dark. Every light in the place abruptly blazed on.

"We're in time for the show," he told the girl. One sweep of his leg was all it took. She was on the floor, he dropped on top of her, and, damn, she smelled *good*. Especially there on the side of her neck . . .

She wasn't interested, kept squirming and fighting. She tried to knee him, but he shifted and slapped that out of her. Women just didn't know what was good for them. He'd have to show her. A little of this and that, and she'd settle down; they all did. First, get that coat open, now push up the dress, see what this one had for him.

She hissed and clawed his face, and the sharp burns from her nails cut through his haze of good feeling. He pulled away, startled.

Get off her!

Who was that? He looked around, but no one was near.

"Nelly, get away—*now*!"

Someone had used Whitey's own voice to yell at the girl. What in hell—?

She slipped out from under him. He tried to grab at her, but something slowed him down. He was only able to catch her ankle. He twisted and pulled and was on top of her, this time pinning her hands. He could smell her terror and his blood and by God, it was *good*.

A sudden stab of pain on the left side of his head came out of nowhere.

Get off her, dammit!

His vision fluttered, and for a moment he couldn't move. The girl pushed her way clear, rolling.

He shook off whatever it was, found his feet, and got in front of her again, keeping her from running. She was within reach, but he hesitated.

Let her go.

"Why should I?"

Because this is wrong.

"What the hell's that mean?"

Back away. Let her go.

"Who are you? Ramsey?" It didn't sound like Ramsey's voice, and it was close, as though someone were speaking right in his ear. Where were they? This wasn't the cabin.

She darted past him, and that seemed to break the spell. He caught and dragged her close, her back pressed to him. She bent forward, fighting, but he wrapped one arm around her body to hold her tight and pulled her head to one side with the other. He nuzzled her sweet throat. He heard her blood roaring, felt its thrum with his lips. He wanted to bite into that taut flesh and just *taste* her—

"Whitey!" A man's bellow cut across the room.

He paused, annoyed. Escott was just coming in, but stopped short, one arm raised, something in his hand.

What is it with all the guns?

Whitey threw him an exasperated look. Before he could speak, Escott fired.

The bullet went high and wide, but Whitey recoiled at the sound. The girl squealed, getting away.

Escott took her hand, and they retreated up the hall. Whitey wavered over who to deal with: the little humdinger or the shooter who needed to be taught a lesson. Never pull a gun unless you can kill on the first shot.

Might as well take care of him. Chase off the distractions, then he could show the sweet thing how to have a real party.

The lobby was a mess: blood on the floor, broken glass, what a sty. Broder, shaking his head like a punchy boxer, was only just picking himself up. He'd be trouble once he got rid of the cobwebs. Mike seemed to be waking, too, blinking, confused. What'd happened to him?

The girl was back in the arms of the old lady; Escott was in front of them both, gun pointed squarely at Whitey.

This was ridiculous. Whitey tried to tell him as much, but it was hard to talk. Those damned bees were buzzing so loud a man couldn't hear himself.

Escott yelled at Mike, his words distorted.

"Not done with you yet," Whitey promised the girl, winking.

Yes, you are.

He heard that clearly, despite the bees. It sounded like his own voice, but that was crazy.

"Whitey!"

My name's Gabe.

But he turned his head.

Mike was fully awake, his gun aimed and steady.

Whitey knew he could stop him again. A quick glance, a single sharp order, and he could—

No more.

He looked steadily into his brother's eyes. Mike could only see the monster, though. Gabriel *made* it hold still and used its voice.

"Do it, Michael."

"I don't want this," Mike whispered.

"I know." The monster forced Gabriel to take a step forward, then another. "But it's all right."

"Stop."

"I can't." One more, and he'd grab that gun and feed it to Mike the hard way. "Now, Michael."

"I—"

"*Now, dammit!*"

Mike's gun roared. In midreach Whitey felt another kick—this one much harder—against his chest, but he fooled them all and kept standing. He had a new hole in his suit, high on the right side. Fresh blood spilled out, and there was a corresponding flow down his back.

He threw a grin at Mike. "What you got in that thing? Rock salt?"

He coughed. It hurt.

He thought to draw a breath and couldn't quite fill his lungs. Must be a cold coming on. Another cough. A knot of blood splattered on the floor. He stared at it, wondering how that had happened.

The air was too thick, that was all. Too thick to breathe. He didn't need to, anyway. Good party trick, impress the girls.

There was a pressure around his chest like a steel ring; it was shrinking tight against his ribs. That wasn't right . . .

"Mike?" He was smart. He'd know what to do.

Whitey felt feverish. Sweat popped out over him. His body was baking inside his hot skin.

He clawed at his tie, dragging it off, tore at the top buttons of his shirt. Still too hot. He fumbled with the suit-coat buttons, but his fingers weren't working. Tremors jerked through them and up his arms. One of them was bleeding. What the hell? He couldn't feel it. There was that awful pressure squeezing his chest, though. What was happening?

"Mike?"

But his brother didn't speak, didn't move.

"I forgot something. What is it?" He'd spoken clearly. Mike had to have heard.

Whitey felt another coughing bout coming on. A bad one, so bad that his legs couldn't hold him. He awkwardly folded to his knees. Then the floor came at him. He tried to push it away and only ended up on his back again. The ceiling spun, the lights there too bright.

Broder started in on him, kicking him. That was what it felt like. But he kept well clear. Whitey's body thrashed and spasmed all on its own. Convulsions. They were tearing him apart.

He bit his tongue, tasted blood, heard gagging noises. His body stopped flailing on the floor, but the poison was still in him, oozing through his blood. The growing pressure around his chest would crush him from the inside out.

He became aware of the others, one in particular, the shivering girl with the dark hair. He reached toward her, though she was too far away.

She whimpered, clinging to the other woman.

The monster was scaring them. That was wrong. He pulled his arm back. His clutching hand turned into a fist, and he drew it tight against his aching chest so there was no chance of accidentally touching her. He nearly echoed her whimper, but shut it down. Show weakness, and Sonny would beat it out of him. The bastard could *smell* it.

Gabriel couldn't remember the beatings, but the monster did. The monster *loved* Sonny.

The steely pressure on his chest worsened, slowly crowding out his lungs. He had to say something, say it quick before his air was gone. He gasped like a fish, trying not to cough.

Where was she?

His sought her eyes, willing her to—

Look at me!

He managed to croak her name. She looked up, and he put his last effort into it; desperation got him past the surface mask to the soul inside. Vital, but damaged, trying to heal, hardly able to limp from one day to the next—how could she live like that?

I hurt you. I'm sorry . . . I'm sorry.

But his lungs were crushed flat.

He couldn't get the words out. He never would.

He stopped moving altogether. The feeling was much like his day sleep, his active mind trapped within a dead body.

He heard weeping. That would be Nelly Cabot, crying in her mother's arms.

"It's over, honey," the older woman murmured. "It's all over. He can't hurt you anymore."

It was true. The monster was gone.

Gabriel was alone.

HE drifted in the red shadows behind sealed eyelids.

People were nearby, but he was detached from their concerns like a stranger overhearing a private conversation. It was interesting for the moment, but he had no real care for the goings-on around him.

Someone put a hand on his throat, fingers resting on the pulse point for a long time.

"He's dead," said Broder.

Michael muttered a curse and walked away a few steps. His shoes crunched against broken glass, then there was the slosh of liquid. He choked on his drink and cursed again, and it almost sounded like a sob.

No one spoke for a time. Gabe had the impression they were in some kind of shock.

Mrs. Cabot broke the silence. "What was the matter with him? He go crazy? How could he move so fast?"

"The drug did that," Escott promptly answered. "Cocaine can be a very powerful stimulant."

"He used the stuff," said Michael, his voice thick, "but not all the time. He kept it quiet. If you didn't know to look, you just didn't know. But the last year . . . he got bad. He'd go off on 'fishing trips' to shoot dope. That's what he called them."

Mrs. Cabot snarled in disgust.

"Ma'am, I'm sorry. I thought he was only hurting himself. I swear, I did not *know* about your daughter. Broder should have told me."

"Why, so you can blame my girl?"

"No, I—"

"We don't want nothin' more to do with you. Just leave us alone."

"Yes, ma'am. I promise."

"One of you get us home, and that's the end of it."

"I'll drive them," said Escott. He was over by the bar now.

"What are you doing?" Mike asked.

"Your brother has no need of it." There was a rustle of shuffling paper. "I'm sure the ladies won't mind a small monetary compensation for the hell they've been put through tonight."

Mike grunted.

The door was opened. "Ladies, if you would? The green car just around the corner."

They shuffled past Gabe's body. Cold outside air flowed over him.

"Will you have sufficient time before I return?" Escott asked.

"He'll be gone," Mike said.

"You've made arrangements?"

"You could say."

The door closed. Shortly after, a motor turned over. A car rattled past the front entry and faded.

Mike must have been holding his breath. He choked out another curse and had another drink.

"It had to be done," Broder rumbled.

"Why'd I have to be the one to do it?"

"Just how things work. Stay here, get drunk. I'll deal with him."

"It's a two-man job. He's my responsibility. You shouldn't have kept quiet about this. Should have told me."

"Seemed like the right thing to do at the time."

"Him shooting the dope I could deal with, but not him hurting women like the old bastard."

"I kept an eye on him. If he stepped out of line, I was gonna—"

"Kill him?"

"Tried to. Would have saved you from it."

"But . . . he seemed to want me to do it. Did you see? At the end?"

"Yeah, Mike. He knew. He was crazy-sick like you said. No cure for that kind of thing. It's over now."

Neither spoke after that. Broder went outside briefly and returned, then Mike shut the lights off. The red shadows went black.

They lifted Gabe's body and carried him into the cold, dropping him heavily into . . . he wasn't sure what until the trunk lid slammed down. The car grumbled to life, and they began moving. Start-stop, start-stop, they must be hitting every signal between here and . . . where were they going?

Gabe couldn't bring himself to worry about it. He floated within the boundaries of his skull and decided being dead wasn't too objectionable. At least he wasn't having those dreams. That might change when the sun came up, but again, it just wasn't important. They hit a smooth road, and he drifted off.

The car began to jolt and jounce, sometimes skidding.

It was enough to wake Gabe from his long doze.

His chest itched. So did his left shoulder. He couldn't move to scratch either annoyance, though he tried hard to do so.

Damned drug. He was bogged down in its sluggish flow.

A sharp turn, and, though the car crawled along, the jouncing increased. His inert body slipped about in the trunk, unresponsive.

They stopped, the motor died, its growl replaced by the sound of wind sighing through pine boughs.

He was back in that dream of absolute peace and calm. He was safe. Here there were no monsters wearing his face to trouble him or anyone else.

After an indeterminate time, he was taken from the trunk and carried a distance. They left him on his back on raw, bare ground. He floated in cold shadows while the others got on with their own concerns.

None of it had to do with him, even when the first heavy wedge of damp earth slapped over his face.

19

FLEMING

THE third night I awoke weak, cold, and shaking, with the hunger like a gunshot wound in my belly. It had never been this bad before.

Dugan was upstairs snoring, a short, heavy rasp, as though even in sleep he breathed faster than normal. When I yelled his name, the snoring abruptly ceased. After a minute the springs squeaked, and he paced unsteadily back and forth.

Last night he'd fallen into a pattern of first feeding me, draining away my blood to drink, followed by another feeding—four or five times. He kept up the assurance that this would speed his transformation, and it was clearly having an effect on him. Toward dawn he was unnaturally restless, with so much energy thrumming through him I thought his heart would give out. He took that as evidence his procedure was succeeding.

I'd continued my dying act and hoped it would remain an act. He was careful to replace my lost blood, so when the sun rose, I was in reasonably good shape considering the situation.

Plodding down the stairs, he put the light on, and it took time for my dazzled eyes to adjust. What I saw scared me.

Now I looked at my left wrist, which was covered with many more thin welts where he'd cut me. The son of a bitch had been drawing off blood while I slept. That was why I was so sick.

Dugan looked the way I felt. He was unshaved and drawn, his sweat-sheened skin had a yellow tinge, and that rotten-fruit smell was more pronounced. I wondered if he'd noticed. Though his wide-open eyes were not flushed wholly red the way mine got after feeding, they were bloodshot and muddy. His movements were jerky, hands shaking, fingers nervous. He looked exactly like an alky caught short on booze.

My blood had to be killing him, consuming him.

"I've kept up my end," he said brightly, holding another milk bottle within my view. "Straight from the Stockyards—less than an hour old."

My corner teeth were out. I was hurting for it. I'd have taken anything then, including human blood from an unwilling donor.

Solicitous as a nurse, he lifted my head, allowing me to drink from the glass he'd filled. I finished it quick, but the belly pain didn't cease.

"You're draining me during the day," I said.

"Only to speed my transformation process. Have more, have all you want. I went to considerable trouble to obtain this for you."

I shut up and finished that bottle and the second one he fetched.

Dugan had been careless, letting me know we were less than an hour's travel from the Stockyards. That covered a lot of area, of course, but I filed the information away with other details I'd gleaned about my location, which was definitely the basement of a house. I was able to pick up certain noises unique to a home: the hum of a refrigerator, the rumble of an oil heater, the plumbing, and sometimes the click of an electric light.

I heard no traffic, but being belowground might have to do with that. Earth and concrete make for great insulation from the outside world.

Throughout the previous night, I'd paid attention to each sound, trying to distract myself from the constant pain, sometimes succeeding. Once he put on the radio to listen to a news show, giving a snort of disdain whenever he didn't like what was said. The rest of the time he paced back and forth or was writing, to judge by the frequent scratch of his pen. If he had so much to say, why didn't he just get a damn typewriter?

As the blood saturated my body, the sickness slowly faded, but I demanded more.

"Where are you putting it?" he asked, surprised.

"Losing ground."

"What?"

I glanced toward my mangled wrist. "You don't give me time to heal. I need more than you take just to recover. More than that to stay alive."

He almost sounded defensive. "I didn't do it that often."

The day feedings terrified me. If his thirst got the better of him, I might not wake up tomorrow night. "Enough to kill me if you don't . . . oh, God . . ." I trailed off into a groan and submerged into my dying act.

"I'll get another bottle," he said and left. He stumbled on the stairs on the way up, caught himself, and shot a quick, self-conscious look back. My eyes were mostly shut, so he was a blurred figure through my lashes, but I'd seen. This flash of insecurity was good. I had him worried.

He let me empty the third bottle with a fourth standing ready before doing his little cut-and-drain operation. Tonight, he gulped the beakerful with alarming speed and relish. When his shuddering subsided, his eyes were fever-bright and much redder than before. The whites were nearly gone.

Maybe he *was* turning into a vampire, just no kind I'd ever heard about. I fought to maintain listlessness.

"I'm feeling so much stronger," he said, swinging his arms around. "I've never been so energetic. I'd been looking forward to acquiring the ability to influence weaker minds, but it never occurred to me that my physical being would be so greatly augmented."

He sniffed at the untouched bottle of cow's blood, took an experimental sip, and grimaced. Apparently it wasn't to his taste yet.

"I should be fully changed by now," he said. "Perhaps you were right about it taking longer. I'm very sorry, but you'll have to remain here. But I'm optimistic—today I had to go out, and though it was cloudy, I wasn't at all comfortable in the light. That's progress, though it is rather short of the comalike state you fall into."

How much of that was self-suggestion, I wondered.

I mumbled for more blood. He cheerfully complied, chatty now, telling me about his goals once his little experiment was completed. He was excited about leaving Chicago and moving up in the world. First he'd have to deal with his criminal record. He was a wanted fugitive, and that had to be fixed.

"The police and court papers should be easy enough to destroy. Then I shall talk with everyone concerned with the case. I'll persuade them to completely forget me—even your English friend won't recall anything of it. Neither will that woman whose deficient offspring I kidnapped. She'd be better off without such a burden, you know." He sounded speculative. "So many things to do once I have your abilities. I shan't waste them, though. The world is going to improve significantly because of me."

Oh, brother.

But he could be right. Say he went to Washington and started doing an evil-eye whammy on anyone he chose. Though its influence wasn't permanent, I'd read enough history to know that one man in the right place at the wrong time could change things. For good or ill was up to the man. In Dugan's case, I couldn't really imagine how bad things could get.

How I hated his voice. I looked around for the other me. He was out of view. Dammit, I wanted his company. *He* could listen to the idiot; I wanted to hide in that summer day again.

Maybe Dugan was only blowing hot air to entertain himself, but his plans were too detailed.

Without referring once to it, I also understood he would kill me despite his promise to the contrary. I'd known that from the moment he first showed himself; this simply disposed of any lingering delusion. He couldn't set up anywhere and feel secure with me running loose.

I had a black moment, wondering how he'd carry it out. He could drain me completely by accident or do it on purpose. Or would he resort to the traditional stake and hammer, followed by a beheading just to be sure?

Bobbi would think I'd walked out on her because of her going to Hollywood. She'd never know.

Escott would think I'd gone off my head again and run away to kill myself.

They'd never find me.

My friendly doppelgänger appeared just then, scowling down. "You going to feel sorry for yourself or do something?"

I'm open to suggestions.

"You know what to do." He talked right over Dugan's blather.

A better hint, please.

He pointed at my right arm.

It's hard to pretend to be at death's door while at the same time trying to observe what's going on around you. I kept my eyelids at half-mast, looking straight ahead and unfocused, but still managed to see plenty whenever Dugan turned his back. Not that there was much to notice at the moment; my view was blocked by another glassful of blood, which I drank. I was feeling full now, but made no objection as Dugan poured another. While he was busy, I let my head loll to one side.

The L-shaped rod was still in place, the handle pointing in the same direction, my arm a ragged mess around the wound. A glimpse was enough, then I straightened back so he wouldn't notice.

I finished the next glass. The milk bottle was empty.

He gave me a long, considering look. "Tell me about that female of yours. How do you feed from her?"

What the hell? "None of your damn business."

Dugan's eyes flashed amusement, and I instantly regretted speaking. I shouldn't have reacted at all. Dear God, if he went after Bobbi . . . I wanted to rip free and strangle him. At the last second I changed the expression of the impulse and out came that maniac laughter again. There was no humor in it, and it sounded even more disturbing than before.

He backed away. Good, I'd scared him.

I let the laughter die and shut my eyes. Let him think I'd passed out.

He trotted energetically upstairs and slammed the door. Soon water was running, a lot of it, as though for a bath. The sound just might be enough to cover things if I ended up screaming.

I checked my right arm again. Sometime during the day a miracle had happened.

Healing had taken place, and the dried blood had concealed it. The skin was no longer adhering to the metal, trying to mesh to it, but had shrunk back from the rod. Not by a lot, just a fraction. It fit snugly enough, almost exactly the same as an earring wire through a woman's pierced ear, but larger in scale.

The important thing was that the wound had closed, and I was no longer bleeding.

I'd had the right idea last night when I'd tried to rip free, just not the strength or a reserve of blood to draw on. It had been too soon. My body needed time to figure out that the metal wasn't going away and had to be accommodated.

Now I slowly lifted my arm, working it along the threads a little at a time. It was awkward, and my muscles cramped. I told them to shut the hell up.

My arm couldn't twist to the point of getting the bone over the angle, but I got enough leverage to start bringing the end of the rod around. It came reluctantly, one inch, two, then it gradually swiveled into place, pointing at my head.

More twisting, and it burned like blazes, and suddenly I was pulling my arm off the damned thing.

No need to breathe, but I was panting, half from pain, half from triumph. I kept looking at my freed arm, fearing it was another hallucination. The hole was ugly as sin. I wasn't crazy enough to make up anything that bad; it had to be real.

Moving was painful. I'd not done much more than shiver and twitch the last two nights. Every joint was brittle and popped, but I made myself roll over to the left. My other arm was still pinned, the skin sealed to the rod, but I had momentum going, mental and physical.

I grabbed the handle and pulled it sharply straight up. The threading provided friction for my grip. Back, forth, back—the thing snapped and came away. I yanked my bleeding left arm up, unaware of my howling until I smothered it. That would bring Dugan running.

As soon as flesh lifted clear of the metal, I tried to vanish.

Nothing.

Goddammit. Now what?

I threw the blanket off and tore at the ropes binding my legs. The muscles burned at the sudden movement.

My hands no longer clawlike, the fingers were now swollen and clumsy. The rope was too thick to break casually unless I got some slack to work with, but Dugan didn't know anything about knots. He'd coiled the rope around and around, wrapping me like a mummy, immobilizing to a man lying flat, much less effective when he was vertical. All it took was to push everything down to my feet.

It was more painful than it should have been.

There were spots of blood along the length of my trousers, making the material stick to my skin. Then I looked closer. It was just too easy to put myself in Dugan's place and figure out what he'd done. I didn't have time to fix it; the basement door swung wide.

He was partway down, a bottle in hand. My yells must have made him think I needed another feeding.

The shock on his face when he saw me lurching toward him was sweet to see—then that smug smile came back. He'd planned for this. If I'd somehow gotten free on the first night, he had prepared for it.

He threw the bottle, missing me. The glass broke; the contents splashed everywhere. He whipped around and up, and I was right behind him. He was in time to slam the door in my face. I spent a couple seconds yanking it open. That gave him what he needed, the opportunity to get to his revolver.

I ducked back, and he wasted one of his six bullets when it struck somewhere to the side of where I'd been. Like Kroun, I couldn't vanish. Getting shot now could truly be fatal.

"I can stay here all night, Mr. Fleming," Dugan announced. "Until the dawn comes." He tried to sound bland and bored, but couldn't pull it off. He was breathing too hard.

My view from the basement was limited: an unadorned wall within arm's reach, part of a hallway. I had no idea how far it went in either direction. He sounded close, only steps off. I could charge him blind and collect a bullet, hopefully not in the head. Satisfying as getting my hands around his throat would be, I could not risk the damage.

I slipped back down the stairs, looking for anything to even the odds. My legs complained with vicious sharp pains, but those were nothing compared to being pinned to that table.

Which was indeed a huge Victorian thing, too large to get up the stairs and throw. I grabbed smaller stuff: empty milk bottles from the floor.

"Fleming, I don't expect you to be reasonable, but if you would just think a moment, we can easily revolve this. We can come to an arrangement that will be mutually beneficial. I have a great deal of cash . . ."

He'd stolen it from that misguided girlfriend. No thanks. He was moving, edging closer to the door. I reclaimed the stairs, and keeping all but my arm inside, blindly flung one of the milk bottles down the hall. It crashed and shattered, I immediately followed it up with the second, then risked a look. He was in the act of dodging, but fired at me and struck the ceiling. Two bullets wasted.

He knew how to shoot, but aiming is a skill. Some naturals can point and hit the bull's-eye; most need hours of practice. His planning hadn't taken into account that I'd hit back. I hurled an empty at him like a cannonball.

He dodged that one, but not the second. By then I was halfway out in the hall and able to put some pepper on it. The heavy glass container got him square in the chest. He staggered back, and I took the opening.

I was wobbly and hurting, but made a solid tackle that rattled his teeth. We rolled in broken glass and pummeled each other, and I heard a maniac laughing and cursing. I shut him up once I realized it was me. Dugan still had his gun, but I had a grip on that hand, keeping him from firing.

He threw some good punches, and their force was a surprise. Drinking my blood had improved him. He'd gotten stronger and faster, but he was unprepared for frenzied desperation.

However much thought I'd put into how to kill him, I wasn't thinking now. Brutal instinct to survive was running this show. He was a threat, I had to make him harmless.

I slammed pile drivers, one after another, to his gut, and that broke him. He couldn't draw breath and sagged in place. I wrested the gun clear, pushed away, and scrambled upright. He gasped, clutching at me, but I made sure he saw where the muzzle was pointing, which was right in his face.

Eyes wide, he stopped; it must have penetrated that I wasn't going to shoot him immediately.

I was tempted.

We stared at each other, me unnaturally still, Dugan puffing like a runner, his face sweaty and more yellow than red from exertion. I let him catch his breath, listening to his heart as his lungs sawed air. It was going too fast even given the circumstances. Whatever benefits he'd taken from my blood, it was devouring him from the inside out.

"Pliers," I said, my voice uncannily gentle, but then I wasn't what could be called winded from the fight. I was pissed as hell and working to keep in control.

The remnants of his ingrained smile gradually distorted into a confused expression.

"You'll have tools. I want pliers."

He must have thought I planned to yank his fingers off—not that it hadn't occurred to me—and hesitated. He was visibly thinking.

I roared "pliers" at him, and he got moving.

We were in a small room, perhaps meant to be used as a parlor or for dining. It had a long and ancient sofa, a table and chair, a radio, and on the floor, an open suitcase of jumbled clothing. He'd picked this room closest to the basement door to set up camp.

I was not surprised by the large collection of origami animals spreading across one corner of the floor like a lost herd. He'd been very busy with his fountain pen and green ink, so many profound thoughts to record.

This room opened directly to a kitchen, with a box of tools on a counter by the sink. They were new, as though he'd bought them all at once from a hardware store. He'd likely gotten the threaded rods at the same time.

With me keeping him covered and giving specific instructions, he gingerly got the pliers. His hand shook so violently he dropped them. He glanced at me and bent to pick them up again, getting a better grip.

That rotten-fruit smell had taken on a more familiar tang that I knew to be fear. He had no idea what was coming next. I was tempted to keep him hanging, but this wasn't the time or place.

I sat on the sofa, grunting as I stretched my legs out. The blood spots on my pants were more than simple stains.

He was a grating, insane, self-important bastard, but give him credit, he'd planned this one through. If I somehow freed myself from the table, this was his insurance to keep me anchored in flesh, allowing him time to either escape or wound me enough to restrain again.

The spots on the trousers were nail heads, not bloodstains. While I'd been in my day sleep, he'd pounded the metal into my legs right through the cloth.

I pointed to one of them, then at the pliers in his hand. "Pull it out."

"Wh-what?"

"You put 'em in, you pull 'em out. Make it fast, and I'll let you keep your ears."

He knelt, made an effort to still his shaking, and did as he was told. He gripped a nail head with the pliers and pulled hard.

I hissed, and made an effort not to shoot him. The damned nail was a good two inches long. And I'd been able to *move* with all those in me? Jeez.

"Next one," I said, my voice thick and harsh.

He repeated the operation, faster. I hissed again, and once more did not shoot. That was moderately encouraging to him. "Mr. Fleming, I'm sure we can—"

I suddenly grabbed his hair with my free hand, twisting his head around almost to the breaking point, and shoved the gun hard against his nose, the muzzle half an inch from his left eye. "You say another word—*one more goddamned word* . . ."

No need to finish. He got the idea and continued in sweating silence.

The next few minutes weren't fun for either of us. I had to endure his ham-fisted surgery, and he had to not talk. Suffering was likely equal for both parties.

When the last nail came free, it was better than Christmas.

I wasn't there anymore. My poor body vanished into that sweet, gray, healing nothingness.

Dugan gave a surprised yelp, falling back. I could imagine him looking around in confusion, wondering what would come next.

He bolted.

I heard a door jerked open, there was one in the kitchen, and swooped myself that way, following his panicked breathing as he pelted toward some goal.

A car, as it turned out. I went solid right behind him as he scrabbled at its door handle. He screeched in panic as I caught his collar and spun him to the ground.

My mind was very clear now that the pain was gone. In a glance, I took in the back of a small, plain house, trampled snow, the little yard surrounded by tall, overgrown holly bushes. They blocked the view of whatever lay beyond and worked better than a brick wall for concealing everything within.

This included two holes in the middle of the yard, one long enough to hold a body, the other smaller, located several yards from the first. Both were deep. I was surprised Mr. Genius had applied himself to so much physical labor.

Dugan's legs weren't supporting him, but he tried to run anyway. His version of instinct was trying to get him clear, but I wouldn't allow it. I dragged him toward the larger hole and let go just at the edge. He sobbed and rolled around to face me, hands pawing the air, begging. I still held the revolver.

He was not a pretty sight, his groveling made it worse. I'd been here before, on the edge of murder, and there is no satisfaction to killing a man, however deserving. Dugan's death would just create another dark burden for my tattered soul to haul around for however long I walked the earth. I had too many of those. No need for more.

I'd throw a good scare into him, tie him up, remove all trace of myself from this place, and drop him at the nearest police station. He had to pay for all those deaths. A judge and jury were needed, not me.

"*Please* . . ." he said.

Then again . . .

"That—" I told him "—is another goddamned word."

20

KROUN

A slow, dull pounding awakened Gabriel. The vibration of each impact thumped against his cold, cold body, irritating him to no end.

Can't a man get some sleep?

Apparently not. The heavy, regular thumps continued, getting louder. He tried to roll away from it, pulling a pillow over to cover his ears, but was unable to move. That was when he became aware of the weight pressing him. Evenly distributed so he had no sense of being crushed, it held him solidly in place, like a bug suspended in amber. Strangely, he did not find that to be alarming.

Thud. Thud. Thud. Like God knocking on a malleable door, coming closer, closer.

Gabe was unsure whether that was a good thing or not. After some thought he leaned toward the more negative assessment, certain that God had debts to call in. Better not keep Him waiting. Gabe pushed against the weight, managing to wriggle a little. He tried to take a breath to speak and got a mouthful of dirt.

Oh, cripes, not again.

The pounding stopped when he made a sudden frenzied shove that caused earth to shift above him. The weight fell away from one of his arms, and he clawed free air.

A hand grasped his wrist and pulled.

He emerged spitting and blind, frantic to escape his second grave. He shook off the help, scrabbling up and over the sides, not stopping until he was yards from it. He rubbed his eyes clear, catching impatient glimpses between blinks.

Snow. Trees. River. Sleet. Wind. Lead gray sky. A flashlight on the ground, its beam toward the disturbed grave. A man standing by the hole. Lean and angular body. Dour face.

Despite the bone-freezing sleet, he was in shirtsleeves, sweating. A shovel lay discarded on the broken ground. The man held a large revolver now.

Gabe rubbed his face, his fingers gritty, and stared at the company.

"What—what *is* it with all the guns?" he asked.

Escott aimed down the sights like a duelist. "That depends, Mr. Kroun. Who are you tonight?"

What a damned stupid question. "Who do you think?" He spat more dirt.

Escott picked up the flashlight and pointed the beam at Gabe's face.

"Hey!"

"Open your eyes," he snapped.

He made it sound important. As Gabe found himself unarmed, he complied as best he could. The light seemed to pierce right through his skull—which began to thunder inside. He grabbed a clump of snow from a drift and pressed it against his head.

"You done yet?" he growled, squinting.

"Normal as can be expected." Escott switched off the light.

"Huh?"

"Your eyes. Last night what little iris you had vanished entirely. I don't think the others noticed, not that it matters to them now."

Gabe stayed put, applied another snowy compress, and began shivering in the wind. "You wanna fill me in? 'Cause I'm thinking you're nuts."

Escott slipped the gun into its shoulder rig and retrieved his suit coat, which he'd hung on a low branch. "You're correct in that assessment. It can be the only explanation for why I'm here." Next he drew on his overcoat. He left both unbuttoned, his revolver within easy reach. "What do you remember of last night?"

"You pulled a gun on me again. That's pretty vivid."

"And?"

Gabe shied away from more, but couldn't ignore the holes and blood on his mud-covered suit. "Mike shot me," he muttered.

"What about your actions leading up to that point?"

He wanted to put off thinking about that until his head pain eased. At this rate it might never happen. Sleet flecked his face, and the wind flayed his exposed skin. "Where the hell are we?"

"A place familiar to you."

Cripes. This was his lucky night. "How'd you know they'd take me here?"

"I asked Mr. Strome to wait within sight of the club and follow your brother and Mr. Broder when they departed. He tracked them to this dismal spot, then phoned me when he could."

"You set me up. You knew they'd kill me."

"Yes—though I did not foresee the method. I suppose your brother was trying to make it painless for you. Injecting an overdose of cocaine should have rendered you unconscious. Instead, there were some unexpected and singularly unpleasant consequences before you succumbed."

His memory on that was disjointed. Someone else had been running the show except toward the end. He'd asked Michael a question and gotten no answer.

"You set me up," he repeated.

"Because it was the right thing to do." Escott had an edge in his tone that stated he was immune to reproach. "There is a terrible darkness in you. We saw Whitey Kroun last night, and he is a monster. Have you any control over him?"

He winced at the word *monster* and that someone else used it so accurately. "If people left me alone, I'd be just peachy."

"You can't, then."

"I—"

"Yes?"

"I did. A little."

"Indeed?"

He rubbed his numb hands. "I was scaring the girl. Tried to tell her I was sorry."

"For scaring her? Just for that?"

What more do you want? "It wasn't me. I'm not like that. The dope pulled that out. It's over."

"You're certain?"

"What kind of proof can I give you for that?" Exasperated, Gabe looked around. The hole he'd crawled from wasn't his original grave. This one was much closer to the river.

"Where's Ramsey?"

Escott nodded toward the right. Farther into the trees was the mound of black earth. There had been changes since Gabe's visit. Someone had tamped down the top and arranged large river stones over it into the shape of a cross.

"How'd you know which one to dig up?"

"Yours was unembellished." Escott grabbed the shovel, bracing it upright against a tree. "I suppose your brother thought God wouldn't have you."

"He was right."

"Come along, Mr. Kroun. I've not yet decided what to do about you."

That made him pay attention. "What do you mean?"

"Pick yourself up." Escott said it the way someone else might say, "Time to settle the bill."

I hate this place.

With less effort than anticipated, Gabe got to his feet. His day's rest in the ground had restored him. His scratches were gone, and the chunk torn from his shoulder was filled in, no longer hurting. There was a scar, but it was well healed. Another day, and it might be gone entirely; the same went for the hole in his chest. His head continued to throb, probably a hangover from the dope.

Following a well-trampled path in the snow, Escott trudged toward the clearing and the dark cabin. Gabe did not want to go there.

The hinges creaked, and Escott left the door open. Inside, he lit a few candles. Shadows jerked and quivered, as though surprised by the intrusion.

I should have burned the dump when I had the chance.

Gabe forced himself up the step and in. The wind followed him, carrying the whirring sound of the pines singing to themselves. He slammed the door on it.

The cabin looked smaller and meaner. The bloody, mold-eaten blanket and mattress had been thrown back on the bed. Gabe scowled and sat on a bench as far from it as possible. A fire in the potbelly stove would be good, but take time to start, and he didn't want to linger any longer than necessary. Escott obviously had some things to say. Let him get it out, then they could leave.

"You talked to Mike," prompted Gabe. He tried to not look at the bloodstains by the bed. Escott had to have noticed them.

"At length."

"He pay you off?"

"He did not. After a call to Gordy to establish my bona fides, I persuaded Mike to accept my help and silence in exchange for the truth of what happened in this cabin."

"What'd he tell you?"

"It was Miss Cabot's story that convinced me you needed to be dealt with. She and her mother were present. Broder had been hiding them from you in Cicero. What you did to that girl . . ."

Gabe made a cutting motion with his hand. "Never mind that."

"No, I will not." Escott's voice lowered, taking on a harsher tone. "You crossed a line."

"*Shuttup.*"

Surprisingly, he did. Escott used a candle to light a cigarette, smoked it to the filter, and stubbed it out.

During that pause, Gabe tried to fit things together with this new information. He couldn't. "Ramsey was supposed to kill me, thought he had, and the girl was in the way, a witness. All I wanted was to find out if she was okay."

"She's as well as can be expected. Perhaps her mother is right, and she may find some shred of peace now that you're dead to her."

"But I *couldn't have*—"

"Mr. Kroun, you don't remember your death or what led to it, not one moment of it. Please have the courage to face the truth: Ramsey had no orders from anyone to kill you; he just couldn't stomach what you'd done to that poor girl."

"I did nothing! There's *no* way I'd have hurt her. You got that yet?"

Escott was silent for a long moment. "You absolutely believe that."

"It's true."

"It is not true, yet you believe it. Were that not so, you would never have hypnotized her last night and demanded she tell her story again. That would have damned you on the spot, but you tried anyway, thinking she'd exonerate you."

"Listen to me . . ."

"No." Escott cut his gaze away and pulled out his gun. "None of that. Try to put me under again, and I will shoot you. Look at the floor. Now."

That was stupid. He did as he was told. He was fast enough to rush the man, but it would put a stop to learning anything else. Escott would fire, and that might bring the monster out. Gabe was angry, but he didn't want to risk killing Escott.

He put a hand on the side of his pounding head and wished for more snow. "All right . . . what did she say?"

"You're ready to hear the truth?"

"Just tell me."

"Very well. Two months ago you did hire Miss Cabot's services as a companion for what you termed a 'fishing trip.' She understood that much and went willingly as the money was good. Ramsey drove and turned a blind eye; that was his job. You stopped at the asylum to show her off to your father, then continued on to Wisconsin."

Gabe's shivering abruptly ceased as heat crept up his neck and face. He was ashamed of what he'd done even if he couldn't remember it.

"This cabin was not the warm winter lodge she'd been led to expect. Soon as you arrived you gave yourself an injection of your chosen poison, then gagged her to keep her quiet. I shall not repeat what followed, only that it was brutal and went on for some while. Ramsey waited in the car as ordered, but when she managed to get rid of the gag, he heard her screams and came running. He burst in, did not like what he saw, and shot you dead."

Sickness rolled through him; Gabe shook his aching head. "You're wrong. I could never do that to a woman."

"Why would she lie?"

"I don't know." God, it hurt. "Keep going."

"Along with a hysterical girl, Ramsey had the problem of how to explain your death to your brother. Fearing the reception of that news would result in his own swift demise, he decided to get away and make himself scarce. He said as much to Miss Cabot, telling her she should do the same."

"Did she kill Ramsey?"

"Yes. Miss Cabot was in a bad state, fearful for her life. She knew how things worked in your world and had little trust that Ramsey would just let her go. By then she really was a witness to murder or at least a justifiable homicide. Perhaps he said something to make her doubt him. She said it was self-defense. She took the car back to the brothel."

"Why not to her mother?"

"Didn't know where to find her. The girl had fallen in love with some man when she was fifteen, run away, and some years later wound up working in that house. The madam there called a doctor for Miss Cabot, and since you were involved, he, in turn, called your brother."

Gabe risked looking up. "Then Mike knew all along?"

"No. It happened that Mr. Broder answered the phone. He took the next train to Chicago to sort out the mess. It was he who eventually found Mrs. Cabot and got her daughter home again. He paid her a sum to keep quiet. If she had any trouble, she was to phone him, which she did when you arrived unannounced at her diner. Her trunk call to New York got her message passed on to him here, and he came running."

That explained the car crash and grenade-throwing. "Why help her? What's his stake in this?"

"Because he is at heart a decent man."

"Decent? The man's a piece of walking granite."

"Who still had pity for the girl and wanted to spare your brother from having to deal with you." Escott let that sink in. "He found the broken grave and Ramsey, but you were missing. He buried Ramsey and left. Thereafter, he was careful to keep an eye on you. Broder accepted the story you yourself put about—that you'd been grazed by a bullet."

"Okay, some of that adds up, but not the rest. Not what happened here. Nelly was hysterical, she mixed things up. Or she was afraid of what Mike might do to her. She figured out a story that would keep her alive. She's not the first dame to accuse a man of—look, just *get* me to her. If I can put her under for five minutes, you'll hear the truth."

Escott stared, thinking maybe. One-handed he pulled out another cigarette and lit it with a candle. He kept the gun's aim steady. "It's truly lost to you, isn't it? Not just what happened that night, but everything. Otherwise, you'd never say that."

A hot spike hit that spot on his skull. Gabe flinched.

"You insist on your innocence because you don't remember who you were."

Gabe managed a snort despite his pain. "What gave you that idea?"

"I also had a long talk with Gordy. Jack mentioned you'd been getting information from him, then making him forget. I found that a little prodding on my part brought back some recollection of your conversations. It was clear to us both that you had no memory of who you used to be before that bullet hit your brain."

"That's crazy."

"Why deny it?"

Because it was weakness. Show that, and they ate you alive.

"You wanted details concerning your death, but with it came the ugly facts about the life you led. That's why you let Jack know certain things. You craved the truth but knew there might be consequences. If at some point you remembered and turned back into what you'd been, then you'd need someone who could keep you in check. Who better than another vampire?"

Gabe stood and walked out of the cabin, his knees shaking. He scooped more snow and pressed it to the white patch, but the agony wouldn't stop. His head felt too full. Sleet ticked down steadily, freezing, leaving a crust on everything. It stung his face, clinging to his eyebrows and lashes until his vision blurred.

He sank onto the icy step, holding tight to the porch support post. He wanted the cold to take him, freeze him solid so he wouldn't have to think or feel. Maybe Escott could simply bury him again, let the earth cover and blot him out forever.

He heard Escott's step behind him. The man passed by and stood in the blowing sleet, finishing his cigarette, letting it fall to the snow. "This way," he said, heading toward the trees.

Gabe felt too dizzy to walk, but made himself move.

Escott stopped on the other side of the black mound, looking down at its cross. "You weren't even meant to be here."

"Why is that?" Trying to distract himself out of the pain he searched for anything familiar, anything that would spark his memory.

"Miss Cabot said Ramsey scavenged the place for something with which to weigh your body, planning to sink it in the river."

"Not bury me?"

"He changed his mind when he found this grave ready and waiting."

Gabe looked up. "What?"

"You heard."

"But who put it here?"

"You're being unnecessarily obtuse, Mr. Kroun. You dug it yourself."

He just couldn't see. "Why?"

"For *her* body when you were finished with her."

That was too much. "No. Absolutely not."

The wind swept his words into empty darkness. Bare branches clacked around them, sleet hissed, and the pine boughs made sad music.

But from his last visit he recalled the familiar feel of a shovel in his hands. The blade cutting into the earth, regular as a machine, he was used to such work, took enjoyment from it.

Now he knew why.

Just as Sonny had murdered his wives, Whitey Kroun would murder his little hired humdinger . . .

He sagged, unable to deny, unwilling to accept. Ice crept down the back of his neck. He didn't want to know any more. This was too much.

Shivering, he turned toward the cabin.

Escott stood blocking the path. "Not yet. There is still a debt to pay."

Gabe spread his hands. "But I don't *remember*!"

"If you did, I'd kill you myself."

"*How* can I be responsible if I don't remember?"

"Your victims do."

That hit Gabe as hard as one of Sonny's slaps. "Wh-what?"

Escott pointed.

He rubbed sleet from his eyes. Peering, half-expecting to see Ramsey's ghost drifting between the tree trunks, Gabe only saw more snow. There were footprints wandering here and there in the clean drifts. Escott had been exploring, but his tracks were filling in.

"There and over there and that one . . ." Escott said, still pointing.

Gabe couldn't see anything but trees and snow and—

God . . . no . . .

The many layers of white fall covered several low mounds scattered over a wide area, softening their lines, but their shapes were unmistakable.

No . . . no, no, no . . .

Gabe staggered back, blundered against a trunk and held on to keep from falling. He turned away, doubling over. There was nothing in his cramping belly, but it twisted inside out regardless. He retched and gagged, staggered a few more steps, then doubled over again, unable to stop. He coughed bloody spittle, choking.

"Kroun!"

No more. He had to get away from that voice, that name, away from this hellhole.

Sleet blinded him. He kept going.

His legs seemed on fire as he slogged through deeper and thicker snow. The burning surged upward, tearing into his chest. It closed with a rush over his head, cutting off the wind. He leaned into the flames as they started to tug him down. Blistering hot, yet exquisitely cold. He was going to hell where he belonged.

Then something strongly grabbed one of his arms and, half-pulling it from the socket, hauled him back from the flowing abyss. He had no strength to fight. His feet tangled, he tripped, and abruptly body-slammed against rocky ground.

He lay stunned, blinking sluggishly, eyes swimming. Tears or melted sleet, he couldn't tell.

Escott stood over him, panting from some recent exertion. He was soaking wet and cursing, the invective aimed at Gabriel.

"On your feet, you idiot," he finally snarled.

Gabe dragged himself upright. He was soaked, too. He'd run himself straight into the river. "Why'd you stop me?"

Escott pointed again, up the easy rise, past the cabin, toward—"Those women—they had families, friends, people who need to know what happened to them. *That* is your debt. You will pay it before you leave this life."

It was insane . . . how could Escott expect him to—

"We'll sort something out."

Was he a mind reader? "You're gonna help me?"

"I'm helping *them*."

"Why?"

"Someone has to. Whitey Kroun was a very sickening fellow, perverted, dangerous, without conscience, and thoroughly deserving of his fate when it overtook him."

Dizziness washed though him again. *No more, please . . .*

"He died far too quickly and easily for his crimes."

He scrabbled for more snow, pressing it to the spot of agony on his head. It burned, gradually cooled, and left his fingers white and numb.

"Then you rose from the ruins. *Tabula rasa*—a clean slate."

"Not so clean." With flaws. So many dangerous flaws.

"But I believe you want to do the right thing. You just don't know how."

"'S crazy."

"You saved my life, Mr. Kroun. If you will allow, perhaps I can help save yours."

Gabe had forgotten the hospital, what he'd done for a stranger. Things made better sense now. He began shivering again, more violently than before. His clothes were freezing to his skin. Escott looked no better, but still waited for a reply.

Gabe didn't know what was expected for a moment, then understood. "You're crazy, you know that?"

Escott gave a nod and held out his hand.

But I can leave. He could do that. Just walk away. He could bolt and disappear himself quick enough. Leave the state, leave the country.

But maybe . . . maybe this would make the pain go away.

He had to chance it. No plan. Deal with whatever came, whenever it came, and hope for the best.

He put his hand out and sealed his deal with another madman.

"It's cold, Mr. Kroun, we should leave."

"Don't call me that. I'm not him anymore, never again. Gabriel. Gabe's fine."

▲ 21 ▼

FLEMING

Dugan's hideout was the last of four similar small houses on a narrow road that continued south through empty fields; in the distance were enough lights to indicate a town. The two farthest houses showed lights, the nearest was dark. He'd picked a great spot for privacy.

To the north was Chicago, its glow against the clouds unmistakable and reassuring.

Mindful of how Dugan had acquired his last lair, I looked for graves and was thankful when nothing obvious presented itself. There was a rickety shed in back, empty, dirt floor undisturbed, a faded FOR RENT sign leaning against one side. The house itself was empty of furnishings except what he'd apparently brought himself. He must have gone legit to better keep his head down.

Putting the revolver on a kitchen counter, I gave myself a preliminary wash in the big sink, getting most of the blood and grime off my face and arms. The water was even hot.

He'd been intent on bathing, too, before my interruption. The bathtub had water in it, but it was draining away around a leaky plug. I quelled an urge to fill the thing and dive in.

His shaving things were balanced along the edge of the sink. I felt my beard, considered for less than a second, and left. I didn't want to touch any of his stuff if I could help it.

First things first, I found the rest of the blood supply he'd brought for me in the fridge: a dozen quart milk bottles filled to the brim. I snagged one and drank it straight down. My healing and the fight had taken it out of me, and even after my drink I still felt a general weariness.

That, I told myself, would fade with time. He'd given me his worst, and I'd beaten him. Maybe tomorrow night I'd get the shakes or cringe at a bad memory, but I'd worry about it then, not now.

Next I had to clean things other than myself, and it wasn't easy going back down into that damned basement. It stank of blood and terror. I made an effort not to breathe the rusty sweet stench.

The table must have been brought down in pieces; it was that big. He couldn't have managed it on his own otherwise.

The two rods stuck up as I'd left them, one with the handle broken off. I looked underneath to see how he'd worked it and saw that there had been a reason for the threading.

The lower part of the rods extended about a foot and a half below the table, and he'd filed the ends to points, the easier to pierce my arms. There were two thick metal squares with half-inch holes drilled in their centers firmly screwed to the underside of the table. Each rod went through that hole, held firmly in place with thick nuts and washers. Without the plates to spread the load, I might have been able to pull the rods out from the wood. Hideous, simple, and it worked.

I wanted to burn the table, but that would not be practical. Instead, I removed the rods, leaving the table with the holes and reinforcing plates as a mystery for anyone who happened to come down here next. The rods, rope, and my packet of earth went into the car. I kept the butcher's apron out.

The basement had a cement floor with a drain and over in a corner was a faucet. Cold water, but it did the job once I found a bucket and an ancient mop. I threw water over the table and swabbed it down, on top and underneath. My blood had soaked into some spots, but given time would turn into unidentifiable stains.

After the table I threw water on the stairs and floor, mopping them down. The porous cement would not scrub clean, but most of the red stuff went down the drain, and the place looked less like a slaughterhouse. The mop head remained bloody however much I rinsed it, so it would also go in the car.

Upstairs, I swept up the broken glass and put it in the bucket. I carried his radio, toolkit, and the bottles of animal blood to the car. He had a crate in the trunk, and the bottles fit neatly into it with no chance of spilling. This must have been how he'd carried them in the first place.

I searched his suitcase, finding bundles of money, spare clothes, newspapers, and most of a ream of writing paper, but nothing to indicate his identity.

On his writing table was a bottle of his favorite green ink ready to refill his favorite fountain pen.

In his neat, machinelike hand, he'd covered one sheet of paper with personal observations about his experiment—me. I didn't care to read more, and found matches left forgotten in a kitchen drawer. I crumpled his latest thought into a ball, and gathered up all the origami animals, carrying them to the kitchen sink.

They made a nice blaze for a few long minutes. I unfolded and fed them in one by one until the green was consumed by black, then crushed the ashes to dust. Running water flushed the last of his poisonous thoughts away for good. The sink had a scorched area, but that would be someone else's problem.

I squashed his clothing into the suitcase with his shaving gear, the paper and ink—everything he'd brought—and put it in the car, keeping one of his shirts. I used it to rub down every surface in the house I could remember touching and a few more besides just to be careful. I used it like a glove to pick up the revolver again, wiping it, too, then thoughtfully switched off the lights. The doorknobs got a final swipe as I went outside.

My arms were still bare, what with the sleeves having been cut away, but I didn't feel cold. I'd worked up a good sweat from all the work.

There was one last job to do, and I'd allowed for the fact that I might not be able to finish it.

Dugan lay flat on the ground next to the grave he'd dug.

I'd shot him. He was dead.

For now.

I didn't know if he would stay that way.

After all the blood he'd drained from me, I sure as hell wasn't going to take any chances.

I looked at his corpse, and all I could feel was relief. Guilt, regret, fear of being caught, even satisfaction—all the varied emotions that people experience when they murder another human being weren't there for me. I was only relieved that it was over.

Maybe that meant another piece of my soul was gone, burned away like his writing. Or maybe I was in some kind of shock.

Then it was a *relieved* kind of shock.

I dropped the revolver into the hole and tossed the shirt aside in case I wanted a rag for later.

His shovel was on the ground next to a pick he'd used to break up the tough earth. He was no expert at grave-digging, but he'd made it and the smaller hole very deep. All the energy and strength he'd taken from me had had to go somewhere.

I stooped and got the shovel. It still had the price written on the handle in grease pencil.

Last job.

It was a bad time to stop and think, but I realized I didn't know just how to do what needed to be done.

One short moment of consideration later, I turned him on his face. His body was flaccid and oddly heavy. Was it already repairing that bullet hole in his heart? I had no sense that there was anything left of him. There is an awful emptiness to the dead. You expect them to notice and react to your presence. It's unsettling that they don't.

Of course, it's even more unsettling if they do.

Two-handed, I raised the shovel and brought it straight down like a guillotine blade on the back of his neck. It sheared through the bones and flesh, biting into the earth beneath. His head did not roll away. Appalled that I'd even thought of it, I had carefully banked snow around him to prevent any such motion.

There was, not surprisingly, a great deal of blood. Much of it leaked into the ground, but a lot splashed onto me. I'd put on the butcher's apron, though, tying it low to cover my legs and shoes.

I kicked his body into the longer hole. It landed chest up.

Snapping the pick handle in two over one knee, I vanished, went down in the hole long enough to ram half of the splintered length of wood into his heart, took off the heavy apron, and shot swiftly clear.

Solid again, I quickly stumbled away and threw up.

My legs gave out. I fell on all fours in the snow, heaving and whooping and finally sobbing, though my eyes were dry. The emotional reaction caught up to me sooner than expected. I rode it out like a storm, letting my body have its way so I could eventually function again. On an intellectual level I'd done what was necessary, but certain horrors are harder to deal with than others.

Nausea anchored me in place for some time, blotting out even the cold, wet snow as I lay curled on the ground, groaning and miserable.

Once more I conjured that perfect summer day, but it was less perfect now. The stock-tank water was uncomfortably cool, and gray clouds crowded in, dulling the blue sky. Bobbi and Escott were nowhere in sight.

My doppelgänger loafed under the shade tree, hands in his pockets, his expression sympathetic.

For the first time it occurred to me that doppelgängers in legend were supposed to be evil things. They brought calamity, chaos, and worse to those unlucky enough to see theirs.

Maybe he was the real Jack Fleming, and I was *his* doppelgänger.

The other me gave a sardonic snort, shaking his head, showing a brief grin.

"Don't be a pill," he said, then walked away.

I blinked awake. What the hell did that mean?

Ah, crap, I'd think about it later. I was freezing.

I scattered snow over the mess I'd made and went back to the long hole. Dugan's body was still in it, showing no signs of resurrection. I shoveled dirt in, enough to discourage scavengers, then regarded the smaller hole.

Clearly he'd dug it as a place to bury *my* head when the time came. It would be easy enough to toss his in, but I felt a reluctance to do so. There was no excuse not to use it, but from there I went up against an unexpected streak of superstition.

I had a nightmare picture of Dugan's body blindly lurching from its grave to go digging up its head.

That would *not* happen . . . but sometimes it's okay to give in to a mild case of irrationality. If it makes you feel better, why not?

My irrationality was sufficiently strong that it gave me the stomach to slam the sharp end of the pick through the back half of Dugan's head. Can't say I felt better, as the nausea returned in force, but the action removed all doubts that Dugan would somehow revive. His ghost might haunt me, along with the sound his skull made when the bones shattered, but everyone else was safe.

I shut the impaled remains in the rickety shed along with the swabbed-down shovel. In a couple days I'd call the cops and complain about intruders in the house and a bad smell coming from the shed. Of course they would be revolted by the headless corpse and the obvious violence that had taken place, but that couldn't be helped. They would eventually identify Dugan from his prints or what was left of his face and unofficially close a few files.

Someone would have to make an effort to find his killer, of course. That was of no concern to me so long as they didn't come knocking on my door. If that happened, well, I had plenty of friends who would provide me with an alibi, no questions asked.

Keeping my head low, I drove his car past the two occupied houses at a sedate, everything's normal pace, and continued north.

The city gradually embraced me, fields giving way to sidewalks and houses and traffic; I made brief stops to clear the car of evidence. Most of it went into an incinerator near the Stockyards that I'd used before for getting rid of incriminating things. Dugan's suitcase and that goddamned bottle of green ink went into the fire, along with the mop.

I left the small radio on someone's porch. Did the same again for the box of new tools. Happy birthday.

The blood went into a gutter drain. It seemed to take a long time to pour out, but only because I was worried someone would catch me at it. Though it was wasteful, I wasn't hungry. The empty bottles and threaded rods I shoved into trash cans behind a closed diner along with the bucket of broken glass.

The car emptied bit by bit until only the bundles of cash remained. In a few weeks I'd mail the money back to the woman it belonged to with the hope she'd wise up about her choice in boyfriends.

Cleaned out, my prints wiped away, I left the car across from a police station and slunk off into the shadows before anyone noticed.

I was still in a scary-looking condition and avoided people. A beat cop noticed me and started coming in my direction, but I vanished into an alley and sped along for a block before re-forming again.

Needing clothes and a cleaning up, I slipped into a closed men's store and helped myself to one of everything, leaving the tags and more than enough cash on the counter.

A few streets over I found a hotel. Not wanting to startle the night clerk, I floated up the outside wall and sieved into an empty room on the top floor. There I stripped and scalded clean in the shower bath.

With much relief I noted that there were no permanent scars on my arms or my wrist where Dugan had cut me. The old ones left by Bristow were still present, but they didn't bother me as much now.

I had no shaving gear, but the rest of me was clean and grateful for the new clothes. I shoved my rags down the hotel's own incinerator chute and left five bucks in the bathroom for the maid to find.

Doing a plausible impersonation of a respectable citizen, I hired a taxi from the hotel stand, and got a quick ride to Lady Crymsyn.

The lights were on. Myrna must be awake. I paid off the driver and strolled across the street, checking both ways for anything more dangerous than myself.

The front door was unlocked. I listened a moment. A radio played, and a woman was singing along with the music.

I pushed in. Bobbi was at the bar with several stacks of paper scattered over it. She was in deep study over something but looked up the moment the door opened.

Her eyes widened as she stared me up and down, but I couldn't read anything of what she was thinking. I let the door shut softly behind and stepped in, unsure of my reception. She shut off the radio.

"I'm back," I finally said, just to break the thick silence.

"No kiddin'," she replied. "You get your thinking all done?"

Oh. Dugan had left a misleading message on my behalf.
hell or at least in that pit he'd dug for me. "Yeah. All done.'

"Good."

I wanted to *hold* her, make sure she was real, but sensed she
prickly mood. "What's that?"

She rested her fingers lightly on the papers. "Head shots, clip,
and my credits list. It was in the files upstairs. I want to get everythin
order. Lenny Larsen said I'd need to have new photographs, but tha
should wait and have them done in Hollywood."

"He'd be the expert. How are Roland and Faustine?"

"They're fine. He's getting better. So's Gordy."

I nodded, forcing a brief, wooden smile.

God, I felt as awkward as a kid at his first dance. After three nights of
surviving hell's antechamber it was disorienting to be back in my normal
world. It and the people there had no idea of what I'd been through. I had
no inclination to tell them, either.

"What is it, Jack?"

"I . . . I'm just glad to see you. I missed you."

"Missed you, too."

She was waiting for me to work up to the delicate topic of her going
off to make that screen test. I'd promised to think about it. And I had. At
length. It was one of the things that had kept me alive.

It had to wait, though. A car pulled up out front. Probably some late
drinkers hoping the club had reopened. I went to the door to lock it, but
not in time.

Escott, looking like he'd been dragged through Lake Michigan and
hung out to dry in the rain, barged in. He stopped in surprise, glaring.

"Well, it's about damned time you got back," he told me, and bulled
past.

Behind him was Kroun. "Where the hell have you been?" he said.

He didn't wait for an answer but trudged to a chair and dropped
heavily into it. He'd been dragged through the lake, mudflats, *and* some
kind of obstacle course.

Bobbi didn't know who to stare at the most. That made two of us.
"Charles?"

"May I have a whiskey?" he asked her. He peeled out of his damp
overcoat.

She played barmaid. "What happened to you?"

"Minor escapade. Quite stupid and wholly boring."

She shot a glance at me. Neither of us believed him. "Mr. Kroun?"

He held up a grubby palm and summoned some charm for her. "Gabe, ~ase."

"Gabe. What happened?"

He grimaced and brushed his hand over the white patch. "I had some business problems to work out. Got a little messy. I need to lie low for a while. Escott said this joint would be all right." He looked at me.

I gave an "I don't mind" shrug, trusting Escott would explain later.

Something shook inside my chest, fighting its way out. I tried to suppress the urge, but nothing doing, it was too strong.

I started laughing.

Thankfully, it wasn't that scary, maniacal kind, but the three of them stared until I got it under control.

"Sorry," I said.

"We were worried about you," said Escott sourly. He downed his drink.

Bobbi poured him another and growled agreement.

"I wasn't," said Kroun. "But you picked a hell of a time to run off."

"Sorry," I repeated. "Won't happen again."

That stood on its own for a while. I took off my new coat and hat, putting them on one of the stools. No one seemed disposed to start a conversation until the light flickered behind the bar.

"Hello, Myrna," I said. "Good to see you, too."

Kroun muttered something I didn't catch.

"Figuratively speaking," I added.

The flickering stopped. I thought that later, when I was alone, I'd tell Myrna what I'd been through. She wouldn't mind. It wouldn't change things between us.

"What's with the beard?" asked Kroun, rubbing his own unshaved jaw.

"Forgot my razor."

"Jack . . . is that a new suit?" Bobbi came around the bar for a closer look.

"Like it?"

"It's nice."

At the clothing store, the only double-breasted in my size that I could halfway tolerate had been a pale gray number. I felt like an overdressed street sweeper.

"It's kind of light for the season, isn't it?"

"Well . . . uh . . . I heard it's warmer in California."

Her eyes blazed impossibly bright; she gave a laughing shriek and jumped into my arms.

Oh. Dugan had left a misleading message on my behalf. May he rot in hell or at least in that pit he'd dug for me. "Yeah. All done."

"Good."

I wanted to *hold* her, make sure she was real, but sensed she was in a prickly mood. "What's that?"

She rested her fingers lightly on the papers. "Head shots, clippings, and my credits list. It was in the files upstairs. I want to get everything in order. Lenny Larsen said I'd need to have new photographs, but that I should wait and have them done in Hollywood."

"He'd be the expert. How are Roland and Faustine?"

"They're fine. He's getting better. So's Gordy."

I nodded, forcing a brief, wooden smile.

God, I felt as awkward as a kid at his first dance. After three nights of surviving hell's antechamber it was disorienting to be back in my normal world. It and the people there had no idea of what I'd been through. I had no inclination to tell them, either.

"What is it, Jack?"

"I . . . I'm just glad to see you. I missed you."

"Missed you, too."

She was waiting for me to work up to the delicate topic of her going off to make that screen test. I'd promised to think about it. And I had. At length. It was one of the things that had kept me alive.

It had to wait, though. A car pulled up out front. Probably some late drinkers hoping the club had reopened. I went to the door to lock it, but not in time.

Escott, looking like he'd been dragged through Lake Michigan and hung out to dry in the rain, barged in. He stopped in surprise, glaring.

"Well, it's about damned time you got back," he told me, and bulled past.

Behind him was Kroun. "Where the hell have you been?" he said.

He didn't wait for an answer but trudged to a chair and dropped heavily into it. He'd been dragged through the lake, mudflats, *and* some kind of obstacle course.

Bobbi didn't know who to stare at the most. That made two of us. "Charles?"

"May I have a whiskey?" he asked her. He peeled out of his damp overcoat.

She played barmaid. "What happened to you?"

"Minor escapade. Quite stupid and wholly boring."

She shot a glance at me. Neither of us believed him. "Mr. Kroun?"

He held up a grubby palm and summoned some charm for her. "Gabe, please."

"Gabe. What happened?"

He grimaced and brushed his hand over the white patch. "I had some business problems to work out. Got a little messy. I need to lie low for a while. Escott said this joint would be all right." He looked at me.

I gave an "I don't mind" shrug, trusting Escott would explain later.

Something shook inside my chest, fighting its way out. I tried to suppress the urge, but nothing doing, it was too strong.

I started laughing.

Thankfully, it wasn't that scary, maniacal kind, but the three of them stared until I got it under control.

"Sorry," I said.

"We were worried about you," said Escott sourly. He downed his drink.

Bobbi poured him another and growled agreement.

"I wasn't," said Kroun. "But you picked a hell of a time to run off."

"Sorry," I repeated. "Won't happen again."

That stood on its own for a while. I took off my new coat and hat, putting them on one of the stools. No one seemed disposed to start a conversation until the light flickered behind the bar.

"Hello, Myrna," I said. "Good to see you, too."

Kroun muttered something I didn't catch.

"Figuratively speaking," I added.

The flickering stopped. I thought that later, when I was alone, I'd tell Myrna what I'd been through. She wouldn't mind. It wouldn't change things between us.

"What's with the beard?" asked Kroun, rubbing his own unshaved jaw.

"Forgot my razor."

"Jack . . . is that a new suit?" Bobbi came around the bar for a closer look.

"Like it?"

"It's nice."

At the clothing store, the only double-breasted in my size that I could halfway tolerate had been a pale gray number. I felt like an overdressed street sweeper.

"It's kind of light for the season, isn't it?"

"Well . . . uh . . . I heard it's warmer in California."

Her eyes blazed impossibly bright; she gave a laughing shriek and jumped into my arms.